Hummingbirds Know Where to Fly

THE TAKEN SERIES
BOOK TWO

E. C. RODERICK

For all inquiries about this book, contact:
E. C. Roderick
1217 Wilshire Blvd.
P. O. Box 3283
Santa Monica, CA. 90403

Cover Design: Mary Ann Smith

Editor: Candy Leonard

Library of Congress Control Number: 2022924065

ISBN (Ebook): 978-1-7374357-3-0

ISBN (Paperback): 978-1-7374357-4-7

ISBN (Hardback): 978-1-7374357-5-4

Publisher: Sandy Pier Press
Los Angeles, California

Also by E. C. Roderick

1. TAKEN
2. Hummingbirds Know Where to Fly
3. The Pulse of My Heart
4. A Thorn in the Garden

He touched me, so I live to know
That such a day, permitted so,
I groped upon his breast —

It was a boundless place to me
And silenced, as the awful Sea
Puts minor streams to rest.

And now, I'm different from before,
As if I breathed superior air—
Or brushed a Royal Gown—
My feet, too, that had wandered so—
My Gypsy face—transformed now—
To tenderer Renown—

Into this Port, if I might come,
Rebecca, to Jerusalem,
Would not so ravished turn—
Nor Persian, baffled at her shrine
Lift such a Crucifixial sign
To her Imperial Sun.

—Emily Dickinson

Hummingbirds Know Where to Fly

PART ONE

The Wedding

<h1 style="text-align:center">One</h1>

F*riday, November 26, 1756. Concord.*

THIS MORNING the house was a bustle with many special preparations taking place. Evidently, this was going to be an extraordinary event by all considerations happening around me for today's wedding. It was proving to be an experience like I had never known as I watched what was occurring to me. I had awakened to maids waiting on me hand and foot like I was royalty. I wasn't used to this sort of attention at all and as I was being primped, I modestly recoiled when my shift was taken from me and pulled over my head, baring my nudity as a fresh one was being replaced on me.

It was somewhat bewildering to me as I sat sipping my tea and eating crumpets with cranberry preserves at the dressing table, having my hair preened and curled in perfect ringlets into a pleasant coiffed style that wasn't too high over my head. It was arranged loosely, pulled back in a series of three tiers until it tapered down the middle of my back. Pretty little glimmering garnet and gold jeweled pins were placed around my head at every row of ringlets, finishing the labor-intensive hair style. I had to confess, I was rather impressed with the way I looked, since it sort of reminded me of some of the hairstyle images I remembered seeing in antique Vogue fashion magazines from the nineteen sixties of women's beehive hairstyles.

Once my clocked stockings covered my legs, and a beautiful pair of gold buttercream, silk brocade two-inch heel slippers covered my toes, my rose embroidered stays were laced securely supporting my torso. As the strings to my matching rose embroidered pockets placed at my hips were being tied around my waist, I felt like a mannequin being decorated for a high-end clothing boutique window storefront. I fleetingly imagined this must have been what a high fashion model felt like as the particulars of various fabrics were well placed accordingly on her body.

Next a lightweight hoop came over my head and was fastened at the back of my waist, followed by an under-petticoat. When I saw the next petticoat come around me, I was mesmerized by its intricate beauty. It was the same gold buttercream color perfectly matching my shoes. The skirt was separated into two tiers from mid-calf to my ankles among two rows of large, intricately hand-made, lace rosettes embellished with elaborately sewn in pearls positioned around the lace petals on each tier. The silk dupioni material was gathered into pleats beneath the extraordinary lace on the first tier and finished by another row of petite, fine lace, interwoven rose buds. The second tier had a band of pearls and garnet beading, and completed the hem at my ankles just beneath the wide band of white French lace.

Then my stomacher, in the style of *echelle de rubans*, was attached to the front of my stays. I recognized the tartan of the supple silk ribbons climbing the length of the stomacher: Royal Stewart.

"*Ouch!*" I winced. I was suddenly pricked by one of the maid's needles while she completed pinning the gown to the bodice before securing it further to the gown petticoat. My daydreaming thoughts abruptly flew from my head calling me back to the reality occurring before me.

"I am terribly sorry, my lady," said Harriet, the maid who pricked me. Her expression didn't seem all that heartfelt as I noticed her exchanging a certain glance with Elizabeth who was assisting her.

"Oh no," I said worriedly, observing a bit of blood seeping onto the seam of the bodice.

"Never you mind, my lady, nothing is spoilt. It will cover nicely once I conclude the attachment," Harriet assured politely.

"Here," Elizabeth said as she tucked a sprig of beautifully dried, white heather tied together around a pastel blue satin ribbon at the top left side of my bodice between one of the decorative tartan bows.

When Harriet had completed attaching the gown, I stood in front of the looking-glass, primarily awestruck while studying my own transformed image staring back at me as an eighteenth century bride. The gown was unmistakably breathtaking. The dupioni silk gleamed over my frame and offset the more uniform sheen of the buttercream gold silk brocade of my gown petticoat. Lucious crimson, petite rosebuds had been embroidered throughout the skirt and bodice of the gown. The gown's skirt opened at the front from the bodice before the stomacher, separating widely over my beautiful under petticoat, and enhancing my gown petticoat with a buoyant row of lace and glimmering pearls on each side. Flounce sleeves followed a series of four tiers of extravagant French lace until they reached the middle of my forearms. In addition, on each arm, a tartan ribbon was stitched just above my elbow before my ruffle sleeves. The Royal Stewart red plaid remarkably complemented the gleaming gold cream material.

Lastly, a choker of matching lace and pearls was fastened around my neck finishing my transformed appearance.

THE HOUSE HAD EMPTIED as my bridal party arrived at the front door where a silky mink-lined, white velvet cape had been draped over my shoulders adequately shielding me from the cold. I noticed how unimaginably soft the mink fur felt against my neck and cheek as I was given a matching fur muff for my hands.

Mr. Pulst, the footman, opened the door for us, ready to lead us to the waiting carriage just beyond the front door in the snow.

"Right foot first, deah," Mrs. Buckingham said to me the minute I had raised my left foot to step over the threshold into the frigid air.

"Of course," I replied unknowingly and proceeded outside into the freezing, white, quilted landscape on the right foot along with the six pence that had been slipped inside my shoe. I spotted the gray horse that would pull the carriage waiting directly in front of us. It appeared like a beautiful ghost against the icy winter backdrop as it waited in the snowy road in front of the house.

I was rather surprised to see all the onlookers on the side of the road as I rode with my bridal party through town toward the church. It seemed like a significant portion of the population stood on the sidelines merely to catch a glimpse of us when we passed by them. As I peered from my window, I was curious to see the crowd moving on foot following us along the way and my stomach fluttered with butterflies from anticipation. Remembering to breathe, I took several deep, long breaths to control my breathing and curb my nervous anxiety.

It was only a matter of minutes until we had arrived at the front of a quaint whitewashed clapboard chapel called First Parish Church that was not an Anglican parish but Puritan. It was the only church in town and for this wedding occasion today the parish granted the small Anglican minority population the use of its chapel.

Once I had been carefully and properly unloaded from the

carriage, Finley promptly approached and lightly took hold of me around the elbow. His unfaltering light blue gaze skimmed me over with scrutiny. After a fleeting minute, he nodded approvingly and gave me a discreet wink. He then proceeded guiding me along the short path toward the stairs and mindfully assisted me up over the stone steps.

When we reached the top landing of the church's entrance, the droning sound of bagpipes erupted from behind us. The harmonizing music interrupted the muted winter atmosphere, and Finley began steering me between the opened doors inside the church. Although it was a moderately sized chapel, it seemed unexpectedly enormous as I realized all the spectating faces staring at me from the pews. I curiously wondered who all of these parishioners were as my nerves jittered with expectancy. Again, I strove to measure my breathing in order not to become lightheaded and faint, like I'd done yesterday, from the pressure of the impromptu marriage ceremony that I'd already undergone.

In a moment that seemed to have fast forwarded, I had arrived at the front of the church before the pulpit with the clergyman standing before me. Elizabeth had appropriately stolen my cape from me as I caught a glimpse of Leif already staring at me when I was positioned beside him at his right. His flushed face beamed like the sun when I saw a soft smile spreading over his lips. My own lips tilted automatically in response as his extraordinary appearance completely struck me. He was stunningly handsome in full Highland British military dress. His glimmering golden hair was perfectly tied back in a carmine silk ribbon at the nape of his neck and two rows of flawless, pin-tucked curls were horizontally rolled on each side over his temples.

His clean-shaven face allowed his expression to radiate full force among the starch white stock peering from the top ridge of his waistcoat and military coat. His gold gorget reflected the sunlight coming through the side window and glinted in my eyes. The white baldric over his right shoulder matched the lapels on his scarlet coat and contrasted brightly as the brass buttons lining the edge gleamed like gold nuggets beneath the sunbeams radiating through the windows.

The black cross-belt exposed beneath his coat over his waistcoat joined with the belt around his waist, making him appear commanding and stately. I noticed the intricate, gold fringed, officer's knot dangling from the grip of his Highland basket broadsword above the throat of the scabbard mount while it hung from the black belt around his waist over his kilt. The shiny black hide sporran that was fastened around his waist was beautifully crafted from the soft gusset. A nice panel of pleats on the sporran radiated from a decorative scalloped, punched hide apron with matching soft leather tassels tied in Celtic knots toward the end of the sporran was attractive. Finally, the flounce sleeve cuffs that hid a portion of Leif's knuckles as he collected my left hand in his right palm finished his impressive appearance.

So, the service began with Reverend Stansfield opening with a prayer as I carefully arrived before him and attentively stood to Leif's right.

Despite my trying to pay attention to what was happening around me, my mind kept wandering in and out of the ceremony, taking place as flashbacks from my past entered my mind. I kept seeing the ghost of my dearly departed Matt's animated image inside Santa Barbara Mission Church on our wedding day as we knelt before Father Sanchez and all of our family and friends. I remembered the way Matt looked: he was brimming with serious pride, much like the way Leif was looking now as he attentively gazed at Reverend Stansfield speaking in front of us.

The happy and loving life I had spent with my late husband played like a video in my mind. It was an odd feeling, because I remembered how I used to be. I never *dreamed* that I would ever marry anyone else after he died.

I sensed a braided cord binding my wrist over Leif's. When the knot was being tied, Leif proceeded with his vows and placed a simple gold band above the ring he had placed upon my finger yesterday. I noticed this beautiful gold wedding band had been engraved around the face of the ring: *Leif & Sylvina.* Then, it was my turn to place a solid gold band that Finley had passed to me to place over Leif's left ring finger with the same engraving.

Afterward, Reverend Stansfield continued with more stoic words and prayers. When he had finished speaking during this section of the ceremony, I observed Finley come around before me. He proceeded in pinning a Royal Stewart tartan sash over my shoulder with a large, circular, silver badge. The badge was a belted circle enclosing a thistle and on it read: *Virescit Vulnere Virtus*: Courage Grows Strong at a Wound.

Next, Leif turned aside, slightly away from me. He abruptly heaved as he sharply retrieved a substantially large, very dense and threatening looking broadsword from the baldric over his back. My heart skipped a beat as I laid anxious eyes on the glimmering blade when he swung it over himself and carefully placed the tip of the blade upon the chapel floor just between his toes. His voice carried coarsely as he whispered a few words in Scottish. Then, he kissed the cross-guard before laying the weapon flat directly before my feet. I stared with apprehension at the mesmerizing Claymore sword as it gleamed directly before my toes from the encompassing sun rays entering the windows above our heads. I pondered the gesture as my eyes roved absorbedly over the endless Celtic knotting engraved throughout the cross-guard and at the end of the grip around the pommel.

Finally, Reverend Stansfield had concluded the ceremony. After Leif picked up his sword from off the floor and slid it back into its scabbard, he now began leading me through the center aisle as his lawfully wedded wife toward the back of the church among the sounds of following bagpipers. As we paced along the center aisle just before crossing the threshold leading outdoors, I was met by a pretty toddler boy who placed a horseshoe over my wrist. I smiled at his cute little face, thinking it was a strange gesture to do as I gladly received his gift.

When we were leaving the church, I noticed Leif reaching inside his sporran and pulled forth his coin purse. He began tossing gold coins into the snow, and the children rushed to collect the sparkling pieces. I didn't much understand many of the wedding traditions here, but found them interesting and merry as everyone else had who was familiar with them.

Two

It seemed all of Concord had turned out for a wedding celebration despite the cold. Both of the Buckingham houses were overflowing with celebrating guests. Even some of the neighbors had opened their doors for the festivity. Not surprisingly, the British troops quartering in town for the winter partook in the celebration with some wary concerns from the locals.

The grand dining room had been sufficiently prepared for loose dining, since the center of it had been cleared for music playing and dancing. Leif and I sat squished together while eating and drinking among family and close military companions over a stretched table. My conversation with the women beside me was filled with kind and thoughtful advice spoken in minimal suggestive terms regarding my wedding night and how to best submit to serve my new husband. I found it interesting that Suzanna was so considerately dispensing her sisterly advice to me as if I had no idea what to do with a husband in spite of her awareness of my previous marriage experience. Still, it was a bit entertaining to listen to her modestly chirp like a bird about it.

While I half listened to what Suzanna had to say about her husband and their wedding day, the conversation the men were having with Leif caught my attention and shocked me with some consideration. I thought I had been suddenly thrown inside a guy's locker room forced to listen to a bunch of jocks talk shop about women.

"Nae, Seamus, dinnae listen tae a single word Cole has told ye—he has merely ridden bags," Angus joked roughly in hushed tones, and half the left side of the table erupted in coarse laughter.

"Och! Come, now, lads! They are all the same tae me—ye had one, ye had 'em all is whit I say," Cole rebuffed confidentially.

"*Pfft!* Whit does Cole ken in truth? He is fortunate tae have a bag tae ride at all!" Liam ribbed. More coarse laughter erupted on Leif's side of the table.

"Och! Shut yer yaps!" Cole protested.

"It has been quite a while since Seamus had a lass, however. 'Tis likely that he has forgotten whit tae do with one," Roy teased and chuckling snickers flew around them. Leif's ears went hot pink.

"Should ye need any reminding upon whit tae do with yer bride cousin, I shall gladly instruct ye," Liam joked.

"I'll need nae reminding from ye, Liam. Or, from any one of ye other lads fur that matter," Leif responded modestly, although his face had turned beet red from embarrassment.

"Merely be certain ye dinnae wear the poor lass out, Seamus," Finley said under his breath.

"A bonnie face like hers, I would bed the poor lass till she never walked again," Liam laughed some more with the rest of their cousins down the table.

"She would be fortunate tae ken whit a guid ride is all about with ye, Liam," Lachlan joked sarcastically, messing around like the rest. Some more hearty chuckling broke out when he continued to say, "May I also grant ye a bit of advice, Seamus?"

"Hold yer tongue, Lachlan. If ye ken whit is best fur ye," Leif lightly threatened, inspiring abundant laughter to break out loudly between his cousins, embarrassing him further.

I suddenly cleared my throat as I glanced at Leif's scarlet face and shot his cousins a certain disapproving look. Their mouths stretched ear to ear like multiple jokers as they respectfully raised their rum glasses to me. Leif grinned abashedly at me with his crimson cheeks glowing and took a large swig from his glass tumbler. I thought that wasn't a half bad idea and turned toward the glass of port facing me. At the rate my life was going at this point, I felt I could use a good drink right about now anyway. I touched the rim of my wineglass to my lips and began sipping away.

After several wine glasses full, I soon started feeling a lot different and suddenly everything seemed funny. I started giggling at the wig over Mr. Maxwell's head, thinking how very odd that I was in a place where men wore wigs, and at the irony of my new setting. Noticing Mr. Maxwell's wig tipped haphazardly to the left with the part off-center, I wondered if he usually wore it that way or if it was a consequence of him being plain drunk and having accidentally pushed it to the side. In any case, I started imagining how my own family back at home in the twenty-first century would all appear in wigs and the thought struck me with such hilarity, tears emerged in my eyes as I simply started laughing.

Next, Mrs. Bunt caught my attention when noticing her portly finger discreetly lift a ladyfinger from an arrangement of food on a table over to one side of the room. She eagerly stuffed the baked treat into her mouth, smiled and nodded her head. I wondered if she was going to do it again, so I waited with an anticipatory eye. I watched her like a hawk as she quietly paced among the presentation of baked deserts while deciding the next one to sample. Finally, she stopped before a pie, retrieved a tiny bit of rhubarb from it and quickly plopped it inside her portly mouth as she glanced over her shoulder to see if anyone was noticing her.

I couldn't help it; I was giggling for no apparent reason at all. It was amazing how everything around me—my circumstances and all—seemed so ridiculously funny; this twist of fate happening to me was inconceivable and the irony of it cracked me up into complete laughter.

"Whit is raither amusing?" Leif inquired properly as he noticed my silly giggling.

"Um... Well, I was just thinking that I would like to try some pie," I laughed, trying to control myself. He turned a discerning eye on me.

"A bit of pie?" he responded doubtfully.

"Yeah," I giggled.

"Ye dinnae say?" His eyes bounced from me to the wine glass between my fingers.

"Um-hm, I think it might be really, really, *really* good," I replied happily.

"I dinnae doubt it micht be quite delicious," he said while skeptically looking at me.

"What?" I asked guiltily.

"How much wine have ye had already?" he inquired.

"Ooh, c'mon, Leify-poo, I'm just enjoying myself that's all," I giggled, teasing him a little. He gave me a quirky look that I thought was funny, and I laughed some more.

"Weel, dinnae enjoy yerself too much as we still have some time yet before we may depart," he warned. His fingers slipped around my wine glass and he confiscated it from me, placing it beside himself opposite of me. "Furthermore, I mean tae bed ye whilst ye remain of wit."

"Okay, *buddy*," I snickered. "Can I call you buddy? Because we're buds? You know buddies? Right? We're friends, right? Pals?" His eyes abruptly widened and he briskly chuckled with a look of unexpected amusement while lightly shaking his head.

"Aye, we are friends," he agreed quizzically.

"Good. Because you know what?"

"Pray tell."

"I wouldn't have it any other way."

"Nor, I," he said with an entertained expression and sincere tone in his voice.

"Fan-*tastic*!" A strange grin curled his lips as he looked at me, making me giggle more. "Do you want to know something else?"

"Aye. Tell me."

"I think you and I are going to get along just *swell*!"

"Swell?"

"Yeah, splendidly—we're going to get along *splendidly*!"

"I do agree."

"Good! And you know what else?"

"Aye?"

"You're a great guy."

"A great guy?"

"Yeah, a great *man*, you know?"

"Och! Am I now?"

"Yup!" I replied and gave him a wink. He laughed and his face flushed.

"Weel, thank ye fur saying so. I'll have ye ken that yoo're a grand lass," he said frankly and winked back at me. I giggled some more, and he smiled. Music commenced playing around the room: three fiddlers, a bagpiper, a drummer and a fifer. "Come along, loove," he suggested as he enfolded his hand over mine and started standing from his seat at the table.

"What for?" I asked curiously while inspired by the happy look on his face.

"We must dance. Ye ridiculous bird," he said cheerfully as he urged me from my chair.

"Right…" I said, suddenly filled with caution. "But wait a minute!"

"Aye?"

"I can't."

"Whit do ye mean?"

"I don't know how to dance."

"Whit do ye mean that ye dinnae ken how tae dance?" he asked unexpectedly.

"That's what I said—I don't know how," I repeated worriedly, shrugging my shoulders.

"Surely ye must ken."

"Nope. Not at all."

"Ye truly dinnae ken how tae dance?" he asked, apprehending himself before he took me any further away from the table. The look of surprise on his face was obvious as he stared at me with a raised brow.

"Yeah, I don't know," I said, shaking my head absolutely. I suddenly felt very hesitant.

"Nae matter, merely follow my lead," he insisted.

"No! I can't! If it's not a waltz then I can't do it," I told him apprehensively.

"A waltz?" he questioned as his brow briefly furrowed.

"Yeah, I know how to waltz, but I don't know your dance."

"Never ye mind. Simply follow my lead, and ye will be fine," he insisted again. Without any more consideration, he tugged me to my feet and led me from around my seat at the table. Hearing the musicians play a reel in the background, I dubiously followed him as he led me by the hand toward the center of the room before all our happily celebrating guests. As there was absolutely no other choice but for me to comply, we faced each other a few feet away and stood in the center of the room while I nervously anticipated his lead. He bowed, I curtsied and so the reel began...

AFTER ABUNDANT EATING, drinking, dancing among family and friends along with town wedding guests, we sampled wedding cake which closely reminded me of those grocery store holiday fruitcakes found at Christmas time. Except, this one was clearly much better. I'm sure it had to do a lot with the fresh and authentic ingredients, not to mention the percentage of sugar and rum involved in making it.

By this time, the day had grown quite late since dusk had come and gone, leaving the late hours in the night to linger. Leif finally stole me away from the guests, and we started out from the lively venue into the cold, silent snow. I wondered about the handful of Leif's companions following behind us at a slight distance along with the reverend leading the way.

The guest house was overflowing with merrily drunken men from a Highland military company when we arrived. Just as we had reached the doorstep to the front door, Reverend Stansfield prayed at the threshold. Then, Leif swooped, lifting me up high into his formidable arms before passing through the doorway into a foyer full of noisy, cheerful salutations and congratulations from a multitude of soldiers.

"Och! How we all admire yer position, Your Grace!" shouted some faceless rowdy soldier among the crowd.

"Micht ye require any assistance, I shall be honored tae provide my service, Your Grace!" yelled out another. Rounds of laughter swarmed us as Leif continued carrying me through the intoxicated party.

"Sedition will run amongst the ranks, Your Grace, if ye dinnae afford the lads haur screaming entertainment!" someone else shouted and roaring laughter howled throughout the crowded hallway as Leif was making his way through the packed house with me in his arms. More obscene hilarity roared jocularly everywhere around us, and all I wanted to do was shrink away.

"Can you believe that?" I said appallingly, looking at Leif completely shocked as he now carried me up the staircase unfazed.

"Pay them nae mind. They are merely drunkards," he replied, excusing them. I noticed some of the men following the reverend behind us when I glanced over Leif's shoulder.

"Why are they following us?" I asked with uncertainty.

"They are witnesses," Leif said.

"*Witnesses?* For what?"

"Dinnae worry."

Of course, I was worried; I had no idea what to expect with all these strange, rowdy men hanging around inside the house.

It was a matter of seconds when we arrived at Leif's bedroom door, along with some followers behind us, in addition to the reverend. The reverend began offering prayers at the doorway to the bedroom, then moved aside so that we could pass through. When we entered the room, Leif proceeded to place me at last upon my own two feet. He turned toward the crowd peering around the reverend's shoulders at the entrance and politely, but certainly, closed the door in front of their drunk faces.

Suddenly alone now, Leif turned from the door, facing me once he had shut us inside the bedroom, and we simply looked at each other a little blankly. There was a certain level of palpable anticipation between us, and the moment quickly became awkward. Sordid talking, joking, and laughing audibly came from behind the door, and things regarding what was to take place next between us this evening unexpectedly seemed oddly contrived. I began feeling discomfited as I stared back at Leif's reddened expression full of expectation.

"Shall we make ourselves more at ease?" he suggested thoughtfully.

"Um-hm," I muttered self-consciously, too aware of the entire house full of celebrating men just outside our bedroom door. He reached for my hand and guided me away from the door toward the chaise lounge chair where we ceased. We unfastened our capes, and he gathered mine from my shoulders. I watched him lean slightly as he placed our outerwear over the chaise cushions, wondering how we were going to proceed.

"May I?" he offered solicitously, suggesting to help me unpin my stomacher from my gown.

"Yes, thank you," I said bashfully.

"Very weel," he responded quietly, and gave an inhibited little grin. He carefully placed his fingertips over the front of my bodice and mindfully began removing the pins to my stomacher. I stood there close before him with our heads nearly touching as I watched his shaking fingers slowly move to undress me. His ears were extremely pink, I noticed, and I could feel his steady breathing breeze warmly among the lace surrounding my breasts.

After nearly five minutes, my gown had been freed and pulled from my shoulders away from me. The color of his face, while he remained silent, intensified as I now stood still in front of him with my stays and gown petticoat fully revealed. He stepped behind me, proceeding to unlace the cords binding my stays, and in a minute, I was able to pull it from my torso. I reached around my waist to untie my gown petticoat, then started removing my other petticoat when he decided to unfasten his sword belts from around his waist. He turned and placed his sheathed swords over the chaise, then withdrew his scarlet coat from his square shoulders. He hung it in the Queen Anne armoire, then proceeded to unbutton his waistcoat as my hoop fell to my ankles.

Leif's gaze silently turned toward me as I stepped from the hoop around my toes. I didn't think I had ever seen his expression so flushed as I had witnessed at this particular moment. I nervously dropped my gaze from him and sat on the edge of the bed to remove my toes from my shoes. When I had finished rolling my stockings from my legs, I automatically folded them among my hands and moved to place them neatly on the chaise above my shoes on the floor. The stillness in the room between us was thick with perceivable expectation. And, the fact that the house was full of jovial men anticipating outside our bedroom door, did nothing to soothe matters. Instead, I felt like a bumbling jitterbug inside, filled with insecure angst.

As I started away from the chair after placing my stockings down, I discovered Leif observing me and I stopped. His crystal ultramarine gaze was mindful and soft.

"What?" I asked uncertainly, gazing back at him.

"Yoo're bonnie," he said warmly, as he perceived me now standing before him simply clothed in the sheerness of my shift.

"That's very sweet of you to say, thank you," I replied. I felt a draft in the room and caught a chill over my skin. I shivered, and ran my hands down the goosebumps over my arms.

"Och! Forgive me, let me git the fire," he said abruptly and moved toward the hearth. I hopped into bed among the pillows beneath the covers, pulling them up high to my neck like a mummy to warm myself, and quietly watched him stoking the flames in the fireplace from the blankets. When he was finished, he straightened and caught a glimpse of me buried to my neck under them. "Are ye as a bit of ice?" he chuckled lightly.

"I feel like a snowman," I joked.

"We mustn't have ye like so," he replied.

"I never have liked feeling like an icicle," I admitted. A brow arched slightly over one eye as a gentle grin spread evenly over his face. He started pacing across the room toward the bench at the foot of the bed.

"I guarantee ye will presently nae longer feel frozen as long as I'm about tae warm ye," he said expectantly.

"Is that right?" I replied sheepishly, witnessing him pull the stock from around his neck. The collar of his shirt opened, and I could detect the bit of blonde hair peeping from his chest.

"It most certainly is correct," he promised.

"Well, we'll see about that," I teased nervously.

"Aye, ye will indeed see precisely whit I mean." He unfastened the large shiny brass buckle around his waist, and his kilt suddenly unraveled away from himself.

"Uh, I don't know about that," I mentioned unevenly. The same golden eyebrow immediately arched over his blue eye again.

"I reckon that ye are the sort who must have things proven so that ye will believe it," Leif asserted definitely. He stood tall at the foot of the bed peering down at me. His bright white, fine linen shirt billowed out and hung long around his solid masculine frame at mid-thigh. In one simple motion, he pulled his shirt up over his head, and suddenly I realized my first row seat in front of him as he boldly stood completely naked before my very surprised eyes. I couldn't help my unwitting eyes as they compulsively skimmed over his broad, well-defined chest. He was sculpted and beautiful. My gaze passed his navel down to the blonde tuft of hair at his groin and I noticed him.

There was no wonder why I had unexpectedly responded the way I had during the instance he had me intimately on the sitting room floor the other day, as I could see the reason why plain as day right before my eyes. No question about it. He had not been over-looked in this department in the slightest. He was very well endowed, and to view his shaft aroused not yet to its fullest extent, lent some fear to its final potential.

Leif caught me blatantly staring at him and he smiled widely, exposing the pearly gleam of his teeth. I abruptly looked away, totally embarrassed, and sensed his smile widen further. He started around the edge of the bed and slid in close beside me beneath the covers, naked and warm, ready to begin the next phase of our evening.

Suddenly, a knocking was heard from behind the door.

"Come!" Leif responded expectantly, and I shot him a very ill at ease look as the door began opening. I quickly tugged the blankets higher until they were smothering my face, and only my eyes could peer forth to see. It was the reverend striding beyond the threshold, entering our room with the door remaining wide open for anyone else to enter.

"What's he doing here?" I whispered anxiously to Leif. He gave me a strange look as he noticed the way I was tucked under the blankets.

"He is haur tae bless our bed," Leif answered obviously.

"Oh," I replied uneasily. I further heard, to my apprehension, a group of rowdy, nosy onlookers pouring in through the doorway into our room, surrounding Reverend Stansfield. "But, why are *they* all here?" I murmured insecurely.

"They are haur tae witness," Leif informed me.

"Witness *what*?" I was extremely reluctant about this.

"The blessing," Leif answered obviously again.

"And then they have to *go*! Every last one of them! Do you hear me?" I chimed back. Leif stared quizzically at me as the reverend began to speak. We promptly turned our attention toward Reverend Stansfield and listened to his blessings.

Thankfully, the reverend's speech didn't run for too long when he finally turned to leave us. However, unlike Reverend Stansfield, the interfering spectators were slow to leave on cue in their merry drunkenness and loitered some moments afterward with jesting taunts toward Leif. I also caught some teasing directed at me over the way I was appearing with the covers over my head.

"Dinnae worry, lass, if he disnae ride ye weel, try me fur a stallion!" shouted one man. Rounds of laughter shot out across the room.

"Mayhap, a pony ride is whit the lass prefers!" someone else joked obnoxiously.

"She is about to have a stud such as myself! Now, the lot of ye —remove yerselves! Or, I shall have every one of ye horse-whipped!" Leif snapped half kiddingly as he abruptly sprang buck-naked from the blankets without any consideration and began shooing the hullabaloo from the room and out the door.

He quickly shut and latched the door after the last trouble-maker retreated behind the threshold, sealing us both alone securely inside of his room.

Three

"Now, that is better," Leif said with approval as he easily strode back toward the bed.

"A lot," I agreed, completely mortified. I withdrew the blankets from my face and propped myself more comfortably against the pillows. Still, I could hear plenty of racket coming from behind the door while I observed Leif pull back the blankets and slide beneath them next to me again. I was still not quite ready for him and felt very uneasy with a house full of wakeful drunken men just outside our bedroom door.

"Mayhap, we micht speak prior," he suggested as I sensed him noticing me.

"Okay," I agreed, feeling a little relieved. "What do you want to talk about?"

"I reckon I wish tae ken more regarding ye," he said.

"Oh," I replied thinkingly. I wasn't sure what to tell him, or what I *could* tell him without sounding strange, or suspicious. Or, raising questions that I felt I couldn't answer, fearing the outcome.

"Ye may tell me whit ye like," he encouraged.

"Well..." I demurred softly.

"Mayhap, I shall like tae ken about yer parents," he suggested.

"Oh, sure—well—my dad's name was Leonardo Miguel Cielo Esperanza. But, everyone just called him Leo," I disclosed.

"Och—the reason fur yer knowledge of the Spanish language," he responded interestedly.

"Yeah," I replied.

"Whit else will ye tell me of him?" he asked inquisitively.

"He was a military man too," I said.

"Was he indeed?" he inquired, looking at me with noticeable surprise.

"Yes, he was," I admitted.

"I see."

"He was a very good dad," I remembered wistfully.

"Ye waur fond of him, then?"

"Yes, I loved him very much. I remember him being in a good mood all the time—in spite of knowing what war can do to people. I remember he used to take me out on outings many times when I was little—like to the beach or sailing for the day. Once he even took me to the circus—when they were still popular."

"The circus? Whit micht that be?"

"Um, it's a traveling company of acrobats, trained animals, and clowns who perform to audiences in tents."

"Yer father took you tae see gypsies?" Leif's ultramarine gaze went round with astonishment.

"No," I laughed as I looked at the weird look on his face. "They weren't Roma."

"Roma?"

"Yes. They weren't Roma. They were just performers. That's all."

"Och," he replied with a strange expression. "Such entertainment is common from whaur ye come?"

"Yeah. Well, it was popular once—for many years it was."

"I see. Why is it nae longer common?"

"People just began thinking that the animals weren't treated humanely, and so the majority stopped patronizing the entertainers," I answered.

"Och."

"Yes, well, it was a lot of fun up until that happened."

"Hmm, curious... Tell me more about yer father."

"Well, my dad always made sure everything was right with us, just as it should be, you know...? He had a good disposition and always made me feel special. He could always cheer me up whenever I was sad, and he could always make me laugh."

"It seems he was quite pleasant with ye."

"He was..." I drifted for a moment as I fondly remembered my dad. "Once, he brought me a puppy for my birthday."

"Did he?"

"Yeah. I had just turned seven. It was a black terrier and I named him Mickey after Mickey Mouse."

"Mickey Mouse?" Leif chuckled quizzically.

"Yeah."

"Whit sort of name is that?"

"Well, Mickey Mouse is a fictional character in a story," I explained simply. I couldn't very well tell him that he's Disney's mascot; he certainly wouldn't have understood.

"I huvnea ever heard of such a character. And, 'tis a mouse ye say?"

"Yeah," I replied, gently smiling at him.

"Is he a brave mouse?"

"He's witty, silly, and lovable—and, sometimes brave, I suppose."

"He seems a fanciful character."

"He is," I said and Leif smiled enchantedly at me.

"Tell me about yer mother," he wished.

"Well... she was a really good mom. She was very busy, though."

"I see."

"Even though she was like that, she always gave me her attention when I needed her... Whenever I fell and scraped my knee when I was little, or if something was bothering me—especially when I became older—she always made it completely better—particularly when my dad was away on deployment. Or, if I got sick, she knew exactly what to do to help me... She was very easy to speak with, and she always gave me good advice if I had a problem that I couldn't resolve on my own," I recalled.

"'Twas guid of her," Leif acknowledged, intently looking at me.

"Yeah," I replied remotely, longing to hear my mom's voice again.

"Whit was her name?"

"Bernadette."

"French?" he recognized instantly.

"Her mother spoke the language," I divulged.

"Thus is the reason ye ken the language as weel," he easily deduced.

"Yeah."

"Engel is amongst one of yer names," he commented curiously.

"My mom's dad's heritage was German."

"Hessian?"

"Bavarian," I specified.

"I see," he said, more fascinated. "Then, ye are familiar with the German language as weel?"

I shook my head a little. "He never really spoke it—so, I never actually learned it."

"I see... Did ye have any siblings?"

"I had a brother."

"Whit was his name?"

"His name was Kyle."

"Unusual. But, a guid Scottish name," he said, musing for a second.

"Yeah, I suppose..."

"Waur ye fond of him?"

"Yeah, we got along great."

"Quite fortunate."

"Yes."

"Who was eldest?"

"He was six years older than I."

Leif silently nodded his head a bit. He stared at me absorbed, and I perceived him pondering me. He paused, and his mild deep blue gaze cast down on my bandaged left hand where it rested above the covers in my lap. His large palm gently covered my bandage, and his fingers lightly played with the rings he had placed upon my hand.

"Sylvina... It means of the wood," he recommenced gently.

"Yeah," I replied, amazed that he knew the meaning of my name. His eyes returned to mine and a soft smile graced his kind expression.

"Yer entire name is bonnie," he complimented while his fingers continued gently stroking my new rings.

"It's all right, I guess," I replied self-consciously.

"Leilani—I huvnea heard of it till now. Whit does it mean?"

"It means Heavenly baby girl."

"Does it?" He seemed rather impressed or surprised; I couldn't tell the difference.

"Um-hm," I replied simply.

"How bonnie."

"Thank you."

"In which language?"

"It's Hawaiian," I revealed.

"Hawaiian?" he echoed strangely.

"Have you heard of Hawaii?" I inquired cautiously.

"Nae," he said, shaking his head a little.

"Oh..." I suddenly realized, with some regret, that I had slipped in my conversation and had revealed a bit too much.

"Is it a place ye have seen?" he asked peculiarly. I hesitated. I didn't know how to proceed.

"Yes, I've been there," I decided to tell him anyway.

"Och... Do ye speak the language as weel?"

"Not really," I said, shaking my head a tad.

"Whit do ye mean?" he inquired curiously.

"I just know standard things to say—like the way you say hello is, *aloha*," I informed him.

"Aloha," Leif echoed, really fascinated.

"It also means goodbye."

"Does it?"

"Yeah. And, *mahalo* means thank you."

"Mahalo."

"Yeah. And, *i lā maika'i* means have a nice day."

"Is that reit?"

"Yes." I nodded a little. "And, the way you would say 'I love you' is '*Aloha wau iā 'oe*'."

He smiled gently at me. "Tell me how tae say it again," he requested interestedly. "Yet, say it slowly so that I may repeat it."

"All right," I replied. "*Aloha.*"

"Aloha," he echoed.

"*Wau.*"

"Wau."

"*Iā 'oe.*"

"Iā 'oe," he repeated carefully.

"That's it." I smiled at him. He grinned in return.

"'Tis bonnie."

"That's all I pretty much know. Except, I do also know how to say Merry Christmas."

"And how do ye say it?" he inquired, appearing very enthralled.

"It's said like this—*mele Kalikimaka*."

"How bonnie."

"Yeah."

"The language soonds quite pleasant."

"I think so too," I agreed. Leif broke off a moment as he stared intently at me seeming deeply mesmerized and wondering.

"Whaur does Hawaii lie?" he inquired curiously.

"It's far away from here," I hesitated.

"Och," he said while closely gazing at me. He paused for a moment again, appearing meditative. "Heavenly lass of the wood," he said softly after a minute.

"Hm?" I responded vacantly.

"Yer name—'tis whit it means. Heavenly lass of the wood," he repeated.

"Oh, right..."

I observed his eyes drop to the new rings on my wedding finger. He rotated them between his thumb and forefinger as he noticed them.

"Ye switched yer other rings to yer right hand," he remarked, lifting his gaze back to mine.

"Well, I'm married to you now, so..." I said softly to him.

"Aye. Yoo're mine now," he replied gently. "I shall like tae ken about yer departed husband."

"Well..." I paused thinkingly. "I guess—I guess I could say that he was somewhat like you, actually."

"Indeed?" Leif responded amazedly.

"Yeah."

"In whit manner?"

"I think you both kind of share some similar characteristics."

"Is that reit?"

"Um-hum."

"How so?"

"He was genuine, and honorable. His personal character was resilient, and he treated others with respect and dignity... He was always very sweet, loving and kind to me," I remembered. Leif drew my hand over his lap and held it securely in his as he gazed openly at me.

"I vow tae always honor his memory. I shall never treat ye in any lesser manner, Sylvie. Ye are my wife, and ye honor me with the privilege of accepting me," he expressed endearingly. "I am pleased tae live and lay down my life fur ye. I shall always be loyal and true tae ye, and I shall always hold ye dear tae my heart. Ye must ken thaur is nought that I wulnae do fur ye. I shall serve ye with my devotion and honor... and thaur will be nought that will separate me from ye until death—"

"I don't want you to die," I interrupted frightfully.

"Nae, nae—I dinnae foresee that I shall any moment close at hand," he comforted tenderly as he wrapped an arm around my waist and pulled me against him. I nodded my head a little in response. "However, whit I am about tae require of ye is severely grave," he said staunchly.

"What?" I replied curiously, gazing closely back at him, wondering with some uncertainty what he was going to expect from me.

"Ye must swear yer oath never tae lie tae me. I ken occasionally when I have inquired something of ye, ye will tell me it is nought, or ye will hesitate—yet, I ken it is of a matter when ye say it is not. I respect that ye bear much within, and I understand that ye believe ye cannae tell me some things. I can abide by that. Yet never, ever lie tae me," he expressed steadfastly.

I gazed into his compelling expression and easily perceived the candid, serious intensity on his face. I thought his request was fair; I wouldn't have expected anything less from him also.

"I swear I will never lie to you," I vowed.

"Very weel," he accepted completely.

"Will you promise me the same thing?" I asked fairly.

"Indeed. I have always been truthful with ye, and I vow that I shall always be true tae ye," he said earnestly.

"Okay," I consented. I paused for a second, thinking. "May I ask you something?" I started carefully.

"Aye?"

"Do you still believe that I'm a secret agent?"

"Nae," Leif said flatly, shaking his head.

"You don't?" I was fairly surprised.

"Correct," he said, seeming very sure about it.

"How come?"

"Pardon?"

"I mean why?"

"Weel, I ken that if ye waur duplicitous, ye would have previously revealed yerself some time ago," he said.

"Oh."

"'Tis quite difficult to maintain the air of a spy fur some time without prior being discovered through certain behavior."

"Where you testing me?"

"I have been genuine with ye."

"But, you were sort of testing me in order to find out."

"In a manner."

"So, you believe now that I'm telling you the truth about not being a spy, right? Because, it's absolutely the truth."

"I do believe ye arenae a spy. Thaur waur ample opportunities fur ye tae flee us, yet ye didnae. Additionally, I reckon that ye would have never agreed tae wed me if it waur true that ye waur underhanded, fur ye would have valued yer employer over me. Fur instance, ye wouldnae have refused Laird Vaudreuil and alarmed me when I had delivered ye tae him. Ye waur terrified tae be left with him. I also recognized yer air of innocence which disnae correlate with treachery but contradicts it, fur yoo're too unawaur tae ken the tactics of a spy as yer honest decorum in this regard pervades yer disposition through yer mannerism," he explained.

"So, I'm too honest?"

"Aye."

"Oh... Well—I have to say that I'm really glad that you believe me," I said genuinely, feeling relieved.

"I do," he said frankly.

"May I ask you another question?"

"Aye?"

"Why did you want to get married?" I inquired vulnerably.

"I wed ye tae protect ye, certainly," he said apparently.

"Oh…" That wasn't quite the answer I was looking for, and I felt silently disappointed.

"But, I desired tae wed ye also."

"Why, did you desire it?"

"I desired tae wed ye, fur I find ye immensely bonnie," he flattered.

"Oh, well, thanks," I replied ironically. Then, I detected the color in his face begin to rise and sensed his warm palm slipping from my fingers beneath the covers. His fingers discovered the hem of my shift and gently moved beneath the soft material up over my bare calf and knee. He leaned in close, and I could smell the light aroma of port on his warm breath as he began tenderly caressing my neck and chin with his other hand.

"Moreover, I wed ye fur I wanted ye," he revealed to me with some discernible embarrassment.

"You mean you married me just because you wanted to have sex with me?" I asked, slightly put off.

"Aye, I desire tae couple with ye."

"But, we were kinda already *doing it*—if you catch my meaning—before we got interrupted, remember?"

"Indeed, I recall. However, I meant tae bed ye and keep ye all tae myself whether before the wedding or efter it," Leif replied absolutely.

"Is that a fact?" I replied—a little thrown by his candor.

"It most certainly is a fact," he said precisely. "Yet, truly I didnae want tae live in sin with ye, so I wished tae wed ye before God."

"Oh…" I muttered. "Is that it?"

He grinned at me, and I recognized the affection in his eyes. "I wouldnae have wed ye if I didnea care fur ye, *àille dhubh*," he said.

"Oh…" was all I could say, as I was aware of his anticipating lips closely hovering near mine and distracting me.

"Now," he said warmly, letting his hand wander down my neck over the lace flounces bordering my upper torso and continued sliding between my breasts toward my stomach. I felt the hem of my shift rising higher above my leg until his hand found my pubic area and the petite tuft between my thighs.

"*Uhh,*" I gasped unexpectedly when I sensed his finger spreading my labia apart and entering me.

"Shall we continue whit we have started?" he whispered heatedly against my lips.

"Uh, since you insist," I whispered unevenly, incapable of denying my yearning for him.

"I fear that I do insist."

"Then, I guess, what can I say?" I replied, succumbing to his massaging touch.

"Not a contrary word, mayhap." His lips expressively came over mine as his caress left between my legs when his hand began stroking my naked thigh instead. He kissed me with warm, tender, passion when his shaking hands mindfully worked my shift up over my head completely off of me.

When his lips withdrew from mine, he stared at me as his palm gently cupped my breast and carefully began fondling it. I observed his eyes lowering toward his hand gently caressing my areola and nipple. He curiously gazed at the nipple he was carefully catching between his fingers. Then, his palm started drifting downward toward my flat stomach where it splayed and rested. I suddenly felt like I had been put on a bleak examining table as he overtly scrutinized me with roving eyes.

"What are you doing?" I whispered, feeling immensely embarrassed as I shrank away from him and automatically covered my arm over my breasts.

"Nae," he objected warmly.

"I don't want you to look at me."

"Yet, yoo're exquisite."

"Do you think so?"

"Without fault."

"But, I—"

"I want tae gaze upon ye."

"It's not like you've never seen a woman before, though."

"Yet, I have never seen ye till now, and I want tae see ye," he answered wondrously as I felt him coercing my arm away from covering my breasts.

"Still, why must you stare?" I responded insecurely.

"Yoo're mine now—my very own, *ceisdein*, and yoo're bonnie, that is why," he replied endearingly.

I didn't say anything in response except I relaxed my arm a bit, letting him remove it from my bare chest. He then softly lowered his lips and began trailing gentle kisses along my torso over my left breast. His tongue latched onto my erect nipple and ensued with suckling kisses. I instantly began feeling strange all over again. My temperature began rising. My blood turned hot and seared throughout my veins. My breath fluttered as his lips moved over my breast, and when I sensed his large muscular thigh push down between my legs, separating them. His second leg moved, further parting my thighs to accommodate himself when he suddenly released his suckling lips from my breast. Then, he lunged over my mouth with fervent kisses and dizziness spun my head.

"*Huh!*" I gasped abruptly between his kisses when suddenly I felt his shaft spreading me completely open, entering me and filling me from within. He carefully eased himself over me and sheathed himself to the root.

"*Och...*" Leif groaned feverishly. I could feel the heat coming from his shaking breath over my brow as he thrust between my legs. He mindfully withdrew and surged deeply inside of me, enabling me to sense every detail of his formidable shaft pushing against the ceiling of my cervix. "*Ceisd mo chridhe... ceisdein... mo ghaol*," he repeated in scraping tones as he deliberately pumped himself far inside me. He seized my gaze with his keen blue eyes and held me captive to his passion. "Say my name," he grunted heatedly above my lips as he receded from me.

I perceived him: he was powerful. He could be unrelenting. He was compelling me. He was tender and loving. And, he could overtake me at any moment according to his whim.

"Leif," I panted breathlessly between my heightened arousal.

"Aye," he moaned coarsely while withdrawing and surging again. "Say it again," he heaved scorchingly against my lips.

"Leif," I responded impulsively.

"Aye," he groaned thickly and plunged himself deeply once more.

"*Uh*," I wheezed unexpectedly. He seemed surprisingly farther within me when I thought he had already reached my end and could go no farther.

"Again," he grunted roughly upon his measured ebb.

"Leif," I gasped.

"That's it, *mo leannan, ceisd mo chridhe*," he uttered coarsely as he deliberately thrust himself.

Again, Leif passionately desired for me to call his name. I repeated it; so it went with every unhurried retreat and purposeful plunge. I realized as he moved deep within me that he would not have it any other way; he was silently speaking to me, and he wanted me to acknowledge him. The way he propelled himself was profound and stirring. He compelled me to see him; he induced me to be aware of his composition, to understand the nature of his gentleness, the reality of his raw openness, and the virtue of his uninhibited emotion as he freely abandoned himself to me.

With every tender thrust he drove to the limit inside me, he was making me starkly aware of myself and awakened my senses to him. It felt as if the edge of his shaft was methodically pushing past the physical point of my uterus straight into the center of my heart as he was shamelessly making love to me—and, he wanted me to love him back.

"Have I hurt ye?" he whispered worriedly, unexpectedly ceasing in mid movement.

"No—you haven't—why?" I panted, half dazed.

"Thaur are tears in yer eyes," he observed, concernedly as I sensed him tremulously hovering over me.

"Really?" I whispered unknowingly.

"Aye," he confirmed softly. I felt the pad of his thumb gently stroking the corner of my lashes when I realized a teardrop existed.

"Oh, I didn't know," I uttered breathlessly.

"Are ye certain that I huvnae hurt ye?"

"Yes, I'm sure. Please—don't stop."

He tenderly pressed his lips over mine, expressively kissed me with affection and care, and then resumed his visceral motion.

Leif continually drew my consciousness toward his, and I instinctively followed him. My body intrinsically reacted from his swelling touch, and my hips began taking me over as I grew consumed by his intensity. My blood coursed heatedly throughout my veins. I began feeling tingly all over, as if an electrical charge shocked me and pulsed recurrently deep through my abdomen with each thrust. My legs naturally wrapped around his hips, manifestly welcoming him, and incited his response with elevated vigor and strength. I felt as if I were mutating completely into molten liquid inside.

He surged enthusiastically far within, effectively pulling me with him along a vast escalation toward an imminent crevasse. I moaned desperately. I thought I was going to dissolve if I couldn't be released. Instead, he kept me hovering right at the brink of blissful annihilation in a lapse of time.

"*Tha gràdh agam ort,*" he heaved hoarsely above my feverish lips, and he pushed himself to the crest of my cavity. Suddenly, I felt like I was hit by a bolt of lightning from within, setting off a charge stimulating a chain reaction of multiple sensations of convulsing contractions right through the lower portion of my body. An uncontrollable tidal wave overtook me without warning and washed over my senses, sweeping me out into a turbulent sea of rupturing ecstasy. My thighs irrepressibly quaked around his loins as pulsating contractions seized the entire hollow within me. Leif growled coarsely against the side of my neck upon the expulsion of his surging release, and I sensed his groin convulse wildly between my trembling thighs in the wake of our simultaneous climax.

Instinctively, I tightly encircled my legs around him to keep him securely inside of me to receive the full intensity of the shock-waves encompassing me. He groaned again in the midst of his discharge, and I sensed him helplessly overrun just as I had become. We rode our thrilling pleasure-filled reverberations together as it diminished, which landed us both in a cushion of peace.

As reality was emerging around us again, we remained heatedly entwined together in the scope of our aftermath. My breathing was shallow and irregular as I felt him heaving heavily when he collapsed over me. His skin was warm and moist with perspiration as I lightly stroked his bare, broad back. I lay there listening to his breathing and feeling the deep flowing expansion and retraction of his chest resting over me, wondering how this could all be true—staying as we were, lying together connected in ensuing contented, unbroken silence.

AFTER A MOMENT, Leif lifted his gaze to me and tenderly grinned. His lips affectionately pressed over mine, then he bestowed warm kisses over my chin and cheek. He returned looking at me and stared keenly into my eyes, as I noticed his ruddy masculine cheeks were bright red.

"Did I satisfy ye?" he inquired sheepishly.

"Yes, very much," I whispered.

"I am heartened," he responded softly. His gently stroking

fingers caressed my brow until they buried deeply among my loose ringlets. "It greatly pleases me that yoo're mine now," he uttered gratifyingly.

"It does?" I replied mutually, still suspended in a dreamy afterglow while gazing back into his eyes.

"More than ye may ever truly ken," he said while sensing him idly fondling my lengthy curls between his fingers. "I wanted ye the moment I first set eyes upon ye—the day ye came from the wood upon the road as our company marched. I had tae have ye... I kent that I had tae take ye fur my own. So, I gave chase efter ye intae the wood tae steal ye back from the Huron who captured ye... I was determined not tae let ye vanish from me."

"Really?" I responded amazedly, noticing his absorbed expression.

"Aye," he said. "Now I have ye... all tae myself." It seemed he did, and I couldn't refute it. He paused slightly while maintaining his concentrated gaze on me. "*Mo ghaol*," he murmured against my lips, gently kissing me again. He subsequently disengaged himself from me, and I felt myself emptying from him as he shifted off to the side. He naturally wrapped an arm around my waist and pulled me snug against him, fitting me into his side.

The new rings over my finger glimmering in the firelight caught my eye. I reached over and absentmindedly toyed with them while lying in his arms. I remembered the wound on my hand, and I turned my palm over observing the dried blood that had leached and drawn through the dressing. I wondered about it again. Leif's hand moved over my injury as he mindfully enveloped my palm with his and raised it into view. He silently gazed at it for a minute.

"What was this for?" I inquired.

"I made us take an oath," he said.

"What kind of oath?"

"One which bonds us till death."

"Oh... So, a verbal contract wasn't sufficient?" I joked lightly. He shifted a serious glance toward me regarding my faint irony.

"Nae," he said absolutely. "It had tae be done in this manner. Whit is betwixt us had tae be sealed in bluid—it will never be torn asunder unless by God."

"Oh..." I replied contemplatively. "What did you say—in the oath?"

He glanced back at my fingers and the stained dressing among his hand. He began uttering the translation of his words, and they flowed from his lips:

"On this night, never longer two are we. You and I become one. With these words, transformed are we. With this blade, I shed my bluid fur thee.
"Tae thee I pledge willingly: forever my fidelity, my truth, my armor, my service, my honor.
"Never will I cause thee threat. Never will I cause thee harm by a traitorous arm. Never will I forsake thee; tae thee I make this vow from my soul solemnly.
"My bluid tae thine. Thy bluid tae mine. Together we are ever one from this time henceforth.
"Thus, I welcome death mine tae receive, if ever I pass falsely unto thee. For thou art mine tae have and tae hold through God's will fur eternity."

When Leif finished telling me what was spoken in the oath, chills crept bizarrely over my skin. I was fundamentally struck by the literal core meaning of those pledging words. I found it extremely intense, unyielding, and gripping with personal conviction and intent—and haunting. I wasn't exactly sure how to digest, or interpret, the frightening depth of his expression.

"That's pretty profound," I commented dryly.

"Marriage is profound," Leif replied.

"Yes, I suppose it is," I acknowledged while observing him still examining my dried blood stained bandage in his attentive hand. He carefully replaced my palm over my stomach and scooped an arm beneath me, effectively turning me over to face him.

"Thus, yoo're mine now, *àille dhubh*," he declared, closely staring into my eyes.

"I guess so," I said nervously. I sensed his large fingers skimming the back of my hand up along my arm, over my shoulder, passed my clavicle until it rested possessively upon my breast.

"I ken so," he said unwaveringly.

"You do?" I asked insecurely, feeling him fondling my nipple with pleasure.

"I do," he said warmly.

"How do you know that?"

"Weel, I have ye, do I not?" His eyebrow arched, and his lips tilted with a quizzical expression.

"It looks like you do," I replied nervously.

"In which case, I can bed ye upon any occasion that I wish."

"Is that right?"

"Aye."

"Oh?"

"Mayhap at present fur instance."

Leif readily shifted around me, coercing me onto my back again. Looming over me with apparent desire, he wedged his knees between mine, separating them far apart.

"Holy cow! You certainly don't waste any time, do you?" I remarked with a little insecure giggle.

"Yoo're culpable."

"How's that?"

"The way ye make me crave ye."

"How do I do that?"

"By yer charm. Now, come haur," he responded huskily as he gripped his hands around my hips. He abruptly tugged me away from the pillows toward him in the center of the bed, and leaned over me, pressing gentle kisses over my face and lips. I suddenly gasped and he groaned hoarsely as he pushed himself into me. He completely sheathed himself in my depths and filled me to the brim like before.

He began stirring, ebbing and flowing with gentle ease far inside me. I moaned as he moved deliberately. He was arousing my deep emotional response, and we connected; our consciousness fused. We were innately aware of each other. With every thrust my breath fluttered, and my hips responsively met his. He responded and drove himself further into me, endeavoring to reach my pleasurable response. He fed my reaction. I reflected his. I found myself in the midst of a swirling tide of elevating enjoyable angst while he worked to gratify himself and bring about ultimate satisfaction. I spontaneously encircled my legs around his hips, and my palms artlessly flung tightly over his animated buttocks merely to savor the raw sensation of each wanting plunge of his filling shaft.

Suddenly, my depths began rocking my awareness in consuming rapture. My body quaked uncontrollably, and I drowned as my vaginal walls clamped down on him, madly convulsing. He groaned thickly as he buried his face into my long ringlets upon the climatic expulsion of his blissful end. I sensed him throbbing intensely between my thighs and filling me with his essence as it poured from him. I pulsated wildly from within and held him close while interlaced in his seizing embrace, riding the abating shockwaves together.

When reality descended, he collapsed over me breathing heavily into my neck. I enfolded my arms around his shoulders and sensed his heated, damp skin as I hid my fingers in his loose, long, silky, golden strands at the nape of his neck. I kissed his shoulder and listened to his warm breathing as it caressed my neck while we lay there together in our silent afterglow.

"I'm certain ye will be the death of me," he uttered hoarsely against my neck after a passing moment. "Yet, I shall die a blissful man."

"Well, you're a young enough guy. You seem like you'd be able to handle it," I teased brazenly.

Leif's gaze suddenly popped up over mine. He lightly chuckled and shook his head in disbelief.

"Till then, ye will come tae see how precise I can *handle it*, wife," he forewarned jeeringly.

"If tonight is any indication, then, I guess I'm really looking forward to your proving so," I bantered back.

"With pleasure," he responded like a scoundrel and suddenly bent over my neck with a growl, playfully taking a fake bite like a demonic vampire as I squealed. Chuckling, he seized me by the waist and pulled me over him as he rolled onto his back. He raised his hands to the sides of my face and caressed his thumbs over my cheeks, tucking my obscuring ringlets tendrils dangling over my face carefully behind my ears. Still engaged as I lay above him, his hands affectionately roamed down my back over the rump of my buttocks and thighs, then back up again. "*Ceisd mo chridhe,*" he said to me, "let's rest now, *mo ghaol.*"

"Okay," I agreed softly. He smothered his hand in my curls at the back of my head and tenderly compelled my lips down over his for one more kiss. I shifted a little making myself more comfortable over him, and placed my head on his chest just beneath his chin. He naturally wrapped an arm around my waist, securing me over him, and easily crooked his other arm behind his head against the pillows.

I closed my eyes listening to the rhythm of his heart beating soundly within his chest, and I began drifting into a soothing, blissful dream with him still inside of me.

Four

I awakened this morning to the faint touch of Leif's fingers tracing a petite area at the small of my back just above the cleft of my buttocks. I drowsily turned my head from the pillows and faced him. He smiled warmly at me, causing me to smile in return.

"Guid morrow," he greeted gently.

"Good morning," I replied.

"Have I awakened ye?" he asked as his hand lightly stroked my buttocks.

"Um-hm, but it's okay," I said sleepily. He glanced at the area where his fingers were languidly tracing above my tailbone.

"How bonnie ye are," he stated, then mindfully urged me onto my back so now I faced him hovering over me. "Yoo're unique." He seemed struck with intrigue and I smiled at him as I sensed his knees pushing my legs far apart while he maneuvered himself between my thighs.

"Why do you suppose I'm unique?" I inquired.

"I cannae say. Yoo're a mystery tae me," he answered heatedly above my lips.

"Am I?" I uttered with bated breath when he purposefully

adjusted himself and sensed the tip of his shaft at my entrance right before he surged deeply inside of me.

"Ye are indeed mysterious. The only notion of that I am awaur, is I merely ken that I am spellbound by ye, and I want ye—always," he said hoarsely as he rested over me without stirring. "I yielded tae my weakness fur ye the nicht we embraced in the cave when I first pressed my lips upon yers... I kent then that ye understood whit I felt fur ye. Do ye recall?"

"Yes, I remember," I whispered breathlessly.

"Aye..." he groaned as he now began moving within me. "As I kissed ye thaur in the cave, I thought ye also wanted me at that moment..." He attentively fixed his gaze over mine, holding my attention captive. Locking his eyes to mine, he drove himself unbound deep within me, causing me to feel things I never thought I'd ever feel again. Assorted emotions began swelling inside of me that I couldn't arrange or reason with while he unrestrictedly expressed his physical emotions for me. "Do ye want me now, *mo ghaol?*" he heaved warmly, kissing my cheek with meaning.

"Yes," I panted. My hips responded to his motion, and the deep-seated aching for him ensued burning inside me.

"Tell me so again," he desired coarsely. He pushed himself with careful ease reaching farther into my depths with each deliberate surge, compelling me to further release myself to him and forget my mind.

"Yes..." I scarcely uttered.

"Aye, whit...?" he pursued the question as he expressively moved. I was beginning to buckle and surrender beneath him as he intentionally meant for me to subside.

"Yes, I want you, Leif," I admitted, acknowledging my need for him.

"*Aye,*" he groaned hoarsely, searing my ear.

Suddenly, my thighs started uncontrollably quaking and my insides sharply convulsed like crazy amid his moaning as he expelled his hot essence into me. Usurped by my own trembling climatic release, my thighs shook wildly as my cervix pulsated. Contractions radiated in distinct, blissful currents as I sensed him throbbing forcefully between my legs.

Subsequently, Leif abruptly gave way and collapsed over me, succumbing to lifelessness by the peacefulness that overcame him immediately afterward instead.

"Sylvie... Sylvie... *mo leannan*..."

I suddenly roused from slumber in a fog, realizing Leif was leaning over me with concern on his face.

"What's wrong?" I asked confusedly as I drowsily gazed up at him.

"Ye waur weeping in yer sleep," he said softly. He gently cleared my ringlet strands from my brow and stroked the side of my face.

"I was?" I asked strangely.

"Aye."

"I'm sorry. Did I awaken you?"

"Nae matter," he disregarded.

"I didn't mean to wake you," I regretted, feeling silently troubled now.

"Shhh," he hushed and drew me close to him. He fitted me snug against his warm naked body, securely spooning me with him.

I felt like crying and I tried subduing it, but a silent tear crept from my lashes and rolled over my cheek.

"Please don't ever leave me," I beseeched him under my breath.

"I shall perish before ever leaving ye," he said in a soft tone close to my ear. He squeezed me tighter against him and kissed the back of my head.

"I was five months pregnant when Matt died," I sniffled. "I never told you that."

"Ye didnae."

"I—I don't talk about it at all. It's just too hard for me to have to remember."

"Och... *mo ghaol*... I am heartbroken fur ye."

"He risked his life to save me from being run over as we were crossing the street together... He pushed me out of the way so that I wouldn't have gotten hit by the oncoming vehicle... I fell... I didn't realize he had died until after the doctor had told me about my miscarriage," I sniveled as I recalled my worst life experience.

"*Ceisdein...*" Leif lightly clasped my chin between his thumb and forefinger, turning my gaze to meet his benevolent expression. "I can merely imagine the forlorn sadness that has been brought upon yer heart. I ken whit it means tae have lost a loov'd one once my father passed away. Ken that I shall always be with ye. Pray, remember it. Yoo're safe with me. Do ye understand? Yoo're safe. I shall never leave ye," he guaranteed.

He dried away my silent tears from my cheeks with his thumb, then repositioned me on my side. He fitted me close to himself and cradled me in his secure embrace. The knot in my throat began dispelling, and I lay there quietly encircled by him with his arm stretched over mine, realizing that I felt comforted, safe and sound with him.

I lightly sensed his fingers mindlessly playing with my new wedding rings on my finger, and I relaxedly observed his large hand covering mine as he laced his fingers among my own.

"They're really pretty," I commented appreciatively, regarding the rings he gave me.

"Do ye approve of them?" he inquired.

"Yes, very much," I said.

"I'm pleased," he said close behind my ear.

"This one has our names on it," I recognized as I admiringly touched the top band.

"I wished it so."

"That's nice. I like it."

"I had it fashioned in Boston in time."

"Boston?"

"Aye, when Fin departed us in Northampton tae travel tae Boston. I gave him my request tae do so when he was going tae have the papers drawn fur our wedding efter his meeting with Governor Shirley."

"Oh, how nice."

His thumb continued lightly rolling over the rings, and the sensation was soothing. "This one was given tae my father by my grandfather," he disclosed as his index finger touched the ruby one.

"It's really lovely," I acknowledged admiringly.

"I received it upon my father's death," he informed me.

"Oh—I'm sorry that your father's no longer living," I said compassionately.

"I as weel."

"So, you had a good relationship with your father, then?"

"We waur fond of one anither. He was a guid father tae me, and I an obedient son tae him."

"That's really good. You're fortunate."

"I am."

"When did your father die?"

"'Tis eleven years now since his death."

"How did he die?"

"He was murdered."

"*Murdered?*" I suddenly shot up from Leif's embrace, starkly astounded and alarmed. I sat among the blankets staring at him with a bizarre, far-out expression.

"Aye, he was murdered at nicht whilst he slept in his bed," Leif revealed to me.

"Are you serious?" I asked unbelievably, studying the sober look on his face now.

"Unfortunately—quite earnest," he replied gravely.

"I've never heard of such a thing. I mean, I have—but, I've never known anyone to be a victim of such a heinous crime. My

God—that's insane. What happened?" I was staggered by this information, and I blatantly gaped at him with incredulity.

"It was fur political purposes," he said.

"Political reasons?" I questioned unbelievably.

"Aye," he replied and took a considerable breath. He sat up from the blankets and repositioned himself better, propped against the pillows. "Ye must understand. My father was reared favorably by the Duke of York, James Stewart, as an illegitimate son of his... and, as he was treated fondly by the duke, he often traveled with him tae visit his uncle, the king—"

"Wait a minute," I interrupted indelicately, "please excuse my naïveté, but are you telling me you're related to a monarch?" I was stunned, because in spite of Leif's title, nobility did not mean anything to me and carried no weight in the society from where I came. So, I never really considered his position before now.

"I'm related tae several sovereigns, in truth," Leif replied actually. I looked at him incredulously, wondering how this was possible.

"Okay, so, would you be related to Henry the Eighth?" I inquired curiously.

"He is my great, great, great uncle," Leif disclosed. I couldn't believe what I was hearing as I stared at him. It was a surreal feeling.

"I see," I replied in spite of my ignorance.

"Why are ye surprised when ye ken that I am a duke?" he asked curiously. I shrugged my shoulder a little, not wanting to tell him the reason for it. He thoughtfully stroked my bare shoulder with a gentle forefinger before he started to say, "My bluid-line is as far traced tae Robert the Bruce through my father and grandfather, as my grandfather chose tae recognize my father as his son upon his birth in the year of our Lord sixteen seventy one, October thirty first," Leif revealed to me.

"My goodness," I said under my breath in mere disbelief.

"Upon my uncle, King Charles the Second's death, my grandfather, his rightful heir, succeeded the throne as King James the Second of England, Scotland and Ireland," Leif continued explaining. I nodded my head in acknowledgement, trying to seem historically aware. "Ye see, whilst at times my uncle's reign might have been contentious with parliament, he was a Protestant and treaded lightly tae maintain peace betwixt Protestants and Papists. Thaur was much Protestant suspicion over Papists—as it still remains... My great uncle was a religiously tolerant king, and he tried tae have it so that all would be tolerant. However, once the plot tae have him and my grandfather murdered was discovered, the king dissolved parliament and preferred absolutism tae rule with order."

"Um-hm," I replied, closely listening to Leif with interest.

"Hence, when my grandfather succeeded the throne upon his brother's death, he was soon deposed merely three years later by a union of parliamentarians who didnae agree with his primary belief in the Devine Right of Kings, and that he was a Papist amongst other concerns... My father was a loyal son of King James's—he supported and fought with him in battle against William of Orange... But, the king was defeated... and William and Mary took the throne, as ye ken."

"Right."

"Thereafter, my father fled tae France with the king and his many supporters."

"I see."

"Yet sometime later, my father returned tae the Highlands as a silent emissary fur his father tae acquire support fur his return."

"Really?"

"Aye. Efter a number of thwarted attempts tae restore the Stewarts, my father continued tae pursue support fur the Jacobite Cause. A missive had been sent from the Highland lairds that they would unite, and the battle took place at Culloden in forty-five, but the Cause was defeated... The next year my father was discovered in his bed with his throat slit," Leif solemnly explained.

I stared at him, speechless. I could not believe what I was hearing, and it took me a moment to process what he was telling me.

"So, you're a prince?" I asked, suspended in amazement. Leif smiled gently at me.

"Aye," he responded modestly.

"Wow," I muttered.

"Yoo're truly surprised, fur I can plainly see."

"Yes, of course. I never knew. You never told me anything about your parents."

"Aye, I reckon not."

"Yeah—you didn't."

"Yet, ye ken that I am a duke."

"Yes, well—but, still, your title never really registered with me... I just assume that people are simply people regardless of social class. Those sorts of things don't influence me."

"Do they not?" Now, he was the one looking at me with abrupt astonishment.

"Not at all."

"I see..." he replied thinkingly, still appearing quite surprised. "Weel, 'tis just as weel. I'm pleased that ye waur ignorant of my being a prince."

"Why?"

"I would raither have a lass wed me fur the man that I am than fur my wealth and position alone."

"Right. That's very understandable. I would want that too."

"Aye."

"So, do you know who killed your father?" I asked, feeling parched.

"An illegitimate son of the Duke of Argyll," Leif said.

"Was he apprehended?"

"Aye."

"Did the case go to trial?"

"He was never tried."

"Why not?"

"He openly admitted his guilt in the MacDonald court upon his capture whaur the trial was tae take place… and whaur he challenged me in public."

"He threatened you?"

"Aye. He said that I was next tae meet my father's fate."

"Oh, my goodness!"

"Aye… Weel, now, as it was, the guilty man was never tried due tae a MacDonald clansman who rushed him from within the Great Hall before I could reach tae slit the murderer's throat myself. The clansman took the opportunity tae pierce him in the heart instead with his own dirk. My father's murderer dropped dead on the instant, and that was the end of it," Leif remembered.

"Holy cow…" I whispered meditatively, utterly shocked. "So, where were you and your mother when your father was working on your grandfather's behalf?"

"I never kent my mother," Leif replied.

"You didn't?" I was surprised.

"She passed away once I was born," he said.

"Oh, I see—that's really sad. I'm so sorry to hear that," I said sympathetically.

"Thank ye. I have often wondered whit it would have been like tae have knoon her," he said.

"I'm sure."

"Whit I ken is whit my father had told me of her."

"So, what do you know?"

"She was bonnie. She had golden hair."

"Like yours?"

"Aye."

"What else?"

"She was quite young when she passed away—merely twenty years of age."

"Oh! That is very young. But, wait—isn't Finley older than you by several years?"

"Aye, thaur is five years difference betwixt us."

"Really?" I responded with added surprise.

"She wed at fifteen."

"Fifteen?"

"Aye."

"That's very young."

"Indeed."

"What was her name?"

"Ceana Stewart of Atholl. She wed James MacLeod, her cousin, a son of the MacLeod chieftain," Leif informed me.

"I see... So, that's why you and Finley have two different last names," I realized apparently.

"Aye," Leif said, nodding his head a bit. "My mother's first husband caught a fever and perished three years efter she bore Fin."

"Yeah, I remember Finley mentioning that earlier."

"Aye. Weel, my father met my mother soon efter Fin's father's passing when he returned tae Scotland from France upon visiting Laird MacLeod as emissary... and, my mother's uncle merely agreed tae the match upon condition their offspring be reared by him till school age."

"So, you spent part of your childhood with your uncle?" I inquired curiously.

"Aye, I spent a portion of my youth at Donvegan Castle with Fin," Leif said.

"Then, when would you ever see your dad?"

"Upon his visits whilst he pertained tae matters in the Highlands."

"Oh... Well, tell me about your grandmother—your father's mother. Do you know anything about her?"

"I do. Her name was Muirne MacLeod. I was told that she was a young bonnie lass when she met the Duke of York at his court... and, although she was already wed with a young bairn of her own, the Duke of York made her a lady in waiting fur the duchess. Not long efter, he took her as a mistress, and soon my father was born... she perished promptly efter bearing my father," Leif explained.

"That's so sad," I acknowledged sympathetically.

"Aye," he agreed.

I broke off, and there was a slight pause between us. Leif smiled affectionately at me, and I noticed how his eyes always seemed to twinkle whenever he acknowledged me in this regard.

"So," I started again, feeling insecure. "You're a duke—and a prince—obviously."

"By blood I am a prince," he replied with a gentle smile. "I own titles and lands—bequeathed by my grandfather tae my father and bestowed tae me upon my father's death."

"I see—of course," I responded awkwardly, and Leif nodded his head a bit.

"Fin was granted Earl of Kneep upon his father's death," he mentioned.

"Right," I understood.

"Aye."

"So..."

"So..."

"Yeah..."

"Aye... Ye have wed and bedded the Duke of Monteith who happens tae be a prince," he said modestly. I paused momentarily, simply staring at him. "Ye are surprised, I can see," Leif observed.

"Well, yes—I just never imagined it," I replied honestly.

"Nae?" He continued looking at me with significant astonishment also.

"No."

"Och."

"I never knew the details... You never really said anything to me about your family," I said again.

"Aye. I suppose that I didnae."

"You're actually kind of understated about your social status."

"I reckon that I try tae be so."

"Why?"

"I dinnae fancy flaunting my nobility."

"It seems like most people in your position present their social level without any reservation. But, you don't see it that way?"

"Nae... I find whilst my eminence grants me wealth and prominence above others, I feel that I am nae better than any other honest man of lesser stature... and, it has also brought me significant political and mortal peril... 'Tis a misperception tae believe thaur is liberty amongst the landed aristocracy. If I could have the reit tae my wealth and privilege without risking my honor and liberty, then I should be pleased tae have it," Leif explained.

"I can understand that," I acknowledged.

"I believe all men have the reit tae honestly pursue liberty and prosperity without risk of imprisonment or death."

"I certainly agree with that."

"Aye, weel... Do ye realize this discussion betwixt us would be considered treasonous by the Crown?"

"Why? Because we're simply expressing our opinion?"

"Aye—and, I'm a Stewart expressing it."

"Oh... Well, would it shock you if I not only told you that I believe in freedom of speech without reprisal, but also in the right to religious freedom without punishment?"

"Aye, somewhat it does surprise me," Leif replied with a slight grin. "Now I certainly ken that I have a wee rebel upon my hands."

"Maybe so," I joked lightly. A brief chuckle escaped him as a quizzical look on his face lingered.

"I reckon ye and I have been quite informal with one anither upon our first meeting," Leif recognized.

"Yes, I think so..."

"I had made ye an exception once I first laid eyes upon ye in the wood."

"You did?"

"Aye."

"Why?"

"I wanted ye, that is why."

"Oh..."

"I admire that we speak plainly with one anither."

"Yeah, I like that very much too." I paused for a second as he maintained his steady gaze on me. A little grin crept over my face as a self-conscious thought entered my mind. "But—does this mean that I have to call you my lord? Because, I haven't been calling you that."

Leif's blonde eyebrow arched high above his sparkling blue gaze, and the corner of his lips slanted upward.

"As well ye ought not. Regard me as Your Grace, and I am indeed yer laird and master. As such, ye will serve me as I deem fit," he said as he slipped an arm around my waist and coerced me back against the pillows.

"Well, um, what do you deem fit?" I replied coyly. He suddenly rolled over me, causing me to release a nervous giggle while I sensed him pushing my thighs apart with his knee.

"I reckon this fit," he said affectionately as he shifted himself above me. My breath caught when he took his ready shaft and parted my cleft, easing himself fully extended inside of me. He remained still between my legs purely gazing into my eyes with adoration as the pad of his thumb lightly caressed the ridge of my lips.

"What is it?" I wondered.

"It has presently occurred tae me that I dinnae reckon that I ken yer proper age," he said thoughtfully.

"I'm thirty-three," I told him.

"I beg yer pardon?" Leif's eyes suddenly widened as he gazed at me with a gaping expression mixed with utter wonderment and astonishment.

"I'm thirty-three," I reiterated sincerely.

"That cannae be," he responded with sheer amazement. I couldn't help it, but his goofy expression of stark surprise displayed sheerly across his face made me giggle.

"Why? How old did you think I was?" I asked, amused.

"Weel," he started, seeming a little embarrassed.

"C'mon, tell me," I encouraged.

"I reckoned ye were eighteen," Leif admitted abashedly.

"*Eighteen?*" I repeated remarkably and suddenly cracked up laughing hilariously. "Holy cow, you've gotta be kidding me!"

"Quite honestly, it is whit I believed," he responded genuinely.

"I'm sorry—I'm not making fun of you. It's just—that's really funny, since no one's ever told me that before. Wow—I have to say that you've really made my day! Thank you!" I said, trying to control my laughter.

"Yoo're welcome," he replied bewilderedly. "When is yer birthday?"

"It's December twenty-fourth."

"Christmas Eve?"

"Um-hm." I nodded my head while smiling at him.

"Why, it is merely less than a month from the present," he calculated keenly.

"Yeah, I suppose so." I was suddenly amazed by how quickly time was passing since my arrival here, and I stopped smiling.

"Then, we are closely a year and a half apart," he computed swiftly.

"Who's older?" I asked.

"I am eldest."

"So, you're thirty-five?"

"Aye."

"When's your birthday?"

"The day of Beltane."

"May Day?"

"Aye."

"How nice."

"I never imagined that we are so close in age."

"You don't like it?"

"On the contrary—I have a wife who appears as young as a

bonnie maiden, but has scruples as a mature lass. So, I shall not complain," Leif expressed delightedly as if he had scored big and hit the jackpot. I felt his warm hand sensitively stroking the side of my face. His fingers caressed my jaw and chin, down my neck, across my clavicle and around my shoulder along the length of my arm. "How is it that yer skin is smooth as silk?" he wondered marvelously.

"I don't know," I said quietly. His hand moved up toward my face again, and his fingers gently caught my ringlet strands splayed over the pillow.

"Yer tresses are soft as mink—mirk as ebony, and glisten like water beneath moonlicht... and thaur isnae a single flaw upon yer bonnie face," he examined. "Yer eyes smile even when ye do not, and they are as green as fresh spring leaves... It is truly mesmerizing... Yer teeth are perfectly aligned and whiter than pearls—like none I have ever seen—and ye huvnae lost a single tooth... Such fine features thaur are upon ye...Yer bonnie lips are full, soft and round... and the color of yer skin is swarthy, but not like a Negro's and lighter than a mulatto's—thaur is red in it, however yoo're not like the Indian lasses of these parts either. It seems yer coloring is more like golden sand by a desert sea... My word—ye are the bonniest lass upon which I have ever laid eyes."

Leif proceeded moving freely and deeply inside of me with real emotion. He zealously drove himself, and I moaned. I craved him. I wanted him all and completely to myself too. So, I consumed his giving kisses. I eagerly received each distinctive aching thrust he measuredly drove into me.

"*Och*," he heaved heatedly, brushing his lips over mine. "My bonnie, bonnie lass—wife of mine... Ye will not be content unless I award ye with whit ye wish, is that not so?"

"Yes..." I panted very much in escalating need.

"*Mmm*," he groaned in rasping undertones. I was growing anxious and greedy, but he held me gently at bay with every deliberate surge under his control and forced my patience. "Do ye see now how ye long fur me...?" he grunted coarsely.

"Yes..." I panted, catching my breath.

"It will never vanish—we are bonded... I shall have and keep ye. Yoo're mine now—entirely mine, *mo ghaol*. Do ye understand?" he groaned thickly as he keenly plunged himself so far into my depths, I lost my breath.

"Yes," I whispered unevenly, half aware as my thoughts floated away from me.

"Aye," he uttered in a gravelly voice and pumped himself with further zeal, encouraging the physical urgency beginning to consume me.

My breath escaped me as my hips instinctively rocked with his ardent movement. The crescendo was within reach. A little whine fluttered from my lips, and Leif groaned roughly against my feverish neck. All of a sudden, my depths quivered as I was sent into flight filled with ecstasy, and my thighs began uncontrollably shaking during Leif's throbbing release as his essence pumped from him and filled me. In a moment, he collapsed limp, breathing heavily over me.

"Aye... Ye and I agree weel with one anither," he muttered once he returned his gaze to mine. He gave a tender kiss over my lips and withdrew between my legs as he shifted beside me. His arm wrapped possessively around my waist when he gently tugged me close and tucked me against him. His hand rested peacefully over me as it naturally cupped my breast, and I lay there relaxed among the blankets and pillows, spooning safely with him in shrouding calm.

Five

Sometime later in the morning, I awakened from my
slumber with my head comfortably resting on Leif's shoulder, still encircled in his arms. He remained sleeping, and I
lay there quietly looking at him. A portion of his golden head
caught the silent winter sunlight entering the window, and the
loose strands cradling his face shimmered like gilded foil. I was
tempted to lift a finger to the long strands perfectly amassed over
his shoulders. His strands were straight, smooth, and soft as they
lightly flipped between my observing fingers, perfectly supple and
lovely.

I glanced past the beautiful hair around his head and
observed his broad, gently sloping brow. There were already
several faintly inset lines stretching across his forehead which
only became apparent when he appeared surprised. His silky, soft
eyebrows matched his yellow locks. Except, the eyebrow hair
seemed to darken slightly toward the glabella, the part of the
forehead just above the nose between the eyebrows, which made
his eyebrows seem petite. His closed eyelashes were thick and

oddly lighter than the hair upon his head that resembled platinum. Crow's feet were detectable at the corner of his eyes and showed distinctly when he laughed or smiled, brightening his expression with distinguishable heartfelt warmth. I lightly traced my forefinger down the ridge of his flawlessly straight, narrow nose. He had a prominent nose bridge raised high above his face and attractively sloped at a gentle gradient like images of Augustus Caesar's.

My finger carefully rounded the tip of his nose and gently sank into the deep groove of his Cupid's bow just above his upper lip. His lips were slightly full and soft—and rather pink, I noticed. I found them to be very attractive as I continued to trace downward past his bottom lip, across his stubbly cleft chin. His jaw was rugged and square and complemented his high cheekbones.

His chest was large, square, lean, and noticeably cut with muscles. A thin patch of blonde hair covered his upper chest and felt soft between my fingers. I traced his sculpted arm muscles and sensed the smooth, slightly long hair over his forearm tickling my palm.

"Hullo, *àille dhubh*," Leif muttered softly with his eyes scarcely opening. He smiled languidly at me.

"Hi," I said gently, smiling back at him.

"Yer tooch feels lovely," he murmured, gazing at me through the slits of his eyes.

"It does?"

"Mmm, aye... ye indulge me."

"That's nice," I said, sensing the favorable touch of his hand tenderly stroking the side of my naked hip and upper thigh.

"Is it not?" he said sleepily.

My stomach suddenly gave a little rumble, and I realized how hungry I was. The wound on my hand also began to feel sensitive, and I sat up from the covers.

"Ye must certainly be ravenous at present," he recognized, also stirring from the blankets.

"I could probably eat a horse," I acknowledged casually as I started unraveling the soiled dressing from around my hand.

"Fur mercy's sake! We dinnae wish fur that tae occur," he said bizarrely.

"No," I replied amusedly.

"Whit a horrid notion."

"I didn't mean literally."

"I pray not," he said. "I shall prevent any such occurrence and return with a hearty meal fur Her Grace."

"How sweet, but I don't mind getting something for us to munch on," I offered freely while watching him remove himself from bed.

"Nae, nae—I shall be the one tae gather us a meal," he insisted, now standing naked near the edge of the bed.

"It's really no big deal for me. You just woke up, and you were so comfortably lying in bed."

"Thank ye all the same, *ceisdein*. However, I dinnea believe ye will much appreciate being seen by the lads," he informed me as he proceeded wrapping himself in his banyan.

"What are you talking about?" I asked unexpectedly.

"The lads, of coorse," he replied obviously.

"Yeah, I heard you. How can those guys still be here?" I was clearly shocked as I observed him tying the belt to his banyan around his waist.

"They had a festive celebration."

"Obviously. I thought they would've all gone by now."

"Scarcely—they are tae billet haur fur the winter."

"You're joking?"

"I fear not."

"Oh, my gosh…! Well, then I guess we're just not going to have any privacy."

Leif gave me a pitiful grin as he moved to sit on the edge of the bed next to me. I felt his large hands gently coming over my shoulders and caressing them.

"I promise ye shall have ample discretion once we arrive in Boston," he guaranteed understandingly.

"Boston?" This was somewhat of a surprise as I gave him a strange look.

"Aye."

"When are we going to Boston?"

"We shall depart in less than a fortnecht."

"Why?"

"I have property thaur, and I reckoned ye might better prefer the city. We shall come tae reside at *Taigh Gràs*."

"Oh... I guess I would like that. I didn't know that you had property in Boston," I said, considering the nice idea.

"Aye. I acquired it as an investment once I first arrived haur in the colony," he informed me.

"Oh. But, what about Amity? She's made a lot of progress in her learning, and I'd hate to see that suddenly interrupted."

"I shall speak tae Fin regarding it."

"Okay."

Leif smiled warmly at me and affectionately stroked the side of my cheek. My eyes dropped from his to the dressing in my hand over my lap among the blankets still partly covering me. The wound was slightly red and a tad swollen. It hurt only a little, to my surprise, given the depth of the cut. He cupped his palm around the back of my hand and carefully stroked his thumb over the clotted blood along my palm. He lifted the injury to his lips and pressed a tender kiss on it.

"Does it ail?" he asked.

"Not really," I answered.

"I'm pleased."

"I just need to keep it disinfected, and it'll be good as new. We should do the same with yours and change your bandage," I suggested.

"As ye wish—once I have returned with a meal fur us tae eat. Nae wife of mine will wish tae devour a horse in place of a proper meal, or go tae waste without one so long as I'm alive tae forbid it."

He slid his forefinger beneath my chin and drew my lips to his with a tender peck. Releasing me from his little kiss, he then proceeded to withdraw from the room. Almost instantaneously after vanishing behind the bedroom door, an abrupt uproarious round of cheers and applause shouted brazenly throughout the corridor, with more echoing loudly from below on the first floor. The house full of men was unabashed and blatant in their clapping and cheering. Hearing their vociferous approval, I froze sitting in bed. Sudden and deep mortification filled me while I listened to them boisterously praising Leif. I couldn't believe my ears and wanted the earth to spare me by opening up and swallowing me whole.

I swung my feet over the edge of the blankets and took my shift from the foot of the bed where it had been carelessly thrown last night. I tossed it over my head and pulled my arms through the sleeves, then stepped across the room. As I paced toward the privy closet, I sensed the dampness from Leif's aftermath running between my legs, and it abruptly occurred to me that I had surely thrown all caution to the wind. I was fundamentally terrified of becoming pregnant in this hazardous day and age. There were so many perils to pregnancy, and the thought of becoming pregnant now deeply worried me.

There was a real possibility that I could have become pregnant. It had only taken me once with Matt to have conceived. I typically ovulated early after my menstrual cycle, and it literally only took the second day after my period for us to have become pregnant. I swallowed hard, forcing my dry throat to gulp down the alarming realization. I wished that I could have remembered the date of my last period, but I couldn't recall it. It must have been at least a couple of weeks ago, I speculated. If I were lucky, then I could experience my cycle again soon within the next fourteen days. So, I was forced to sit tight, and wait on pins and needles before the end of the month when I'd really know what was actually going on with my body.

In the meantime, I thought it would be wise to exercise some kind of birth control outside of using sheep condoms, which were due to fail for certain—not to mention the fact that it would likely raise an issue with Leif. He seemed the sort of man who would be very disinclined to practice such caution.

Instead, I needed something personal and discreet, and that was not likely to raise any questions. So, I thought of constructing a ring of cycle beads for myself in order to chart my fertility. It was easier to do it this way instead of having to record on paper via the calendar, since the days for me often became confused. Plus, there would be no paper trail to consider, which guaranteed privacy. Also, since I was familiar with using this natural method of birth control with previous success in preventing pregnancy with Matt before we had decided to get married, I presumed that I would have the same secure result in this case now.

WHEN I RETURNED from the privy closet and proceeded to wash my hands in the washbasin over the dresser, I was surprised to see Leif stretched out over the covers already arrived with a large spread of food on a sizable ebony tray placed in the middle of the bed.

"My goodness! It looks like we're having a picnic," I remarked, impressively gazing at the bounty beside him. He grinned at me in response.

"Come haur, then," he said and lightly patted the space next to himself for me to sit on the bed. I eagerly paced across the room and hopped onto the blankets beside him. He poured a mug of apple cider, and held it out for me to take. I received it and promptly sipped. It felt warm going down my throat as I watched him carving slices of cured, salted ham, cheese—of which I still could not yet stomach the dung smell of it and remained hesitant to eat—and bread. He stuck the knife in a bowl of soft butter and spread it over slices of bread. He had even managed a nice, petite jar filled with lemon curd and pieces of our wedding cake.

I gathered several slices of ham and placed them over a slice of buttered bread. Covering the top layers of meat with another piece of bread, I started eating my little concoction, tossing my manners out the window simply to satiate the famished growling in my stomach. Leif stared at me somewhat amused, watching me as he tore into a hulking portion of bread also.

"This is probably the best sandwich I've had in a long time," I said with a stuffed mouth full of food.

"Is that reit?" he said with a quizzical grin.

"Um-hm," I muttered, chewing the food swollen in my cheeks.

"Ye call it a sandwich?"

"Um-hm... only it's even better with lettuce, pickles and tomatoes."

"Tomatoes?" he suddenly questioned with surprise, grimacing at me.

"Yeah," I replied obviously.

"Yoo've eaten a tomato?"

"Sure, I have."

"But, they are poison!"

"No—they're not," I laughed.

"Everyone understands they are poison!"

"Well, I assure you they're not. I'm living proof of that fact. Where I'm from, people eat them all of the time, and they're really very good—especially when they're nice and sweet, fresh right off the vine."

"Ye dinnea say?" He gazed astoundingly at me.

"Absolutely."

"Curious." He simply shook his head in amazement.

"Perhaps, I might cook something yummy for you with tomatoes in it, and then you may see for yourself what you might think of it," I suggested freely.

"Aye—I reckon that I micht be interested," he said hesitantly. "Ye ken how tae cook?"

"Yes—I used to love to cook. It was one of my favorite things to do when I had time to devote to it."

"I see..." he said abstractedly and paused momentarily, musing as he gazed at me.

"So, will you tell me some more about yourself?" I resumed after sipping a bit of apple cider again.

"Certainly," he agreed.

"What part of Scotland are you from?" I asked curiously.

"A place knoon as Skye."

"Oh?"

"It is an island in the Highlands."

"What does it look like?"

"'Tis bonnie. The air is cool and crisp, and the sky is boundless like the sea, which one can see fur leagues uninterrupted, and the land peaks and dips—rolling into grand glens along the way. Thistles garnish the land in the spring, and in August, heather blankets the earth all about."

"Mmm... sounds very pretty," I commented, imagining the beautiful scenery.

"'Tis bonnie haur as weel," he acknowledged, looking directly at me as he said it. I smiled bashfully and broke a bit of ham from my sandwich, placing it delicately into my mouth.

"Do you miss it a lot?" I inquired.

"Aye—in the beginning I suffered a bout of melancholy... However, this is whaur I have come tae reside—and, I am raither fond of it."

"Are you?"

"Aye, I am. Men are more free tae do as they please haur without terrible concern fur reprisals from the Crown should a man differ in opinion with English law."

"I see... Do you want to ever go back to Scotland?"

"Mayhap I micht like tae return one day—tae see it again—with ye, my bonnie American wife."

"That would be nice. I would like that a lot."

"However, I micht be apprehensive over how ye micht fare by voyaging the sea. 'Tis a devil—voyaging the sea. I am not inclined tae ever risk it with ye. Aside from this, I fear all the lads in Scotland will become charmed by yer appearance."

"Don't be so silly," I chastised bashfully.

"I am quite sincere," he replied endearingly. I shook my head a little, feeling self-conscious.

"So, you spent your primary years there, then?" I inquired, aptly sticking to the original subject of discussion.

"Aye, at Donvegan—my uncle's castle."

"Oh."

"He was laird of clan MacLeod. He is, however, departed, and 'tis my cousin who is now laird."

"My goodness..." I couldn't help it, but I was very intrigued. "That part of your ancestry is through your mother?" I guessed.

"Aye, my mother's mother was sister tae my uncle who was chieftain," he said.

"I see."

"My cousin, Norman, is now chieftain upon his brother's passing."

"Oh," I responded interestedly as I began spreading some lemon curd over a piece of bread. "So, when did you start school?"

"I was seven years of age when my father came tae take me away from my mother's family and brought me with him tae France," Leif explained.

"That explains your ability to speak French so well," I construed obviously. I smiled at him, and he smiled in return.

"I was tutored by Benedictine monks," he said, bringing a large mug of cider to his lips.

"You went to a monastery?"

"As a guid Papist lad who would have received a proper education," he said after drinking from his mug.

"Right," I realized. My eyes landed on the burnished Claymore resting over the cushions in the settee. I remembered him placing the threatening weapon flat before me as I stood in front of the reverend in church yesterday during our wedding ceremony. "Did you always want a military career once you finished your education?" I asked curiously, returning to looking at him.

"Nae," Leif said certainly as he replaced his mug on the tray.

"You didn't?" I was somewhat surprised.

"I raither fancied the notion of being a gentleman farmer," he admitted boyishly.

"Seriously?" I automatically smiled at him, taken by the thought.

"Aye, I'm quite earnest."

"Well, why didn't you?"

"I reckon that I didnae have much choice in the matter."

"How come?"

"I was placed in the personal guard of King Louis of France upon the completion of my education by the king's request as a sign of his affection fur my grandfather and father."

"Oh."

"I of coorse had tae accept the king's bidding as it was a display of respect and loyalty as weel as friendship—most importantly— tae France upon my father's behalf," Leif explained.

"Interesting."

"I otherwise would have been considered a traitor tae my grandfather if I went against joining the guard. I also would have been disavowed completely by my father if I had not done so."

"I see."

Leif broke off in contemplation. He seemed hesitant as I could discern him thinking when his glance fell toward bread, he was currently buttering. I waited patiently with my gaze steady on him as I licked the sweet lemon curd that had just fallen off my piece of bread onto my thumb. He lifted his deep blue eyes to me again, and I gave him an inquisitive look.

"I also believed in the Cause," he began pensively.

"What Cause?" I inquired.

"The one tae restore my grandfather tae the British throne," he revealed mindfully.

"Oh—right…" I stared at my new husband at a loss for words.

"Aye," he muttered.

I cleared my throat. "So, there was really no choice—you had to pledge your allegiance to the King of France," I said dryly. Leif slowly nodded his head a couple of times.

"Aye."

"Well, that kinda puts you in a bit of an odd position now, doesn't it?" I recognized.

"Ye micht say so."

"Except, how is it that you're serving in the British army, then?"

"Aye—a bit of a long tale."

"I don't mind—obviously," I joked lightly in spite of the seriousness of our conversation.

"Apparently," he replied, grinning a little too. He took a sip of apple cider and replaced his mug on the ebony tray. "Weel, whaur micht I begin this tale…"

"Start anywhere you'd like."

"I'll tell ye from the moment my father set sail from France tae Scotland back in forty-five," Leif decided.

"Okay," I responded attentively.

"Ye see, I was granted leave from King Louis's guard tae join my father in Scotland. Upon my arrival in Scotland, I discovered that the country was indeed perilously ill at rest. The reit of Stewart succession tae the throne was paramount… The country was divided. Although none will speak of it tae this very day, much of Scotland and Ireland remain loyal tae the House of Stewart.

Nonetheless, the matter, as it was debated, divided men and tore apart families and clans," Leif explained soberly.

"Sounds like the emergence of a civil war," I observed, feeling a little chill creep over me.

"Indeed," Leif agreed. I shuddered. He noticed, and suddenly I felt a blanket coming over my shoulders as he pulled it snug around me.

"Thanks," I said gratefully.

"Aye."

"This is sounding like a dangerous situation."

"Quite."

"I don't suppose there could have been a way to work it out judiciously through the courts?" I inquired as I placed a piece of bread in my mouth.

"Nae."

"I didn't think so."

"Justice is elusive. 'Tis an idealistic notion when absolutism is instituted," Leif said.

"That's true," I agreed, nodding my head a little, anticipating more of the story.

"Men waur forced tae take sides. Nae man was spared from choosing a stand," he continued grimly. My heart was sinking into my knotting stomach, because of what he was revealing to me, and I suddenly wondered more about him.

"Oh my God, you're going to tell me—"

"I never conspired against the English Crown," Leif interrupted abruptly.

"Okay," I sighed with relief, "I thought you were going to tell me that you were an anarchist involved in a coup."

"I never conspired," Leif repeated definitively.

"I believe you," I replied honestly.

"Guid," he said, seeming satisfied. "Although, tae overthrow the Crown was in fashion at the time," he added with a grim expression on his face. Suddenly, I felt my stomach clinch as a chill crawled over my skin again.

"You were obviously sympathetic to your grandfather," I said dryly. Leif silently nodded his head. "And, everyone had to choose sides, you said," I echoed mindfully. He again nodded his head. *My God!* I didn't know what to think—except, I was growing more shocked thc more I was learning about him. "But, you never conspired..."

"Nae. I never conspired. However, it didnae matter," he said realistically.

"Why not?"

"I was a marked man nonetheless by the nature of my bloodline, and the knoon fact that I was also loyal tae the King of France," Leif revealed.

"An enemy of the state?" I muttered, astonished.

"Thus I was considered, though I never conspired against the English Crown. Nor, did I ever take up arms against England," he swore.

"I believe you."

"'Tis true, however—I am a dissenter. My opinions deem me thus."

"I see."

"I am awaur of being watched," he stated straightforwardly.

"By the government?"

"Aye," Leif confirmed.

"But you said that you didn't take up arms or conspire against the government."

"I have made my opinions knoon in certain circles," he informed me.

"So?"

"So?" Leif's eyes widened with surprise as he stared directly at me.

"Well, everyone has a right to an opinion, right?" I said obviously.

"The art of holding one's tongue is a virtue tae master, lest it otherwise git ye killed," he said certainly.

"Can it?" I swallowed the cider hard down my throat.

"Of coorse it can," Leif said absolutely, looking at me with continued astonishment.

"So, were you trying to start something dangerous, then?" I inquired.

"I was a lad with a quick tongue," he disclosed.

"Most kids are quick with their mouths."

"'Tis not a favorable attribute fur one tae have."

"So, you said something some people didn't like. It doesn't mean that you, or anyone else for that matter, should be labeled a terrorist or an enemy of the state by a government because it didn't agree with what you had to say."

"Yet, it does mean precisely so. The Crown may call a subject whit it will like."

"Well, then I guess the Crown would have a problem with me too. My opinions definitely would not be considered Kosher."

"Kosher? Yoo're a Papist." Leif grimaced blatantly at me.

"Orthodox—my opinions, I mean, conventional according to the government," I clarified.

"Och!" he realized. "I micht have tae agree with ye on this account, lass. Ye are a bit outspoken on occasion, I have observed," he said ironically.

"Hey," I scolded flippantly, making light of his words.

"'Tis true, however. One must take care of whit one says, or it will indeed git one killed," he warned.

"Hmm..." I considered. "But, aside from slander and defamation of character, freedom of speech is a tenet I fully support. Whether I agree or disagree with someone's opinion is immaterial by the very fact a person has a mind and mouth to express a thought, and that nature should be respected by the government no less, without fear of reprisal from it," I disclosed honestly.

"Indeed?" Leif looked at me wide eyed.

"Absolutely. It's a fundamental human right," I said definitely.

"Curious," he replied thinkingly. He paused briefly, keeping steady eyes on me. "I wonder whether I have wed a philosopher or a rabble rouser."

"Neither," I answered self-consciously. He drifted into silence again, and I sensed his pensiveness as he gazed at me with his piercing eyes and deliberate grin. "What?" I inquired finally. He shrugged his shoulders a little.

"I believed ye might have been an agent against the Crown when we first met," he admitted to me.

"I know that you thought that I was a spy."

"Aye."

I glanced down at the new piece of bread I was tearing. I was aware of him watching me. I placed the small morsel inside my mouth and slowly started chewing. Then, I lifted my gaze, and our eyes directly met again.

"You said that you didn't think that about me anymore," I said.

"Aye," he said.

"I'm not a spy," I repeated.

"I believe ye. I have told ye so," he replied undoubtedly. I nodded my head a little, certain that he did believe me.

"But—you're a dissident," I realized coincidentally.

"Aye."

"I never would have figured you for a renegade."

"Nae?"

"No. Not at all," I said, shaking my head. Leif paused briefly, appearing thoughtful.

"I apologize tae ye fur it," he resumed regrettably.

"Don't be sorry. I know that you're not a bad man. You're a good guy," I said really. Leif slightly leaned in close and gave me a gentle kiss over my lips.

"Ye have a generous heart, *àille dhubh*," he remarked in a soft voice.

I smiled diffidently at him; he made me feel a bit shy again for whatever reason I couldn't explain. He then shifted back a little, sitting more comfortably in front of me once more over the blankets and proceeded to tear apart a piece of sliced salted ham.

"So, how is it that the government allows you to serve in the military?"

"I dinnea choose tae serve England," Leif disclosed carefully.

"I don't understand."

"It is what I was beginning tae tell ye—about my father."

"Oh, right."

"Once my father and I had returned tae Scotland, my cousin, the prince—"

"Prince?"

"Charles of coorse," he said apparently.

"Oh yeah, of course."

"Aye, weel, Prince Charles, was believed by now tae have landed in Scotland weel outfitted with arms, supplies, and French troops tae reinforce clans willing tae fight against England," Leif started explaining.

"Oh," I said attentively.

"However, since the ship with arms was lost tae the English en route, and although Prince Charles landed safely upon Scottish soil, the lad arrived with nae French reinforcements as promised by King Louis."

"Oh-no."

"Aye. As a result, thaur was little enthusiasm amongst the clans tae pursue the Crown."

"So what happened, then?" I inquired inquisitively.

"My father and uncle, Norman MacLeod, quarreled."

"Why?"

"'Twas over the loss of reinforcements."

"I see."

"A meeting took place with clan lairds who remained sympathetic tae the Cause. Weel, as it was—the lairds quarreled over what tae do... the risk was too great, some believed. Others disagreed, and believed the risk was much greater not tae fight. Nonetheless, as it transpired, a portion of lairds refused tae merely meet with Prince Charles," Leif continued explaining.

"Really?"

"Aye."

"What did Prince Charles say about it?"

"He was outraged, of coorse."

"So, what did he do?" I inquired interestedly.

"He intended tae fight, nonetheless."

"He did?"

"Certainly," Leif said, and then he paused. He glanced at me inquisitively. "Have ye never heard any tales about Prince Charles?"

"Not really," I confessed, shaking my head a tad. Leif's brow lifted high as he stared at me, very much astounded.

"Och... Weel, then, I shall tell ye a bit about him whilst I continue my tale."

"Okay."

"Now, ultimately, the lairds had decided tae forbid their clansmen tae battle since their lands and titles were jeopardized. It would all be forfeited in the event of defeat," Leif informed me.

"That's frightening."

"Aye. However, men who waur supporters enlisted in secret, regardless of this fact."

"Really?"

"Aye."

"Then, you abstained? Is that why you still have your wealth?"

"In fact, most of my wealth has been kept from me by the Crown till I have completed my service tae England."

"Are you serious?"

"Aye, 'tis the Crown's insurance that I remain loyal tae England."

"Can they really do that?" I asked unbelievably.

"The Crown can do as it wishes."

"That's... I don't know—unjust, I think."

"I shall agree."

"So, finish telling me—what happened?"

"Weel, I shall tell ye that I did have the intention tae fight," Leif revealed to me while appearing pensive.

"You did?" I replied, astonished.

"Aye. I remain a Jacobite tae this day."

"But, I thought—"

"I ken. However, my uncle, Laird MacLeod, continued quarreling with my father. He wisnae in agreement that we lads battle against the English as my father had intended."

"I see."

"Fin gave his word tae our uncle against my father that he wouldnae so much as peer across yonder from behind a wee crag tae glimpse at the battlefield. This further outraged my father. It appeared that not enough men would raise arms against King George... Thus, fur me, thaur was nae choice—I had tae do so."

"You were compelled out of loyalty to your father," I realized.

"Aye."

"And, Finley did so out of loyalty to your uncle who fostered him."

"Aye..." Leif broke off in a meditative state of mind for a moment. "How could I abandon my father, my grandfather and my cousin, Prince Charles—rightful heir tae the British throne?" he rejoined.

"I imagine it must have been a very difficult position for you to have been in," I fathomed.

"The Cause was great... Countless Jacobites risked their lives and perished in this enduring struggle tae reit whit was unjust."

"I understand what you're saying," I said as I listened to him. He nodded his head a tad in acknowledgement.

"I dinnae believe in absolutism as my grandfather. Raither, I merely believed in the House of Stewart's proper reit tae succeed the British throne."

"I see."

"Thus, as it came about, Prince Charles persuaded enough men willing tae fight tae raise an army. So, the day I traveled tae meet with the prince tae accompany him tae Moidart, I was unexpectedly apprehended by a group of men. Clansmen had taken me and brought me back tae MacLeod lands, tae the Isle of Skye. I was promptly sealed within my bedchamber within the castle having nae way out," Leif explained.

"My goodness! Who had them do that to you?" I wondered.

"My Uncle Iain's orders," he said.

I paused placing the morsel of bread I had just dipped into the lukewarm squash pottage between my lips.

"You were kidnapped, and held hostage by your own uncle?" I responded in disbelief.

"He meant tae seize the prince as weel, yet Prince Charles was quite weel ahead by a day and weel guarded," he continued. I slowly shook my head in astonishment.

"This is like a movie or something," I remarked incredibly.

"A whit?" he responded, frowning a bit, obviously looking puzzled.

"Never mind," I said unimportantly.

"As ye wish."

"Where was Finley when all of this was happening?"

"I didnea ken whaur he was."

"You didn't?"

"He was forbidden tae see me."

"Really?"

"Aye."

"What motivated your uncle to do that to you?" I asked curiously.

"I reckon that I canna say, precisely," Leif replied.

"That's weird," I said frankly with a little grimace.

"Weel, I truly dinnae ken. Though, I have my suspicions," Leif disclosed.

"Suspicions?"

"Tae put it quite simply, my Uncle Iain ordered it on behalf of Laird MacLeod, my uncle also, as it was most likely done out of concern with securing his own coffers. Ye see, if I had gone tae battle fur the prince, then I surely would have lost all my worth tae the English Crown. Furthermore, if Finley and I had fought along with the lads, it may have been interpreted that my uncle, Laird MacLeod, also approved of the uprising tae which he would have risked forfeiting the clan's lands and titles—all of its wealth," Leif explained to me.

"Ooh," I understood.

"Waur I killed or captured at Culloden, my inheritance bequeathed tae me by my father would have been tae the Crown's benefit instead of returning tae my uncle, Laird MacLeod," he added.

"I understand," I realized. "What happened next?"

"Needless tae say 'twas a mess. Jacobites waur defeated. Those captured by the English waur executed, and England made its presence knoon in the Highlands."

"Oh," I responded uneasily.

"Aye... When my uncle decided tae release me, I learnt Finley had abruptly sailed tae America."

"Really?"

"Aye. Our Uncle Norman had secured him a commission in the British army as collateral tae the Crown—and as a display of his loyalty tae King George."

"Wow," I responded somewhat shocked. "So, is that how you came to serve in the British military too?"

"Essentially."

"Amazing... That's, um, some story—quite intense."

"Aye."

I fell quiet for a moment, thinking. I slowly swirled my spoon around in the porridge I was now eating, watching the trailing patterns emerging as I played with it.

"Your situation must have been—still must be—hard for you," I acknowledged finally after a second.

"I dinnae much think on it, in truth. Not as I have before," he replied as he gulped some cider. I lifted my gaze and looked at him again.

"I sympathize with you," I admitted.

"Weel, I thank ye, lass," he responded kindly, gazing steadily back at me. "I, however, dinnae seek your pity. I shall manage weel enough as I have always done." I nodded a little, understanding him.

"Do you resent it?" I asked.

"Nae," he said.

"You don't?"

"I dinnae, since now that I have ye," he said genuinely.

"Oh," I whispered, struck suddenly shy again.

"Aye," he said softly as I felt his warm hand gently slipping over my shoulder and around the side of my neck. He drew my lips to his and slid an arm around my waist, compelling me close toward him, causing me to knock the tray of food with my knee. He pulled me over him as he leaned back against the pillows and warmly kissed me with growing heat. He rolled over me, fixing me beneath him, and fully caged me with his brawny frame as he pressed desirous kisses over my lips. I sensed his knee unmistakably wedge my thighs apart, and I was well under his spell.

PART TWO

Touching the Ground

Six

November 30th.

Leif and I left for Boston this morning with Amity in our company. Winter was completely upon us with larger quantities of snow having fallen the night before. Fortunately, the clouds had cleared. The sky was crystal blue as the sun shined brilliantly across the white landscape. It seemed there would be no further precipitation for the rest of the day while we journeyed, but navigating through thick blankets of snow-covered terrain was surely not an ideal circumstance for traveling. We journeyed over uncleared roads in a coach with skies that Leif had rented, and I hoped we'd ultimately arrive at our destination without incident as we swayed and bounced unpredictably while gliding along the way.

I took note of the freezing cold outside while gazing through the window. Silence prevailed across the blinding, quiet, winter landscape. Thankfully there was no windchill to add to the additional harshness of the icy temperature. But, it was amazingly warm and cozy inside our coach with us covered in woolen blankets and an extremely large black bear's skin covering our legs. The two leather bench seats facing each other were comfortable and were even wide enough to allow Amity or me to recline for an easy nap if we wished to do so.

I was admiring the encased icicle branches on all the maple, birch, and dogwood trees surrounding us. The light caught their branches like glimmering silver lattices between intermittent sunlight among the towering evergreens, and the woodland scenery appeared beautiful.

My attention shifted from gazing out the window when I realized Amity's resting head leaned lightly against my upper arm. I reached around her, drawing her close against me to keep her comfortably sleeping. Once I finished carefully adjusting her just so with the blankets, I lifted my gaze and realized to my surprise that Leif had been silently watching me.

"I thought you were asleep," I said softly.

"Not quite," he muttered, grinning gently as he sat across from me.

"What's wrong? You're not comfortable?" I inquired.

"Och, aye, I'm comfortable," he said.

"What is it then?" I asked curiously.

"I micht say that ye are tae blame fur my inability tae rest weel," he said in a low voice.

"But, I'm not doing anything to be blamed for something," I replied modestly.

"I dinnae believe that ye must do a thing tae warrant it," he said.

"Well, that's not fair," I responded, recognizing his flirtation with me.

"Possibly," he said.

"Oh, *please*," I replied sarcastically.

"Truly, I wish that I merely could," he said. I stared at him, dumbfounded.

"You're incredible," I said with a mixture of disbelief and amusement.

"Aye, yoo've told me so," he said nonchalantly.

"Okay, you need to stop." I was feeling slightly embarrassed as I detected the playful smirk on his face.

"Fur whit reason must I cease?"

"You're being really silly."

"I am quite earnest, however."

"I don't think so."

"Of coorse I am."

"Ridiculous."

"Ahh, so I am amusing ye, am I not?"

"Not quite."

"I beg tae differ."

"Don't beg too hard."

"Ooo, *cheeky.*"

"Just what are you getting at?"

"I am getting at the apparent fact that I desire tae bed ye, presently," he said bluntly.

"Do you *mind*?" I scolded, shocked, despite myself.

"Not at all."

"Well, I do!" The pearly gleam of his playful grin stretched vividly across his handsome face. "You're awful," I chastised.

"I micht be."

"I think you're being arrogant now."

He chuckled and the grin across his face lingered. "Merely come sit by me." His tone sounded so innocent, I noticed, despite his ulterior expression. He lightly patted the empty space next to himself.

"No," I said, shaking my head.

"Please do—I'm quite alone over haur. Will ye not comfort yer poor husband?" he sulked affectedly.

"Uh, don't you see that we're not *exactly* alone here?" I pointed out the sleeping child I was allowing to rest against my breast.

"I assure ye the lassie is soond asleep. She wulnae ken the

merest thing taking place. I also may remind ye that she is safely quite deaf," Leif reasoned, attempting to convince me.

"You can't be serious," I scoffed unbelievably, though I was amused by him. But, I noticed his eyebrow arch over his eye. "Out of the question!"

"Truly?" He chuckled again.

"Get your mind out of the gutter!"

"Yoo're coldhearted," he laughed again.

"FYI—for your *information*—this is a *G* rated ride," I reminded.

"*G* rated?" Leif grimaced curiously.

"Yes, meaning for a general audience attending. So, I suggest you keep it clean and proper for the duration of this trip, mister," I scolded.

He puffed up like a pufferfish and narrowed his eyes on me. "Och, now ye wish tae claim *propriety*?" he jeered.

"I mean it," I warned.

"'Tis a wee late fur that, is it not?"

"You better not try any of your games."

"Games?"

"I'm not playing."

"Nor am I," he claimed, but I gave him a doubtful look.

"I'm being serious," I said. Leif abruptly paused and stared at me for a second. I could plainly see the enamor on his face.

"It appears that ye micht be quite earnest," he said calmly after a second.

"Yes, I am," I maintained.

"I see."

"Good."

"Very weel, then," he resigned. He grasped his ebony walking stick and suddenly pounded the tip of the silver grip overhead against the ceiling of the coach.

"What did you do that for?" I asked confusedly, sensing the coach now coming to a halt in response. "Why are we stopping?" I asked again, but Leif didn't answer. The coach quickly came to a complete stop, and one of the coachmen could be heard scraping himself off from above. Within a second our compartment door swung open.

"Is there anything the matter, Your Grace?" the coachman inquired concernedly.

"Merely an order of fresh air, Tibbs," Leif informed him politely.

"Very well, Your Grace," Mr. Tibbs replied respectfully, then widened the door. The chill quickly entered from outside as Leif started out onto the footstep. He leaped out into the padded snow near Mr. Tibbs and spun around, peering back inside the coach.

"Come along, lass," Leif urged with a gloved hand stretched out from his fur cloak for me to take.

"But, I've got Amity," I replied apparently.

"Simply tuck her weel aside, and she will be alrecht," he assured.

"But, we just can't leave her," I said reluctantly.

"We shan't be long," he promised. He impatiently wiggled his gloved fingers for me to take.

"All right, just a moment. Let me just notify her in case she wakes so she doesn't get scared," I suggested.

"Certainly," he agreed. I leaned close to gently rouse Amity from her slumber and she sleepily awakened. I communicated to her that her uncle and I were going for a little walk. She nodded her head and closed her eyes again. I glanced out the open coach door feeling the frosty air freeze against my face and glanced at the dormant forest surrounding us.

"Where do you want to go?" I asked curiously, somewhat doubtful about coming out into the cold.

"Merely fur a wee stroll. Pray, join me, *mo ghaol*. We have journeyed fur some time yet, and 'twill do ye weel tae come forth fur a bit of air," he recommended.

I hesitated, but it was true that we had been traveling for about three and a half hours or so with few breaks in between. My legs did feel cramped, I realized. So, I supposed that maybe I could use the stop to stretch my legs a bit and get some fresh air. I only wished outside hadn't been so cold!

I carefully slipped myself away from Amity while she continued soundly sleeping and mindfully repositioned her lying fully extended on the bench. Once I was satisfied with having her sufficiently blanketed, I turned toward the door. Leif carefully seized my arm first, then took my waist and lifted me across the footstep, planting me firmly in the snow.

Mr. Tibbs subsequently closed the coach door, and Leif started leading me away between the trees. The snow-covered scenery was muted all around us and encapsulated us in an acoustical cocoon that seemed enchanting. The snow lightly crunched beneath our padded steps while we leisurely strolled through the dormant forest.

We probably paced along for approximately ten minutes until we came upon an evergreen thicket of pine trees and mountain laurel undergrowth. My kid gloved fingers stayed nice and toasty in my mink muff like the rest of me covered in my matching cape. Except, my toes had grown a little too cool, I felt.

"Perhaps we should turn around now," I suggested, since I was becoming skeptical of my shoes, although they were in pattens.

"In a moment we shall make our return," Leif preferred. He slipped a palm around my elbow and began leading me into the thicket facing us.

"But, I think my feet are getting cold," I informed him.

"Are they?"

"Yeah."

"I assure ye that we shall not be much longer," he promised when we entered the evergreens. He seemed sort of determined, and I wondered what he had in mind.

"Where are we going?" I asked curiously. He stopped walking and turned his gaze to me.

"Do ye suppose this location micht lend better discretion?" he implied.

"Hm?" I responded, a little confused.

"Weel?" He hinting at our sudden seclusion. I glanced around, and we were surely hidden behind a visible curtain of vegetation.

"Well what?" I responded spontaneously.

"I reckon ye micht agree haur will suit ye weel enough as it is quite removed from others," he suggested.

"You've gotta be kidding me," I realized suddenly.

"I am far from jesting, as I told ye inside the coach that I was quite earnest," he said. His demeanor was charming despite the fact that he was trying to seduce me right now.

"Right here? Right now?" I replied in disbelief.

"Aye, presently," he said unequivocally.

"It's *freezing* out here! How can you be serious?" I complained, giving him a ridiculous look.

He suddenly unclasped his fox fur cloak and whipped it off his shoulders and place it down before us over a section of snow.

"Now then, I shall not let ye catch a chill. Ye will warm before ye ken," he said. I recognized the warmth and desire creeping into his expectant expression, and my attraction to him only served my weakness to agree with him.

"I can't believe you. You're a terrible man," I said, sensing the touch of his ungloved fingers gently stealing over the side of my cheek.

"I confess possessing such weakness fur ye," he said in a low voice.

"You can't blame me for it," I said, aware of the effect he was having on me despite myself.

"Aye, yet I can," he whispered warmly as he lightly stroked his thumb against my cheek. He leaned, and I could feel the heat from his breath warming my lips as he hovered close to them.

"You're such a troublemaker," I whispered.

"Yoo're quite fit fur that description, on the contrary."

"But it's just so cold—" I shuddered.

"Now that will be enough, wife. 'Tis time fur ye tae git upon yer back," he murmured as he began sweeping his lips over mine.

"I really don't have a choice, do I?" I sighed against his coaxing lips.

"Yoo're understanding me." He straightened from me and removed his greatcoat from his broad shoulders. He tossed it onto the green shrub next to him and began unbuttoning his navy blue velvet coat.

"You're going to catch pneumonia," I discouraged.

"I'll be alrecht," he disagreed. "Ye best git upon yer back with yer skirts raised," he continued while beginning to unfasten his sword belt.

"Unbelievable." I stood self-consciously before him, still a little hesitant due to the freezing air. Leif's warm expression deepened as his lips spread wide into an attractive smile, exposing the pearly gleam of his teeth. He whipped the sword belt from around his waist, ignoring my hesitation.

"Quit dallying, lass," he urged while propping his sword against a close branch.

"Oh, yes, Your Grace, *anything* you say," I jeered as I shuddered from the weather.

"Begin, then. I shall warm ye weel," he said, throwing a glance at the fur cloak extended over the snow. I peered over my shoulder at the blanket he made and was tempted to move toward it. But, on second thought I turned and looked at him again.

"You know, if you want me on my back so much, then you're just gonna have to put me there yourself," I taunted.

"Och! Is that the way ye care fur it, then?" he laughed, appearing suddenly entertained. I carelessly shrugged my shoulders without another word, except for the daring expression on my face. The clasp securing his pistol belt suddenly came loose, and the belt slid from his firm waist as he drew it away. "Ye ought tae mind fur whit ye wish as it micht very weel come tae pass." He placed the holster on the shrub near the sword with the rest of his belongings. Then, he returned gazing at me. Now, he stood exposed to the frigid elements with only a shirt, waistcoat and breeches on.

"You're going to get sick," I warned.

"Quit yer gab, *mo ghaol.*" He shushed me, and seized the little button to my cape just below my chin.

"I'm serious," I said, regardless.

"As am I," he replied. My cape slipped from my shoulders, and he gently tossed it over his great coat on the bushes. He removed my palms from my muff, and let it fall to the snow. "I do reckon that I perceive a wee grin upon yer face," he noticed.

"What grin?" I asked.

"The one plain upon yer lips," he said, holding a captivated gaze on me.

"I have no idea what you mean," I said dismissively, shrugging my shoulders with an unintentional smirk.

"Aye, ye do. Should ye not, permit me tae explain my intention tae take ye, and do as I please." His voice was husky, I noticed, and he gently snagged me by the waist, drawing me against his body.

"Is that a fact?"

"'Tis most certainly a fact."

"Well, uh—who's stopping you?" I replied unevenly, sensing his heated lips beginning to caress the side of my frozen cheek.

"Not a soul it would seem," he murmured in a gravelly voice. I was struck by the singeing warmth emitting from his skin in this cold winter air as he brushed his kissing mouth across my cheek until they met my lips. My breath was cut short when the sudden thrust of his tongue entered my mouth in a deep rousing kiss. Suddenly, I was beginning to feel a lot warmer, and the frosty air no longer bothered me while receiving his kisses. He was fervent, adoring and ultimately craving with consuming desire. I found myself enjoying his hot-blooded kisses and just as easily returned them; I was so attracted to him that I was unaware of losing myself to him this time outside in the snow.

I felt his hand roving up my back and around my neck until his fingers stole beneath my loose ringlets at the back of my head. His gently massaging palm against my scalp further hypnotized my senses. I reached around his broad shoulders and pulled myself tightly against him, anchoring my body to his. Sinking my palms into the back of his lush, loose hair, I drew myself deeper into his spellbinding kiss.

His palm clutched a handful of my hair and gently tugged my head back, exposing the underside of my chin to his warm lips. His slightly coarse cheek scraped feverishly against my neck as desirous kisses passed between us. Urging me to my knees, he carefully coerced me to fall backward where he pressed me into the blanket against the snow with the weight of his body coming over mine. I felt him wrap a sturdy, ungloved palm around my ankle and stroke beneath my skirts up along my stocking covered leg, until it reached the bare skin of my thigh. Raising my skirts above my waist, he possessively caressed my pubis. My breath shortened as he pushed a knee between my thighs, coercing my legs to part. He reared up a little and invisibly released his breeches while gazing fervently into my eyes. Shifting his long shirttail aside, I anticipated him.

My breath caught in my throat and he moaned when he entered me, fully extended. Sheathing himself to the hilt, he stretched my passageway wide, filling me like nothing I had ever felt before until we'd come together like this for the first time. He locked his cutting, deep blue gaze to mine, and I could clearly see his feverish complexion contrasting his yellow hair. His reddened cheeks glowed, and his face seemed to burn. The potential hunger mounting within him was plainly visible, and I innately felt that this time was going to be different. I simply wasn't so sure about him right now; he seemed a little unusual. I was slightly afraid as I sensed him beginning to stir determinedly within me. He was powerful—and he was intent. He groaned coarsely and the power within him was manifesting.

I got the impression that he wasn't going to be so careful this time as he pushed deliberately and solidly against my cervix, rocking my uterus.

I automatically stiffened and wiggled my hips to move comfortably away from him to adjust the enormous sensation of his shaft moving inside of me. But, he already had me pinned and responded by further fixing me exactly the way he wanted me to be beneath him. He purposefully withdrew, then surged impressively to the root again, and I gasped.

"I'm not comfortable," I moaned apprehensively, aware that it might hurt if we continued like this.

"I swear tae ye that I shall not harm ye, *ceisd mo chridhe*," he promised huskily while he persisted ebbing and flowing with purpose—the whole time fixing his gaze to mine.

Every intentional stroke filled me beyond belief and pushed me a little more past the previous point. The sensation of his precise power brought my senses to the cusp of pain that was not quite fully reached. I moaned, starting to lose myself in the depths of the severe phenomenon he was causing me to experience, which seemed to be stemming from a new and deeper place from within.

"Aye," he grunted heavily as he consciously drove himself far inside me. I lay there staring back up at him, growing aware of the heart of his awareness. I realized with each thrust he was ultimately posing a silent question to me. Unlike before, this question was of a much different nature. This time it was more pertinent to the crux of our relationship and had nothing to do with whether I would simply allow him to make love to me. For the first time, I think, I was beginning to comprehend the essence of his meaning: *will you wholly accept me without restrictions or conditions—without preconceptions—and accept my true core identity for the man that I am?*

I realized the fundamental question he was asking me of myself. To allow him to really claim me as he desired was the quintessential consequence of his constant question. If I truly let go and relented to him, as I was considering, then that meant that I would be completely accepting of him without reservation at the expense of my own self-preservation. Losing control the way he wanted me to would mean for me to give over to him a concrete part of myself that could never be reclaimed by me.

A tingling sensation started happening from deep within my abdomen. My body was naturally responsive to Leif's touch that I found myself submitting to him. I surrendered to him and let him do to me as he desired. He thrust evenly, tenaciously, and intentionally. He was calling my sensibilities to focus on the drowning intensity of his forging drive to seek and claim every undiscovered part of my depths.

Suddenly, a piercing feeling overcame me that felt like electricity shocking me and surged far within me. Uncontrollable pulsations trembled forcefully throughout my abdomen as my cervix pulsed like crazy. He abruptly ceased stirring and kept himself still in my shuddering response to him, allowing me to maintain the full effect of the thunderous palpitations coursing between my legs as my muscles fiercely throbbed around him. I gasped at the shocking sensation, never having felt anything like it before—more than I had ever known. It was euphorically sublime. I was conscious of him perceiving me disintegrate beneath him in the middle of wave after wave of encompassing ecstasy washing over me, drowning my senses without mercy as my insides wildly convulsed around his swollen shaft.

"Aye, that is it," he groaned with satisfaction.

But before my thrilling orgasm was completed, Leif began moving again, reversing the end result of my satisfaction. Instead, he appeared justified and his expression changed. His flushed cheekbones burned bright red and contrasted against his very fair complexion. His lips appeared filled with intense, ruby-red blood, making them distinct against the color of his shoulder-length, golden hair slightly obscuring his face.

He suddenly broke his steadfast gaze over me and sealed his

heated lips over mine. His tongue forcefully plunged between my lips causing my breath to shorten. With a couple of tugs by his hand at the base of my neck, the button on my velvet Brunswick jacket flung open and exposed my skin to freezing air. The sudden cold felt crisp and nice against my warm neck when he abruptly released me from his compelling kiss. He fervently turned my face away from his and lightly pulled my hair from the back of my head, tilting my chin toward his scraping jaw as he continued pressing burning kisses over my neck.

He had become animated and ardently gruff as his lightly stubbled jaw scraped like faint sandpaper over my throat. Fiery lips trailed near my jugular where they feverishly hovered, nipping and sucking obsessively on my tender skin. A moan escaped me at the sensation of his intensely suckling lips causing a little pain. He didn't cease, and I naturally responded to his zealous wanting; I feverishly craved him as if I had been starved my whole life. My thighs wrapped tighter around his hips as my palms anxiously raked over the back of his velvet waistcoat in my desire to bring him closer to me. He replied and lifted his devouring lips to mine again while moving ravenously between my legs. It boiled my blood and stirred my belly like wildfire from within.

Leif took me as he wanted. He enthusiastically seized every kiss, every caress, and every thrust from my body that he could possibly capture to feed his hunger. Without a drop of guilt, I greedily fed my own need as we anxiously used each other to nourish our carnal and emotional starvation. Suddenly, my thighs began shuddering uncontrollably, and the sense of thunder shook my body from deep inside as internal spasms took control of me. He groaned coarsely against my lips as I simultaneously felt him wildly convulse, expelling himself into me.

His warm breath heaved over my lips when he collapsed, vanquished, still throbbing deep between my thighs. I could feel his chest pounding against my breast as my senses were muted by the rapid beating of my own heart. He groaned a little more against my cheek, but soon went silent while fiercely panting.

After a moment, he shifted a little and returned his gaze to mine. I felt the light touch of his fingers delicately stroking the side of my face and clearing a few wayward tendrils of hair from my brow. I could see the tender and affectionate expression on his face as he simply gazed into my eyes. The effect of our lovemaking lingered perceptibly in his gaze as he thoughtfully stared at me. A gentle grin passed over his lips, and I mirrored his smile.

"That, er, was... 'Twas raither remarkable," he murmured.

"Yeah," I whispered, agreeing with him. I had never craved for anybody like that before. I couldn't help but think that was strange... and, I felt some guilt.

He grinned again and gave me sweet, gentle kisses over my lips. Then, he returned to gazing at me and I could see his admiration.

"What are you thinking?" I inquired softly.

"Whit am I pondering?" he echoed.

"Yeah," I whispered.

"I am merely reveling in the fact that yoo're mine now," he said.

"Oh," I muttered, feeling dreamy.

"Aye." He grinned at me.

"I think I like that," I admitted.

"I most certainly am fond of it."

"I'm glad."

His lips curled upward, and the expression on his face beamed with perceivable adoration. He kissed me one more time, and I felt an emptiness between my thighs as he then carefully withdrew from me. He stirred upward and drew my skirts modestly over my knees. Returning to his tall stance, I propped myself up to sit and watched him tucking his fine linen shirttail within his breeches over his waist. He swiftly made his appearance proper again, then leaned and clutched my arm, easily pulling me to my feet.

Turning for his arms, he started replacing them over his body as I began fixing the top button of my Brunswick jacket. I retrieved my cape from the top of his outerwear resting over the green mountain laurel bushes, and drew it over my shoulders. Once he had fixed his weapons over his coat, he snagged his greatcoat and began slipping his muscular arms through the sleeves. I finished clasping my cape closed as our eyes met again with contentment and intimacy while observing each other dressing ourselves.

After a moment, he appeared nearly completely attired. When he buttoned his greatcoat closed, he leaned to gather his fur cloak from the snow and collected my muff at the same time, giving it to me to hold. He swung the massive garment of his cloak around his shoulders and fastened it around his neck, then briefly skimmed me over. Lightly stroking a wayward ringlet tendril from my face, he tucked it behind my ear and appeared satisfied with my appearance. Snatching up his tricorn hat off the laurel branches, he placed it on his head and we were ready to leave.

"Shall we?" he intimated with affection in his eyes.

"Sure," I replied with a little nod and placed a hand inside my muff. Leif turned and started before me, separating the branches for us to get through the small thicket.

In a moment we had cleared the thick vegetation and were now pacing out into the open snow among the massive, ancient woods. I naturally slipped my palm in the opening of his cloak and found his large hand. He turned his glance down at me and smiled warmly. I felt his hand tighten around mine, securing it in his clasp.

"So, this was your idea for a walk?" I joked lightly. His lips tilted wryly.

"'Twas indeed," he replied candidly.

"Shame on you," I teased. His grin grew wider.

"I wouldnae reckon so," he gloated.

"And to think that I thought you had my best interest at heart here."

"Och! I assure ye that I have nought but yer best interest at heart."

"Well," I considered, "all I know is that you want to seduce me all the time."

"Yet, ye mustn't blame me fur wanting ye."

"Why not?"

"Why, I'm a man with needs, of coorse—and, yoo're the bonniest lass I have ever laid eyes upon. Now that ye belong tae me, I can bed ye at my whim," he expressed evidently.

"Oh my goodness!" I gaped, staring incredibly at him. "You're awfully sure of yourself." He smiled boldly at me, appearing confident and proud. "Well, I seem to remember you were quite eager for some hanky-panky lots of times before we tied the knot," I reminded him.

"I meant tae make ye mine whether ye believe it or not. I planned tae wed ye long ago, *ceisdein*," he said. I paused and just stared at him, amazed.

"Seriously?" I asked, seeing the sincerity in his expression.

"Aye, I wanted ye, and I meant tae make ye my wife," he said genuinely.

"Well..."

"Aye?" he prodded.

"I—I'm glad it happened," I admitted softly.

"Are ye?" he inquired really.

"Yeah—I am," I confessed.

"Ye greatly please me," he responded with a heartened look on his face. He paused walking and turned toward me with my hand still in his. With his free hand he carefully caught my chin between his thumb and forefinger. Tilting my lips up toward his, he pressed a kiss over them. When he released me from his kiss, he simply gazed into my eyes with warmth. At that moment, I noticed how the frosty sunlight brilliantly washed over him as he stood where the light easily fell unobstructed between the trees and set him aglow like a heavenly apparition. Indescribably gleaming white light surrounded him, and he appeared encapsulated, suspended in beautiful luminosity. I thought he looked magnificent in that simple moment—like a mystical apparition from a clandestine realm.

He turned, facing forward again, with me beside him, hand in hand, and we resumed pacing through the silent snow among the primitive woods towering over us. The walk on the way back was nice and familiar between us as we quietly crossed over the silent snow. The silence surrounding us veiled the dormant earth in utter stillness. In that fleeting instance, while we walked along, I realized that I was enjoying this exact moment in time being alone with him. I was content, quieted, and comforted. My usual troubled thoughts of someday returning home oddly faded—and, I never wanted to let this moment go. I wanted to keep it perfect with him just like this forever.

Seven

S oon the coach and the three coachmen could be seen at a distance through the trees. A couple of them had dismounted and were lingering around the horses feeding them oats. All three men were talking and having rum while smoking their pipes. When they detected us emerging toward them from the woods, they promptly collected themselves and resumed their driving stations. Except, Mr. Tibbs remained at the front of the cab and dutifully opened the door for us to enter.

"Thank ye, Tibbs," Leif said as we came close to entering the coach.

"Aye, Your Grace," Mr. Tibbs replied politely.

As I returned inside the coach, I noticed Amity still soundly sleeping in the exact position I had left her, with the blankets and bearskin tucked over her the way I had originally placed them. Leif followed directly after me into the coach and intimated for me to sit with him on the opposite side in order to let Amity continue resting undisturbed. I sat myself comfortably on the other bench seat from Amity, and Leif slid over it, seating himself close beside me. Then, Mr. Tibbs secured the door and climbed on top at the back end of the coach. In a moment, we were off traveling again.

The coach drove steadily over the snow, and I felt not too long after we continued our journey that I had grown tired. So, I naturally leaned my head against Leif's shoulder. He swung an arm around me and drew me close against him. While he held me tucked against his shoulder, I leaned into his chest quietly observing Amity resting so soundly on the seat across from us. I admired how sweet and angelic she looked while sleeping, thinking she was such a lovely little girl, and I also started remembering what it was like when I was close to her age; I imagined how vastly different my childhood experience was from hers.

"I reckon yoo're going tae be a fine mother," Leif uttered in a low voice over my head as I rested against his shoulder.

"Thank you, that's nice of you to say," I replied softly as my eyes remained on Amity. There was no question that I loved children, and while that was true, the thought of being pregnant as I felt the dampness from Leif's expulsion slick between my thighs, rather gave me pause to seriously think for a minute; giving birth in 1756 instead of 2017 scared the absolute living daylights out of me as my stomach clinched at the thought.

"I anticipate the day yoo're surrounded by my bairns," Leif said pleasantly. I turned my gaze up toward him, and his embracing palm began gently stroking the side of my cheek. Simultaneously, his other palm slid yearningly over my flat stomach and caressed it. "I shall rejoice the moment ye grow swollen with my bairn inside ye," he said longingly.

"Yeah—that would be nice," I replied, feeling very uncertain about it. Ideally speaking, I felt that I could easily want to have children with him, and if I could bear his child without any mortal risk, or if that would not further complicate this situation I was in, then I would completely do it in a heartbeat. But, as it really was, I was extremely worried about the possibility.

I sensed his palm lightly massaging my flat stomach, and I knew, despite my personal reservations, that he truly expected to have children.

"What were you like as a kid?" I inquired, trying to curb my apprehensive thoughts.

"Och, I cannea say," he replied thoughtfully, shrugging his shoulders a tad. "I reckon that I was a typical laddie in some aspects."

"Typical?" I responded doubtfully.

"I reckon that I was plenty in mischief," he confessed.

"Really? Wait—on second thought that doesn't seem so surprising," I reconsidered ironically.

"Indeed?" Leif chuckled a little.

"Um-hm," I muttered. "What sort of trouble did you get yourself into?" I was very interested to know more about him.

"Nae *trooble* at all per se," he said. I glared skeptically at him. "Weel..." he reviewed thoughtfully, deciding to tell me with a persuaded look. "Thaur was a time as a laddie when I lived with my uncles in the Highlands. Le Duc de Gris had come fur a visit, and a large commemoration took place with fireworks, swans, and recreation. In fact, he had traveled with his own cuisinier. That was the period when I was first introduced tae the delicacies of French cuisine."

"Really?"

"Aye. 'Twas my first experience having a meringue crisp. I also remember particularly wonderful wee sugar grape centerpiece embellishments Monsieur Morelle le Boulanger created that I had pilfered tae taste beneath the kitchen table. It wisnae anything that I had ever experienced at the time—the taste was sweet and heavenly."

"That's not such a bad thing you did," I said actually, grinning at him.

"I reckon not," he agreed.

"Was that all you did? Steal food from the kitchen, and get in the way of everyone's cooking?" I inquired.

"Weel, I reckon that I had committed worse offenses than that," he confessed.

"So tell me," I replied, amused.

"Weel, not long efter the duke's departure I discovered a bundle of remaining fireworks and I took one tae examine it," he started to divulge.

"Oh no," I interjected dubiously.

Aye I was curious about it, as I was a curious laddie. I wanted tae understand how it worked. So, I stole it."

"You did?"

"Aye. I ran off with it and hid behind the barn. Efter I toyed with it fur a while without consequence, I decided tae lecht a spunk, and I lit the match. I dropped it tae the ground and observed it shoot high into the air—only it veered into the window of the hayloft. Weel, I ran off knowing it wisnae supposed tae steer in that direction. So, as I cleared the barn, I heard an explosion and I immediately ceased in my tracks. When I turned tae see whit had occurred, I saw the entire roof of the barn had been abruptly blown off."

"Oh my goodness!" I gasped with astonishment. I straightened from leaning on his shoulder, looking at him really astounded.

"Aye, weel, 'twas quite a colorful display," he remembered.

"I bet it was," I commented. "You're lucky that you didn't loose a hand or blow your head off," I added fortunately.

"Indeed," he chuckled actually.

"So, then what happened?" I asked.

"The barn went up in smoke."

"Of course. What happened after that?"

"Weel, I took off running away from the burning barn like the dickens knowing full weel that when my uncles learnt of it, I was done in fur it. And as it came tae pass, they of coorse did learn of it. My uncle Dermott wisnae knoon fur his compassion, or his guarded temper—he promptly took a paddle tae my crease and whaled upon me something fierce. He tanned my crease quite weel in fact. I was so blistered that I couldnae bear sitting afterward, and had tae eat standing fur a week or two," Leif revealed in a humorous way.

"Oh my goodness!" I gasped in astonishment. I was slightly amused by the way he was telling me his story, but also felt horrible that he had received a severe beating for it. "I'm really sorry about the consequence you received from your uncle."

"Aye, I regretted it at the time as weel. But, I lived tae see anither day," he said.

"How old were you when that happened?"

"Och, about five or six years of age."

"Really?" I was shocked that he was so young at the time to have gotten into such mischief and had received such a harsh repercussion.

"Aye."

"I take it that you weren't well supervised."

"Of coorse I was. I was weel looked efter. I had my aunts and uncles, and I had a nursemaid tae mind me."

"I've never heard of such a thing, though."

"Weel, I was a lad."

"Where any animals killed in the barn as a result of your shenanigans?"

"Fortunately not—the cows waur out tae pasture."

"Oh, lucky for you."

"Indeed—I micht have met my death at my uncle's hand otherwise, as I nearly had with the barn alone having gone up into smoke." I think he was exaggerating—or, maybe not by the sincere way he was looking at me. He appeared truthful, actually, as I continued gazing at him. I shook my head in transparent disbelief in response.

"Sounds like you were a handful," I remarked.

"That is the nature of a lad," he said obviously.

"Well, thanks for sharing. Now that I've learned that you had pyromaniac tendencies as a child, is there any other information you'd like to divulge to me? Because, I really should know what

I've gotten myself into. It's only fair," I replied with a little humor. Leif chuckled, and his eyes sparkled warmly as he gazed at me with some reluctance.

"Thaur are plenty more tales, yet let us leave those fur now as they wouldnae be polite fur me tae tell ye," he considered.

"Hmm... I don't know—I think I need to know more," I said. He paused for a second. The expression on his face was musing and relaxed as he gazed at me.

"Very weel—whit else would ye care tae ken?" he agreed.

"Well, okay, now that we've established the fact that you were a *curious* boy, and besides your education, what else did you do? Were you involved in any sports or anything like that?" I inquired interestedly.

"Och, aye," he replied certainly.

"Oh, yeah? Like what?"

"I'm a very guid archer, ye ken?" he disclosed proudly.

"Really?" I replied amazedly.

"Aye. I am also a guid shot with a pistol and musket," he mentioned additionally.

"That's good."

"Aye. I am also a raither guid horseman."

"Yes, you are," I agreed for sure.

"I use a sword quite weel, furthermore," he said, and winked at me with some suggestion.

"Um, yeah, I suppose you do," I concurred unevenly. His lips noticeably curled upward, exposing the pearly gleam of his teeth.

"I liked tae hunt, and I also liked tae stone put, hammer throw and tae weight throw," he informed me.

"Wow," I responded considerably impressed. "Sounds like you were quite active."

"Aye."

"When I was five my mom—" I unthinkingly started to say but caught myself.

"Aye?" Leif encouraged curiously.

"It's okay," I said dismissively, changing my mind.

"Is it a terrible memory?" he inquired carefully, appearing sensitive toward me.

"No," I assured.

"Och..."

"I was just—I was just going to tell you that when I was five my mom let me take ice skating lessons," I disclose hesitantly.

"Indeed?" Leif responded, lifting his brow with apparent surprise.

"Yes," I said. "I became very good at it when I became older, actually."

"Why, I huvnae heard of such a thing fur a lass."

"I figured so. But, she let me have lessons, and I enjoyed it very much."

"I see." He gazed remarkably at me.

"I suppose now you know what I loved to do as a girl."

"Aye."

"My mom was an unconventional woman," I decided to say.

"Och, I reckon so... And, yer father agreed tae it?" Leif asked, gazing unusually at me.

"He was unconventional too."

"It would seem," he replied curiously. I could discern Leif strangely pondering me as we gazed at each other. I wanted to look away, but he held my eyes to his.

"You don't like that I know how to skate?" I inquired uncertainly.

"'Tis of nae consequence tae me. I merely find it intriguing."

"Oh..."

"Apparently, yoo've had an uncommon upbringing fur a lass."

"Yes."

"Tell me about yer subjects ye have learnt," he requested inquisitively.

"Do you really want to know?" I replied curiously.

"Certainly."

"All right—well, math for one," I started.

"Mathematics?" he inquired oddly, grimacing.

"Yeah—arithmetic, geometry, algebra, calculus, physics, astronomy, geology, chemistry, botany, art and music," I listed.

"Indeed?" He gave me a remarkable look.

"Yeah," I laughed a little, perceiving the strange expression on his face.

"Continue," he encouraged peculiarly.

"Well, there were lessons in logic, philosophy, statistics, biology —obviously—including anatomy," I named.

"Anatomy?" His eyes widened, really appearing shocked.

"Yes," I said.

"Yet these are all male subjects," he acknowledged strangely.

"It was kind of expected of me to learn them," I told him with some uncertainty.

"Was it?"

"Yes."

"How in Heaven's name would ye have had the opportunity tae learn anatomy?"

"I told you that my dad was in the military, do you remember?"

"Aye."

"Well, he was a military trauma surgeon, and he encouraged me to learn as much as I could about everything medical."

"Och," Leif considered, appearing obviously amazed also. "It remains most curious that ye would have been educated in such a manner."

"You don't agree with it?"

"On the contrary—I am not offended. Yet, I dinnae ken whit I reckon of it in truth. Despite it, I do indeed find it quite curious that ye have knowledge in mathematics, science, and reason as thaur is nae place fur a lass tae ken such subjects."

"Oh... Well, I tend to think that they're subjects that are good for everyone to know. My parents believed in me having a well-rounded education.”

“Hmm. Yet, aside from language and music, did ye learn any other subjects of the feminine sort?”

“I’m actually a fairly good cook.”

“Och, aye. I recall ye telling me about yer ability tae cook.”

“And, I know how to sew too.”

“Is that reit?” he responded, appearing pleased about this knowledge about me.

“Yes, it is.”

“Och, of coorse—how I forget that ye used yer ability tae sew my leg upon my injury.”

“Yes.”

“Those subjects are certainly agreeable. Yet, yoo’re not skilled at a horse,” he recognized.

“No—I suppose—I just never had the time to really learn it. It’s just one of those things, I guess,” I replied insecurely.

“Och, weel we shall see tae it that ye master the art of riding a horse,” he said, also implying something else.

“If you think so,” I grinned bashfully.

“I think it best.” Leif smiled boldly at me. I sensed him gently slipping my glove from my left palm. He carefully lifted my finger-tips to his warm lips then drew my palm back into view, admiring it between his caressing hand. “Yer fingers are so fine,” he scruti-nized. “Ye dinnae seem tae mind laboring a wee bit with yer hands, do ye?”

“No—not really.”

“Hmm...” A pause ensued between us, and I felt a second set of fingers seeping into my ringlets. They began fondling my locks as I perceived him mulling over me. “I huvnae ever met a lass like ye, Sylvie,” he said. I diffidently smiled at him, feeling a little awkward.

“Well...” I started, “I haven’t met anybody like you either.”

“Nae?” he replied genuinely, appearing captivated.

"No," I said.

"I feel unique in that case."

"You are unique," I told him.

"And, I am certain thaur isnae a lass like ye in all the heavens above," he said. "'Hear my soul speak: the very instant that I saw ye, did my heart fly tae yer service.'"

"Are you quoting Shakespeare?" I recognized.

"It summons my heart." He smiled dotingly at me. I smiled back at him, observing his face becoming ruddy with affection. He drew me close again and leaned me against his broad chest. I let my head rest comfortably against his shoulder again, enjoying the sensation of his caressing fingers through my loose curls.

"So, what was it like for you as a little boy when you went to live with your dad in France?" I continued asking.

"Och..." he responded thoughtfully, "I reckon 'twas fine."

"Was that the first time you had really gotten to know your father?"

"Aye."

"What was it like seeing him?"

"I recall him being impressive, courtly and grave—primarily."

"Oh."

"He was not anyone with whom I was familiar."

"Um-hm," I muttered, understanding him.

"I knew he was an intelligent man, and brave. Later, I learnt he was ambitious as weel."

"I see... Was he happy to see you again?"

"He was pleased."

"What was he like with you?"

"Polite."

"Was he affectionate?"

"He was moderate.."

"I see."

"However, I sensed that I should never cross him."

"Really?"

"Aye."

"So, he kind of scared you?"

"In spite of his reasonable fondness of me, when a laddie I witnessed his wrath on one occasion over a correspondence he had received. Therefore, I knew never tae cross him," Leif disclosed to me.

"Oh," I replied, intently listening to him.

"He wisnae the same as my uncles. He was controlled and measured with a temper weel guarded. Yet, when his temper was loose, he was a cold and calculating man—save fur the exhibition of his unguarded wrath over the correspondence I recall him having received," Leif said.

"I see... But, did the both of you have a good relationship with each other?" I inquired.

"I reckon we had a respectable bond," he answered.

"That's good," I acknowledged.

"Yet, I shall treat my own bairns in a different manner," Leif stated earnestly.

"Oh? In what way?"

"I shall adore them with great affection instead," he said.

"That would be really nice."

"Indeed."

"Well," I reconsidered hesitantly, "I suppose that'll be fine so long as you don't wind up spoiling them rotten."

"Alas, how micht I help myself, as they will come from ye?" He smiled at me with such affection, my heart skipped a beat.

"You're silly." I nudged him in the ribs a little and could feel my cheeks warming since I knew he could see them blushing when I glimpsed at him. He lightly chuckled and gave me a little wink, evidently amused by me.

"Ye need not be modest," he said.

"I'm not," I differed self-consciously.

"Are ye not?"

"No."

"Hmph."

Though I refused to glance at him again, and decidedly kept my gaze on Amity still sleeping, I knew that he was grinning at me.

"So where in France did you live with your dad?" I asked, returning to our original topic of discussion.

"My father took residence in Versailles," Leif informed me.

"How lovely," I recognized. "I imagine, though, there must have been some culture shock for you?"

"A curious way tae express it—aye, 'twas quite unusual. I say 'twas raither beautiful—the food, the dress, the music... even the air was beautiful. *La beauté est partout dans la cour de ma cousine*," he recalled. It occurred to me just now that, albeit through illegitimacy, Leif was biologically King Louis XV's cousin. He was first cousins once removed with Louis XIV and second cousins with Louis XV to be exact as I continued to learn. Quite frankly, I was silently stunned and imagined myself having a coronary attack the more information I kept learning about Leif. I didn't respond as I listened to him speak about his family. Instead, I just remained as I was, resting close against him quietly listening. "'Tis whaur I learnt my most courtly manner," Leif concluded.

"I see. Didn't you say that you were also educated by Benedictine monks there?"

"Aye."

"When did you leave for the monastery?"

"'Twas a month later from when I became acquainted with my father. My father instead had me tutored daily by a monk at our residence as he came tae visit us."

"Oh... Your mother?"

"Aye?"

"You said that she died when you were born?"

"Aye."

"Do you sometimes wonder about her?"

"Certainly, I ponder her upon occasion. Yet, I have this—" Leif broke off, abruptly reaching beneath his cloak and greatcoat. He retrieved a timepiece from his coats. He pushed the back panel off to the side, and it opened. A miniature portrait painting of a fair-skinned, blue-eyed, blonde-haired girl with pink lips had been captured. "This is my mother," Leif said, passing the image to my hand for me to see. I straightened from his shoulder and gazed at the pretty likeness. I supposed she couldn't have been more than twenty years old, and I was captivated by her youth as a wife and mother.

"She appears very pretty," I acknowledged.

"My father bestowed it upon me when I entered my cousin Louis' guard," he told me while thoughtfully looking at her like-ness now in my hand.

"I see," I replied, examining the image. "I think you really favor her."

"Aye, I have her fair hair raither than my father's," he commented.

"Your dad had dark hair?"

"His was quite swarthy indeed—more brown than black, unlike yer own ebony locks."

"Oh," I replied attentively. "How old did you say she was when she gave birth to you?"

"She was twenty."

"Twenty," I echoed pensively.

"Aye."

"Do you know what happened to her, exactly? Did she become sick after you were born?"

"Nae..." Leif hesitated. I looked expectantly at him, wanting to know.

"What was it?" I prompted carefully, sensing him.

"She couldnae withstand the birth," he revealed tentatively.

"Oh..." I responded fearfully.

"The physic had tae retrieve me from her womb lest I would have perished as weel," he said.

"Oh my gosh!" I gasped horribly. My mouth suddenly went

dry, and a bone-chilling sensation crept up my spine sending a shudder throughout my nerves. "I'm sorry," I said as I carefully clasped the image closed over the watch and handed it back to him.

Leif quietly gathered the ornate, glinting gold timepiece from my fingers and returned it beneath his coats. I was shaken by the thought; for all I knew I could be pregnant right now, I thought—and, there was no way of knowing about it until I got my period which I had lost track of. *God, how I wish I could get my hands on a prompt pregnancy test right now.* But, then if I found out that it was too late—then what? All these disconcerting thoughts swiftly arrived and swirled around in my mind, sharply reminding me of my birth control predicament.

"However," Leif began again, "I was told that my mother was of a delicate nature. She had succumbed tae a number of illnesses as a lass."

"Really?" I uttered uncertainly.

"Aye. Although yoo're quite fine and slight, I dinnae see that yoo're fragile as many other lasses like my mother. Yoo're soond and sturdy. Yoo're well made. Yoo've got a guid, wee rump upon ye. Yer hips are wide enough—fit fur bearing bairns," he assessed assuredly, observing me. I returned my gaze to his, suddenly feeling like he was describing a cow or some other kind of livestock animal.

"Well, I'm glad you're so confident," I said, embarrassed.

"Aye, weel, 'tis the truth. 'Tis anither reason why I desire ye," he replied confidently.

"Seriously?" I questioned.

"I ken yoo're guid fur bearing my bairns," he said.

"Okay..." I replied awkwardly. "Well—I hope that I have more to offer to you than just popping out litters of children," I said nervously.

"Aye," he agreed, grinning comfortably.

"Good."

"It wouldnae be half correct without the favor of yer conversation, and the pleasure of yer company," he said genuinely.

"You're so sweet."

"I'm pleased that ye do find me agreeable."

"Well..." I paused for a second, then admitted, "you kind of make it easy for me to find you so pleasant."

"How very kind of ye tae kindle my heart by saying so," he said with a heartened look. I felt his hand gently return caressing my ringlets between his fingers. I sensed him enjoying the feel of my hair as he carefully toyed with it. I think perhaps two and a half inches had been added to the length since I had arrived here. It hung low past my shoulders, resting at breast level. "Yer tresses are not at all dull, but free... soft and gleaming as silk. So fine yer locks are," he examined again.

"Really?" I responded unusually, gathering a ringlet between my own fingers and bringing it into view.

"Aye," he scrutinized.

"Oh, well, I don't know," I said with a little shrug. He leaned slightly, and I felt his nose bury within my locks. He sniffed long and deep, then straightened and appeared to muse some more.

"What did you do that for?" I asked curiously.

"I wished tae smell ye," he answered plainly.

"Why?"

"I dinnae ken," he replied. "I reckon that I'm fond of yer scent."

"Oh..."

"I still cannae place it—'tis an unusual aroma... quite strange, but pleasant. I fancy it."

"You do?"

"Aye. I enjoy drowning in yer aroma."

"Okay..." I replied strangely. "I think you're being a little strange right now."

"Indeed?"

"Yes."

"I reckon that I micht with ease say the same of ye," he noted jokingly.

"Not really."

"Quite so," he rejected, shaking his head a bit as I noticed the slight grin slanting his lips. I felt my own lips begin mirroring his before I glanced down at my cold palm resting in my lap. I decided to return my chilled hand inside my kid glove, and our conversation drifted into silence for a moment as I wiggled my fingers back inside of it. But, I thought of something else to ask him, and I shifted my gaze back to him.

"Did your dad ever remarry?" I inquired.

"He didnae," Leif said, lifting his gaze from my adjusting palm and returning his eyes to mine.

"Did you sometimes wish that you had a step-mother in your life as a child?" I was curious about knowing more about him— particularly when he was a child and what his family was like.

"Weel, my father had several mistresses," he mentioned nonchalantly.

"Really?" I responded, extremely surprised.

"Aye."

"A harem?" I couldn't help but feeling shocked in spite of my awareness of how the shameful world went around.

"I wouldnae say so," he disagreed.

"Well, how many?"

"I cannae say—several of which I am certain. Five, I do recall whilst I was a laddie."

"*Five*?"

"Aye," Leif replied naturally.

"I'd pretty much say that's a harem," I responded scandalously.

"Nae. Not at all." He chuckled, apparently amused by my reaction.

"Then you explain it to me, because I don't know about that," I insisted.

"Very weel, I shall. My father, from what I kent, loov'd women and indeed cared fur them. Whilst he wisnae exclusive tae one or the other, he was continuously guid tae them. He treated them weel at the time he was engaged with them—gave them gifts when they deserved it, traveled with them and minded them," Leif divulged.

"But neither one of them was good enough to marry," I presumed disapprovingly.

"He had his wealth tae protect," he said.

"He didn't trust them?" I gave him a strange look.

"Nae," he replied frankly.

"Oh... well, what kind of women were they that he felt like he couldn't trust them?"

"The sort which desire position, power and wealth above all else."

"I see..."

"'Tis a common trait amongst many women," he said obviously.

"Not just women. There are plenty of men that desire that too."

"Aye, yet I am referring tae women as I am speaking through a man's experience with regard tae his position. 'Tis through a man's position which offers a woman's stature." I nodded a little in response, uncomfortably considering his perspective. "However, thaur was one—Lady Philippine, who remained my father's mistress fur the longest period till his death. I believe he was fondest of her," Leif explained.

"Why was he fondest of her?" I asked curiously.

"She was wed tae Lord Allard. Unlike the others, she was of nobility and shared much in common with my father. My father once told me that she desired nought from him but his loove. She and my father waur fair tae one anither—and I recall that she was pleasant, and courteous tae me. She was devoted tae my father unlike the others, and continuously treated him with genuine kindness. He regarded her well... She was most like a mother tae me whilst I was in France," Leif remembered.

"I see... well—it seems like it was actually a good thing for you to have had someone like her in your life while growing up if she was loving toward you," I recognized in spite of what he was saying.

"Aye."

"Do you still stay in contact with her?"

"We correspond."

"That's nice. Does she have any children?"

"Nae."

"Oh. So, you're really like a son to her."

"I reckon."

"Hmm... That's nice."

Suddenly, a little yawn overtook me, and I realized that I was tired. I naturally leaned against him and placed my head on his broad shoulder again. Leif drew me snug against him and wrapped a securing arm around me. The coach lightly swayed, and it started pacifying me. I sensed his lips tenderly pressing against the side of my head, and his warm breath caressing my temple. He began softly singing a gentle, soothing melody, I thought was nice. The lyrics pertained to a man who asked why his love was forlorn due to the thought of his leaving her, and the man expressed that he could never leave her no matter what occurred because his heart was hers.

The rocking motion and Leif's lovely, soft baritone pitch were lulling me nicely. In a moment my eyelids grew too heavy, and I closed them as I began to drift toward a nap.

Eight

It was late in the evening when we arrived in Boston. The night sky was clear, and the moon was glowing brightly above us. It illuminated the snow pack in blue fluorescence all around as we made our way through town. Flaming lanterns lit areas along the roads as I recognized brownstones lining the streets. However, I didn't recognize any of the buildings as we rounded the corner to one of the streets, and a bizarre feeling came over me as I realized again the time period in which I was stranded.

We seemed to keep straight for a bit until we turned left and continued straight again for a little while longer. It soon seemed the buildings had grown scattered around town; the area had grown slightly rural, and the street lanterns had gone as we moved along. A handful of scattered houses littered the dark location with windows dimly lit by firelight. We turned again and rode through a gap in a row of fences up a lane cleared from trees.

Soon, a substantially large brick mansion came into view, and the road curved toward the front where we had finally stopped. I peered out the window and discerned several individuals waiting outside by lantern light in the frost before the front door steps. They appeared to be household staff. A man promptly came forth from the steps and approached our coach. He swiftly unlatched the door and pulled it open.

"Good evening, Your Grace. Safe journey I pray?" The man said politely to Leif.

"Guid evening, Quinn. Aye, our journey went weel," Leif replied cordially as he stepped outside into the snow-covered ground.

"Very well, Your Grace," Quinn replied in a deep Bostonian accent.

"It appears that ye have remained fit, Quinn," Leif remarked.

"Aye, Your Grace. No illness amongst us yet," Quinn said.

"Och, grand!" Leif replied while attentively turning and slightly leaning back inside the coach with his hand stretched out for me to take. I slipped my gloved palm into his proffered hand, and he helped me emerge from the coach out over the snow. I noticed the air smelled significantly different. I could taste the salt in my throat as I breathed in the icy air with the strong scent of wood burning chimney smoke mixed in.

"This is my wife, Her Grace, Duchess of Monteith," Leif introduced me politely.

"Your Grace," Quinn acknowledged me with a gracious bow.

"Quinn is my steward and valet," Leif informed me, shifting his gaze back to me.

"Oh, very nice to meet you Quinn," I said genially.

"A great pleasure, Your Grace," Quinn replied to me.

"My niece has accompanied us, Quinn," Leif informed him.

"Aye, Your Grace," Quinn returned to Leif.

I glanced back into the coach where Amity remained seated still and quiet. I gently motioned to her, and she stirred away from the bench toward my guiding hand.

"My niece is deaf and dumb. She will use the bell tae call as need be," Leif stated to Quinn as I was drawing Amity near to me.

"Very well, Your Grace," Quinn said.

"My wife has taught our niece tae express with her hands, as she will continue to instruct her on how tae read and scribe. My wife has made splendid progress with our niece. Our niece is far from dull of wit," Leif expressed factually.

"What a blessing," Quinn replied.

"Indeed it is, Quinn." Leif lightly seized my elbow with his steady hand and proceeded guiding me toward the front steps where the rest of the domestic staff remained standing while bundled from the cold in their outerwear, waiting for us.

Leif began introducing me to them: Elijah, the footman who was promptly called by Quinn to collect the luggage, Faith, Remember, Humility and her daughter Annabelle were among the cooks and scullery maids, Mercy—who stood out to me as the one black individual among the staff and very young looking of about sixteen—was introduced to me as my lady's maid while Prudence, Sarah, Mary, and Mabel were introduced as the rest of the maid staff. Jonah and his young adolescent son, Samuel, were the coachman and stableboy. They all greeted me with kindness, and I thought that they were all very nice individuals. There were a number of grounds keepers I later learned existed along with gardeners, gamekeepers, and casual male staff.

"Oh!" I gasped unexpectedly as Leif suddenly swept me off my feet high up into his robust arms when we reached the landing above the front doorsteps. "What are you doing?" I uttered breathlessly, surprised by him.

"I am presently taking my bride indoors," he said obviously.

"Oh," I laughed lightly, as I recalled the old tradition.

"Aye," he muttered warmly against my ear while crossing the threshold into the mansion. He paused in the rich, golden yellow ochre, distemper painted foyer and eased me back down to my feet as the household servants ensued indoors after us.

"Thank you," I said bashfully to him, hearing the front door quietly shutting behind us. Leif simply grinned at me, obviously pleased. With everyone inside now sheltered from the cold, the servants promptly dispersed except for Mercy who remained among the three of us standing in the foyer. I thought she seemed particularly nice even though this was my first introduction to her; she had a familiar appearance to me that made me feel more natural around her. Perhaps it was the characteristic of her mocha complexion I recognized as common from where I came. She had nice features that were considered quite attractive among the general twenty-first century American population. She also seemed attentive and dutiful, giving me the distinct impression that I could trust her, and that we could become friends. I also thought that she might be repressing a unique bit of mirth as I noticed the twinkle in her raw umber eyes. I thought that I might likely relate to her well, and so I also believed that she and I would get along very well together.

"Mercy, presently show us tae our chambers," Leif requested politely.

"Yes'm, Your Grace," she responded and began through the corridor up the staircase. Leif gestured for me to follow Mercy before him. I took Amity's hand into mine, and we started pacing after Mercy with Leif following us. We followed her up the grand staircase, and as we rounded the steps to the first landing on the staircase, I noticed a grandfather clock loudly ticking in the corner. I took note of the time which read nine o'clock as the clock simultaneously chimed and turned my gaze ahead, minding my skirts as I stepped upward. When we reached the top landing, Mercy led us through a relatively long corridor followed by a series of shorter passageways toward the back of the house by an alcove that had a window bench seat and showed us the door to the left where we all paused.

"Thank ye, Mercy," Leif said when she turned facing us again.

"Yes'm, Your Grace," she replied and curtsied.

"Now, introduce Miss Amity tae her chamber and mind her as she rests fur the nicht. My niece cannae speak. Nor can she hear, thus mind her weel, Mercy."

"Yes'm, Your Grace," Mercy replied respectfully. I automatically turned to catch Amity's attention and explained by signing to her that she would go with Mercy, who would tend to her by placing her in bed. Amity appeared a little reticent to leave me, since we had bonded so well over the close period of time that we had spent together. So, I also encouraged her not to be afraid and informed her that Mercy would be very kind to her. Also, if she needed me, then I gave her permission to knock on our door anytime for our attention. Amity nodded her head as she understood me. She relinquished my hand, then began following Mercy back through the corridor.

Leif glanced impressively at me as he proceeded to turn the door handle in front of us. I watched him open the door to our bedroom, and I proceeded inside before him when it was opened.

"Whit did ye convey tae our niece?" he inquired curiously while closing the door behind us.

"Just that everything is all right—she should go with Mercy who's going to be very nice to her, and put her to bed. And, that if she felt she needed us, then she could come get us any time she wanted," I informed him.

"Och," Leif replied, impressed.

The master bedroom smelled freshly painted in pastel Egyptian blue and snowflake-white along the wainscoting stretching a third from the baseboards up along the walls around the room. A mahogany four poster, light mint green silk damask canopy bed was detected at the back of the room, askew in the corner near the right of a pair of French doors leading out to a small balcony. The mattress noticeably looked very inviting with all the well-fluffed matching light green silk damask pillows distributed near the mahogany headboard. Drained from traveling, all I wanted to do was sink myself into those pillows and slumber beneath the down covers for the whole night.

I moved my fingers to my neck and unfastened my cape as I glanced around the new room. I immediately thought it was a nice place. Although at first glance, it appeared slightly modest from my standpoint, but for Colonial era standards it was extremely extravagant as my gaze fell to the large cream and crimson Oriental area rug covering the hardwood oak wide-planked floors.

"Is this really your house?" I inquired surprisedly, sensing my cape being slipped from my shoulders by his fingers.

"Aye, it is *our* hoose," Leif corrected. I smiled at him. "Do ye fancy it?"

"Yes, very much," I answered, impressed.

"I'm pleased. Welcome tae *Taigh Gràs*," he said, while I was noticing that the room was quite spacious. In fact, it was probably more spacious than an average modern day urban bedroom of eleven by twelve. Instead, it seemed much larger than that. I guessed it might have been closer to eighteen by twenty-four.

"What does that mean?" I asked simply.

"Grace hoose," he answered.

"Oh, that's nice." He smiled gently at me. "Grace house," I repeated.

"Aye."

"Why is it named that?" I wondered.

"I named it *Taigh Gràs* in hope that in time our Heavenly Father would bless me in this hoose with a wife and bairns," he said.

"Oh..." I suddenly felt my cheeks grow warm and I glanced away from him. "I didn't know that you had any other property other than the one in Northampton," I said, returning my eyes to his steady gaze.

"Aye," he said. "I obtained this property upon my initial arrival and station haur, as a result of my cousin, King Louis, having generously released my French inheritance without further obligation efter my father's death."

"Oh," I realized, looking around some more at the well painted walls and luscious moss green velvet drapes drawn over the windows. "That was very nice of him to do that," I recognized.

"Aye," Leif said. He paced toward one of the Chippendale armoires and hung my cape.

"So, this was an investment property?" I asked.

"Aye, 'twas my first intention. I thought tae make it a boarding hoose, but had since changed my mind in hopes of wedding one day. I meant for the hoose in Northampton tae be a country retreat and this one tae be my primary residence. This is also whaur I come when I have business haur in the city tae mind."

"I see," I replied. Leif began removing his fur cloak, and I kicked my heel from my slipper, removing my chilled toes from my shoe.

"Och, I'm quite expired," he commented while removing his other coats. "Certainly ye must be weary as weel."

"Yeah, I'm pretty done," I admitted tiredly, deciding where to place my muff until I thought to simply place it on the large Queen Anne dressing table.

"Then, let us retire at last," he suggested as he started unbuttoning his waistcoat.

"Sounds good." I moved to place my shoes out of the way near the armoire. Leif was certainly ready for bed; he easily removed his sword and pistols from around his waist and began swiftly removing his breeches. He tossed his breeches over the back of the upholstered Prussian blue, silk damask Chippendale wing-chair by the wall close to the other armoire. Now only dressed in his long white, billowy, fine linen shirt hanging mid-thigh, the black silk ribbon holding his hair back in a ponytail swiftly came undone, and he placed the ribbon carelessly over the night stand. He briskly combed his fingers through his loose straight blonde strands, tidying the strays over his head, and then reached an arm behind his back, easily tugging the shirt over his shoulders and head, mussing his hair all over again. He briskly stroked his hair back down as he now stood before me entirely unclothed and unabashed in his broad, lean, sculpted naked form.

Noticing me struggling with the ties to my stays once I had

removed my Brunswick gown, he strode toward me, stepped behind me, and gently cleared my long locks away from my back, draping them around the front of my shoulder.

"Such a pity," he remarked softly while I sensed him carefully tugging at the back of my stays.

"What's a pity?" I asked drowsily.

"The many loops and ties," he said, unfortunately, with a low, concentrated voice while standing close behind me.

"I know," I agreed, feeling the light warm steady stream of his breath caressing the back of my neck. After a moment, I sensed my ties loosening and I could breathe well again.

"Thaur!" he said as he successfully loosened the last lace from the loop and freed me from the garment.

As I was about to step away from him in order to place my stays next to my muff on the dressing table, he enfolded his arms around my waist, keeping me still with my back against his brawny chest.

"Aye," he muttered with his lips pleasingly hovering barely above my neck.

His arms shifted, and I felt his hands slowly rove up my waist. He heatedly pressed his lips against the nape of my neck while his hands found their way comfortably possessing my breasts. Suddenly, my toes left the floor as I found myself being scooped up high in his formidable arms. I recognized that particularly strange sensation coming over me again when his warm, tender kisses covered my lips.

"I thought you were tired," I murmured between his kisses.

"Indeed I am. However, I prefer tae be entirely worn fur a guid nicht sleep," he said in a low voice.

"Really?" My breathing was uneven as he strode with me toward the bed.

"Aye."

Sensing myself being lowered among the pillows, he carefully placed me in the center of the bed and hovered over me while kissing me. Wedging a knee between my thighs, separating them, he made room for himself and my blood began to heat me. His hand meandered over my stocking-covered leg, forcing my shift to wrinkle upward. I felt the warm touch of his hand on my bare skin when he leaned up from kissing me as his hand roamed far up my thigh. It passed my hips, high over my flat stomach, above my breasts until I realized my shift was being pulled over my head completely off me.

He paused and held my gaze for an unspoken moment, tracing a finger mindfully over my lips down along my chin. His finger continued trailing down my neck when it reached between my breasts and meandered beyond them. It passed my navel, then arrived at the private patch of hair between my legs. He cupped his hand over my pubic area and held it for a second. Then, I sensed his large fingers separating my cleft and he found my clitoris. He began gently massaging it. I lightly moaned at the dizzying sensation and with anticipation, he shifted over me while rubbing his thumb between my cleft, intensifying the heat coursing my veins.

Then, I felt a finger sliding inside of me and began stroking from within, causing me to gasp. Another finger carefully eased into me, and I felt him stretching me open as he moved his fingers, proceeding to spread my entrance wide apart. I moaned again, deliriously for him, sensing the large head of his hard shaft kissing the beginning of my passageway.

"*Och*," he groaned and I gasped when the enormity of his organ entered me. He completely buried himself between my thighs. Remaining still, fully extended within me for a moment, filling me to my core, he gently held the side of my cheek with his warm palm, forcing me to gaze up into his eyes. He throatily started saying something to me in Scottish in affectionate tones. It seemed he was saying something substantial; he was absorbed, intense, authentic, and affectionate. Then leaning, he passionately covered his lips over mine, muttering while kissing me, "*Mo ghaol... ceisd mo chridhe... Tha gràdh agam ort... Tha gràdh agam ort... Mo ghaol bith-buan... mo àille dhubh... mo leannan.*"

My pubis pressed against him and my thighs snugly wrapped around his hips, securing him close. I arched my pelvis against his when he groaned and began stirring. It didn't take long before I was enveloped in rapture from the glorious rhythmic sensation he was pledging to me as he thrust.

In a moment, I succumbed to wild spasms consuming me, and he buckled simultaneously upon his throbbing release. He growled as we climaxed together, then collapsed over me. Breathing heavily against my neck, I sensed the strength of his pulsing groin slowly diminishing while holding him in my arms.

When Leif calmed, I felt him withdraw, leaving me empty as he shifted comfortably onto his side. He whipped the covers over us and tugged me close against his warm body. Cocooned beneath the blankets now, I slid my palm over his enfolding arm and entwined my fingers between his. Consumed in bliss after the exhilaration of climatic pleasure, his hand contracted around mine. I closed my eyes and my soul was quieted as I began drifting into slumber at last.

Nine

Sometime very early in the morning, I awakened needing to use the privy closet and carefully stirred from Leif holding me beneath the covers. When I had finished, I quietly closed the closet door, and noticed the faint golden hue in the room as new daylight seeped beneath the soft moss green, velvet drapes. I silently paced toward the windows and mindfully peeped around the drapes through the large uneven glass window. The sky faintly transitioned from dark Prussian blue and violet, to a hint of gold at the brink along the horizon. I could see nearby a small pond frozen over surrounded by a snowcapped clearing. Beyond the clearing lay a dense collection of dormant maples with a scattering of green pine trees among them. I scanned the landscape toward the right and saw a large white blanketed hill cleared of trees. My gaze dropped below and landed on a distant road dividing our property from the scenery beyond.

After peering out the window, I turned and unexpectedly realized Leif staring admiringly at me from across the blankets.

"Did I awaken you?" I asked apologetically.

"Nae," he said softly. A lazy grin curled his lips as he gazed relaxingly at me from the pillows. "Did ye see the Common and Beacon Hill out yonder?" he asked casually.

The Common and Beacon Hill...? A complete shock went through me. They were not recognizable! The areas were completely undeveloped—appearing nothing remotely the way I had remembered them.

"Uh, yeah—I saw," I stammered.

"We shall go thaur fur a sleigh ride, if ye wish."

"Yes, that'll be fun," I agreed.

"So be it." He smiled at me as I simply stood nude before him, feeling inwardly discombobulated over my temporal dislocation as I was suddenly reminded of it again. "I reckon yer stockings waur terribly forgotten," he noticed. I glanced down at myself and realized that they were indeed left on over my legs. I didn't think anything of it, since my legs were always prone to getting cold in the winter anyway.

"It's not so terrible," I said.

"Aye, it is," he disagreed with an implicit expression on his face. He patted the empty space on the bed next to him for me to rejoin him beneath the blankets. I noticed the glint in his eyes as I moved away from the drapes and slid next to him beneath the covers. Shifting onto my stomach, I propped my cheek over my folded arms on the pillows, facing him. He stared admiringly at me as I gazed back at him. His hand gently stroked wayward tendril ringlets from my brow off to the side, placing them behind my shoulder. He returned caressing the side of my cheek, and I sensed the pad of his thumb lightly stroking the curve of my eyebrow.

"How did ye come tae have such emerald eyes?" he inquired, mesmerized.

"My dad had green eyes," I answered softly.

"Did he?"

"Yeah," I whispered.

"And yer hair?" He collected a thick ringlet between his thumb and forefinger, propped it in view and watched it naturally curl around his finger.

"The color is my father's. But, the curls and the texture are from my mother," I informed him.

"Whit hue was yer mother's?"

"Her's was red."

"Roy?" His brow lifted high with surprise.

"Yeah."

"Whit about yer mother's eyes?"

"Blue."

"Och... And, yer skin?"

"A mixture between my mother's and father's."

"Yer father was swarthy, then?"

"Yeah," I replied, nodding my head a little.

"Och..." His lips curled subtly upward, and the expression on his face was pleasant as he seemed to be thinking. He gently stroked the top of my hair all the way down toward my bare back beneath the covers. "Exceptionally bonnie," he said softly while appearing meditative.

Then, I felt the blankets being removed from my shoulders and off my backside. His fingers lightly moved my ringlets away from my shoulder, trailed down my spine, grazed the cleft of my buttocks and faintly slid further between the crevice amid my private tuft of hair between my thighs. I suddenly took a little breath when I sensed my labia spreading apart and an unexpected finger sliding inside of me. I immediately shut my eyes, sensing his probing touch. It slowly pumped inside me a few times, then withdrew and traced back up around my buttocks where his trailing fingers splayed possessively across one of my cheeks. I felt his soft lips tenderly lean against my bare shoulder at that moment. His lips affectionately meandered over the back of my ribs along my spine until they reached the small of my back where I felt them stop.

I then sensed him carefully removing my stockings. Shortly

after, my ankles were bare and he rolled me onto my back so that I faced him now. He made way for himself between my thighs, and I felt the head of his engorged organ gently stroking my entrance when he opened me on his surge into me, filling me completely.

He was an amazing lover, I thought, as he moved affectionately among my thighs. He was organic, uninhibited, free with his emotion, and indisputably real. He could compel me as he desired, and I was like putty in his hands as he made love to me.

LATER, I had awakened to find myself alone among the billowy blankets. The bedroom had been noticeably quiet and tidied from our scattered clothing. Leif was nowhere to be seen in the room. It seemed he might have already gotten dressed and started the day. So, I stirred from beneath the covers and crossed over the cream and crimson Oriental area rug on the oak floor toward the newly delivered chest by the door. As I passed the dressing table, I noticed a sheet of parchment and turned to get a better look at it:

> December 2, 1756
> My Dearest Sylvie,
> I have immediate business to attend about town and shall return not before long to dine with you this morn.
> Your Most Loving Husband and Devoted Servant,
> Leif

I was glad to know that we were going to eat together, and I carefully folded the note. I went to the chest and opened it looking for my journal. I found it at the bottom of the trunk and retrieved it. Opening it, I thumbed through the leaflets for a good spot and safely tucked my letter between the pages intending to keep it for always.

Afterward, I located a fresh winter gown and placed it over the Prussian blue silk cushioned bench seat at the foot of the bed. But first, I was going to freshen up and went to the privy closet. I reached for the pitcher and poured water into the washbasin. I screeched and shivered a bit as I splashed the frigid water over my face, and when it uncontrollably streamed down my bare neck and breasts. Hurriedly dabbing the soap into the water, I scrubbed vigorously in all the important spots on my body just to get through this miserable attempt at a bath, wishing that I had the advantage of running hot water. When I was done, I quickly toweled myself dry. Returning inside the bedroom, I snatched up my clean shift and slipped it over my head, onto my body, urgently desiring the warmth of some clothing as I began to dress near the warm hearth.

I still wasn't used to having help when it came to dressing myself, but it was difficult to lace the stays around my torso alone. So, I had one that was fashioned to lace both front and back, called a pair-of-bodies, where I had access to the laces in front for ease of fastening it by myself. I slipped on my stockings, then placed my slippers on my feet prior to lacing up my stays. Next, I proceeded to put my pair of pockets around my waist. Afterward, I tied my under petticoat around myself and fixed my hip-pad over my waist. I then put on my full-length woolen under petticoat and silk neckerchief. Next, I tied my silk gown petticoat around my waist and pinned my silk stomacher. Finally, I pinned the rest of my gown to my stomacher and tied it to the gown petticoat. At last, in about twenty minutes, I was finally properly attired and missed the days when I could just throw on a pair of jeans and a T-shirt in less than half the time.

I emerged from the bedroom into the corridor and unexpectedly discovered Amity sitting patiently, perfectly like a cutely attired doll, on the window bench in the alcove to my left. She noticed me and turned her blue eyes up at me. I waved hello, and she sweetly waved back.

"Have you been waiting for me?" I signed to her.

"Yes," she motioned.

"Not long, I hope?" I signed again.

"Long," she signed back to me.

"I'm so sorry," I told her. She smiled adorably. "Sweet girl," I voiced softly as I gently caressed her cheek and leaned to kiss it. As I straightened, I continued signing, "Have you seen your uncle?" wondering if he had returned yet.

"No," she responded.

"Okay," I said aloud to myself. Then, I had an idea about what we could do together while we waited for him to return, and I communicated, "Look at the house?"

"Yes," she signed back to me, appearing quite pleased about the idea.

"Great!" I signaled in response. A bright smile lit her cute, fair face. "Let's go," I motioned to her and held out my hand for her to take. She slipped her little hand into mine and we were off to exploring the house.

We started through the corridor, and it seemed Amity wanted to show me where her room was first. She led me through the hallways passed the staircase I remembered climbing last night and guided me into a very nice sized twelve by twelve bedroom with fresh, light rose, distemper painted walls divided by snowflake-white wainscoting all around the room. There were plenty of windows all around which let in daylight and cheerfully lit the area. Pink silk drapes hung open over the windows, and positioned at the back of the bedroom was a small mahogany four poster bed with a matching silk canopy. A small beige, French area rug lay center in the room upon the wide oak floor planks. I expressed to her that I thought it was a very nice bedroom, and I asked her if she liked it to which she communicated, "Yes."

When we had finished exploring her room, we stepped out into the corridor again and noticed the door to another room directly next to hers. We entered it and agreed that this room was also nice. It appeared to be a nursery with several wooden and tin toys, including several wooden dolls also placed on a shelf at the back of the room. There were a couple of little chairs centered in the middle of the room around a black bear skin rug.

Near one of the windows was a small letter desk with a petite well of ink and a quill that rested next to it. A larger writing desk meant for an adult was positioned beside it. I thought this would be the perfect room to use for studying with Amity as I peered out the second story window. I discerned the barn and stable not too far away from the mansion near a pasture surrounded by snow covered evergreen trees, and the Atlantic Ocean not too far beyond.

Amity tugged on my sleeve intimating for us to continue with our exploration. We left the nursery room and went straight across behind the staircase, discovering another bedroom beyond the stairs. This room was larger than the last two, roughly fifteen by twenty I was guessing with sap-green painted walls, and was clearly prepared for a guest given by the plain décor and basic room essentials. This room didn't quite hold our attention as much. Nevertheless, I still thought it was a nice bedroom also.

The two of us decidedly exited this room for the second staircase located at the back of the corridor near my bedroom once we returned through the corridors in that direction. Instead of going downstairs we went up a narrow, winding staircase to the third level. Four more rather spacious bedrooms were positioned on each side of the staircase at the top landing and seemed approximately the same in features. It appeared Leif's office was also on this level as it was discovered at the back of the corridor. I strode through the hallway and glanced out from one of the windows, discovering our orientation toward the road outside. I was really amazed at how many bedrooms this house had as I counted there were at least eight, so far, not including the servants' quarters which were located in another house on the property that I would later discover. I reconsidered my initial impression and recognized that this house was certainly grand in its own right regardless of era.

After exploring the third level, Amity and I went back down the stairwell passing the second landing until we came to the first floor. When we arrived facing the front door in the foyer, we could have gone either right or left. Amity wasn't sure which way she preferred to go... left, she abruptly decided and we crossed the hallway.

Entering a doorway, we discovered a very spacious dining room. A large, nicely lacquered, ornately carved oak dining table with twenty lush, Egyptian blue, silk upholstered, English Chippendale chairs surrounding it was centered in the room. I discerned that the table didn't appear to have originated in America also and instead came from Europe due to its French Rococo design.

As I glanced around the dining room, I thought it was very pretty. It was decorated with light green damask wall paper, and a low hanging crystal chandelier just above the center of the table which magnificently charmed the room. A large decorative, hand tufted, crimson and mauve Oriental area rug covered most of the hardwood planked floor beneath the dining table. It reminded me of the one Leif also had in the master bedroom. Lastly, ornate valances corresponding with the walls covered the top of the numerous windows surrounding the room, allowing brilliant sunlight to enter, leaving the room in cheer.

Amity tugged on my sleeve suddenly calling my attention back to her. I followed her out of the room across the hallway into the opposite room, and we explored the drawing room: another good-sized room that was attractively embellished with a strong European influence, painted in a rich light toned sienna and contrasting snowflake-white wainscoting along the walls.

When we left the drawing room, we abruptly met Mercy at the bottom of the front staircase holding a bundle of mildewed laundry.

"Good morn, Your Grace," she greeted respectfully with a curtsy, appearing stunned to see me.

"Good morning, Mercy. How are you this morning?" I asked amiably.

"I is doin' jus' fine, ma'am," she replied demurely.

"I'm glad to hear it," I said, smiling at her. But, Mercy's eyes nervously skimmed me over.

"I beggin' yo pardon, Your Grace, but you gone dress yoself," she noticed anxiously.

"Yes," I said, noticing her disconcertion.

"Lawdy!" Mercy expressed under her breath, appearing very worried.

"What's wrong?" I asked concernedly.

"His Grace—ain't gone be at all pleased wif me," she said. Her brow furrowed and she bit her bottom lip, appearing very uneasy and it made me worry too.

"Why not? I don't understand," I replied, confused.

"He gone reckon I'm a bad lady maid, ma'am," she said.

"That's not true," I guaranteed calmly, trying to soothe her concern.

"He gone git rid o' me, an' I won' have no wheres else ta go." She started crying in front of me and I felt worse about her concern, and for this sudden situation that arose.

"No, he won't. He wouldn't do anything like that—it's all right," I assured her.

"Save, you must calls upon me ta helps you from now ons, Your Grace—if you don't mind my sayin' so. His Grace is gone be most displeased wif me if he learns I ain't mind'n you none propa," she said tearfully.

"I promise he won't be upset with you," I reassured again, now also troubled by her obvious consternation. "You don't have to worry about anything. Please, believe me." I couldn't help but find her unexpected fear and sensitivity over my having dressed myself very odd, and I wasn't quite sure how to help her except soothe her with my words of confidence. Her reaction was so strange to me that I found myself placed in an unusual position due to being caught off guard as I tried consoling her. I believed she was overreacting as I stared at her in bewilderment.

"Please, Your Grace, allow me ta wait upon you," she pleaded.

"Sure—of course. I'll let you know whenever I need you," I stammered.

"Thank you, ma'am. Thank you," she responded gratefully, appearing to calm herself now. "I beggin' yo pardon presently, if I may be excused as I am seein' here to this bad laundry," she requested.

"Yes, absolutely," I said easily. She quickly curtsied and abruptly continued on her way, rounding the banister and vanishing through the corridor in the opposite direction. I remained standing there in suspension, thinking how incredibly odd for her to have such an extreme reaction over something I believed was so minor, clearly stumped.

Amity tapped my arm and motioned, "Look more." I nearly had forgotten that she was standing next to me observing until she grabbed my attention again, and I looked at her suddenly.

"Okay," I gestured back feeling distracted. Amity started off again, and I followed her.

We discovered the sizable kitchen with Humility, Annabelle, Faith, and Remember in it, easily preparing the morning meal. I directed Amity out of the way of the cooks and we left the kitchen for another room to explore. After we discovered the grand ballroom, we continued to the back of the house where we explored the sitting room and large sunroom. The sunroom was my favorite part of the house, since it was brilliantly bright with all of the surrounding windows from wall to wall completely letting in warm cheerful daylight.

I plopped myself in a rose damask silk upholstered wing-chair facing the snow-covered vegetable and floral gardens, and Amity copied me by tossing her small self into the chair next to mine. We both sat next to each other, gladly gazing out the windows. She excitedly pointed out to me a couple of squirrels prancing in the snow just outside the window. She was clearly entertained by them. They did look a bit silly dancing around in the snow with acorns stuffed to the max in their mouths, and I giggled a little too.

I faintly heard Elijah open the front door. In a moment the sound of boots clunking robustly over the hardwood floors advanced through the corridor toward us. I glanced over my shoulder when the sound became obviously audible, and recognized Leif entering the room, approaching us. I bobbed up from my seat, glad to see his strapping, fresh, attractive golden appearance in his billowy, ivory white fine linen sleeves, cream and gold silk brocade waistcoat, beige breeches, and boots.

"Good, you're back!" I expressed happily. I easily stepped to greet him as he strode deeper into the room.

"I am, *mo ghaol*," he replied. I freely wrapped my arms around his neck, and he leaned in, embracing me around my waist as he took me in his arms. I instinctively kissed him lightly over the lips, and when I withdrew, I noticed his expression had suddenly flushed. "Forgive me fur having delayed our meal together."

"Oh, it's okay," I said easily, smiling gladly at him. His lips warmly curled upward in response. His crystal blue eyes also sparkled with pleasure as I sensed his forefinger gently tap the tip of my nose, causing me to smile even more. He then glanced at Amity, still seated quietly in her chair, and absorbed by the jumping squirrels in the snow right outside one of the windows. "How have ye and our niece been diverting yerselves this morn?" he inquired.

"We decided to explore the house," I informed him.

"Och, splendid!" he replied acceptably. "I pray that ye may find *Taigh Gràs* tae yer liking."

"It's great!" I told him, quite impressed with the New England mansion.

"I'm pleased," he responded accordingly. "Weel then, let us presently collect Amity and take our breakfast."

"Good idea." I promptly strode back toward Amity and slipped a gentle palm over her shoulder. She glanced up at me, and I expressed to her that her uncle had arrived. She glanced over her shoulder to see him standing patiently for us to leave the room, then returned her glance to me as I explained that it was time for us to eat. She stood from her chair and slid her little hand into mine, and the three of us left the sunroom for the dining room to enjoy breakfast together.

Ten

During breakfast, Leif asked if I was interested in accompanying him on a journey through town, because he had to make another errand after our meal. Of course, I gladly accepted his invitation; it was an opportunity for me to tour the city and see the sights. So, when we had finished eating, he followed me upstairs back to our bedroom to collect our outer garments. I also needed to place my pattens over my slippers due to the winter weather, so I collected them from the floor beside my armoire and sat on the plushly cushioned foot bench waiting for him to help me slip them over my shoes, while he gathered his pistol belt from one of the chairs. He turned from the chair with his belt in hand and noticed me waiting patiently for him just when he started wrapping the holster belt around his waist. Instead of securing it first around himself, he replaced it in the chair and strode toward me. He knelt before me and took my ankle in hand, ready to assist me.

"Leif?" I started as I was observing him gather one patten into his hand.

"Aye?" he responded, shifting his gaze up to me.

"Will you tell me something about Mercy?" I asked.

"Aye, whit do ye wish tae ken?" he responded casually.

"Well, I noticed her dialect," I mentioned.

"Aye," he said nonchalantly.

"Do you know where she's from, originally?" I inquired.

"Aye, the lass was born in Virginia," he answered.

"Virginia?" I echoed in amazement.

"Aye." He nodded, returning his attention to my ankle as he began slipping my patten on my shoe.

"Well, that's a bit of a ways, isn't it?" I asked curiously.

"Indeed."

"It's so far for her."

"I reckon so."

"So, how did she come here under your employment?"

"Weel," Leif considered thoughtfully. He secured my patten on the first foot and started doing the same with the second. He didn't say anything as he worked my other patten over my shoe; he seemed to be thinking for a minute. When he easily finished securing the second patten, he straightened from kneeling to sit next to me on the bench, and I curiously looked at him. He sat in his typical fashion with his sturdy knees separated and palms resting over his muscular thighs whenever he meant to have a considerate talk. "The lass is a runaway slave," he finally disclosed to me.

"Seriously?" I replied suddenly, looking at him with an openly shocked expression. I was sharply stunned to learn that she was in bondage when I believed her to be free like anyone else who was supposed to be according to my expectations. I would have never thought that anyone I knew would ever be enslaved, and for her to be working for us while enslaved was deeply troubling to me—particularly because he and I had discussed the issue of slavery before we got married. "Is she still a slave?"

"Aye, the lass is," he said, seriously looking at me. Now, I was even more troubled, since I believed we both believed that it was an abominable institution.

"Oh—I see... What happened to her? How did she come here?" I asked pensively.

"Her proprietor was slain in a dual with swords," Leif began informing me.

"Oh, my God!" I responded abruptly, further astonished, covering my palm over my mouth in appall.

"The victor acquired her proprietor's property. Mercy claims that her new master was a callous man in general who was unmerciful, and indecent tae the slaves. Thus, she ran off with several other slaves and escaped as far north as Maryland Colony till she was captured by anither man who wouldnae return her but held her tae sell. I met the man, at a canteen, who attempted tae sell her tae a brothel holder fur British troops haur by the wharf. I knew whit it was all about regarding him, and it didnae bode weel with me—her fate was in deeper peril as she would have been further mistreated and made tae whore. Thus, I purchased her, and she has since been in my possession," Leif explained to me.

"I see..." I felt really uncomfortable about this unexpected news. "So, then, you own her now?" I asked perturbedly.

"As I do all of my servants," he said naturally.

"Oh..."

"They are all indentured. I have permitted them an allowance in order that when they receive their freedom in time from me, they will have obtained sufficient means fur independence," Leif said.

"I see..." I said abstractedly. "So, this is a temporary position for Mercy also?"

"Aye." Leif nodded.

"Hmm... But, you told me that you didn't believe in slavery," I reminded him.

"'Tis true that I dinnae agree with the wickedness that slavery brings," he said, earnestly looking at me.

"Except—you have them," I pointed out hypocritically.

"I do." He nodded his head, admitting it.

"Why?"

"They have been fated tae servitude and are most vulnerable tae the inherent evils of it. If I'm able tae protect them whilst they are in my charge, then I shall do it," he said unquestionably.

"I see," I replied meditatively as I held his steady gaze. "But, you don't have to own them. You could free them instead."

"I shall not."

"Why not?"

"I shall do nae such thing. 'Twould be cruel. Not at present shall I do so, fur they are most vulnerable and need my protection," he said.

"Protection from what? May I ask?"

"From slaveholders and traders who would recapture them intae servitude before they would have a chance at living a free life that would be warranted."

"But, couldn't you just give them papers or something like that to prove their freedom in case that should happen?"

"It isnae as simple as ye perceive it tae be, *mo ghaol*."

"To me it is."

"Yoo're not properly understanding the matter."

"I think I do understand it."

"Nae, it seems that ye dinnae realize that the issue is perilous. 'Tis a difficult matter and isnae a simple one as ye may like it tae be."

"Why not?"

"Firstly, I shall bring tae yer attention that the papers of which ye speak can be stolen and burnt. Secondly, my slaves will be left destitute and fall intae servitude once more if I waur tae merely free them before they can prove their self-reliance. I cannae afford that upon my conscience. Many freed slaves land in desperation, fur they are forbidden tae lead lives that will lend tae their sufficient means fur independence from their masters—as I am certain ye may weel ken already. As such, I shall not contribute tae their plight when I have the ability tae properly provide fur mine in my own charge."

I considered what he was saying. From what I read in his expression, he really did believe that he was offering them sanctuary, and he meant no ill will toward any of them in the least bit. So, I carefully started to say, "Well—I suppose that is very generous of you." But I was absolutely in disagreement with him on this issue. There had to be a way where we didn't have to have slaves working for us.

"Whit is it?" Leif scrutinized me with his transfixed eyes.

"I—I just don't agree with the concept of slavery," I told him frankly. Leif merely nodded a little, appearing deeply pensive like I was. I nodded a little too, still thinking. I was conflicted over the fact that he owned people while my affectionate feelings for him ran considerably deep. I didn't know how I could reconcile this serious contradiction. I shifted my gaze down to the rug at my feet while tucking my loose ringlets behind my ear.

"You said to me that you thought slavery was an abomination," I reminded him.

"It is," he said.

"Then I don't understand you."

"I also told ye that I hoped fur one day waur all men would be free tae self-determine their own lives without reprisal," he reminded me, too.

"I remember that."

"Aye, weel—I am in fact a slave also, Sylvie. Mayhap ye never considered my military service tae the Crown as me being placed into bondage as I was in truth pressed into it. The yoke of the Crown has many in servitude as it has me also by the neck. Should I not perish in battle fur England, then I shall strive tae attain my liberty from the Crown—however long it micht take," he said. I suddenly realized that I never considered the fact that he was also actually trapped into servitude by the government as he served in its military, and this realization, which made me shift my perspective regarding him and placed him into a new light.

"I'm sorry that I didn't consider your position with the government," I said delicately. He nodded his head in acceptance. "Well..." I drifted off as I considered my disturbed thoughts, still feeling highly uncomfortable that he had slaves working for us and about his own bondage to the government.

"Aye?"

"I guess that explains it," I remarked contemplatively.

"How do ye mean?" Leif inquired curiously.

"Well, Mercy was really upset earlier this morning," I told him.

"Whit ever fur?" He gave me an odd look.

"Because she saw that I had dressed myself, and thought if you —I don't know—for whatever reason found out about it, that you'd be angry with her and send her away. But I told her that you wouldn't ever do that," I disclosed to him, feeling awful that Mercy had become so upset about it.

"Och, weel," Leif considered as he thoughtfully looked at me. "Why did ye not call upon her, however?"

"Well, I don't know. I suppose that I just thought I could dress myself. It doesn't bother me to dress myself. I'm an abled bodied person, you know?"

"Despite that fact, she is haur tae wait upon ye—and, ye must let her," he said. I bit my lip and automatically gave him a reluctant glare.

"I don't know..." I shrugged my shoulders a little, disinclined to have anyone helping me. Leif studied my hesitation.

"I can have it instead, if it is whit ye prefer, tae have a white lass be yer maid," Leif offered sincerely.

"Oh no!" I gasped. I buried my face in my palms in sheer mortification.

"Weel, I dinnae wish fur ye tae be affronted," he suggested honestly. I suddenly let my hands fall from my face as quickly as I had put them up and utterly stared at him with incredulity.

"*Affronted?* Why on earth would I be affronted?" I asked ridiculously.

"I dinnae ken," he replied earnestly. "I merely reckoned it micht be whit ye prefer."

"What I prefer," I echoed, thinking again.

"Aye."

"Well..."

"Aye?"

"I don't prefer anybody. I'd rather that we just not have any slaves—to be honest with you. I can't help thinking the way I do about it. I don't agree with it. I think it's wrong to own people."

"Yet, they wulnea be dismissed, Sylvie," he said certainly. I looked at him, contemplating him some more about his intentions. I was also aware that we were heading for a disagreement, and although I didn't want for us to argue, my conscience kept pressing me.

"But Finley doesn't have slaves," I pointed out to him.

"He had a number of them in fact," Leif said without any reservation.

"He did?" I felt my eyes widen in shock as I learned this about his brother.

"Aye."

"I never knew that."

"I reckon not."

"What happened to them?"

"They waur stolen by Indians when we waur away upon duty."

"They were?"

"Aye."

"When did that happen?" I asked, stunned.

"Some years efter Governor Shirley had the fort built near the Hoosic."

"That was some time ago," I realized.

"Aye."

"But I thought there hadn't been any raids since the Abenaki came down the river the last time you told me about it when we were in Northampton."

"Aye, yet thaur was once anither event efter that occurrence when Fin and Beth waur newlywed. Abenaki returned over the river and stole into Northampton. They raided the village whilst Fin and I waur stationed in Albany."

"Oh..." I swallowed dryly. "You never told me about that happening."

"I didnae care tae frighten ye," he said. I nodded slightly in response, feeling significantly uncertain as I acknowledged him. "So, Finley hasn't had any slaves since then?"

"He replaced a few, but didnae recoup the loss."

"But he didn't have any slaves when I was staying there, though."

"He didnae. The several that he had waur struck with fever and perished whilst we waur in Albany," Leif explained. "Therefore, Fin had none when ye waur residing with us in Northampton."

"Oh... But the ones you have—will they ever be free?" I asked.

"If they so choose tae save their allowances adequately in order tae have some means. Without it, should I free them presently, it is as I said—their fate is subject tae either destitution or certain slavery whaur they micht easily land in a harsh state of affairs with anither master who isnae God fearing."

"God fearing," I echoed.

"Aye."

"I think if anyone really feared God, they wouldn't have slaves to begin with," I said. The expression on Leif's face turned grave.

"Yoo're unaware, *ceisdein*. Many men fear God though they own slaves. Dinnae be blindly pious."

"I'm not being that way."

"Certainly, ye are."

"I'm just saying that slavery is evil."

"Inherently, I do agree—as money is the route tae all evil. Yet, we confront such temptation in ways that are not simplistic. Fur example, I have wealth, therefore do ye deem me an evil man?"

"No—absolutely not."

"Then, pray, understand the complexity of these matters and dinnae be judgmental."

"Hmm," I sighed. "I don't mean to be judgmental. It's just that owning people doesn't sit well with me. I mean, if you freed them, couldn't they gain employment instead where they could freely support themselves?"

"Proper employment is scarce and merely meant fur those with a skilled craft acquired through apprenticeship," he pointed out. I pensively nodded. "So..."

"Yeah?"

"Are ye certain of Mercy, then?"

"Well, I... Never mind... I suppose that it doesn't make a difference right now at this stage in time, I guess... yeah, it's all right, I suppose—Mercy's fine, she's all right, I like her. She's very nice," I accepted with silent disappointment.

It was pointless for me to pursue this issue any further with him, I realized. I had remembered just now that the colony of Massachusetts had not abolished slavery until its constitution took effect during the American Revolution in 1780, and that it would be some time before sentiments about the issue would change. Still, it was incredibly frustrating for me to be here during this time where the institution of slavery was accepted. It went against my moral standards and my customs. How could I change this fact, or make a difference that was meaningful, that would not jeopardize my own safety along with Mercy's? I mean, if I refused her as a servant to me, would Leif sell her? Would she be traded for someone else? Would she be made to work harder for us if she wasn't sold? I had no idea what Leif would do, or what could actually happen to her that might lead to her severe detriment. But then again, while I continued thinking, there could be a possible solution: why couldn't she simply be freed and still work for us? That way the choice would be hers if she decided to leave or stay.

As I returned looking at Leif and studied his grave eyes, I perceived the unlikelihood of such a proposal to him. The adamance in his expression was clear. I realized then, once again, that not even I carried any rights since I was second class due to the fact that I was a woman. The issue pertaining to women's rights wouldn't even be addressed until after the abolition of slavery for several decades to come. So, I was stuck. Stuck in this new reality that granted no leeway or opportunity to make my opinions and actions carry any weight in society. This greatly disturbed me, but I didn't know what I could do to make my situation more palatable according to the liberated traditions that I was accustomed to. I felt resigned and trapped.

"Then ye agree tae let her wait upon ye?" he insisted.

"Yes, of course," I relented. I didn't like that he had people as possessions. But I could clearly see that furthering this discussion was going to lead into a big rift between us as we butted heads on this issue, and I didn't want that to occur at all; my dear feelings for him outweighed any potential for disagreement with him. All I wanted for us was to get along and live in harmony. So, I gave him a little smile and he slightly nodded in concert as he kept staring at me.

"Very weel," Leif said, seeming satisfied with me. "Now, let us collect ourselves, and have a merry outing." He decisively stood from his seat beside me on the foot-bench and stepped toward the chair to collect his pistol belt.

WE CLIMBED INTO THE HORSE-DRAWN, open sleigh and nestled close together, covered warmly in our outerwear, blankets, and bearskin cover. I sank my gloved palms inside my muff and kept it resting comfortably on my lap beneath the bearskin. I was excited to ride in the open winter air with Leif to explore the city despite my earlier conversation with him. I looked across from us where Amity was seated and noticed the delight on her face too. This was going to be quite fun, I thought. I glimpsed at Leif, and he caught my gaze. I smiled at him, and he smiled in return when the next thing we knew, our driver, Jonah, started the horse and the bells around the horse's neck began jingling as the sleigh whizzed off with us in it.

As we made our way off the property, we exited onto the white snow-fluffed road headed north. We passed a small brownstone school house and several scattered dwellings. I was beginning to get the feel for the layout of the area as we rode along. It was surely a small town at most rather than a city; it was more rural than urban. We passed along Common Road and to the left of us were small ponds frozen over, seen in the clearing. While continuing our way, I also noticed off in the distance gallows perched on a hill in the clearing. My blood instantly chilled, and the chill crawled over my skin, forcing me to realize again the period in which I found myself.

I shifted my gaze ahead to the road we were traveling on as it turned into Common Street at the point of Beacon Hill. Within a block or two, Common Street had suddenly changed into Tremont Street at the corner of the church to our right, and to our left was the cemetery. At the next block, we turned right on Queen's Street. We continued along for several more blocks, and the brownstones began to collect together interspersed with stone masonry buildings. Soon, the Old South Meeting House emerged midway at the intersection of Cornhill Street and King Street.

The sleigh turned right along Cornhill Street where we passed a collection of closely gathered brownstone establishments and residences. At the next block, was another large intersection where the State House fell in sight in the middle of the street to our right. We veered right through the narrow passage between the State House and other buildings and continued some more on our way.

When the street suddenly widened, the name changed to Union Street until we turned right again onto Middle Street. Shortly, Faneuil Hall fell into plain sight to the right of us and between the buildings across the way, adjacent to us, the marketplace could be discerned. My heart galloped with excitement as I was utterly awestruck by realizing that I was witnessing in real time the live historical context of the major significance of these famous landmarked buildings in American history.

I glanced around and unexpectedly noticed Leif's musing gaze on me. I grinned nervously at him, conscious of his awareness of me.

"It's really nice to be in a city again," I commented pleasantly as the sleigh came to a halt.

"Aye," he agreed thinkingly, with a look of intrigue on his face.

"We've stopped," I noticed.

"We have arrived," he said. He straightened from his seat and easily leaped from the sleigh. Proffering a hand to me, I slid my palm into his and he gently pulled me forth, clasping me firmly by the waist as he swung me out of the sleigh. My feet firmly planted in the snow, and I watched him turn to retrieve Amity. After collecting her from the sleigh, I sensed his palm wrapping around my elbow when he guided me across the walkway. Up a few steps, he reached for the handle to a door, and we entered a milliner's shop where the mantua maker was also employed.

Three women attendants with attentive gazes and an inquisitive stare from a young woman customer promptly turned in our direction as we made our entrance. I noticed the woman customer was being fitted for a pretty gray bonnet with blue satin ribbons and petite, white silk flowers on it.

"Oh! Good morn to you, Your Grace," said the matriarch of the shop in an extremely polite tone as she attentively rushed over toward us.

"Guid morrow tae ye, Mistress Dunn," Leif replied courteously. "I shall like tae introduce tae ye my wife, Her Grace, Duchess of Monteith," he continued.

"I am most honored to make your acquaintance, Your Grace," Mrs. Dunn said pleasantly and bobbed a curtsy before me.

"This is our niece, Miss Amity. Her experience is an inaudible one, yet she has the ability tae communicate weel with Her Grace," Leif said.

"What a blessing," Mrs. Dunn replied sympathetically.

"Indeed," Leif agreed.

"Pray, how may I assist you this fine morn, Your Grace?" Mrs. Dunn inquired, gazing attentively at Leif.

"Her Grace requires several new gowns—two of which must be ball gowns," Leif said.

"Most certainly, Your Grace," Mrs. Dunn responded cheerfully.

"Aye, and our niece will have two modest gowns made fur herself," Leif included.

"Splendid! We shall commence straight away," Mrs. Dunn replied enthusiastically, ready to please it seemed at any cost.

"Very weel," Leif replied adequately, then turned toward me. "I shall take my leave from ye haur fur Master Dunn's tailor shop across the street. I shall have my sleeves adjusted."

"All right," I agreed pleasantly. He subtly winked at me and smiled. Then, he dipped his head toward me, and I curtsied politely in front of him, understanding the custom.

"Your Grace," he said kindly to me as he straightened.

"Your Grace," I replied equally to him, understanding how I should address him in public. I then observed him turn away from me and pace toward the threshold as he replaced his tricorn hat over his head before disappearing out the door.

I returned my gaze to the women inside the shop who were peering inquisitively at me when I felt Amity's small hand slide between my fingers once I removed them from my muff. I gently wrapped my palm around hers while we gazed at the women who were curiously looking at us.

"Won't you please come, Your Grace?" Mrs. Dunn nicely invited me.

"Yes, thank you," I replied politely. I proceeded following her deeper into the shop as I noticed that she was short and plump with a very fair complexion highlighting her gray hair and bright rosy cheeks, and seemed extremely friendly.

"Please meet Miss Harriet who is newly arrived from London merely last month before the first snow," Mrs. Dunn introduced me to her as she properly gestured toward the young blonde woman getting the pretty bonnet fitted over her head. I supposed that Miss Harriet couldn't have been any older than twenty, as she gazed interestedly at me.

"It's nice to meet you, Miss Harriet," I acknowledged pleasantly.

"'Tis quite nice to make your acquaintance as well, Your Grace. How do you do?" Miss Harriet greeted kindly.

"Very well, thank you. And you?" I asked.

"Quite well also, I thank you, Your Grace," she said nicely.

"I'm glad to hear so," I responded kindly. I was distinctly aware of having to force myself to realize my most elevated manners in this close situation and hoped I'd be well received.

"This is your niece, one understands," Miss Harriet commented inquisitively.

"Yes, this is Amity," I replied, introducing my new niece to her.

"A pity she cannot hear, for she appears a cheerful creature. But you are good to her, one may see," Miss Harriet expressed politely.

"Yes, of course" I said primly.

"Pray, might we have tea together? I have longed for dainty company since my arrival. I am kept such alone whilst I remain with my brother, Lord Brighton, as I await the arrival of my betrothed, Lord Overland," Miss Harriet explained.

"I see. Well, certainly, Miss Harriet, let's have tea together. That will be nice," I agreed.

"Thank you. You are most kind," Miss Harriet responded graciously with graceful diction in her English accent.

Mrs. Dunn led us to a table with several chairs for us to sit. As tea was being prepared by one of the shopkeeper girls, Amity sat patiently and well behaved observing me examining various fabric prints and illustrated gown styles in what appeared to be in a catalogue. Once Miss Harriet had decided on her sort of bonnet, she approached and placed herself in the empty seat across from us at the table.

One of the shopkeeper girls properly arranged tea before us, and Miss Harriet delicately proceeded preparing herself a cup as she took the sugar nips and broke off a piece from the sugarloaf and placed it into her teacup. I daintily retrieved a scone on a petite porcelain plate and carefully layered it with cranberry preserves, then placed it before Amity for her to have.

"She is indeed a dear creature," Miss Harriet commented as she was observing Amity beginning to quietly eat her scone and preserves.

"Thank you, Miss Harriet. My husband and I are very fond of her," I said.

"I wonder, if I might inquire, if Your Grace is not from near London as I notice a unique accent from you?" she asked.

"Actually, I am not originally from London. Nor am I from anywhere else in England for that matter," I replied politely.

"I see. From were, then, does Your Grace originate?"

"I am from a place that's quite far from here, in fact."

"Indeed?" she replied amazedly as her blue eyes widened accordingly.

"Yes," I said.

"I find it most fascinating."

"You do?"

"Why, yes—I have never left England till now. To arrive in

Boston is a much different experience than from what I am accustomed. It makes for quite an exciting adventure, I believe. I have even heard about the savages who live amongst the wilds of the wood beyond these parts. I find it quite interesting, and I shall like to see one of these savages of which I have heard speak," Miss Harriet explained innocently with noticeable but prim enthusiasm.

"I perhaps might recommend that you not wish for such an encounter, Miss Harriet. The wilderness is presently an unpredictable and dangerous place—especially for one not quite native to this land," I warned delicately.

"I see. Aye... Mayhap, you are correct," she considered thoughtfully. "However, one continues to remain curious... Nonetheless, then I shall pray to our Lord God that He is merciful to my betrothed, Lord Overland, upon his journey from Albany to meet me here in Boston without peril. Lord Overland has corresponded with me and described the thick wilderness which lies beyond. He even wrote to me that he has seen these Indians as he has battled against them and the French upon the frontier. Therefore, I shall continue to pray for his welfare."

"Yes, that would be wise," I agreed.

The conversation paused briefly as we both took a sip from our teacups. I observed Miss Harriet as she daintily replaced her cup upon the saucer and demurely stared at me for a moment.

"Might I inquire if it is customary for ladies of your origin to wear hair in your manner? I find it most unique and becoming," Miss Harriet asked interestedly.

"Yes, it is preferred this way from where I come, I suppose. Actually, if I'm being rather honest, women wear their hair in all sorts of styles from where I come. There is no standard, really," I said sincerely, as I thought how I had fixed my hair this morning. I had parted it in the middle and set two crystal floret pins on each side of my head. The pins gathered a bit of hair away from my face while the remainder freely cascaded in thick Shirley Temple style ringlets past my shoulders.

"There is no standard?" she replied curiously, lightly touching her own stylized ringlets to her coiffed hairstyle.

"No, actually. But there are a number of popular hair styles women choose to wear," I said.

"Oh, aye, I see... If I might say to Your Grace, that I find I quite admire your appearance, for I have not known anyone with your beauty. It is most refreshing," Miss Harriet said before she took a bird's bite out of her scone.

"Thank you, Miss Harriet. You're very kind. I also admire your appearance, and I believe your Lord Overland will be very pleased to see you," I replied graciously.

"Thank you, Your Grace. You are most kind also," Miss Harriet said, then sipped a bit of tea again. She placed her teacup back over her saucer and ventured shyly to say, "It seems His Grace is quite generous with Her Grace."

"Yes, he's quite kind," I acknowledged.

"I merely pray Lord Overland will treat me with such kindness once we are wed," she disclosed hopefully.

"Oh, I don't see why he wouldn't," I replied encouragingly.

"But, we have not yet been acquainted with one another save for a few correspondences," she revealed.

"Oh, I see... Well, perhaps you might give yourselves the opportunity to become better acquainted once he arrives in town to see you," I said.

"Aye, mayhap," she considered. "Yet, I realize that I am being quite bold when I must confess to you that should he appear anywhere similar to His Grace, then I should be *most* pleased." She smiled bashfully.

"Begging pardon my ladies," Mrs. Dunn interrupted mirthfully without consideration as she smiled boldly at us, "but would any one of our own husbands appeared as Duke Monteith, we would all be *most* pleased."

The three other shopkeeper girls, Gertrude, Anne and Prudence, giggled in response. I felt my cheeks suddenly become warm as I nearly choked down my tea.

"A man such as His Grace would satisfy any woman who might have eyes to see," Mrs. Dunn continued precociously in good-nature with the shop girls giggling quietly in the background. "Her Grace is most fortunate to have His Grace for a husband. 'Tis quite clear in his dashing appearance that he is indeed *smitten* to have his new wife, as many of us have long wondered when he would wed. It also quite seems that Her Grace is pleased with her new husband, if I dare say so."

"Would you say this might be true, Your Grace?" Miss Harriet inquired.

"Um—well, yes, I suppose," I admitted abashedly, feeling placed on the spot.

"See there? A man's appearance counts for some," Mrs. Dunn said with a knowing smile.

"I do find that I share Mrs. Dunn's sentiment," Miss Harriet agreed as the shopkeeper girls kept giggling.

"Whilst all children are a blessing from God, I shall also continue to boldly endeavor to say that a man's appearance will also let a woman know whether she cares to bear his children given the choice, by the by. Yet, I reckon you, Your Grace, have no quarrel over this where His Grace is concerned, would you not say?"

"Well, I didn't give it much thought when we got married, I suppose," I responded uneasily.

"Indeed?" Mrs. Dunn laughed.

"Not really," I replied demurely.

"Be that as it will, for we are not blind. Pray excuse my outspokenness, yet, the Lord Almighty willing a joyous thing to anticipate that you will be round with your husband's child soon to celebrate all of His blessings." Mrs. Dunn continued optimistically.

I quickly stuffed my mouth full of scone and began chewing. When the food in my mouth soon began to dissolve and once I had swallowed it, I quickly changed the subject of conversation by asking Mrs. Dunn to tell me something about the design of the gown in the illustration before me.

JUST WHEN WE had concluded our business in the milliner's shop, Leif arrived and retrieved us from it. We returned to the sleigh and made a stop at the Knight's House Tavern for some hard cider to warm our bones. However, unlike Leif, I still couldn't quite stomach the strength of the beverage, because it was too strong and reminded me too much of hard liquor. So, like Amity, I settled for a small bowl of hot chowder and tea before we hopped back into the sleigh and returned home to *Taigh Gràs*.

LATER THAT NIGHT I lay in bed beside Leif with his arm enfolding me close against him. The plaguing troubles that continually kept my consciousness unsettled and wakeful at night as the thought of returning home to the twenty-first century suddenly vanished, leaving me calm and unworried. I felt content, emotionally restful, secure, and kept. Tonight, I realized for the very first time since I came here, while I was silently observing the moonlight glow between the drapes in our bedroom, that my mind was empty of all compunction and finally still with peacefulness. I gently enfolded my palm around his and seized it close to my breasts against my heart, and I felt his warm breath coming over the back of my head as his lips quietly pressed upon it in a kiss before drifting to sleep.

Eleven

A few days later I was very relieved, nearly overjoyed, when my menstrual cycle came. I quickly decided then to devise a ring of cycle beads and use them as a measure of birth control. I was aware of the natural contraceptive through a friend of mine who was a homeopathic medical practitioner in Los Angeles, and she had informed me about this system as a method she had used. Given my experience with Matt, I believed the method probably would be highly successful if done correctly. According to the Institute of Reproductive Health at Georgetown University, which developed the method, the success rate could be as high as in the ninety percentile range for accuracy. Also, with my success at having used the method when Matt and I were together before we had decided to have children, it proved to me its ability to work. So, this course of action to use this method of birth control was an easy decision for me to make.

MOST OF MY time during the day was spent tutoring Amity in the nursery. The room decor was further enhanced with juvenile furnishings along with a new bookcase and blackboard. Amity seemed to be thriving very well under my tutelage, and now we were progressing with the written alphabet. It was so fulfilling for me to work with her and to witness her development in her ability to communicate, which would in time lead to further academic exploration.

One afternoon after we had completed our lessons and as Amity often trailed off to keep the maids or the cooks company, I stepped outside into the winter air for a walk in the snow. The air was cold and crisp as I peacefully paced over the frosted ground through the field. The nearby pine trees were heavily covered with snow, and the sky was a cool gray. Daylight lit the scene in monochromatic tones of washed-out light blue and dark gray, I observed as I was admiring the scenery while pacing along.

Catching me unexpectedly off guard, Leif suddenly stole alongside me just as I was about to cross the road toward the Common.

"Oh! Hi," I gasped, glad to see him walking beside me.

"Did I cause ye fricht?" he asked regretfully.

"No," I replied.

"Guid, fur I wouldnae wish tae do so tae ye," he said.

"You didn't," I reassured him. He grinned at me and I smiled at him. "I thought you were still in your meeting with the governor."

"We have completed our business," he informed me.

"Oh."

I noticed his eyes seemed much bluer than usual. They sparkled like deep sapphire orbs, and I thought they were lovely. Bundled to the neck with his coat and scarf, his ruddy expression warmly beamed as he smiled down at me.

"Whaur about are ye headed?" he inquired.

"I don't know. I thought I'd just take a walk in the Common now."

"Och. I wish tae accompany ye."

"Sure, that'll be nice."

We started together crossing the road toward the Common in comfortable silence, glad to be among each other's company. It was a nice stroll together as we paced over the clearing. The snow level was fortunately not too deep to withstand, and the white scenery enveloping us all around was still and inaudible. The watch house and powder house could be discerned perched on a mound off in the distance, as we wandered across the clearing, I recognized.

In a little while, we had aimlessly wandered among a thin row of barren maples near a small pond where several older boys were squealing and laughing, plainly having a good time, while they wildly chased each other on ice skates across the frozen pond. I stopped to watch them with admiration as they scurried and skirted crazily around each other all over the ice. At one point in the chase, some of the boys dashed from one end of the pond toward the other side to steer clear from the one boy chasing them all. But the chaser caught up with one of the fleeing boys and grabbed him by the coattail. The one who was caught suddenly whirled around. The boy who had apprehended his friend by the coattail unexpectedly lost his balance and was sent flying off to the side until he crashed full force over the snow bank, landing smack dap faced down planted in the snow.

"Oh, my goodness!" I gasped in surprise, uncontrollably bursting out with laughter. I abruptly covered my mouth with my hand, guiltily entertained, trying to subdue my giggling.

"Are they not foolish lads?" Leif chuckled also, observing the boys bowling over with laughter across the ice.

"Totally ridiculous!" I laughed.

"Those are lads fur ye—always thaur fur one's enlivenment," he said, chuckling.

"No kidding!" I laughed some more.

"May our Lord Almighty comfort me if I should become a father tae a lad," he remarked amusingly. I turned my humored gaze up to him.

"Why do you say that?" I inquired.

"Weel, I shall never have a moment's peace due tae a lad's continuous antics. It will be quite fortunate should he survive his entire youth by the foolhardy he will likely commit." He gazed wistfully across the pond at the boys.

"Then do you prefer having a girl?" I asked curiously. He turned his eyes toward me, meeting my gaze.

"Ahh, tae have a lass will be the lecht of my eyes. Yet, whit am I tae do once she will wed? I shall be struck with heartache as she will have her own bairns and nae longer be my precious wee lecht," he said. I thought that was very sweet of him to say, and it attracted me even more to him.

"She would always be your light—no matter what," I said. He simply smiled at me in response. "So, what are you going to do? It seems there's no choice between the two."

"Apparently, it therefore is the case. I shall enjoy either lad or lass all the same and take my blows as they come," he said with a warm look on his face. I felt my lips easily curl into a little grin, and I removed my hand from my muff, sliding it around his arm.

"That's fair."

"I reckon so." He smiled back at me as I tugged on his arm a little.

"Let's go," I urged lightly.

We started away from the pond, leaving the boys to their rambunctious playfulness. Arm in arm, we meandered around the Common for a while longer. We talked nicely with each other as we strolled along the way, and I found myself really enjoying the present deepening connection between us.

"We shall have the governor along with a few distinguished guests fur Christmas Eve dinner," he mentioned.

"Christmas Eve?" I echoed unexpectedly.

"Aye," he replied while gazing at me.

"Isn't that next week or something?" I realized, surprisingly.

"Nae, in slightly less than a fortnecht."

"I didn't realize how close we are to Christmas. Time's passing by quickly, it seems."

"Aye, 'twould seem so... I shall like fur ye tae consider a menu, *mo ghaol*," he requested.

"Sure, no problem," I agreed, thinking with shock at the time imperceptibly passing by me.

"Very weel," he responded, seeming satisfied.

"Oh!" I had a sudden thought that hit me on a whim.

"Aye?"

"Do you think that we may have a Christmas tree?"

"A Christmas tree say ye?" He strangely looked at me.

"Yeah." I gazed at him with enthusiasm.

"As do the Hessians?"

"Yes!" I said eagerly. He broke off a moment, grimacing while staring weirdly at me, though he seemed to be considering the idea.

"Weel... I have never observed Christmas with a tree."

"You haven't?"

"I cannae say that I have."

"Then, you're missing out. So, let's have one."

"The thought is novel. I am uncertain of it."

"Oh pretty please! With sugar on top," I pleaded playfully.

"I beg yer pardon?"

"Pretty please with sugar on top," I repeated.

"I huvnae ever heard such an appeal." He suddenly appeared entertained as he gave me a little grin.

"Of course you haven't," I teased.

"Weel, as yoo've quite irresistibly sugar sweetened yer appeal, I haven't the faintest heart tae say nae."

"Thank you! I'm thrilled!" I happily squeezed both my arms around his robust bicep, I was still holding. The quizzical expression on his face suddenly transformed into full diversion as a wide smile spread over his lips.

"Ye quite continue tae surprise me, *mo ghaol*." He secured my grip around his arm with his other gloved palm.

"Do I really?" I asked as it began flurrying around us.

"Aye," he said certainly.

"Well, that's good, isn't it?"

"Quite guid."

"Great! At least I'm not a bore."

"A wit?"

"You know—boring. At least I'm not boring to you."

"Och. Ye could never be that tae me even if ye attempted it."

"Nice. Well, you're not close to being a bore to me either."

"How comforting."

"I guess in that case we're a good match for each other after all."

"A match that is ideal," he said. I smiled at him and my heart warmed. "Now, let us return indoors before we shall catch our death," he suggested. I suddenly realized that I had grown somewhat chilled and thought that he was right to have us return inside the house.

I agreed and released my hand from his light clasp. Turning from him, I promptly started trotting through the snow back toward the direction of the house. I glanced over my shoulder, seeing him being left behind. "Well? What are you waiting for, slow-poke? Let's go!" I called back to him.

The expression on his ruddy face unexpectedly piqued as his brow lifted high. He chuckled at my taunt and leaped forward, suddenly darting after me in the snow. He began chasing me, and I found myself laughing breathlessly as I strove to stay ahead of him. I heard him panting and chuckling close behind me, and I glanced back over my shoulder at him when I discovered him only a slight distance from me. Aware of him closely chasing me, excited me to escape him. I strove to pick up my pace, feeling that at any moment he would overtake me and snare me.

We weren't that far away from the house anymore as we kept running together, and soon one of the back doors leading inside came within tangible sight. But despite my approaching the door, the distance ironically seemed to remain slightly too far as I quickly advanced with him closely jogging after me. When finally, I lunged, my hand caught the door handle and I swung the door wide open, dashing inside out of the freezing cold air with him short on my heels.

Whizzing through the corridor, some of the servants were caught off guard, and I accidentally crashed right into one of the maids carrying an armful of fresh linens.

"Oh! My goodness, Prudence! I'm so terribly sorry!" I gasped suddenly, realizing that I had haphazardly knocked the white linens out of her hands and onto the floor, sullying them. I abruptly knelt and hurriedly gathered the material off the floor. "I'm so sorry for spoiling your work. Please don't worry about it. Just set these aside, and I'll take care of it. Leif's chasing me! He's as bad as a kid!" I panted excitedly as I sloppily returned the disheveled linens to her.

"Aye, Your Grace," Prudence replied, blatantly shocked. Anxiously glancing over my shoulder again, I saw Leif hastily approaching, seconds away through the corridor.

"Oh! I don't want him catching me!" I giggled nervously.

"Aye, Your Grace," she replied again, now holding the messy bundle of linens in her arms. Without another word to her, I immediately took off, hurrying once more through the corridor.

At the foyer, I rounded the banister and dashed up the grand staircase as quickly as I could without tripping over my skirts. Hastily gathering my gown, petticoats and all, above my knees, I frenetically continued up the stairs with Leif now closely pursuing me—all the while aware of his audible chuckling behind me.

Whirling along the passageways toward the back of the house, I burst inside our bedroom and shut the door behind me. The weighty sound of his boots over the hardwood floors suddenly slowed as they continued approaching. I decidedly hurried into the privy closet, hiding myself, and remained standing motionless, except for the wild panting escaping me—hoping that I was well hidden from him.

The door to our room was heard opening, and his footsteps slowly steadied and followed inward into the room. The bedroom door closed and *clicked* shut, and his heavy heels audibly thumped over the hardwood floor with even, measured steps, as they paced evenly around the room. But, I thought I heard them cease just beyond the opposite side of the privy closet door where I was hidden. I caught my breath, striving to stem my uneven breathing, but I couldn't seem to get a grip on controlling it from rapidly escaping me.

He seemed to pause for a moment just beyond the door, and my eager eyes watched the door handle, anticipating him opening it and discovering me. Except, his steps surprisingly started away from the door and seemed to pace away for a distance. Then, I thought I heard the bedroom door opening and closing again. Next, the room became quiet. Still, I waited silently in the privy closet—just in case he hadn't gone yet.

It seemed that he might have really left the bedroom, and the coast was presumably clear from him, I thought. So, I quietly turned the door handle and carefully pushed the door scarcely ajar to peer out into the room. Scanning the room as best as possible from my vantage point, it appeared that Leif might have left the bedroom, failing to discover me. But I noticed his coats, including his waistcoat, tossed in the chair opposite of me. Realizing that he'd made himself comfortable, I wondered about it.

With a little caution, I let the privy closet door open wide and came forth into the bedroom, believing myself safe from his capture. But just as I came into the room, the privy closet door abruptly whirled shut behind me when an imperceptible arm reached around my waist, grabbing me. An excitable screech escaped me as I instantly recognized Leif pulling me taut against his sturdy frame.

"*Och!* Now I've caught ye! Ye cannae hide from me, lass," he said playfully with a beaming expression.

"Oh yeah?" I laughed, noticing his Cheshire Cat smile.

"Aye," he replied unequivocally.

"I just didn't find a good enough hiding spot," I said, laughing some more.

"Thaur will never be an appropriate location fur ye tae hide from me, fur I shall always discover ye. Do ye not already understand?" he chuckled. He was significantly flushed, and the color of his laughing eyes was the deepest blue I'd ever seen. They glittered like crystal gems as he laughed, attracting me warmly to his mirth. He unfastened the clasp to my cape, and its heavy weight slid from my shoulders to my feet.

"What are you doing?" I asked, sensing his attraction to me also.

"Whit does it appear as though I'm doing?" he asked me instead as he began removing my scarf from around my neck.

"Um, well, I don't know," I stammered. His fingers wrapped around the buttons to my Jesuit jacket and began carefully unfastening them.

"Weel then, I reckon that I must show ye," he replied in a low, warm voice. I recognized the look in his eyes and I started feeling diffident in front of him.

"I guess so," I muttered. It seemed to never fail how shy and uncertain he could make me feel when he wanted me like this. He patiently began removing the many bits and pieces from my garments. I glanced up at him, observing the gentle grin over on his face. "You know, you don't have to undress me all the way if you don't want to," I suggested.

"Och?"

"Well, there's just so much stuff to bother with." I pointed out my attire, and all the attachments holding my gown and petticoats together.

"I want tae see ye," he said as he continued undressing me.

"Oh..."

"I am fond of observing ye."

"You are?" I giggled nervously, somewhat surprised to hear him say so.

"Aye," he replied when I felt him tugging the pins loose from my bodice.

"Why?"

"Yoo're bonnie."

"You think so?"

"Indeed."

"That's sweet of you to say."

"I like tae behold ye when I am with ye."

"You're making me shy." I felt slightly embarrassed that he admitted this to me even though I couldn't explain why.

"Am I?" he asked with a crooked grin.

"Yes, you are," I muttered.

"Ye charm me further."

"Why?"

"Ye entice me in ways that yield my will." His posture straightened when he finished unpinning the last pin to my stomacher, then he began untying my gown skirt and it fell to my feet upon the last loosened tie. I sensed Leif's fingers gently clasping my chin, forcing me to gaze up into his eyes. "Ye mustn't hide yerself from me, *àille dhubh*," he said.

"I'm not hiding," I replied.

"I fear ye understand my meaning." He ceased undressing me further while he stared steadfastly at me for a moment. I could perceive him purposefully searching deep into my gaze.

"Okay," I acquiesced.

"I shall forever want tae behold ye," he said meaningfully.

"Really?"

"Aye."

"Why?"

"I care tae gaze upon ye as we couple."

"Why, though?"

"I adore the way ye appear when I tooch ye."

"Oh," I whispered.

"Aye," he said softly, and gently pressed his lips over mine. Consequentially, I found myself scarcely aware that I had been undressed with merely my shift remaining over my naked frame. His touch began affecting me with an aching between my legs as he gently began kissing my lips. Feeling myself growing strange again, he gathered me up into his arms and placed me on the bed.

Twelve

One afternoon Leif entered the nursery just as Amity and I were completing our last lesson for the day.

"Oh, hi," I responded, glad to see him coming through the door.

"Hullo, *mo ghaol*," he said.

"Are you joining us?" I inquired.

"Aye, if I may."

"Sure, of course."

He strode toward a leather chair not too far across from us at the desk. This was actually the first time I remember Leif exclusively attending our lesson and observing what it was all about.

Amity and I continued scribing alphabet letters and assembling them into simple three letter phonetic words to sign their meaning. Leif sat quietly observing us for the entire rest of the time while he restfully smoked his pipe.

After about an hour, Amity's lessons had been completed, and she began asking me a question as I reached for our learning materials to gather from her writing desk.

"Whit is she communicating tae ye?" Leif inquired interestedly as he was observing us.

"She just wants to draw on the chalkboard a bit," I informed him.

"Is that permitted?" he asked oddly.

"Well, she's concluded all of her lessons—very well, I might add. There's no harm in it," I said.

"Och." He nodded a little, then I returned my attention to Amity as she was still gazing at me for my answer to her.

"Yes, you may," I signed and verbalized simultaneously to her, answering her question. She smiled at me and happily retrieved a piece of chalk when she began marking on the chalkboard.

"I shall like tae say a word tae her," Leif requested of me.

"Of course," I responded naturally. I gently called Amity's attention to her uncle.

"How micht I tell her that I am pleased by her achievement?" he asked me.

"Oh, that would be like this…" I demonstrated the articulating hand motions step by step for him to follow, and Leif interestedly began mimicking my hand signals. The message began registering on Amity's face as she modestly watched her uncle complete his communication to her. When he had completed following my lead, communicating to her what he wished to say, she responded demurely using her own signs with a sweet expression on her face.

"Whit did she say?" he asked curiously turning his gaze to me.

"She said, 'Thank you, Uncle. You are kind,'" I translated. Leif pulled the pipe from his lips and grinned, impressed. He straightened from his chair and delivered a kind little pat on top of Amity's head before he whimsically tapped the tip of her petite nose with a gentle forefinger. She smiled at him and turned back toward the chalkboard to continue drawing.

"There you have it," I said contentedly.

"Aye, very weel," he agreed as I turned to straighten the nursery. I returned a portion of our educational materials and art supplies in their rightful places over the desks and on the book shelves. Leif lingered around as I was tidying up the area and when

I leaned to collect the quill and inkwell from the side of Amity's desk to place on mine, Leif's palm stole gently around my neck. I turned my gaze up to his and smiled.

"I desire yer presence in my library," he said softly.

"Are you lonely for me?" I joked bashfully.

"Quite lonely," he said. I liked the way his eyes were glimmering just now, and noticed his lips curving into a boyish grin.

"Well," I started, "perhaps I'll be so generous to indulge you with my most precious time."

"Ye are most gracious, Your Grace."

"Anything for you, Your Grace," I responded. I naturally bobbed up on my toes to lightly press my lips to his for a quick kiss. "Now scoot so that I can finish tidying all this stuff up." His eyes suddenly widened and he grinned. He appeared simultaneously surprised and amused as a smile spread wide across his face.

"Very weel, *mo ghaol*," he replied good-naturedly.

"I'll see you shortly," I said.

"Aye." He pressed a light kiss on my brow, then turned and proceeded toward the door. I observed him vanishing out of the room, and at that moment, I was unexpectedly aware of how much my feelings for him had run deeper than I believed they would have ever ventured to go. *As if I couldn't fall any harder for him than I already have.* It excited me to the core of my heart and it frightened me a little too.

After I had concluded replacing all the learning supplies where they belonged, I strode toward Amity, still delighting over the chalkboard to gain her attention. I informed her where I would be if she needed me and that she had the rest of her time free to amuse herself. However, since it was a bright sunny day, I instructed her to remain in the garden and not to wander too far off if she desired to play outside in the snow for a little while. She nodded in acknowledgement as she understood me. After giving her a little kiss on her small cheek, I left the nursery room for Leif's study.

Climbing the staircase winding up to the third floor, I arrived in the corridor leading me to the entrance to his library. I entered it finally and discovered him at the back of the room by the window sitting at his large writing desk, currently stuffing fresh tobacco inside of his pipe. His gaze instantly lifted from what he was doing, seizing onto me as I crossed over the threshold, and the expression on his face suddenly brightened.

"Yoo've arrived at last," he said.

"Was I long?" I asked as I continued toward him.

"Merely according tae my heart," he replied. I smiled at him, taken by his sweet temperament.

"Sorry," I apologized.

"Yet, I'm contented now."

"Good."

"Come." He encouraged with a slight wave of his hand for me to approach him at his desk. He finished stuffing his pipe just as I arrived, standing before him seated in his large, leather wing chair. He lightly seized my palm in his hand and looked up at me from where he sat. "It will please me if ye waur tae read tae me," he requested fondly as I felt the pad of his large thumb tenderly stroking my knuckles.

"Okay," I agreed easily.

"Ye please me."

"What would you like for me to read to you?"

"Anything ye wish." He gestured to the stuffed built-in bookcases lining the back wall. Books filled the shelves from top to bottom, along the large wall.

I moved away from him toward the many books and briefly scanned the wall from one end to the other before moving forth to peruse the selection. I didn't know where to start—actually—as I strode closer toward the extended bookcases. So, I just randomly picked a place in the wall and began examining the titles: Plato, Aristotle, Socrates, Cicero, Marcus Aurelius, Boethius were among the list of many works I had first skimmed over the shelves. Newton, Leibniz, Buffon, Voltaire, and Swift stood out among others—a far more esoteric and eclectically arranged collection of literature than what would have been found in my own bookcase. If I weren't updating myself with the latest issues of American medical journals, science magazines or *National Geographic,* the *New York Times* or *Wall Street Journal,* then it was most definitely romantic novels, tabloids or fashion magazines I was interested in reading.

My eyes landed on Shakespeare, and I finally pulled forth a publication of his sonnets—a selection that wasn't too intense or required such heavy thinking—I preferred right now. I strode over toward the sofa and sat making myself comfortable as I gathered up my skirts to stretch across the seat. Leif had just lit his pipe while I thumbed through the pages. He began puffing away, filling the room with a smoky sweet scent. I had decided on the sonnet *Let Me Not to Marriage of True Minds Admit Impediments.*

"Och! Very guid—Shakespeare, a favorite," Leif recognized instantly as I read the title. So, I started to read while I lay comfortably stretched out over the sofa.

I glanced up from the pages and viewed his expression when I had completed the sonnet. He smiled affectionately at me, appearing pleased and contented as he puffed on his pipe. I returned his smile before dropping my gaze back to the words in my lap and read some more from a different sonnet.

After a while, I peered up from the pages again and discovered him seemingly having dozed off with his long legs stretched out over the ottoman before him. Noticing the smoking pipe remained cradled in his relaxed palm over his lap, I stirred from my seat, replacing the book into the bookcase, then quietly paced toward him. I reached for the smoking pipe in his hand and snuffed it out. Then, I took the tartan blanket resting in the corner of the window seat and carefully spread it over him, covering him well, since he remained slightly away from the burning fireplace.

Deciding to return to the books, I curiously perused through some more publications until my eye caught a volume of published

Rembrandt etchings. I retrieved the collection from the shelf, and strode back to the sofa, making myself comfortable on it again.

Opening the volume in my lap, I began studying the beautifully etched images. I found them absolutely captivating—the way the lines merged and diverged, appeared and vanished at the same time, and the way they became thick and thin with ink in various places. The images seemed to appear exactly the way a marvelously skilled free hand drawing would have appeared and lacked any of the stiffness innately characteristic of printmaking. Instead, each image seemed to breathe with life on its own. I became mesmerized by the beauty of every print presented. The portrait studies were fantastic, I thought. Every idea of emotion carried on any of his subjects' faces was perfectly captured and connoted the exact meaning of a particular feeling.

But then I stumbled upon another image which struck me as somewhat surprising. It was quite a bit unlike the first many I had been looking at of portraits, idyllic provincial scenes, and religious depictions. This one, I noticed, represented a scene that was, well, rather intimate, to put it politely. Still, even though I was no stranger to certain intimate sexual depictions of people in art and literature, I was actually quite shocked that the famous Rembrandt Harmenszoon van Rijn decidedly chose to depict this particular image.

Depicted in the image, I recognized a young woman happily perched on a canopy bed completely nude with her legs spread far apart as a partly shirt-covered, bare buttocks man was obviously in the middle of committing a love-making act with her. The way it was depicted, however, made me wonder if it was actually pornographic, or if it was considered merely artistic. I couldn't decide... Certainly, as I continued to think about it, if the crafted image had been a photograph instead of an etching by hand, then it reasonably could have been placed in the erotica category. But, the thing about it that truly caught me off guard, since I had to do a double take and looked closer at the image, was that the man in the middle of his sex act was peering over his shoulder at the viewer where his blatantly gloating, brazen, smiling gaze could be detected as the great artist himself.

"Oh my gosh!" I gasped laughing in utter surprise, believing it was absolutely hilarious that the artist would make himself public like this.

"At whit are ye looking, lass?" Leif asked unexpectedly. My gaze instantly shot up from the image I was examining to Leif when I realized that he wasn't so much asleep as I had originally believed.

"Um, nothing," I stammered, slamming the book closed. He adjusted himself more alert in his chair and looked doubtfully at me. "Oops! Did I awaken you?"

"Aye," he replied lazily.

"I'm sorry," I said sincerely.

"Nae matter," he dismissed. "Now, tell me whit amuses ye?"

"Nothing really," I replied with a little shrug.

"Pass it over tae me," he insisted, briefly motioning with his palm for me to bring the book to him.

"It's only Rembrandt's etchings," I assuaged guiltily.

"I shall have it." He gazed doubtfully at me again as I stood from my seat and started crossing the room to give him the book.

"I didn't realize that Rembrandt could be rather explicit in his art," I commented casually.

"Aye, mayhap," Leif replied suspiciously as I held the book out for him to take. The book slipped from my fingers when he took it. "Have ye discovered something captivating?"

He slightly waved the book back and forth in the air within his clasp, giving me a certain look.

"Well, nothing unusual, I suppose. I just never realized that Rembrandt appeared to have been quite a passionate man," I acknowledged, actually.

"Aye, so," he acknowledged.

"Yeah," I responded simply.

"*Hmph.*" I noticed a wry grin coming over his lips. "Show me whit it is that ye have discovered that has brought ye tae this sentiment," he said bluntly. He held the book out to me, and I perceived the quirky smirk on his face.

"All right," I said unconcernedly. I took the book from his grip and searched the pages. When I finally found the print again, I returned the book to him for him to view the etching.

"Och," he responded, recognizing the image. He lifted his gaze from the page and our eyes met. "This is whit ye saw?"

"Um-hm," I muttered inconsequentially.

"I see..." He paused for a second, appearing thoughtful. "Whit do ye reckon of it?"

"I don't know. It's different, I guess," I said, shrugging my shoulders.

"Weel, I shall tell ye whit I reckon of it," he said.

"Yeah?" I looked curiously at him.

"It isnae fur yer bonnie eyes tae see," he said shortly and immediately closed the book. "Now," he continued while placing the publication possessively over his desk, "should I catch ye viewing this book again, then I shall do tae ye the perceived act Master Rembrandt committed in that particular etching," Leif warned. I couldn't help the large smile spreading over my face.

"Is that a threat?" I responded unbelievably.

"Provoke me, and ye will see," he replied undoubtedly with a twinkle in his eye. I gaped incredulously at him and shook my head a little.

"Well, it's not like you haven't already done to me what he did in that print," I returned smartly with an openly ironic look on my face. Leif's cheeks creased as a wide grin spread over his face.

"Quit yer gab, *àille dhubh*, or I shall do it tae ye again this moment," he threatened again, giving a mischievous smirk. I stared incredulously at him and rolled my eyes.

"You're incorrigible," I said flatly.

"I micht agree accordingly as it pertains tae yer regard," he responded smugly.

"Huh!" I giggled, shaking my head a little again.

"Now," Leif started calmly, "I shall be most pleased if ye waur tae serenade me." I hesitated while pursing my lips with light consideration. "Pray, will ye not? 'Twill greatly warm my heart."

"Well, since you put it that way. I suppose that I will." I gave him a teasing look.

"Thank ye." He smiled, winking at me also.

"You're lucky I like you."

"Ye neednae remind me so, as I dwell upon it every wakeful moment."

"Goodness! You're killing me with kindness." I leaned toward him and pecked my lips over his. He smiled again when I straightened from him. He then leaned around his chair and retrieved the cittern concealed on the opposite side of himself.

"So, what should I sing?" I asked as he passed the instrument over to me.

"I shall like tae hear the bonnie melody yoo've been humming of late," he requested. He straightened himself from his chair and gathered a different nearby chair. He brought it toward the chair where he was sitting behind his desk and placed it before himself. Intimating for me to sit in it, I moved toward the new chair.

"Have I been humming?" I inquired surprisedly, proceeding to sit in the chair close to him that he had provided me.

"Aye, ye have," he replied while replacing himself in his chair across from me at his desk.

"Oh—I hadn't realized."

"'Tis a charming melody."

"I can't remember it though."

"How is it possible that ye cannae recall it as yoo've been humming it every morn fur the past sennight?"

"Really?"

"Indeed."

"Well, could you remind me of the way it sounds?" I requested.

"Alrecht, I reckon I micht attempt it," he responded uncertainly. He began humming a portion of the melody.

"*Ohh...*" I suddenly recognized it. The melody was *Lullaby* by the Dixie Chicks. I was really surprised that he had recalled it so well, and that I had been obliviously humming the song without realizing it.

"Ye recall it, then?" he asked.

"Yes," I said, sort of regretting that I had been overheard singing it.

"In that case, I wish tae hear it," he insisted. I didn't think that I could have backed out of his request—especially because of the intently interested look on his face he was giving me right now.

"All right," I agreed. After tuning the instrument, I set my fingers in playing position over the cittern strings. I began melodically strumming and plucking the sound of a soft rhythmic lullaby tune according to the introduction. Subsequently, the lyrics gently came forth from me. Leif maintained an attentive gaze on me, sedately listening to the lyrics as I softly sang the song...

When I had finally finished singing, he didn't immediately respond but instead tranquilly gazed at me in thought for an extended moment. I decidedly laid the cittern flat in my lap now that I had completed singing to him, wondering what he was thinking.

"That was a *most* bonnie ballad," he said at last.

"You liked it?"

"My spirit has risen tae new heights. Thank ye, *ceisd mo chridhe*," he said gently. He leaned forward carefully, catching my chin between his thumb and forefinger, and pulled my lips toward his.

"You're welcome," I responded when he released my lips from his kiss.

"Pray, serenade anither tae me," he requested.

"Another?"

"Aye. I shall enjoy it very much."

"Whatever suits you." I repositioned myself back in my chair and placed the cittern in playing position. I started plucking the strings, and it nearly sounded like a soft, soothing banjo as I began to gently sing *I Will* by The Beatles...

As I concluded singing the song in a soft country style, Leif stared at me, appearing pleased.

"Quite bonnie," he said when I had finished and I smiled at him. "Yoo're too delightful." He leaned back in his chair again when I unexpectedly noticed a violin propped on a stand behind him.

"Do you play the violin?" I asked, surprisedly.

"Aye," he replied with an inspired look. "I shall now play fur ye as weel," he said eagerly. He reached around himself to pick up the instrument from the stand. He straightened with it in hand and leaned to collect the bow. Then, he moved around me and paced to the center of the room where he stood facing me.

I adjusted my chair to face him more suitably, interested and excited to hear him play. He tuned the instrument a little and then easily swung the violin upon his left shoulder beneath his chin, resting it securely over the chin-rest. With his right hand, he set the bow above the strings. He pulled the bow down commencing a brilliant pitch to flow forth and swallowed the room in a beautiful concerto. I listened enjoyably as he clearly mastered the instrument and commanded the lustrous allegro pitches of various tones belonging to Bach's *Brandenburg Concerto No. 3.*

He indulged me as he beautifully played the entire composition. When Leif had completed playing his violin, I was very much taken by pleasant surprise.

"That's fantastic!" I responded suddenly with enthusiasm, clapping my hands.

"Are ye partial tae it that much?" he inquired diffidently as he brought the violin to rest-position.

"It was great!" I responded again.

"Yer favor is weel received," he said with a self-effacing smile. I impulsively left my seat and paced toward him after carefully leaving the cittern on the chair.

"I didn't know you played," I said interestedly.

"Aye."

"When did you first learn to play?"

"Since I was seven years of age."

"When you went to France?"

"Aye."

"How nice." I glanced down from him to the violin he was holding and lightly stroked my fingertip on the smooth wood over the curving scroll. "May I see it?" I asked, turning my glance back up to him.

"Certainly," he responded freely. He removed it from beneath his arm, allowing me to hold it. It was an absolutely beautifully handcrafted musical piece, I recognized. The wood was smooth and shiny, with rich overtones of gold, and deep coffee undertones uniformly sequencing each other along the wood grain of the instrument's body. I naturally swung the violin between my chin and shoulder and rested my jaw on the chin-rest. It seemed a little large, I thought, but I could manage it. I turned my glance to Leif and noticed his quizzical expression.

"May I see the bow too?" I asked.

"Whit are ye about, lass?" he inquired skeptically.

"Please?" I asked. He pursed his lips, appearing to consider briefly, then decidedly passed the bow to me. "Thank you."

"But, this is not a musical instrument meant fur a lass," he noted, apparently doubtful.

"My dad used to fiddle," I mentioned freely as I gripped the frog of the large bow.

"Aye, as many men do ken how tae do," he said obviously. He watched me set the bow over the violin strings and started chuckling. "Yoo're behaving most inanely at present." I noticed the absurd grin on his face.

"Will you just let me try?" I asked harmlessly. He paused and momentarily gazed at me with some consideration.

"Och—I reckon I micht permit ye tae try yer hand at it," he consented. He oddly shook his head a little, though. But I suddenly sensed him gently seizing my bow-hand and carefully placing it in the exact position over the strings. He subsequently stepped away a bit and sized me up and down. "I reckon yoo're in the correct stance."

"Okay," I replied readily as he stood across from me with folded arms over his broad chest.

"Weel? Attempt tae play," he instructed doubtfully.

"I am," I responded simply. I precisely pulled the bow down on the open **A** string, skillfully running up through a quick scale and back down it again. Upon finishing, I promptly drew the bow away from the last **A** string and returned my gaze to his. He stood there transfixed, utterly gawping at me with perceivable unexpectedness clear across his face, obviously completely stunned. "This violin has an amazingly beautiful ring tone," I observed, extremely impressed. "Is this a Stradivarius?" I asked curiously.

"Aye, it is," he said, as he continued gazing flabbergasted at me.

"*Wow...*" I amazingly drew the musical instrument away from my shoulder and wondrously looked at it for a moment. Then, fitting the violin back between my shoulder and neck, just out of curiosity, I wanted to know what it sounded like some more. So, I started playing the *Kaiser-Waltzer* opus 437 by Johann Strauss— one of my favorite compositions. Although the music piece was ahead of its time, it was the one I was most familiar with. Since my favorite classical musicians were Strauss, Beethoven, Chopin and Tchaikovsky—who were all from the Romantic period—it left me less familiar with the present-day Baroque period. I was also a fan of George Gershwin and his brother, but that was pushing modernity too much, I thought.

The music sounded so lovely to my ears, as I drew and pushed the bow long and short in various areas in the rhythm of an emotional, celebratory, lighthearted waltz. The bow bounced with staccatos followed by my plucking fingers over the strings in certain locations within the musical piece. I was really enjoying myself as I played until I had finally completed the whole movement. As I pulled the bow long, extending the last end of the final note at last, I drew the violin away from my neck and tucked it beneath my arm to rest-position.

Leif had decidedly taken the seat in which I had been previously sitting while I played the violin. I observed him leaning back in the chair with an elbow propped on the armrest and fingers clasping his gaping square chin, appearing completely awestruck. I paced quietly toward him, extending his musical instrument to him for him to take from me.

"Thank you," I said politely as I held forth the violin and bow for him to receive.

"Certainly." He appeared abstracted with wonderment. I sensed his violin slip from my grip as I returned his gaze, wondering what he was thinking.

"Whit sort of piece was that ye played?" he asked in amazement.

"It's a waltz," I replied.

"A waltz?"

"Yes."

"Och, aye, I recall ye mentioning such a dance at our wedding —of which I am unfamiliar."

"Yes, that's right."

"Why, I huvnea ever heard quite a piece. Does it have a name?"

"Yes, it's called the Kaiser-Waltzer," I revealed.

"The Emperor Waltz?" he translated.

"Yeah."

"And, who composed it?"

"Johann Strauss."

"But, I have never heard of this composer," he replied, shaking his head somewhat puzzled.

"I know—he's a little obscure at the moment."

"I see..."

"What's the matter?"

"'Twas unusual," he expressed as he spectacularly gazed at me.

"Do you really think so?" I asked insecurely.

"Most certainly." He got to his feet, towering erect and silently strode back behind his desk to return his violin to its stand, offering no further comment. After he secured his violin back on the stand, his eyes shifted to me again. "It appears yer father was a fine fiddler," Leif rejoined at length.

"He was okay," I acknowledged.

"I huvnae ever heard of such a musical piece," he commented curiously again.

"Are you saying that you didn't like it that much?" I guessed, unfortunately, as I tried to understand his response.

"On the contrary—'twas brilliant!" he responded. "I am quite taken by it in truth."

"I'm glad."

"Yet..."

"Yet, what?"

"'Twas lewd," he replied candidly.

"*Lewd?*"

"Aye, quite obscene."

"*Obscene?*" I echoed, affronted, giving him a remarkable look.

"Indeed."

"It wasn't at all like that."

"It most certainly was."

"Why do you say that?"

"'Twas overt," he said with a tone as plain as mine as he stared directly at me.

"So?" I folded my arms at my breast, feeling shortly disagreeable.

"Weel, I have never in all my years witnessed a lass master a male instrument. Nor, have I seen a lass play melodies with a particular passion as ye do—and, I must say that I am astounded," he expressed evenly. But I was suddenly feeling a little less than calm myself, and I frowned at him.

"So, you don't like the way I play music?" I asked, surprisedly, gazing at him with a perplexed look.

"Merely it isnae the common proper way," he said plainly. But a quizzical look suddenly came over his face, accompanied by a slight smirk.

"Fine," I said, insulted, turning away from him, ready to leave him alone in his study. He suddenly reached for me, clasping me around the arm and apprehended me from stepping away from him. Carefully spinning me around to face him, he drew me near while shifting his position to now comfortably leaning against the edge of his desk.

"Dinnae be cross with me," he entreated as he mindfully possessed my arm.

"Why not? You said that I was obscene," I said irritably.

"I said nae such thing. I merely observed the manner in which ye play music. It is merely out of my inquisitiveness that I said so, as it is certainly curious—yet, I am not slighted by it. Raither, I find it intriguing, fur I am quite captivated by yer mannerisms," he said honestly.

"Oh..." I muttered, still disgruntled. He coerced me closer by positioning me between his parted knees. I sensed his hand stealing around my side and rest securely on my waist as he endeavored peering at me in a mollifying manner.

"My bonnie wife is a consummated violinist tae my wonderment," he ventured genuinely.

"Just a little," I murmured, slightly less annoyed.

"More than a little, I say," he acknowledged in an assuaging manner. "I am continually charmed by ye, *àille dhubh*. I adore all that ye do, and all that ye are. I have never met a lass like ye, and I find ye far above the rest in many ways. Therefore, take mercy upon yer dear husband who meant ye nae harm."

I stared momentarily into his ultramarine eyes and perceived the pathetic conciliatory expression on his face that closely reminded me of a cute, guilty, little boy desperate not to receive punishment.

"All right," I caved, assuaged.

"That is better," he replied, satisfied. "It pleases me quite weel that we may speak plainly tae one anither," he added.

"I'm glad about it too," I agreed calmly. He seized my chin between his thumb and forefinger and drew my lips over his.

"How sweet ye are," he muttered against my lips when he barely withdrew from his kiss. Returning his lips to mine, he sealed them with another warm kiss. "Is it not nice now betwixt us?" he remarked softly between our lips.

"Um-hm," I muttered, feeling better again.

His lips began trailing affectionately over my chin, passing lower along my neck. They discovered the rounded mound at the top of my bodice where he bestowed plenty of tender kisses. I thoughtlessly toyed with the black satin ribbon gathering his blonde locks into a queue and naturally drew it loose. His golden hair fell loose over his shoulders, and my fingers sank into his silky strands. Firmly held within his warm embrace, Leif lifted me from my feet and propped me onto his desk, snugly planting me against him as he stood before me.

The sensation of his heated lips on top of my round breast sent a strange, warm, tingling feeling throughout my body. I anxiously ran my palms through his gilded hair as his soft, heated lips were trailing up my neck again. My skirts pushed up high around my thighs as he wedged himself between my knees, forcing my thighs to spread far apart. His breath was heavy and hot over my skin, boiling my blood and making me dizzy. I recognized his desire as my wanting fingers impatiently stroked the back of his head while kissing him back. I liked very much that he wanted me, and I kissed him with the same heat in return.

"Aye," Leif moaned coarsely between our kisses. "I permit ye tae be overt with me as ye please, *àille dhubh*... Do tae me as ye will. I shall not mind." I sensed him adjusting his breeches when suddenly he carefully coerced me on my back over his desk.

"*Uhh!*" I gasped suddenly, aware of the tip of his swollen penis at my entrance. Spreading me apart, he entered my body, and solidly filled me from within.

"I permit ye tae be free with me, Sylvie. Do ye understand?" he groaned thickly as he stared transfixed at me.

"Yes," I uttered shakily, strangely a little winded.

"Aye," he muttered, brushing his lips against mine with soft kisses, and began stirring inside of me with pointed enthusiasm. "Ye may do tae me as ye will..." He groaned roughly between a strong thrust which caused me to sharply gasp. "I shall not mind... *mo ceisdein. Tha gràdh agam ort...* Do ye not understand me, *àille dhubh?*"

"Yes..." I whispered shakily.

"Guid," he rasped. He immediately yanked my hips with a little force against his groin. I instantly groaned, sensing him firm and unyielding at the farthest point from within. He abruptly pushed against my cervix and caused a little pain. Moving with mounting desire, the pleasure was beginning to take him over. Fully conscious of what he was causing me to feel, I succumbed to him and melted in his hands.

Thirteen

Advent was well underway. Signs of the Christmas season had emerged in simple handcrafted evergreen laurels, decorative door wreaths, and burning candles in the windows, or flaming torches in the front of houses around town. The decorations were far simpler and less abundant than the busy modern adornments that were popularized by commercial decorations consisting of electrical lights, trimming nearly every house in modern times. The illuminated Nativity Scene, the humungous inflatable Frosty the Snow Man, animated Rudolph, Santa Claus, dancing penguins, and blowing snow globes which lit and adorned virtually every front lawn were absent this year. Even the community brightly ornamented Christmas tree in the center of town or above tall buildings, the illuminated hanging snow flake decorations dangling across power lines over bumper-to-bumper commuter traffic, and audible Christmas music over the speakers through the bustling shopping malls and on the radio were noticeably missed by me.

Instead, it was quiet—noticeably quiet. The true intention of Christmas was clear; it was graced with humility and observance. This is not to say that it was not a festive time, because it was a time for joy and cheer. It was merely modest. Much of Advent centered around fine meals and visiting with family and friends.

I realized the weighty task Leif had given me when he informed me of our hosting the governor along with some other notable guests within the community for Christmas Eve dinner; I had to organize a proper menu and establish a presentation. While I felt some pressure under the circumstances, I was considerably more excited over arranging the event with festive pleasure.

I had just completed hanging the Christmas wreath that I had created on the front door. I stepped away to examine the look of it as it hung on the door and was quite pleased with my handy work, liking its spiraling red and green apples between petite pinecones. Rings of holly accented by red and yellow berries with dried lavender and white Queen Anne's Lace—all of which nestled in a circular bed of large evergreen pine tree needles—the wreath was finished with a large deep scarlet, velvet, bow at the center top.

Objectively, I thought the front of our brick mansion looked nice with all the windows adorned with garlands of long pine branches framing the bottom window panes, overflowing onto the sides. They were embellished with red apples and green pears resting on a center bed of large holly leaves at the top. I had asked several of the groundskeepers to finish helping me arrange the lower windowsills with a string of thick holly garlands and they willingly took over to assist me in completing the task. After the garlands had all been arranged and fixed against the windowsills, I stood back in the snow admiring all our festive work and thought the house appeared attractively completed.

"Och! 'Tis quite bonnie," Leif said suddenly from behind me as he unexpectedly appeared the moment we had finished decorating the house. I abruptly spun on my heels, happy to see him.

"Do you really like it?" I asked.

"Aye, most certainly. 'Tis the grandest hoose in town," he replied.

"I'm so glad that you like it," I said, glad that it met his approval. I suddenly realized that he had come from walking in the snow bearing a sizable Christmas tree that he had just cut down. Impulsively throwing my arms around his neck, I tightly embraced him. "You remembered the tree!"

"Aye," he chuckled. His face suddenly flushed, I noticed, when I caught a glimpse of his eyes as I lightly pecked his lips.

"Thank you!" I said, slightly pulling away from his mouth to gaze into his sparkling eyes. His cheeks immediately deepened into a redder hue and creased when a broad smile swept his lips.

"Certainly. Now whit shall I do with it?" he asked curiously. I released my arms from around his neck and slid from his chest back down to my feet onto the snow, then glanced at the end of the cut tree trunk.

"Well, you might want to nail a couple of flat strips of wood on the bottom of it in a crisscross fashion—to make it stand upright," I explained as I pantomimed the position of the strips on the end of the trunk.

"Och, aye," he understood instantly. "Alrecht. I shan't be long."

"Okay."

He started away from me and paced along the side of the house until he vanished around the corner and headed toward the back of it, where the wood pile and chopping block were kept between the house and the gardens. When he disappeared, I decided it was past time for me to dart out of the frosty cold air, and I ran inside the house for warmth.

I unraveled my scarf and unbuttoned my cape as Mercy promptly appeared to retrieve my belongings from me.

"Thank you, Mercy," I said appreciatively.

"Yes'm," she replied as she collected my things in her arms and turned to tend to them.

I returned to the kitchen where I had last seen Amity watching the cooks who were busy following my instructions on how to prepare the menu. I thought it was a good time to finally put my own culinary art skills to use. I had learned from a Le Cordon Bleu chef who offered a culinary arts summer camp in Los Angeles in which I had enthusiastically participated while a grad school student on summer break.

I had at last decided on a menu that was more familiar to my taste, and so the cooks were dependent on my knowledge to get it right. Preparations started days before the celebration due to the required abundance of food needed to properly present to our guests. Given the limitation of certain spices and other ingredients, there were some things I was forced to simply substitute that I knew would work. In doing so, the ultimate result of the prepared food was noticeably richer than usual. But that was just fine, I believed.

We were in the process of retrieving an abundant amount of freshly roasted cocoa beans from the Dutch oven and began removing the cooled beans that were spread over the table from their husks. I had an assortment of chocolate recipes that I was happy to use; they were recipes that I had learned from my father's sister, Aunt Aidia, who acquired the knowledge from their Puerto Rican descended grandmother, which had been passed down to her from her mother. My Aunt Aidia had taught me the process from scratch when I was a young girl. The chocolate recipes had been among some of her most popular baked items, her customers had the fortune of enjoying them from her neighborhood bakery in the Bronx.

"Och! Haur ye are," Leif said immediately when he suddenly discovered me working in the kitchen.

"Hi!" I greeted him cheerfully while dumping hot roasted cocoa beans fresh from the Dutch oven out onto the stretched pine table, and began evenly spreading them around for them to quickly cool.

"It is delicious in haur," he remarked captivatingly. "Whit is it yoo're creating?" He gazed curiously at what we were doing in the kitchen and noticed the beans I was spreading around. He strode toward me at the table, keeping my attention.

"Chocolate," I answered.

"Chocolate!" he responded interestedly. He reached for a roasted bean and snatched it between his fingers. "Och! 'Tis scalding," he scowled and abruptly released the bean to the table.

"Careful! They're just out of the oven," I warned him. "Are you all right?"

"Aye," he replied easily.

"Good."

"Whit will ye do with this chocolate?"

"It's a surprise."

"Is it?"

"Yes."

"'Twill pain me tae wait."

"I won't let you suffer for too long," I teased.

"How merciful of ye." He feigned sadness with a meager pout, making him look boyish. I smiled at him, shaking my head a little. "Will ye pause momentarily and have a glimpse at the tree?" he suggested expectantly.

"Oh, yes!" I agreed eagerly. I quickly turned to the cooks to see if they needed any further instructions. They were easily cracking and winnowing the cocoa beans, and I thought that they didn't need my help at this moment. Amity noticed me, and I signed to her to gather the couple of baskets on the shelf in the corner of the kitchen. She promptly gathered them by the handles and began following me and her uncle out of the kitchen. We paced through the corridor toward the back of the house until we entered the sunroom together where Leif intimated toward the windows. I peered through them overlooking the bright white snow-covered gardens and discovered, to my delight, that he had perfectly fixed the blue spruce Christmas tree upright. I glanced away from the tree and smiled at him as he stood next to me, feeling really glad about what he'd done for me. "Thank you so much! It's so great!" I responded, clasping my hands together to my heart.

"Yoo're pleased, then?"

I perceived the gladness in his eyes as we looked at each other. "Absolutely!"

"Very weel. Micht that be all?"

"May we bring it inside now?"

"Bring it indoors?" he asked strangely.

"Yes, of course."

"Does it truly belong indoors?"

"It does."

"As ye wish. But, whaur will it be placed?"

"The living room is always a good place for it," I replied.

"The drawing chamber ye mean?"

"Yes."

"Then, I shall git it indoors tae suit ye."

"Thank you," I responded, happily clasping my hands together before my breast again. Leif's cheeks creased as a bright grin spread over his face and his ultramarine eyes sparkled like brilliant gems. He winked at me, then turned toward the door leading outside, and I felt warmed.

Deciding to leave the sunroom with Amity, we waited in the drawing room for his return with the Christmas tree. In a moment, he burst inside, bustling from the cold into the house with the large spruce tree and entered the drawing room from the corridor. He asked me where the tree should be placed within the room, and I suggested that it be positioned at the back of the room away from the fireplace by the window where it could be seen from outside. He was happy to oblige and after he had arranged it just so, we all stood in the center of the room away from the tree to gaze at it. I admired it very much and thought it was just as it should be as it reminded me of the joyful times I had spent with my family this time of year.

While I thought of my family, the feeling of missing them

came over me again, and I began feeling wistful. I wished that I could see and be with them once more right now, as the thought and prospect of ever returning home was more than bleak. It was likely impossible given my lack of understanding of how I arrived in this century to start with.

"Does it please ye, *ceisdein*?" Leif inquired as he turned his attention to me. I shifted my gaze up toward him and smiled.

"Yes, it does, very much. Thank you," I replied.

He grinned at me, then turned his gaze back to the tree and stood with me, thoughtfully staring at it.

"Oh! How could I forget?" I remembered suddenly. I carefully gathered one of the baskets Amity was holding into my hands.

"Whit is it?" he inquired curiously.

"I almost forgot all of this," I said, holding up the basket for him to see.

"Whit have ye?" He inquisitively peered into the basket, getting a glimpse of the contents inside of it. "Wee, bonnie gingerbread men." He instantly recognized the basket overflowing with the sweet spice cookies.

"We have to decorate the tree now," I suggested.

"Embellish it?"

"Yeah."

"Truly?" He looked at me with a mixture of intrigue and curiosity.

"Of course—c'mon," I encouraged him.

He followed me back toward the tree as I held the weighty basket full of gingerbread cookies. I signed to Amity for her to join us with the second basket as she had been watching me and waiting for my instructions. She promptly approached me at the tree. I set my cookie basket down on the floor beside my feet, then reached inside the basket she was holding to retrieve one of the strands of decoratively strung popcorn and cranberry garlands, interspersed with dried lavender, that Amity and I had created for the tree.

"How micht this appear upon the tree?" Leif asked as he strangely collected a portion of the strand into his hand.

"We'll just spiral it around on the limbs from the top toward the bottom," I simply informed him.

"Och." He nodded and initiated by catching the embellished garland in his hand, beginning to place it over the boughs from the top and winding it down around the tree.

When all the decorative garland trim had been nicely wound around the tree, we added paper chains on the limbs. Afterward, I drew forth a single little gingerbread man that Amity and I had made and decorated a couple of days ago for our decorations. I dangled it in view between my fingertips from a portion of red yarn looped through a hole punched out at the top of the gingerbread man's head. With it in hand, I went for the tree and easily found a place for it to hang over a bough. Then, promptly returning for the next gingerbread man, I gave it to Leif for him to have a turn at hanging it on the tree. He glanced simply at it and gave me a questioningly look.

"Well?" I urged.

"Och, aye," he realized and followed my lead. I also gave another to Amity, encouraging her to join in on the fun, and she happily accepted the cookie decoration that I had offered to her. She randomly placed her decoration on the tree while Leif took a second longer to decide where to place his ornament. Once he found a suitable place for it on a limb, he returned for another ornament in the basket, and the three of us started enjoyably trimming the tree. "Is this amongst yer customs?" he inquired interestedly as he gathered another gingerbread man in his hand and hung it.

"Yes, it is," I replied while I was hanging mine.

"I find it merry," he said.

"You do?"

"Indeed."

"I'm glad that you like it."

"Verily."

"It's always been my favorite thing to do this time of year since I was a tiny tot."

"Truly?"

"Yeah."

"How pleasant."

I smiled at him, and he grinned at me too. We continued decorating the Christmas tree for a while longer; I had made a ton of gingerbread men, large and small, to cover the tree in place of the decorative glass, sparkling crystal, shimmering silver—or gold-plated lovely keepsake ornaments that I remembered having in my time and were readily available in every store. Instead, I had decided to be creative this year; gingerbread men were cute, easy, and simple to make in large batches, and I thought they would nicely suffice.

Finally, Amity hung the last gingerbread man on the tree. Next, I collected the angel I had made from a collection of large walnuts and white linen. I had wrapped the linen cloth over the walnuts, and tied a golden silk ribbon around the nuts to secure them in order to form the head while the rest of the material draped loosely and hung free for the body. I sewed some gray goose feathers on the back to create the wings and fashioned a petite wreath from golden Queen Anne's Lace around the head for the halo.

"Yoo've made a bonnie wee angel as weel?" Leif instantly recognized, charmed, as he noticed me holding it. He drew it away from my fingers to see it better.

"Yes," I replied.

"Why, 'tis most charming!"

"Thank you. Will you place it on top of the tree for me?"

"Aye. 'Twould appear tae be a proper place fur it," he said while examining my crafted angel in his hand.

He was taller than the sizable tree, and I watched him carefully stretch a long arm out over the top of it with the angel in hand.

The angel's skirt fell perfectly around the tree's panicle as Leif placed it on top. He then stepped away from the tree and paced toward me as I stood in the center of the room, a fair distance from it. Now standing close beside me, he also observed our newly trimmed tree as Amity remained resting on her knees over the floor in front of it, looking up at it.

While standing there next to Leif admiring our first Christmas tree, I felt excited to celebrate this Christmas with him despite missing my family; it was our first celebration together and I wanted it to be special. Even though I also missed the illuminating electrical lights beaming from the boughs, and all the shiny sentimental keepsake ornaments that I had collected over the years, I had decided that this tree was as lovely as all the others in my past. It was simple, naturally attractive, and just as strongly conveyed the warmth of the festive Christmas season.

"It is quite grand," he commented.

"It is nice, isn't it?" I agreed.

"Indeed... I reckon that I favor yer tradition." I glanced up at him and discerned the pleasure in his expression.

"I'm glad that you're fond of it," I said.

"Whit shall we do next?" he inquired with more anticipation.

"Well, I suppose that's it," I replied, believing that all of the decorations had been placed on display accordingly.

"Och."

"Oh! Wait! I haven't hung the garland over the banisters yet," I suddenly remembered.

"Very weel. I shall manage it," he responded willingly.

"Really?" I asked, looking unexpectedly at him.

"Aye."

"Are you sure? You've done enough already—I know that you're kind of busy with other things."

"'Tis nae trooble at all. Whaur micht I find yer garland?"

"It's in a basket in the closet down the hallway."

"Och," he responded, eager to assist me and promptly withdrew from the drawing room. I heard his boot heels audibly diminishing over the hardwood planked floors as they paced through the corridor, and I smiled to myself, feeling it so nice to share this tradition with him.

As the sentiment warmed me, I picked up the empty baskets and gathered Amity's attention from the tree. Leading the way, she followed me out of the room and we continued with all my culinary preparations being made in the kitchen, which I had in mind for creating a successful holiday celebration.

Fourteen

Christmas Eve had arrived. I peered through the window outside this holiday morning as I was being dressed. The day was cheerful and overcast as flurries fell lightly throughout the silent wintery scene. I felt jittery inside as Mercy was tying the petticoats around my waist. I had realized that this dinner event was essentially going to be my introduction to the top echelon of Boston's modest society, and I hadn't given the idea much thought until today. It nevertheless was in fact a relatively significant ordeal to have to experience, and I was simply quite worried about my presentation. I wasn't really familiar with many individuals belonging to Boston's elite, and I worried about making a good first impression for Leif's sake upon meeting these people.

Furthermore, although some months had passed since my arrival here, I still understood that I was more like a square peg in a round hole here, and I sensed that people had the ability to perceive it. So, the pressure for my Christmas Eve celebration dinner to succeed without a hitch was especially intense for me to realize—particularly because of Leif's exclusive social and military prominence. I not only had to make a nice impression, but had to make an extremely good one. The more I thought about it, the more my spirit jittered; with all the time I had invested in this undertaking, I had no choice but to get it right.

I glanced at myself in the dressing table looking glass and noticed my reflection. My hair pleased me, since I chose to finally wear it completely up in a style that was unique to my taste. I thought Mercy did a very good job at arranging the curls in large overlapping streaming loops resembling a well-crafted loose braid which never seemed to end; it coiled around my head from the crown to the nape of my neck. I thought my hair nicely reminded me of how I might have worn it on the day I was first married to Matt.

I also thought I really liked the gown I had designed. It was different. But, Leif hadn't seen it yet, and I wondered if he might not actually take to it because of its modernity. I examined it while Mercy was skillfully pinning the bodice to the rest of the gown. It was unquestionably pretty, I thought, in light smokey pink, gold embroidered, brocade silk. The bodice was fitted, which was in typical fashion for the period, but the stomacher was invisible to the whole portion of the bodice as it was designed to appear like a whole piece of material around the torso, like in contemporary styles I used to know. Therefore, the top portion of the gown appeared crisp and sleek with unaltered lines, except for the striking pearl and crystal beaded, decorative, solid four-inch, frost gray colored sash encircling my entire waist which appeared like a belt.

The neckline was a deep sweeping, slight rectangular shape that crested at the edge of my shoulders, nearly simulating an off-shoulder look. It was trimmed with the same frost gray colored, beaded sash around my waist that was reduced to a two-inch thickness and perfectly complemented my neckline.

My sleeves were a slim three-quarter inch length and simply trimmed with an inch of the same frost gray silk sash minus the beading. A large bow was set at the back of the cuffs adorning each arm. Rose patterned lace flounces emerged from the cuffs and flowed in waves to my wrists.

The bodice was straight, instead of typically dipping in front, and encircled my waist where the rest of my gown was attached. I had been mulling over while designing this gown whether to have a hoop at all. If I were to have had it with a hoop, I thought, it would look more appropriate with an **A** line hoop rather than the common oblong shaped ones that protruded straight out from the waist according to eighteenth century fashion. But hoops were altogether difficult for me to freely move and feel comfortable in. Furthermore, according to the material and style of gown I had been anticipating, I decided to ultimately forego the hoop altogether. It might have made the gown appear simpler in comparison, but I was after a particular look.

So, I had the skirt fashioned in a full, free flowing **A**-line. The silk hung beautifully as the fabric hitched in various areas to create asymmetrical bustles all around. It quite appeared to me like a flowing waterfall of glistening soft muted pink silk taffeta. Lovely gray and white silk ribbon roses peeped from the tucked folds within the bustles and sprinkled the gown with cheer. The skirt opened as usual in the front to reveal my simplified smokey pink, silk, gown petticoat that hung free and slender, slightly fitting my form. It beautifully accented the entire gown embellishing my figure. My hem hung nearly to my toes rather than commonly just below the ankles. The design was reminiscent of a 1950's style ballgown, and I believed it to be a suitable bridge between the current dress style and the upcoming regency style of gown.

Overall, as I viewed myself in the looking glass, I was really pleased at the results—especially with the small train in back which precisely finished the gown in the manner I liked—and, I thought that it could respectably suit any glamorous red carpet event.

"Och!" Leif said unexpectedly with astonishment as he suddenly entered the bedroom. He interrupted us when Mercy had completed attaching the last pin to my bodice and started tying the rest of the gown to my gown petticoat.

"Thank you, Mercy," I said kindly as she had skillfully finished tying the gown.

"Yes'm," she responded and quickly curtsied before promptly retreating from the bedroom, leaving me and Leif alone together.

"Guid heavens! Whit is this *mo àille dhubh* is wearing?" Leif inquired with surprise. My eyes shifted to him as the door was closing to our room. I could perceive the plain wonderment in his gaze as he stared at me.

"Well?" I asked. I was a little nervous to hear his opinion. "Is it all right?"

"Ye appear quite fine," he replied.

"Do you really think so?"

"Indeed!" he responded superbly. "Remain—permit me tae examine ye," he insisted earnestly, pacing toward me. I stayed still as he approached, and he started slowly circling me for a quiet moment. When he arrived, facing me again, he ceased and continued to roll a scrutinizing eye over the front of my gown. "Is this yer fashion?" he inquired finally.

"Yes," I replied demurely.

"Hmm... But ye have forgotten yer hoop, have ye not?" he asked curiously.

"No—I haven't," I replied with an uneven little grin.

"Ye have not?"

"No."

"Och..."

"The gown is supposed to be this way."

"Is it?"

"Yes."

"Yer hem is a bit long, is it not?"

"I don't think so."

"Will ye not trip upon it?"

"I'll be all right."

"Yoo're certain?"

"Yeah."

"I see," he said and thoughtfully paused. "Weel, I huvnae seen anything quite like it. I reckon ye carry it weel, fur it is most becoming upon ye."

"Thank you." I felt myself relax and I smiled a little at him.

"Ye appear splendid," he concluded sincerely. He grinned at me. It was large and confident, making him appear obviously very pleased about my appearance. He lightly clasped my chin with his thumb and forefinger then leaned in close and kissed me softly on the lips. I smiled at him again as he withdrew from me, feeling slightly less jittery than before. His hand fell from my chin and lightly seized my fingers. "Come, ye must momentarily sit haur."

He guided me toward the dressing table and placed me in the seat before the looking glass. I observed him turn away from me and pace toward his armoire, admiring his brilliant appearance also. His golden head gleamed like liquid rays of sunlight against the Prussian blue velvet coat over his broad, square shoulders. His attire today was a French design. The coat was intricately embroidered all around along the trim from the high collar down the front along the sides and around the coattails with small, smokey pink, crème posies. There were glinting topaz gemstones encrusted in the center of each flower. The matching trim encircled his large five-inch cuffs and attractively correlated with richly detailed embroidered smokey pink and crème posy blooms over his gray, silk waistcoat. It perfectly complemented the grey pieces in my gown. Along with his corresponding solid Prussian blue velvet breeches, white stockings and black buckle shoes, thick swirling flounces around his sleeves and neck, fashionably suited the era and further enhanced his strikingly handsome, masculine appeal.

Leif opened one of the armoire drawers and withdrew what appeared to be a slender but wide, rich cherrywood, ornately carved box. He closed the drawer, then closed the armoire doors before turning toward me with the object in hand. As he was returning to me, I silently observed him in the looking-glass on my dressing table. When he arrived, standing close, he placed the box askew directly before me on the table. I could now clearly see that the box appeared to have been an exquisite, antique example of fine woodworking craftsmanship. Actually, not only was it recherché, it looked distinctly aged in fine condition as I continued to study it with my eyes—perhaps many decades old.

He started opening it with the lid facing me, and I was abruptly rendered speechless as he drew forth what was obviously an extremely valuable piece of jewelry. He carefully lifted the weighty, shimmering gold, swirling filigree choker necklace. It had one three-inch large oval, ruby crystal cabochon resting in a gold setting with swirls linked by petite, enamel florets and filigrees of two flanking medium sized rubies in the same setting. While a petite teardrop pearl hung from each filigree joint, the large center stone carried a one and a half inch, lustrous, teardrop pearl.

I watched him string the radiant jeweled piece around my neck and sensed the heaviness come around me as the gold felt a little cool to the touch against my skin. I stared stunned at the jeweled piece around me while he was fixing it at the nape of my neck.

"Leif—" I started as I felt him secure the clasp from behind.

"Aye?" he responded before lifting his eyes to catch mine in the looking-glass. "Och! Yer beauty crushes my sovereignty," he said softly when he immediately seized my reflection with his eyes. I sensed his hands gently come over my shoulders as he was very pleasantly admiring me.

"Leif," I started again.

"Aye, *mo ghaol*?" he said warmly.

"I think—I think this might be a bit extravagant, wouldn't you say?" I asked unnaturally.

"Indeed," he agreed.

"I mean—" I stopped short in order to turn from the looking glass and really look at him face to face.

"Whit is it?" he inquired gently, noticing my hesitation. I

sensed him delicately seize my chin and faintly stroke the side of my cheek with his thumb while gazing down at me.

"It's just that—well, it's *beautiful*, absolutely without question —*gorgeous*, and I'm truly grateful—more than you know. It's extremely thoughtful of you. Thank you tremendously—really and truly—from the bottom of my heart. Except—but, I think it's too generous of you for me to have. I'm so sorry—I don't feel like I can wear this. It's too great a gift," I expressed awfully.

He looked at me with a mixture of sudden surprise and puzzlement. "My dear, Sylvie," he started soothingly as his lips faintly tilted into a half-grin. "Pray, receive my gift. Ye are indeed a lass of virtue. Ye honor me as my wife, and it is my wish tae bestow upon my dear wife all the gifts I desire fur her tae have, however significant they micht be. Happy birthday, *mo ghaol*, and Merry Christmas."

"Thank you," I said very appreciatively. "But..."

"But?"

"It's just that I didn't get you anything—well, I made you something for Christmas, but it hardly compares. It's laughable relative to this, really," I responded inadequately. I noticed his lips curving into a grin and his eyes were warm and receptive. He appeared heartened.

"Ye neednae concern yerself. I shall admire any gift ye micht ever furnish me, even if it is a mere kiss. Fur that it comes from ye, makes it the grandest gift of all," he said. All of a sudden, I felt overcome with emotion as a knot had quickly formed in my throat, and my eyes began stinging with saltwater.

Why oh why did he have to say such things? Because, now I suddenly found myself weeping; he was so loving, genuine, and good to me all the time, and it simply made me want to forget about my past and be here with him always. I was starting to think that I might not want to ever give him up—ever; even if it meant that I would never return home.

"Why must ye weep, *mo ghaol*?" he cajoled.

"I don't know…" I sniffled.

"Ye dinnae ken?" he replied, appearing perplexed. He whipped out the handkerchief from his breast pocket in his waistcoat.

"Because of you," I sniveled. I felt like a blubbering idiot. But, I just couldn't help myself from crying.

"Am I at fault fur this unhappiness?" He appeared visibly puzzled and regretful as I felt him carefully blotting away my tears with his handkerchief.

"Yes…" I sniffled.

"Och, I shall weep as weel should I pain ye," he said. He meant it; I could perceive his sincerity. Still, it sounded a little strange and made me sort of giggle briefly. "Thaur, it isnae so terrible efter all, is it?"

"Yes, it is—because you make me want you all the time, and it isn't fair… It's just not. It's a terrible… terrible thing what you do to me—and, it's not right." I continued whimpering.

"Och! Is that it, then?" he chuckled. Now, he seemed struck by slight amusement. But, I wasn't happy at all, because I was torn by him and missing my family.

"It's not funny," I sniveled.

"Weel, it certainly isnae wrong. Are ye not awaur that I am indeed yer husband?" he replied.

"You're making fun of me," I wept.

"Weel, I find this disclosure of yers tae be quite heartwarming," he said amusedly.

"Of course you do. It's not fair," I sniveled ironically.

"I believe it is reasonably fair. It is quite appropriate. Should this be the root of yer unhappiness, then I shall gladly continue tae be responsible fur yer reproach of me. Indeed, I welcome it," he said with a coaxing look in his eyes.

I sighed. "Why do you have to make this so hard?" I asked, allowing him to wipe my damp eyelashes from tears.

"Weel," he started, turning slightly solemn. He crouched over his knees, and he was now gazing eye level at me. "Micht that difficulty lie with the notion that I loove ye, Sylvie?"

"You love me?" I looked at him with such surprise.

"Aye, I loove ye," he said unequivocally. I stared back into his deep gaze and noticed the intensity in his rich blue eyes. I felt ashamed for having asked the question as I stared back at him.

"You do?" I responded meekly.

"Of coorse I loove ye, Sylvie. *Tha gràdh agam ort,*" he said tenderly. I simply stared at him, suddenly realizing that he had been telling me that he loved me in Scottish for a while now without my knowledge of knowing what he meant. Suddenly, I felt immensely foolish for ever doubting how he felt about me while I listened to him speak to me. "I loov'd ye the first I ever laid eyes upon ye. Merely, I reckon that I would have told ye that I loov'd ye back in the wood the day we first met, but ye wouldnae have believed me, because ye waur scared," he said gently. "And, when we at last came together in the hoose in Concord on Thanksgiving Day, I expressed my loove fur ye, as I do indeed loove ye with all my heart." At that moment, things seemed to suddenly stop for me. Everything went quiet as if the world stood still, and all I recognized was the concentrated depth of the genuine sincerity in the exposure of his heartfelt words.

He loves me.

"Oh... That's very nice to hear," was all I could scarcely say as I gazed at him through watery eyes. Then, I started stupidly crying again, because I didn't realize that he had felt that way about me from the beginning, and I felt foolish, and I was immensely touched.

"Now, now, thaur," he hushed warmly as he blotted away my tears again.

"You are so, so nice—and sweet... I'm so sorry for making a mess of myself like an idiot," I blubbered.

"Yoo're quite far from an idiot," Leif responded absurdly.

"Well—my feelings for you run extremely deep too. I'll have

you know," I admitted as I wiped the tears from my blurred vision with my fingertips while he also continued dabbing my eyes dry with his handkerchief.

"Therefore, I am greatly moved," he said softly as he closely gazed at me. The pad of his thumb tenderly stroked my moist cheek when my watery gaze met his warm eyes. "As it seems tae appear in our case, would ye not agree that it is quite fair fur us tae want the other?"

He was right, I thought; I accepted the truth of our feelings for each other with a little smile and a mere nod.

"Yes," I confessed after a second.

"Aye," Leif upheld. He leaned in very close and softly pressed his lips over mine. "*Mo ghaol,*" he muttered gently as our lips parted. "Now, let us leave these tears and have a bit of cheer on this fine Christmas Eve," he urged and resumed patting my face dry.

"Okay," I responded, feeling calmer.

"That is far better," he said, approving my refreshed appearance when he cleared my tears from my face. "Now," he continued as he straightened from crouching, "permit me tae complete my gift tae ye."

"All right," I whispered humbly as I observed him carefully tugging the little knob from the middle section of the wooden box when a small drawer opened. As he drew it forth, a pair of corresponding gold dangling earrings with sparkling, round, ruby cabochon gemstones set in gold filigree complimented by a lustrous white, teardrop pearl came into clear view. He gathered one of the pair between his fingers and dangled it out to me for me to take. I was so impressed by its beauty that I was nearly afraid to take it from him.

"Ye have pierced ears," he said.

"Yes, I do."

"Have these tae adorn yer ears now."

"Thank you," I said gently as my fingers faintly brushed his while grasping the astonishing earring piece from him.

"These jewels once belonged tae my mother," he said. "My father bestowed them to her upon their wedding nicht. Now they are yers," he informed me and tenderly kissed the side of my neck.

"Thank you," I responded affectionately.

"Aye," he replied with the same gentleness.

I moved my fingertips to my ear and finally removed the Tiffany & Co. pink tourmaline teardrop and diamond earrings I had first worn the night I had vanished—and, the only other thing on my person besides my wedding ring from Matt that reminded me of my past.

I proceeded to slide the new earring through my pierced ear and noticed the exquisite piece dangling magnificently, altering my appearance along with the chocker necklace around my neck. After I placed the second earring in my ear, Leif pulled forth a third and final compartment from the case revealing an impressive tiara swirling with abundant diamonds and rubies all around that completed the set. I observed it come over my head as he precisely placed it on top of my crown. I simply sat there at my dressing table staring at myself in the looking glass in utter suspension as I was amazingly adorned in relic jewels.

He leaned close behind me and said softly against my ear, "*Tu es la plus belle femme,*"

"Thank you," I replied softly.

"This was given tae my father's mother by my grandfather, King James the Second," Leif disclosed in a low voice. I could feel his breath sweep warmly against the side of my neck as he gently spoke into my ear.

"Really?" I gasped, utterly flabbergasted.

"It belongs tae ye now," he said gently.

"Leif—" I started as I swung my shocked gaze around from the looking glass to directly look at him.

"Aye?"

"I—I don't know what to say."

"Say nought."

Instead, I simply stared closely into his deep ultramarine eyes, struck speechless, and sensed his lips come over mine in a single warm kiss.

"Thank you," I muttered against his soft lips, and felt his mouth curving upward over mine. He subsequently withdrew from me and straightened to his full height. He gazed admiringly at me for a minute, and smiled with satisfaction.

"Come," he urged as he took my hand in his and helped me from my seat to stand. The expression on his face was brilliant and full of blithe while he continued gazing at me. The sides of his cheeks creased as a radiant grin swept across his face, and a shy little smile tilted my own lips when I looked at him also. "Micht we observe the desserts prior tae our guests' arrival?" he asked.

"Yes, of course," I replied, inspired by him; I was feeling much better now, and was happy to indulge him.

"Very weel," he said.

WE ENTERED the grand dining room together, and I discerned the large mahogany dining table attractively set for twenty guests with our finest French porcelain, silverware, and crystal goblets. The desserts were prominently displayed around the room over mahogany dessert tables and flint glass plates, except for the ice cream that I had made, which was to remain chilled in the ice cellar until served immediately after dinner. The servants appeared crisp and clean and ready to be summoned at any moment as they moved throughout the room completing the dessert displays. Everything looked exquisite, I thought, and I was happy at the appearance of my desserts.

"Och! Whit is this magnificent creation haur?" Leif inquired interestedly as he spotted the three-tier cake sitting near one of the windows in the room.

"It's a dulce de leche buttercream fondant cake," I informed him, following him to the table with the cake on it.

"Is that whit ye call it?" he responded wondrously.

"Yes," I replied as we both came to stand near it.

"'Tis magnificent!" I was amused to see him so fascinated by it. "Is this truly yer creation?"

"Yes," I said.

"How did ye manage it?" he asked without removing his eyes from the cake.

I explained how I created the dulce de leche and the cake batter. Next, I revealed how I made the white buttercream frosting covering it, and the required technique to get the frosting perfectly smooth in order to create a plaster appearance. Lastly, I disclosed to him the way I had constructed the very realistic smokey pink and lavender fondant rose bouquet and leaves embellishing the entire top tier. A series of three large rose clusters positioned on the sides of the second and first tier, offset each other. I had also devised a series of intermittent light mint green vertical fondant stripes in varying widths along the bottom and top tiers while the center second tier remained solid buttercream without fondant. A complimenting light pink fondant ribbon sash flawlessly encircled the base of the bottom buttercream tiers with adorning pearl drops. The cake was finished with a final bow at the base on the bottom tier, completing the details.

"Do you like the way it looks?" I asked.

"Most certainly!" A pointed finger unexpectedly caught my attention as I noticed it slowly making a beeline approach toward the buttercream frosting. I abruptly slapped it down, immediately catching Leif's attention off guard.

"Don't touch!" I scolded.

"But, it appears delicious!" he chuckled foolishly.

"Not yet," I warned.

"Och!" he grumbled immaturely. But then his eyes attentively landed on the large five-tier porcelain platters filled with petite fours *glacés* decorating the table in another corner of the room. "Och! Petite fours!" he suddenly recognized with more captivation. He promptly left me at the cake table and directly strode toward the embellished tower of petite fours. "How bonnie! Have ye created these as weel?" he asked, turning and admiring me.

"Yes," I responded, charmed by his reaction.

"I am unawaur that ye possess talents as a culinary chef!" he said with delight. I couldn't help grinning demurely. "They are quite bonnie. I huvnae seen any of this sort," he said while examining them.

"You mean the frosting?"

"Aye, reckon."

"I see." I observed him gladly gazing at the pretty little cakes with pleasure. They were attractively frosted in pastel pinks, blues, lavenders. and mint green. I was able to extract the colors from preserves by liquefying them. Once I had colored the confectioners' sugar mixed with maple syrup, I glazed the little cakes and decorated some of them with tiny white and pink swirls. Others had yellow stars, and colorful pearl drops resembling polka dots over them.

"How waur ye inspired?" he inquired while maintaining his attracted eyes on the cakes.

"I used my imagination, I suppose, and found a way to create them," I replied, shrugging my shoulders a little.

"Remarkable."

"I also made crème de cocoa pudding," I informed him, indicating the surrounding dishes on a different table.

"Did ye?" His eyes became even wider when he caught a glimpse of the filled little dishes and clearly reminded me of a child in a candy shop. I couldn't help smiling at him.

"And, also chocolate dipped vanilla cookies," I added.

"Whit are they?" he asked innocently.

"I'll show you," I said eagerly, abruptly leaving him standing by the petite fours for the next table displaying the little cookies on small, beautifully hand painted floral porcelain dishes spread over another table. Arriving at the table, I turned my gaze to him and called his attention from the petite fours to show him these new cookies.

"Och, aye." He strangely sounded muffled with a mouth stuffed full of something when he responded, and appeared exactly like an extremely pleased chipmunk with swollen cheeks full of goodies. He was obviously chewing as he made his way toward me when I realized he had stolen a treat.

"Leif!" I exclaimed as I rushed toward him. "What are you doing?"

"'Tis most delectable!" he said mutedly as he was chewing and swallowing the evidence when my eyes instantly found the gaping space between the petite fours on the fourth tier.

"You're not supposed to do that! You'll have to wait—they're for the guests," I chastised, giving him a disapproving glare.

"Yet, I huvnae harmed a thing," he assuaged guiltily. I simply gave him a certain rejecting maternal look. "They are *most* delicious. I have never experienced one so heavenly," he said coaxingly.

"What am I going to do with you?" I shook my head a little, perceiving his endearing, childlike persuasiveness as he stared at me.

"But, I am a guid lad in truth. If ye wouldnae agree?"

"I suppose, then, I'll spare you from a time out." I couldn't help the crooked grin curling my lips as I started repositioning the little cakes over the fourth-tier platter to cover the missing space.

"Whit is a time out?"

"Sneak another treat, and you'll find out."

"Och! I fear ye as a mother," he joked half earnestly. I giggled a little, and his sparkling eyes smiled, warming my heart to the brim.

Just as I had set the petite fours straight again, Amity had entered the room dressed in her darling best dressed attire in white, teal ribbons and bows, and wispy lace flounces. Leif and I both turned our attention toward her as she approached us with a cheerful smile and expectantly looked at us both.

"Och! See who enters and joins us," Leif commented kindly as Amity came to stand directly before us. Leif smiled at her and affectionately pinched her little nose. "Aye, yoo're particularly bonnie this morn, lassie," he remarked.

Amity glanced up at me and signed to me with innocent anticipation, wondering if she could participate in today's festive celebration. I promptly turned to Leif and translated, "She wants to know if she may stay with the adults today."

"Ahh, I reckoned as much. Alas, she may not remain," he said, though the expression on his face was kind.

"Well, why not?" I asked perplexedly.

"'Tis a Christmas dinner ball," he answered obviously.

"Okay?" I questioned, not understanding him.

"It isnae traditional, of coorse," he said.

"Of course it is—Christmas is especially for children's participation. Who else would it be for?" I differed politely.

"*Ceisdein,* it is merely not customary fur children tae participate with adults. 'Tis particularly a formal event and 'twould be inappropriate. Surely, ye ken this tae be true," Leif explained courteously.

"But, it's Christmas time—time for cheer and love. She won't be disruptive, if that's what you're worried about. You know how well behaved she is. She's very good—and look she's so excited for it. She's all dressed and everything. We can't disappoint her. It would be sad to do that. Please just let her attend? I promise it will be all right. Please?" I pleaded, given the disinclination expressed on his face. He momentarily paused, and gazed thinkingly at me. I could perceive him pondering the option, and he didn't seem inclined to be persuaded by my appeal. "Please?" I asked him once more. He didn't easily respond, but I began sensing that he now might possibly yield. "I'll have her by my side well supervised. I promise you, she won't be in the way. It would make me sad if she were left out of the festivities and ignored."

"Whit am I tae do with ye as ye conflict me? She mayn't socialize with our guests," he said.

"Why?"

He held up a silencing finger in the air. "However, she may very weel visit with ye before they arrive, and she may indeed delight in the feast and share in desserts till her heart is content."

"So, she'll eat without us then?"

"Although 'twill be highly irregular fur her tae be permitted tae do so on such an occasion, I shall permit her tae dine with us. Yet, once she has completed her meal, she must promptly retire tae her bedchamber tae sleep—she mayn't partake with our guests thereafter," he insisted. He also sighed a little as he was resigned to the decision he had made to suit my wishes for Amity's sake.

"Thank you," I said appreciatively, and naturally reached on my toes to peck him softly on his cheek.

"Aye, so be it," he acquiesced.

"You're so sweet," I replied delightedly.

"Aye, weel, recall that ye said so regarding me the next time ye decide tae give me whit ye call a '*time out*'," he joked.

"Oh!" I unexpectedly yelped when I suddenly felt my backside receive a hearty slap from him. He winked and grinned at me, then strode across the room where the chocolate cookies had been prettily arranged among the nuts, raisins, dried apricots, and citron slices. He snatched up a cookie and arrogantly plopped the whole bit into his mouth before he continued on his way out of the room.

"Delectable!" he voiced satisfactorily as he chomped on the cookie right before he fully left the room and glanced over his shoulder when he brazenly winked at me again on his way out.

I watched him in shock as he audaciously disappeared past the doorway, and at that moment, I realized that Amity had been lightly tugging at my palm for an answer to her question, and my attention returned to her again.

"Your uncle said that you may stay for a little while," I communicated to her. She suddenly wrapped her arms around my waist and tightly squeezed me with delight. I reciprocated her embrace and bestowed a little kiss over the top of her head as both of us were merry for a Christmas celebration.

SOON, guests began arriving, and the house took on the full festive air of Christmas holiday blithe. The delicious aroma of special food, drink, clinking goblets and pleasantly animated voices echoed throughout the first floor. We were hosting some rather esteemed guests from the community this evening, and it was a pleasure for me to meet them as they were all very pleasant and accepting of me. I found them to be quite interesting in particular ways while Leif and I were properly receiving them into our home.

Governor Spencer Phips was an aged man I fathomed to be relatively in his seventies. He seemed to be a well collected Englishman and was a veteran of the political arena. He appeared fairly genuine, typically moderate, and generally sociable. He was no doubt a very well-educated man with a unique practical life's perspective. He had newly assumed being governor of Massachusetts Bay Colony two months ago in place of Governor William Shirley on account of Governor Shirley's recall to England by the Crown on the unfortunate accusation of treason. Given what I had understood from Leif, Governor Shirley was a reputable man who aimed to build honest coalitions between the colonists, the Indians, and England against France and its Indian allies. The fate of Governor Shirley did not sit well with me once I'd learned of his ill-fated circumstances, and I hoped—as I was naive to the laws of England—that he ultimately would be vindicated from his tribulation of being falsely accused as a traitor.

Among our other guests was the local General Winslow, commander of provincial troops, until the despised Lord Loudoun's arrival into the colony as he assumed all colonial regiments under his command and unceremoniously dismissed the general. General Winslow appeared to be an older man in his fifties also who was thin and of average height towering between five foot seven and a half inches to five foot eight inches. Regardless of having been dismissed by Lord Loudoun, General Winslow still held great interest in the war with France and was greatly esteemed by the provincials and their commanders. Furthermore, although seemingly earnest and stern, he nevertheless also appeared moderate and even tempered with politeness. According to Leif, General Winslow and Lord Loudoun were at great odds personally and professionally, and had many open disagreements.

"'Tis my great honor to make your acquaintance again, Your Grace," General Winslow politely addressed me, bowing as he remembered me from our meeting at Fort Edward earlier this past late summer when I was newly taken into captivity.

"Thank you, General Winslow. It is very nice to see you again as well," I replied when he straightened from his bow as Leif and I were receiving him. He had a stiff, proper manner about him as he then turned from us and moved toward the other congregated guests in the drawing room.

There were several more off-duty military brass serving in the general's regiment who also attended, namely Colonel Jonah Shea and Major Ephram Hawkins and their wives. There was Mr. Nathanial Hewitt, a local publisher, and his wife, Mrs. Annabel Hewitt, who unconventionally assisted her husband as editor for his circulating periodical. I actually found her to be one of the most interesting women among our guests as we later engaged each other in genial conversation. I learned some things from her about the local political scene and the rhetoric expressed among the locals. I found her extremely fascinating, because what she discussed revolved around current affairs involving the colony and

England, which was closely experienced in real life and was unrevealed in history books familiar to me.

There was also, Lord Brighton and his sister Miss Harriet, whom I clearly remembered from before when we first met at the milliner's shop on my first visit in town, and with whom I had become better acquainted since that time. Lord Overland accompanied them, and I assumed that his journey from Albany went well, since now he and Miss Harriet were getting better acquainted in person.

The matriarch Lady Brigham and her grandson, Mr. James, and her granddaughter, Miss Sarah, who all seemed quite modest and pleasant, now entered the house. Soon following were Lord and Lady Capshaw. Businessman and political influencer Mr. Thomas Hutchinson and his wife, Mrs. Margaret Hutchinson, and the Reverend Thomas Beebe and his wife, Mrs. Elizabeth Beebe simultaneously entered the house.

Finally, but not least, there was also a very young and handsome Mister John Singleton Copley, the engraver and artist who I knew would one day make a name for himself as one of America's first and greatest painters. I was impressed that he was now actually in my presence as a young living vibrant gentleman. I had seen his magnificent and impressive paintings hanging on display at the New York Metropolitan Museum of Art, Los Angeles County Art Museum, among my own Alma Mater's art museum, and at many other art locations spread throughout the country where I was from. His beautiful paintings portrayed a wondrous period in America's past that was since long gone in my day.

"He's going to be a magnificent artist one day," I whispered in amazement to Leif as Mr. Copley proceeded to make his way toward the gathered guests.

"Aye, I reckon he is quite accomplished at present already," Leif agreed. He discreetly smiled at me and gently seized my elbow as he finally led us to join our guests.

Fifteen

It was nice to see guests admiring the desserts as conversations swirled around the festive atmosphere. A number of our guests seemed noticeably impressed by the desserts displayed in the dining room, since a crowd had gathered by the frost-covered window near the fondant cake displayed on a small dessert table in the corner of the room.

"I shall speak tae the governor and General Winslow at present," Leif muttered attentively against the side of my head as we observed our delighting guests in the room.

"All right," I agreed. He gathered my fingers among his hand and raised them to his lips, gently kissing the back of my hand.

"Your Grace," he said once he drew my hand away from his kiss.

"Your Grace," I acknowledged politely. He bowed and I curtsied in response before he left me alone to mingle with our other guests. I returned to observing the many individuals crowding the cake, eagerly anticipating the first reviews as the dessert was soon to be tasted after dinner was served.

"This is a most glorious presentation, is it not?" proclaimed one of the ladies hidden in the surrounding crowd, admiring the cake.

"Indeed! What sort is it?" Lady Capshaw asked.

"One is not certain. Nonetheless, it indeed appears to be delicious! I also do wonder what it might be named?" Mrs. Hewitt voiced curiously.

"Why, 'twould likely be a cake, I would presume. Though I am unfamiliar with the nature of this one," Lord Overland said.

"Aye, a most deliciously appealing one at that. Her Grace's cooks appear to be extremely talented," Lady Brigham complimented.

After overhearing some of the guests' compliments, I modestly turned away from them, feeling very satisfied of their enthusiastic observations as I meant to mingle with other guests who were less distracted by the cake, and who appeared to be on their own. I strode toward the dessert table prettily displaying petite sweet potato and apple pies while on my way. The pies were surrounded by intermittent decorative fondant flowers over the table with an attractive collection of chocolate bonbon truffle pieces I had made. I too looked forward to a little bite from a piece of truffle after dinner just to enjoy the familiar taste that I had missed for so long.

Young Miss Harriet noticed me while I had almost passed this dessert table. She glided near and stood at the table with me as she daintily glanced at the plated treats. She ventured to strike up a conversation with me, and we chatted cordially with each other for a good while. She informed me of Lord Overland's fortunate arrival from Albany, and how they were becoming pleasantly acquainted. Overall, it seemed she and Lord Overland were going to be a suitable pair. He was young and eager to please, and he appeared taken by her which seemed to calm her nerves a bit. I ultimately didn't think there would be a problem between them as she was worried for so long that they might not be compatible. I was pleased to see that she was apparently relieved when she told me how well they were enjoying each other's company when he would come to visit with her and her family at their mansion on Tremont Street.

"Might I say that this is the most cheerful dessert that I have ever seen. I very much anticipate experiencing it," she complimented amiably after our discussion about Lord Overland when referring to the little plated chocolate bonbon pieces presented on the round table by the wall where we were standing.

"I very much look forward to your trying some of them and hope that they please your palate," I said, smiling at her.

"Do they have a name?" she inquired unknowingly.

"They are cocoa bonbons," I informed her.

"How delightfully exotic!" she replied enthusiastically.

"I would agree!" Miss Sarah unexpectedly added as she appeared beside us with her grandmother, Lady Brigham.

"Thank you, Miss Sarah," I responded politely.

"My grandmother and I find the cake most enjoyable to view, and we do look forward to tasting it," Miss Sarah said in her London accent.

"Well, I hope that it suits you well," I replied.

"I am certain that it will," Lady Brigham interjected confidently.

"We shall like to thank you for all of these appealing desserts upon display. One can hardly wait to indulge—if I may be so forward to inform you," Miss Sarah said agreeably.

"Well, you're very welcome. I hope that you will enjoy them," I replied pleasantly.

"We have never seen a cake designed in such a manner. What might it be named?" the matriarch Lady Brigham inquired modestly with the same London intonation as Sarah's.

"It is called dulce de leche," I disclosed to them.

"Dulce de leche," Lady Brigham echoed thoughtfully.

"Yes," I replied.

"How very curious. I have not heard of such a flavor. I imagine we shall enjoy it, immensely," Lady Brigham said.

"Given by its favorable appearance, I am certain that we shall," Miss Sarah said.

"I'm very glad that you will be trying it, and I hope that you will find it enjoyable, ladies," I said cordially.

"Thank you, Your Grace," Lady Brigham replied.

"Please, I insist, make yourselves welcome and sample all that is presented once our meal is soon served," I said.

"Thank you," Miss Sarah said eagerly.

"Of course," I replied.

I politely excused myself from the ladies after some more light conversation with them, and proceeded making my genteel rounds among all the guests. Leif was finally spotted in the drawing room near the Christmas tree with the governor and General Winslow as they stood conversing. It seemed they were making brief references about the tree as they glanced intermittently at it.

"Och! Indeed, 'tis my wife's fancy," Leif said discernibly as I moved toward the male guests surrounding him. They were chuckling as I arrived, standing next to Leif. "Och! Speak of my angel!" Leif responded suddenly, noticing me. I think I might have taken him a bit off guard by my sudden appearance due to the unexpected, but cheerful look he gave me. "Haur is Her Grace presently, spying upon me," he said lightheartedly, inciting the other two men to laugh also. "Will Her Grace not tell these sirs how she had twisted me about tae bring this monstrosity indoors?"

"It's true—I'm a great torturer of arm twisting. I nearly tweaked His Grace's arm off entirely before he cried out for mercy and acquiesced to my Christmas tree demand," I bantered. Chuckles gusted between the men.

"'Tis quite a merry sight, I must say," General Winslow said, referring to the tree.

"Aye quite. What a novel notion," Governor Phips agreed.

"Thank you," I replied politely.

"I fear, sirs, that Her Grace has rendered my sense of soond nature entirely unfit, fur I am easily manipulated by her will," Leif reparteed as he continued to refer to the tree.

"His Grace grants me too much credit. He is sweet and kind, naturally," I said modestly.

"I shall correct that it is Her Grace who is most generous in nature as she has granted me the privilege of becoming my wife," Leif replied certainly.

"Your Grace is most fortunate to have Her Grace for a companion," the governor said to Leif.

"Aye, for we are able to perceive well that His Grace is most fond of his duchess," the general agreed.

"And, we shall all agree that Her Grace is indeed most generous to hostess such a splendid Christmas dinner ball," the governor added kindly.

"Thank you, Governor Phips. You are very kind. I entreat you both to be welcome and merry. Enjoy our many delights this evening," I expressed politely.

"Thank you, Your Grace," the governor responded cordially.

"Aye, thank you, indeed, Your Grace," the general corresponded.

DINNER WAS ANNOUNCED, and our guests were encouraged to gather into the dining room and sit at the large, stretched dining table. As plates had been served, soaring compliments traversed among our guests over the oven roasted turkey basted in salt, sugar, vegetable stock, pepper corns, allspice, and ginger with added steeped aromatics of apple, onion, cinnamon, rosemary, and butter combined in a bread stuffing. Pleasant reviews continued over the honey glazed ham with cloves garnished with rosemary and salted buttered oven roasted potatoes, and sautéed brandied sweet potatoes. Following these courses were boiled lobsters, light pastry covered cod fish fillets embellished on a bed of lightly buttered peas, provided with pumpkin soup and butter-milk rolls—all of it served with goblets of Madeira. Finally, finishing the multi-course meal was my special butter pecan ice cream.

I glanced at Leif at the far end of the table as I sipped a bit of my Madeira while vaguely listening to the surrounding conversation between Miss Harriet and Miss Sarah. Leif seemed to be really enjoying himself as he dined and conversed with the governor, Lords Stanton and Capshaw. As he was conversing, he caught my eye and subtly raised his crystal goblet to me with a warm smile and I perceived his endearment. I naturally returned his smile before placing my spoon full of ice cream between my lips. Suddenly, an audible sound of clanking silverware against crystal rang out and quieted the chatter between our guests when the governor emerged standing from his chair.

"I shall like to thank the Duke and Duchess of Monteith for this invitation of merriment," the governor proceeded to say. "And, for delighting our palates with a grand arrangement of delectable cuisine that I have had the great fortune of sampling. Such cuisine quite recalls to mind a French chef I once had the privilege of meeting who magnificently created cuisine for the English emissary to France. Therefore, might I request that you send my compliments to your cook for creating such a delightful meal?"

"Indeed, governor, I am certain Her Grace will be most pleased tae accept your compliments, fur it is she who has permitted her own recipes tae be created fur this afternoon's dinner ball," Leif proudly informed him.

"Is it so?" the governor responded with utter surprise as he had suddenly shifted his gaze across the table toward me.

"Thank you, governor," I said politely.

"Indeed, Your Grace. It is with immense pleasure that I say to you that you have greatly enriched my evening with this fine dinner," the governor said, very impressed. He commenced a round of applause, then resumed sitting in his chair. When the applause diminished, I was aware of impressed eyes all on me from around the dining table.

"You are certainly very kind, Governor Phips. I would like to thank you all for attending our Christmas gala and for helping make this a very merry occasion. Please, enjoy your ice cream," I said modestly. The governor nodded his head with a gentle smile in acknowledgement and I smiled in response.

Soon, conversations recommenced around the dining table when I unwittingly glanced from my dish of ice cream and noticed Leif quietly gazing at me from the opposite end of the table. A relaxed grin curved his lips as he brought his crystal wine goblet to them and sipped. When he lowered his goblet again on the table, his hand lightly encircling the base of his goblet while he kept his eyes on me. I noticed a certain admiring look in his gaze and my cheeks felt suddenly warm. I grinned at him before dropping my gaze toward the last bit of ice cream in my dish, feeling shy in front of him for some strange reason.

ONCE OUR MEAL had been completed, guests congregated leisurely in the drawing room, sitting room, ballroom and dining room among more conversation, desserts and spirits. I remained with Leif in the sitting room as we conversed with Mr. and Mrs. Hutchinson. Listening to the conversation of politics taking place between them seemed to fade in and out at times for me while I stood there silently intrigued by the moment. The festive scene surrounding me appeared like a snapshot from a distant time, and I was daydreaming about the difference between my era and theirs.

"*Mo ghaol?*" Leif gently called me, unexpectedly interrupting my thoughts.

"Yes?" I responded suddenly.

"I shall like tae request a melody upon the harpsichord," he suggested.

"Oh!" I replied surprisedly, as I consciously shifted my gaze between an interested Mr. and Mrs. Hutchinson, and Leif. "Forgive me, but I have not rehearsed," I said uncertainly. I was quite unwittingly put on the spot, and felt uncomfortable about it. I was familiar with the piano, not the harpsichord, and didn't know how I was going to properly play it.

"'Tis quite alrecht. Play as ye micht," he encouraged.

"But I—well I—" I stammered.

"I am quite certain ye will play weel," he said confidently.

"All right, I'll do my best," I agreed courteously, realizing there was no room for me to decline without seeming rude. I turned away from him and our guests and paced toward the harpsichord near the Christmas tree, hoping not to embarrass myself as well as him in my attempt at playing this unfamiliar instrument. I self-consciously approached the seat before the musical instrument and carefully slid over the petite bench facing the beautifully painted keyboard. I sat there for a second, looking blankly at it as I wondered how I was going to approach this challenge—fully aware that Leif and his closely surrounding guests had their full expectant attention on me.

As my eyes skimmed over the small keys, the thing I initially noticed was how minuscule the keyboard actually was. While a piano had eight octaves, there were only four and a half facing me. *Where is middle C?* I wondered about it. I glanced over the keys and instantly recognized the keyboard format, but I wanted to know where middle C was as it was referred to on the piano. So, I simply pressed the C key before me not exactly anticipating it to sound like the note I was seeking, but merely to gauge where middle C might be. I discovered quickly that middle C was two octaves up, and the present C key before me was the fulcrum of this keyboard. Later, I learned that this key was called Great C.

Now that I had some semblance of the keyboard layout before me, a piece that I used to play frequently for Matt came to mind. It was a favorite of his, and one of the few Baroque harpsichord pieces I used to play for him on the piano. But I hadn't touched a piano in three and a half years since he had passed away, and I knew that I was going to be somewhat rusty now.

I was relieved though, to see sheets of music by Johann Sebastian Bach propped against the music rest and searched through the printed parchments. Finally, I found *Prelude* from *The Well-Tempered Clavier* and adjusted the music sheet before me. I glanced insecurely over my shoulder toward Leif and noticed him still steadfastly observing me. He gave me a confident nod, and I turned my uncertain gaze back to my fingers. I positioned them over the black painted wooden keyboard and took a little breath.

I tapped the keys and started to play. The keys felt different to the touch, I instantly noticed—not like the expected cool smooth ivory or plastic covered piano keys I was used to. I noticed that the sound was rather light until I swiftly realized that I had to push the keys harder than normal unlike over a piano, because the resistance on the harpsichord was stiffer. I also noticed that the keys themselves were a lot slimmer than usual, and I had to concentrate on not tripping over them.

Oops! I had pressed a key too hard, and it knocked the harpsichord. I nonchalantly moved to recover as I continued playing. While I corrected myself, it became apparent to me that there was a noticeable shallower key dip than from the piano. Each finger had to articulate the sound unlike over the piano where I could sometimes just fling my fingers over it and get away with it. Still, overall, as I moved through the music composition, I grew more confident and no longer needed to rely on the printed music sheet in front of me since the memory of it started flooding my mind again.

Once I had completed playing, I found myself surrounded by some of our guests attentively listening. I unwittingly noticed some of our young male guests flushed in the face and briefly wondered about it as it curiously struck me. But, a nice round of applause sounded out while I straightened from my seat, and I felt better about my entertaining performance over the harpsichord. I politely nodded in appreciation and offered to one of the ladies to entertain us on the instrument before making my way through the crowd. I located Leif standing alone now at the back of the room, leaning against the wall quietly enjoying a goblet of Medeira while I moved toward him.

"Ye play quite bonnie, *mo ghaol*," he complimented when I approached and stood near him. His tone was affectionate and the look in his eyes was warm.

"Thank you for saying so. But it was a little imperfect," I said self-consciously.

"It is of nae consequence. 'Twas weel done," he assured.

"Still... I could have played better with some practice," I muttered.

"I am certain 'twas perfectly done tae our guests' appreciation."

"You're very sweet to say that."

"'Tis my favorite composition ye played," he disclosed to me.

"Was it?"

"Indeed."

"Oh, I'm glad that I played it then."

"I wish fur ye tae play it again fur me whilst we are alone." He gazed adoringly at me and I smiled at him, feeling bashful again.

"Of course," I said. His grin lingered, and it heightened the strange shyness I was feeling around him.

"Is Her Grace delighting in her ball?"

"Yes, it turned out well, I think. What about you? Are you enjoying it also?"

"Aye, much, indeed. It has been a long time since I have enjoyed myself in this manner."

"Has it?"

"Aye."

"Oh..." I fathomed that it was because he had been alone and soldiering for so long. "Well, I'm really glad that you're having fun now."

"Indeed I am pleased, *ceisdein*," he responded. "Now if merely I micht have the indulgence tae share a dance with ye, then I would be most satisfied."

"Oh, yes! That would be really nice, wouldn't it?" I agreed, when I realized that I hadn't hired a quartet for our festive event, as the thought had completely slipped my mind. "I can't believe that I completely forgot to hire a quartet. That's a big slip on my part, isn't it? I don't know how I could have forgotten it," I said disappointedly.

"It is of nae matter," he pardoned.

"Sure it is—it rather makes the party, I think," I differed.

"Nae, 'tis Her Grace who makes the cheer grand during this ball," he said. I automatically responded with a diffident smile. "Yet shall I consider having nae music play is of nae concern. Fur if we had music and we should dance pursuing against custom in these parts, 'twould bring us a bit of scandal," he warned.

"Would it?" I responded, astonished.

"Most indeed," he answered. "'Tis already noteworthy that we are openly celebrating Christmas as it were, fur it is not normal tae tradition."

"Really?" I was rather surprised to learn this.

"Aye."

"Oh, I hadn't realized, actually... Not celebrating Christmas is sad, though. Why wouldn't we celebrate like this?"

He smiled gently at me in response. "If merely we waur in Virginia, mayhap we micht indulge ourselves differently with such open enlivenment as dancing included in our ball."

"Virginia?"

"Aye."

"Hmm—maybe... but, I'm not fond of Virginia," I considered.

"Aye, I reckon ye micht not be," he regarded. "Yet, as I ponder, mayhap celebrating Christmas in Virginia with a dance may prove to be unusual as weel in spite of the colony's customs being in more alignment with the king's. In which case, I reckon we ought tae merely dance amongst ourselves in private haur in Boston."

"That sounds like a reasonable option," I replied coquettishly, inferring his meaning and his face grew ruddy. A wide corresponding grin creased his cheeks as it spread across his handsome face, and I felt the temperature rising in my own cheeks. I couldn't hold his steady gaze any longer, because I knew he could see the warmth on my face. So, I glanced away from him and observed one of our lady guests delightfully playing the harpsichord instead.

THE DINNER PARTY carried late into the evening until our guests finally began departing. I had Mercy place Amity to sleep much earlier in the evening, and it wasn't until I glanced at the clock that I realized how late it had actually become. The chimes tolled eleven o'clock which made a complete sixteen-hour day for me. It occurred to me that I was fairly spent. I sought Leif in the sitting room before the fire, sharing a glass of brandy and pipe smoke with the general during a seemingly serious discussion. I overheard a tidbit of it as I entered the room: something to do with Fort Oswego and Lord Loudoun's neglect which led to the fall of the fort to the French, and how Lord Loudoun was pointing the blame at Governor Shirley.

Leif ceased speaking when he suddenly noticed me approaching him and General Winslow. He promptly straightened from his chair and stood tall as I strode closer toward them. General Winslow's gaze also abruptly shifted from the discussion they were having and accordingly ensued standing from his comfortable chair as I neared them both.

"Your Grace," Leif responded attentively to me.

"I'm sorry for interrupting, but I think that I might retire if Your Grace doesn't mind," I said politely.

"Aye, of coorse," he said kindly.

"Thank you," I replied. He took my palm into his hand and gently placed a kiss over the back of it "Goodnight, then," I said modestly.

"Goodnecht, *mo ghaol*," he said.

"Goodnight, Your Grace," General Winslow said deferentially to me.

"Goodnight, General Winslow," I replied politely to him, and the general graciously bowed. I lightly curtsied in front of Leif before turning to depart from them. As I was leaving the room, Leif and the general recommenced their conversation and I was glad to finally retire for the evening.

But there was one more thing I had to do before finishing my day. I had to conclude distributing Christmas gifts to the servants. The gifts included petite fours and petite mint chocolate truffle bonbon candy that I had made and had nicely wrapped in silk gauze for them. When I was delivering their gifts to them, it struck me uniquely by the way they had pleasantly reacted to my gesture; they were shocked—to put it simply. Completely stunned and grateful when I presented them with these Christmas gifts, I realized that not only had they not been expecting a special gesture from me, but maybe they had never received any kind of gift before in the past. They seemed genuinely happy to receive presents, and it was heartwarming giving them a bit of joy this season. After they had thanked me, I started out of the kitchen ready to leave for my own bedroom at last. As I was exiting the kitchen and started through the corridor, however, I overheard some of the cooks remarking to each other about what I had done.

"Why, can you imagine that?" Humility said with astonishment in her voice.

"I ain't seen no lady like her," Mercy said with the same amazement.

"Indeed! What kindness to grant us gifts!" Annabelle said.

"Aye, have you any notion from where she come?" Prudence inquired.

"I ain't have the merest notion. Yet, she certainly is most kind," Annabelle said.

"I reckon quite unusual for any other lady—in manner and appearance," Humility added.

"Agreed," Prudence said.

"She's quite pleasant, is she not?" Mary interjected.

"Indeed! Have you not seen how His Grace fancies her?" Sarah said. Giggles flittered between them.

"Aye, His Grace will war for her on any little slight, certainly," Humility said.

"Did Her Grace not say also that we shall all have a respite tomorrow for Christmas Day?" Annabelle inquired amazedly.

"She did that!" Remember expressed delightedly.

"What will you do for yourself on Christmas Day, then, Prudence?" Annabelle inquired.

"I mean to sneak to my young John Henderson and join him for church," Prudence responded merrily. More giggles flittered throughout the corridor.

"Do not let His Grace discover you sneaking off," Remember warned Prudence.

"I shall be most discreet," Prudence said carefully. The conversation between them faded as I continued making my way through the corridor for the staircase.

Once I returned to my bedroom, Mercy surprisingly met me first at the door to my room ready to assist me with removing my gown and helping me into bed. We entered the room together and I was relieved that I could soon place my head against the pillows.

"You had a mighty fine day today, ma'am," Mercy said to me as she was unpinning my gown.

"Yeah, I think everything worked out nicely for the party today. Thank you so much for all your hard work, Mercy."

"No bother, ma'am." I smiled at her and she gave me a demure little smile in return.

"So, do you have any plans for yourself tomorrow on Christmas Day?" I asked. She shook her head. "You don't?"

"No, ma'am."

"Don't you have a best friend? Or someone like a significant other that you could spend the day with on your break?" I inquired curiously. She suddenly appeared extremely bashful and shocked that I had asked her that particular question as she hesitated answering.

"You meanin' a beau, ma'am?" She asked sheepishly.

"Yeah."

"No ma'am."

"So, there's no one that you like especially?" I pried a little. She gave me a subtle grin and her eyes seemed to sparkle with a secret. "Ooh, so there is someone special." Her wistful smile spread more prominently across her face as she was working to remove my stomacher from my torso. "What's his name?"

"It be Jerome, ma'am."

"How nice. Tell me about Jerome."

"He belongs to the Crawfords."

"Does he?"

"Yes'm."

"What else?"

"He's creole from the West Indies."

"Is he?"

"Yes'm."

"Well, that makes him interesting."

"I reckon so, ma'am."

"So, he knows how to speak French?"

"Yes'm, that he do know how to do." She lifted her gaze to me once she had removed the last pin from my stomacher, and I discerned the slight upward tilt of her lips as we were speaking about him.

"Do you like that he knows French?" I asked. She shrugged her shoulders.

"I like it fine. It sounds nice to my ears."

"It is a nice language," I agreed, smiling at her. Mercy lowered her eyes and started untying my gown from my petticoat. "Is he nice?"

"Verily."

"Well, that's very good."

"Yes'm."

"Maybe, you might see him tomorrow, then?"

"No, ma'am. I won't be doin' so."

"Why not?"

"He won't get no time for a reprieve tomorrow. His masta ain't lenient as His Grace is. So, I must bide my time ta see him on Sunday at worship," she said.

"Oh, I see... How old is he?"

"He be twenty years of age," she informed me. I nodded a little, remembering that Leif had told me that Mercy was close to seventeen—still too young to court but old enough to have a secret crush on someone.

"Well, maybe you and Amity could spend a relaxing day together tomorrow instead."

"I reckon I shall, ma'am."

"That might be nice for both of you. Maybe you could show her some of your needlepoint work. Amity enjoys doing that kind of craft also, and you're very good at it. You could probably show her a thing or two. I know she would appreciate you showing her how to do something new with it," I suggested.

"That seem like a pleasant notion, ma'am," Mercy considered, as she was now starting to remove my gown from my shoulders.

"You know, since you are so skilled with your embroidery, you should consider going into business for yourself," I said. She suddenly looked at me blatantly stunned, and I wasn't sure why. "Well, you could do that one day, you know?"

"Business? Me? Do business?"

"Sure. Why not?"

"I beggin' yo pardon, ma'am—but, I don't reckon so."

"Why not? You could do it if you wanted to."

"How could I do business?"

"Well, you could embroider for people and get paid for it."

"I must ax His Grace fa permission in orda for me ta do somethin' like that, mustn't I?

"Oh... Must you?"

"Why, of course, ma'am."

"Right—of course." I hadn't considered this protocol before and suddenly felt a little out of place for making the suggestion, recognizing perhaps I shouldn't have brought up this topic.

"Truth be told, ma'am, I is too busy with my chores ta try a thing like that. I also know His Grace won't allow me," she said with clear certainty.

"How do you know that he would say no to it?" I asked, regardless. She gave me a confounded look. "Have you ever asked him?"

"Well, no, ma'am. I haven't. Course I never thought of such a notion neither," she said.

"I'm sure that he would listen to you if you asked him about it."

"No, ma'am."

"Why not? It's a good idea, though."

"I ain't certain about it, ma'am. I s'pose you know what is proper for me."

"Hmm," I muttered, wondering how it could not be proper?

"Besides, it ain't my place, I already know so," she said.

"Who's to say that?" I muttered again.

"Beggin' yo pardon, ma'am?"

"Are you afraid to ask him to allow you?" I asked curiously. She cast her eyes down from me to the ties she was untying on my petticoat and hesitated answering me. "You don't have to be afraid to ask him, Mercy."

"Yes'm."

"The worst that can happen is that he would in fact tell you no. But he would never get upset with you for asking."

"As you say, ma'am. But, beggin' yo pardon, I ain't knowin' 'bout no business."

"But that's something you can learn about doing."

"Can I?"

"Sure, you can. If you wanted to."

"I see... Beggin' yo pardon again, I don't know 'bout this notion 'bout business. Seem important and I ain't thinking I can manage that."

"I know it sounds like a frightening idea. But you could learn how to do it one step at a time just like in anything else you've already learned to do."

"Seem important."

"It is important."

"Too important fo me."

"That's not true. You're important, Mercy—so, you should be able to do important things."

"I just as soon reckon that what I do fo you is suitable," she said with pride.

"I appreciate everything you do for me. It means a lot to me," I replied sincerely.

"Then, my business is right here with you, ma'am. Ain't? What I do fo you is important—the way I sees it. Excusin' my boldness in tellin' you so. I like servin' you fine. I hope you ain't gettin' rid o' me," she said worriedly.

"Not at all, Mercy. I'd never get rid of you." I could see that she wasn't understanding the significance of my point of view and I didn't wish to push her into doing something she was not yet ready to do—or had any interest in doing at all.

"Well, if you ever wanted to do something like make a business out of your embroidery, just let me know and I could arrange it for you," I said, and her eyes went wide for a moment. She nodded her head a little and didn't respond otherwise for a second.

"Yes'm. Thank you, ma'am. But, I won't be needin' no such thing when I know what I am doin' right here with you is just fine —if you is pleased wif me."

"Of course, I'm pleased with you."

She demurely nodded her head in response. "Even so, I thank you all the same when I know you is certainly kind ta me," she said modestly.

"Well, of course. It was only a thought," I replied just as she removed my stays from my torso. I felt a little awkward for having mentioned such an idea to her. I didn't anticipate her negative response to my novel suggestion to her. Instead, I thought she would have been receptive to the fresh idea of owning her own business, and feeling a sense of independence and some pride in that fact. But, her response told me that I was wrong; that she was proud of the work she was already doing and was content with her status. *What's going on?* I don't quite understand... *Did I step on her toes? She seems uncomfortable... Why is she so upset? I don't want her to be upset with me... and, I didn't mean to rock the boat. Maybe —did I overstep my bounds regarding my role here?* I wasn't sure.

As I thought about it, I wondered in actuality: *what right did I have to disrupt her conscience and force a change in her position when she told me that she was content with herself?* As surprising as that was for me to learn from her, I unexpectedly realized that I might have been arrogant with her if I demeaned her in any way by imposing my perspective upon her when it was her right to feel the way she did about herself—despite her point of view that I perceived as narrow due to the advantages I knew existed in my era which brought me a broader perspective on a person's right to freedom and the pursuit of happiness.

As I was beginning to learn, Mercy had no social, emotional, or financial network here that could help her. Things that I realized I had taken for granted in my era. Instead, she had no one she could rely on. She was alone.

She smiled at me and I smiled at her in return while thinking about all of this when my thoughts were called away from my contemplation as I realized that now I was dressed merely in my shift and gladly undressed. After hanging my gown in my armoire, Mercy then moved to stoke the fire in the fireplace before leaving me to finally rest for the night. When she had finished, I thanked her and she curtsied before departing the room.

At this moment, nothing felt better right now than to get into bed and slip beneath the down blankets and surrounding pillows. My tired eyes landed on the light mint green damask canopy draping around me from above, and I reflected on the day's festive event before falling into slumber. I was glad about the effort I had made in organizing a successful party, and that the Christmas celebration had gone so well, as I buried myself cozily between the covers and closed my eyes at last. My mind began emptying and settled quietly while relaxing when the last thought that entered my mind was hearing Leif's voice floating in my head: "*I loove ye, Sylvie,* before I was finally carried off to sleep.

Sixteen

Sometime in the middle of the night, or very early in the moonlit morning, I was vaguely roused from slumbering and found myself in a foggy state of mind being lightly smothered with gentle kisses over my neck and lips. Sleepily, I opened my eyes and discovered Leif directly hovering above me, smelling warm and sweet of brandy wine as his lips pursued tenderly kissing mine. A stifled moan escaped me as I sensed him already erect and hard.

"Aye..." he muttered heatedly against my lips now that I was alerted to him between my thighs prodding my entrance open. Before I was fully conscious of it, I felt him suddenly surging deeply into me, causing me to gasp and moan. He ebbed, and I gasped again as he flowed, taking me by surprise. I caught his amorous grin in the moonlight glowing closely beside me from the windows as his heated breath caressed my brow. "Have I awakened ye now, wife?" he groaned unevenly.

"Yes—you have," I whispered shakily, feeling him completely in motion within me as the head of his shaft pushed against my cervix, electrifying my uterus and sending my blood coursing like lava through my veins. "I thought I was dreaming," I moaned.

"Did ye?"

"Yes..."

"Of whit was *mo àille dhubh* dreaming?" he inquired thickly. I paused between another gasp, fully sensing the pressure of his powerful presence filling me.

"I was dreaming..."

"Aye?"

"That I was at the beach... wading in the warm ocean. It was bright—and sunny, hot—like summer. Something snagged my ankle—and—it pulled me... pulled me under far beneath the water. It was enormous... and frightening—like a dragon. I couldn't breathe beneath the water. It was overwhelming... and—it—began to take me," I uttered between my shaking breath.

"It began tae ravish ye as I micht be doing tae ye reit now?" he breathed heatedly just over my lips, stirring prominently between my thighs.

"Yes," I moaned.

"*Hmmm...*" he groaned coarsely. "A sea serpent, was it?"

"I suppose so..."

"Yoo're sweet as waterweed tae such a beast. Ye say he frightened ye?"

"He was very scary."

"Is that not a pity?"

"Yes—I think so."

"I shall not have ye afraid."

"How could I not be scared?"

"I shall take ye from yer frightening silky and have ye fur my own... and, ye will ken that yoo're safe with me," he said. I smiled between moaning in response. He groaned heatedly against my neck and the deep-seated aching for him between my thighs grew more intense.

He had already raised my shift above my breasts and was now removing it over my head completely off me. His succulent lips came down over my erect nipple and he began teasing it with his tongue. I arched to his touch as I stroked my palms over his lean bare back, wanting him, yearning to pull him closer and deeper into me. I moaned and was suddenly stifled when he abruptly sealed his lips over mine and thrust his tongue into my mouth.

When he finally released me from his powerful kiss, he surged vigorously into me, bringing himself to climax, when suddenly, my thighs began quaking and I was hurled into a euphoric cloud beyond the world surrounding me. My cervix thunderously throbbed sending electrifying convulsions throughout the walls of my depths, and I found myself now drowning in a swirl of ecstasy. I sensed him pulsating between my legs, which heightened the wild sensation I was already feeling as my insides vigorously clamped down onto his shaft. He groaned heavily while we drowned together in rapture, embraced in each other's arms.

Carefully collapsing over me, he began bestowing small kisses over my lips, cheek, and brow as I felt his heart rapidly pounding through his heaving chest. His heated breath breezed over the side of my neck when he fell to rest and still within my arms.

We lay there in bed quietly listening to each other's heavy breathing for a moment. Then, I sensed his withdrawal from my depths and the release from his expulsion between my legs escaped me, dampening my inner thighs when he carefully shifted beside me. Feeling his warm stream draining from me, not a single contrary thought entered my mind. Only the residual feeling of euphoria kept me soaring.

Leif drew me snug, fitting me against his chest, and his arm embraced me with a hand naturally cupping my breast. Relaxing my arm over his as we spooned, I peacefully lay with him, listening to the sound of his breathing finally settling into the first rhythms of slumber.

"Ye waur splendid yesterday," he muttered unexpectedly into my locks at the back of my head.

"I was?" I whispered, surprised to hear him speak right now when I thought he was drifting to sleep.

"Aye."

"Thank you. You were really nice too."

"I couldnae remove my eyes from ye at the dining table."

"You couldn't?"

"Nae... Ye were also brilliant at the harpsichord."

"Do you really think so?"

"Aye."

"Thank you. I'm glad that you really enjoyed it."

"I quite did."

"That makes me very happy."

"I dinnae ken whit I shall ever do."

"What do you mean?"

"I fear that I cannae keep my hands off ye... It seems that I want ye more each day—and, I cannae help myself... I merely crave tae tooch ye always. My desire fur ye is great. Forgive me..."

"It's okay."

"Forgive me—I dinnae wish fur ye tae ever fear me."

"There's nothing to forgive. I don't fear you, so don't worry," I assured softly. He pulled me even closer within his embrace.

"*Mo ghaol bith-buan, Tha gràdh agam ort, mo Sylvie bhrèagha,*" he whispered closely behind my ear.

"What does that mean?"

"It means my eternal loove, I loove ye, my beautiful Sylvie."

"Really?"

"Aye."

"Oh..." I realized softly. "*Mo ghaol.*" I tried saying it the way he said it, but I lacked his finesse.

"Aye. *Ceisdein.*"

"And, what does that mean?"

"It means question."

"Question?" I responded oddly when a yawn overcame me.

"Aye, nearly the same as darling in English."

"Oh... So, what does *àil-àille dhubh* mean?" I asked curiously, as I tried staying awake.

"It means black beauty."

"I see."

"*Leannan*," he whispered behind my ear.

"*Leannan*," I repeated.

"Beloved," he said tenderly.

"Beloved," I echoed.

"Aye."

I gently entwined my fingers within his and fastened them snug. He tenderly secured my palm in his grip. It then fell quiet between us again as we lay there together in the silent darkness spooning in each other's arms, merely listening to the intermittent crackling wood in the low burning fireplace. It wasn't long thereafter that I contentedly closed my eyes and drifted back to sleep.

THE WINTER MORNING light flooded through the windows, illuminating portions of the pillows in glowing whiteness. Drowsily opening my eyes, I gently rolled to my side facing Leif. The sunlight washed over him in rays of gilded luminescence. I simply remained quietly lying next to him watching him sleep as I slowly roused from my own slumber. Resting silently for a while, just staring at him as he continued sleeping, I admired his long golden hair, prominent razor-straight nose, and soft, slightly full pink lips.

He stirred among the blankets, and his eyes opened. They always seemed extremely dark blue in the morning and turned to almost deep, ultramarine gray during the day, depending on the light. He gazed at me, and a smile graced his fair face. His palm gently came over the side of my cheek, and he lightly stroked my brow with his thumb. His fingers moved carefully around my neck, delicately stroking my ringlets off my bare shoulder. I sensed his palm gently caress my entire arm and move beneath it to steal around my waist when he drew me close and began lightly stroking my naked back.

"Guid morrow," he muttered softly with an indolent smile.

"Good morning," I whispered. "Did you sleep well?"

"Aye, and, ye?"

"Yes, I did," I replied, feeling his warm palm carefully caressing my buttocks while he smiled at me in response.

"I reckon today is Christmas Day."

"Yes, I suppose it is."

"Merry Christmas, *mo ghaol*," he said.

"Merry Christmas."

"Whit shall we do this fine day?"

"I don't know." I shrugged a little.

"Weel..." Leif started thoughtfully, "I reckon we micht rise in order tae first attend King's Chapel."

"I think—I'm wondering, if you won't mind—would it be all right if I wished for us to just stay here today instead?" I ventured hesitantly.

"Hmm... I understand, since it isnae a Papist chapel your reluctance tae attend," he said understandingly.

"I just want to stay here with you."

"A notion that soonds quite tempting," he said as he seemed to be reconsidering the choice. He grinned affectionately at me and I smiled back at him.

"Good, because I'd like that very much," I said softly, still aware of his hand caressing my waist and backside.

"Mayhap, I micht grant yer desire tae refrain from doing so this day. However, we mayn't miss church on the morrow or the following Sundays henceforth," he specified.

"Why not?" I inquired unknowingly.

"Why, I shall be pilloried, of coorse," he replied with a look of surprise.

"Pilloried?" I gave him an equally astounded look.

"Aye."

"Seriously?"

"Weel, I would most likely pay the fine instead of experiencing the shame and embarrassment of it."

I nodded a little in response, silently shocked that he would be penalized for not attending church. I looked at him feeling disappointed inside, because I could sense his reluctance for abandoning church today by the disinclination in his thinking gaze.

"I reckon it micht suit us fur this once today," he said leniently after a moment of consideration. I immediately smiled at him and impulsively wrapped my fingers over his slightly scratchy jaw to kiss his lips. When I withdrew my lips, I rested my head back on his muscular shoulder. A grin swept evenly across his face making his expression appear easy-going. He shifted slightly upward onto his elbow, displacing me somewhat deeper among the pillows. "Now, why did ye do such a thing?" he asked. He cupped the back of my head and shifted me by the waist with his other arm, adjusting me beneath him as he caged himself over me.

"I guess I just wanted to," I said as he locked me beneath him and propped his elbows by my head.

"Is that reit?" he questioned warmly.

"Yeah," I replied, recognizing a certain expression in his eyes.

"'Twas raither pleasant of ye." He began pressing gentle kisses over my brow to the tip of my nose and over my cheek.

"What are you doing?" I giggled a little, feeling the tickling sensation of his scratchy jaw within the curve of my neck.

"Whit does it appear tae ye that I am doing, Your Grace?" he coaxed.

"It seems you're being naughty again," I giggled some more, beginning to feel strange.

"Am I now?" He continued enticing me with his warm lips over my heated skin.

"Yes, you are."

"Alas, how can I cease whit ye have commenced? Fur, I have assured ye that I have little resolve regarding yer influence upon me," he said. His lips moved down past my neck between my breasts and caressed toward the right.

"*Uhh!*" I gasped suddenly when he caught my nipple between his teeth. He began adoringly suckling me, warming my blood, and causing me to grow dizzy with burning need for him.

Suckling for a moment, I felt the cool air waft against my moistened breast when he released his ravenous lips from it and started trailing lower with continued admiration toward my navel where he sealed it with a fervent kiss. Then, his kisses moved lower until I realized he had buried his lips within the tuft between my legs.

"Och!" he wheezed abruptly as I instantly slammed my knees closed against his head.

"Don't!" I gasped unexpectedly, suddenly sitting up a little from him as I propped myself on my elbows against the surrounding pillows.

"Whit is it?" he inquired unknowingly, looking up at me from between my thighs, caught off guard.

"Oh, gosh—I'm sorry," I said suddenly as I quickly covered my face with my palms, feeling utterly embarrassed.

"Whit is it?" he inquired again. I could sense the concern in his voice.

"I can't do that," I muttered mortifyingly through my fingers, not wanting to look at him.

"Whit is the matter?" He obviously sounded confused and a little surprised.

"Ugh! It's— " I broke off. *How on Earth can I tell him this?*

"Aye?" he pressed carefully with apparent curiosity in his voice. I hesitated telling him. "Will ye not look at me?" he requested. I sighed apprehensively and reluctantly let my fingers fall from my eyes, humiliatingly looking at him. "Do tell me."

"It's just that—well, I haven't washed yet—and I—I haven't exactly shaved down there," I divulged, completely mortified.

"I beg yer pardon?" A queer grin crept over his face as he gazed quizzically at me.

"Well, I haven't had the chance to bathe from last night and to shave—and, I just didn't think—" I broke off realizing his unexpected laughter as he bizarrely looked at me.

"Why in Heaven's name micht ye ever shave yourself?" he laughed absurdly with an illogical expression. He was entirely red-faced from laughter, making me feel even more embarrassed and shy of him.

"Well—it's kinda customary where I come from," I revealed self-consciously.

"Is it?" He was still humored and simultaneously looking strangely at me.

"Yeah," I murmured. "Besides, isn't it what the French do too?"

"Nae," he said flatly.

"Oh."

"Why micht ye do such a thing?" he asked curiously again after he had calmed himself from laughing.

"Well, it's sanitary," I replied obviously.

"Sanitary?" he questioned meaninglessly.

"Yes!" I highlighted, a little annoyed.

"Och! Yoo're behaving quite unreasonably," he declared.

"No—I'm not!"

"Aye, ye most certainly are."

"But, I—"

"Och, quiet yerself and quit yer dither!" he interrupted. "Now, come haur and let me pleasure ye," he asserted with an abrupt grip around my ankle.

"No!" I squealed. But he suddenly yanked me back down toward him among the blankets with resolve.

"Leif!" I screeched reluctantly. "You can't!"

"I can—and, I shall," he maintained, and pried my thighs apart.

"What are you doing?" I exclaimed abruptly as he suddenly buried his face between my legs.

"I'm smelling ye, of coorse," he said, sounding muffled among my private tuft of hair.

"Oh! Do you have to do that?" I exclaimed again, sheerly embarrassed. I wanted to recoil, but he had me fixed on the bed.

"'Tis quite natural fur me tae do so."

"No it's not!" I squealed.

"Certainly it is! 'Tis whit animals do."

"So you're a dog or something like that now?" I gasped horridly. He chuckled, and his breath hotly caressed the pubic area most sensitive among my thighs.

"I fancy that I am a lion," he said plainly.

"Holy cow! Give me a break! You're an awful lion, then!"

"I fancy that ye reckon me awful," he chuckled.

"Ugh!" I sighed as it seemed pointless to contradict him.

"Ye smell—weel, I reckon that I dinnae ken. Yet, it isnae foul—raither, I reckon ye smell quite nice—lovely in truth—nice enough fur me tae—"

"*Ahhh!*" I screamed, utterly embarrassed. I slapped my palms over my face, covering my eyes in desperation wishing to merely dissolve from the earth. I heard him laughing again between my legs.

"Yoo're quite foolish!" he chuckled as he popped up from my thighs into view once more.

"I'm not!"

"Aye, ye are."

"Well, look what you're doing to me!"

"I huvnae done a thing tae ye yet."

"Yes, you have!"

"Not yet," he laughed.

"Well, don't do anymore!" I squealed anxiously.

"I'm not done with ye," he said certainly, appearing blatantly mischievous.

"Yes, you are!"

"Hardly. Now, adhere tae yer vow and obey yer husband as I grant ye awful pleasure!"

"Unbelievable!" I responded exceptionally, perceiving a wicked grin curving his lips. Then, he intentionally dipped back down between my thighs. I gasped, suddenly sensing the thrust of his intruding tongue beginning to tickle my clitoris when he spread my labia wide apart with his fingers. "I can't believe you're doing this to me," I wheezed embarrassedly, as I was quickly aware of the unusual hyper sensation he was creating within my cleft.

"*Mmm*, yoo're fine," he heaved heatedly between my thighs.

"*Huh!*" I huffed as the feeling between my legs completely focused my attention in an extremely unusual way. I wanted him to stop, since the playful sensation was uniquely intense and too much to bear. But he continued to thrust and stroke his tongue over and around my clitoris, which caused over excited stimulation and consequently forced my awareness to that one particular focal point on my body. He found my entryway, and shoved his tongue inside as he also danced it around my opening. I moaned. The feeling he was quickening between my thighs started to give rise and caused me extreme pleasure.

His mouth moved over my clitoris again and he gently began to suck and slowly stroke his tongue around it. I thought I would die by the wild sensation he was forcing me to feel. It was euphoric and rendered me helpless, paralysing me while causing swelling between my thighs. I moaned again and sank my fingers into the back of his gilded hair, desiring his inspiring lips to consume me, completely.

"*Ahh!*" I choked unexpectedly when suddenly a concentrated tingling sensation bolted from my clitoris, and shot straight up through me. It began throbbing wildly, sending a rapturous feeling to course powerfully between my thighs. The sensation was utterly stupendous, that gasps escaping me.

"Aye," Leif muttered, suddenly covering his mouth over mine

in a strong kiss. I wondered how he knew how to do that to me when he simultaneously entered and filled me, completely. The sensation he just made me feel was unique and was an orgasm I hadn't ever felt quite like before. It was sharp, quick, and rattled all of my nerves to the core, leaving them raw. I felt that I caught on fire and I wanted more.

He began pumping himself with fervor inside me, and I had grown so moist for him that I could hear his shaft thrusting in and out of me. It seemed I was going to keep climaxing as my body pulsated while he drew and pushed himself into me. He was commanding my body in a way that I didn't know could possibly be done by anyone—whether I was in agreement or not. I felt myself swimming among throbbing shockwaves on each thrust that kept me in a state of ecstasy as my cervix ached for him, causing me to tremble. He continued moving rapturously within me and in a moment he groaned thickly. Breaking upon his release, he shuddered against me and expelled himself into me with elation, as I sailed down from my multiple orgasms.

As I sensed his throbbing wane, he stilled himself above me until he stopped pulsating completely. Then, he gently collapsed over me panting heatedly within the curve of my neck as he kept me cradled in his embrace.

While peacefully laying entwined in each other's arms, listening to each other breathe, my stomach gurgled, embarrassing me a little and spoiling a perfectly nice moment. He lifted his warm gaze to mine and I smiled.

"Yoo're hungry," he recognized.

"A little," I replied softly.

"I shall inform cook that we shall presently take our morning meal," he said willingly as he was about to pull the cord on his side of the bed to ring the bell for one of the servants.

"But, she's gone," I said. Leif gave me an unexpected look.

"Whit do ye mean?" he asked with a confused expression.

"Well, I gave all the servants the day off," I informed him.

"Did ye?" He was definitely surprised to learn that I had taken this liberty as his eyes widened.

"Yeah—for Christmas—I thought it would be nice if they could celebrate the day with their families and friends," I said.

"I see... Yet, their family and friends are haur at *Taigh Gràs*. So, whaur micht they otherwise go?"

"Nowhere, I suppose. Just spending time at their own quarters without a bother." I shrugged my shoulders a little with indifference.

"Without a bother?"

"Yes. Except, Mercy is still here since she hasn't anyone to spend time with, so I thought that she could simply amuse Amity," I continued informing him.

"Is that reit?" I nodded. Leif seemed to ponder my decision as we gazed at each other. "Hmm... I reckon that is most generous of ye," he mused, and placed a gentle kiss on my brow. "Therefore, the hoose is empty?"

"Yes."

"Thus, who micht prepare our proper meal?"

"I thought you would," I incited playfully.

"Truly?"

"Yeah," I said, smiling at him.

"Hmph! In that case, I micht hunt a stag fur ye, and roast it in the open fire," he taunted.

"Forget it! I think I have something better up my sleeve," I replied reluctantly, remembering the unfavorable time I had spent so long in the wilderness in the beginning of my captivity.

"Have ye now?" he chuckled briskly.

"Yes," I said definitely.

"I shall delight in the delectable remains of last dinner," he desired.

"Sure—if you'd like. Or, I could make you something entirely different," I suggested also.

"Micht it take a moment tae prepare?" It didn't seem he was inclined to wait for a meal to be cooked since he apparently didn't have the patience for it right now. I saw that he was as hungry as I was.

"Not at all," I assured him.

"Certainly? I realize that yoo're quite famished as weel as am I."

"Yes, it's quick and simple—and, very good."

"Whit micht it be?"

"Let me up, and you'll see."

"Och, very weel," he acquiesced, then stirred from me, pulling himself from between my thighs. I sat up from the pillows and first escaped into the privy closet to cleanse and refresh myself. Once I was finished and returned to our bedroom, I reached for my shift smothered between the blankets. Tossing it over my head, I pushed my arms through the sleeves, immediately covering my nudity before stepping toward the chair near my bedside for my lavender, silk dressing gown resembling a modern-day woman's housecoat. I slipped my arms through the sleeves and wrapped it over my shift, keeping myself warm from the coolness that had settled in the room.

After Leif decided to visit the chamber pot and follow my suggestion to rinse his hands in the washbasin, he gathered his nightshirt and covered his muscular naked body with it. He easily slid his silk embroidered, light blue banyan over his shoulders, which very much reminded me of a man's long Asian style house robe. Once we slipped our toes into our slippers, he followed me out of the bedroom downstairs to the kitchen.

"The house is far silent," he mentioned as we both entered the kitchen.

"I like it this way," I said.

"Why so?" he asked peculiarly.

"Because, it's just you and I alone together," I said naturally.

"Och."

"Now, go sit over there while I make you something special to eat," I suggested as I pointed to the stretched servants' table.

"Aye." He slid over the bench at the pine eating table and observed me as I paced around the kitchen collecting the iron skillet and some ingredients.

The stove was fortunately still burning, I noticed. So, I placed the skillet over the wood burner, and the pan started heating. There were remaining eggs left in the basket over the counter, so I took a few. I quickly minced a couple of onions and chopped winter green beans. Then, I swiftly cracked open the eggs over the bowl. I whisked the eggs and poured a tinge of milk into the bowl. Next, I plopped a wad of butter into the skillet and it sizzled, releasing the wonderful smell of a beginning morning breakfast cooking that I gladly recognized.

I first sautéed the green beans and onions, then removed them from the burner when they began sweating. Next, I poured the scrambled eggs into the hot skillet, and the eggs began to fry. Shortly it was time to add the goodies, so I sprinkled in the freshly diced sautéed ingredients along with some small chunks of cheese. Once the ingredients were enfolded within the eggs, I easily removed it from the skillet and placed it on the first plate. I swiftly made a second one and then thinly sliced several pieces of ham, lightly frying them like Canadian bacon. In a minute, the butter-milk biscuits from yesterday were lightly toasted from the Dutch oven and dressed with strawberry preserves on each half.

With a tinge of salt and ground pepper added over the eggs, I placed the ready-made plates on the table and carefully slid a plate over to Leif.

"Whit is this that ye have prepared?" he inquired amazedly as I grabbed some fresh pewter cutlery that the servants used for their meals from one of the counters.

"It's an omelet," I replied pleasantly, observing him examining the encasing egg with curiosity.

"Och, it smells appetizing," he acknowledged when I seated

myself across from him at the table. I noticed him peculiarly gazing at it a little as I started a knife and fork to mine.

"Try it," I encouraged him.

"Aye." He took up his cutlery and cut away a small piece of omelet. He placed the small portion in his mouth and chewed. "'Tis quite guid!" he said with surprise.

"Do you really like it?" I asked.

"Aye—truly," he insisted while shoveling a new fork full into his mouth. I smiled automatically at him, inspired by his reaction.

"Great," I said, placing a bit of my own omelet on my fork between my lips.

"How waur ye inspired tae create it in such a manner?" he inquired once he swallowed and began scooping more omelet into his mouth.

"It's a common breakfast recipe where I'm from," I disclosed to him while chewing a small portion of food in my mouth.

"Is it?"

"Yeah." I nodded a little as I swallowed my food, then momentarily glanced away from him toward the food on my plate as I started cutting my omelet again.

"I see..." he replied thinkingly. "Weel, it is quite palatable." I lifted my gaze and our eyes met again.

"I'm glad that you like it," I said, observing his warm laid-back expression. He released my gaze and concentrated on eating his food. A comfortable silence ensued between us as we enjoyed eating our breakfast together alone in this big empty house.

Once we had finished eating our omelets, I urged him to remain sitting with me at the table for a few minutes longer as I made tea. I also took the moment to heat something else that was extra special in the oven that I had made especially for him earlier the day before yesterday.

"Whit have ye got thaur now?" he inquired curiously while watching me. I shifted my gaze from the oven just as I was retrieving the item warming in it and looked at him.

"It's supposed to be your Christmas present," I revealed inadequately.

"Is it?" A look of sudden excitement and surprise lit his sparkling deep blue eyes.

"Yes, but, like I said—it doesn't compare remotely to the presents you've given me," I said. I retreated from the oven and strode across the kitchen with the warm item cradled in a folded cotton towel between my hands and placed the beautifully baked chocolate cake on a plate on the table before him.

"Och! Whit could this be?" he asked, intrigued.

"It's my attempt at giving you something for Christmas," I said.

"Why must ye ridicule yourself? Did ye not make this particularly fur me?"

"Yeah. I did."

"In that case, it is as I have told ye. Fur, as ye made this glorious creation precisely fur me, makes it a gift that I shall greatly cherish."

"Okay," I accepted and smiled demurely at him.

"Very weel," he said, satisfied. "Now, let us have a look at this creation haur." He eagerly returned, gazing at the petite, piping warm cake and examining it. As he was looking it over, I poured us cups of tea before returning to my seat across from him at the table. He collected his fork between his large fingers and glanced at me with some expectation.

"Go on," I urged him. Anticipatory, I gazed at him, waiting for him to take his first bite from the special cake before placing my teacup to my lips. Leif slightly raised his fork to me as in a toast before dipping it into the delicious-looking, petite chocolate cake.

"Och!" he gasped, surprised with amusement as the molten chocolate center began oozing forth when his fork broke the moist sponge. I smiled with expectancy when he proceeded scooping up some of the molten cocoa and fluffy chocolate sponge with his fork. He placed it all into his mouth at once, and his eyes abruptly widened with pleasure.

"Well?" I gazed at him, waiting for his response.

"'Tis heavenly!" he said amazedly once he swallowed the warm cake.

"Good!" I giggled a tad, amused, and satisfied that he liked what he had tasted.

"Is this magnificent bread common as weel from waur ye come?" he asked.

"Yes, it is. It's my Aunt Aidia's recipe. It's called a chocolate lava cake," I informed him.

"Och!" He dipped his fork into it again and took another large bite. "'Tis *most* magnificent!" he said again, perceivably impressed.

"Thank you," I replied.

"Many thanks tae ye, of coorse!" he insisted. I was taken by his enthusiasm and smiled as I sipped more of my tea. "Micht ye take a bit of it as weel?" he invited me.

"Okay." He held out his fork to me with a bite-size portion of cake on it, and I carefully snagged the piece of cake as he placed it gently between my lips. The taste of it was really very good, I agreed; it was just the way my Aunt Aidia had made it. I smiled at him as I savored the delicious chocolaty taste of the sponge cake mixing with molten fudge in my mouth.

"'Tis grand, is it not?" Leif attested.

"Yes," I agreed.

"Aye, yoo're a master culinary chef," he said, very impressed. I noticed his lips indolently tilting as he seemed to be thinking of something else when he went for another bite of it. Silence ensued for a moment as we started comfortably enjoying eating the cake together, but I wondered what he was thinking. "Did ye like whit I did tae ye earlier—whilst we were in bed?" he inquired, suddenly interrupting the quiet between us.

"Huh?" I responded unexpectedly, awkwardly returning my gaze to his. The expression on his face seemed a little sheepish.

"Did ye fancy the manner in which I pleasured ye?" he asked again. I noticed the visible redness in his face, and I abruptly felt the temperature in my own cheeks begin to rise. Suddenly, I felt a bit warm and shy.

"Um—well—yeah, I suppose—it was really nice," I said abashedly while I simultaneously moved a wayward ringlet strand from the side of my face, and tucked it behind my ear. I couldn't maintain my gaze on his steadfast eyes looking at me, and embarrassedly averted my gaze away from his toward the cake we were eating.

"Ye reckon so?" he asked.

"Uh—yeah—definitely." My eyes automatically returned to his, and I discerned a wide grin sweeping his face, making him appear exultant. But then it slightly disappeared as he seemed to closely ponder some more.

"Did yer first husband ever do that tae ye?" he wondered.

"Um—well, yeah, I suppose—a few times, he did," I said self-consciously.

"Did he?"

"Yeah, I guess so," I responded, feeling slightly uncomfortable about the topic.

"Did ye like it?"

"Well, I—why are you asking me this?"

"I reckon that I wish tae ken," Leif said plainly.

"Oh... Well, I guess, that I liked it—yes," I admitted.

"Did ye?"

"Um-hm," I muttered awkwardly, simultaneously filling my mouth with cake.

"Och..." He thoughtfully nodded his head a little and paused. His gaze shifted from mine down toward the cake he was continuing to eat. He was quiet while he ate it, and I sensed his remoteness from me as he seemed abstracted by his thoughts. I swallowed the small portion I was eating and sipped some more tea, observing him. I replaced the teacup over the table from my lips and thought for a moment, also, feeling the need for him to hear something from me.

"You know," I started unevenly as I nervously stroked a few of my ringlets behind my ear again.

"Aye?" he responded, returning his calm gaze to mine.

"I think I might have—I'm not sure now—but I think I might have told you this already," I stammered as I was thinking of telling him a little secret of mine.

"Aye?" he encouraged.

"Well—I think you and my first husband share some of the same attributes," I disclosed thoughtfully.

"Och, aye." Leif nodded a tad, remembering my telling him this earlier in our relationship.

"Yeah—it's very strange," I remarked.

"Why do ye reckon?"

"I don't know—I can't exactly explain it... it's bizarre, really... He was loving and really cared for me, and was good to me—everything like that. We got along great, and it was easy—like us, the way you and I get along so nicely... I think the reason why he and I got along so well was because we had known each other for a while before we got married."

"Aye."

"But..."

"Aye?"

"I was just going to say that you and I—I don't know—we haven't known each other long and... and that I really feel a unique connection with you, though—in spite of it. It's so strange—it's like I've always known you, even though I haven't... and I can't explain why. I guess, I just feel comfortable around you, and I really like it. It makes me feel so nice. I'm glad about what you and I share. It's different—and it's very special," I admitted, feeling scared of my deepening feelings for him.

"Aye."

"Do you know what I mean?"

"I do quite ken whit ye mean," he agreed.

"You do?"

"Indeed... I feel it also—that ye and I share a unique union."

"Really?"

"'Tis as if I have knoon ye my entire life. Yet, I huvnea knoon ye at all till recently."

"Yeah, that's right," I replied amazedly. As we gazed at each other in amazement, I felt some fear destabilize me, because I didn't want to lose him like I had lost Matt—especially since my bond with Leif for some inexplicable reason felt deeper. I couldn't explain this, and it truly frighten me.

"It comforts me tae ken this from ye," he said. Leif reached a hand over mine. I took his fingers among my own and naturally began caressing them.

"Even though you and Matt share some characteristics, like the way we get along, I know that you are also very different from him. So, I don't compare you to him, because I admire you for who you are and for the unique connection we share together," I said.

"Aye... I am my own man," Leif said.

"I know... Still, you should know that the same strong feelings that I had for him, I also have for you too," I revealed.

"Do ye?"

"Yes. I do."

"It is quite nice of ye tae tell me so."

"I didn't know that I could feel this way again for anyone else —and, um... it's very unexpected... and, uh, a little frightening for me, you know? Because, it feels a lot more intense this time— stronger, with you, I mean," I told him honestly.

He nodded attentively in response. My gaze fell from his toward the gold wedding band encircling his finger on his left hand, and I remembered placing it on his finger during our church wedding. The memory, while it kindled my heart, was also surreal. He straightened the dessert plate before himself and my attention was drawn to him again.

"So..." I started, but drifted into not saying anything else.

"I have a confession," he began instead.

"What is it?"

"Weel..." The hue in his cheeks rose and his face flushed. He seemed abashed and I noticed his expression become obviously ruddy the more I gazed at him while he hesitated.

"Yes?" I urged sensitively.

"I, er, I have had my share of several lasses in the past—as I'm long since a military man—only, I huvnae ever knoon one like ye in all my travels—in all of my life," he said.

"I remember you telling me that you've had some experience with women."

"Yet, I huvnea knoon one like ye," he repeated. I nodded a little in response. "Aye. Yoo're a wonder."

"Am I?"

"Indisputably. The moment I laid eyes upon ye, I kent that I wanted ye fur my own in a manner like none other. I was going tae keep ye and make ye mine. Do ye recall my saying so tae ye?"

"Yes."

"Aye, fur it is most true. I intended tae have ye. I loov'd ye the moment I saw ye come from the wood." Leif paused momentarily and simply gazed at me with a genuine expression. I could also see the love and hope in his eyes.

"That's extremely nice," I said unevenly.

"I wisnae going tae let ye loose from my secht when I first laid eyes upon ye, fur ye stole my heart and chained my soul... I am haur fur ye, Sylvie. I am haur tae protect ye, and tae care fur ye so long as thaur is breath in my body. I shall always keep ye safe," he vowed again.

"I know you will," I replied softly, sensing the gravity of his full devotion moving me to the verge of tears. I bit my lip and swallowed the knot down in my throat.

"I shall lay down my life tae keep ye from any harm," he swore fundamentally.

"Well—I don't want anything bad happening to you. It's a bit extreme to say, don't you think?" I expressed worriedly.

"Nae," he said, irrefutably shaking his head.

"But, you could get hurt."

"I pray that I shall not."

"You don't have to fight over me."

"I must—if the time will ever arise."

"I don't want you to ever be in that position."

"Yet, ye belong tae me now—yoo're mine, my wife. It is my duty tae protect ye. I swore my oath tae ye through words and in bluid, and I shall honor ye with my life," he said directly.

"Leif—" I stifled my breath, curbing my emotions.

"Indeed, ye neednae be troobled, *ceisdein*. I promise that nae harm will befall ye. Ye have my name, my wealth, my protection and my loove. I shall never forsake ye," Leif promised. He seized my fingers within his then brought them to his supple lips and kissed them. Unable to speak, I secured my palm around his as he drew his lips away from my knuckles. It became quiet between us again, and we remained there sitting together at the table for a moment longer. My thoughts absorbed me again. *Why are we so compelled toward each other? What have I gotten myself into? He says he loves me... I know now that he really does. What will I ever do if I lose him too? I can't go through that again—especially with him; I don't have the strength...* "Och!" he suddenly said, interrupting the calm between us along with my contemplation.

"What?" I replied curiously as he unexpectedly began removing himself from the table.

"I mustn't forget," he responded eagerly.

"Forget what?" I looked strangely at him, not knowing the reason for his sudden change of course as he swiftly straightened to his feet from his seat on the bench at the table.

"Merely bide as ye are, and I shall promptly make my return," he told me.

"Okay," I replied simply, pushing away my pending tears over our conversation. I curiously looked at him as he easily strode past the entrance and vanished out of the kitchen.

In roughly a couple of minutes, he returned holding something within his arm, not readily discernible. I strangely observed him striding toward me until he stood close beside me and sat next to me on the bench. I wondered what he was concealing as I tried peeking at what was hidden in his folded arm.

"Oh my goodness!" I said excitedly, unexpectedly surprised as my eyes landed on a brand-new pair of ice skates he was presenting to me in his hands.

"Merry Christmas, *ceisd mo chridhe*," he said.

"What made you?" I gasped, astonished. I turned my gaze from the skates to his crystal blue eyes, taken by his generosity.

"Ye had expressed tae me that ye liked tae skate upon the ice when ye waur a lassie. Thus, I reckoned that I shall grant ye a pair," he said.

"This is incredibly sweet of you. I can't believe you."

"Weel, I wish fur ye tae be pleased with me."

"Thank you," I replied softly. My vision was becoming blurry as my eyes began to water. I quickly wiped away the emerging tears from my eyelashes, not wanting to become consumed by my emotion for him.

"Are ye pleased?" he asked.

"Yes—very much, thank you. It's very nice of you—really nice," I said unevenly, and smiled at him. His cheeks creased as he grinned at me in response and his eyes were warm with affection. "I really wasn't expecting another gift—particularly one like this."

"I'm awaur of it." He reached his fingers over my brow and delicately moved my ringlets from my eyes and tucked them behind my ear.

"I think you're trying to spoil me," I realized.

"Conceivably," he said. I grinned bashfully at him, and his eyes twinkled confidently. "Do ye wish tae use them?" he asked.

"Yes," I said, of course. Although, as I gladly stared at my new pair of skates, I thought that they seemed a bit dubious. They were weird looking, initially reminding me of the pair the film character Pippi Longstockings had skated on in a particular movie, except maybe slightly less fantastic. On a normal pair of figure skates where the toe-pick would be, the blade instead extended out and curved a bit past the tip of the toe. And, unlike the blade reaching a bit past the heel on a modern skate, it instead stopped abruptly just beneath the heel of the boot. The boot itself didn't seem to go further than the ankle, and I was skeptical of the amount of support one might get while skating in them.

"Shall we go presently, so ye may skate?" Leif rejoined encouragingly.

"Yes," I responded willingly, nevertheless. "But, I wish for you to skate with me too."

"I have a pair also," he said.

"You do?"

"Aye. Although I huvnae skated since a laddie."

"Oh."

"Shall we, then?"

I nodded. He gathered the skates from the table into his hands and proceeded to stand from his seat once he helped me from sitting to my feet. Moving away from the table, I followed him out of the kitchen excited to have a bit of outdoor fun with him.

RETURNING TO OUR BEDROOM, we proceeded to change from our nightwear into proper clothes ready for the cold.

"Whit is that yoo've got upon ye now?" Leif asked with surprise, suddenly noticing me as I was buttoning the front of my newly tailored trousers.

"Pants," I said apparently.

"*Pants*," he repeated questionably.

"Yeah," I replied.

"Is that yer word fur breeks?" he asked strangely.

"Sure."

"But yoo're a lass!"

"I know."

"Merely sailors, or tradesmen and male laborers, slaves also, wear breeks—not lasses—particularly not gentlewomen. And, *never* one that micht be a duchess would ever wear such a garment!" he said exceptionally.

I glanced at my reflection in the looking glass and gazed at my nice updated version of slim fitting, boot-leg, lavender, velvet trousers that I had designed along with my crème color, brocade waistcoat over my slender white linen shirt.

"Oh, I don't look so bad," I disagreed.

"But ye appear as a lad!" he protested.

"Oh, c'mon." I laughed. "You're being ridiculous!"

"Ye accuse me of being ridiculous?" His brow lifted high, staring preposterously at me.

"Yeah." I laughed again.

"Waur in Heaven's name did ye come upon that garment? Did the Mantua maker fabricate them?"

"No, she didn't."

"Then, who?"

"Mercy made them for me. Aren't they great? I'm so excited to have them!"

"Did she?"

"Yes, she did such a fantastic job! Don't you think? She's so sweet! I like her so much."

"I cannae permit ye tae go outdoors appearing quite like a lad, Your Grace," Leif insisted.

"Oh now," I giggled again as I swung my matching lavender velvet caraco over my shoulders and peered at myself in the looking glass again with satisfaction.

"Whit do ye mean, '*oh now*'? There is nae hilarity about me," he disagreed absurdly.

"Yes, there is." I continued giggling, simultaneously deciding that I also liked the tailored look of my caraco jacket; the fabric loosened into gradual **A**-line pleats at the waist and flared from my waist until it hit just at the hip. I thought I looked rather smart and fashionable—quite business like.

"I am far from humorous at the moment," Leif continued.

"No—you're not," I re-asserted, returning my smiling gaze to him.

"Does it appear so?"

"Yes."

"Och!" He scoffed unbelievably.

"Look, you know *very* well that I'm not a guy," I said, coaxingly patting the side of his face with a gentle touch.

"Weel, I thank the Lord Almighty fur that yoo're not a lad," he replied, mocking me.

"See?" I pointed out as I modeled my outfit before him. "My suit jacket even flares a little and makes me look quite feminine."

"Och, aye, quite feminine as yer shape is revealed!" he grumbled ironically. I stepped closer to him and stood on my tiptoes as I placed a nice quick peck over his lips. "Och, I see—ye make nice with a wee kiss, do ye?" he jeered. I merely smiled at him, then moved toward the armoire for my newly fashioned riding boots. "Yoo've also got boots now, do ye?" he scrutinized with a ridiculing glare. But then, his gaze suddenly turned quizzical as he lightly shook his head while watching me slide my foot into the first boot.

"Of course," I said obviously. "They're better for my feet—especially in the snow."

"Indeed," he teased.

"What's good for the goose is good for the gander," I said.

"Och!" he laughed out loud. "A goose is quite different than a gander, *mo ghaol*."

"Right—well, obviously, but you know what I mean," I said.

"I reckon that I micht quite fancy the gist of yer meaning," Leif said ironically as he skeptically glared at me.

"All right, then—*voila!*" I said indifferently just as my second heel popped into place inside my boot.

"*Voila!*" he echoed.

"You don't fool me," I scoffed and he chuckled. The expression on his face relaxed into an easy curious smile.

"Scandalous," he uttered under his breath, lightly shaking his head. "Very weel, then—observing how obstinate ye are and that I huvnae the heart tae reprimand ye fur it momentarily, let us go before I do have a change of thought upon it," he consented at last. He briefly sighed and shook his head again with a resigned look.

ONCE WE COLLECTED OUR OUTERWEAR, Leif gathered my palm into his, then grabbed the skates from the floor and led us out of the room through the house for outdoors.

When we entered the white winter scene, we snowshoed across the deep, freshly fallen snow out over the clearing. Chimney smoke filled the frosty air and rose against the cloudless, cold blue, winter sky. Once we crossed the road, it took us several minutes longer to trek across a portion of the Common toward a thicket of towering viridian-green pine and blue spruce trees. Soon the pond where Leif and I had witnessed the group of boys skating a couple of weeks earlier came into view. This time the ice was empty of skaters, and it would just be me and him alone together having the frozen pond all to ourselves.

I followed Leif between the trees toward a log at the frosty shore where he decided for us to sit. He set the skates in the snow beside his foot and reached for my leg, straddling it across his large, muscular thigh. He proceeded easily, removing my boot and fixing my toes inside the small skate boot, securely lacing it. When he completed securing my second foot in the skate, he began placing skates on his own feet.

Once he was ready, he stood before me and naturally assisted me to my feet, eager to lead me out onto the ice. I carefully stepped out onto the slippery surface with him aiding me by the arm, excited for this experience.

"*Whoa!*" I gasped, laughing immediately as I almost suddenly lost my balance. Leif swiftly secured an arm around my waist to keep me from falling, accidentally causing me to collide ungracefully into his chest.

"Och!" he chuckled as I abruptly crashed into him. "Are ye alrecht?"

"Yes!" I laughed, rubbing my nose.

"Guid," he chuckled.

"These feel a little different than from what I'm used to," I said inadvertently.

"Do they?" he asked, looking curiously at me.

"Yeah."

"How micht they otherwise feel?"

"A little less awkward, I guess."

"Och."

"Let me try," I suggested interestedly as he was helping me along.

"As ye wish," he agreed and fixed his grip around my arm. He began mindfully moving us away from the shoreline with me in tow. As we ventured farther out into the middle of the frozen pond, it seemed Leif had us both stably gliding around the ice.

"Hey," I started in amazement.

"Aye?" he replied, glancing down at me.

"You seem to be pretty good at this," I observed, rather impressed.

"Och! Not as skillful as I once was as a wee lad," he said.

"But, you still are," I complimented.

"Thank ye." He warmly winked at me before turning his gaze ahead again as he guided us over the pond.

I noticed how nice and still the frosty air was as we moved through it. It broke frigidly over my face, freezing my cheeks while breezing through the chilly air when I found us having gone far out past the center of the pond. As we stroked along, I began to feel more comfortable in these strange pair of skates. I discovered my center and realized that they felt more like hockey skates than figure skates. I simply had to remember that I didn't have the safety of a toe pick to catch me, or the back blade extension to rest my weight on. But, after a moment of getting acquainted with my new pair of skates, I naturally was compelled to weave a few swizzles. I worked my blades in a familiar fashion by driving the edges on each foot hard into the ice with single footed undulating curves.

"Och! It seems that yoo're indeed quite skilled at this!" Leif remarked surprisedly, noticing my moving feet.

"Oh, I don't know..." I differed self-consciously. I stopped my foot work and started stroking regularly again.

"Let me see ye do that again," he insisted curiously.

"Do what?" I asked thoughtlessly.

"The movement ye waur making with yer feet," he said.

"Oh," I realized quickly. So, I obliged him and did it again. Leif suddenly ceased skating, stopping us short. I returned my gaze up to his and he appeared visibly impressed.

"Quite extraordinary," he said remarkably, inciting me to smile.

"Will you like for me to show you something else?" I inquired willingly.

"Aye," he said cautiously. "Merely take care," he warned additionally.

"I'll be careful," I agreed as I thought to remove my cape. I unhitched the clasp around my neck and drew the cape from my shoulders. He naturally took it from me and draped it over his arm as I moved off away from him and began skating without him. I deliberately started stroking in long concentrated strokes around the ice. There was no way that I was going to attempt anything serious like complicated jumps or spins that I regularly knew how to do with confidence. In these archaic boots and blades that offered little support, it would be suicide, I acknowledged. So, I continued gliding around concentrating on manipulating my edges as I dug into the ice with my blades carving out curves along the way. I moved forward and backward interchanging my feet one after the other before balancing on a single foot and controlling my curves.

After a moment of warming up, my maneuvering grew more confident. So, I began picking up speed. I practiced front and backward crossovers in a large figure eight across the pond. After a moment, I decided to take a section from a routine I used to do and began fancy footing it across the ice. When I had concluded maneuvering through that particular arrangement with success, I decided to continue dancing my feet over the ice from the same routine. As I ended that segment, I felt glad that I was able to accomplish it. So, I moved through more choreographed arrangements. I had come to a certain section in the choreography requiring complicated combination jumps, so I curiously substituted very minimal bunny hops and petite waltz jumps for the powerful multi-twirling loop and axel jumps.

As I was dancing across the ice, I discovered that I could actually jump a tiny bit if I remembered that I didn't have a toe pick to catch me and instead land on the flat blade with my weight evenly distributed over it. Still, it required a bit of a mindful effort. Then, I finally decided to transition into a combination spin by first deleting the layback spin, because I was terrified to try it just now. So, I selected to cross over backward and wound up into a slow rotating camel spin then changed it into a fast sit spin and concluded with a perfect scratch spin.

When I ceased twirling, I immediately stroked back toward Leif, still standing where I had left him, and stopped short just before him. He stared speechlessly at me with an utterly mesmer-ized expression and slightly gaping lips. I met his eyes with expecta-tion as I smiled at him.

"Why, I huvnea ever seen anyone so accomplished upon skates!" he remarked exceptionally. I giggled and panted while I was recovering my breath from the exercise. "That was *exquisite.*"

"Really?"

"Aye, ye waur bonnie," he expressed fantastically.

"Was I?"

"Most certainly!"

"Thank you."

"I have never witnessed such a manner of skating. Ye waur marvelous as ye moved about." He continued staring at me full of wonderment.

"Thank you" I replied again as my breathing was becoming more settled.

"How have ye learnt tae do such a thing?"

"I had a very skilled skating teacher once when I was a little girl," I reminded him.

"Indeed."

"Yes."

"Stunning."

"Did you like it?"

"Indubitably!"

"Would you like for me to skate a bit more for you, then?"

"As ye wish," he said wondrously.

"All right," I agreed, feeling glad that he was so impressed by me.

I turned away from him again and pushed off the ice ready to accomplish some more interesting maneuvers for him. After several more minutes while playfully prancing around the ice, showing off, I mechanically slipped into my comfort zone building up momentum and leaped into the air into a simple double salchow. However, I didn't realize my mistake until I was in midflight. I suddenly crash-landed, impacting over the ice, falling square on my bottom and skidded uncontrollably for a second over the pond.

"*Sylvina!*" Leif abruptly yelled from a distance across the pond. His blades were heard quickly scratching over the ice as he swiftly advanced from behind. I shifted around and glanced over my shoulder at him, quickly approaching me as I began moving over my knees to stand. Shortly, he arrived and anxiously gripped my arm, drawing me straight up from the ice onto my feet. "Are ye hurt?" he asked extremely worried.

"No—I'm fine," I said actually.

"Yoo're certain?" he asked again, appearing skeptical and enormously concerned.

"Yes, I'm perfectly fine. See?" I dusted myself off from the snow on my legs and backside, showing him that I was stable again on my skates and not the slightest injured. Nevertheless, he momentarily scrutinized me, scanning me all over with his eyes to see for himself.

"Thank Heaven. It appears that yoo're indeed not injured," he ascertained, greatly relieved, still appearing seriously alarmed though.

"I've taken a lot harder bumps than that," I joked lightly.

"Ye gave me a bit of a start."

"I'm sorry that I frightened you."

"Yoo're not tae do that again, do ye understand?" he forbade with distress.

"You don't have to worry. I know how to jump and land. I also know how to fall without getting hurt," I tried explaining, attempting to calm him.

"I dinnae care fur whit yoo're saying. I forbid ye tae jump upon skates ever again, lest ye break yer neck and kill yerself, permanently leaving me forlorn my remaining years," he said, obviously distraught.

"All right, all right." I gazed at him with caution.

"Ye must promise me so," he insisted.

"Okay—I promise I won't jump like that again on these skates," I agreed, discerning the firm look he was giving me.

"Very weel," he said seriously, appearing acutely satisfied. "Now then, I reckon we have had enough diversion fur today."

"But, we haven't been out here that long. Can't we just stay for a little while longer?" I asked hopefully.

"I dinnae reckon 'tis wise," he said.

"Please?" I pressed persuasively. "Just for a little bit longer may we stay?" He pursed his lips a little, hinting consideration as he gazed staunchly at me. Given the earnest look he was giving me, I wasn't so sure he was going to relent as he pondered for a second.

"Very weel," he agreed after he briefly thought about it.

"Great! Now, we can keep having fun."

"Aye. Yet, not fur much longer shall we remain. Church will end soon and I dinnae mean fur us tae be discovered."

"Okay," I understood. A small but kind smile eased over his worried face, changing his expression; he seemed better at ease now and ready to finish enjoying our outing together today. I slid my gloved palm over his, and he clasped it as he enfolded his hand around mine.

We started off together again, stroking calmly over the icy pond. The ease between us was quickly reinstated as we enjoyed each other again while gliding over the sleek surface in this silent snow-covered scene encapsulating us.

TONIGHT, I lay in bed awake for a little while resting closely next to Leif as he held me wrapped in his arms. Listening to the soft rhythm of his breathing was nice and lulled me while gazing at the entering moonbeams glowing in our room from the windows. The fire in the fireplace burned low and softly crackled. I was remembering some of my joyful moments with him today and realized, despite the simplicity of the holiday, it was actually one of the best Christmases that I could recall ever having had in a long time.

And with that thought, I finally closed my eyes. But, vague images of my family and friends came to mind and for the first time I wasn't troubled by it; I distantly wondered how they were going about their daily lives, and I hoped that they were all well—because in actuality, as I admitted it, I was well too. It then occurred to me right now that I was doing just fine here regardless of my fading desire to return home, even though many times my thoughts still settled on my family. While the feeling to return home continued, it was no longer a feeling of intense desperation to escape from here. Somehow, someway, the urgency to return to my previous life was no longer in the forefront of my mind, pressing me and evoking severe sadness for the longing of home.

Instead, I unexpectedly discovered that I was oddly no longer frightened by this realization as I also understood that I was living in centuries past. Now, I felt contentment and was consoled by this fact, because—as I continued realizing it—I was safe and happy with Leif; a feeling I thought would never come to me again.

Seventeen

❧

Since Christmas Eve, Leif and I had been quite social with a full visiting schedule. It seemed my dinner ball had made quite an impression and rumors about it had quickly spread with high reviews throughout town. I found myself in good standing among members of Boston's small demure community elite and was surprised, and grateful, that I had been well received.

On New Year's Eve we had spent visiting the governor. It was a mirthful dinner ball with many pleasant guests that lasted well into the evening. A bonfire and torches had been lit at night in celebration for the quickly approaching New Year. We had all gathered in the illuminating night snow around the burning fires in front of the governor's mansion, anticipating the chimes from the bell tower to ring. Everyone glowed like dancing red and orange shadows amid the brightened fire-lit night as we gathered around. In a moment the bells tolled twelve times and simultaneously musket fire and pistols shot out. Surrounding gunfire *cracked* audibly into the frigid midnight air, alarming me a little; I hoped as the musket balls shot high into the vanishing night sky, that as they returned raining downward, none of us would unexpectedly get hit in the skull with one and killed.

"Happy New Year, *mo chridhe*," Leif said quietly to me, calling my attention away from the men shooting their guns.

"Happy New Year," I responded, noticing the endearing expression on his glowing face from the bonfire in front of us. He gently grasped my fingers and raised the back of my gloved palm to his lips. I smiled and when he drew my palm away from his lips. I slid my hand around his arm and stood closely with him in the snow, silently watching the erupting bonfires as everyone was cheering in the new year. We continued listening to the gunfire as clinking crystal wine goblets broke in toasts among jubilant guests while bells rang throughout town. It was nice standing there with him, holding onto him in the muted shadows of the freezing night air, watching the scene. It felt normal, real, and serene—as if we were meant to be together like this just so in this place in time.

NOW THAT JANUARY was well underway, the festive days of Christmas waned. Leif and I frequently escaped together to the frozen pond for clandestine afternoon outings on Sundays after attending church while the day of rest was observed throughout town. Sometimes we escaped earlier during the week when boys were in school, because the ice would be empty and free for us to enjoy alone.

One afternoon after returning from skating, we entered the back of the house and the scent of sweet tobacco pipe smoke wafted strongly as we started through the sunroom, leaving the cold outdoors for warmth and shelter. An unexpected visitor was immediately recognized sitting in the large wing-chair across from us as we advanced through the room.

"Och, Fin!" Leif suddenly said as he receptively greeted his brother with a hearty pat on his shoulder, very glad to see him again.

"Hullo, Seamus!" Finley responded as he heartily patted Leif on the shoulder too.

"How micht ye be, brother?" Leif inquired gladly.

"Quite weel enough, lad," Finley replied the same way.

"Och, guid," Leif said.

"It appears that I dinnae have tae inquire efter yer welfare as I can plainly perceive that ye are in strapping health," Finley said.

"Aye, weel..." Leif suddenly turned a bit flush in the face when Finley's gaze promptly bounced over to me standing slightly behind Leif.

"Hello, Finley," I welcomed nicely, extending my hand for a warm handshake or maybe a fair hug. Instead, he seized my hand and politely kissed the back of it. I felt a little awkward inside since I still wasn't quite used to the customs here.

"Hullo, Sylvina," he greeted amiably.

"It's nice to see you again, Finley," I said. I was sincerely glad to see him and wondered how he and his family were doing, since it had already been several months ago since we last saw each other.

"'Tis quite nice tae see ye as weel, lass," he responded kindly. He caught a glimpse of my trousers, and a puzzled, scandalous, look came over his face.

"How is Elizabeth?" Leif suddenly inquired, and Finley redirected his attention back to his brother.

"She is quite weel," Finley responded easily.

"I am glad tae learn of it. And, the lasses?" Leif continued asking.

"They also fare weel," Finley answered.

"Guid tae hear so. Bonnie as ever, I reckon," Leif said.

"Och, aye, they are. I must concur," Finley replied.

"I'm certain of it," Leif agreed. There was a little pause between the brothers as Finley glanced questionably at my pants again.

"Would you like some tea?" I offered politely to them both, trying to curb Finley's scrutiny.

"Aye, I'll take it, thank ye, lass," Finley said actually as his eyes bounced from my pants to my eyes again. I was certain that he didn't approve of the way I was dressed and it made me feel slightly self-conscious.

"All right," I replied. I started away from them intending to have it prepared, a little relieved to escape Finley's judgment.

"Have it sent tae my library, *mo ghaol*," Leif requested, calling my attention to him from behind just as I had started my way out of the sunroom. I arrested my steps turning around to acknowledge him.

"Sure," I said politely as I easily looked at him. He tilted his head at me in response and I bobbed a little curtsy in reply before spinning back around on my heel, resuming my exit for the kitchen.

"Let us go tae my library, shall we?" Leif suggested to Finley, as I continued pacing past the threshold into the corridor.

"Aye," Finley said as his voice resonated into the hallway.

"Very weel," Leif responded gladly with the same resonance. I heard them beginning to pace out of the room a distance behind me.

"Do ye permit yer woman tae wear breeks?" Finley asked Leif strangely.

"Weel, er, she fancies them fur when we skate about upon the pond," Leif replied unnaturally.

"Ye permit her skate like the lads as weel?" Finley questioned oddly.

"Aye," Leif said simply.

"Indeed?" Finley responded, sounding critical of it.

"Aye."

"Curious."

"Och, she can do it quite bonnie like, however," Leif justified.

"Can she?" Finley asked with surprise in his voice.

"Aye, she knows how tae whirl magnificently about," Leif said impressively.

"Is that reit?"

"Aye."

"Highly irregular. I micht have reckoned that ye wouldnae have fancied such boldness in a lass as it waur. Let alone permitting yer wife tae be so," Finley said strangely.

"'Tis harmless—I reckoned," Leif said.

"Yoo're poised fur scandal," Finley warned.

"Nae novelty," Leif acknowledged ironically.

"Mayhap..." Finley mocked. "Yet, thaur are lads about, are they not?"

"Nae. 'Tis a clandestine affair," Leif responded.

"Och," Finley replied simply as I rounded the corner heading toward the kitchen, losing the tail of their conversation.

PRUDENCE ASSISTED me in delivering the tea to the brothers as she set the nicely arranged silver tea service tray over the stand in Leif's library. Once the tray was properly placed, presenting crumpets and strawberry preserves, I thanked her and she curtsied before she proceeded out of the room, leaving me to serve it to them instead.

I started preparing the brothers' tea while they lightly conversed. As I snipped off a couple of petite pieces from the sugarloaf into one of the teacups, I happened to glance up from stirring the tea with the sugar in it and noticed Finley examining me again while Leif was searching through some parchments over his desk. I smiled meekly at Finley, and he responded with a modest grin that was not offensive. I cast my eyes from him down to the tray of food before me and returned my attention to preparing tea.

"Ah, haur it is!" Leif said abruptly, finally satisfied that he had found the sheet of parchment for which he was searching. I glanced up again, and Finley shifted his pondering gaze to Leif as he began approaching the empty chair next to his brother.

When I had finished preparing tea for them, I strode toward Leif now seated beside his brother and informed him that it was ready for their taking.

"Thank ye, *mo ghaol*," he said.

"You're welcome," I replied. I leaned slightly and naturally delivered a gentle kiss on his cheek. He suddenly flushed and unevenly glanced at the tea I was properly positioning over the stand. Finley noticed his brother, I happened to discern, before glancing away from them both to serve them their tea. When I lifted the teacup and saucer from the tray and passed it to Finley, he politely received it from me and gave me a pleasant grin that was sincere.

"Thank ye, lass," Finley said kindly.

"You're welcome, Finley," I said.

"She is quite bonnie, Seamus," Finley commented, shifting his attention directly to Leif as he complimented him regarding my presence.

"Och, aye," Leif agreed simply, with discernible color in his cheeks. He briefly caught my glance when I moved back toward the platter over the stand to position the crumpets, butter, preserves, and cheese for them to receive.

"It appears wedded life suits ye, brother," Finley fathomed openly.

"Aye," Leif said.

"Quite nicely, I expect," Finley said, looking at Leif with a determining expression.

"Aye, quite nicely," Leif echoed modestly.

"I expect so," Finley implied with a chuckle. I quickly glanced over my shoulder at both of them, and my eyes landed on Leif. He seemed distinctly ruddier and reticent about their light discussion.

"Micht we have a look at this parchment haur?" he interjected, holding forth the paper to Finley.

"Aye, of coorse," Finley agreed, taking the parchment from him. I caught Leif's glance as I placed the last dish in the right location over the table. He subtly nodded his head, and I curtsied in reply. Turning toward the doorway, I moved out of the room into the corridor for the staircase.

"Yoo've done weel, lad," Finley mentioned as his voice echoed past the open door into the corridor.

"Aye, thank ye," Leif replied, sounding modest as his voice carried also.

"She is quite changed," Finley remarked.

"Ye reckon so?" Leif asked.

"Aye."

"Och."

"She is cheerful."

"Aye—she is."

"She's nice fur ye, then?"

"Aye, indeed, she is quite nice."

"Is she as feisty?"

"She has settled quite nicely."

"Guid. Ye tamed her, evidently."

"I reckon."

"'Tis a benefit nae doubt."

"Aye."

"Ye bedded her weel, I micht reckon in that case," Finley commented with a chuckle. I heard Leif chuckle too, although he sounded bashful. I stopped abruptly in my steps just as I was about to start down the staircase, suddenly filled with embarrassment.

I instantly did an about face, ready to burst through the library and chastise them for talking about me in that manner. But on second thought, I stopped short just before the entrance and hesitated. I quickly thought about the consequences if I acted on my rash impulse in a display of anger and after a second, I ultimately decided not to enter the room and confront them. So, I just as quickly turned back and resumed my way through the hallway and down the steps, leaving them to their male conversation, entirely peeved.

However, later that evening while Leif and I were lying next to each other in bed, he was in the mood for some affection, as usual. But I abruptly slapped his hand away from me when he cupped my pubic area with his palm.

"Och!" he gasped out of surprise, quickly recoiling his eager hand from me. He unexpectedly looked at me. I rolled my eyes at him, no way in the mood for his attention.

"You're not allowed to touch me," I said absolutely.

"Why in Heaven's name not?" he asked with a puzzled expression.

"Never mind. Let's just go to sleep—I'm tired," I responded irritably, and rolled onto my side, no longer facing him.

"Yoo're being churlish presently," he determined. He reached an arm around me and rolled me over to face him again. "Now tell me whit is the matter with ye? Why are ye cross?" he asked with a straight-forward expression.

"Do you really want to know?" I replied frankly.

"Aye."

"Fine—I'll tell you."

"Pray, do."

"I heard you and Finley talking about me," I disclosed plainly.

"Of whit are ye speaking?" He gazed at me with confusion.

"Earlier today in your library—I heard you guys talking about me," I said grumpily.

"Och! So, ye are a spy indeed, then," he taunted.

"Stop it—I'm not a spy—and you know that already," I said, annoyed.

"Then how have ye heard anything that was said about ye?" he joked. He propped himself on his elbow and hovered over me, gazing steadfastly.

"It was by accident as I was coming from your library after serving you tea," I explained.

"Och." His brow raised slightly.

"There—now you know. Goodnight," I concluded abruptly and turned over onto my side away from him again.

"Yet, I huvnae finished with ye." He shifted me back around with certainty in order for me to look at him some more. "Come now." He gently started stroking my brow. "I apologize that ye overheard our discussion. Yet, 'twas innocent."

"It didn't sound innocent to me," I disagreed.

"However, it was indeed innocent," he insisted genuinely. "Fin is quite fond of ye, ye ken?"

"He is?" I responded, surprised.

"Certainly he is."

"That's news to me."

"How can it be when 'tis the truth."

"Because he's grumpy to me. That's why."

"He is mindful of ye, because he regards ye weel. He reckons that yoo're quite bonnie."

"I've heard."

"He also reckons that yoo're most kind."

"Really?"

"Aye."

"I suppose that's nice of him."

"He also believes that ye have a noble heart, and that yoo're quite intelligent fur a lass."

"For a lass?" I frowned at him.

"Aye."

"Would that mean I'm smarter than a dog, but stupider than a man?" I questioned sarcastically as I continued glowering at him.

"Pardon?" His brow lifted high on his head with surprise.

"You heard me."

"Aye. Yoo're being impudent," he scolded lightly. I didn't respond because I could perceive the slight pang of hurt and annoyance in his eyes when I realized that he was being genuine with me.

"Sorry," I decided to say despite the anger I was feeling.

"Forgiven. I shall continue tae inform ye that Fin most importantly believes that we are a guid match fur one anither."

"Really?" This bit of news struck me with consideration and suddenly softened my hurt feelings.

"Aye—and, that is guid of him tae say."

"I suppose that it is."

"He is pleased that I have ye. He also told me that he is pleased that he listened tae my request tae keep and wed ye efter I stole ye back from Fort Carillon," Leif informed me as he remained gently stroking my brow.

"He is?" I asked thoughtfully, beginning to feel better again.

"So, ye see?" He leaned in close and tenderly pressed his lips over mine. "Thaur was nae harm meant in our discussion."

I suddenly became appeased when he lifted his gaze to mine again after his kiss.

"Okay," I realized, now feeling a bit contrite. I sensed him lean another soft kiss over my brow this time.

"Micht ye forgive me, however, fur rumpling yer spirit?" he asked as he proceeded to benevolently give tender kisses on my cheeks and lips.

"Yes, I forgive you," I responded calmly, falling under his coaxing spell.

"Thank ye," he muttered warmly over my lips.

"You're welcome," I whispered back.

He moved over me, and I sensed him separating my legs with his sturdy knee as he generously covered me with affectionate kisses upon my cheek and lips, causing me to forget that I was ever disgruntled with him in the first place.

Eighteen

It was pleasant having Finley visiting with us as it had been several months since Leif had seen him. The brothers had missed each other quite a bit, because they spent all their time together now. It was nice seeing them rekindle the unique sibling bond that they shared, and it made me wistful for my own brother as I admired their connection. Finley was also very pleased to reunite with Amity. He was entirely impressed with how far advanced his niece had become in her communication skills and all the other areas pertaining to her education. He was plainly stunned, and Leif was particularly proud of me for all that I had accomplished with her as he explained to Finley the immense learning work Amity and I had undertaken together.

Thoroughly impressed, Finley began asking Amity all sorts of questions regarding her stay here with us as I communicated to her his desire to know about her. She expressed to her Uncle Finley all that had happened to her with particular excitement over having attended the Christmas dinner ball due to Leif's leniency. Finley was no less surprised by this in a non-offended manner and liked her telling him all about it as he was charmed.

A few days later, Leif told me the additional reason for Finley's visit. He mentioned to me during breakfast this morning that he and Finley were to partake today in an assembly convened by the newly appointed Royal Governor, Thomas Pownall. While I found this information curious, I was really not piqued with interest to delve into a conversation regarding this meeting because I didn't find it concerning. So, I quietly continued eating my breakfast while he and Finley continued discussing their optimism over the meeting and the politics surrounding it.

ONCE LEIF and Finley went to the center of town to attend their meeting with the governor after breakfast this morning, around midday I had completed my lessons with Amity, then wandered around the house looking for Leif hoping to share tea with him and Finley. But I noticed that they were nowhere to be found and assumed the meeting was still in progress, and therefore he and Finley had not yet returned. So, I decided to occupy myself with some exercise and ventured out into the biting cold alone, and headed for the frozen pond to skate.

WHEN A COUPLE of hours of skating enjoyment had passed, I decided to return to the house as flurries began falling silently from the dark gray sky. Finally returning inside from the Common, it seemed Leif and Finley had not yet returned from their meeting. So, I decided to take my tea alone in the sitting room and read the *Boston Gazette*. It was my first time taking a moment to read a local newspaper here, called a broadsheet, and I noticed right away that it was simply laid out with only occurring facts.

Subjective reporting, sensational editorials, the glitz of entertainment news, gossip, fashion, and colorful advertisements, were completely missing from this typical publication. Except an obituary did in fact exist. But, accounts of what was occurring in the rest of the colonies instead influenced the news. The war with France dominated the print with detailed accounts of what various regiments had undergone in their battles across the frontier against the French, and a list of their Indian allies terrorizing English settlements across the colonies. The news did not seem good. In fact, given the reported accounts, it very well appeared that England was losing the war—badly. The paper also briefly announced the new sitting Royal Governor, Thomas Pownall, in place of the interim Governor Phips, for Massachusetts Bay Colony.

After some time had passed reading the broadsheet, I found myself growing a little tired of reading and I simply closed my eyes just to rest for a second. But I must have dozed off for some time while reclined over the settee, because I was suddenly awakened by Leif's voice carrying past the foyer as he entered the house with Finley. Their boots were also heard heavily thumping over the hardwood planks when they entered the sitting room, while in the middle of a discussion. They both apparently seemed peeved when my eyes began focusing on them from sleep as they paced deeper inside of the room. I shifted from the settee, wiping my sleepy eyes, and turned my attention to them.

"Och! Hullo, *mo ghaol*," Leif greeted, appearing slightly less annoyed as he suddenly noticed me sitting up from the settee. He approached me and gave a small kiss over my brow.

"Hi," I said softly and sat appropriately in my seat.

"This is an abomination, ye do realize?" Finley snapped, openly disgruntled.

"Aye," Leif agreed in the same moody manner.

"Lord Almighty, how do they expect tae win militia support if they further strangle our liberties?" Finley disparaged.

"I dinnae ken," Leif said as he irritably ran his fingers through his loose hair. "'Tis an utter mess—the entire state of affairs."

"Aye," Finley agreed unflappably.

"What's wrong?" I inquired curiously.

"Loudoun is it," Leif said.

"Oh..." I realized, suddenly feeling a little apprehensive about knowing Lord Loudoun was the reason for their anger.

"And now we have Pownall, our newly appointed governor, who will act accordingly with threats," Leif informed me.

"Threats?" I asked.

"Aye," Leif answered. "He is nae different than Loudoun, and presently we are cursed with him also."

"We shall take up matters with the Council," Finley suggested abruptly.

"Aye," Leif agreed. "The sooner, the better."

"Indeed. I dinnae believe the justices of the peace will support these new measures," Finley said.

"I dinnae believe it either. I shall not be forced tae billet the dregs under my roof! I have a wife tae protect—and women servants in my charge as weel," Leif said, visibly incensed.

"Correct—as weel do I," Finley agreed.

"Aye, thaur are enough fresh barracks haur fur them tae use instead of pressing this encroachment upon us," Leif pointed out.

"As weel as thaur remain enough in Albany and New York Town," Finley added.

"Aye, I have already shown plenty of courtesy by billeting them upon my property in Northampton. I'll not go any further than that," Leif said.

"As I have soldiers quartering too thaur presently at *Taigh Bheinn* fur the winter whilst my family and I are visiting Elizabeth's kin in Concord. Nae doubt this will sit weel amongst others," Finley fathomed.

"Indeed."

"Nor will it sit weel when word spreads that lads will be sent tae the lines without Assembly permission," Finley stated further.

"Aye, this is most troobling. It clearly appears that diplomacy disnae exist with the governor," Leif said as he rubbed his palm over his forehead appearing quite disturbed. "I dinnae foresee mili-tiamen agreeing tae fight under these circumstances. Thaur is even much decent and desertion amongst our own men. And, I am sympathetic tae their plight."

"Agreed. We must tread carefully, however, lest we are accused of treason," Finley warned.

"I realize," Leif replied.

I was beginning to get a much better sense of what was taking place here and a terrible feeling settled over me. I felt frightened and I wasn't sure about what could potentially happen to us which left me with a firm sense of foreboding.

"What would happen to you if you didn't quarter anyone?" I interrupted, concerned. Leif and Finley unexpect-edly turned their attention to me. A faint sigh escaped Leif and a surrendering look crossed his face. Leif strode toward me and sat next to me. He propped his elbows over his spread knees and appeared slightly hunched as he gazed steadily at me with a serious but assuaging expression on his face.

"Ye neednae concern yerself, *mo ghaol*," he assured. Except, I could see in his eyes that he didn't wish to tell me everything. It seemed he didn't want me to worry about politics and what was happening with the war. But I was concerned.

"I want to know," I said.

"Ye mustn't be troobled," he said calmly.

"But, what would happen to you if you didn't do it?" I requested again. Finley paced slowly toward the warm hearth and rested his arm on the corner edge of the marble mantlepiece with noticeable pensiveness.

"I micht be imprisoned—tried fur treason, mayhap," Leif informed me.

"That can happen to you?" I was surprised to hear him tell me this.

"If Loudoun orders it and I dinnae comply, when he learns of it, he will see fit tae have me court martialed waur such charges will be levied upon me," Leif explained.

"I don't understand how that could happen to you. I mean you have clout, don't you?" I responded unbelievably.

"This isnae my grandfather's Crown. Nor, that of my great uncle's." He sighed. "Whilst I do bear some influence, I am not in King George's favor till I complete my service tae him."

"Right. But you can still bend the king's ear, can't you?" I asked.

"Not if the work of politics are against me," he said.

"It seems so lopsided and unreasonable," I said unjustly.

"Reason is a novelty. Merely recall Governor Shirley's current predicament as he is currently being tried fur treason," Finley reinserted himself into the conversation.

"Aye, and Loudoun and I share hostilities toward one anither. He would be pleased tae see me hanged as he is familiar with my political opinions," Leif said grimly.

"Then why not just go ahead and house the military troops if it ultimately means keeping you safe and intact? I'd rather have you alive than dead," I said honestly.

"*Ceisdein*, I regard that ye care fur me, but indeed it is fully not within my inclination," Leif said unequivocally. I suddenly remembered the frightening time I had encountered at the farm back in Northampton when I was nearly raped by a couple of English soldiers, and I immediately understood his position on the subject. I silently nodded as I gazed back at his contemplating eyes. "I'll take my chances outside Loudoun's terms, if I must," he resolutely concluded.

"We micht garner a meeting," Finley urged as he was also appearing extremely pensive with a furrowed brow.

"We ought," Leif agreed.

I continued sitting there on the settee when Leif stood from sitting next to me and paced toward the fireplace near his brother. He reached for the poker on the side of the hearth opposite from where Finley was standing and began stoking the flames while I merely sat in my seat listening until they concluded their conversation. They decided their next course of action would first involve an undisclosed meeting consisting of like minds living in town. While I perfectly understood the brothers' position in this matter, I couldn't help the deep skepticism I also held for Lord Loudoun; from my own personal encounter with the man, I was certain that he was dangerous to cross, and I didn't want Leif remotely endangered by him. Furthermore, the idea that Leif was not at all inclined to give into Lord Loudoun's quartering edict here in Boston internally made me distinctly uneasy, striking me with dread.

A WEEK LATER, a secret meeting had taken place between certain members of society here in town, and a decision had been made to assemble a public town hall meeting that included the justices of the peace. Transpiring from the assembly, an agreement had been reached among the justices: it was determined by them that the Crown was acting unlawfully toward its colonial subjects. Therefore, the justices would not enforce the Quartering Act. Additionally, it was found that to draft men into the militia and send them outside of the colony without Assembly consent, was a violation of law and unreasonable. As a result, the justices would not uphold Lord Loudoun's harsh edicts against deserters.

It was a victory for Leif and Finley and for the community for not having to quarter, and an additional victory for the colony at large regarding the action of deserting militiamen. As a result, Leif seemed better eased over the prospect of not accommodating soldiers in our house. But he and Finley still were not exactly satisfied as I had discovered one late evening when I intended to bid Leif goodnight and turn myself in for bed.

Anticipating Leif to be found reading in his library, I had

stumbled upon overhearing a conversation between him and Finley among several other unknown men gathered in his library as I approached through the hallway on the third floor leading to his library. The discussion revolved around Fort Oswego. It seemed to be a bitter sticking point for many in the room. They were discussing the tactical failure by Lord Loudoun regarding the fort, and were voicing anger that it had fallen to the French General Montcalm. According to the men's discussion, it seemed that particular fort was a key asset for strategic defense against France. But now that Lake Ontario was dominated by the French due to the fall of the fort, the opposition had a far stronger position against the British.

A Lieutenant Colonel Bradstreet was also mentioned in the conversation, which further incited cynical reactions around the discussing men. Apparently, they were further outraged over the fact that Lord Loudoun had dismissed Bradstreet's troops after Bradstreet delivered much needed provisions to the fort's garrison without Lord Loudoun's instructions. Furthermore, Lord Loudoun was incensed as a result of Colonel Bradstreet having delivered news of Fort Oswego's imminent peril upon his return from the fort after having delivered the provisions to the troops there. As I continued listening, it seemed Lord Loudoun had effectively turned a deaf ear to Bradstreet's urgent intelligence and dismissed him, in addition to all his troops, just like he had done to General Winslow.

"It would benefit immensely if Lord Loudoun exercised a bit of tact and showed restraint towards us. In which case, we might better advance against the enemy," said an unknown man, apparently embittered.

"Indeed, he has successfully waged war against us rather than upon the enemy and has quite disaffected us residing here that we might rather lose to the enemy," said another stranger, also candidly irate.

"He is a tyrant in favor of the Crown's hostility toward us!" came forth an angry voice.

"'Twas initially agreed that we would have control over our own militias, but His Lordship has usurped that agreement," someone else charged resentfully.

"Indeed! Usurping our militias and inflicting brutality upon us is unwarranted! It decisively defeats the effort for our success against France and her Indians!" someone other strange man said.

"Aye, 'tis a response that the Crown favors," Finley interjected disdainfully.

"Mayhap, we must move tae have him recalled," Leif suggested.

"Recalled?" someone questioned.

"Indeed," another man agreed.

"Aye, indeed! We might draft an initiative," someone else agreed.

"Whit do ye reckon, Seamus?" Finley asked his brother.

"I shall not say that the notion has not already occurred tae me far sooner than now," Leif said frankly.

"Weel, then?" Finley anticipated. There was a pause and silence ensued through the corridor where I had ceased approaching as the library went silent.

"I shall take the responsibility tae form an initiative," Leif replied finally, resuming the conversation.

"Alrecht. My brother will draft a proposal," Finley said. "Are ye lads in agreement with this motion?"

"Aye," the men said in turn.

"Then, we shall reconvene tae discuss the draft," Finley said.

"Once it is approved, we sign it, and I shall have it delivered tae the king," Leif said.

"Aye," the men agreed.

"I shall promptly correspond with Master Pitt in London in conjunction," Leif said.

I slowly backed away in the hallway and turned around, deciding not to disturb the meeting. When I entered the bedroom ready to retire for the evening, I felt hopeful after hearing this conversation and thought maybe they could actually successfully remove Lord Loudoun from the continent. I wasn't sure how they were going to achieve this goal, but the idea of it lent a glimmer of optimism. And, I thought if they did succeed, then we finally might all be safe from him.

Nineteen

A month later, Finley left us to return to his family in
Concord after it seemed he had concluded his business
in Boston. Once he had gone, Leif began attending a
number of meetings—most of which were private and took place
in certain men's homes who were of similar political minds.

Early one morning while he was away to one of these meetings,
I slipped outside to skate over the pond. I had been skating around
for a while enjoying myself, when I happened to notice a solitary
man in a black tricorn hat and cloak standing at a distance by the
embankment among the trees. It seemed that he had been
watching me dance around the ice for a while. At first glance I
believed it was Leif, and I gladly waved at him from afar across the
ice. But he didn't wave back as he kept watching me, and it oddly
struck me when I realized that he wasn't who I thought he was. So,
I turned back around feeling somewhat foolish about my mistake
and skated off to resume prancing some more around the pond.
When I curiously glanced over my shoulder in his direction, I
noticed that he'd suddenly gone, nowhere to be seen as I scanned
his previous location.

Later when I returned indoors, I met Leif for some hot cocoa that I had made in place of tea, and we sat enjoyably together in front of the fire in the sitting room. After he indulged me in a game of chess, I sat comfortably stretched out across the sofa with my ankles stretched over his lap quietly observing the crackling fire burning warmly in the fireplace. His palm was lightly caressing my foot, nicely relaxing me as I was finishing my hot cocoa that had grown lukewarm after our chess game together.

"I thought you might have visited me at the pond today," I mentioned casually as I was enjoying his foot massage over my toes.

"Och, nae, I apologize, *ceisdein*. I couldnae escape duties today," he said regretfully.

"It's okay. I thought you had come, but realized it was someone else," I said.

"Was someone else thaur?"

"Yeah."

"Och..." he responded abstractedly as he seemed to ponder.

"He disappeared right after I noticed him," I said.

"Did he?" Leif replied curiously with a furrowed brow while gazing at me.

"Yeah, he was no longer there when I looked again in his direction."

"Hmm... A tad odd, I reckon. Ye must have struck his curiosity whilst ye skated about the pond."

"Maybe so."

"Regardless, I shall be certain tae join ye the next time ye wish tae venture fur a bit of diversion upon the pond."

"That would be nice."

Leif gave me a shallow grin and subsequently shifted his gaze from me to the burning fireplace. He stared at the roaring flame in it, appearing to brood as his fingers stopped caressing my toes and stilled comfortably on my ankle stretched over his lap. I observed him prop an elbow over the arm of the sofa and place a meditative finger above his upper lip. He was definitely thinking and appeared unsettled.

"Are you all right?" I inquired, concerned.

"Hm? Whit is it, *mo chridhe*?" he replied, suddenly returning his eyes to mine, interrupted from his thoughts.

"You seem a little bothered," I said.

"Och…" He sighed a bit and was now looking at me with his full attention instead of at the raging fireplace. "I fear that I am displeased over whit I have only recently learnt," he disclosed.

"What's wrong?" I curiously looked at him, wondering what had gotten him annoyed and brooding.

"Pownall threatens tae penalize the magistrates fur allowing deserters tae go free if they dinnae choose tae promptly enforce the edicts," he said.

"Oh." I gave him an unfortunate look.

"'Twill only serve tae anger the militiamen and cause desertion and mutiny. Thaur wulnae be any unification amongst our forces if thaur isnae a reasonable resolution fur the militia and British. As Loudoun wulnea consider the militia, those men wulnae respect him. 'Twill make battling the French far more difficult. And tae further impede the guid will of men and tae complicate matters, I have also learnt Loudoun intends tae occupy the city with troops tae impress quartering," Leif said disconcertedly.

"That's illegal, though," I disputed.

"He has overruled whit is legal haur as it appears that we are clearly under his jurisdiction," Leif recognized unfavorably.

"He's an autocrat," I scoffed with a note of disgust in my voice. Leif cocked an eyebrow at me. I wasn't so sure he approved of my tone.

"A tyrant, ye mean?"

"Yeah."

"Aye," he agreed. "I'm certainly not in accordance with his absolutism."

"Seems there's no choice, though—at least right now, anyway."

"I mean tae curb his actions," he said with earnestness, gazing steadily at me.

"How?" I responded cautiously.

"He isnae leading the war weel whilst being a threat tae us haur. Even though he is a personal nemesis of mine, he is also an utter menace tae the lot of people haur," he returned.

"What are you going to do?" I inquired uncertainly.

"I'm in the process of putting forth a proposal, but 'twill take some time before it reaches the correct officials in London. Therefore, I am required tae devise a more immediate initiative. Yet, I huvnae reckoned the complete details of the matter. I must see tae it with members of the Assembly tae understand whaur we micht effectively stand," Leif pensively informed me.

"I see…" I said thinkingly.

"Dinnae worry, *ceisdein*. 'Twill be alrecht," he promised.

"I'm not worried," I said. I believed him and had faith that everything would be all right just as he said despite my initial concern. I gave him a little smile as a vote of confidence, and a gentle grin passed over his lips also. He reached for my fingers and enfolded them in his palm as he brought them to his lips. After placing a kiss on my fingertips, he tenderly held my hand.

"My brave *àille dhubh*," he said admiringly. "How have ye come upon yer heroism that I so deeply admire in yer nature?"

"I'm not at all brave," I disagreed.

"Yet, ye are. Ye have faced fear and never once did ye ever tell me that ye waur afraid—not even the moment ye wept in my arms efter we had escaped the Algonquin war party giving us chase when we fled Fort Carillon. Ye must ken that ye give me much strength that wulnae otherwise exist if it waur not fur the way ye care fur me," he said meaningfully.

"I'm really glad that you feel the way you do—because I do very much care about you," I said, and smiled at him again. But this time it was gentle and honest, as he touched my heart while I held his steadfast gaze. The expression in his eyes was deep and heartfelt, and compelled my shyness as he kept gazing at me with such penetration.

When Leif finally released his eyes from me, he drew the back of my hand to his lips again and planted a soft kiss on it. I shifted from reclining on the sofa and straightened upward next to him. I leaned my head on his solid shoulder and naturally cuddled against the curve of his broad chest. Wrapping an arm around me, he held me close and I sensed his lips press against the top of my head. Silence followed between us, and we sat together on the sofa near the hearth simply snuggling and relaxing before the warm animated fire crackling in the fireplace for moments longer.

THE DAYS SEEMED to roll into weeks, and weeks blurred into months. April was now already here. Lent quietly passed us by, and Easter came and went with reverent observance.

An outbreak of the flu had occurred, and some of the servants, including Leif and Amity, had succumbed to the illness. My attention had been redirected to medically caring for them in addition to our servants who had fallen ill. Given the course of the illness, it was proving to be a moderate episode lasting several weeks between everyone afflicted. And while weeks were spent dealing with the draining impact of the virus, I was glad to finally witness everyone safely recovering after a dreaded while of my exhausting round the clock care for them.

Except now my worry remained with two-year-old Daniel, the youngest member of our household, son of one of our maids. It seemed that he was experiencing a hard bout of congestion and was minimally taking in nourishment. I spent several long days and nights observing him. I focused on reducing his temperature with lukewarm baths and assisting his airways by keeping them clear of mucus with minimal funnel drips into his nose of saline solution that I had concocted. It was also important to ensure that he was sustaining an adequate hydration level. So, I made sure that he was drinking adequate amounts of herb tea and lemon water, and chicken soup that I had especially made for him. After a week of concentrated care, his proper hydration level stabilized, and his appetite came back with a vengeance: a very good sign!

One day while the effects of the flu were certainly subsiding, I decided to take the opportunity to venture to the marketplace with Mercy accompanying me to obtain some things that I needed. A noticeable number of British troops were walking the streets. It seemed as though more of them had newly landed as I was making my errands around Boston. Among one of my final stops was to the apothecary. When I had at last exited the establishment out onto the brick-laid walkway and started pacing with Mercy up the block, I was unexpectedly alerted by someone attempting to gain my attention.

"Yes?" I asked, apprehending my steps. When I turned around, I noticed a young English soldier who acquired my awareness.

"I beg your pardon, milady," he said not so nicely.

"Yes?" I asked again in a civil tone, although I was skeptical of him due to his tone toward me.

"This eya is fer you, milady," he said unceremoniously and abruptly held out a wax sealed letter to me.

"What is it?" I inquired curiously without taking it.

"It is fer you, milady," he repeated, insisting that I take the note from him.

"Whom is it from?" I asked. He wouldn't answer. In that case, I decided to accommodate him and curiously received the small, sealed, folded parchment from him. As I gathered it from his hand, he suddenly turned away and began pacing back down the walkway in the opposite direction. "Just a moment!" I suddenly called out to him, but he didn't respond. Instead, he kept casually walking farther down the street. I impulsively cracked the carmine wax seal and unfolded the note to see what it was about. Still standing on the walkway, I swiftly began reading:

7 April, 1757

Mistress Arboles,

I submit to you a gracious request for an interview with you to-morrow. I ask that you please my request to avail yourself to me by ten o'clock next forenoon. I quite anticipate our meeting with pleasure and thank you as a favor to me to make my appeal.

With Most Sincere Kindness and Friendship,
Earl of Loudoun

Lord Loudoun...? How does he know that I'm here in Boston? How did he find out? And why is he asking to see me?

Suddenly, my carefree mood changed as this note did not bode well with me at all. In fact, I felt quite intimidated and dread came over me. I hadn't seen this man in months and thought he would have forgotten about me by now. Obviously I was very much mistaken. I wondered what he wanted with me, because I wanted absolutely nothing to do with him and had hoped that I would never see him again in my life.

After escaping him once before, I was certain he was furious about it, and I wasn't entirely confident that Leif could protect me from him a second time. I was hardly inclined to freely walk into the lion's den belonging to Lord Loudoun on his request and become trapped by him again in his quarters. So, I was a little more than shocked to have received this note from him as I also suddenly wondered how his messenger knew how to recognize me in order to deliver it to me in public.

Is Lord Loudoun spying on me...? A chill ran down my spine at the thought.

I shortly folded the message and glanced up from the piece of parchment I was holding. I quickly spotted the soldier again walking through the crowd and was going to catch up to him.

"Excuse me, Mercy, please wait for me here—I'll be right back," I said thoughtlessly as I suddenly pardoned myself from her.

"Yes'm," she obliged, though she appeared rather surprised that I was abandoning her. I quickly dispensed a couple of the packages I was holding into her already full arms and hastily took off walking through the strolling pedestrians. In a moment I had caught up close enough behind the soldier to be tactfully audible to him.

"Excuse me," I discreetly called after him, knowing that he could hear me. I wasn't sure, but it seemed he wasn't going to promptly respond as I continued pacing closely after him. He picked up his pace and began walking more hurriedly through the pedestrians on the walkway. "Excuse me," I said again, walking hastily after him. He suddenly stopped short, spinning around on his heel completely facing me and bent mockingly into a ridiculous, ceremonious bow.

"Aye, milady?" the soldier said when he straightened and looked directly at me with a rude smirk. I was somewhat insulted and incensed by his uncalled for rudeness. I glared at him unimpressed and suddenly I found my nerve.

"Hey," I started boldly, "you tell *El Jefe*, that brilliant boss of yours, Lord Loudoun, that if he wants to meet with me, then he may do so through my attorney by court order." The young soldier's eyes abruptly widened with stark surprise, and he appeared significantly caught off guard by my abrupt response.

"Aye, milady," the soldier replied mockingly, regardless. Then the rude smirk reappeared over his grimy face, and he glared derisively at me as if he knew a secret. "If I may confess to ya. Dare I say that ya are a vision most lovely—particularly when ya skate about the pond, *milady*," he sneered—stressing *milady* in a deriding tone—as he leaned in toward my face to tell me confidentially. He stared at me for a second longer as I noticed his eyes glance down at my lips before returning to meet my eyes again. "I overheard His Lordship speaking of ya once. He said that ya 'ave the most enticing mouth he 'as ever seen on a lass. I find that I strangely agree wi' him. Good day to ya, milady." He then abruptly turned his back to me and restarted pacing away along the walkway in the opposite direction.

"Dipshit," I scoffed under my breath, definitely irritated by him. But I was more so appalled at Lord Loudoun's unscrupulous audacity to try communicating with me as if all was well after he propositioned me and attempted holding me hostage while threatening to jail me if I refused his demands. The soldier right at once slightly turned his ear in my direction after my expletive, and I knew that he unintentionally had heard me. But I didn't care.

I spun around over the walkway feeling hot under the collar, oddly no longer afraid of Lord Loudoun now and returned to Mercy still waiting for me right where I had left her. I realized then that Lord Loudoun couldn't touch me even if he wanted to unless he flat out kidnapped me, and I didn't see how that could possibly happen. So, I felt confident against him, and I returned to pleasantly finishing my last errand with Mercy before returning to *Taigh Gràs*.

WHEN I RETURNED from the marketplace, I discerned the voice of an unfamiliar man coming from the drawing room at the front of the house behind an ajar door. I heard Leif responding to the gentleman after his statement when I took a quick peep through the crack of the door and realized then that Leif was in the middle of an important private conversation. Choosing not to disturb him, I decided to wait until later to show him the note given to me by the soldier at the marketplace. So, I tucked the note back into my pocket and started back through the corridor.

Later at dinner as I sat close to Leif at the head of the dining table across from Amity quietly eating her peas, I was listening to him express further discontentment over the latest injunction imposed by Lord Loudoun.

"Now that the ports have been blockaded, commerce is at a standstill," Leif said meditatively.

"That's really going to hurt the economy," I recognized certainly.

"Aye, men will suffer," Leif said.

"Are these orders from Lord Loudoun determined solely by him?" I asked.

"Aye, the Crown has sanctioned his discretion in terms of defeating the French," he said.

"At the expense of everyone's civil rights?" I responded unconscionably.

"As it seems."

"Well, that's a fine formula for social unrest, isn't it?"

"Indeed..." Leif paused momentarily as he took some rum from his crystal tumbler and placed it back down on the table in front of him again. I sensed he was thinking when he continued to say, "I shall lose a fortune due tae this blockade."

"Personally, you mean?"

"Indeed. I have investments in several commodities that trade betwixt haur and England—also with Canada and Hispaniola."

"You do?"

"Aye."

"I didn't know that."

"I reckon not, as I huvnae told ye till presently. I'm a merchant as weel as a soldier whilst my ships sail the seas."

"Oh—I see."

"Aye, weel, I didnea see it pertinent tae inform ye of it as it disnae pertain tae yer matters. Nonetheless, I shall now have ye ken a bit of my business. My sugar, tea, fur, timber and copper investments are now threatened because of Loudoun."

"I didn't realize that."

"I ken."

"How badly are we going to be affected?"

"We shall be sorely affected should he succeed. Yet, I pray not by much if I can help it. Men have livelihoods that must be sustained. Trade must continue lest we all become impoverished and pitiable."

I nodded a little in acknowledgment, thinking also. "Is this where you get most of your income while the government still holds your inheritance?"

"Aye."

"Oh... What do you think you'll do now so that we don't lose everything?"

"I am promptly uncertain. But I promise ye that we shall not become impoverished. Loudoun's machinations be damned. I have heard other merchants encourage smuggling as I met with one prominent merchant today, who claimed that he will proceed with his business through the illegality."

"Really?"

"Aye."

"Oh..." I considered the merchant he must have met with was the one I had heard him talking to when I returned from the marketplace today. I wasn't sure how I felt about the idea of Leif smuggling his goods into the territory. There were in fact numerous reasons why I didn't actually favor the idea: smuggling was lawbreaking, and I didn't like the idea of breaking the law under any circumstances. But, as I was forced to realize these circumstances, we were under unusual and dire conditions, our livelihood depended on Leif's business success. What was more, I worried for Leif's security and didn't want him to place himself in peril with the law, or with Lord Loudoun. "Whatever you do decide to do, Leif, please be careful. I don't want you getting caught doing something secretive that could land you in jail."

"Dinnae be concerned. I shall be prudent at any cost," he assured me. I nodded in response. "I am most prudent regarding my affairs, nonetheless, so not tae suffer hardship. Yet, Loudoun has raised the stakes, and I must outwit him... I shall not let him corrupt whit is legal haur."

"You plan on stopping him?"

"Indeed, I do."

"How will you do that when he's got the government supporting him?"

"I shall find a way tae prohibit him. He wulnae thwart me fur too much longer," he said indisputably.

A pause ensued as he reached for his tumbler and took some more rum from it. The note that I had received earlier today came to mind, and I wondered about the most appropriate time to make him aware of it. I wasn't certain if this was it, but since we were on the topic of discussing Lord Loudoun, I thought this time might be reasonable. So, I reached into my pocket and pulled forth the note I had received from him earlier today.

"Well, it's said that when it rains, it pours—and, I don't mean for it to pour any more than it already is, but I really think that you need to know about this," I attempted informing Leif as I placed the message over the table with the broken seal facing up and carefully pushed it toward him.

"Whit is this?" he inquired strangely.

"A soldier gave it to me today when I was at the market with Mercy," I informed him while watching him grasp the small parchment between his fingers. He opened the note and started reading it. His expression was emotionless as his eyes easily rolled over the parchment. But, when he lifted his gaze and met mine, I could swiftly discern the silent disdain in his eyes.

"I forbid him," he said immediately with a scowl on his face. "I say! He is truly impudent! Evidently, he's got spies out fur ye. I shall see promptly tae this matter in the morn. Ye neednae be concerned by it any longer," he guaranteed coolly. Suddenly, the scowl on his face vanished and he appeared emotionless and cold again. The frigid look on his face was frightening. There was something I observed in Leif's expression that seemed to hold an unearthed potential to be extremely volatile if ever fundamentally threatened, and it unsettled me.

"Okay," I said meekly, trusting that he was going to keep me safe from Lord Loudoun.

He grasped my fingers into his hand and drew the back of my knuckles to his soft lips, placing a pacifying kiss over them. When he drew my hand away, the expression on his face was assured and earnest as his deep blue eyes returned to mine.

PART FOUR

Tender is the Heart

Twenty

The thaw had finally come. Abundant fresh periwinkle and lavender lilacs appeared in full bloom everywhere. Their sweet, heady scent perfumed the air, enhancing the fresh scenery with brilliant colors. The green grass grew tall, and wildflowers rippled endlessly over the clearcut land in the temperate, lightly blowing breeze. Bright pink blossoms covered the black cherry trees like confetti. Birch and maple leaves dressed the tree branches in intense sap-green hues beneath the brightly shining sun. Spring was here and time moved accordingly.

I was watching Leif galloping around on his horse in the field from our second story bedroom window early this morning. He bounced on his horse beneath the new daylight in suitable undress with breeches and merely a white linen shirt, appearing to enjoy himself as he rode. His hair was untied, and shone like a golden corona in the sunlight. The strands bounced over his shoulders while he moved through the open air. He moved gracefully with his horse in galloping circles and in straight lines back and forth, rounding about again before changing course once more.

While watching him, it occurred to me that I hadn't thought about my previous life in weeks now, and also discovered that I was no longer quite as homesick. At the same time though, I realized that the memory of my family and friends, along with the life I had led before, had grown distant in my mind and it had become hard for me to perfectly recall their faces. I was beginning to forget everything that had been important to me, and the thought of it eerily struck me with fear.

I instinctively moved away from the window, and went to my dresser. I opened the bottom drawer and began rummaging through my belongings, searching toward the bottom at the back. In a second, my fingers anxiously grabbed the small wooden case I was looking for, and I retrieved it from the back of the drawer. Opening it, I discovered my cellphone again that I had successfully kept concealed for many months and pressed the activation button. As I had expected, the battery had completely discharged and I stared at a dead screen. I had only hoped this once that I might have been able to revisit the stored images of my mom and dad, my brother Kyle, and my sister-in-law, Dakota. Saddened by the knowledge that I would never see their faces again, I was forced to rely on my fading memory of their images.

Despondent, I replaced my phone back inside the case and securely hid it again, tucking it away unnoticeably back inside the drawer. Resigning myself to the idea that images of my family may never be seen again, I sighed, close to tears. Heartsick, I closed the drawer and paced back toward the window, peering out again. My eyes returned to Leif, still on his horse, cantering around the field at a moderate distance from the house. After taking a moment to collect my emotions, I moved away from the window again and decided to dress.

With Mercy's help, I was soon properly attired, and I decided to make my way outside in search of Leif, where I had last seen him. When I approached the field, I discovered him a mere distance away, dismounted and slowly leading his horse toward the stable. I hurried across the slightly tall green grass to meet him, and he noticed me approaching. He ceased walking, and I picked up my jogging pace, eager to greet him.

"Hi!" I said to him, arriving slightly out of breath. I was happy to see him and smiled.

"Guid morrow tae ye, *ceisdein*. How micht ye be this fine morn?" he welcomed with an affectionate tone that I had grown accustomed to hearing from him.

"I'm fine," I said. I reached up for his lips and gave him a nice little kiss. His cheeks creased as he smiled at me. "How are you?"

"Quite weel, indeed."

"That's nice." I naturally slipped my palm into his, and we started walking together hand in hand with his horse trailing behind us."Happy birthday," I mentioned.

"Och! How kind of ye," he said, appearing suddenly surprised and smiled at me.

"Well, I have a surprise for you," I said.

"Have ye now?"

"Yes, I do."

"Ye neednae have troobled yerself, however," he said modestly.

"It was no trouble. Besides, I wanted to."

"Ye tickle my heart." His charmed expression warmed my affection for him.

"Here," I said gently. I withdrew my palm from his to retrieve a red velvet pouch from my skirts and carefully gave it to him.

"Whit micht it be?" he inquired interestedly.

"You'll have to open it to see," I replied. He gave a curious look and stopped pacing. I stopped walking too while observing his fingers drawing the silk cord around the yoke open.

"Och!" he exclaimed when he unexpectedly discovered the gold timepiece, I had fashioned for him.

"I know that you already have one, but do you like it anyway?" I asked.

"Aye, it is most lovely," he replied with a pleased expression as he noticed his clan badge engraved over the cover. His thumb stroked the engraving then pressed the small clasp, and the cover popped open. He turned it fully open noticing the inscription inside. His lips quietly began reading, "Tae my beloved husband, Leif. Ye will remain in my heart fur all time. Happy Birthday. All my loove, yer loving wife, Sylvie." Leif turned his gaze back to me, and I discerned the warm sentiment in his eyes. I felt him tenderly clasp my chin with his forefinger and thumb when he lifted my chin to his and gave a soft kiss over my lips. "Thank ye, *cuisle mo chridhe*. I shall forever cherish it," he said meaningfully.

"You're welcome," I replied with the same affection. He tenderly kissed me again. When he released me from his kiss, he carefully replaced the watch into its velvet pouch and tucked it securely in his breeches' pocket.

"Come," he urged. He gathered my hand in his and began walking again, leading me with him. "I have a surprise of my own fur ye."

"What do you mean? You're the one with the birthday today, not I," I said as he was leading me with him and towing his horse behind us once more.

"Simply come along," he urged pleasantly again, and we continued heading in the direction of the stable. When we arrived at the entrance, he first hitched Blaze to the post before the trough near the stable by the paddock. Then he proceeded, leading me inside the stable to a stall that was once empty, but now a beautiful, shiny-haired, rich cappuccino colored filly stood.

"Oh my goodness! She's gorgeous!" I exclaimed amazedly.

"Indeed, she is," he agreed.

"Where did you get her?" I inquired, as I carefully stepped closer toward the new horse to stroke her shiny coat.

"I acquired her from the Hutchinsons as they waur seeking a buyer fur her," he informed me.

"Wow," I replied under my breath, entirely impressed while caressing her silky smooth coat. "She's a beauty all right."

"Ye like her, then?" he asked.

"Oh, of course I do," I responded enthrallingly when I unexpectedly noticed her green eyes.

"She has eyes like yers," he mentioned while observing me examining the new animal.

"I just noticed so."

"She belongs tae ye now."

"Are you serious?"

"Most certainly."

"Oh my goodness! You're giving me a horse?"

"Of coorse, I am."

"I can't believe you. That is—I don't know what to say. How very sweet of you. Thank you, Leif." I turned my gaze from the horse back to him and met his smiling eyes. He was leaning lazily against the sill to the stall and I couldn't help smiling widely at him.

"Weel, I reckoned 'tis high time fur ye tae have a horse of yer own," he said.

"I don't know what to say—you've totally surprised me," I said, significantly touched.

"Ye neednae say aught. Save, ye micht wish tae consider a name fur her," he said.

"Right, well," I responded thoughtfully turning my eyes back to the young horse. "Um, I'm not sure what to name her..."

"She has a bonnie disposition—quite spirited also. I reckon like ye."

"Really?"

"Aye."

"Well, lets see, then... In that case, I think I'm going to call her Oakley. It seems to fit her well, I think."

"Oakley?"

"Yeah."

"Whit sort of name is that?"

"I'm naming her after Annie Oakley," I informed him.

"Who is she?" he inquired curiously.

"She was a cowgirl," I said automatically.

"A cowgirl?" he responded oddly, grimacing a little.

"Yeah."

"Whit is a cowgirl?"

"A woman who herds cattle."

"Indeed?"

"Yeah."

"How curious. I huvnea heard of such a woman." He looked at me strangely and I knew that he had no idea what I was talking about. But I didn't care, because he'd made me so happy and all I wanted was to be able to just be my complete self around him.

"But, she was more like a sharpshooter," I said.

"A sharpshooter?" he repeated, appearing obviously shocked this time.

"Yeah," I giggled a little, amused by his sudden reaction.

"Are we speaking of a lass?" he inquired confusedly.

"Sure. She was quite good at it," I added.

"Och…" he replied with a mystified look on his face, also now. "Weel, if ye fancy the name, I reckon so be it."

"I think it's perfect."

"Very weel, then."

"I'd like to ride her."

"Why not efter we first take our breakfast meal?" he suggested.

"Okay," I agreed.

"Come along, then." He easily gathered my hand in his, urging me away from my new horse and led me out of the stable for the house instead.

ONCE WE HAD FINISHED our breakfast together, I decided to change my attire into something more suitable for horseback riding. I dressed myself in a slightly altered version of a riding habit that included the usual jacket, but had my favorite style trousers instead of skirts. Once I quickly slipped my feet into my boots, I darted outside to meet Leif as he had returned outdoors before me. He was waiting for me by the stable with our horses already saddled and ready to go.

"Are ye certain ye dinnae wish fur the side saddle instead?" he asked, doubtfully looking at me.

"Yes, I'm sure," I said positively.

"Alrecht." He didn't seem wholly convinced as he observed me sliding my left boot into the stirrup. I felt him clasp my waist, assisting me as I started to pull myself up over my new horse. In one relatively easy move I was up swinging my right leg over the saddle and was comfortably mounted.

"That's better," I remarked.

"Is it?"

"Yes," I said confidently.

"Alrecht, then," he accepted, then turned toward his own horse, Blaze. In a single motion he adroitly whirled himself high up over his horse and soundly straddled his back. "*Tick, tick,*" he clucked the inside of his cheek, urging Blaze forward. I lightly tapped my heels into Oakley's sides, and she easily responded matching Blaze's relaxed pace out into the open field.

We paced comfortably alongside each other as we rode our horses in the warm spring sunshine. The air was nice and mild. It smelled richly fragrant of lilacs everywhere with a mixture of green earth and coastal saltwater. Hummingbirds fluttered by the flowers and fed from them. A light breeze gently wafted over us between the intermittently shading maple trees. I had quickly discovered that Oakley was a very easy and responsive horse to ride. She and I seemed to get along rather nicely, and I decided that I really liked riding her as we continued onward.

After a while of walking our horses along, I wished for a little bit more fun and started Oakley on a sudden trot, leaving Leif behind without warning, except for the playful grin I had given him as I passed by him. Within a second, he was effortlessly trotting Blaze beside me. I glanced at him, and he had a cheerful twinkle in his eyes when he winked at me. I laughed, feeling lightheartedness, and abruptly took off again—this time into a gallop—leaving him behind once more. But he swiftly caught up with me again, and we subsequently found ourselves playfully racing each other on our horses through the grassy field. We beelined across the open green until we finally came near a band of pine trees at a slight distance ahead where we began slowing our horses into a light jaunt before they came to an easy stride.

"Jesus, Mary, and Joseph!" Leif laughed audibly as we halted beneath the large heavy bows of a pine tree. I was laughing too— excited by the exhilarating fun we were having. "Ye appear quite capable riding astride without me," he chuckled, appearing very impressed by me.

"Yeah—well, I think I do have the hang of it," I laughed.

"Yoo're a bit like a spark upon that new horse of yers." He was grinning from ear to ear, and I giggled some more, enjoying myself with him immensely. "Ye best take care lest ye lose balance and fall tae the ground, however."

"I think I can manage," I replied despite his warning.

"Yoo're a novice."

"Even so, can you keep up with me?"

"With ease."

"Well, let's see if you can really match me old man," I playfully teased.

"Old man?" His brow immediately raised in surprise as he snorted.

"That's what I said!"

"Who are ye calling an old man, wee lass?"

"You!"

"Och! Is that reit?"

"Yeah!"

"I reckon that ye micht not speak tae me in such a manner,

lassie, lest I turn ye across my knee and tan yer backside," he threatened mischievously.

"Oh! You'd never do such a thing!" I laughed flippantly.

"Would I not?" he taunted with a wicked glare. The rakish expression on his face made me giggle again.

"No—you wouldn't," I replied.

"Press me," he jeered.

"Not if you can catch me first!" I abruptly urged my horse onward, away from him and took off with Oakley again racing past the band of trees out into the clearing, leaving him behind once more. But he swiftly appeared alongside me and matched my speed, and we were playfully galloping together over the green grass.

We enjoyed ourselves tremendously together with our horses for a while until we arrived at the pond in the Common where we had skated in the winter. Here is where we decided to dismount our horses and let them drink some water before tying their reins around a young blue spruce trunk.

Leif found a shady spot for himself beneath a substantially large pine tree slightly away from the bank and relaxed against the trunk while I remained close to the horses, fondly stroking Oakley. I haphazardly spotted a smooth pebble by Oakley's front hoof next to the gently sloshing shoreline and leaned to gather it into my hand. I examined it for a second, noticing its pretty green veins inside the black matrix, then tossed it into the water and watched it skip across the pond.

When the pebble sank on the second skip, I turned my gaze over my shoulder toward Leif sitting behind me, and realized he was staring at me with a pondering expression. I knew he was contemplating me, and I smiled and gently waved at him. A reciprocal grin pleasantly eased over his lips, warming his gaze, and causing my stomach to flutter with butterflies. I moved from the water, leaving the horses at the tree by the shore, and lightly jogged toward him. When I arrived, I casually sat close beside him while he continued gazing at me as I made myself comfortably sitting next to him. I glanced away from him for a second toward where the horses were standing by the water just to calm my excitement and to repress my strangely emerging shyness around him before shifting my eyes back to him.

"What?" I ventured asking curiously as his eyes penetrated mine. He shrugged a little, seeming a bit reticent or bashful. "You're staring at me."

"I am."

"Why?"

"I care tae."

"Oh... But I can tell that you're thinking."

"I am merely considering my elation fur having decided tae return fur ye and take ye back from Fort Carillon," he said.

"Oh... Well, I'm certainly happy about that too," I replied.

"Also—I am joyous that I merely found ye, *àille dhubh*."

"I feel the same way." I smiled at him, feeling happy and diffident at the same time.

"I can nae longer perceive my life without ye henceforth," he said.

"Well, I neither can see my life without you now too," I admitted. At that moment, I realized that I felt it was true; my feelings for him had unavoidably materialized and were significant. They were real and had gone far deeper than I had ever first imagined, or thought that they could have ever taken any deeper root than they already had. It occurred to me that what I felt for him was more than the novelty of infatuation, intrigue, or sexual attraction. Instead, I recognized that I had fallen hard for him and was fast in love with him, and the love for him grabbed inside me beyond any love that I had ever experienced before—and, it excited me to the point of fear.

"Yoo're merry," he perceived.

"Am I?"

"Aye."

"Oh, well…"

"It becomes ye."

"Thank you," I said self-consciously. I thoughtlessly twirled the gathered ringlets in my ponytail among my fingers as I brought them around my shoulder. An inspired grin noticeably spread evenly over his face, and I unintentionally realized that I had inadvertently revealed myself to him, and he could see right through me now. The temperature started rising in my cheeks and I started feeling warm all over. I nervously glanced away at the swarm of geese landing and splashing over the pond as they touched down from flight into the water.

"Come along, *àille dhubh*. We best start our return," Leif urged and stirred from his resting place at the base of the tree trunk. He straightened to his feet and reached for my hand, drawing me up to stand also. He then turned for our horses and I followed him toward the tree where they were hitched. Unhitching Oakley first, he passed her reigns to me then gathered Blaze's reigns and unhitched him also. Holding the reins to our own horses now, we began our way back from the pond on foot, crossing the green clearing as we walked beside each other, leading our trailing horses.

"Leif?" I started thinking when I began picking lilacs along the way back from the Common.

"Aye?" He turned his gaze down toward me.

"Do you ever contemplate the universe?"

"Pardon?" He gave me a strange look.

"You know? Do you ever think about the universe?"

"Yoo're inquiring whether I ever contemplate the stars?"

"Yeah."

"I reckon on occasion I have pondered their beauty. Why do ye inquire?"

"Well, I was just wondering if you ever thought about the universe and how we fit in it."

"Curious…"

"I know."

"Weel, I dinnae believe that I have considered it of late. Whit a unique question. Whit ever made ye think upon it?"

"I was just wondering why we're here—on this planet, at this time—you know?"

"Och..." He kept gazing at me a little strangely, but I could see that he was sincerely considering my question. "Weel, God has placed us haur tae love and tae serve one anither as we first honor Him."

"Hmm... Yes, well, but why though. Why us—you and me—why of all the places in the universe, why do we exist right here right now in this moment in time together?"

"This is a novel and complex question, is it not?"

"I know."

"I reckon that I huvnae ever considered this stirring question in truth. I cannae presume tae ken the will of our Heavenly Father. Yet, I might reckon the reason fur our being haur at present is this is the moment upon which God has chosen fur us tae be."

"Yes, but why us—you and me, specifically?"

"Ye and I, precisely?"

"Yeah."

"Hmm... Weel, I humbly presume that the Lord Almighty wishes fur ye and I tae be one with one anither."

"Yeah—I suppose so..."

"I believe that He has graced me with ye. I mean are ye not an angel? Did ye not fall from Heaven when we first met?"

"What?" I gave him an innocent look as my heart suddenly ceased in my chest in the span of a beat as he was flattering me. I was trying to tell him that I was from the future, but I suddenly thought that he would think that I was crazy... and call for a physician to come examine me. I didn't want to frighten him at all. So, I lost my nerve to broach the subject further.

"'Tis whit I think of ye—my angel—and whit I thought of ye upon first we met. That God Himself blessed me with ye this moment in time upon our meeting," he said. I merely stared at him at a loss for words, but he smiled softly at me. "I dinnae believe in happenstance, but in the will of God as it pertains tae us and all other matters. 'Tis through His grace that ye belong tae me. And, I am most humbled by it. Ye are my angel, Sylvie."

"So, you believe that it was supposed to happen—that we meet?"

"As I had prayed long and hard fur a unique lass who would not merely steal my heart but cherish it also so that I may take her fur my wife and live in harmony with her, I believe His Almighty has heard my prayer."

I was struck by his words. Maybe we were supposed to be together like this, I considered; maybe he's the reason why God allowed the earth to open and swallowed me whole through time, landing me in this place to meet him—to take me away from my consuming depression surrounding Matt, to slap me in the face just to force me to see and to believe in the undying nature of love found with another man. *Who really knows?* All I knew was that I was here now and I loved Leif like no one else—and I was scared to admit it for many reasons: one being that I didn't want to forget about Matt. But, Leif had more than replaced my grief over him at this point as our lives had become entwined and were growing inextricably bound with each passing day—and I understood my life had irrevocably changed for the better.

I smiled affectionately at him in response and silently slid my hand around his robust arm, linking my arm with his. He took his other hand and squeezed my fingers as he grinned at me with a heartened expression. He then shifted his gaze ahead as we continued walking with our horses, and I kept thinking about how much I loved him.

As we kept walking back toward our property, I had gathered a lovely bouquet of fragrant lilacs. It wasn't long before we had returned to the stable, and Leif took our horses toward the nearby enclosures. He let them loose in separate paddocks before a pile of fresh hay. Blaze and Oakley began nibbling on some of the grass, and I followed Leif inside the gable roof stable all the way toward the back until we arrived at the ladder leading up to the hayloft. He effortlessly stepped up the ladder into the high elevated loft, and I easily followed him. Just as I had peered over the platform, he invisibly seized my arm and simply hauled me up perfectly level on my heels inside the loft.

"Micht ye bide fur me haur till I return?" he asked.

"Sure," I replied easily.

"I shan't be long," he promised.

"No problem," I said.

"Alrecht, then."

I decided to make myself comfortable and perched myself upon a bale of hay. Reclining over my stomach, I propped myself over my elbows while reaching for a piece of straw. I placed my fresh lilac bouquet next to myself over the hay and stuck the bit of straw that I had snatched up between my lips. I lightly gnawed on it when I noticed Leif removing his white linen shirt over his head. He swiftly tugged it over his shoulders, revealing the solid form of his muscular chest, and tossed it on a mound of hay near me.

"I shan't be long," he promised again.

"Okay," I said without a bother.

I watched him turn from me and start pacing toward bales of hay closer to the edge of the loft. He leaned and took a hefty load within his sturdy grip, tossing it over the hay lift. A muted *thud* sounded as the weighted bundle hit the lift. He turned, leaning for the next load to toss over as I admiringly watched him effortlessly move the dense piles over the deck. After a minute, he finished and strode back toward the ladder, starting to climb down it, and shortly disappeared when I rolled onto my side, facing the opposite way to gaze out the stable window, hearing the hay lift moving downward.

When I looked out the window, Blaze and Oakley were seen just below, close to the entrance of the paddocks still chewing hay. Shifting my gaze from them, I was at once taken by the surrounding scene; I had a panoramic view of the entire town from a distance. I could see all the way out to the deep blue Atlantic Ocean and discerned ships docked at the wharfs. As I panned around, I recognized some of the layout of the town, and closer in the distance were plenty of sheep grazing peacefully in one of the clearings in the Common. A massive flock of ducks suddenly flew overhead, quacking loudly as they swarmed by. I suddenly averted my gaze from the glare of the sun and coincidentally recognized Leif now down below from me at one of the troughs drawing fresh well water and pouring it into the trough for the horses.

After he finished, he splashed himself with clean water from the well bucket, refreshing his face and neck, then vanished beneath the gable. That's when I noticed Blaze and Oakley were no longer by the fence. Instead, they were off roaming inside their paddocks with six of our other horses also roaming and trotting around. And as I continued gazing out the window at the peaceful panoramic scene, I grew lost in my quiet thoughts, enjoying myself right now.

Until I recognized Leif's arm stealing around my waist as he imperceptibly snuck close behind me and reclined next to me, interrupting my view as I turned my attention toward him.

"Was I long?" he inquired quietly into my ear as he kissed my temple.

"No," I responded gently as he rolled me from my side onto my back to face him.

"Guid." Now hovering directly over me, he removed the straw I was nibbling on from my lips and grinned at me. Smiling at him in return, I noticed his fair skin glistening from the water he had splashed over himself, and his hair hung long and damp in front of his shoulders, obscuring his face a little. I carefully moved some of the damp strands off to the side behind his ears. My fingers naturally continued moving over his moist shoulders, delicately caressing his firm, powerful arms, and I smiled some more at him.

He leaned, gently pressing his lips over mine and began kissing me with affection and growing warmth.

"*Leif*," I said faintly, feeling a strange current rising in my blood.

"I need ye, Sylvie," he said heatedly against my neck.

"I know," I replied, feeling dizzy while drinking in the enveloping drowning scent of earth, sweet tobacco and male perspiration covering him.

"*Och, ceisd mo chridhe*," he muttered against my warm skin. I sensed his fingers moving over the buttons attaching my stomacher to my riding jacket. He skillfully unfastened my jacket, exposing my stays, and slid a hand between my fashioned camisole and my naked breast. He pulled the material down from my breast, revealing it completely, and his lips moved from mine and trailed past my chin and neck down toward my breast, which he was caressing. As he was kissing me, he caught my nipple between his teeth, and I anxiously whined, anticipating him. My aimlessly moving hands sank into his luscious locks, and I found myself wanting to be quickly satisfied as the aching between my thighs grew intense and my blood began boiling, making me feel hot all over.

His drawing, tugging, suckling lips finally released my nipple and wandered heatedly over my abdomen, and I sensed his fingers striving to loosen the buttons fastening the front of my trousers until they had completely come undone. He abruptly lifted his kisses and impatiently tugged my trousers down off my waist, quickly exposing my pubic area.

"I dinnae favor these breeks in the merest," he said with dissatisfaction, as he continued removing my trousers completely off my ankles.

"What?" I said anxiously, a little confused.

"These breeks—are trooblesome. I forbid ye tae wear them," he chastised playfully while struggling with them over the heel of my boot.

"Sorry," I laughed a little.

"As am I," he agreed ironically, and I laughed again. I felt him tug one last hard yank, and they were finally removed entirely from my lower half. "At last!" he chuckled. "Now then," he said huskily, shifting aside. I watched the buttons holding his breeches closed coming loose, and in a moment, they fell from his hips. He rolled onto his back and suddenly scooped me up from lying on the hay, compelling me to lie over him. He coerced my thigh around his hips, and now I was kneeling astride him half unclothed with my camisole, pair-of-bodies, and stockings. I unexpectedly looked at him, and he met my gaze with a rakish smirk.

"What are you doing?" I asked as he began unlacing my pair-of-bodies and hastily tossed the garment to the side in the hay.

"Untie yer locks," he demanded meaningfully. So, I reached my fingers around the back of my head and drew the ribbon loose, obliging him. My ringlets suddenly flowed long and free over my shoulders. My hair had grown significantly longer after having gone many months without a usual haircut, and now it hung far down my back as I moved my hair behind my shoulders. He gently entwined his fingers among my ringlets and delicately caressed them down over my shoulders, bringing some tendrils over the front of my camisole. His fingers traced along the top ridge of my camisole over my breasts when he began lifting the garment off my torso until it was entirely removed from me, and tossed it into the pile with the rest of my clothing beside us.

His eyes returned to me again and were leal and penetrating. I felt I couldn't shift my gaze from him as he held my eyes locked to his. Holding his fixed gaze with transparent feeling, I sensed his wandering hands lightly meandering over my bare arms, encircling my waist, and roaming up toward my breasts until he cupped them. He caught my nipples beneath his massaging thumbs and rolled them fondly between his fingers and caressing palms. He was driving me crazy with the need to have him inside me as his roving palms heatedly moved over my slim belly and seized my hips, gripping them firm with determination. He shifted me precisely over himself and fitted me at the pinnacle of his swollen penis. His large hands gently guided my hips down on him, and I felt his shaft spreading me open with burning anticipation.

"*Mmh*," I moaned as I slowly eased over his forceful organ and carefully sank down on him. The sensation of him filling me was expansive and solid—indescribably bold—causing me to ache with anticipated bliss.

"Aye," he responded in a low, husky voice. The penetration was unusually deep, I realized, as I settled completely over him. He was a big man and the uncommon sensation caused my breath to flutter, as I wasn't certain about this particular position; his shaft was long and wide, pushing against my cervix with extreme force as if it was going to burst through my uterus. So, I sat motionless for a moment resting on him, careful of myself in order not to feel pain, while his strong hands gripped securely around my hips. I wasn't used to him like this. I knew that if I moved the wrong way, pain would be felt and I didn't want to be uncomfortable as I sought pleasure from him. "Demonstrate tae me accordingly how ye micht ride this stallion," he insisted heatedly.

I smiled unevenly at him, slightly uncertain of myself. But he started rocking my hips in a slow, deliberate motion, and I could feel him in a new way—entirely articulate—as he boldly filled my body. My breathing was hard to control as it kept stealing from me when I felt him grinding into my cervix and pushing against my uterus, causing my belly to ache with heated pleasure. He continued rocking me, and the uncommon sensation was profound—inciting me to shudder a bit as he moved me. But after a moment, my body instinctively began taking over, and I began milling my hips tightly against his, feeling him rubbing against my depths and shoving high into my belly with distinction.

"*Aye*," Leif said coarsely, sensing me as I moved over him. I felt a palm lessen its grip around my waist and move toward my belly when he pushed his hand against it while carefully grinding myself upon him. Maintaining his gaze, I perceived the far-reaching running depth of his adoration for me emoting from his stare. I suddenly recognized myself; I saw my reflection in his eyes, and something breached within my consciousness. All of a sudden it had become emotional for me while I continued rocking sublimely over him. I loved him, and I wanted to tell him so. My affection for him erupted my awareness; I knew nothing else from here forth as I adored him with my body—professing my commitment to him, my love for him, and giving myself completely to him; I willingly gave to him my foundation and entrusted myself to him in all that he had promised me: to keep me safe and secure, to love me, to cherish me—for always.

His palm stole gently around my neck as he quietly wiped a silent tear from my cheek with the pad of his thumb while I concentrated my eyes onto his. I lifted my fingers and brushed the light hairs of his forearm until I covered the back of his hand with mine as he tenderly caressed the side of my face. Sweeping my lips inside of his palm, I fondly pressed gentle kisses over it, then drew it away from my lips and entwined my fingers between his. With my hand interwoven with his, I held on, riding him to the point of my delicious dissolve. Conscious of the expression in his unwavering eyes, deep and silent—connected—my heart swelled for him even more than I thought was ever possible and began drowning in a sea of aching hunger and stinging desire for him to awaken my depths where he'd touch my heart.

Then, suddenly, the core between my thighs began violently convulsing, and I moaned audibly as I was hurled off a steep cliff into ecstasy. My thighs simultaneously trembled with my cervix and vaginal walls as I reach my zenith. I was filled with euphoria at the abrupt sensation of my walls clamping down and pulsating around his thick shaft. Consumed by this marvelous feeling, I didn't want it to end. Seizing, I wanted to capture every ecstatic wave washing over me. Trying to freeze the feeling of him inside of me, I quaked uncontrollably as my insides screamed with pleasure.

But I was distantly aware of the gravelly groan eluding his lips while drowning in a whirlpool of transcending euphoria that encapsulated me and swallowed me whole.

At once drained, after gliding down from my orgasm back to reality, I collapsed breathlessly over Leif's heaving chest, and it was only then I sensed his groin pulsating beneath me. I buried my head in the curve of his neck and kissed his heated skin as he finished. I sensed his large hands now warmly kneading my buttocks while I listened to his heated breath escaping him. His heart was pounding hard and I could feel it against my breasts.

I lifted my gaze to his, feeling a warm river seeping from me as we remained connected. A smile spread indolently across his doting face. He raised his fingers and carefully moved my ringlets obscuring my face off to the side, over my shoulders. Delicately seizing my chin with his thumb and forefinger, he pulled my lips down gently over his. After our kiss, I returned, gazing into his soft eyes as I lightly caressed the side of his smooth shaven, masculine jaw, admiring him so deeply.

"I love you, Leif," I whispered finally, admitting my true feelings to him.

"Do ye?" he responded tenderly, still caressing me.

"Yes. Truly."

"Ye warm my soul, *ceisdein.*" I smiled gently in response, suddenly feeling overcome with emotion. He raised his thumb and cleared a teardrop from the corner of my eyelashes. "I adore ye as I have adored nae other," he said. "My angel. Dinnae weep, *mo ghaol.* I dinnae wish tae see ye weep, *mo leannan,*" he continued endearingly as we closely gazed at each other, then kissed my brow.

"All right," I said faintly, agreeing to curb my quiet tears; I never thought I could love anyone so intensely the way I loved him.

He drew my lips over his again and amorously kissed me while solidly embracing me in his muscular arms. When he released me from his kiss, I leaned over and rested on him with him still inside of me, cuddling my head in the curve of his neck and shoulder.

Splayed over him like I was, we rested together quietly holding each other for an undetermined period. I sensed him grow flaccid in our contented embrace and I didn't want this moment between us to end.

Although the air surrounding us was tranquil and pacifying, I was wide awake, listening to the drum beat of his heart as his chest rose and fell with every breath he took. For the first time since having arrived here and after several years of living in somberness from Matt's death, I felt that I had finally landed securely upright with my feet soundly planted on the earth in this place in time with me joyously touching the ground.

As I rested here with Leif holding me securely in his arms, my mind settled and my heart soared with elation; it occurred to me just now how happy I truly was.

Happiness is only illusive when you refuse to experience it. Right now, I'm happy, and I refuse to let it go.

Twenty-One

One day I took Amity and Mercy with me to the marketplace to buy a few things. I was really hoping to obtain vanilla beans and a few Caribbean and Indian spices, but it seemed I was quite out of luck this time since the blockade had taken full effect. The economy was beginning to suffer, because trade was nearly at a standstill. People were beginning to feel economic pressure as the price of bread had skyrocketed and protests in the streets were beginning to occur.

As I was going about my business in the marketplace, I noticed several men pilloried in the center of the square for having used profanity and one other for having publicly kissed his wife before the front door to his house. When I glanced around, I happened to realize a young boy, who couldn't have been more than thirteen, pilfering fish from a stand just as I had exited the baker's shop. I had given Amity and Mercy a few guineas to treat themselves at the mercantile across the square, and they hadn't yet returned as I was observing the owner of the fish stand noticing the boy stealing from him.

"*Thief!*" shouted the fishmonger, pointing out the boy as he rounded his display of seafood on the stands to apprehend the boy. "*Thief!*" the fishmonger shouted loudly again, sharply drawing attention to the boy. The boy immediately took off running away from the shop and darted fast in my direction, bumping unpredictably straight into me. He unexpectedly looked stunned at me, then dashed around me. The fishmonger still excitedly yelled after the boy, and I decidedly hurried toward the fishmonger.

"Here," I said intentionally and passed him a couple of shillings. He looked at me with surprise and confusion. "For the fish," I said apparently.

"Thank you, milady," he replied respectfully, appearing caught off guard. He promptly bit the coins and waved the authentic pieces at me with satisfaction.

"No problem," I responded automatically and quickly turned my attention around noticing the commotion on the street coming from behind me. I thoughtlessly reacted and paced quickly toward the disturbance. As I made my way through some of the onlookers, I realized that the boy had been promptly apprehended by soldiers. I recognized one of those soldiers being the one who delivered Lord Loudoun's note to me several weeks ago. I was rather put off when I realized he was the one holding the squirming frightened boy by the ear.

"Well, look eya! We caught ourselves a thief, lads!" the soldier taunted among his surrounding companions, drawing sneering chuckles from them.

"Let me go!" the boy cried, obviously frightened. The soldier abruptly tugged on the boy's ear, causing him to suddenly cry out in pain. More mocking laughter came from the other six surrounding soldiers. The soldier holding the boy brutishly punched the fish from the boy's arm and stomped on it with his heel to bits on the ground. I unthinkingly made my way through the apprehensive onlookers and approached the soldier callously holding the boy.

"Hey, is that really necessary?" I questioned with concern as I arrived before this particular young soldier. He suddenly looked at me, coincidentally recognizing me also.

"Why yes it is, milady. This lad eya was in the midst of pilfering fish," he said scornfully, still holding the boy by the ear. I noticed the dubious look on the soldier's face as I boldly returned his skeptical glare. I was now also aware that I had all of his companions' attention along with the congregated bystanders who were fearfully witnessing what was taking place.

"What is your name?" I inquired directly to the soldier. He hesitated briefly with a mocking expression.

"Why, 'tis Lieutenant Henry Wells, if milady is so desiring to know," he said in an unfriendly manner with a wry grin. He winked at his friends, and they chuckled.

"Well, Hank—oh excuse me—do you mind if I call you Hank?" I asked, disregarding him. He failed to respond except for the unexpected look on his face as he then narrowed his eyes on me. "I didn't think so," I continued, "It seems there's been a misunderstanding with this boy. You see, the badly decimated fish now on the ground by your hand was indeed paid for."

"Is that so?" he questioned skeptically.

"Yes," I said flatly.

"'Tis not my understanding of this circumstance at all," Lieutenant Wells said.

"Well, it's a fact that there's been an error," I replied.

"So *Your Grace* says," he jeered.

"It is what I say, and you may let him go now, since he hasn't offended anybody. You may verify it with the fishmonger also that the fish was paid for," I said.

"Look eya, lads, it seems milady is quite confident in her assertion. Is she not most *charitable*?" he joked. Sarcastic sneering chuckles went around his surrounding friends as the boy whined again in pain by his grabbed ear Wells was continuing to hold.

"Let him go. You're hurting him," I said, observing the callous way he was holding the boy.

"I cannot do what milady wishes. The matter will be taken by my superior," he said directly. He impatiently began walking away from me, taking the boy away with him.

"Wait! You can't do that," I disagreed suddenly. Lieutenant Wells abruptly laughed and stopped short, turning his glaring eyes on me once more.

"Why not?" he questioned jeeringly.

"Aside from the fact that he's a juvenile, you didn't witness him stealing it. The fish was paid for. You don't have probable cause," I said. He glowered at me with affront.

"'Tis not a matter for you to decide, milady," he said cynically. He turned from me and started taking the boy away with him again. "By the by," he abruptly recommenced, momentarily seizing his steps once more and turned his gaze to me, "what does a lady mean when she says the word, '*dipshit*?'" he asked pointedly with blatant disrespect. Gasps suddenly whizzed around among the surrounding appalled onlooking bystanders.

"I imagine she would mean someone like you," I said calmly in spite of my rising temper.

"Seize her!" he shouted uncouthly. A guard among his companions invisibly grabbed me from the side by my arm.

"Take your grubby hands off me!" I exclaimed as I simultaneously yanked my arm free from the guard, shocked that I was being taken.

"Seize her!" Lieutenant Wells ordered in a volatile voice again. I was abruptly grabbed again and secured with force this time.

"How dare you! You let me go this instant! You haven't the right!" I protested irately as I tried wiggling from the soldier seizing me with a solid, firm grip.

"Since milady has decided to take interest in the lad, she may accompany him to visit my superior officer about the matter," Wells ordered discourteously.

I suddenly found myself enclosed by seven troopers along with the boy. Observing that I had no other choice, we were marched all the way across town...

WHEN FORT HILL came into plain sight, and I realized that we were about to enter through its gate, a sinking feeling came over my stomach. Leif wasn't going to be pleased about this happening to me in the least bit, I thought, as we crossed the gate and entered inside the fort. A sea of redcoats swarmed the grounds. I gathered a new fleet had freshly landed as a stream of fresh faces appearing disoriented and anticipatory were presently entering and checking in after us as we moved through the grounds. We rounded the stockade when I realized the boy and I were being separated.

"Where are you taking him?" I asked the apprehending soldiers, concerned for the boy. But I was duly ignored by the guards and instead marched inside quarters by Lieutenant Wells and one other trooper. We approached a guard posted in front of one of the doors, and Lieutenant Wells knocked on the closed entrance. A muffled voice on the other side beckoned the call. He opened the door, and I was coerced to walk inside the room with him.

When my eyes unexpectedly landed on the high-ranking officer seated behind his desk in the middle of writing a correspondence, my heart skipped a beat with fear and my blood froze in my veins. I realized to my utmost shock that I had been easily delivered squarely into Lord Loudoun's hands.

Once he had shortly completed scribing the last word on the parchment before him on his desk, he lifted his gaze and instantly noticed me. He recognized me on the spot as he moved his quill to the stand and left it. My heart rate suddenly skyrocketed the moment he met my gaze.

"Well, well, who micht we have haur, lieutenant?" Lord Loudoun inquired knowingly with an ironic tone.

"The Duchess of Monteith, I have reason to believe, Your Lordship," Lieutenant Wells answered.

"The Duchess of Monteith, have we now?" Lord Loudoun responded particularly as he maintained an unwavering gaze on me. He moved to stand from his chair behind his desk.

"Aye, milord," Lieutenant Wells said.

"Very weel, lieutenant, ye may take yer leave," Lord Loudoun instructed. Lieutenant Wells sharply bowed before spinning about face and promptly left the room with the door shutting behind himself. Instant dread came over me as I remained standing alone in Lord Loudoun's tall, imposing presence. The last place I would have ever picked to be was in the same space with this man again. "Pray," Lord Loudoun commenced calmly, politely gesturing to the empty chair against the wall near the side of his desk.

I hesitated; I didn't know how to read him.

He seemed different this time—more docile, or polite—less threatening, maybe, I supposed. I couldn't put my finger on it. But I could see that he was calculating—that, I knew for certain— given my experience with him the last time we had met each other.

"I fear that I dinnae have a court order for this visit as ye have requested, madam. Therefore, I pray that this visit wulnae land me in a predicament with yer barrister," he said with a wry grin. The look on his face appeared ironic if not flat out jeering. I remained silently standing before him not knowing how to respond. "Pray, will ye not have a seat? This is a friendly visit, is it not?" he asked graciously.

"Yes—I suppose it might be," I replied, feeling very uncertain of him. I decided to move across the room to sit in the chair he offered me.

"Thaur now... We are friends, are we not?" he asked easily, appearing quite collected. I didn't respond again, except simply looked at him quite ill at ease. He bewildered me somewhat, because he was acting as if he had never done anything to ever harm me. I watched him with skepticism as he calmly replaced himself comfortably in his seat behind his desk. He precisely turned his chair to directly face me. "I must say that I am surprised and pleased tae see ye, Your Grace. Is it now? First, I wish tae offer my felicitations tae yer new marriage," he said politely.

"Thank you," I replied in the same polite manner, still dubious of him. I quickly wondered how he knew that I had gotten married and was stunned that the news had traveled to him so soon. I hoped Leif hadn't gotten himself into trouble with this man because of me when I knew that he had particularly risked his life to save and protect me from His Lordship.

"I must also say, that the news of yer wedding came tae me as raither a great astonishment," he said.

"Did it?" I responded emotionlessly, trying to control my fear of him.

"Indeed," he said. "I didnae realize that ye had captured His Grace's attention. But, once more it is not difficult to fathom the reason fur His Grace's interest in taking ye fur his own. Yer beauty strikes any man who micht have eyes tae see," Lord Loudoun complimented.

"You flatter me," I said politely.

"It is quite the truth, madam. Now that His Grace has wed ye, I find myself at a loss," he said in a regretful tone. But he arched an eyebrow and looked skeptically at me as if he were actually suspicious.

"At a loss?"

"Aye."

"From what?"

"From ye, of coorse."

"Oh."

"Thaur has been a question gnawing upon my mind about yer escape from me. Quite simply—how did you manage it?" he asked bluntly.

I cleared my dry throat a little, trying to assemble my thoughts without implicating Leif. "Well, I—I convinced the guard you had posted at the door to let me get some fresh air outside for a moment. How else would I have been able to escape your quarters?" I replied, hoping he'd believe me. A sardonic smirk twisted his lips.

"Hmm… Aye. Ye charmed my guard, of coorse. A simple recourse fur a lass of any tae flaunt her appeal," he said. "My men are easily taken by women. Yet, ye are not ordinary. Why, as I confess, even I continue tae be bewitched by ye. Therefore, I cannae quite blame the imbecile fur losing ye, though he was flogged fur his disobedience. I ought tae have supervised ye myself by never letting ye out of my secht. Alas, my business tae oversee with my aid-de-camp at the time forced my releasing ye intae the hands of the incompetent fool." I didn't respond to his twisted compliment and instead simply gazed at him, wondering how I was going to escape him this time. "Do ye ken that I had heard many tales of the beauties who reside in these colonies before I had come tae assume my position haur?"

"I'm unaware of it," I replied mindfully.

"Och, weel—the tales are vast," he said with a thin smile.

"Oh," I said simply.

"Yet, I was uncertain of it till I had seen it myself—and, whit I have seen has greatly pleased me," he disclosed. "However, ye are most unique in appearance, mannerisms, and in intelligence. Truth be told, madam, I meant tae release ye upon the French once I had turned ye toward my friendship, primarily. Ye must understand that my affection fur ye wouldnae have been lacking. Bending ye tae my will would have been a great pleasure of mine as weel as ye would have found tae yer agreement, I assure ye. We micht have worked beautifully in tandem should ye have chosen tae come under my employ. Ye as my spy would have granted me much insight, and would have been a most beneficial situation tae ye accordingly. Ye would have been a great asset tae the Crown, indeed."

"I see," I replied dry mouthed.

"As I said, 'tis my loss. Yet nae loss tae ye, fur one can perceive that ye may be content with His Grace instead."

"I am."

"Double crossing him may lead ye tae yer ruin, however. Where I could have protected yer duplicity."

"Why would I ever betray him? I'm not a spy."

"Hmm... so you say."

"Because it's true."

"Whether ye are, or are not, remains to be seen," he said. "However, I do realize that I cannae help my regard fur ye. Ye have charmed me... Indeed, ye are certainly fetching. Therefore, I am quite struck. Permit me to inquire. Ye do claim tae originate from Pennsylvania, is that not so?"

"Yes." I nodded a little.

"Intriguing. I have also heard the creole lasses in Hispaniola tae be alluring," he implied as he gazed directly at me with a mining expression.

"I wouldn't know," I replied, feeling underscored.

"Would ye not indeed?"

"No."

"Och, aye, how micht ye be awaur if ye originate from Pennsylvania. 'Tis foolish of me tae believe otherwise. Weel... If any man would know of such lasses, 'twould be men like the Duke of Monteith. He micht have a notion regarding the lasses of Hispaniola."

"Why do you say that he would know anything about the women there?" I asked strangely.

"He is familiar with the slave trade, evidently," Lord Loudoun said casually.

"What do you mean?" I asked, very much puzzled, as I was clearly in doubt.

"Why, he is, in fact."

"I don't think so."

"Of coorse ye wouldnae understand. Men do not commonly

discuss their business affairs with their wives," he said nonchalantly.

I swallowed hard, feeling very uncomfortable about what he had just told me about Leif before saying, "Actually, my husband and I have a candid relationship. He tells me everything."

"Does he?" Lord Loudoun inquired in an unusual tone, looking surprised.

"Yes, he does, in fact," I replied certainly, trying to maintain some semblance of impassiveness.

"How uncommon." His haughty gaze turned curious.

"Who's to say what is common and what isn't as it pertains to people's personal relationships," I said thoughtlessly.

"Hmm... I micht find it captivating tae meet a woman with whom I micht speak sensibly—one like yerself, I imagine." He paused momentarily, and his cool blue eyes noticeably scanned me over. I noticed his gaze narrow a bit on the trousers covering my legs and briefly settle on the boots over my feet. I crossed my ankles feeling somewhat uncomfortable, and the expression on his face changed subtly. A shallow grin crossed his thinking expression, and I wondered what sort of thoughts were passing through his mind. "Ye are much changed, madam," he resumed curiously. "Bonnie as ever, tae be certain, as I gaze upon ye—even in breeks. Permit me tae say that yer visit tae me comes as a great surprise—particularly, efter nae response tae my invitation tae ye was given, but a mere suggestion of my obtaining a court order so that we may peaceably meet... Be that as it will, thaur are nae hurt feelings amongst us. I shall assure ye. Now, reveal tae me tae whit do I owe the pleasure of yer company?" he said in a businesslike manner as he continued scrutinizing me with his eyes.

"Actually, I was coerced to be here by your Lieutenant Wells involving a situation that had occurred at the marketplace," I informed him, noticing his light blue eyes that reminded me of hard topaz gems.

"Whit occurrence micht that have been?" he inquired evenly.

"Well, I'm afraid there's been an unfortunate misunderstanding. A simple one, however."

"Och?"

"Yes, it occurred at the marketplace with a boy. It was believed that he was pilfering fish from one of the fishmongers—but, you see, it was paid for."

"I see," Lord Loudoun replied unemotionally.

"Yes, and he was nevertheless apprehended by your soldiers and brought here. So, I'm here to testify to the fact that the fish was paid for, and I'm requesting that the boy please be released from custody to be sent home to his parents," I appealed politely, despite my discomfiture as I now stared at this man.

"I see," he responded coolly with his hands folded over his desk.

"The fishmonger can verify it also," I added.

"Can he?"

"Yes, he can. I doubt that he will press charges against the boy."

"Weel..." Lord Loudoun considered as he held his fastened gaze on me. "Ye are correct tae visit me over this matter, as I do have complete authority tae return the lad tae his family. However, ye micht perceive me in a bit of a quandary."

"A quandary?"

"Aye."

"What might that be?" I asked.

"It pertains tae the fact that we are currently at war, as ye weel know. And, quite simply, we need men tae fight," he said plainly.

"I see."

"Micht ye be awaur of how old the lad tae be?"

"I would guess not more than thirteen."

"Och, a perfect candidate tae serve the Crown."

"But he's just a child," I rebutted disapprovingly with concern.

"He is a suitable lad," he said.

"But, what does a child know about war?"

"I imagine he knows naught about it, as do all the lads when they first enlist. Yet, one micht be surprised at how weel a lad in his position might survive in battle when it remains that he fight or be killed," he said callously as he propped an elbow on the armrest of his chair.

"Still, don't you think that is unreasonable? To draft him is immoral," I differed. Lord Loudoun paused momentarily and brought a thinking forefinger above his thin upper lip as he was now staring frigidly at me.

"I reckon I micht applaud yer effort in the lad's defense. Ye are quite generous tae do so," he said.

"Thank you—but I think anyone with a conscience would do the same thing," I replied modestly.

"Mmm..." he responded thinkingly. "I micht consider the lad's release."

"Thank you," I said, feeling a modicum of relief.

"If ye waur tae join me fur tea. Only if."

"Oh... For tea?"

"Aye," he said.

"But, my niece and maid were left at the marketplace—they don't know where I am. Besides, my husband will be looking for me soon also," I said, attempting to change his mind and finding a way to exit his office.

"It wulnae be fur long. I promise yoo'll not be missed," he said.

"I don't know," I said doubtfully.

"Pray, consider it. The lad will be released into the bosom of his family should ye grant my wish."

"Is that a promise?" I spontaneously asked. I couldn't believe that I was considering his option when all I wanted was for the boy to have his freedom, and for me to immediately return to the marketplace.

"I shall give ye my word. The lad will have dinner with his family tonecht," Lord Loudoun guaranteed.

I considered the heartless general for a moment. It was

strange, although he was unyielding and calculating, he didn't seem too threatening right now as I sat across from him at a close distance, examining him also. His mannerisms and tone were polite, but he was blackmailing me with the boy to keep him company. Seeing that I hadn't a choice even if I wanted to leave and reject his invitation for tea, I couldn't abandon the child into his hands knowing he hadn't a care in the world for him and counted him as just another body to serve in the war against France.

As we gazed at each other for a moment while I was considering his offer for tea, I suddenly noticed the appeal his mistress held for him; he was nice-looking, polished with good manners and intelligence. On the surface, it seemed he wouldn't harm a fly. But, push him a little and one would quickly discover they were already snared into his trap before anticipating it and realizing it too late for escape.

"All right," I consented at length.

"Splendid," he said charmingly. He reached for the beautiful porcelain teapot on a silver tray over his desk. I watched him in silence as he quietly prepared two cups of tea. When he finished, he kindly passed a cup over to me.

"Thank you," I said, receiving my tea from him. My fingers accidentally grazed his hand as I took the cup from him, and he grinned.

"Indeed, my pleasure," he said, appearing distinctly charmed. I placed the rim of the cup to my lips, and carefully sipped the lukewarm tea. When I drew it away, I noticed him watching me. "I am quite pleased tae have this opportunity tae meet with ye again, I shall confess," he began.

"Really?" I asked inquisitively.

"Indeed."

"Why?"

"My missive tae ye was sent in hope that we may meet again in order fur me tae clear any misunderstanding betwixt us. Tae put it plainly, I feel that we got off on poor footing the last time we had met."

"Yes, we did. I'd agree."

"Aye, weel, I micht have been a bit harsh upon ye," he admitted.

"Yes, I think so."

"Mayhap, ye micht be so generous tae forgive me?" he inquired. But I didn't respond. "I have wished fur a new meeting with ye fur quite some time that micht prove more pleasant than the time before," he said.

"I see," I said, doubtful about that. I sipped some more tea from my cup as he kept watching me.

"I wish fur us tae be friends. Sincere friends," he said.

"Do you?" I returned my gaze to him as I placed my teacup back on the saucer balancing perfectly over my knee.

"Indeed."

"I hadn't considered that option."

"The possibility ye mean?"

"Yes."

"I see. However, it would greatly please me if we waur nicely acquainted. Would ye not consider the prospect, as ye micht find it a benefit tae ye as weel?" It wasn't a request he was asking, but an expectation he was forcing on me that was a demand.

"Fine," I said politely. I granted his request, understanding that if I didn't, he was likely to threaten me in some way. And, I basically wished to hasten this interview without provocation, given our previous meeting together.

"Splendid," he responded adequately.

"You know, quite frankly, I wasn't expecting that you would be in town. So, I'm also a little surprised to see you," I said while also observing him sip some tea from his cup. He returned his teacup over its saucer on his desk. He grinned widely at me and I could see his yellow incisors that made him appear slightly less handsome.

"I have arrived in Boston tae meet with the governor," he informed me.

"Oh."

"Thaur is much business which needs discussing betwixt us."

"I see."

"Yet, my journey haur tae the city was fortunate without any rain."

"That's lucky," I said and he grinned at me in response. "From where were you coming?"

"Why, I have arrived from Albany," he said politely.

"Oh…" I sipped a bit more from my teacup. He quietly observed me sipping more tea for a moment, and all the while I was wondering how soon I could escape his office for my return to Amity and Mercy before it had gotten too late and they'd begin worrying about me—if they weren't already.

"I have been told that ye are quite skilled at ice skating," he recommended pensively. I was surprised that he would have known about my recreation.

"Have you?"

"Aye. Raither accomplished, as a matter of fact."

"I see—well, yes, I am familiar with the sport."

"I didnae believe how expert till I was told that I ought tae witness ye fur myself. Lo and behold—I was indeed taken by yer accomplishment."

"Thank you." It suddenly dawned on me that he had spied on me at the pond back in the winter, that day I was alone on the ice when Finley had come to visit us at Tàigh Gràs. "When I was there skating, I waved, thinking you were my husband watching me. Did you see that?"

"You waved at Lieutenant Wells instead."

"Oh." I swallowed dryly.

"Ye didnae see me at all when I had witness ye on an occasion whilst ye waur alone again, fur I was hidden behind a tree. As much as I would have liked tae have spent more of my leisure observing yer talent, I could not sustain sparing more time than I already had. My duties pressed me, ye see."

"I understand."

"My business hinders my leisure quite a bit. You must enjoy the recreation raither weel tae acquire such skill."

"Yes, I enjoy it very much."

"'Tis quite unusual fur a lass tae be as sheer as the lads—particularly fur one as yerself," he said contemplatively. "I must say that I find it curious that His Grace permits his wife tae be so bold by being incongruent tae the norm of a lady." Lord Loudoun's gaze briefly scrutinized my trousers.

"Well, he and I have a pleasant understanding," I said.

"Do ye, indeed?"

"Surely, why not?"

"Why not?" he echoed meditatively and smiled wryly. "It appears His Grace has nae qualm with the notion of scandal regarding yer unique attire as he inhabits this city with Puritan dolts."

"Puritan dolts?" I echoed, slightly frowning at him with offense.

"Aye. Although, His Grace would be remitted tae scandal even in London amongst the most libertine should his wife be discovered attired in breeks."

"Really?"

"Why, of coorse!" he laughed, inflating my insecurity overall as I was beginning to wonder about my appearance.

"Well, I don't know about causing any kind of scandal as it pertains to my husband's reputation."

"As ye say. Yet, permit me as I say that presumably ye micht not be concerned of it as His Grace is quite libertine."

"What do you mean by that?"

"Exactly as the word would imply."

"My husband has morals."

"Exemplified in yer attire. Ye neednae be coy with me, Your

Grace. Or, abashed. In one manner I am a libertine man myself. Therefore, yer husband and I have some commonality betwixt us regarding our own affairs with our weaker counterparts. 'Tis simple fur ourselves tae bend tae the will of women when we are blinded by their appearances, causing us tae ignore our own sense of mind."

I gave him a weak smile, not liking what he was saying and instead attempted changing the subject. "So, you've been in town this whole time, then? Since the winter?"

"Of coorse I have. Do ye not recall my missive tae ye?"

"Yes—well, I thought that maybe you had traveled between then and now."

"Nae. I have been haur all along," he informed me. I suddenly swallowed hard and my throat felt very dry. I realized then that he had surely been spying on me and suddenly I felt exposed to him. A lull in the conversation momentarily ensued. "Och! I shall like tae share something with ye," he remembered unexpectedly and shifted a little in his chair to pull open the top drawer to his desk. He retrieved an attractive pink silk-covered box and held it out before me to see when he opened it. It was filled with little mounds of solid chocolates. "Pray," he urged kindly for me to take one.

"Thank you," I said, carefully wrapping my fingers around one of them.

"They are from Denmark, and they are splendid," he said.

"Are they?" I said, impressed.

"Indeed, have it. I promise that ye will desire anither," he guaranteed. I plopped the small chocolate piece inside my mouth and let it melt like silk over my tongue.

"Mmm, it is rather good," I acknowledged once I swallowed it.

"Have anither," he offered nicely again.

"Thank you," I said politely and retrieved one more. He withdrew the box and closed it, setting it aside over his desk in front of the tea tray. I calmly glanced away from him and noticed a chess game stand rather close in the corner ready for play. I admired the beautifully carved stained wood pieces over the board from where I was sitting while enjoying the second piece of chocolate in my mouth.

"Are ye familiar with chess?" he inquired, noticing me.

"Yes, actually," I said, returning my gaze to his.

"Certainly?" he responded, intrigued.

"Yes."

"Weel, then, micht we give it a round of play?" he encouraged with a spark of amusement in his eyes.

"Sure—if you'd like," I said, understanding his demand and feeling compelled to remain seated as I feared his temper.

"Very weel," he replied and stood tall from his chair. He stepped from around his desk and carefully collected the game table, then placed it before me. Next, he retrieved his chair from behind his desk and closely seated himself directly across from me. He let me start with the white pawn, and soon we found ourselves in the middle of a game. The conversation was lacking while we played together; you could hear a pin drop. But not too long into the game, however, I had captured his rook and he chuckled, seeming amused. "Ye have raither surprised me at this chess game. I perceive that ye present a talent fur it," he said while grinning at me. "Yer husband has taught ye weel."

"Actually, I learned from my father who was a master chess player," I revealed to him accidentally.

"Was he indeed?" Lord Loudoun responded with piqued interest.

"Yes, he used to travel around playing in chess tournaments with other people when he was very young," I said.

"Indeed?" he inquired surprisedly.

"Yes—that was before he went into the military, though," I said a little nervously.

"Is yer father a military man also?"

"Yes—well, I mean he was one."

"He is departed?"

"He's no longer with me," I replied, nodding a little.

"My commiserations."

"Thank you."

"He has taught you how tae play raither weel."

"Thank you."

"'Tis curious, however," Lord Loudoun responded meditatively. He paused for a moment as he captured my knight. "Micht I offer ye a spot of wine in place of yer tea that I am certain ye will find more pleasant?" he asked interestedly.

"Well, I really need to be getting back to my maid and niece," I reminded.

"Pray, won't ye indulge me? Merely a spot, and I shall have ye returned straight away," he insisted.

"I really should go." I hesitated staying any longer than I already had with him; it was also getting late and I needed to leave.

"Will ye not simply please me fur a bit longer? I do indeed enjoy yer company," he said. It was discernible that he was not going to yield and something in my gut told me to remain in order to satisfy his wish. Seriously conflicted, I thought of his eminence and ability to detain me regardless, and Leif immediately shot into mind; I considered His Lordship's ability to pawn me in order to ensnare Leif to his detriment as a result of his having rescued me from His Lordship's clutches from before in the past.

"Perhaps a small glass would be all right," I acquiesced despite my reservations. I was trying to think of a way not to offend him while manipulating him into letting me leave without consequence.

"Splendid," he responded. His Lordship shot up from his chair and moved toward the decanter on the other side of his desk. He pulled up a small wine glass from the cabinet below and poured a glass of glimmering claret wine. He strode back toward his seat at the chess table, then passed the filled wineglass to me as he retrieved my teacup from me. I took a little sip of wine and swallowed, thinking I might take another sample of it. I subsequently took another larger sip and decided this was probably the best wine I'd ever tasted in my life. It was smooth, flavorful, and aromatic like nothing I'd encountered before. I sipped some more fully enjoying it, aware of his watchful eyes on me as I drank.

"Will ye have anither?" he inquired as I drew the emptied wineglass away from my moistened lips. I didn't think that I would have so quickly finished my wine when I realized that not only had I been quite parched, but my nerves needed settling too.

"Yes, please," I agreed. He easily replenished my glass, and I started sipping some more from it. After my third glass, I started feeling a bit giddy and more relaxed in his company. The wine obviously had gone straight to my head since I hadn't much of anything to eat this whole afternoon and I was starving now. "Oh! Look! It appears I've taken your other knight! I think you're in trouble now," I giggled, entertained by our chess game.

"It micht appear so," he grinned. But something about his grin seemed superficial to me as his gaze was thinking. "Perhaps, we micht play anither game fur our entertainment."

"But this is a good game that we're playing now," I objected.

"Indeed. We may return tae it, if ye so wish—once we have completed this subsequent game which may strike your fancy even better," he said.

"What do you have in mind?" I inquired curiously.

"'Tis a language game," he said.

"A language game?"

"Aye. I say a word in one language, and ye try tae guess whit language tae which it belongs," he instructed.

"Okay, that sounds like it might be fun."

"It may very weel be to our interest."

"All right," I agreed easily, taking a little breath.

"Shall I begin?" he asked.

"Sure," I said.

"*Bonjour*," he started, intrigued.

"French," I said easily.

"Très bien! Now ye give it a try," he encouraged.

"All right—*Buenos días*," I said.

"That would be Spanish," he said effortlessly. "*Guten morgen*."

"German," I recognized.

"Sehr gut," he said amusedly.

"Ok, what about—*Bom dia*," I said interestedly.

"Portuguese," he said curiously.

"Yes!" I said.

"*Buongiorno*," he said.

"Oh, that's easy—Italian," I said swiftly. "Name this one—*Ni hao*." He seemed suddenly stumped with a quizzical look on his face. "That's Chinese," I disclosed lightheartedly to him.

"Chinese?" he said looking at me with unexpected surprise.

"Yes. *Yeoboseyo*—that's Korean. *Konnichiwa*—that's Japanese. What about Indian, though—how would you say hello in Hindi?" I asked curiously, thinking aloud without any thought to the languages I was saying.

"I have heard that is said to be—*Namaste*," Lord Loudoun said coolly.

"Oh, right! Of course—*Namaste*—I should have known that already," I remembered in a silly manner as I giggled a little.

"Should ye have?" he questioned, now observing me with visible suspicion in his eyes as they narrowed on me.

"Uh, well, I don't actually *know* all of those languages—just the simple things. That's it, really," I said uncomfortably.

"I see," he said skeptically. The conversation rather suddenly dropped dead like a lead weight to the ground. I suddenly felt extremely nervous. I finished my wine as he fixed an examining gaze over me again while I realized the most uncomfortable silence that I had ever experienced in my life. "I wonder if ye micht kindly grant me some insight intae ye Americans," he recommenced evenly, appearing grim now.

"What do you want to know?" I asked cautiously.

"It appears the subjects living haur have a strange mindset that I dinnae quite fathom."

"Oh?"

"Aye. I wonder why ye subjects should demonstrate such obstinance when the Crown has moved tae protect ye?" he inquired evenly.

"Well, I wouldn't say that we're merely obstinate," I said carefully.

"Whit micht ye name it, then?"

"I think the people here feel as though their validity has been disregarded. It seems, well, people have been living peacefully here for a number of years, and suddenly feel usurped without a voice to be acknowledged," I divulged.

"Is that yer opinion?" he inquired.

"Yes—I believe so," I said.

"Hmm... Yet, I dinnae believe that provides fur any mere excuse tae not behave accordingly to the rule of the king's law," he disagreed. "Whit is yer opinion on that account?"

"Well—except, that's the way people are feeling—and, perhaps if some diplomacy were to be applied between the English government and the people here, it might foster some kind of cooperation," I ventured to say honestly.

"Do ye truly believe so?" He chuckled ironically.

"Yes." I was wary to see him amused, and I wondered what he was going to say next, as I felt I was walking a tightrope in front of him.

"I am quite disinclined tae believe it. Do ye realize that I have set a blockade out tae sea?"

"How can anyone not? The price of bread is unbelievable," I said despite my fear of him.

"Not my concern. I have found it tae be the only way tae git subjects tae adhere tae the rule of law. Whit is more, do ye realize they still defy my orders? I have recently arrested shipping smugglers en route tae Hispaniola only the day before," he said gravely.

"Is that so?" I responded with some surprise—and misgiving.

"I shall make ye awaur that I shall place every man caught smuggling from these ports under arrest and hang them fur treason," he said.

"I see," I said, swallowing dryly. His light blue eyes were frosty and hard. I perceived no humor in them now.

"I have knowledge that yer husband is in business and has vessels," he indicated earnestly. He paused for a moment and seemed meditative as he continued gazing at me without reservation. I supposed that he was waiting for my response. But I simply remained quietly seated before him not knowing what to say. "Waur ye not awaur that I micht know this about yer husband?"

"No." I shook my head a little.

"Then, ye are surprised by my knowledge of it?"

"Yes—I am."

"Did ye not inform me earlier that ye share a unique understanding with yer husband?"

"Yes."

"Then, ye are awaur of his commerce?"

"I—I don't think so—because we don't discuss his business frequently—or in detail."

"Puzzling... particularly when ye stated that ye and he share a unique understanding with one anither."

"Well—I just mean generally speaking."

"Pray, permit me tae further enlighten ye in this case. Why, I shall have ye awaur that I have only recently intercepted a correspondence from a highly regarded merchant reit haur in Boston. The correspondence reads of his continuation tae supply his buyers in Canada with copper. I also am awaur that yer husband trades in sugar from the West Indies, as weel does he trade in copper tae Canada. Are ye certain that ye are unawaur of that, madam?" I didn't respond immediately; I wasn't sure what to say again. He was glaring at me with sudden harshness and was making me very nervous to answer him. "Weel?" he prompted seriously.

"I'm unaware of it," I lied.

"Hmph. Then, consider yerself presently informed about yer husband by me. He's an industrious man having learnt his business weel from slave traders."

"Slave traders?" I looked at him with exception.

"Aye."

"What do you mean? He doesn't sell people," I said for certain.

"He has knowledge of the trade as 'tis a common and lucrative business."

"I think I'd know if that is his business dealing."

"How micht ye know if ye say that ye had no notion of his trading specifics, as ye have newly been informed of his sugar and copper trade by me?" he asked, stumping me for a response. "Given yer reaction, I micht presume ye are indeed ignorant of yer husband's business ventures, and that ye are not as awaur of him as ye have claimed tae be. Or, ye know how tae feign grandly."

"Well, I know that he wouldn't have any sort of business involving human trafficking, trading or selling people. Slavery is an evil business and my husband is not an evil man."

"Hmm. Yoo're quite outspoken regarding yer opinions. Furthermore, yoo're contradictory as ye do own slaves. Be that as it will, ye ought tae cary the sentiment that because a man owns slaves disnae deem him malevolent. Be mindful as ye cast yer stone, I do suggest. Why, a man isnae spawn of the Devil fur having such property.

"Whit deems a man immoral is when he breaks God's Commandment, or betrays his Sovereign by abandoning the proper laws of the Crown. In this case, as for example, the merchant I spoke of whose correspondence I have seized has committed an offense against the Crown through his deceit by smuggling guids intae Canada. This is an act of treason as we are at war. Now that I know yer sentiment upon slavery, whit is yer sentiment upon the punishment fur treason?"

"The correspondence that you intercepted—does it belong to my husband?" I asked instead of answering his question.

"It is instead from a close ally tae yer husband. Should it have come from the duke himself, thaur would have been grave consequences that certainly would have affected ye. I am weel awaur of the nefarious business dealings involving yer husband. He is in a high stakes enterprise with me now that I am enforcing the blockade. I doubt fur yer sake that the stakes couldnae be higher, would ye not agree?" I didn't respond; I thought better not to. "Mayhap, it micht be wise fur ye tae disclose this bit of information tae yer husband, that he is gambling with his life. It would be a tragedy if ye waur tae be left widowed a second time due tae his folly should he be caught dealing in treasonous affairs, do ye not agree?" Again, I didn't respond; I was completely caught off guard by his accusation and threat against Leif. But he continued to say, "Should this case occur with yer husband—that he be apprehended fur treason—ye will have nae one tae blame but him for it. He appears to be acting in a most imprudent manner in yer regard." His Lordship paused shortly, seeming to consider his thoughts as he stared fixedly at me when I noticed his hard eyes soften a little. Then he continued to say, "Do address me by Jonathan, as ye and I are friends of the ideal sort. Therefore, bear in mind that should ye ever need a confidant, pray think upon me. I would imagine that ye micht have need to confide in someone other than yer negligent husband who would prove tae be more attentive tae yer needs than he. Should ye find the desire tae confide in me—about yer husband, or in anything else fur that matter—I shall be pleased to be at yer aid... Of coorse, as it greatly pleases me to be your ally in whitever matter which may arise, do understand that I am truly not yer enemy but am a dear admirer who will sacrifice his—"

Without warning, the door abruptly burst open and Leif barreled his way like a tornado inside the room.

"*Bloody Hell!* Whit in *damnation* are ye meaning with my wife, Loudoun!" Leif charged angrily, steamrolling his way forth toward His Lordship. The general abruptly stood from his seat and uneasily postured himself, appearing significantly bamboozled by Leif's sudden confrontational appearance. "Ye and I have already discussed that my wife will be left be!"

"It is quite innocent, Your Grace. I was merely enjoying a spot of tea with Her Grace, that is all," His Lordship said coolly, noticeably displeased about the interruption.

"I have warned ye once, Your Lordship. I shall not do it again. Dinnae cross me!" Leif expressed vehemently in a bellowed tone, slamming his fist unanticipatedly hard on the general's desk, rattling the inkwell and tea. I jumped a little at the sudden sound of his crashing fist and His Lordship stiffened. Leif straightened, glaring visibly incensed at him, gnashing his teeth as he continued measuredly saying, "Ye have nae business with my wife. Any matter ye have with me may be personally addressed tae me and settled by me alone. Is that clearly understood?"

"Ye have made yerself quite clear, major. I shall remind ye of yer *rank*!" The general seethed and loathsomely narrowed his eyes on Leif. "I shall also warn ye tae tread lightly with me, fur ye indeed forget yer place!"

"And you forget yers, *Your Lordship*! Ye have made it quite personal betwixt us. If ye so much as lay a finger upon my wife— cross me then, fur I shall challenge ye, and I'll kill ye," Leif said in a cold, steady, calibrated voice, swearing it to the bone.

The pallor in Lord Loudoun's face drained completely white, and I noticed him swallow hard.

"Ye are in contempt! Treason is rife, Your Grace. Threatening yer superior officer warrants punishment! Hanging from a rope may be yer fate. An end I shall welcome!" Lord Loudoun caustically warned Leif again.

Leif detestably scowled at him before abruptly stepping away from him and swiftly came toward me. He firmly clutched my arm and easily tugged me to my feet, rapidly steering me out of His Lordship's office. He guided me outside into the courtyard and speedily urged me inside our carriage. In a second, the carriage jerked into motion and we were shortly off returning on our way to *Taigh Gràs*.

As I sat across from Leif riding in the carriage on the way back to our house, I was aware of the silence between us while he sat there remote and brooding in his displeasure. This was the first time I had ever known Leif to become visibly angry, and it made me feel recognizably uncomfortable. I was wondering what deep-seated problem it was between him and Lord Loudoun to make him have such an extreme reaction toward him; I just couldn't understand why Leif lost his temper as he did a minute ago. I knew he would have been upset, but I just didn't know to what extent. Noticing Leif abstracted as he sat with me in silence, sort of frightened me; he said that he would *kill* His Lordship. He meant it. I wasn't used to that kind of talk at all, and it *really* unsettled me. I didn't want him murdering anyone, or doing anything rash that would jeopardize his freedom, his safety or his life because of me.

The whole way back to *Taigh Gràs* was ridden in silence, and I was aware of Leif remaining silent once we entered the house also. He passed me by to go up the staircase without a word while I was being greeted by a very worried Amity and Mercy, along with other women house servants. Once I had answered all their frantic questions and calmed their concerns, I left them and hurried up the staircase seeking Leif. I presumed that he had gone to his library. So, I made my way around the house to the third floor. When I entered the study, I found him sitting on the sofa stuffing his pipe with fresh tobacco. I closed the door behind me, and I mindfully approached him while he was preoccupied. He didn't acknowledge me when I arrived, standing before him as I saw that he was clearly absorbed in his troubled thoughts.

"Are you mad at me?" I ventured asking with uncertainty.

"I beg yer pardon?" he responded in confusion, suddenly called away from his brooding as his eyes abruptly bounced up from his working fingers to me.

"Are you mad at me?" I repeated cautiously.

"Do ye mean whether I am angry at ye?" he inquired strangely.

"Yeah," I said.

"Of coorse not, *mo ghaol*. I dinnae ken how I could ever be crossed with ye," he said, shaking his head. "Come." He waved a hand at me, urging me to approach him. I proceeded, stepping closer toward him and stood directly before him. He reached for my hand and benignly took it into his.

"I was just trying to help a young boy at the market. He was starving," I started explaining.

"I ken all about the scene today at the marketplace," he said.

"You do?"

"Aye. Amity and Mercy found me at Master Otis's office and informed me of whit had occurred tae ye. Several other witnesses went in search fur me also and told me whit had transpired once I was discovered outdoors with Amity and Mercy from Master Otis's office," he said.

"Oh," I realized.

"My guid wife—has a heart of gold," he said. "Now, sit by me."

I shifted aside from where I was standing in front of him and sat close beside him on the sofa.

"I'm glad you knew where I'd been taken," I said gratefully.

"I'll be damned if he harms ye. His impudence is most disconcerting tae my mind," Leif said with a pensive look on his face.

"He didn't try anything. He just spoke to me," I informed him.

"He has nae business with ye in the merest," Leif said factually, still visibly irate. A brief moment of silence ensued between us as he glanced away from me and looked down at the pipe, he was stuffing a minute ago in his hand. Instead, he set his pipe aside on the tea stand beside him on the opposite side of me and untied the black silk ribbon binding his hair into a tail at the back of his head. He placed the ribbon on the tea stand also and raked his fingers through his shoulder-length hair as he continued brooding.

"You know, His Lordship told me something while I was in his office," I started thinkingly also.

"Whit did he say tae ye?" Leif asked sharply with lingering displeasure as he returned his attention to me, locking his eyes onto mine.

"It was about you," I said.

"Indeed."

"He gave me a warning."

"A warning?"

"He said that men have been arrested and hanged for smuggling."

"Aye, I'm awaur of it having happened."

"He said that he knows all about your shipping business too."

"I am not a wee bit surprised."

"He also told me that you had experience in the slave trade."

"Did he?"

"Yes, he did."

"I expect that is true."

"Are you serious?" I responded, literally aghast.

"My involvement wisnae as a trader or a profiteer. I was posted as a soldier in Guinea tae assist in manning a fort thaur in the territory," Leif disclosed.

"Oh," I replied, struck by surprise nevertheless.

"It was my first commission in the British army."

"Was it?"

"It was punishment from the Crown."

"Punishment?"

"Aye, I told ye about Culloden, do ye recall?"

"Yeah."

"Weel, it was alleged that I was seen upon the battlefield upon the Jacobite side, although my uncle was certain tae keep me from joining the fight. So, the Crown sent me tae Guinea as cause fur reparation. I reckon 'twas better than imprisonment, being tortured and losing my head over the battle," he explained.

"I should say so," I said, agreeing with the last part of his statement. "But, you said serving here was your punishment."

"Aye, my uncle petitioned the Crown tae have me banished haur instead—till war was declared by the Crown against France, then I was reinstated tae serve England in the army once more. And so, ye see, the Crown still has my servitude till I have completed proving my loyalty. Till this dreadful war is at last done in order that I have my entire wealth restored tae me from the government, then I shall be a free man."

"I see..." I said and pondered the fact he also was considered a slave to the Crown. "So, you've been banished here?"

"Aye."

"Is that why you told me that there was nothing left for you to return to in Scotland?"

"That is the reason." He nodded a tad.

"Oh... I didn't know the extent of your punishment."

"I reckon not."

"But you still have your property over there—and your titles also," I said, trying to understand the way nobility worked and all of the politics involved.

"My dukedom remains intact—at present—so long as the Crown disnae punish me further."

"I see... How do you manage all of your properties in Scotland in your absence?"

"My uncle Norman MacLeod sees tae it and keeps me abreast of my affairs regarding it." I nodded in response. He paused again and leaned over his spread knees as he rested on his elbows. He clasped his hands together and stared at them in silence for a moment longer. "Does it trooble ye that I ken the slave trade?" he suddenly inquired when he returned looking at me. His eyes were sharp and steady, but open with sincerity as he searchingly looked at me.

"No. It's not as though you were a trader," I said honestly. "It's really unfortunate that it is legal, though. Human beings are not meant to be commodities to be traded."

He didn't say anything to my reply. Instead, he simply looked at me unresponsive. Whether he agreed with me, I wasn't sure. But I could perceive him thinking. I glanced down at my fingers mindlessly twirling the wedding rings he gave to me, thinking for a moment also.

"You know," I started mindfully, still gazing at my rings as I broke the pensive silence between us.

"Aye?"

"Why did you really marry me, Leif? I just really want to know," I asked meekly. I returned looking at him and noticed his furrowed brow, obviously giving me an odd look.

"But, ye already ken my reason, as I have told ye," he said.

"No. I don't know why." I demurely shook my head.

"Whit do ye mean? Of coorse ye ken why." His voice was mild, but the expression on his face was perturbed.

"My complexion is olive compared to yours and not too far from Mercy's, actually. You could have easily chosen to marry a girl who's as fair as Constance and avoided the attention altogether."

"I could have done so, aye. Yet, I chose tae have ye instead, because it is whit I wanted. I want ye and nae other lass. I dinnae care that ye are swarthy. Yoo're bonnie tae me, and I assure ye that I am not the only man who agrees. Laird Loudoun fur instance would certainly agree, if ye are not already awaur of it—he is one of many who fancies ye." The expression on his face turned sullen with detestation. "Ye could have skin like ebony, and I would still claim ye fur my own," he said.

"Oh," I muttered, feeling embarrassed.

"Thus, apparently I wed ye because I loove ye. Do ye understand at last? I wouldnae risk my position unless I did so."

"Okay... I'm sorry—I didn't mean to make you upset. I'm just concerned because people seem curious about my heritage and—"

"Of coorse one is curious about ye. Nae one has seen a lass with the likes of yer beauty."

"You're flattering me in spite of everything."

"I'm merely stating the truth."

"But, people can be strange about things sometimes."

"I dinnae care about whit is upon the minds of others regarding my affairs. My affairs are solely my concern, not the affairs of others. 'Tis no one's business how I determine myself," he argued definitively. "Ye bring me joy, and I loove ye. That is all thaur is tae it."

"Well..."

"Aye?"

"For the record, I love you too."

"That is whit matters most tae me," he said. He wrapped an arm around me, drawing me close against the curve of his chest. I smiled a little at him and curled up on the sofa placing my head on his shoulder. I began resting contentedly next to him as he reached for his smoldering pipe again.

We drifted from further speaking with each other, and he seemed to have calmed down a bit from his encounter with His Lordship as he began smoking his pipe. But the tension in his shoulder I was resting on was still discernible, and I knew then that his anger with Lord Loudoun may never truly wane from him. So, I worried about Leif in this regard and hoped that nothing detrimental would ever transpire against him involving Lord Loudoun.

We didn't talk about Lord Loudoun anymore after that. The conversation between us seemed to close the topic; I understood that Leif was determined to protect me from him and I felt secure in this knowledge, knowing how much Leif loved me.

PART FIVE

The Crucible

Twenty-Two

Since my last encounter with Lord Loudoun, Leif was less inclined to let me out of his sight to be sure that I was out of harm's way. He was always ready to escort me around town whenever I needed to go on errands, guarding me like a precious gem. I think normally I would have found such behavior not only odd, but intolerably suffocating. But Leif truly seemed to care for my well-being, and I thought his genuine sincerity in doing so was endearing. So, I tolerated his mindfulness.

Early one morning, I eagerly rushed into his library seeking him to join me on a morning horse riding jaunt. I discovered him by the window at his desk, gravely skimming over a correspondence.

"What's the matter?" I asked, quickly noticing the weighty expression over his face as he was reading at his desk.

"Guid morrow tae ye, *ceisdein*," he greeted kindly nevertheless and straightened from his seat. He met me as I approached him with a gentle kiss on my brow.

"What are you reading?" I asked curiously, sensing his concern.

"I have received my orders from Laird Loudoun," he said with a serious expression.

"You did?" Suddenly, I was struck with dread. "What are your orders? Are you staying in town?"

"I am not."

I always knew this uncertain time would come. But I had pushed the idea of his deployment to the back of mind like it didn't exist—and now the reality of it was here, staring at me right in the face.

"You're being sent away?"

"Aye," he said, seeming hesitant.

"Well, where are you supposed to go?" I asked, realizing our serendipitous time here together was coming to an end.

"I'm tae leave fur Fort William Henry the day efter tomorrow," he disclosed.

"Day after tomorrow?" I echoed, feeling disenchanted and worried, holding his steady gaze.

"Aye," he said.

"But, that's so soon—and so far away." I was also hit by an intensely horrid feeling that sank inside the depth of my bones.

"'Tis raither soon and a fair distance, I shall agree," he said with a note of regret in his voice.

"Can you postpone it? Or, at least request for orders to be posted at Fort Hill so that you can stay local?" I asked anxiously.

"I fear not."

"Well, can't they send you somewhere else that isn't so far away?" Remembering a major historical fact about this fort, I knew it ultimately fell to the French. Except, I couldn't remember for the life of me the details of what had happened to it, or the time frame of when it took place—and this severely unnerved me.

"I cannae petition Loudoun fur me tae be sent elsewhaur. He will forbid it. I'm certain my abrupt transfer from Boston tae the frontier is his punishment tae me fur my slight tae him. Regardless, I shall not grovel tae him fur new orders. These orders he has given me are whaur I'm tae be sent—though we shall be separated." Leif explained resentfully. I stood there in front of him feeling very distressed while looking at him. "Come tae me, *mo ghaol*," he urged as he noticed the expression on my face. I worriedly wrapped my arms around his brawny chest and he embraced me. "'Twill be alrecht, lass," he said, gently assuaging me.

"No—it's not," I said, fearful.

"I shall be alrecht," he assured. His voice was calm and soothing, and I felt as though I wanted to relax in his arms as he embraced me, but my concern for him was in the forefront of my mind.

"I wish that you didn't have to go." He slightly drew from embracing me and lifted my chin with his fingers to see my face. "I won't let you go," I promised wholeheartedly, still holding him. A remote smile slightly buoyed the grim expression on his face.

"Ye inspire my heart. I swear tae ye that I shall soondly return," he vowed solemnly.

"You can't leave me," I replied, realizing that he could be killed and that I could possibly lose him forever. I just couldn't let that happen. "You can't leave me here alone."

"I shall not leave ye alone. I'll return—yoo'll see," he assuaged me.

"Wait a minute! I could go with you!" I suddenly thought.

"It wulnae be possible," he discouraged quickly.

"Why not?"

"Foremost, yoo're the Duchess of Monteith, mistress of *Taigh Gràs* with yer own affairs tae mind. Aside from this fact, 'twill merely be too perilous fur ye tae join me. I cannae risk having ye with me at the fort, fur thaur are many terrible risks tae ye. I shall never forgive myself if I let anything ill become of ye," he said decisively.

"But, you said that you'd be all right, though" I countered, nervous about him leaving me. I couldn't begin to imagine living here without him; he was my foundation here.

"Aye, I shall be. But, yoo're a lass, *ceisdein.* Anything can befall ye. Aside from this, additionally, 'twould be irregular fur ye tae join me," he said.

"Still, I'll be all right. I'll just stay out of the way," I persisted.

"'Tis impossible. I wulnae have it," he responded steadfastly. "Ye micht be with my bairn as we speak. I cannae have ye in such a state at the fort. Or, whit if by chance ye git bairned whilst we are thaur? Certainly not—I'll not risk ye or the bairn if it will be the case."

I sighed, dissatisfied and distressed, realizing the unwavering position to which he was adhering. He frankly was not going to budge on this issue. I didn't know what else to do, or how else I could convince him to change his mind. So, I withdrew my embrace around his broad chest and wiped the moisture accumulating in my eyes.

"Okay," I accepted.

"It pains me tae see ye weep," he said.

"I know. I'm okay. I've just never been good with deployments, you know? Because of my dad and everything—when he had to deploy too," I said meagerly.

"I understand," he replied, appearing sympathetic as he gazed at me.

"I'm sorry—I don't mean to make this any harder than it already is."

"Dinnae apologize fur caring fur me."

"Well, I understand it's your duty, and you have to go. So, I'll be all right, too." I forced a weak smile.

"My brave lass," he said softly. He covered the side of my cheek with his palm, and I lifted my fingers to his as I pressed my palm on his, not wishing to let his hand go. He gently stroked a tear away from my eyelashes with the pad of his thumb and kissed me tenderly on the lips. When he withdrew, he stared back into my eyes, heartened. "Nonetheless," he started again with reconsideration in his tone, "I realize that I cannae have ye remaining haur in the city in my absence."

"Why not?" I asked confusedly.

"It has grown particularly unsafe with the many troops about. Also, regarding Laird Loudoun, I dinnae want his clutches near ye. With my absence from haur, I cannae protect ye from him fur as long as he remains in the city. Whilst he remains at Fort Hill, he is bound tae make contact with ye again as he has set his sechts upon ye. Should ye ever encounter his company again, I am certain he will harm ye one way or anither. Recall the warrant he had fur ye?"

"Yeah."

"'Twas merely voided because we wed. Yet, his interest in ye has not waned. He reckons ye micht be useful tae him in more ways than one. I shan't have ye near him under any circumstances."

"But you just said that I have the house to look after."

"I realize so, and ye shall—from afar," he answered.

"From afar?"

"Aye."

"How?"

"Ye will be in contact with Quinn through correspondence, of coorse."

"Oh, but—"

"Pray, listen as I huvnae completed explaining to ye that I have sent word tae Fin fur ye and Amity, along with yer maid, tae remain with Elizabeth and her family in Concord till my return."

"Oh."

"Ye will be safe thaur fur the duration of my absence, and ye may correspond with Quinn tae ensure the guid state of *Taigh Gràs* in my stead," Leif informed me authoritatively.

"Okay," I replied, slightly relieved that I likely wouldn't be bumping into Lord Loudoun again any time soon because of my new location.

"I shall escort ye safely tae Concord. Then, I shall take my leave the next morn tae Fort William Henry," he informed me.

"All right," I replied faintly as my mind settled on his departure from me once more.

"Now," he continued on a moderate note, "micht I share a bit of cheer with my bonnie wee wife tae lift my spirit before we shall depart?"

"Yes—that would be nice," I agreed, forcing my troubled feelings aside. "But, you have to promise me one thing?"

"Whit micht that be?"

"That when your tour of duty is over, you have to retire from the service," I requested.

"It depends upon the Crown," he said.

"Oh... right." I nodded regretfully, remembering his predicament.

"Now... Whit shall we do together this morn?" he asked. I shrugged a little as I thought about what we could do together.

"Well, I was thinking that we could go for a horseback ride."

"Och, that shall be nice fur us."

I was still disheartened over the realization that I was going to lose him in too short a time to Fort William Henry. I was never fond of military life in general given my experience as the daughter of a military trauma surgeon. I wasn't born yet to remember my dad's service in Vietnam, but I clearly remembered what it was like when he left for the first Gulf War. Later, he was in Iraq for the first eight years of the Second Gulf War until he settled as a burn specialist at the VA hospital in L.A. So, I had some familiarity with this. I never dreamed that I would have become a military wife like my mom. Now knowing how she must have felt facing my dad's departures, it hit me especially hard.

Still, I decided for both our sakes to remain strong about the prospect of him leaving, and I pretended to be cheerful whenever I was in his company.

A DAY LATER, at dawn, we started out of Boston on our way to Concord. Leif had left strict instructions for Quinn in case our property was forced to quarter troops in his absence, and informed him that any matters regarding our property may be addressed by me.

I rode out in the open astride Oakley alongside Leif. He was mounted tall and grand in full military dress, cantering comfortably before the three coaches where Amity and Mercy remained seated inside. It was a full day's journey by the time we had arrived in Concord at dusk. Finley and Elizabeth welcomed us with open arms along with her extended family. We reconnected well with them and had much to catch up on as we informed them of the latest news from Boston. And, they were amazed and impressed with how much Amity had grown and had advanced in her education. Leif and I were equally surprised by how much our remaining three nieces had grown as we gladly listened, interestedly, to all their innocent tales. And, I was happy to see that the girls had reunited and reacquainted themselves with each other while we also shared gifts that Leif and I had brought from Boston for the family to enjoy.

We spent time after tonight's dinner sharing in their delight over our gifts from Boston while Leif and Finley conversed over port wine and pipe smoke with Mr. Buckingham and his son, Earnest. While it was nice being reunited with Elizabeth's family, I couldn't shake the cloud of Leif's departure from my mind as we continued enjoying the family's company after dinner.

But later that night, I lay in bed cuddling with him peacefully enjoying his lightly stroking hand over my arm while dreading our coming separation. I also sensed that he was likewise awake thinking in the dark.

"I wish you didn't have to go," I whispered against his bare shoulder.

"Aye," he whispered back.

"Are you afraid?" He suddenly turned his eyes to mine, and I could see the shadows dancing over his face in the candlelight. His eyes appeared like coal orbs in the dark, and the cleft in his chin seemed deep set in his square jaw.

"I give ye my oath that I shall return tae ye," he vowed softly.

I responded with a little smile. "I believe you mean that... but, I'm still afraid for you," I said.

"Come haur," he said gently and rolled me over his chest so now I lay stretched over his body, facing him. I felt him gently bury his fingers in my ringlets and stroking them away from my brow. He placed my curls behind my ears and shoulders as he gazed adoringly at me. I leaned and gently kissed his lips. His hand began caressing the back of my ringlets as I kissed him, and he pulled me tighter against him, kissing me in return. I quickly sensed him as we were kissing; the innocent kiss I had given him changed as his desire erupted, and I naturally returned kissing him in kind. "Ride me," he said between our kisses while his hands wandered heatedly beneath my shift over my bare thighs until he removed my garment off of me.

I COLLAPSED over Leif's heaving chest listening to the sound of our heavy breathing and buried my head in the curve of his perspiring neck, feeling his rapid pulse against my brow as he remained embracing me tightly in his arms.

"*Tha gràdh agam ort*," he said in a soft voice.

"I love you too," I whispered.

"I shall never leave ye."

"You better not." I tried curbing the tear slipping down my cheek.

"Shh, now... shhh... *mo ghaol bith-buan*," he whispered in assuaging tones as he kept kissing my damp eyelashes. I couldn't bear the thought of him being away from me. He was the only reason worth living here in this era. If he were prematurely taken away from me by death, then I'd be devastated again and left in a worse state of mind than I had been when Matt died. Without Leif in my life, there would be no reason for me to stay here. Instead, I'd make it my life's mission to find my way back home to be with my family again and forget about this place.

When I soon calmed from being upset, I simply remained lying stretched over his body while resting my head on his broad chest, hearing his strong heartbeat calming me. The lullaby of his beating heart soothed and consoled me until I closed my eyes and rested my weary mind as sleep disconnected us.

THE NEXT MORNING, I awakened among the pillows and realized Leif had already gone. I was disheartened and started wondering what I was going to do with myself now that we were apart. But my eyes focused on a large, lovely collection of lilacs and honeysuckles, the kind hummingbirds are attracted to, tied into a fragrant bouquet with one of his black silk ribbons he used for his hair, resting on top of the pillows beside me. I rolled to my side, reaching to gather the bouquet. I drew the pretty, fragrant collection of flowers to my nose, drinking in their beautiful, heady, sweet scent. When I removed the flowers from my nose, I noticed he had also left a note on the pillow. I grasped the small parchment between my fingers, and began reading with fondness as his warm voice resonated in his written words:

> 10, May 1757
>
> My Dearest Sylvina, My Love, My Heart,
> I long too soon to behold your bonnie face and to lay a kiss upon your sweet honey lips. I shall carry the thought of you, darling of my heart, in my every wakeful moment and dream of holding you

every night as I await my homecoming with eager-
ness. My soul will rejoice to hold my missing heart
that I have left behind. By our Heavenly Father's
will, I have faith that I shall lay eyes upon you
once more. Trust in our Lord Jesus Christ that he
will hear my prayer and deliver my return to you.
    Your Most Loving Trusted Servant, Your
Devoted Husband,
    Leif Charles Seamus MacLeod Fitz-James
Stewart, Duke of Monteith

I folded the letter and sat up in bed, realizing how much I already missed him too. I wondered what my days were going to be like now without him. I didn't much like the thought of it as I dwelled. I knew that I was going to be constantly consumed with wondering about him despite our ability to correspond. I was going to perpetually think of what he was doing at any given point in time, considering if he was in good health or harmed, as I hoped and prayed for his safety. Although I wasn't clear on the details, I ultimately knew the fate that would come to this fort. The knowl-edge of it sent icy shivers down my spine and turned my blood cold, making goosebumps appear on my skin.

Now that I had gotten married to this man and had fallen in love with him, I thought that it was completely unfair—and abso-lutely made no sense—that I could potentially lose him too. The realization settled in my mind that I couldn't risk losing him. I wasn't about to stand idly by and lose someone else that I cared deeply about if I could help it. *I would be damned if I did.*

I came to a clear decision and removed myself from beneath the blankets. I paced toward the traveling trunks situated in the corner of the room. Unlatching one of the trunks, I began rummaging through my packed belongings until I found my keep-sake box which had everything endearing that he had ever given to me that I had collected. I opened it and stored my latest letter and flowers given to me from him. When I replaced the box far below inside the trunk and closed the lid, I recognized his Claymore lying flat above one of the trunks. I moved to grasp it. It seemed to weigh a ton. I unraveled the tartan cloth protecting it and revealed the engravings on the hilt. I trailed my fingers over the clan inscription on the pommel and followed the engravings around the grip while I pondered what I meant to do.

When I finished thinking, I carefully rewrapped his sword and struggled a little to move it aside from the trunk in order to searched through the luggage which had my clothes inside. Once I found my clothes, I started dressing, deciding not to die longing for his return.

The Lord helps those who help themselves, I told myself.

After placing my pair-of-bodies around my torso over my camisole, I quickly tucked my fitted shirt into my riding trousers and buttoned my pants around my waist. I fixed my riding jacket over my shoulders, securing the bodice, and stepped into my boots. After I tied my hair back into a loose ponytail, I hurriedly started packing as lightly as I could. When I had finished, I glanced at the clock on the mantelpiece and noticed the time read ten-thirty. It was already late in the morning now. I didn't know exactly when Leif had left and guessed he must already be far up the road, presuming he likely left at dawn. I wasn't sure how much of a lead he had, but it was far enough, I expected. I had to hurry if I was going to catch up to him by nightfall.

I scooped up one of my silk ribboned straw hats, tied it around my head, snatched my two large satchels, and made a mad dash out of the house for the stable without saying a word to anyone in the household—except for the note I had written and had slipped beneath Elizabeth's bedroom door, letting her know of my travel plan.

When I had arrived at the stable, I swiftly located Oakley in her stall and proceeded preparing her for the journey.

"What do you mean, Sylvina?" Elizabeth asked suddenly as she unexpectedly made an appearance from around the corner of the horse stall, catching me off guard. Evidently, she had discovered and had read my note sooner than I had anticipated.

"Oh! Good morning, Elizabeth," I said as I was in the process of anxiously saddling up Oakley.

"You mustn't take your leave," she said, appearing clearly surprised and confused.

"I need to be with Leif," I said, preoccupied with buckling the saddle.

"I shall very much miss Fin also, but it is best that we remain. Trust in our Lord God, for you will see—they will come back to us," she assured with concern on her face that I perceived had more to do with me and my intention rather than to do with our husbands.

"But I have to go. It's important," I replied. Her brow knitted as she clearly didn't understand or agree with me.

"'Tis imperative that you remain here with us. Ill may fall upon you—'tis not wise to travel unescorted as you are well aware."

"I'll be all right."

"You cannot be assured."

"If I leave now, then I'll catch up to them hopefully before sunset."

"I do not understand. What is causing you such urgency to take leave?"

"They won't be back unless I go," I said inadvertently just as I had finished the last buckle on Oakley's saddle.

"You must not speak in this manner, Sylvina. God has their fate," Elizabeth said with disapproval.

"I know He does."

"Then, what do you mean?"

"I mean to make sure they come back to us safe and sound," I responded determinedly.

"Fin has always come back to me, and so will they both return should it be God's will. I don't understand why you will depart. You are being unwise."

"It might seem like it. But I'm actually facilitating their safe return."

"How can that be?"

"Please believe me."

Elizabeth sighed, appearing not only obviously worried but frustrated with me also. "Have you forgotten Amity's reliance upon your tutelage?"

"I realize that—but, she's far enough along now where she can communicate by writing a little bit to you. Besides, when I get back, she and I can resume where we left off in our learning."

"This is most irregular."

"Perhaps it is."

"Have you not thought that you will not assist our husbands, but be a burden upon them? Do you not realize this? It is not our place to meddle in such affairs when we are not our husbands. We have our own affairs to mind. Goodness me, Sylvina! Ponder it momentarily, fa Heaven's sake! Have you not forgotten that you and I have duties? What business is it of ours—my being a countess and you a duchess—to involve ourselves in war is outlandish! We must set a respectable standard by adhering to it. We are well regarded and must avoid straying which would lead others to their detriment. We would be blamed and scandalized if this should occur. Surely you have pondered this, have you not?

"For the love of our dear Lord and Savior, I do realize that you are willful and have your convictions which stem from a noble mind. Yet, you should not wish to pick up a rifle and battle, fa you will welcome a fight that you will not win. I implore you to reconsider yourself," she expressed.

"I once saw a murdered family lying in the field by their

home on the frontier and all I could think about was how their deaths could have happened. Maybe they wouldn't have suffered such a horrific end to their lives if they hadn't lived so far out in the frontier. But I like to think that if I had arrived soon enough before they died, maybe I could have helped ease their suffering. I don't plan on fighting. I plan on saving lives," I said.

"I don't understand how you will do so. Should you take your leave from us, you may very well soon realize that you will have to guard yourself in the path of war but discover that you cannot as you are vulnerable. Not even camp followers have the ability to protect themselves. Thus, I inquire of you, how will you save our husbands from battle when they are the ones who guard us?" she asked.

"I don't know," I replied honestly.

"Then, you must remain here."

"I know that you don't understand me. But I'm going to try to help them. You'll see. I mean to bring them both home safe and sound."

"By imperiling yourself?"

"I have to."

"I do not know whether you are brave or daft, Sylvina."

"It's fair to say that I'm just stubborn."

"Aye. I can clearly see so."

"I don't mean to trouble you. I'm sorry, but I've gotta go, Elizabeth. Please excuse me for rushing our conversation and for my sudden departure, but I've gotta catch up to them now before it gets any later." I had finished securing my horse's saddle along with the bags and moved her into the aisle. Elizabeth sighed, appearing obviously skeptical and thwarted as she relented from further discussing the matter.

"You are not wise," she said, stepping aside from me as I shoved my boot into the stirrup and swiftly mounted Oakley.

"I know you feel that way. I don't expect you to understand

me, and that's all right. Please, don't be offended—I just need to help them when I know that I can."

"Your obstinance may prove to be your undoing."

"Please trust me."

"Pray to God, Sylvina," she said. I gave her a gentle smile in response. "I shall also pray."

"Thank you. I must go," I replied.

"As I cannot seem to press reason upon you, I beseech you—do take care," she said uneasily while nervously observing me sitting high on my horse ready to leave.

"Yes, thank you—I will. You also take care and be well." I carefully began maneuvering Oakley away from her down the aisle toward the large opening of the stable.

"Godspeed," she said anxiously.

"Thank you."

"God bless you, Sylvina."

"God bless you too, Elizabeth," I replied. Then, Oakley and I exited the stable. "*C'mon, girl,*" I uttered lightly to my horse. Oakley suddenly took off galloping over the wide clearing along the Buckingham property belonging to Elizabeth's parents out onto the open road heading west.

SHORTLY OUT OF CONCORD, I was now galloping alone on the narrow road among the woods. I was suddenly thankful that there was sun instead of rain, and I pressed onward hoping to reach Leif before dark. The air was temperate, but the sun was warm, and the bugs were buzzing out in force.

I had galloped away until I slowed Oakley to a light trot. I didn't want to drive her too hard, although she seemed all right to take it. Instead, we kept on our way moderately cantering and stopped a few times for short breaks to relieve myself and for her to drink from the streams before continuing on the path. I was entirely focused on just getting to Leif that I couldn't think about anything else. Nothing else mattered to me but him.

The day had grown long and still no sign of the brothers. I wondered how far they could have conceivably traveled, and I was beginning to think that I should have spotted them already by now. As dusk finally began settling, I started second-guessing myself, thinking perhaps this wasn't the best idea to travel like this alone. I didn't want to sleep outside by myself in the woods, vulnerable to only God knew what was out here.

Elizabeth was right to point out my vulnerability; I'm not armed and can't protect myself if I had to. I didn't even think of bringing a knife with me. How unbelievably stupid of me; how could I let that slip my mind...? I should be all right, though—at least I hope so—if I just keep going. Hopefully it won't be much longer before I run into their company along this road...

So, I continued onward along the only road leading me west from Concord at sundown, feeling quite ill at ease.

THE MOON WAS OUT BRIGHTLY SHINING NOW, illuminating the path as shadows fell among the forest. Suddenly, I thought I heard something crack among the trees, and I abruptly stopped Oakley in her tracks. I quieted her and listened all around with misgiving and alarm. As I listened around me, softly speaking voices were emanating from behind the trees at a distance beyond the road. I discerned they were men speaking and laughing—a number of them, I thought. I tried honing in on their location when I unexpectedly noticed campfires flickering away between the trees.

Dismounting, I mindfully led Oakley by the reins off the forested path and started among the trees. Quietly pacing with her in the direction of the firelight, I was very much hoping this was Leif's camp.

I crept forth for a short distance intending to spy on the camp to see if I might recognize him or Finley among the group when I abruptly heard two distinct invisible *clicks* at close range around my head.

"Who goes thaur?" said a man suddenly in front of me. I sharply gasped, intensely frightened, realizing I was looking down the barrel of a readied pistol.

"Hold on, lad," said another man at very close distance who also had his pistol drawn on me. Abruptly pushed backward by one of them, I noticed a man stepping out of the darkness into the moonlight directly in front of me. He was hard looking, gaunt in the face, and did not at all appear friendly.

"Who are ye?" he asked cut-and-dry.

"I'm looking for my husband," I said, suddenly parched. I swallowed hard while looking at him.

"Ooh, yoo're a lass are ye?" the other man inquired from the darkness, stepping into the moonlight also. He was tall and beefy with a full beard obscuring his face. He was imposing as he crowded my personal space. At the same time, an indistinguishable hand reached out and clutched my chest, groping my breast.

"Hey!" I gasped, suddenly jumping back, and slapping the intrusive hand off of me.

"Aye, she's a lass indeed," chuckled the beefy one who confirmed the fact.

"I'm looking for my husband," I said again in spite of my fear of these two unfamiliar men.

"Yer husband?" the skinny ugly one questioned doubtfully.

"Yes," I said, trying to conceal my unease.

"Och, mayhap I could be yer husband, lass. I reckon yoo're raither a looker," the fat one laughed jeeringly as I discerned their pistols being pulled away from my head.

"Who micht yer husband be?" asked the skinny one with suspicion.

"The Duke of Monteith," I said.

"The Duke of Monteith?" the beefy one echoed with blatant surprise.

"Yes," I replied.

"Ye are his duchess?" the skinny one inquired with shock in his voice.

"That's correct," I said. The two men glanced at each other, then at me, glaring with the whites of their eyes glowing in disbelief.

"Beggin' yer pardon, Duchess. We waur unawares," the skinny one stammered regretfully.

"Can never expect who is who at nicht, ye see? Pray, forgive us lads. I'm Thomas and this haur is Simon," the hefty one said.

"How do you do?" I asked politely, feeling better now that we had been introduced to each other, and that I had finally discovered Leif's company.

"We are weel, Duchess, seein' haur it is merely ye out in the wood," Simon said.

"I heard His Grace speak of ye earlier today," Thomas recalled.

"He's here then? In camp with you?" I asked hopefully.

"Indeed he is," Simon confirmed.

"Will you please take me to him?" I requested as I anticipated seeing him.

"Aye, Simon will show ye tae him, as I must remain tae keep watch," Thomas indicated.

"Yes, certainly—thank you, Thomas," I said gratefully.

"This way, Duchess," Simon suggested politely.

"Thank you, Simon," I said as I started following him through the shadows between the trees, towing my horse.

"Aye," he replied simply as he continued leading me through the undergrowth.

In a few minutes, the scent of campfire was strong, and it became clearly visible through the trees. No tents were pitched in the camp. But, a rather large number of British uniforms were relaxing and talking across the site. There was intermittent chuckling from the soldiers between ale, smokes, and decks of cards around the bright campfires. Heads turned questioningly as I passed by the camping groups of men.

"Who have ye got with ye, Simon, eh?" one of the men asked curiously, sitting on a collapsible stool in the middle of a card game.

"Appears tae be a laddie with him," suspected his buddy, also playing cards. My eyes suddenly spotted Finley emerging across one of the fires slightly farther inside the camp. He was stuffing his pipe while sitting on a log, talking to some companions.

"Nae, 'tis the duchess come fur the duke," Simon responded without looking at his wondering companions as we passed them.

"The duchess?" one of the card players responded audibly with apparent surprise. I noticed Finley abruptly look up from his pipe in my direction. He stood from his seat on the log as he recognized me approaching from around one of the fires. Finley quickly advanced toward me and met me, appearing perceivably shocked at my unexpected arrival.

"Hullo, lass," he greeted, looking stunned.

"Hello Finley," I responded, feeling very alleviated that I had found the correct camping group.

"Is something amiss?" he inquired concernedly.

"No, everything is fine," I replied, shaking my head a little.

"Och," he said with some detectable relief. He didn't seem to know quite how to respond to seeing me after his alleviation, except I sensed that he didn't approve by the sudden change in his expression. He gave Simon a quick nod. Simon promptly turned away from us and vanished behind the blazing fire-pit when Finley abruptly blew a quick sharp whistle. Shortly, Leif was detected emerging from the bushes seemingly having just completed relieving himself, since he was in the middle of fastening his breeches around his waist. I was so happy to see him again as he started advancing toward Finley. But while he approached, there was discernible shock in his expression when he realized I was standing next to his brother.

"Yer wife has come tae ye, Seamus," Finley said flatly, visibly disapproving now. Leif unexpectedly glanced at Finley, and Finley gave Leif an incorrigible look in response. I suddenly felt Leif grip me by the arm. He instantly guided me away from Finley and the rest of the men, and paced me far enough away out of earshot until he abruptly stopped us at the edge of camp.

"Why did ye not listen tae me, lass?" he asked immediately with glaring disapproval in his voice.

"I had to make sure you were all right," I explained.

"But, I am weel, as ye can plainly see," he said surely.

"But, I—"

"I cannae have ye with me, lass. I have told ye already that ye mayn't follow me," he interrupted.

"But, I can help," I rebutted.

"Ye dinnae understand. I must see tae it that ye are returned tae whaur ye belong."

"No, I belong with you—where ever you go," I said anxiously. Leif paused momentarily, thwarted as he raked his hand through his loose hair. Visibly frustrated as he sighed, even so, I sensed him gently clasp the side of my cheek and tenderly stroke it with his thumb.

"Pray, *mo ghaol*, be a guid lass and listen tae me. Ye must return tae Concord at first lecht," he said earnestly.

"I can't."

"Dinnae be petulant."

"I'm not being petulant."

"Indeed ye are when ye dinnae listen tae me and disobey. Ye mayn't remain with me as I have already told ye."

"Look. I understand. I know that you have your concerns about me being with you. You think I'll get hurt or something."

"Aye, ye very weel micht. I cannae take that risk with yer welfare."

"Well, I agree about your concerns. They make a lot of sense."

"Then, ye will abide by me and do as expected. Yoo'll return tae Concord. Lord Almighty—whit if yoo're bairned? I cannae have ye or the bairn placed in any perils by being with me."

"But, I'm not pregnant."

"How do ye ken that yoo're not yet bairned?"

"Because I just finished having my period."

"I dinnae understand."

"You know—that time of month for me. It came and went."

"Ye speak of when ye bleed?"

"Yeah, so... I'm not pregnant. I would know if I were."

"Regardless. Ye wulnea remain."

"The thing is, is that I know medicine, though. I know things others don't know—I can help. I can be of assistance. I'm an asset, because I can benefit those who might get hurt. I can help you," I said, suddenly trying to convince him. He paused again for a moment. I could perceive him pondering in the moonlight, and all I knew was that I didn't want to turn back—that I had to stay with him. "Please... I can help you. Let me be useful to you this way. I can possibly save lives," I said again, but he continued to remain silent. "Isn't that worth something?"

"Not at the expense of yer possible injury, or getting killed," he said seriously.

"I won't get hurt or killed. I can help people. I can help you," I insisted.

"I reckon that micht be true," he acknowledged finally, still seeming not wholly convinced. "Yet, I dinnae believe it wise. 'Tis perilous fur ye. I wulnae have ye in such a circumstance. Yoo'll not risk yerself in the wilderness or at the fort. I shan't have it."

"I won't be a liability. I promise you."

"Ye cannae make me such a vow when ye will have nae control over the perils that are guaranteed tae occur."

"But I know medicine very well. I'm extremely well trained. I'm a really good doctor. I can help—and, like I said, I won't get in the way. I'll just work in the hospital assisting the injured. Please let me come with you—please," I repeated imploringly. He paused momentarily and didn't say anything as I sensed him thinking some more. At length he released a heavy sigh and shook his head.

"Soldiering is hard work, lass. I would have thought that ye waur not keen on the fact efter yer experience trekking through the wood last summer."

"Well—I'm not that frail after all."

"I reckon not. Nonetheless, a soldier's life is unappealing—particularly fur the lass who may accompany him."

"But, I'm not a weakling. Haven't I already proven that to you? I mean if I just knew how to fire a pistol, I'd be as good as Annie Oakley and would be able to protect myself if I had to, since you're so worried about me."

"I raither not have ye handle a pistol lest ye accidentally blow yerself tae kingdom come. Ye best put that notion out of yer bonnie wee head reit now."

"I'm just saying that I can learn to withstand the rigors of what you experience as a soldier."

"Nae. I ken all too weel whit men can withstand whilst thaur are plenty of lads who fall by the wayside due tae the hardships of war. I am certain that any lass would find it unbearable. Ye cannae withstand it."

"Yes, I can."

"Ye cannae. Ye huvnea the notion of wit yer saying. Ye dinnae ken the hardship of it."

"I could probably endure some of it, though. I know what it's like to hike for hours and camp for an undetermined length of time. Remember?"

"Yoo'll miss the comfort and security of our home more than ye ken if ye join me. Ye dinnae understand it at present, yet thaur are unforeseen trials that would nae doubt cause a lass tae weep day in and day out."

"Well, what about all of the camp followers, then? Don't

they seem to be able to cope? I mean, I wonder how they manage with all the challenges they face too. It seems that if they can't handle the difficulties, then why aren't they forbidden to join the soldiers? What do they have to offer that the soldiers can't already do for themselves? It doesn't make any sense to me otherwise."

"Do ye not ken whit the purpose of those lasses are?" He sounded rather surprised in the dark shadows between the trees.

"No," I said, shaking my head.

"Imagine a harlot," he said bluntly.

"Oh..." I felt a modicum of embarrassment all of a sudden as I realized his meaning. "Well, regardless of their companionship interests with the troops, those women still have to meet the challenges that the soldiers face also. So, really, what's the difference?"

"Jesus, Mary and Joseph... Whit am I tae do with ye, *àille dhubh*?"

"Let me come with you."

"Ye came all this way fur me, did ye?"

"Yes." I nodded my head.

"'Tis not wise."

"You already told me that."

"Aye..." He broke off, seeming to think again as his eyes never wavered from mine.

"Please..." I implored him once more. He sighed and raked his fingers through his loose hair again.

"Dinnae tell me that ye wulnae return tae Concord."

"I won't go back."

"I kent ye would say so. I closely have it in mind tae haul ye back tae Concord myself."

"But, you won't."

"I huvnea the opportunity. I need tae be in Albany promptly instead. However, I can have anither lad escort ye."

"Please—don't."

"Whyever not?"

"I'll just follow you again," I said. The moonlight caught the smirk on his face and a light chuckle eluded him.

"Yoo're obstinant—as obstinant as an ass, *àille dhubh*."

"I don't mean to be one," I lightly joked. But he didn't laugh now.

"I ought tae turn ye upon my knee and tan yer backside fur not minding me," he said seriously. "However, ye do ken how tae reason."

"So, does that mean I can stay with you?"

"Aye. I reckon so," he finally permitted, slightly nodding his head in accordance.

"Thank you," I said, relieved, and abruptly wrapped my arms around his broad chest. He released me from my embrace and firmly took me by my shoulders as he stared directly at me without any hint of humor. I could easily discern the sternness on his face in the moonlight, and it completely grabbed my attention with a little fear.

"However, ye listen tae me," he continued earnestly.

"Yes?"

"Listen weel. Ye must stay with me at all times. I must ken whaur ye are always. Ye mayn't simply wander off as ye are free tae do whilst at home. Ye must never leave my secht—ever. Ye must listen tae whit I tell ye and do it. Do ye understand me?" he instructed unyieldingly. His low voice came forth noticeably firm and sounded extraordinarily serious in the dark shadows surrounding us.

"Yes, I understand. I'll do everything you say," I promised.

"Alrecht," he said adequately. "Come," he concluded and started leading me back inside the camp. He returned walking with me and guided us toward Finley while he remained standing pensively smoking his pipe by the log where he was first sitting.

"So?" Finley said, turning pointedly to Leif when we arrived at him.

"I have permitted her tae stay," Leif informed him.

"Yoo've whit?" Finley responded with sheer disapproval as his brow raised high on his head.

"She knows how tae heal," Leif reminded.

"I say! Whit will ye do if she gets hurt?" Finley asked disagreeably, now glowering at Leif.

"I shall see tae it that she will not," Leif guaranteed.

"Och! How micht ye manage that?" Finley responded preposterously.

"I shall see tae it," Leif repeated without question. Finley said something to Leif in Scottish. Leif responded in the same language. They went back and forth for a moment, obviously disagreeing with each other.

"Quit thinking with yer cock, Seamus! Yoo'll have us all killed!" Finley shot back entirely disgruntled.

"She remains and 'tis final!" Leif retorted.

"As a blockhead would respond!" Finley insulted, suddenly storming off while muttering irately in his native tongue. I was pretty sure he was swearing up a storm as he left Leif standing alone with me. Finley disappeared around the campfire toward the opposite side of camp when Leif subsequently turned his gaze to me. "Ye must be full of hunger by now."

"Yeah—actually, I am," I realized meekly.

"Let's git ye fed, then," he suggested shortly.

I followed him toward the campfire where he sat me down on a stool. I watched him prepare a tin plate of venison and bread. He passed the portion to me and sat beside me as I delicately began tearing bits of the meat apart with my fingers. I thought the smoky flavor tasted pretty good and reminded me a tad of smoked beef. The bread was hard as a brick, though. Good thing I didn't wear dentures, I thought, as I was struggling to bite a piece off of it.

"Permit me," Leif urged as he took the piece of bread from me. He pulled out his canteen and doused it with rum. He handed the piece of bread back to me when he sufficiently covered it, and it was noticeably softer when I received it from him. After several bites of the drenched bread, I believed I was satiated from eating, and it occurred to me that I was very thirsty. Observing me, he held out his wooden canteen for me to take.

"No thank you," I said.

"Ye need it," he said.

"I can't—it's too much," I replied.

"I ken yoo're not fond of it, but ye need it. 'Tis all I have fur ye," he said, urging me to take the canteen.

"Why don't you ever carry water?" I asked strangely, reluctantly taking the canteen from him. I forced myself to chug a bit of the rum and quickly drew it from my lips, cringing at the burning bite of the alcohol as it went scorching down my throat.

"Water can kill ye," he said factually.

"Excuse me?" I laughed a little, giving him an absurd look as I immediately started feeling warm from the alcohol.

"It certainly can. Moreover, rum will keep ye warm on cool nichts like this," he said, not much amused. "Come, now—I reckon ye have had yer fill fur tonecht."

He took my plate from my lap and tossed the remaining bread into the fire. Then he clasped my arm and pulled me to my feet before leading me away from the flames. I followed him a few paces away from the campfire when he stopped in his steps and leaned to grab his satchel and blanket that he already had sprawled out over the ground for the night. He continued walking with me, relocating to a more secluded location in camp behind shrubbery and a cluster of young trees. He dropped his satchel to the ground and spread the large blanket out at our feet.

"We shall bunk haur tonecht," he said.

"Okay," I agreed simply. I proceeded lying down over the blanket and he positioned himself behind me. He flung the blanket over me and cocooned us close together. I sensed him roll to his side, and he wrapped an arm around my waist drawing me into his secure embrace. His hand roved up over my abdomen and finally rested splayed over my heart, naturally cupping the place over my breast when he fitted me snugly against his spooning body. I squeezed my hand over the back of his palm, locking my entwined fingers with his, and I felt him silently press his lips over the back of my head.

The night air was temperate and calm with a faint sound of the towering trees above rustling their heavy boughs in the delicate breeze. The audible sound of infinite crickets creaked around us, and fireflies intermittently flashed all around us as they danced in the night air. I soon closed my eyes listening to the night's sound and began drifting in a dream with Leif holding me in his arms, feeling comforted and satiated.

Twenty-Three

At daybreak the camp stirred with men pacing around collecting their belongings, readying themselves to move out. In approximately a half hour, we were setting out on the road continuing due west.

I rode on Oakley alongside Leif mounted high on Blaze at the end of the procession line. Finley rode tall in military fashion on his horse in the vanguard as it was clear that the brothers were in disagreement with each other and cared not to share in each other's company for the time being. But after a while, Finley dropped behind the traveling troops until he reached us at the back of the procession and rode beside Leif. He started talking to Leif in Scottish and Leif responded in their language. Their conversation sounded even toned, but serious also. It didn't seem they were arguing anymore and that things were settling between them as they conversed. I ventured a glance toward Leif during their discussion and happened to glimpse at Finley as he coincidentally caught my eye while insinuating me. I realized then that I was most likely the topic of their conversation, and felt somewhat uneasy about it.

When they had finished speaking, Finley urged his horse

forward and returned to the front of the line. Leif rode quietly beside me after Finley returned to his position while I was feeling uncomfortable that the brothers had quarreled because of me.

"I'm sorry for causing an argument between you and Finley," I said finally, interrupting the silence between us. Leif suddenly turned his gaze to me and looked a little unexpected.

"Och, never ye mind, *ceisdein*. We shall recover fair enough," he assured with an appreciative look.

"I hope so," I said.

"Certainly," he promised and winked reassuringly at me. I smiled a little at him, believing him, but still troubled by it. "The men are presently weary. We shall cease momentarily fur a respite. Can ye hold fast fur a bit more?"

"Yeah, I think so," I replied, undoubtedly feeling tired right now also.

"Alrecht," he said adequately.

Soon, we arrived at a rushing brook and finally dismounted our horses for a break. The men marching were pleased to settle for a while to rest their tired feet and to take a smoke along with a drink. Leif led our horses to the stream for them to drink from it, and while they were drinking water, he reached inside one of the saddle bags, pulling forth his wooden canteen. He uncorked the lid and gulped all that was left inside of it before kneeling over the rocks at the stream to dip his canteen beneath the rushing water, filling it to the brim. In a moment, when he was done filling it, he straightened and handed the weighty canteen to me.

"I think I remember you saying water can kill you," I reminded as I took the canteen from him and started gladly drinking the cold, crisp, fresh water from it. An amused eyebrow arched high over his eye.

"This is rushing water. I meant still water," he clarified.

"Really?" I replied skeptically.

"Aye."

"Well, in that case, you should probably know that one

hundred percent proof alcohol that you like to drink so much can kill you too," I remarked with a mocking expression on my face.

"Is that reit?" he responded dubiously.

"Yes, it is—actually."

"Hmph! Weel, I shall enjoy it before it kills me."

"You have a reason for everything you do that's harmful to you."

"I dinnae perceive it being harmful tae me the least bit. Yet, I micht reckon that my enjoyment of ye has the near same merry affect upon my spirit more so, and that I shall indeed die a happy man," he professed ironically. I smiled at him and took a final sip of water. I drew the canteen from my quenched lips and passed it back to him. He refilled it to capacity, corked it, then attached it next to one of the large saddlebags on his horse.

Afterward, he proceeded pacing mindfully over the boulders lining the silt bank, and I followed him upstream. Some of the rocks were large and slippery from lichen and moisture by the water covering them. He lunged for me, firmly grabbing my wrist and assisted me over the larger, more treacherous rocks.

After some pacing and climbing up stream, he decided to cease going any farther at a little inlet tucked by a thicket of vegetation displaying fragrant lily-of-the-valley clusters. I glanced behind and discovered us slightly hidden at a distance from the rest of the infantry. But, if we sat behind the large rock facing us, we would be completely concealed from them all.

"Ye may refresh yerself haur, if ye wish," he suggested.

"Yes, thank you," I said gratefully.

Leif leaped up and placed himself sitting above on the large overlooking rock facing me. He watched me remove my gloves and twirl my long ponytail around into a tight bun. I then began unfastening the buttons holding my riding jacket closed. When the buttons were undone, I removed my jacket and shirt from my shoulders, exposing my pair-of-bodies and fitted white camisole style undergarment as I went to the stream to lightly bathe.

I bent over the streaming water at the edge and splashed the frigid water over my face, refreshing my dusty pores. The water felt sharp and stimulating over my warm skin as I rubbed the dirt from my moistened face and cleansed beneath my arms. When I had finished, I straightened and released my ponytail from my bun, then stepped back toward him while he was observing me as he held my belongings over his knee.

I reached to retrieve my shirt and riding jacket from him, and re-concealed my torso. When I had completed fastening my jacket closed, he stretched forth a hand for me to take and briskly hauled me up over the rock to sit with him. We sat with our backs to the company downstream talking comfortably with each other. The conversation was light between us, and I was glad to be with him on this journey. He was a good story teller, I believed; he always seemed to have a way with words that invariably drew me inside his tale that had me smiling or laughing out right. I was aware of him watching my reaction to him as he told his stories, and I think he seemed to get a kick out of my reaction to him, as he responded with further inspiration to make me laugh.

I leaned to collect a small bouquet of lily-of-the-valley flowers as our conversation naturally waned, and I sensed his hand covering mine. He held it and drew it over his lap, gently possessing it. As he was holding my hand, I gazed out over the sparkling creek, listening to the rushing sound of the water quickly moving by, while quietly sitting with him. A nice feeling came over me while being with him in this serene, primitive landscape. An intrinsic awareness opened my senses and everything seemed as it should be—as if the universe had been balanced and set into harmony. It didn't seem like anything could go wrong—and, the feeling deeply comforted me.

"I fear my weakness fur ye, *mo ghaol*," he started meditatively, interrupting the tranquility between us.

"What are you talking about?" I asked oddly, turning my attention to him as I smelled the fresh, sweet, waxy aroma of my bouquet in hand. He shifted his gaze from overlooking the water and met my eyes.

"I worry about ye being with bairn whilst yoo're with me," he expressed, really concerned.

"Oh…" I realized uncomfortably.

"I dinnae have sheep skins with me," he said realistically.

"Oh…" I replied again, feeling uncertain about this conversation.

"I dinnae ken how I micht prevent it in this case," he considered.

"I see," I said subtly, knowing I had knowledge of my birth control method and wondering whether to reveal it to him finally. Sitting with him now, I began considering my growing guilt over the fact that I was secretly regulating my fertility cycle, and the promise I had made to him about never to lie to him. While truthfully, I had never told him a lie while married to him, the notion that he wasn't aware of what I knew about it turned it into deception. I knew that wasn't fair, and therefore it wasn't right of me. Particularly being my husband, I was aware that he had a special right to his choice too. So, I decided to reach inside the side pocket of my jacket. "I thought about it too—so, I made this," I said to him as I showed him the ring of beads that I had created.

"Have ye?" He appeared puzzled as he glanced at the beads.

"Yeah," I admitted softly as I handed them to him.

"Whit is this?" he asked curiously, gazing at them in the center of his palm.

"Beads," I replied.

"Aye, I can plainly see. A ring of them."

"They're called cycle beads," I disclosed.

"Och," he responded unknowingly. He had a questioning look on his face as he examined them between his large fingers.

"It's a measure of birth control—another way to prevent pregnancy," I continued revealing.

"Och," he responded naïvely. He strangely scrutinized them as he inserted his fingers through the ring and fondled the beads with his thumb.

"It's quite effective—almost one hundred percent," I said.

"Och," he replied distractedly as he confusedly scrutinized the ring of beads. I noticed his expression becoming flush and he seemed reticent—almost embarrassed—as I watched him examining them. "Micht it go about my cock before I bed ye?" he inquired abashedly.

"No!" I gasped all of a sudden, inadvertently giggling in response. He quickly seemed put off. "I'm sorry—please forgive me. I'm not making fun of you—I just didn't expect you to say that," I said sincerely.

"Och," he accepted.

"It's for me. It helps me keep track of my menstrual cycle—you know, every month," I explained.

"Ye mean when ye bleed?"

"Yeah."

"I see." He seemed relieved that it wasn't meant for him to use as he was now gazing intently at me.

"You see, each bead represents a day," I pointed out and started explaining to him how it worked in simplified terms.

"And it is efficacious, ye say?" he inquired amazedly once I had finished explaining the method to him.

"It's very effective," I assured.

"Curious..." He glanced meditatively back at the beads still in his hand for a moment before returning his gaze to me. "It appears harmless."

"Yes, it's completely safe," I validated.

"I see." Even though he said this, he nevertheless seemed abstracted by the novelty of it as he paused for a second longer, looking down at the beads in his hand again, seeming to ponder the concept. "I reckon 'tis wise of ye tae have considered it," he recommended, breaking the little lull between us.

"Well, I knew it was a concern," I said.

"Aye," he said remotely.

"So—now, it should be all right," I said, considering him.

"I micht not be concerned, then?" he asked, focusing again on me as he returned his gaze to mine.

"No... we don't have to be," I verified. Leif silently returned the collection of beads into my palm, and I tucked them back inside my pocket, aware of him watching me.

"So be it," he rejoined decidedly, fixing unwavering eyes to mine when I returned looking at him from my pocket. "I reckon 'twill be suitable—fur now."

Suddenly an abrupt whistle sounded out from behind us. Leif glanced over his shoulder and noticeably waved once.

"'Tis time fur us tae take our leave, *àille dhubh*," he said, turning to me as he proceeded straightening from his seat over the rock.

"All right," I said. He leaned for my arm and pulled me upward, assisting me to my feet. He then turned, beginning down the boulder, and I followed him with his help while pacing carefully back over the rocky path downstream to re-join the men.

When we arrived at our horses, Leif decided to tether Oakley to Blaze. He subsequently lifted me high over Blaze and swung himself with swift ease over his horse, mounting himself firm behind me. Now that we were sharing his horse, he gently urged Blaze to move forward after the last contingent line of men and followed them back onto the road.

WE HAD JOURNEYED for a long while now. The swaying motion of Blaze's movement and the rhythmic sound of his clucking hooves over the dirt began lulling me. Leif had fixed a securing arm around my waist since our departure, and I now succumbed to leaning my back against his broad, firm chest while resting my head against his shoulder. At which point, I sensed him softly leaning his slightly stubbled jaw on the side of my head as his muscular thighs unintentionally rubbed against mine when he began humming. I felt his breath against my skin as he lightly hummed a gentle melody in my ear, and my eyelids grew heavy. After a moment it seemed like weights pulled them shut and in a second, I was drifting to sleep.

I gathered that I had dozed a good little bit, since Leif carefully awakened me and I discovered us now stopped off the road. We broke for a moment at this time in order to simply relieve ourselves and then continued onward along the path going west.

FINALLY, we had arrived at a small clearing before a pond where the men set up camp for the night. Of the men, Leif was the only one who had pitched his tent as the men were settling before nightfall.

Soon twilight came upon us when the colors in the sky quickly turned into darker tones, and different hues of changing blue, purple, orange, and gold over the horizon gleamed by the setting sun.

The sun had set quickly and darkness was now surrounding us when I entered the tent ready to lie my weary self down over Leif's blanket on the ground. As I finally rested on the blanket inside the privacy of his tent, the contingent of men sat around campfires talking and gambling with drinks and pipe smoke like they had done the night before. I could hear Leif and Finley not too far away among the others talking as friends beyond the canvas drapes, and it seemed that the brothers had put aside their differences and resumed their benign demeanors toward each other. While listening to them converse, I kicked off my boots ready to rest, getting comfortable at last, glad that things were pleasant between them again.

Twenty-Four

Within two more days we had arrived deep inside the Connecticut River Valley. I was quickly reminded after joining Leif on this journey of how rough traveling could be as we trekked seemingly endlessly on foot and on horseback through the rising elevation. But this time, unlike the last, it seemed a lot more achievable now that I was contented with Leif and had my own horse.

When we entered the Berkshires and Fort Massachusetts came into view between the trees in a wide clearing at the Hoosic River, I instinctively knew with distinction that we were close to the area where I went missing. But, the compulsion to return home was strangely almost nonexistent as the distant memory of my former life seemed hazy in my mind. Although I still considerably missed my family and friends along with all the modern technological conveniences in my era, it rather felt like a boat drifting by me in the fog, and I oddly didn't care that I was missing it, because it wasn't mine to catch at this time to return home.

It rained hard the day we arrived at the fort and heavily into the night with lightning and thunder. There were few barracks at this fort, so I slept on a narrow cot with a thin hay mattress while Leif and Finley slept on the floor. Many of the other men were packed in like sardines in other tight quarters, unfortunately—sometimes six or ten to a small compartment.

It continued to rain well into the next day and into the following days, inhibiting our ability to travel, which impeded our next arrival time. Therefore, it seemed we would be held up here for several more days due to this bad weather.

A WEEK PASSED before the rain ceased, and the sun shone again before we were able to push forth to Albany.

In roughly a day and a half, we had finally reached Albany from Fort Massachusetts, and I was glad to arrive in a populated town again as I remembered this place from my previous experience here last summer when I was first transported to this era. It was dark by the time we had ridden into town and arrived at Fort Frederick where Leif and Finley checked in with their troops. Once the commanding colonel briefly concluded business with the brothers, all the men were left to find quarters, and I arrived with Leif and Finley at the Rasmussen's residence.

Mr. and Mrs. Rasmussen pleasantly welcomed us back into their home when we entered their foyer from outdoors once we were received by their footman. Mr. and Mrs. Rasmussen were especially surprised, but politely complimentary, when they immediately learned of Leif's marriage to me and offered kind congratulations. But as they did so, I remembered their daughters—particularly Grete, their eldest—as the daughters were presently greeting us in their well-coached, modest manner, listening to the revelation of our good marital news being discussed with their parents once we had been shown into the drawing room.

My eyes circumstantially landed on Grete when the color simultaneously drained from her rosy cheeks as she learned of Leif's dissolved bachelorhood due to me. She narrowed her mean eyes on me and started sniveling, ultimately storming out of the drawing room up the staircase in a complete tizzy with her comforting sister, Elsa, who was close in age, following her. A sudden thick uncomfortable silence descended in the drawing room, and I unexpectedly looked at Mr. and Mrs. Rasmussen with regret. They appeared clearly chagrined and were at a loss for words, momentarily. Mr. Rasmussen shot his wife a stern look, and she nervously glanced at him before her worried eyes bounced toward me.

"Bitte, I beg your pardon, Your Grace. Our daughter is quite sensitive to such matters," Mrs. Rasmussen apologized to me with perceivable mortification.

"Ja, she is quite a fool. She will be reprimanded for her rudeness, Your Grace," Mr. Rasmussen said to Leif as he looked at him uneasily.

"Aye," Leif agreed.

"Ja, I shall see to her punishment immediately," Mrs. Rasmussen said as she nervously glanced at Leif also.

"It's quite all right, really," I replied understandingly instead. I was caught off guard by Grete's sudden distraught reaction and by her parents' strict response to her. I inadvertently glanced at the brothers; they both appeared absolutely emotionless over the issue.

"Danke schöen, Your Grace. You are most kind," Mrs. Rasmussen responded gratefully to me.

"Surely you needn't worry," I replied.

"We do not tolerate insolence. Our daughter will first apologize to Your Graces before she is punished. Bring Grete to me, promptly," Mr. Rasmussen ordered his wife. Mrs. Rasmussen suddenly curtsied before us and immediately left the room.

As we remained in the drawing room waiting for his wife to return with Grete, not a word was said between anyone as discomfiture filled the air. It wasn't long before Mrs. Rasmussen appeared again with Grete pacing in front of her into the room. Mrs. Rasmussen brought Grete to stand directly before me as she faced her father and Leif, who was sitting beside me and Finley in chairs.

"Apologize this instant, Grete!" her father ordered irately.

"Ja, Father," she said meekly, with tears still streaking down her ruddy face. Her irritated blue eyes shifted toward me. "I beg your pardon, Your Grace. Please have mercy upon my soul by granting me forgiveness for my rudeness to you. Pray, do not believe that I am not pleased by your matrimony. I wish you much happiness," she strove to say without sniveling.

"Yes, of course, thank you. It's very nice of you to say," I replied politely.

"Now, remove yourself from my sight, Grete," Mr. Rasmussen said again in the same irate manner.

"Ja, Father," Grete complied spiritlessly. She bobbed a quick curtsy and swiftly turned out of the drawing room, leaving us.

"See to her punishment, Mistress Rasmussen," Mr. Rasmussen demanded of his wife.

"Ja, Master Rasmussen," Mrs. Rasmussen abided by her husband and properly excused herself from us. After the apology, Mr. Rasmussen seemed to collect himself from his irritation as the matter was still being settled with Grete's ensuing punishment.

I wondered how the eighteen-year-old girl would be punished as I considered that she was far too old to receive any kind of actual reprimand. However, as I reconsidered the strictness of this family, I hoped the punishment for her would not be too severe and suspected that a verbal chastisement was what she would receive. But soon a scream and audible crying was heard coming from upstairs, and I knew that she got more than a simple tongue lashing from her mother. I was suddenly stunned and unsettled by this as Mr. Rasmussen was indifferent to the wailing coming from upstairs when he ordered a couple of their maids, Hope and Mary —who I'd remembered from the last time I had visited the Rasmussens—to properly show us to our rooms for our stay this evening.

❆

As Leif and I were settling in our room for the evening, I sat at the dressing table in my dressing gown combing out the deep tangles collected in my ringlets, fairly disturbed over the violent punishment Grete had received from her parents. While I was striving with some frustration to detangle my hair, I determined that it had grown far too long than what I had been accustomed to and realized that it was high time for a normal haircut. Fussing over my hair, I unexpectedly noticed Leif's reflection in the looking glass staring at me as he relaxed in bed smoking his pipe from across the room.

"What?" I responded modestly.

"Yoo're bonnie," he said simply while watching me.

"Oh—this hair is driving me crazy. I need a haircut," I sighed flippantly.

"Ye will do nae such thing," he forbade appallingly.

"Why not?"

"Yer hair is as it ought tae be. 'Tis bonnie, and yoo'll not crop it," he said certainly. I saw myself appearing ridiculous in the looking glass as my curls were now frizzy.

"I look like Bozo," I said, frustrated with myself.

"Bozo?" He grimaced, appearing puzzled.

"Yes."

"Who micht he be?"

"A stupid jester."

"Och!" he chuckled. "Do ye realize all the lasses desire hair like yers?"

"No—they don't."

"Aye, 'tis indeed true, fur they certainly dinnae have tresses that curl naturally like yers. They must sleep with rags tied about their heads tae mimic such locks."

"How do you know?" I asked. He arched an eyebrow over his sparkling ultramarine eye.

"Why, I have already told ye of the lasses I have seen in my past, and that is the manner in which they trained their hair in order tae style it similar tae yers," he said. I suddenly raised an eyebrow also as I gazed at him, looking at me in the looking glass.

"Right. How could I possibly forget about your past beautiful exploits," I said sarcastically.

"Dinnae be jealous."

"I'm not at all jealous."

"Ye ought not be. They could never match yer beauty. As fact would have it, every lass that I have encountered with ye haur in these colonies all desire tae be as bonnie as ye. Their beauty pales in comparison tae yers."

"You're flattering me."

"I am truthful."

"But, there are plenty perfectly pretty fair haired, blue eyed girls all around that get quite the attention," I countered ironically.

"They are all merely the same," Leif said, unimpressed.

"Still. I'm the odd ball here."

"Being unique is a blessing. It places ye in a category that cannae be surmounted by those lasses who envy ye."

"You're really kind, but you don't have to stroke my ego when I can plainly see what the beauty standard is."

"I am not speaking frivolously. Regardless, the lads as weel as the lasses all ken who the fairest is. Whit is usual disnae intrigue those who appreciate whit is unique, and I fur one dinnae fancy a common well-bred lass, fur they bore me. Save the Indian lasses who are irregular, and are raither a fricht if they are not praying," he said. I laughed, outlandishly looking at him; *they are a fright? I disagree. And, who could ever frighten him? Especially a girl?*

"Whatever. You're nuts." I nervously looked at him.

"*Nuts?*" He gave me a weird look.

"Yeah—you know, coo-coo—*looney*—I mean, like a lunatic."

"Och, aye!" He suddenly laughed. "Weel, I assure ye that I am entirely in command of my faculties, and do reckon the lasses envy ye."

"Hmm... I'm not sure what to say, except I don't wish to be envied," I replied while observing his reflection contentedly puffing away on his pipe in bed.

"Yet ye are, as ye ken that Grete disnae like ye," he resumed after several puffs of smoke.

"We all know that," I said obviously.

"The reason fur it being that yoo're bonnie—plainly simple. 'Tis the same reason why Constance didnae like ye."

"That's absurd."

"Those lasses wish tae tear yer hair out if they had the opportunity," he said actually.

"Good grief! Do you know how ridiculous that sounds?"

"Nae, when it is the truth."

"Seems unbelievable. Are you sure they'd do that?"

"Certainly."

"I've never known anyone to behave that way."

"I have seen plenty lasses curse anither over jealousy due tae their fondness fur a particular lad. Thaur was a lass that I kent who hexed her rival over a lad she fancied."

"Really?" I asked, surprisingly.

"Och, aye. She placed a hex upon the lad instead and the next day he dropped dead in his tracks."

"What do you mean?"

"She cursed him tae spite the lass who loov'd him and hexed the lass as weel so that her hair fell out."

"Are you serious?"

"Quite."

"So, the guy just suddenly died?"

"Aye."

"Well, maybe the poor guy was in bad health and had a stroke or heart attack—something like that."

"The lass cursed him. That is whit occurred tae him, as she

promptly sent him tae his grave. And, as fur the other lass's hair, it indeed fell out."

"Well, I don't think Grete is the type to cast spells on people."

"She mayn't be a witch, however she micht ken one who would place a hex upon ye in her stead."

"That sounds absolutely asinine. Grete is clearly upset, yes, but I don't think she's unreasonable like that."

"Reason has nae meaning when it comes tae matters of the heart."

"I suppose that's true. But, I seem to think that her reason for being upset has less to do with me and more to do with you because she likes you and has a huge crush on you, and found out that we're now married when she didn't expect it," I said obviously, still trying to work the tangles from my hair. "You've known her longer than me, and she likely held some expectations regarding you."

"She micht have. I regret that her feelings waur hurt. 'Twas never my intention tae grant her false hope. However, did ye not see the manner in which she glowered at ye when she learnt of our matrimony?"

"Yes, I saw."

"Aye. She detests ye as the lass reckons that I wed ye fur yer beauty and is jealous of ye fur it," Leif said frankly.

I suddenly stopped brushing my ringlets, furrowing my brow. I turned from his reflection to look directly at him.

"Is that the real reason why you decided to marry me?" I asked ironically, feeling a bit annoyed.

"'Tis one reason," he divulged casually.

"Uh-hu."

"Also, since I wanted tae bed ye."

"Uh-hu."

"Which is quite marvelous, I say. Micht ye not agree?"

"Oh, sure..."

"And, fur yer wit."

"That's good—don't suppose you'd want a dull wife," I said sarcastically.

"Indeed, not," he replied with certainty.

"Well, that's fair. I wouldn't want a stupid husband for sure," I said flatly. He suddenly choked on his smoke for a minute, and coughed a lung as he chuckled. I noticed the color in his face had risen bright red once he recovered from coughing and returned a look of unexpected surprise. "Serves you right for smoking," I chastised.

"I beg yer pardon!" he chuckled again, sounding hoarse.

"It's not nice to beg," I teased.

"I say! Yer cheek is too much, lass!" he scolded lightly. I laughed and he smiled at me. "Yet," he resumed, seemingly collected again, "amongst other reasons ye already weel ken fur my wedding ye, I shall have ye ken the other reason fur why I did so is because ye and I agree with one anither in many respects. I otherwise wouldnae have found such agreement with any other lass but ye."

"That's nice of you to say," I realized.

"'Tis the truth."

"You're very sweet."

"I am naught of the sort. Yet, ye are indeed most sweet."

"Well, to me you are." I gazed thoughtfully back at him in the looking glass again when I decided to replace the brush over the dressing table and quickly finger comb my long ringlets. It seemed to do a much better job setting the curls back into shape. When I was satisfied, I stood from my seat at the dressing table and paced toward Leif to join him in bed. "You know?" I started as I removed my dressing gown, exposing my short shift that hung above my knees. I climbed over the mattress and settled next to him beneath the quilts.

"Aye?" he responded interestedly.

"You might want to put out that pipe before you burn the house down," I recommended.

"Och," he realized, appearing disappointed a little.

"I doubt the Rasmussens have fire insurance," I said.

"Fire insurance?" he repeated with a puzzled look.

"Yeah—property insurance. I suppose it's all the same thing here," I guessed.

"Och." He gazed quizzically at me.

"Or does that kinda thing not exist?"

"Och, it does. Merely, I would be the insurer," he said.

"Well, I don't see how that would do anybody any good if you've burned us all to a crisp, including yourself," I replied.

"Och!" he scoffed.

"You think I'm kidding."

"'Tis alrecht. I shall see tae it that it disnae occur," he dismissed nonchalantly while still puffing happily on his pipe. I gave him a certain look of disapproval. "Alrecht then," he resumed thoughtfully, pulling the mouthpiece from his lips and held his smoldering pipe in midair right above his upper lip. "Whit do ye propose other than whit I am currently enjoying tae entice me from my smoke?"

"Huh," I sighed, looking at him ridiculously.

"Weel?" he insisted, maintaining his questioning gaze on me.

"Geez, you are hopeless." He was looking at me with an incorrigible smirk, and I fathomed the hint he was giving me.

"I reckon that we have already established that notion about me," he said.

"Fine," I said, feigning annoyance as I slipped further back among the pillows. He arched an eyebrow and cocked a larger smile, looking very rakish. "Do as you will," I consented, giving him permission.

"Now that will greatly please me," he agreed and promptly snuffed out his pipe. He placed it over the nightstand beside him, subsequently blew out the candlelight but left the dimly burning oil lamp alone on the mantlepiece, slid further beneath the blankets and moved closely over me, caging me beneath him with his muscular body.

❄

EARLY THE FOLLOWING MORNING, I rode into Fort Frederick with the brothers where they had joined the rest of their regiment. It included companies of approximately two hundred men that we had originally traveled with from west of Concord. The number of men had visibly expanded to an impressive number of what I presumed had to be roughly five to six hundred men.

After an hour of organizing, a large mass of redcoats ensued, moving out, marching on foot to the beat of a thumping *rat-a-tat-tat* over loud snare drums that shook the air. As infantry lines began moving into order and falling out from the fort through town, several officers gathered at the back end of the last procession line. When Leif aligned Blaze beside Oakley, I noticed some women mixing alongside some of the troops intending to join the arduous journey north. I wondered if these were camp followers that Leif had informed me about during our earlier conversation as I was observing them mingle with some of the men.

As I was watching everyone organize themselves into marching lines, I glanced at Leif who was acknowledging Finley while he was aligning his horse with Leif's on the other side. The commanding colonel was also arranging his horse behind the brothers when he noticed me. He appeared to be a fit, clean-shaven man in his mid-fifties, and I quickly assumed he was a rather hard man, given his razor-thin lips, blunt square-cut jaw, aged broad brow that set his face emotionless—the kind of man the military always loved to use in order to carry out merciless war campaigns to ultimately benefit the nation's advantage over the enemy. Despite his appearance, he still owned a genuine sense of commanding civility and refinement, which elevated him beyond the brutality I was sure he was capable of commanding others to commit.

"My lords," the colonel greeted his majors as he positioned his horse behind them.

"Colonel Monro," Finley replied in step with protocol.

"Colonel Monro," Leif ensued with the same rigid demeanor. I detected the brothers exchange reserved looks. "This is my wife, Her Grace, Duchess of Monteith," Leif continued to introduce me to the colonel.

"Indeed?" Colonel Monro questioned with slightly raised fury brows. He shot a cool glance at me. "Your Grace," he said in acknowledgment to me.

"Pleased to meet you, Colonel Monro," I replied politely.

"A pleasure," the colonel responded. "Do ye suppose, Major Monteith, that fort living may not be suitable for Her Grace tae experience?" Colonel Monro inquired straightforwardly, addressing Leif in a stout manner.

"Her Grace is quite knowledgeable in the art of healing, Colonel. I reckoned that her skills are second tae none, and will be a benefit tae the lads who micht be injured," Leif said evenly.

"Is that so?" Colonel Monro questioned with surprise.

"Aye," Leif confirmed.

"In that case, major, as I thank ye for her charity, let us pray that Her Grace will indeed remain well, and that it not be a decision we may later regret," Colonel Monro implied coolly in his Scottish brogue. I glanced at Leif as he remained impassive. He emotionlessly gazed forward over the heads of the immediate abundant troops still standing before us from the seat of his tall horse.

"Indeed," Finley said, agreeing with the colonel.

"I'm certain Her Grace will be of great value tae us, sir," Leif reiterated confidently.

"At whit cost, however?" Colonel Monro replied with a pensive expression that appeared dour.

"I have permitted her joining me in order that we may benefit from her healing skill as I am awaur that we huvnae a surgeon amongst us," Leif said instead.

"Is she raither knowledgeable in the art of healing?" Colonel Monro asked.

"Significantly, Colonel."

"Wulnae the hardships of living within the wilderness amongst soldiers try Her Grace too hard, major?"

"She is a fit woman, Colonel. I do recognize her strength, and fathom she will suit our need fur a surgeon whilst we await the time being before we acquire a proper one."

"In which case, let us pray that we obtain a surgeon soon tae spare Her Grace from any hardship at all from the trying duty that will be imposed upon her welfare whilst she may face peril," Colonel Monro said with a note of disagreement in his voice.

"Aye, Colonel," Leif acknowledged while keeping his stalwart gaze looking forward at the troops ahead of us. But Finley slid Leif a sidelong glance, and I continued to sense from him that he still didn't agree with my presence. Instead, he carried the same skepticism belonging to the colonel expressed on his face, although the differences between the brothers about me had been seemingly resolved.

Subsequently, the troops in front of us began moving out, and we started our horses. We exited the stone archway at Fort Frederick and moved through town with an entire battalion on foot and horseback headed north.

Within minutes we were out of town and now marching deep in the dense primitive forest. The forest was overwhelming as it enveloped us along the way on the path. The spring air was mild and fragrant with mountain flora, moss, and damp earth while thick patches of poison ivy blanketed the base around the trees beside the road. Beams of bright yellow sunlight entered intermittently among the sky-scraping trees and illuminated the thick vegetation in gold.

The trek was long with few breaks in between, and I had a sense that the journeying was going to be rough all over again from the moment I first arrived here. Colonel Monro was determined to arrive at our next destination in due time, so the men pressed onward—and this time I felt more mentally prepared to endure this hardship.

WE HAD COVERED many miles by the time the sun dimmed and the forest became completely shaded. Having traveled a distance past Fort George as it was currently overrun with soldiers, we bypassed it for another camping location until we soon came to a clearing around a small lake where we were finally able to break, and the men were able to set up camp for the night. As I dismounted Oakley my legs felt like gelatin, and my rear-end felt like pins and needles poking me. Leif gathered Oakley and Blaze by the reins with me following him and led them toward the water for them to drink where he hitched them around a low hanging tree limb.

After securing our horses, he recommended that I sit on a nearby rock by the horses as his tent was being pitched. I sat contentedly observing the teeming men settling into camp as other tents went up and campfires were started. They easily began relaxing, talking and telling raunchy jokes, which caused outbursts of ruckus laughter everywhere among them. The soldiers were also quick to undress and brought out their long shirttails over their breeches when moving around camp with things to do before nightfall.

The women who had accompanied us were mostly camp followers and some maids who laundered and cooked for the regiment as cauldrons went up over flames. Abundant amounts of water were poured into them with heaps of potatoes and carrots thrown in. Some empty boots were laid over the camp site as the guys made themselves comfortably gathered on stools or easily sprawled out over the ground in their collective groups.

The site buzzed with activity as I detected the wagoneers parking loaded wagons. Men began unloading some of them. Boxes of ammunition remained in the wagons as the horses were unhitched from them and tied to trees or posts that had newly been erected. While watching the men from my vantage point, I noticed a man fixing and shining boots in front of his tent at a distance, when my gaze also landed on one man who had already attained a tin plate of beans, which reminded me of my own hunger as my stomach angrily growled. It seemed he had lost his spoon, or maybe he never had one to begin with, and creatively made do with a rusty broken hinge from a chest as a substitute—which struck me as unsavory. I glanced away from him and discovered several other men shoveling large mounds of soft earth into a heaping pile as they dug a deep hole. When they had completed it, I distastefully turned my gaze as one of them uninhibitedly tugged his breeches down to his knees, raised his shirt and crouched his bare bottom over the pit ready to have a bowel movement.

"Come along, *ceisdein*," Leif said, suddenly catching my attention as he now stood directly beside me. I stood from my seat over the rock and followed him inside our newly pitched tent, glad that I would be able to settle in now. When I entered the tent, I noticed how he had it nicely arranged for me to relax in private as I glanced around myself. I automatically went over to the blankets ready to lie over them, realizing how tired I was in spite of my hunger.

"Thank you," I said kindly, glimpsing over my shoulder at him standing by the entrance.

"Certainly. I shall feed ye now," he said.

"All right," I said, nodding my head also. A gentle grin tilted his lips and he winked at me before turning for the entrance where he stepped behind the drapes and vanished from sight, returning outdoors.

Alone now, waiting for his return, I moved toward the blankets and crouched as I proceeded to lay over them. As I peacefully began relaxing and listening to the rowdy male voices from outside surrounding me inside the tent, my mind began to wander. I started remembering my family and I wondered about their wellbeing; I knew they were grieving for me, but I wished they could know that I was well—and, that I was happy here because of my new husband.

My new husband... The idea of it still sometimes catches me by surprise, and my family would be completely shocked if they knew that I had gotten married again. Astonishment would be an under-statement—really. They'll be either hurt or excited by it—I have no way of knowing; if I had eloped in my era back at home, my parents would be undoubtedly upset with me and likely not accept my new husband the way I'd wish. But that is irrelevant now. My life is defi-nitely my own without them here to emotionally support me, and if I could tell them what I'm feeling, I'd tell them that I'm glad that I'm married to Leif.

Being stranded here is frightening; I still have no idea how I got here—and, I still feel very much out of my element... but out of all this chaos, I'm no longer alone. I have Leif now; I wasn't sure if we could be happy together, but it seems we are. My homesickness also seems to have waned—surprisingly—and as I've prayed about it, I think I now know why I might be here: hope. I've been given that blessing again by God through being thrust back into time. So, this is my new life now, being with Leif—and, it's so strange, but I never thought I could be happy living here...

Suddenly, Leif returned through the curtains inside the tent, distracting my thoughts as my attention landed on him. I noticed that he had no food in his hands to share.

"Is it all gone?" I asked regretfully.

"Nae, I have it fur ye. Raither, it remains outdoors with mine as the lads wish tae see ye—if ye dinnae mind visiting with them fur a wee bit as we eat. Then, ye may retire as ye wish," Leif preferred.

"Okay," I agreed, believing it was probably my duty to dine with the men. As I followed Leif out of the tent, I gasped with happy surprise as my eyes unexpectedly discovered Angus, Derek, Roy, Fearghus, Lachlan, Bearnard, Liam and Cole standing several paces away from the tent waiting to see me. I couldn't believe that I hadn't noticed them earlier, and it completely stumped me for a moment. Leif told me that they were part of the artillery unit, and they were far ahead of us in line over the road as they rode their horses.

They each greeted me with genuine kindness, and if I could—like in normal times—I would have given them each a big embrace. But propriety held me back. As we exchanged pleasant greetings, it was also very nice to see that they all appeared well and in good spirits.

Once we finished greeting each other, Leif led me away toward a chair. I gladly took my place at the portable table next to him and Finley once he had seated himself before enjoying dining with his reunited cousins along with Colonel Monro. Conversation was lively around the table as we dined on salted ham, potato stew and bread. This was the first time since leaving Northampton for Concord to witness our wedding back in the fall when the brothers had encountered their cousins, and it was a nice scene to see as they all sat around the table enjoying each other's company again.

After a while of dining and polite conversation, lantern light and campfire took the place of daylight as abundant fireflies bounced around us at the table. The night air was mild and smelled of thick campfire smoke. It reminded me of the times I had gone camping with my family as a girl and the thought made me wonder fondly of home again. But my thoughts of home didn't linger for long when I caught Leif glancing at me as he was smiling and laughing at the table while engaged in conversation with his companions. He subtly winked at me and I diffidently reciprocated his gesture with a smile which seemed to highlight the laughing grin already on his face.

AT LAST, when the evening had grown late and conversation around the table became calm and lax, I decided to politely excuse myself, bidding goodnight to everyone at the dining table and returned inside the tent. Leif thoughtfully had the tent pitched among some tall bushes for my privacy, so I placed the flickering lantern over a small stool unconcerned about my undressing shadow being projected onto the canvas screen.

When I had undressed down to my camisole, I slipped beneath the blankets and rested my weary head on the pillow, instantly closing my eyes and drifted to sleep.

Sometime much later during the night, however, I was gently roused from slumber as I sensed Leif sidling carefully beneath the blankets, warm and nakedly close beside me, and quietly drew me inside his nestling arms.

"What time is it?" I muttered as I naturally snuggled against him, hearing the crickets creaking audibly all around us outside.

"Midnecht, I reckon," he said softly behind my head. I sensed his fingers gently moving my loose ringlets behind my shoulder away from my face as he lightly stroked my cheek with the pad of his thumb. He pressed his lips on the top of my head, giving me a small kiss.

"I'm glad we're together, Leif," I sighed drowsily.

"I too," he replied. Silence ensued, and it was tranquil. His fingers trailed from my cheek over my shoulder when his palm slipped beneath my arm and cupped my breast where it stilled and held me. Placing my palm over his, I entwined our fingers and his hand contracted around mine. "Goodnecht, *mo leannan*," he said quietly among the stillness in the night.

"Goodnight," I whispered, listening to the sound of his light restful breathing which helplessly returned me to sleep.

<h1 style="text-align:center">Twenty-Five</h1>

L ate afternoon the next day we arrived at Fort Edward. The large stone fortress was flooded with redcoats camped both inside and out of the stone walls and stockade. The premises seemed rather lax in general with sutlers selling provisions while abundant whisky jugs, broken pipes, empty boots, and misplaced tools were left haphazardly on the grounds every which place. Drunken soldiers chuckling while playing cards, or publicly making out and having sex with camp followers, rather embarrassed me.

A disturbance had erupted between a pair of men within a gambling group as I was following Leif and Finley together with Colonel Monro toward the officers' barrack. It seemed one soldier had accused the other of cheating, and a precipitated fight had broken out between the two men with no one quickly intervening to squelch the disruption. Instead, the area cleared around the fighting men as their onlooking buddies cheered and jeered at them. Leif suddenly seized my arm with a solid grip, steering me closely along with him to keep me from becoming separated from him and mowed over by more men bulldozing their way around us to witness the fight.

Finley pushed the door open, and we entered inside the barracks following Monro. Immediately met by Colonel Frye, General Webb's second in command here, he mechanically greeted us and began logging Monro's arrival with his officers in place as he sat at his desk. Once military protocol was completed, we were escorted to our quarters by Lieutenant Hops.

Remaining inside our room as Leif left to retrieve our belongings, I glanced around our quarters, realizing this was really no picnic in the park, and I sighed, biting the bullet of this experience, thinking Leif might have been right about his hesitation on letting me join him. I paced toward the window and peered out of the uneven glass panes, observing the crowd outside. I supposed the fight had been settled as one guy was left bloodied on the ground and was currently being picked up to his unstable feet by a buddy of his. Relative normalcy seemed to have resumed after that.

As I studied my new surroundings through the window, I observed across the courtyard not too far away, a soldier obscenely grab a young buxom maid over her breast and lasciviously squeeze her backside as he blatantly planted a kiss over her lips before letting her go on her way. I automatically covered my mouth in appall understanding Leif's concern.

After a few moments, however, Leif returned with our belongings and proceeded to arrange the room appropriately for temporary stay.

ONCE WE HAD TIDIED ourselves for dinner from the outdoor dust, we went to the dining quarter and sat at the table with Finley, Monro, Frye, and some other lower-ranking officers, including the cousins. After a tenuous moment of waiting for the appearance of the fort's general to join us in dining to no avail, Colonel Frye impatiently proceeded to tear off a piece of salted ham and place it over his plate. Colonel Monro ensued, and so we also began preparing our plates with food to eat.

The conversation between the men was superficial and respectable, but also stilted. At one point during our meal, however, the conversation abruptly ceased as a man emerged from the next room haphazardly dressed with his shirttail completely out over his breeches and open at the chest exposing gray hairs. He appeared slightly drunk and disheveled. He languidly paced toward us at the table and took his seat at the head of it. I also noticed his wig was misplaced over his head as it was crooked with the pin-tucked curls to one side and the queue covering one ear. A young maid was also detected entering the room from the same door while she was fastening the front of her short-gown. She uneasily glanced at all of us as the man put out his cheek for her to kiss. She gave him a quick peck and scurried nervously out of the room.

"General," Colonel Frye said to the man.

"Aye, Frye?" he replied, appearing distinctly annoyed.

"Your wig, sir," Colonel Frye indicated. The high-ranking officer carelessly proceeded, straightening his wig and easily poured himself a drink of rum. "General Webb, Colonel Monro has newly arrived from Albany with his majors, the Earl of Kneep and the Duke of Monteith with his duchess, captains, and lieutenants," Colonel Frye introduced. General Webb promptly glanced up from the tumbler he was filling with rum and placed the decanter directly in front of himself.

"Colonel Monro," he addressed in a London accent with etiquette and continued with the same manner down the line. "Your Graces, my lords, captains, lieutenants—welcome to Fort Edward. It is good to see that you have arrived intact."

"Aye, thank ye, General Webb," Colonel Monro replied stoically as General Webb started gulping down his rum.

In a second Webb's tumbler was emptied, and he promptly refilled it. He hastily drank down his second glass, then fixed himself a poor plate of food. I immediately didn't think he appeared in perfect health, actually. Although he remained fairly handsome for a man appearing in his fifties, his weight seemed slightly low for a man of his age and height at five foot eight inches. Also, his blue eyes appeared sunken with dark circles around them and he seemed apparently unrested. He was restless while meagerly eating the scant food on his plate and looked abstracted as he remained detached from the conversation at the table. It appeared that he had a nearly unnoticeable strange little tick when he blinked. He often brought his handkerchief to his brow and patted it dry from perspiration before drinking more from his tumbler. It seemed he was striving to calm his unsteady nerves.

His eyes inadvertently caught mine as I was discreetly examining him from across the table. He held my gaze for a second before I broke off to slice a bit of wild turkey on my plate and placed the piece between my lips. Subsequently, I now sensed his emotionally distant eyes attentively scrutinizing me as I passively ate my food with my gaze cast to my plate and to the other men who continued conversing around the table.

"May I say to His Grace that Her Grace is quite lovely, and that I fortunately have been granted leave of my melancholy as a consequence of her pleasant company at the table," Webb asserted, unexpectedly interrupting everyone's conversation.

"Thank ye, general. I reckon my wife has such an effect on bairns as weel," Leif replied pointedly—which struck me a little strangely; I don't think he took the general's remarks too kindly as the general was enthrallingly staring at me. Colonel Frye briskly chuckled and quickly curbed it with a swift swig of rum from his tumbler.

"Well, I shall say that it is quite meaningful to me, and I shall thank you for it, for I am gratified. Given the state to which I have been rendered as a consequence of what I have witnessed, I doubt any man or *babe* will be as fortunate as I," Webb insisted and suddenly stood from his seat appearing a little wobbly as he looked directly at us. "Duchess, my lords and officers, I shall presently excuse myself to see to pressing matters at hand," he concluded absentmindedly. He started from the table, pacing unsteadily toward the door and disappeared behind it.

Leif and Finley exchange dubious glances as the conversation resumed normally around the table after General Webb's departure, and I continued wondering about the general as my doubts remained about his overall health.

I LAY in bed watching Leif undress and mindlessly gazed at the round silver scar high on the front of his right thigh, below his groin, left from the arrowhead I had removed from him when we first met. He towered naked beside the bed checking his armed pistol. When he was satisfied, he placed it over the stand near his pillow at minimal arm's length.

"Do you think General Webb is all right?" I asked concernedly as I felt the mattress shake with him entering over it.

"I reckon that he is not fit," Leif judged, turning the covers off his body, since it was fairly warm inside our room.

"He's a heavy drinker," I observed.

"Of coorse he is. He is a man," Leif said indifferently as he settled comfortably on his back and pulled me close against him.

"Yeah, but he's dependent on it."

"He is a military man. Of coorse he depends upon it."

"Yeah, but you're not an alcoholic."

"An alcoholic?" Leif grimaced, appearing questioningly.

"Yeah, it hasn't negatively impacted your judgment so that you can't make sound decisions. You're not dependent on it to function."

"Och, I understand," he said. Except, the curious expression on his face remained. I contemplated for a moment as I lay in his arms, facing him. "I promise ye that I shall not allow myself tae become an alcoholic," he said, sensing me. I automatically smiled a little and lifted my gaze to his. I gently caressed the side of his solid jaw and thoughtfully looked at him.

"You're so sweet," I said affectionately.

"Ye neednae worry about my over indulgence in booze," he guaranteed.

"I know," I said, believing him.

"Now rest yer weary head," he urged warmly. I replaced my head over his shoulder and observed the light extinguish in our room when he blew out the candle in the lantern. His arm subsequently came over me, securing me, and I closed my eyes to finally sleep.

"*DAMNATION!*" Leif audibly cursed suddenly with stark alarm, abruptly thrown from sleep and awakening me with horror as a result.

"What's wrong?" I gasped, terror-struck, as aggressive pounding sounded loudly against our room door from behind. The abrupt sound sent frosty chills throughout my body and stimulated my sudden awareness with the cool sting of fresh adrenaline coursing my veins. Leif invisibly lunged for his pistol, simultaneously leaping out of bed in the surrounding blacked out space. The hammer on his pistol caught the moonlight entering the window and illuminated the cold metal.

"Madam! You must come with me! You must come now! His Grace—your lord, madam, is slain upon the field!" abrasively shouted out a shrill male voice in absolute horror.

"Who's that?" I asked completely aghast, seeking Leif's appearance in the darkness as relentless pounding kept coming through the door.

"Madam! Madam! You mustn't remain! The French! Saxe is

advancing! The slaughter is great! You must come away with me at once!" The hollering came through the door again with more pounding.

"I reckon 'tis Webb," Leif distinguished. I finally discerned Leif's figure through the dark. He was pointing his pistol directly at the door.

"Webb?" I echoed bizarrely, frightened for certain.

"Aye," Leif replied collectedly as I heard the pistol being replaced over the stand by the bed. He reached for his long night-shirt and threw it over his head, immediately concealing his nakedness.

"Oh! They have come, madam! You will parish, do you under-stand! Keep them away! I must keep them away! Escape is our only means! Let us go! Let us go!" Webb continued shouting wildly through the door, then abrupt scuffling was heard. Suddenly, the sound of fast pacing footsteps took off, running through the corridor and swiftly diminished into silence.

Leif's shadow moved across the room until he was illuminated while passing through the moonbeams entering the window before he reached the door in darkness. I heard him twist the door handle.

"Where are you going?" I asked suddenly with sharp concern.

"Latch the door. Dinnae permit anyone tae enter till my return," he directed instead.

"But, where are you going?"

"I must see tae Webb."

"Really?"

"Aye. Now, do as I say."

"Okay," I agreed. I shimmied hastily out of bed and darted across the floor toward the door where he was standing. He promptly opened it and disappeared into the dark corridor. I shut the door after him and locked it.

After waiting nervously for several minutes behind the door, I decided to put my ear against it to see if I could hear anything. The door was solid oak and made it very difficult to detect any soft sound coming behind it. So, I strode toward the bed and sat anxiously on the edge, anticipating Leif's brief return. But as time passed, it appeared he wasn't going to return so soon, and I was forced to wait with anxiety for an undetermined time.

Holding my nervous breath as I waited a while, a sudden knocking came from the opposite side of the door, and I hurried toward it.

"Who is it?" I asked.

"Leif, *ceisdein*," he answered in a muffled tone. I quickly unlatched the door, and he entered the room. I was relieved to see him again while wondering what was occurring.

"The general seemed kinda violent. Is everything all right?" I asked concernedly as he latched the door after himself.

"Aye," he said calmly. Relief swept over me as I discerned him now pacing across the floor toward the letter desk. He sparked a flint stick with charcloth into the tinderbox, and after a minute of blowing on the smoldering cloth he lit the candle in the lantern. His shadow slowly disappeared from darkness as he emerged in the orange glow from the flame, standing perfectly visible in his nightshirt.

"What happened?" I asked.

"Webb appears tae have had a sort of fit recalling a battle in which he had fought," Leif conveyed tiredly.

"Oh, my goodness!" I gasped awfully.

"He battled at Fontenoy," he informed me.

"Oh," I replied unknowingly.

"'Twas a heroic battle."

"I see."

"Many lads perished."

"Oh, how horrible."

"Aye."

"I can't imagine... That must have been really awful to have experienced."

"Indeed."

"So, then he has PTSD," I realized.

"I beg yer pardon?" Leif asked. His brow furrowed, making him appear confused.

"Post traumatic stress disorder," I informed him, unfortunately.

"Do ye mean soldier's heart?"

"Yes, I suppose so."

"Och," he realized as he nodded a tad.

"So, where is he now?" I inquired worriedly.

"He is resting within his quarters at present." Leif adjusted the tin door to the lantern so the light dimmed rather low.

"Oh…" I watched him move away from the door and pace toward the bed as I stood in the middle of the room, wondering curiously about General Webb and sympathizing with his emotional burden.

"Fin restrained him as the surgeon administered laudanum tae him," he continued explaining as I began following him back to bed.

"He did?"

"Aye."

"My gosh…"

"I reckon that Webb will rest quietly now and wulnae recall the events of tonecht in the morn."

"Probably not since he was given laudanum," I replied while sliding beneath the blankets again.

"'Tis because of him Fort Bull nae longer stands," Leif disclosed as he was now placing himself in bed and positioning himself close to me.

"What happened to Fort Bull?" I asked curiously.

"He had it burnt tae the ground."

"Really?" I responded, gazing unbelievably at him.

"Aye."

"Why?"

"He reckoned the French waur advancing through Mohawk Valley, and raither not permit the enemy tae seize the fort, he chose tae destroy it."

"Oh, wow!"

"Aye."

"That's disconcerting."

"'Twas tae prevent the enemy from easily seizing Oneida Carry, according tae Webb. Yet, that isnae the end of it."

"It's not?"

"Nae. He then had trees chopped down tae fill Wood Creek in order tae prevent the enemy from crossing it, but made it impassable fur us and has hindered us in our own advancement."

"He seems certainly delusional," I recognized uneasily.

"Aye, it seems tae be so."

"Why don't they just retire him, seeing how unstable he is? He needs to be out of this environment—out of commission—completely."

"It isnae as simple as ye seem tae perceive it tae be, *mo ghaol*. He will serve fur as long as the Crown needs him, and that will remain till he is maimed or deceased. 'Tis also a means fur him tae earn a stipend," Leif explained realistically.

"I see," I said, somewhat dissatisfied by his answer; that Webb should be used in an expendable fashion made me pity him and annoyed by the government. Leif sighed tiredly as he brought fingers to his eyes, squeezing the tear-duct corners while pinching the perfect bridge over his nose. He momentarily withdrew his fingers and turned his gaze to mine.

"I shall be most pleased once we are left tae ourselves tae live merrily as we did in Boston," he said.

"We will," I promised.

"Aye, we shall," he agreed.

It became quiet between us in the tiresome night, and I moved my head over his shoulder with my arm wrapped around his chest. He kept me close in his arms as he began falling to sleep. I remained awake for a while longer, though, listening to the beating of his strong heart and the light sound of his restful breathing as he respired. The resonance of Webb's terrible voice kept coming to mind, forcing my wakefulness: *"His Grace—your lord, madam, is slain upon the field!"* sent my blood running cold and unsettled my soul, as I wondered if this was an omen to come.

Twenty-Six

It took us about a day from Fort Edward before finally arriving at Lake George without incident, at which time Colonel Monro assumed top command of Fort William Henry from Major Eyre—the fort's architect and one serving as commander of provincial troops here. Now that the location was secured by the British in addition to the already stationed provincial garrison, the area teemed with roughly nineteen hundred men.

Unlike Fort Edward's well-built stone fortress, Fort William Henry was rustic. Built of logs, peat, and mire, it nevertheless sprawled as a well-made and slightly roomy fortress at the end of the lake. Our quarters were sufficient and made for bare-bones, doable living with the added comfort of a full-sized, straw-filled, raised mattress over a sturdy bed frame, tea table and chairs, a writing desk and armoire.

I was pretty much designated to the makeshift infirmary inside one of the barracks established especially for my medical practice. The original hospital barracks, along with all the other outbuildings, had been burned to the ground, resulting from an earlier French raid and were currently being reconstructed. I was not permitted to wander anywhere else around the grounds without Leif's escort—unless I wished to retire to the officers' dining quarter or to our own room to rest.

Monro seemed to run a tight ship, because the men were continually kept busy with their tasks and duties, which included perpetual fort mending due to a significant outer portion of the fort having been damaged by fire. The men worked hard repairing the imperative boats that enabled them to move up and down the lake. Also, another sloop was being heavily constructed that would serve as a gunboat. It was a far different perception than from what I'd witnessed at Fort Edward and to some extent at Fort George.

Every day Leif routinely collected me from work to join him for a leisurely walk around the premises when he broke from his duties. It was typically our only time to visit with each other during the day and was my much-savored time to take my mind off work. It also stifled my growing feeling of cabin fever, since I was newly confined to this very different restrictive style of living.

While we were returning to our barracks, we passed a group of laundresses scrubbing and wringing loads of laundry over troughs of water. We meandered through a row of hanging white sheets tousling in the warm breeze and passed by a maid folding a fresh, dried sheet into a large basket. We made eye contact, and I naturally smiled at her.

"Hallo, milady," she said meekly.

"Hello," I replied nicely, recognizing that she couldn't have been any older than eighteen, maybe. But there was something in her appearance that made her seem much more aware of things than she otherwise would have been at her age. "How are you today?" I inquired, pausing my walk with Leif.

"As well as can be expected, I thank you," she replied as she straightened from placing the freshly folded fabric into the basket. I noticed then that she was pregnant. I wondered how far along she was and made a reasonable estimate between seven or eight months into her third trimester.

"You're expecting?" I asked pleasantly.

"Aye," she replied, seeming modestly pleased.

"That's so nice," I said.

"Aye, milady," she responded.

"You're husband must be really happy," I said.

"My husband passed in the winter from consumption, milady," she disclosed regretfully.

"Oh! I'm so terribly sorry. My condolences to you."

"Thank you, milady."

"Are you alone here, then?" I asked concernedly.

"Nay, Private Henderson has been quite kind to me." Her cheeks suddenly flushed further than they had already presumably due to her working in the outdoor heat, but I assumed that it wasn't due to the warm air.

"I see," I said, noticing her overall pleasant demeanor.

"Thank you for your concern, milady," she said demurely.

"Yes, of course—please tell me your name."

"'Tis Betsy."

"It's nice to meet you, Betsy. I'm Her Grace, Duchess of Monteith."

"I'm begging your pardon, Your Grace. I'm unawares. A pleasure to make your acquaintance, Your Grace," she said demurely. I smiled kindly at her and she curtsied before me with her eyes cast to the ground.

"Please be careful with yourself, will you?" I suggested considerately when she straightened and returned to looking at me.

"I shall. Thank you, Your Grace."

"Well, I won't keep you any longer from taking care of your laundry. Have a nice day, Betsy."

"Good day to you, Your Grace," she said politely. I smiled at her again and she bashfully glanced toward the ground again. I think she was a little surprised by my friendliness toward her, which made me feel slightly awkward as I was still struggling with how I actually fit into this place.

As I resumed walking away from her with Leif, I felt bad about her husband's untimely death and for the precarious state she was currently in. I could imagine being in her position as the realization closely impacted me. Furthermore, not only did I feel sorry for her, but I was also worried about her wellbeing.

"Are ye alrecht, *ceisdein*?" Leif inquired inquisitively, noticing me as we continued approaching the barrack.

"I've never delivered a baby before," I admitted anxiously, turning my gaze up to his. Leif suddenly ceased walking. I stopped too, looking at him with worry.

"Ye huvnae ever?" he replied, utterly surprised.

"No."

"I presumed 'twas one of the many tasks ye seem tae already ken how tae do."

"No," I replied uneasily. "I don't know what I'm going to do."

"Alrecht—dinnae be troobled," he said collectedly.

"But, I don't know what I'm going to do with her when she goes into labor. I have no experience at it. I'm not an obstetrician," I said apprehensively. Leif paused pensively, scratching the side of his head.

"I can assist ye, I reckon," he considered thoughtfully.

"What? How?"

"I once brought a lamb from its mother."

"A lamb?" I looked at him unexpectedly as I felt my brow knit.

"Aye—and, a foal anither instance," he added.

"But, they're animals."

"I reckon 'tis nearly all the same, is it not?" he replied logically.

"Well, I—" I hesitated. To deliver someone's baby was going to be a highly unusual circumstance for me, because I'd never done it by myself before; it was a long time ago when I had interned and experienced a delivery. Furthermore, we were in the middle of nowhere and we were at war...

To do it here in this harsh and primitive environment was an extra challenge that I was going to have to face. I was going to be responsible for the safety, health, and wellbeing of both Betsy and her baby—and as I thought about that, I was suddenly a little gun-shy to uphold my obligation as a physician knowing there was no escaping what was expected of me. I felt extremely pressured to achieve this alone. Nevertheless, since I was forced into this new challenge and would have to succeed without question, I under-stood my moral imperative while worrying about the outcome.

"Dinnae be concerned, I shall assist ye at the appropriate moment," Leif confidently assured me.

"I don't know, I just think anything can go wrong. Besides, you're so busy with all of your responsibilities," I said realistically.

"'Twill be alrecht," he insisted. I sighed, thinking what actual choice did I have but to aid her with my medical expertise despite my fear, and if Leif was offering his assistance to me then the thought of him doing so did lend a modicum of comfort and secu-rity to me.

"All right," I said uncertainly.

"Are we contented now?" he inquired.

"Not really."

"I can plainly see it. Come—let us get a meal inside ye. Yoo'll feel better efter ye eat." He gently took my elbow and led me with him inside the barracks.

I SAT at the letter desk inside our room entering patients' records inside my journal after having mended my last patient early this morning. The soldier had suffered a broken thumb over a wood plank caused by a nail and hammer. I had recorded a number of soldiers that had come into the infirmary with wounds caused by construction as they rebuilt the outer buildings. As I was entering information into my medical journal, I heard the door to our room open and glanced up from writing at the desk when Leif passed through the doorway.

"Micht ye care tae come away with me this morn?" he asked as he entered the room and strode toward me.

"Yes, of course! Where are you going?" I expressed eagerly. I promptly returned my quill inside the inkstand and looked at him with anticipation.

"I reckon 'tis a guid day fur a horse ride," he said.

"Seriously?" I couldn't believe my ears. "You mean we're actually going to get out of here for a while?"

"Aye," he said, nodding a bit.

"Great!" I responded, clasping my hands together with delight. A wide smile easily spread over his enlivened face. "Where will we go?"

"A bit south of haur fur a reprieve as I have a moment tae spare from duties."

"Sounds good!"

"Let us go, then," he urged promptly.

"Righty-o matey!" I expressed enthusiastically as I simultaneously straightened from my seat and removed myself from behind the desk.

A brisk chuckle eluded him with an unexpected quizzical look. "Come along, lass," he exhorted, ridiculously shaking his head. I giggled too, excited that we were going to have a break from the confinement of this place and followed him out of the room.

Shutting the door after me, I paced with him down the steps out of the barracks across the grounds to the stables where I had discovered our horses readied for us to mount. I tossed myself astride over Oakley as Leif skillfully swung himself high on top of Blaze in one swift, easy move. Quickly settled on his horse, he began moving Blaze away, and I started across the yard with Oakley easily trotting comfortably alongside him. We exited the fort grounds and started over the trail headed in a southern direction.

The air was noticeably balmy and slightly humid. The sky was a bright, rich, cobalt blue and there appeared not a single white cloud suspended in it. We were quick inside the forest and the trees seemed like skyscrapers touching the stratosphere with their pinnacle tips. The sunlight was stronger than usual and even lit the shade within the forest to brighter tones of green. The air was fragrant with wild flowers all round, and an infinite swarm of beautiful, intensely colored, yellow, black, and gold tiger moths whirled around us as we cantered through the cluster.

Woodpeckers knocking against trees resonated throughout, and an unseen animal moved overhead a tree limb, stirring fine debris into the air. The particles appeared like shaved gold dust in suspension through the sunbeams as it rained down on us while we galloped through. An eagle screeched from somewhere soaring high above our heads, as I noticed hummingbirds fluttering around seeking nectar from surrounding wild honeysuckles.

It was just us riding out among the woods over the quiet road. It seemed we were encased in a scene that was far removed from what was ordinary and made sublime by the virgin beauty encompassing us all around. It encapsulated us in a clandestine world that seemed permanently undiscovered by anyone else. It felt supernatural and enchanted. I surrendered my memory of the former life I had once lived and was fully present in this moment, feeling truly happy while riding alongside Leif.

We rode for an undetermined time until we had reached a flowing stream and decided on dismounting our horses. We paced for a short distance downstream along the edge, then let the horses drink from the rushing water and feed on fresh grass before we hitched them to a nearby tree. After, I followed Leif a short way further along the riverbank, arriving at the end of the water drop-off over the edge of a not too distant waterfall. It was a beautiful location—remote and secluded.

I gazed down over the moderate drop as the breeze created by the surging water forcefully tumbling over the edge, and stirred mist into the air everywhere around us. A lagoon had been carved out below by the waterfall, and drained into the ravine ahead. I moved with Leif out onto a ledge of an outcropping slate step as we were exploring.

"I shall like tae bathe. Do ye care tae wade?" he expressed hopefully.

"Yes, of course!" I responded eagerly.

"Splendid! Let's go!" he replied. "Take care, however, alrecht?"

"Okay."

He winked at me, then started carefully leading me out over slippery wet layers of sheeted slate rock downward toward the lagoon. I mindfully followed him along the steep incline over each predictable stone step as water rushed thunderously beside us, dampening our hair and clothes. The outcrop protruded approximately halfway into rippling down pouring water, and the rocks were sheathed in running moisture. Leif eased his way first across the unstable platform, then stretched a hand out for me to take. As I was carefully making my way toward him around the bend, a sudden gush of water kicked my heel from under me, and I abruptly lost my footing. My hand uncontrollably slipped from his grip, and I screeched as I unexpectedly flew off the rock. I whirled in the air swiftly downward at a distance and plunged deeply into the cold water below. The distorted sound of my abrupt surge into the water covered my ears beneath the surface as bubbles obscured my vision all around.

I quickly began propelling myself up toward the surface when all of a sudden, I heard a second distortion of bursting water drive beneath me, inciting more bubbles around me and obscuring my view. I immediately recognized Leif's sudden clasp firmly around my waist as he promptly ensued strongly tugging me upward with him. Being powerfully yanked along, we finally breached the water's surface with both of us gasping and panting for air.

"*Christ!* Ye ceased my heart with fricht!" Leif panted alarmingly. He maintained a steady hold on me while soundly treaded water, propelling me toward the shore.

"Yeah! I didn't expect to fall!" I coughed as he swam me along with him.

"I thought I lost ye," he said breathlessly with clear panic on his face.

"It's okay," I panted, "I know how to swim."

"Do ye?" he replied, struck with sudden surprise.

"Yeah—I was a junior lifeguard once," I disclosed instinctively.

"A lifeguard?" he questioned, sounding puzzled. "How is it that ye would guard men?"

"No, I guarded swimmers so they wouldn't drown."

"I beg yer pardon?"

"Never mind—I know how to swim."

"Thus, if I waur tae release ye, I shan't lose ye?" he asked, very reluctant to let go of me while holding me tight.

"Yeah, I'll be fine. You don't have to worry," I assured. But he still hesitated releasing me. "I promise I won't drown."

"Certainly?"

"Definitely."

He slowly lessened his grip around me, and I thrust away from him once his firm arm slipped from my waist, easily beginning to swim through the water. He swiftly swam up close, stroking alongside me just in case, I supposed, until we reached the silt shore at the base of the lagoon where a cave had been carved out of the rock.

As we emerged from the water and paced over the saturated silt shore, we arrived standing in the shade inside the arching rock just barely out of the sunlight. I started wringing out the water drenching my hair when I realized Leif's obvious expression of wonderment.

"I have never knoon a lass who could swim," he said with astonishment.

"Really?" I asked, looking at him equally surprised.

"Aye," he attested.

"Oh."

"I am in wonder... Yoo're drenched now," he said, observing me wringing out my hair.

"So are you," I giggled.

"I reckon so," he acknowledged, glancing at himself.

"So, let's go for a swim," I suggested obviously.

"As ye wish," he agreed as a pleasant smile eased over his lips, dispelling any hint of prior concern.

"Great!" I began unfastening my petite riding jacket while he began laying his wet weapons over the rock.

Next, I started removing my saturated boots. Unbuttoning his sopping wet cardinal coat, he tugged it off his square shoulders with a little force. It fell to the ground like a wet mop as I tossed my jacket in the same condition next to his and proceeded to unlace my pair-of-bodies from the front once I had removed my shirt. In a minute, Leif had his cream-colored military uniform waistcoat removed, and I easily slid my fashioned, sheer camisole off my torso over my head completely exposing my breasts. I realized Leif was warmly smiling at me as I let my soaking camisole drop from my fingertips to the rest of the growing pile of drenched clothing at our feet. Also observing him unclasping the pistol belt around his waist, he pulled his shirt over his golden head after untying the white stock from around his neck. Then, I pulled my riding trousers down from around my hips and they fell to my ankles before stepping from them completely unclothed.

As I subsequently moved toward the rock, Leif was watching me while he began removing his breeches, and I began climbing the steps over the rock wall surrounding the chilly pool near the waterfall.

"Ye ought not be up thaur too high, Sylvie," he warned audibly as I worked my way up the rock, reaching the ledge I had intended to perch myself over.

"It's all right," I replied confidently, gazing down over my shoulder at him and seeing him at a slight distance below now standing entirely naked with signs of concern on his face.

When I reached the ledge, I moved out onto it and stepped toward the ridge with water from the waterfall rushing down over my feet. I curled my toes, positioning myself at the ridge and leaped off the rock, diving perfectly straight. I torpedoed deep beneath the water and promptly turned about, thrusting myself up easily back to the surface. I spotted Leif at the edge of the shore staring over the water at me, gaping with an expression of sheer amazement.

"Come on in—the water's great!" I yelled elatedly as I was easily beginning to breaststroke through the pool.

"Aye!" he replied, sounding completely mesmerized. He swiftly placed our clothes over the rock in the sun for them to dry, then rushed, splashing into the water, swimming freestyle toward me. When he nearly arrived at me at the center of the pool, I playfully re-submerged myself and whirled around beneath him swimming dolphin style in the opposite direction at a distance.

When I returned to the rocky wall, I pulled myself from the water over the rock and climbed it again to the diving ledge. He beguilingly watched me while he swam toward my direction.

"Geronimo!" I screamed right before diving head first in perfect form into the water. Instantly plunging into the cool, deep, fresh water, I turned around and swam up toward the surface and swiftly emerged, completely delighted. "Did you see that?" I laughed.

"Aye!" Leif chuckled, impressed. He was clearly amazed as he swam up to me. "I huvnea ever seen such a thing!" he laughed also. "How do ye ken how tae leap off in that manner?"

"I learned when I was little," I said, smiling at him. He stared at me with bright, cheerfully smiling eyes. "I'm going to do it again! Will you watch me?" I said excitedly, feeling much like a kid.

"Aye!" The sun radiated over his golden, damp head and he looked delightful.

"Okay," I panted. I submerged beneath the water again, eagerly swimming dolphin style, returning toward the same rock. Arriving at the rock once more, I moved over the slate and reached the ledge a second time. "Crazy Horse!" I belted out as I leaped off this time, feet first, plummeting down like a missile into the water.

When I breached the surface, I swam up to him while he easily treaded water. He was chuckling, red with delight and I was completely inspired to please him.

"Whit are those expressions ye holler as ye leap?" he asked wondrously. I shrugged my shoulders.

"They're just names, or things to say to give you the guts to do something exhilarating like that," I panted while treading water with him.

"Och." He didn't quite understand, but he was still smiling widely.

"Are you going to try?" I asked. We were closely buoyed in front of each other panting and laughing.

"Shall I?" he wondered.

"Are you a 'fraidy-cat?" I teased. He laughed and the crow's feet around his eyes emerged as water gleamed over his face.

"Ye cannae goad me, *sìthiche*," he said while smiling at me.

"Well?" I instigated. He stared at me now with a smirk. I couldn't decide if he was considering doing it, or if he was considering me.

"Yoo're entirely a mischief-maker," he said.

"I'm not!" I laughed.

"Aye, ye are." He suddenly dipped beneath the water and swam away in the opposite direction toward the rocks. He easily hauled himself dripping wet out of the pool and scaled the wall until he came out over the ledge where he positioned himself. "Are ye observing me, *àille dhubh*?" he called to me as I observed him from the water a distance below.

"Yeah!" I replied eagerly, locking my attention on him.

"Then haur I go!" He suddenly jumped off, tucking his knees to his chest while tightly clasping his arms around his ankles.

"Cannonball!" I screamed freely for him as he flew through the air, plummeting downward. He splashed forcefully into the water, and I squealed, laughing as a wave of moisture swept around me. He swiftly materialized close to me, and we were both laughing excitedly.

"Did ye see me?" he asked breathlessly, completely amused.

"Yes, of course!"

"I heard ye holler," he said, chuckling.

"You did?"

"Aye!"

"Well it's all part of the fun!"

"'Tis most refreshing!" His bright face was brimming with delight and it really inspired me. "I shall do it again."

"Really?"

"Aye!"

"Okay!"

He swam away again and emerged from the water at the rock wall. I cheerfully watched him move up the rock until he came out over the ledge and readied himself.

"Crease ahoy!" he shouted, leaping off. I screamed, laughing hilariously, watching his bare, colorless buttocks airborne, plummeting downward, and splashing into the water. When he surfaced again, he was obviously struck with utter enthusiasm.

"That was brilliant!" I laughed as he swam toward me.

"Ye fancied it?" he laughed also, looking thrilled.

"Yeah! It was great!"

"Let us do it together, then?"

"Sure."

"Splendid!"

Leif started stroking back toward the wall, and I followed him through the water. He leaped out of the pool onto the slightly overhanging rock and turned around for me, stretching a helpful hand out for me to take. I took his palm, and he effortlessly hauled me forth from the water and over the slate platform. Scaling up the steps together, we soon reached the ledge. I followed him out onto the overhang and stood beside him with our toes curling over the edge. The air faintly moved through the surrounding evergreens above the lagoon, and the sun was warm and brightly shining down on us.

"Whit shall we belt this time?" he asked, glancing over to me.

"Um—I don't know. What do you think?"

"Whit if we micht say—'away we go'?"

"Oh, like Peter Pan!"

"Who is Peter Pan?" he asked curiously with an interested look on his face.

"He's a fictional character in a story. He could do anything."

"Anything?" Leif's eyes widened with a remarkable expression.

"Yeah, he could fly, and do anything he wished. Except, he couldn't leave Neverland," I said, thinking of the fairy tale.

"Whit is Neverland?"

"It's the place where he lived."

"Och," he said, looking at me with noticeable fascination.

"So, is that what we're going to say?"

"Aye."

"Okay."

"Are ye prepared?"

"Yeah."

"Alrecht, then." He took my hand and wrapped his palm securely around mine. "Upon the third count."

"Okay," I agreed. He counted in time, and on the third measure we simultaneously hurled ourselves airborne over the ledge. Hands interlocked, we screamed with all our might, "Away we go!" heading swiftly downward. We plunged into the water and impacted together, surging far below the surface with glittering bubbles streaming all around us. Hands still entwined; we began propelling ourselves back up to the surface.

"Tremendous!" Leif gasped jubilantly when we came up for air. Sparkling beads of water streamed over his gleaming gilded head while dangling crystal droplets hung over his platinum lashes, and he glistened beneath the sun.

"Yeah, that was fantastic!" I laughed. The thrill was unmistakably on his face. It didn't seem he could stop laughing.

"I shall like fur us tae merely swim about now," he suggested, releasing my hand at last.

"Sure, let's go!" I agreed cheerfully.

We swam around the pool together, playfully chasing each other for a time. At one moment, I was easily doing the breaststroke across the lagoon ahead of him until I reached a submerged slate step, and buoyantly propped myself over it. He swam up to me, and I playfully splashed him, wetting his face, catching him off guard. He laughed heartily when I noticed his arm coming toward me, and I suddenly pushed off the rock away from him, intending to steal away from his capture. But he quickly grabbed my ankle as I attempted to swim from him and pulled me toward him, causing eddies to roll over me. He drew me close and detained me with an inescapable clutch around my waist while both of us were laughing and panting together.

While settling from our laughter, I perceived his compelling expression as he gazed absorbedly at me. A pleasing smile relaxed his chuckling face and he looked spellbound.

"From whaur do ye truly come, mermaid?" he inquired in a warm tone.

"Far, far away from here," I answered in a soft voice as I naturally wrapped my legs around his lean waist and floated like a feather before him.

"Aye, I micht reckon so," he suspected. His hands moved down from my waist over my buttocks. "Ye free my heart, *àille dhubh*."

"Really?"

"Aye."

"Well—isn't that nice?" I replied, smiling at him.

"Quite." He securely seized each side of my hips and gently

buoyed me as he positioned me where he had wanted me to be against him near the protruding rock surrounding us. "I fear ye."

"You fear me?" I giggled, ridiculously looking at him.

"I do."

"Why?"

"Yoo're honest."

"Oh... Is that bad?"

"Ye ken nae bounds."

"Are you saying that I'm wild?"

"Aye."

"But—I'm not wild, really."

"Then whit are ye?"

"I'm just what you might call happy-go-lucky," I said.

"Happy-go-lucky, eh?"

"Yeah."

"Whit a curious way tae say that yoo're free-spirited."

"I am free-spirited."

"I'm weel awaur of it," he replied.

"So, what does that mean for you?"

"I reckon that I must tame ye."

"Tame me, huh?"

"Aye."

"Well how are you going to do that?"

"I have my ways, lass."

"Is that right?"

"Certainly."

"Wow, you sound awfully confident about yourself."

"Indeed, I am quite assured." A large grin swept across his face, enhancing his smiling eyes, and creasing his cheeks, making him appear allured.

"Well, we'll see about that," I said, smiling back at him.

"'Tis my duty tae tame ye."

"Your duty?"

"Aye, it most certainly is."

"Oh, well, we'll see about that."

"Ye doubt me then, do ye?"

"Yes, very much," I laughed.

"Yoo're cheeky." He was smiling so warmly at me that my stomach began fluttering with butterflies as I also began feeling warm all over.

"Cheeky," I echoed, surprised by his teasing.

"Quite."

"I'm not at all cheeky."

"Yoo're nothing but pert."

"Hmm, well—obviously you must like it."

"How do ye reckon?"

"Otherwise you wouldn't have married me."

"Och! Weel, ye micht have a notion thaur."

"Of course I do, silly."

"Come haur ye impish thing." He pulled me close, and I sensed his shaft solid and erect between my thighs.

"Umm—I think the only rascal around here is you."

"*Rascal!*"

"Uh-hu."

"Ye slight me," he said with amusement.

"What's funny?"

"Ye have an irregular way with words."

"I know. I remember you telling me so once before."

"It charms me."

"It does?"

"Aye."

"Well, I guess that *is* funny."

"Ye have bewitched me." He gazed enthrallingly at me and suddenly I was feeling bashful along with the growing ache between my legs.

"Oh, stop," I said playfully. He chuckled and his face radiated.

"Why must I cease?"

"Because."

"Because, ye say?"

"Um-hm."

"That isnae a proper answer." His lips tilted, and the smirk on his face highlighted his extremely handsome looks. I felt him seeking the cleft between my thighs with his engorged penis when he found my entrance. He slowly surged inside of me and I suddenly moaned, sensing the full articulation of his shaft filling me. "Now that answer micht suffice," he said huskily. I gasped shakily, securing my arms around his neck in a full embrace. "Och, aye," he responded heatedly against the side of my moistened face. "Do ye see the effect of yer charm upon me and the trooble it causes me?"

"I didn't realize that I wielded so much power."

"More than ye ken," he groaned. The water felt really cold all of a sudden, and my breath fluttered.

His hands started roaming up my back beneath my soaking wet locks to the back of my head and over the sides of my cheeks. He gently clasped my face and began kissing me with heat. Sensing his desire had grown noticeably greater, warmed me further. I naturally parted my lips when his impassioned tongue thrust forth filling my mouth in an excited kiss. His kisses were strong and possessive, and I returned his warmth with nearly the same force, realizing my own insatiable hunger for him.

Dissolving in his embrace, I leaned back releasing my grip from around his broad shoulders and tightly clutched the rock protruding directly overhead. His palms firmly gripped my buttocks, fixing me close against his groin, and I snuggly wrapped my legs around his lean waist. He began moving, and the water lapped gently around my suspended breasts. My hips took over and started rocking over his groin as he met each rock with an easy thrust, surging magnificently between my thighs.

"Oh, Leif," I muttered with bated breath, immensely enjoying the sensation of his powerful shaft thrusting into me, filling me like no one else possibly could.

"Aye," he groaned.

"*Uhh*, you feel so good," I scarcely uttered while disintegrating in the heated experience he was causing me to feel deep inside of my belly.

"As do ye," he moaned against my mouth. "I want tae drown inside of ye."

"Please."

"Please whit?"

"Do it to me. Drown inside me."

"I am, *mo ghaol*. I am."

"Don't stop."

"I shan't. I shall perish deep inside of ye," he groaned. "I adore yer cunt. Och, how I desire tae remain inside of ye fur as long as I draw breath."

"*Uh*," I gasped as I was climbing toward the summit. "I can't stand that you feel so good..."

"Ye drive me tae oblivion... I ache fur ye... I want tae devour all of ye... Ye are truly sublime... How I wish tae penetrate yer soul. Do ye ken how blissful my cock is when 'tis inside of ye?"

"I have an idea," I panted deliriously.

"Ye will ken precisely how adulated it feels when it touches yer heart," he moaned.

Without warning, an abrupt *bang* erupted the silent ambience. It resonated throughout the entire area like a huge firecracker, immediately arresting Leif in mid motion within me. Simultaneously, an invisible object violently pelted the water very close by and rained droplets right next to us. In one movement, Leif abruptly withdrew himself from between my thighs and powerfully swung us both around the outcrop for cover. The scent of gun smoke was immediate. My heart catapulted into my throat with my skyrocketed pulse as I simultaneously noticed the color had suddenly drained from his face. Distinct alarm was impressed upon his expression, and I sharply feared for our safety.

We were completely vulnerable, since Leif was unarmed. His

weapons rested in the sun by the cave on the opposite side of us around the outcrop where we now hid. I supposed his pistol wouldn't have been much use to us at the moment anyway, since it had been soaked in the water when he dove in to rescue me. Aware of the danger facing us, I didn't know how we were going to escape without being harmed.

Suddenly, laughter broke out from somewhere unseen at a distance and echoed throughout the lagoon. Leif had my back snug against the rock that was protecting us when he mindfully peered around me over the edge of the boulder in the direction of the discharged gunshot.

"Alrecht, lad! Ye may come out now!" Finley was recognized shouting at Leif from afar over the crest across the lagoon. I was suddenly struck with immense relief as embarrassment quickly replaced my fear.

"Bloody Hell!" Leif shouted back at Finley with noticeable dissatisfaction, appearing significantly rattled as he slightly released his tight, protective grip around me. He located Finley standing visibly above at the crest. I peeped around the rock too with my heart still wildly racing and discerned all of their cousins laughing up a storm at our expense.

"Damnation, lad! Yoo're fortunate 'tis merely we who discovered ye raither than Huron!" Finley responded unamused.

"Ye needn't have fired upon me!" Leif yelled back, not at all pleased.

"How else was I tae gain yer attention?" Finley replied obviously.

"Firing in the air would have been appropriate!" Leif responded angrily.

"I dinnae reckon so! Ye deserved it reit whaur it landed close tae ye tae teach ye a lesson! Ye could git yerself and yer bonnie wife killed out haur, seeing that ye huvnae already thought upon it!" Finley chastised.

"Ye micht have caused us injury nonetheless!" Leif pointed out outrageously.

"Listen, brother, I dinnae mind ye taken yer pleasurable reit with yer woman, but ye mustnae be dimwitted about it!" Finley expressed apparently.

"Dimwitted!" Leif countered.

"Aye! Ye went missing from the fort without word! None of us kent whit the devil became of ye! So, we went seeking fur ye, of coorse! We at last discovered yer horses abandoned up stream and reckoned something ill befell ye!" Finley yelled.

"Aye, now yoo've discovered my whereaboots weel enough! Ye see that I'm fit, do ye not?" Leif responded ironically.

"We apologize fur interrupting yer *fit* business, Seamus!" Angus jeered laughingly.

"I'll have ye flogged fur it, Angus!" Leif scoffed irritably.

"Yoo're thinking with the wrong head, Seamus!" Liam also mocked with laughter.

"I shall have you hanged by yers, Liam!" Leif jibed back.

"Alrecht, that will be enough, lads!" Finley interrupted. "The gist being, Seamus, we dinnae ken whaur in damnation ye had gone!"

"Alrecht! I reckon yoo're correct!" Leif recognized guiltily.

"Aye!" Finley responded absolutely.

"*Crap*," Leif hissed abashedly.

"Ye have duties that cannae be neglected! Do ye recall?" Finley pressed.

"I realize!" Leif replied awkwardly.

"Alrecht, then—it cannae occur again! Is it clearly understood?" Finley said determinedly.

"It wulnae take place again!" Leif agreed.

"Very weel, then, brother! Now git yer arse out of the water and back tae the fort!" Finley ordered with discernible satisfaction.

"Do ye lads mind, then, granting me a private moment fur my

lass and I tae properly attire ourselves?" Leif requested in humiliation.

I recognized Angus saying something audible in Scottish, and the men laughed boisterously. Cole added a remark, and they all rowdily laughed even more. Leif then shot back in their language with a wise-cracking tone, and I heard the guys grumble a little, seemingly mildly annoyed. Derek said something, and they all laughed rambunctiously again.

"What are they saying?" I asked curiously.

"Ye dinnae ken?" Leif returned his attention to me.

"No, of course not," I said.

"Guid. 'Twill remain so," he said.

"Oh, so then it must be bad," I guessed with a quizzical smirk.

Roy voiced something audibly, and the guys continued laughing noisily. Leif's face suddenly flushed bright red. He looked really embarrassed.

"What did he just say?" I asked defensively.

"It isnae fit fur yer ears," Leif said, then suddenly responded back quite audibly in Scottish that sounded like a very dirty jab back at them. Roy grumbled between persistent laughter among the rest of his cousins as they proceeded retreating from the lagoon and made themselves invisible inside the woods. "I beg yer pardon, *ceisdein*. We must now take our leave," he said to me with an apologetic look on his face.

"It's all right," I said with some regret.

"I promise tae redeem myself tae ye later," he guaranteed with an optimistic expression.

"Okay," I giggled slightly, and he gently pecked his soft lips over mine.

"Let's go, then," he said, urging me to swim with him away from our concealed location. I proceeded following him around the outcrop to the shore by the cave. When we arrived at the cave, Leif had me covered in the shaded grotto when he thoughtfully passed me my damp clothes first before he began dressing himself.

Soon, when we had dressed, and I began carefully following him up the steep outcropping slate steps over the slight cliff facing us away from the waterfall. After several minutes, we finally climbed over the crest and started hiking our way back up stream on the opposite side from which we had originally come.

Not too long from where we had climbed over the crest, Finley and the rest of the guys were spotted through the trees on the opposite side with our horses as we continued slightly farther upstream. Finally, we had reached a location ahead in the stream where it had grown shallow and where there were easy stepping-stones. We carefully crossed over the stones and doubled backed along the reverse side of the flowing water. At last, the men could be seen easily talking, already mounted on their horses waiting for us.

"Och! Thaur ye are, Seamus," Finley recognized as we were closely approaching.

"Aye," Leif replied and customarily took me by the waist as he effortlessly swung me up over my own horse.

"Let's go—we have nae time tae spare," Finley said, appearing distinctly imposing on his horse.

"Aye, I reckon we best make our return," Leif agreed, sounding guilty, and briskly whirled himself high over Blaze.

"Move out, lads," Finley commanded.

We started through the woods. Soon, we came through the thick vegetation onto the open road returning north. It took some time, journeying back to the fort, since we had gone a ways south. Daylight had grown less intense, and the shadows on the ground were long. Leif rode alongside me as he and Derek easily conversed with each other for an extended amount of time along the way. Finley and the rest of the men rode at ease ahead of us, joking and chuckling among each other. It was apparent that the men were in good spirits, and it was nice to observe.

By the time we had returned to the fort, twilight was upon us. We entered the courtyard and met the stablehands ready to take our horses from us. As we walked the grounds toward our barrack, the men separated and wished each other goodnight. Leif and I continued with Finley in the direction of our barracks where the dining barrack was also located. When we entered the dining chamber, Monro and Eyre were in the middle of dining. They promptly gazed at us from the table and politely acknowledged us. The men respectfully greeted each other with Monro not appearing acutely too pleased.

"Colonel, Major," Leif acknowledged respectfully as he distinctly looked at Colonel Monro and then at Major Eyre.

"Your Grace, Your Lordship," Monro replied equally to both Leif and Finley.

"Your Grace, Your Lordship," Eyre responded courteously.

"Pray pardon my error, Colonel. It wulnae occur again," Leif assured, particularly with distinction as he stood in good form before the colonel.

"Indeed, it will not, Major Monteith. I needn't remind ye of yer duties as ye ken a reprimand will be in order upon yer next offence," Monro said adequately with a strict expression.

"Aye, Colonel," Leif replied culpably. Colonel Monro subsequently motioned with a hand toward the empty chairs at the table. "Pray, take yer proper places at the table and fill yer stomachs."

"Thank ye, Colonel," Leif replied respectfully.

Leif and Finley moved toward the table, taking their seats, and I followed sitting next to Leif after he pulled a chair out from the table for me to sit. Then, we filled our plates and began to eat.

<h1 style="text-align:center">Twenty-Seven</h1>

One evening while we were completing our dinner, the easy conversation surrounding me at the dining table was suddenly disrupted as the door abruptly burst open with three men unexpectedly entering. We were startled as our attention immediately turned toward the men advancing inside the barrack. One man was Private Edwards and the other two were strangers, seeming to have been marooned. They were gaunt, wearing shredded clothes and reeked of filth as they stared disheveled at us.

"Edwards," Colonel Monro acknowledged with alarm while gazing at the two foul looking men.

"Lieutenants Smith and Miller, Colonel," Private Edwards introduced to Monro.

"We have just arrived from French captivity, sir," Lieutenant Miller informed Colonel Monro.

"Aye, from Fort Carillon," Lieutenant Smith said.

"Dear Lord, men!" Monro acknowledged sympathetically.

"We must inform you of news of Montcalm's growing assembly," Lieutenant Smith started in a noticeably hoarse voice.

"He has acquired the allegiance of the Chippewas, Mississauga,

Menominee, Potawatomi, Winnebago, Sauk, Fox and more," Lieutenant Miller continued.

"Damnation! That does not already include the Abenaki, Huron, Caughnawaga, and Ottawa he has pledged," Eyre added with steep concern.

"He has amassed closely two thousand Indian warriors assembled at Carillon," Lieutenant Smith informed us exhaustedly.

"Two thousand?" Monro echoed unbelievably.

"Aye," Lieutenant Miller confirmed dryly.

"How many men total do ye reckon?" Monro inquired.

"Nearly eight thousand—from what we know," Lieutenant Smith estimated. My spoon accidentally slipped from my fingers and resonated as it crashed upon my plate when I heard this frightening news. I glanced at the men talking, unintentionally catching their transient attention as they resumed discussing.

"*David Jones!* That's a force," Monro recognized with apparent perturbation.

"We must dispatch a courier tae Webb," Leif said promptly.

"Aye. I must see that this information reaches Laird Loudoun also," Monro said additionally. "Alrecht—thank ye, lads. Edwards, see tae it that these lads are weel fed and tidied."

"Aye, Colonel," Edwards responded and showed the escapees out of the dining chamber.

"I shall have scouts dispatched immediately," Monro determined. "Ye lads take rangers with ye on patrol as Eyre will do."

"Aye," Leif said. I suddenly turned anxiously from the food I was merely staring at on my plate, and my eyes uneasily bounced between the discussing men in the room.

"May I request yer charity, madam, tae mend those poor men?" Monro asked immediately, turning his gaze to mine.

"Yes, of course," I responded automatically, feeling quite parched as a result.

❄

AFTER MY MEAL, I went to the infirmary and examined my newest patients. They had absolutely suffered some brutality given their malnourished and dehydrated states. There were also some notable abrasions over their faces and backs, along with their recognizable exhaustion. Given their weakened states, I was amazed that they had been able to travel such a recognizable distance to reach our fort, and I wondered how they had managed it. However, other than from what I had observed after examining them, these men seemed likely to recover after some rest and proper nourishment once I had tended to their wounds.

THIS MORNING I had awakened alone in bed. Leif had risen much earlier to endure a scouting mission north around Lake George. I could only hope that he and the others would remain unscathed. So, I was forced to merely wait the time of their return with dread until I saw them again, hopefully unharmed.

Later today, I was walking through the open corridor headed toward the dining quarter after visiting my newest patients who were mending from their escape from the French fort, Fort Carillon, when I unintentionally began overhearing a conversation while passing along my way. Monro and a couple of other men could be heard conversing in his office through an open window as I rounded the passage close to the dining quarter.

"How many?" Monro inquired with discernible alarm in his voice.

"Twelve have, sir," informed an unnamed man.

"Any others ye may suspect that have come down with the pox?" Monro inquired.

"None others, sir."

"This is a plight," said another man in an alarming tone.

"Aye... The men are from which regiment?" Monro asked gravely.

I suddenly arrested my steps just as I was passing the colonel's office and without forethought entered through his doorway into the room.

"Our regulars belonging to one of the companies from Albany," Captain Walsh said.

"Damnation!" Monro responded disconcertingly.

"We have a scourge upon our hands, now, sir," Captain MacGregor realized.

"Regrettably," Monro responded thinkingly.

"They have to be quarantined in order to control the outbreak," I interrupted suddenly, calling their attention abruptly to me. "Are you sure it's only twelve so far?"

"Er, aye, Your Grace," Captain Walsh verified uneasily as he unwittingly realized that I had been standing among them in the middle of their discussion. Monro, along with the other two joining officers, had a caught off guard look due to my unsolicited insertion into their conversation.

"Madam," Monro protested.

"Well, you all are talking about a highly infectious viral outbreak, and in this case, then they must be separated outside the fort right away," I said. Monro didn't appear too convinced, however. "It's the only way to prevent an epidemic—if one hasn't already begun."

"I'm weel awaur, Your Grace, of the grave consequences of the plague," Monro responded categorically. "Yet, I cannae permit ye tae be imperiled."

"With all due respect, Colonel, time is of the essence in situations involving radical disease outbreaks as in this instance. An immediate quarantine must be established in order to stem the spread of the virus, and I am capable of overseeing the appropriate medical care that these infected men should receive," I assured confidently.

"Whilst I can plainly perceive that ye believe in your abilities to heal, madam, and as the fact remains that yer husband isnae present tae speak on his wife's behalf, I doubt quite much that His Grace will approve of Her Grace's assistance in this case," Monro said.

"But, they'll stand a great chance of dying otherwise," I explained seriously.

"I shall not risk the guid state of yer welfare, madam," Monro declared.

"I appreciate your concern, Colonel—I really do, but my husband would absolutely understand, and have no qualm with my helping those poor men. I assure you. However, I don't mean to step on any toes here—so forgive me, but I know how to help those men if you'll let me. Otherwise, you can pretty much bank on the fact that we're at the beginning of a widespread epidemic here without any way of containing the contagion, which then means we've really got a disaster on our hands, won't we?" I rationalized frankly.

Monro and the two captains stood around gawking at each other in silence until their eyes settled with astonishment on me. I suppose this was the most I had ever expressed to the colonel, in addition to my having been so candid about it that presumably caught the men by surprise.

Monro cleared his throat. "I have given my orders, Your Grace, tae which ye will also abide. Now, the ill will be isolated from the fort. Captain Walsh, see tae setting a hospital outside the fort straight away," he commanded clearly.

"Aye, Colonel," Captain Walsh replied.

"Captain Daniels, inform Corporal Jennings that he is tae have the ill transported tae the new hospital," Monro ordered, turning his attention to Captain Daniels.

"Aye, Colonel," Captain Daniels responded.

"Her Grace is welcome tae continue tending tae the injured within the fort," Monro commanded unyieldingly. He glared resolutely at me and respectfully dipped his head toward me in a stiff bow. I acknowledged him likewise with a stilted grin and decided

to depart his office. I turned out of the room completely dissatisfied about his decision. I was somewhat incensed, actually; not
having the freedom to do what I knew exactly was appropriate for
those suffering men rather chaffed and frustrated me. Who knew
when Leif was going to be back so that I could convince him to let
me attend to those men? And, the fact that I even needed to
convince him to allow me to do so, irritated the heck out of me. In
the meantime, those infected men were going to very likely suffer a
doomed fate.

I irritably dwelled on this situation while walking through the
open corridor and knew that I would continue to fixate on the
matter throughout my remaining day as I went about my medical
activities within the fort.

Afterward, I entered the dining quarter and decided that I was
not in a sociable mood when I recognized some of the officers
partaking in their meal. So, I returned to my room and chose to
have afternoon tea there; at least I could take the time to organize
my medical records while I ate.

After tea and once I had finished organizing my records, I went
to the hospital barracks, still very concerned over the outbreak and
for those men infected. Nevertheless, I monitored my newest
recovering patients as well as mended several sprains and lacera-
tions on others. One guy had thrown his back out by lifting heavy
wood planks and was designated motionless on a cot until further
notice per my instructions.

By the end of the day I had cold compressed and wrapped a
cranial contusion along with suturing an open laceration caused by
a saw over the forearm, removed a nail from the bottom of a foot,
and shoved a recovered front tooth back into the mouth of a
hysterical man who had knocked it out due to a fall from a ladder
—which would not have been successfully reinserted into the
patient's mouth if it were not for the help of a jug of rum and two
other soldiers holding the distraught man down.

I finally went to bed not particularly glad that the day was done. Leif was on my mind, of course. He hadn't yet returned like I had hoped. Instead, I lay in bed wondering about his safety and his proximity from the fort. I pondered how soon I'd see him again until I couldn't stand another moment of wakefulness and finally fell to sleep.

THREE DAYS HAD GONE by with no word or sign of any of the men who ventured on the reconnaissance mission, and to my dismay, no medical care for the twelve quarantined outside the fort ill with smallpox.

However, as allowed, I spent those days busying myself with others injured and recovering within the fort walls, along with updating my medical journal as I sat quietly in my room, disturbed about the medical disaster upon us.

VERY EARLY ON the twelfth morning at sunrise, I was roused from slumber as I drowsily noticed Leif quietly coming into the room. He sat in the chair near the wall, facing me at the opposite side of the room, and proceeded to take off his muddied boots.

"Hi," I muttered sleepily from across the blankets.

"Och! Hullo, *cuisle mo chridhe*," he greeted with a gentle voice. "Forgive me, I dinnae mean tae awaken ye."

"It's okay," I replied lazily, very glad to see him again as I started sitting up from the pillows. "Oh my God!" I gasped suddenly, realizing the huge blood stains covering the entire front of his waistcoat. It also covered his entire shirtsleeve over his left arm. He straightened from the chair once he kicked off his second boot.

"Thaur isnae any cause fur alarm, *mo ghaol*. 'Tis not mine," he reassured calmly. He promptly began removing the soiled waistcoat from his torso. The sight of it sent a frigidness throughout my body as fear gripped me. I swallowed dryly, wondering where it came from.

"Whose is it?" I asked uneasily.

"It belongs tae Abenaki braves," Leif answered as he took off his waistcoat and started removing his sullied, bloodstained shirt also.

"Oh," I said aridly.

"We waur discovered near Crown Point and at Fort Carillon. We waur attacked closely the entirety upon our return by bands of Abenaki, Huron, Nipissing, and Ottawa till they waur ambushed by the Rangers at which time we turned and laid into them somethin' fierce," he disclosed.

"Oh my goodness!" I responded, sharply unnerved.

"I took a few scalps of my own, and a number of Indian warriors witnessed it," he revealed, appearing a bit wired as he recounted his experience.

"Really...?" I uttered dry-mouthed.

"Thaur was a brave who micht have come efter me, but he ceased dead on his heels. He merely perceived me with a look of trepidation and didnae approach. So, I continued tae fight with the rest of the lads, fending off our attackers till they waur either dead or had retreated back into the wood," he explained, strangely excited.

"Oh my God," I responded faintly, observing his unusual hyped up demeanor. I remembered seeing a similar vicious look in his eyes once before, when he captured me from the one Huron brave stealing me away when I first arrived here in this era.

"It was either he or I tae be scalped, and I was *damned* if I was gonnae lit him take mine. We did manage, however, tae locate the sawmills at Carillon. I'm certain Monro will be pleased tae learn of it."

"Yeah, I suppose so."

"Still, he wulnea be too pleased tae learn how thick the wood has grown with the enemy."

"I imagine he won't. It's definitely disconcerting news."

"Aye—weel, Providence proved tae have me brought soondly back tae ye, and fur that I'm certainly grateful."

"Thank God for sure. I'm really glad that you kicked ass, and you're back now safe too," I said, seriously worried about what could have happened to him. Leif chuckled unexpectedly, looking at me as he dropped his breeches from his waist and pulled them off.

"Ye have a wicked mouth upon ye, lass," he scolded.

"Well, what do you expect? I'm around a bunch of foul mouth soldiers all day long," I said obviously. He chuckled again.

"Aye, I reckon it micht be my fault," he acknowledged and splashed himself down with fresh water from the washbasin on the table near the looking-glass to cleanse himself. "Although, I do seem tae recall that ye waur a feisty one from the start when I found ye."

"So? You don't seem to mind," I teased faintly. I comfortably rolled over onto my stomach among the blankets, turning my cheek into the pillows as I still gazed at him while he continued cleansing himself.

"Do I not?"

"Yeah, I don't think so."

"Och! Who has given ye that notion?"

"You, of course," I mocked, peering at him through the pillows. He caught my eye while he lightly patted himself dry with a fresh cotton cloth. I noticed a light beard had started growing around his jaw. It changed his appearance and made him look rugged.

"Weel," he said musingly with a slightly amused expression, "it appears I micht have tae remind ye of yer proper manners haur with me." Then, he climbed into bed and pulled me close. "I have missed ye," he muttered deeply as his supple lips gently brushed over mine.

"I missed you too," I responded softly. He lifted his gaze to mine, and now I could see him perfectly in the new morning light entering the windows.

"I reckon ye have," he believed.

"Yes, very much... I'm so glad you're safe. I've been so worried about you."

"I shall always return tae ye, come whit may," he vowed and sealed it with a warm kiss over my lips. "Come whit may," he swore again and affectionately pressed his lips over my brow this time.

LATER THAT MORNING while Leif continued sleeping, I decided to sidle from his loose embrace and dress in my dressing gown. I was ready to place myself at the writing desk to begin updating medical records from the day before.

About an hour later, I had nearly completed everything to my satisfaction when I heard him lightly stirring among the pillows. I glanced over my shoulder at him to find that he was already awake from his deep snooze and had been admiring me from the covers.

"Oh, you're awake," I said spontaneously.

"Aye," he responded indolently. "Whit are ye doing over thaur, *mo chridhe*?"

"Just working—filling in medical records, nothing really exciting, I guess," I said mundanely.

"Nae, I meant why are ye not haur in bed with me?" he asked.

"Oh, well, I didn't want to disturb you while you slept, since I couldn't sleep anymore," I said.

"Come haur." He slapped the covers beside himself.

I smiled, simultaneously shaking my head at his insistence. Straightening from my papers at the desk, I strode toward him, resting against the pillows and slipped myself back into bed next to him.

"Who permitted ye tae part from me?" He seized my waist and drew me snug against him.

"No one," I said, looking ridiculously at him.

"Precisely," he said and drew me close beside his chest. "Now, this is quite appropriate."

"Glad you're satisfied," I said facetiously.

"Indeed." He suddenly slapped my bottom with the palm of his hand.

"Hey!" I yelped.

"Och! Quit yer gab and merely lie peaceably haur with me," he insisted, lightly tapping his finger over my lips. I satirically looked at him, and he shushed me again, relegating my head comfortably lying on his shoulder. We lay relaxing together nicely, cuddled in bed for a period without really having anything to say to each other. It seemed he was at peace for the moment, but my mind kept wandering.

"Leif?" I began, quietly breaking the stillness between us while playing with the light hairs on his chest.

"Aye?" he responded lazily, turning his calm gaze to mine.

"How long were you in Africa?" I inquired spontaneously.

"Africa?"

"Yeah. You said you were there once."

"Aye."

"So, tell me then."

"Very weel. I arrived the year forty-seven and was posted thaur fur four years," he said.

"For four years?" I echoed, amazed.

"Aye."

"That's a long while," I recognized.

"Indeed it was," he agreed grimly.

"What was it like over there?"

"Why do ye wish tae ken?" he inquired softly while curiously looking at me.

"I guess I'd just like to know, really."

"I would never wish fur ye tae ken whit I ken of it," he said candidly.

"Why not?"

"I dinnae reckon ye ought tae ken."

"But, you can tell me—it's okay," I gently pressed. He released a faint sigh appearing somewhat discouraged and reluctant. "Please? I would really like to know—that's all."

"Alrecht," he acquiesced, "then, I shall tell ye that it was the worst place I had ever visited upon earth."

"Why?" I asked strangely.

"I was commissioned into service by the Crown tae secure a fort from the Portuguese, and tae assist traders from pirates," Leif disclosed miserably.

"Oh..." Suddenly, I felt a little guilty for forcing him to remember his past, given his grim response.

"It was a lonely, abandoned place... terribly hot and rain-filled. 'Twas wretched. I didnae understand many ways... Thaur was much cruelty all about," he recalled.

"What kind of cruelty did you see?" I inquired, incapable of helping my curiosity.

"Too abundant fur ye tae understand," he said.

"But, just tell me something," I requested.

"I witnessed seduction, banditry, rape, murder—unusual afflictions perpetrated by men—merely tae name but a few. I reckon that I had witnessed all the begotten ills committed by man and nature in a single place," he said with a very bleak expression clouding his face.

"Oh..." I muttered.

"The thirst fur riches is evil, ye ken?"

"Yes, I know."

"Greed turns any man's soul tae the Devil."

"I believe so."

"I have come tae truly understand that men indeed abandon morality and honor tae satiate their lust fur wealth and power."

"Strictly in and of itself, yes, I agree—not everyone is like that though."

"Hmm... I am uncertain of whit ye say."

"Well, you haven't abandoned your integrity. So, I think I've just proven my point."

"I dinnae lust fur power, however."

"That's probably because you already have it."

"More than other men, aye. Yet, I dinnae strive tae advance my privilege."

"No, you don't," I agreed. "But some people have aspirations of power so they can do good things for others who are less fortunate."

"Yer perspective is unique, *àille dhubh*, fur most men yearn fur power—plenty lust fur it—and therefore submit tae greed tae fill their own interests. The less fortunate remain at the mercy tae men with noble hearts removed from lust and whose consciences serve God. Those men are yet few and hold nae earthly wealth."

"Do you really believe so?" I asked, wanting to understand his vantage point.

"I certainly do. Ye must understand that whilst I was in Guinea I witnessed terrible atrocities as a direct result of men's insatiable desires."

"I see..."

"The Negro men delivered other Negros intae white merchant hands as they waur tempted tae trade them fur mere trinkets. Traders luring them fur their own wealth... Once they waur captured by venturers, the Negroes waur deposited intae cages and dungeons—quite inhospitable fur any living soul. The lot of them perished before setting sail tae America, fur many of them waur kept from ever seeing the lecht of day fur a year—or more..." Leif paused and rubbed his fingers over his troubled brow. "Sailors, guards, merchants took Negro women fur their own pleasure always... Their cries—one never heard a thing like it," he remembered. I could perceive as I simply listened to him speak, that this experience he had undergone really seemed to have impacted him in an acutely negative way.

"I guess you couldn't really do anything about it, could you?" I realized awfully.

"I became boozed with rum one nicht... and, I picked a quarrel with a soldier I had witnessed ravishing a Negro lass—och, she was quite young... twelve or thirteen years, I reckon. I dinnae recall whit occurred with my words but merely that I lost my wits, and I laid my fists into him quite guid—kicked his teeth in, closely killed him... I reckon 'tis fortunate that he didnae perish, or I would have been charged with murder and shot tae death. My last recollection micht have been that godforsaken place. I thank the Lord Almighty that it didnae transpire tae be the case," Leif expressed.

"I'm very glad that didn't happen to you too."

"My captain was none too pleased with me, however," he said.

"What did he do?" I asked.

"He imprisoned me fur two months."

"Two months?" I was shocked.

"'Twas squalid in the heat whilst I was in the cell. No room tae merely move—hot inside like an oven with little tae drink or eat."

"Oh my goodness!"

"I reckoned then indeed I micht perish efter all. I had grown weak and ill from bloody flux. I am quite surprised that I had survived the voyage back tae England upon my captain releasing me from prison fur my return, at last," he said.

"That sounds so terrible," I replied horribly.

"I shall never wish tae revisit that place fur as long as I have breath in my body," he avowed.

"I don't see how anybody could ever want to in that case," I acknowledged.

Leif shifted a bit over the mattress, displacing me a little from resting on his chest. He gazed at me as he covered his palm over the side of my cheek and gently stroked the arch of my eyebrow.

"Do ye understand now whit the business of slavery means tae me?" he asked specifically.

"You hate it," I perceived.

"'Tis loathsome. Ye ken that I loove ye?" he continued truly.

"Yes—I know you do," I understood meaningfully.

"Ye must never doubt it," he insisted and softly pressed his lips on my temple.

His lips remained close, lightly sweeping the side of my head as he pressed tender kisses on me. I could feel the light breeze of his warm breath caress my temple as silence ensued for a moment.

"What did you think of this place when you first arrived?" I decided to ask. He stopped kissing me and returned his gaze to mine, locking his eyes on me.

"I reckoned it tae be mysterious and unusual," he said.

"Oh. So, did you think you would like it?" I asked curiously.

"I wisnae certain. However, Fin seemed tae favor it. Of coorse, he met Elizabeth straight away, so since he favored it, I reckoned that I micht as weel."

"Oh."

"I found it tae be simple haur. I reckoned the people tae be modest and decent. The way of life haur is principled and sincere —and, I find it honorable."

"Do you dream of ever returning to Scotland?"

"I shall always hold Scotland dear tae my heart. Yet, thaur is little that remains fur me thaur presently. I have still a bit of land thaur, as ye ken, that I rent tae tenants, that is all. It isnae enough fur my return tae dwell even if I waur not banished haur," Leif reflected.

"I see."

"I met ye haur, and I took ye fur my wife haur. This place is my home now. 'Tis whaur I want fur us tae remain tae live out our lives."

"I'm glad that you feel fulfilled here."

"Aye, indeed, I do." He tenderly bestowed a kiss on my temple again. "However... I shall never risk a voyage with ye across the sea even if I waur free tae return tae Scotland."

"Why not?"

"Sailing is perilous."

"I guess it would be," I considered actually. I felt him stirring slightly away from me and noticed him reaching for the attractive timepiece I had given him for his birthday. He seized it between his large fingers and lifted the cover, opening it to read.

"Och," he muttered regrettably.

"What time is it?" I asked.

"Nearly eight o'clock," he replied. He replaced his timepiece over the stand near his bedside. "I must rise tae tidy before I meet Monro."

"Okay," I realized as he reluctantly removed himself from me when getting out of bed. I sat up against the pillows, crisscrossed my legs, and observed him moving across the floor toward the washbasin. He added fresh water from the ewer into the basin and took the nearby soap in hand. He dipped the bar into the water and began lathering his hands very well with it. I admired him while watching him beginning to spread frothy suds over his jaw. His lower face quickly appeared as if whipped cream had smeared all over it. He dabbed his hands dry on the towel and took the hand-held looking glass into his hand and held it in view before his face. Gathering the straight edge razor in his other hand, he placed the blade at a slight angle against his cheek. The edge began scraping down, and the creamy suds vanished with the hair over his jaw.

"Will you please talk to Colonel Monro for me when you meet with him?" I started.

"Whitever fur?" Leif replied curiously as he shaved.

"Well, unfortunately, there's been a smallpox outbreak among—"

"Smallpox!" he interrupted abruptly with alarm struck on his face. He simultaneously ceased shaving and stared wide-eyed at me.

"Yes," I said.

"Are ye certain?" he asked with sharp uneasiness.

"Yes, I heard Colonel Monro talking about it with the captains," I informed him.

"*Lord Almighty!*" he expressed, startled. He let his busy hands fall to the table with the razor and the looking glass over it. "Do ye ken how many?"

"Twelve men—Monro has them quarantined from the fort to isolate the spread."

"Guid. Has anyone else been afflicted?"

"No one else so far that we know."

"Och, thank the Lord Almighty."

"So far so good at least—the gestation period is a little over a week and a half, however. Until then, we won't really know where we stand with the outbreak."

"I see..." Leif fathomed, visibly troubled by this news.

"But the thing is, is that I must be allowed to tend to those who are infected otherwise they'll most likely die," I said.

"Surely, indeed not!" he said, adamantly opposed. "It is certainly out of the question."

"But I can help them."

"This is a most unfortunate revelation, but I shall not permit ye tae visit the plagued in this case."

"But, I'm the only one here who can see to their medical care."

"Ye may not. I shall not permit yer welfare tae be compromised in this case knowing full weel whit the outcome will be. My answer tae ye is nae."

"I can't become infected though."

"That is utterly preposterous—of coorse ye can become plagued with the pox. I have knoon it tae take a six-foot-tall man down and bring him tae death's door. Listen tae me, *àille dhubh*, I ken ye fancy yerself quite resilient—and come tae reckon it reit now, ye are unusually fit fur a lass—but, this plague can overcome ye before ye understand it."

"Still, I'm telling you that I can't get sick from it."

"How is that at all possible?" he questioned quickly with an atrocious look of skepticism.

"Well," I started thinking fast, "I just won't."

"Aye, ye can, and ye will if I let ye be so careless."

"No—I won't. You must believe me."

"Why must I? It is unreasonable."

"Because I'm telling you the truth," I said anxiously. Leif paused for a moment.

"How can ye be certain? Fur, I am most certainly not," he resumed.

"I'm immune."

"Immune? I dinnae understand."

"I have a resistance to the disease," I revealed carefully. Leif stared at me with an impossible look.

"Ye dinnae appear tae have suffered the curse of the plague, so how can it be?"

"I was immunized when I was a ba—" I suddenly stopped myself.

"Aye?" he anticipated urging me to continue. I sighed a little, quickly trying to figure out what I was going to say to him. I thoughtfully clasped my hands together and looked him right in the eyes.

"It's very difficult to explain. I know that's not a good enough answer for you right now, but I'm just asking you to please trust me. You asked me to never lie to you, and I'm not lying to you when I'm telling you right now that I can promise you that nothing will happen to me if I were to treat those infected patients," I expressed sincerely.

"I dinnae understand how it is possible," he replied perturbedly and paused shortly. He was suddenly in thought, and as he was thinking, he still seemed gravely disinclined.

"I won't get sick. Nothing will happen to me. I promise. Please, Leif—believe me," I persisted carefully.

He released a heavy, reticent sigh and paced toward the bed. He sat on the edge next to me and took my hand into his.

"I dinnae ken whit tae reckon," he said honestly.

"I know what I'm talking about, Leif. You have to believe me."

"Ye seem quite certain."

"That's because I am."

"How are ye so certain, Sylvie?"

"I wish I could just tell you, but you wouldn't believe me if I did."

"Would I not?"

"No—you wouldn't. Trust me. I know what I'm talking about."

"I see," he responded pensively.

"It's too hard right now to tell you... Maybe one day I'll talk to you about it—but right now... I just can't."

"'Tis difficult fur me tae understand why ye wulnea explain yer reasoning tae me. Yet, I vowed tae ye that I wouldnae press yer secrets," he said, meditatively staring at me.

"I wish you'd believe me though—like I believe you."

"It is merely that I dinnae ken whit will become of me if ever I lost ye, Sylvie," he said, looking very concerned.

"Well, I don't want to lose you either, and you're at risk here—especially now because of the outbreak. You have to let me try to contain the spread if I can and treat those infected. You won't lose me. I promise," I swore. I placed my palm over his shoulder and stole my fingers over the back of his neck beneath his loose hair that had now grown three inches past his shoulders.

"I shall never forgive myself if ye grew ill and left me," he said again.

"I would never let you know that burden," I replied. Leif paused momentarily. I could see him thinking very seriously as the look on his face was stern while he kept his eyes locked onto mine without speaking. I realized my commitment to him through my promise, and I discovered right now that I meant to never break it. "Do you believe me?"

"Aye—I do believe ye. 'Tis strange that I reckon ye are telling me the truth about yer invulnerability tae the pox despite that I dinnae understand how it can be so," he said appearing very puzzled. I sensed his intense desire to know how I could be resistant, but he didn't press.

"Thank you," I said relieved. "Thank you for believing me—and, for respecting my perspective." I leaned and kissed him on the lips. I noticed some of the suds over his top lip had been smeared off when I withdrew.

"It best not be the last time ye lay yer lips upon mine. Do ye understand?" he warned.

"It won't," I promised.

He lightly stroked away the transferred frothy mustache above my lip with the pad of his thumb.

"Alrecht, then—I shall inform Monro. He wulnae understand my decision, but I shall convince him," Leif said.

"Thank you."

"Aye. I best not regret it, *àille dhubh*."

"You won't."

"I dinnae intend tae lose ye." He looked steadfast at me, silently connoting his meaning in addition.

"I know. You don't have to worry."

Leif nodded a little and straightened from the edge of the bed. He paced away from me, while I remained on the bed and crossed the room back to the basin where he started shaving again in silence.

I quietly watched him, recognizing how firmly attached he had become to me, and if something bad did happen to me, then I knew for certain that he'd become extremely forlorn. I didn't want that to ever happen to him because my feelings for him were mutual.

He soon completed shaving and began dressing. When he was

done, he strode toward me, still relaxing over the blankets, and placed a kiss over my brow.

"Be a guid lass," he said with an insinuating look.

"Yes indeedy, Your Grace," I razzed lightly in spite of the heaviness of our preceding conversation.

"Yoo're a *ribhinn bheadaidh*," he scoffed looking distantly amused.

"What's that?"

"It means impudent, shameless nymph," he said frankly.

"Oh."

"Yoo're sweet nonetheless." He lightly tapped the end of my nose. "Now mind yerself and remain out of trooble."

"I never cause any trouble," I said exceptionally.

"The mere notion that I want tae bed ye reit now is troublesome enough."

"Well, that's not my fault, obviously."

"Indeed, it most certainly is yer burden."

"How's that?"

"'Tis due tae yoo're being pert. Now, I must see Monro."

"All right."

"I'll later fetch ye fur tea."

"Okay."

He winked at me, then turned, crossing the room, and vanished behind the door as he stepped outside.

Twenty-Eight

I started treating the twelve men infected with smallpox immediately after Leif had convinced Monro to let me see to their proper medical attention. Leif was correct about Monro's reservation over the matter. But, the authorization, however, couldn't have come any sooner given the twelve days that had already passed. I wasn't sure in what state I might have found the ill men as Leif escorted me to the isolated medical camp.

"I don't recommend you come any further with me, Leif," I suggested, taking precaution as the white canvas tents came into view. "It's highly infectious as you know."

"Aye," he acknowledged concernedly. "Yoo're certain of this?"

"Yes. It's all right."

"Then, I shall bide fur ye haur."

"Okay," I agreed. I resumed walking without him through the woods and approached the camp. As I advanced toward one of the tents, I noticed Corporal Jennings, who had survived the illness and remained deeply pockmarked from the affliction, in the middle of digging a wide hole in the ground.

"Your Grace! You must not be here," Jennings warned nervously, noticing my unexpected appearance.

"It's all right, Corporal Jennings. You needn't worry. I've been granted the opportunity to aid the men with the medical care they need by Colonel Monro," I said. He didn't seem at all persuaded, since he remained visibly uncomfortable seeing me.

"Yet, it is a bad state here, Your Grace. You will become ill," he warned.

"Like you, I'll remain unaffected too," I said. "See, His Grace is standing right over there between the trees watching us." I turned slightly to the side and pointed to where Leif was standing at a distance between the trees. Jennings looked and spotted him far enough away, staring directly at us.

"I see His Grace," Jennings observed cautiously.

"All right, then, will you please bring me to date of the men's status," I requested professionally. Jennings looked a bit rattled, obviously shocked and confused that I'd been granted permission to be here. "Please?" I shifted my heavy medical bag into my other hand as I stood before him, waiting for him to update me.

"Aye. Temple and Brady did not survive the fever, Your Grace," he informed me with a muddled expression.

"Oh..." I said remorsefully. "That is disturbing news. I'm so sorry to hear about them."

"Aye, Your Grace. 'Tis quite unfortunate," Jennings agreed. "If you should need assistance tending to the others, pray do call. I am in the midst of digging their graves."

"Yes, thank you, Corporal Jennings."

"Aye, Your Grace," he acknowledged with a short nod also. I turned toward the closest tent and entered it. Four men were easily noticed lying on blankets over the ground with two blankets unoccupied now. I opened my medical bag and promptly began making my rounds examining the patients. Their fevers were extremely high, I noted. They coughed, vomited, and moaned with severe aches and pains similar to flu symptoms. They all appeared to be in close phases of the disease—most likely having contracted it during the same period.

I had Jennings help me attempt to reduce their fevers with lukewarm body compresses. I used mustard wraps and other topical medicinal herb concoctions like mint, basil, and yarrow ointments to subdue body aches as well as low doses of ipecac for a decongestant. I had also devised a mild solution of salt potash and zinc to assist in maintaining hydration, along with an Angelica brew to aid in reducing fever. The men in the second tent appeared in nearly the same condition, so Jennings and I continued with the same treatment.

It took a long while to nurse the ten remaining men. I concluded my first day attending them by feeding them a simple chicken broth for nourishment. After scrubbing my hands and nails down with a thick soapy boar brush in a bucket of lukewarm water, I removed my soiled apron and hung it over a tree limb.

"Thank you, Your Grace, for your mercy," Jennings said modestly the minute I was about to depart the hospital camp.

"Thank you, Corporal Jennings. Of course, it's no problem—anything I can do to help. Thank you for your good assistance," I said.

"Indeed, Your Grace is most welcome," he replied respectfully.

"I'll see you tomorrow."

"Aye, Your Grace."

Jennings politely bowed his head, and I automatically reciprocated a simple acknowledging smile before resuming my departure. I left Jennings as he stoked the campfire, feeling myself quite drained from my work today. Advancing part way through the woods, I found Leif resting on the ground, relaxing an arm over a raised knee with his back against a tree trunk, aimlessly staring at the long pine needle he was twirling between his fingertips. He noticed me advancing toward him and straightened to his feet, tossing the pine needle to the ground.

"Weel?" he wondered gravely.

"Brady and Temple didn't make it," I said.

"Och, that is dreadful tae hear," Leif responded unfortunately with a horrible look.

"Yeah," I agreed. "But the others seem like they might pull through once the fever breaks."

"How long till that occurs?"

"It should be in about two more days."

"Och," he said. "Then, the dreaded pox will appear."

"Right," I said.

"'Tis a terrible pity."

"It is."

"Are ye ready tae return?" he inquired.

"Yeah," I said. We started together through the trees making our way back to the fort. "I need a bath," I blurted, thinking aloud.

"Then I shall have it drawn fur ye," he offered.

"Thank you," I said gratefully as I gladly thought about sitting in the small copper tub in our room to refresh at last.

"My clothes also need to be boiled just to be safe."

"I shall see that is done."

"But I should probably handle my own clothes. I don't want anyone to become infected by them. My clothes aren't sanitary anymore."

"Very weel," he agreed.

DESPITE LEIF'S supportiveness regarding my providing medical care to the infected soldiers, I could sense his unspoken uneasiness and apprehension pertaining to my best interest in doing it. Every day since the first day he had escorted me to the quarantined camp site, he continued to do so for the duration—parting from me at the buffer zone and meeting me again at the same location like clockwork.

The fever broke as anticipated in the next couple of days, followed by the rash and developed pustules all over the skin. The disease had peaked at its highest propensity for transmission with oral lesions and leaking pustules releasing large amounts of the virus from saliva and dermis pus. It was a horrifying disease to be dealt with. To particularly witness its occurrence first hand reinforced in my mind the fortunate miracle advantages of modern medicine to which people were all accustomed in my time period, and I was deeply regretting the lack of it now.

Monro had ordered some days earlier all the bedding and clothing belonging to the infected to be discarded and burned as a precaution. By day sixteen, it was observed with good fortune that no one else from within the fort had acquired the illness while the ones in isolation had progressed to the final stages of their affliction with scabs developed all over the lesions. The scabs had caused a tremendous amount of itching and irritation, making the afflicted vulnerable to flesh infection. So, Jennings and I applied a calamine solution I had concocted to ease the itching, and stave off infection. Later I introduced Epsom salt wraps to help clear the skin, which worked somewhat and seemed to leave the blemishes slightly less noticeable as they healed.

WHEN TWENTY-FIVE DAYS HAD PASSED, I finally gave Monro the all-clear notice. He was quite gratified by the news, not to mention how extremely relieved Leif was to learn of the favorable outcome, also regarding my own unaffected health. I sat at the dining table eating dinner with Leif, surrounded by officers listening to Monro grant me a positive review of my efforts, the evening the surviving ten men returned to the fort.

"Thank you, Colonel Monro," I said demurely after he praised me. I glanced at Leif when he caught my eye and proudly looked at me as the sound of clinking spoons against glass tumblers chimed around the table in recognizable applause. "Thank you, I only did what anyone else would do if one could," I said self-deprecatingly, feeling very self-conscious.

"Well done," Monro said admirably. "I presume His Grace is quite pleased with his wife's achievement."

"Indeed, Colonel," Leif responded proudly.

"Aye," Monro echoed and took a swig from his glass of rum. Everyone else seated around the table ensued with a drink of their own, then the conversation turned to other business as full dinner plates were being consumed.

I sat eating quietly while listening with interest to the latest events taking place. None were thrilled over the fact that every patrol mission up to Fort Carillon had been impeded by terrorizing Huron, Potawatomi and French bushwhacking our surveyors along the way. Apparently, Monro had underway the construction of several serviceable boats, finally near completion, and a plan that was to be executed in mere days.

The operation was to sail up the lake toward Lake Champlain where Fort Carillon rested at the foot of the lake and burn out the enemy's sawmills. It seemed to be a sensible strategy that would be a component enabling our position to be at an advantage. Leif and Finley were to lead the dangerous charge. My heart skipped a beat just as I had placed my teacup to my lips when Monro ordered them to do it. Instead of taking a sip of tea from my cup, I replaced my cup over the table, listening more to the conversation, abruptly worried that Leif and Finley would leave this fortress again to go on another dangerous mission.

A sharp unsettling feeling overcame me. I was daunted by the idea of them going on such a mission, and the fear was distinctive. After what had happened in their last reconnaissance mission, and knowing what I knew now about the other failed spying attempts, I didn't want either Leif or Finley participating in the objective this time around.

I wanted to jump into the conversation right now, but I consciously forced myself to bite my tongue as I was constrained to silence knowing it was not my place to speak. Instead, I remained silently attentive in angst while continuing to listen to their conversation.

As I sat there at the table hearing them speak of this mission, I realized that I had to wait to talk to Leif about it in private. But my soonest chance to discuss it with him seemed remote, and my case for dissuading him I knew wouldn't be convincing. Still, I was going to try my best to influence him, and hoped I'd be successful.

LATER, after dinner, I sat in the chair by the window in our room, combing my hair, thinking about the best way to broach the subject with Leif. He hadn't returned yet from relaxing with a game of cards and enjoying a smoke with Finley and some of their other pals that included their cousins. I couldn't decide on how to mention my feelings and concerns about their new mission without sounding illogical or completely unreasonable.

The small mantel clock chimed, and I glanced at it over the fireplace noticing the time. It was getting late in the evening. I straightened from the bench and moved away from the window to place my comb back on the nightstand. I crossed the room toward the door and stepped outside onto the landing directly before the threshold and decided to pace down the staircase. Strolling past several quarters, I rounded the corner to the dining quarter and peeped inside through the open window, seeking Leif to talk to him. It appeared vacant inside, so I wandered toward the front of the barrack and entered the room simply to see if the room was actually empty.

The loud sound of fiddling came through the door that had been left wide open as I checked the room. Discerning the area to be truly cleared from a single soul, I turned for the doorway and exited the officers' dining room. The music band was detected animated in the middle of the courtyard, stomping their feet to the rhythm of their dancing fiddles, fifes, and drums. Laughter and cheers roared among the sizable congregated crowd encircling the band when I noticed several couples dancing to the tunes moving around each other in quick steps as they hooked arms and crisscrossed their partners similar to a country square dance. It seemed everyone was having a good time.

I started pacing again alongside the barrack in the opposite direction from where I'd come until I found a quiet spot at the corner between the barrack buildings and leaned against the wall, enjoyably watching the lively crowd. The melodies were buoyant and fun, and could inspire anyone's foot to tap.

While admiring the dancing crowd, I noticed a wobbling soldier with a mug in hand totter toward a barrel a slight distance from where I was standing. He bent to sit, except he missed the edge of the barrel by an inch and unexpectedly fell square on his backside onto the ground, losing his balance off to the side as he suddenly landed. He effectively spilled the remaining portion of his drink from his mug when he tilted onto his back sprawled over the dirt. I wasn't certain if he was groaning out of pain, or out of being in a drunken stupor, as I was just about to leave my nice secluded spot to check to see if he was all right.

"Crap!" he hissed, apparently angry at himself for having spilled his drink. A faint laugh escaped me despite myself when I quickly realized that he hadn't injured himself in his fall. He was apparently too drunk to even notice me standing only several paces behind him, watching.

"Och, haur ye are," Leif muttered unexpectedly into my ear from behind me, startling me a little. I suddenly turned, noticing pearly teeth gleaming on his shadowed face.

"Hi," I responded lightly.

"Whit amuses ye?" The warm, sweet scent of wine was on his breath.

"That guy over there is totally wasted." I gestured to the soldier now sprawled out flat on his back over the ground as if he had been hit by a train.

"Och, he does appear tae be a waste," Leif said, also observing the drunk soldier.

"He misjudged where he was supposed to sit on the barrel and fell flat to the ground instead," I sniggered.

"Did he indeed?" Leif slipped an arm around my waist pulling me from the wall.

"Yeah," I said as he released my waist and took my hand into his instead.

"A pity whit too much spirits can do tae a man."

"Yeah," I laughed lightly. Leif chuckled a little too.

"Micht ye please me with a dance?" he asked agreeably.

"Sure," I replied gladly.

"Grand."

He bowed and I curtsied. Suddenly, he had us dancing in private a slow reel to the lovely protracted melody of a single fife and second soprano in haunting Irish Gaelic.

As we repeated the steps in the middle of our dance, we gently took each other by the waist and rotated together. We released each other and he took my hand. I unthinkingly altered the move and slowly twirled beneath his extended fingers, ending up close against his chest as I wrapped my arm around his lean waist.

"Whit motion was that?" he inquired, intrigued.

"An old disco move my mom and dad used to do together when they danced," I answered.

"I dinnae reckon that I am familiar with it," he said in a curious tone.

"I don't suppose you are." I smiled easily at him.

"And whit is it we are presently doing?" he inquired with captivation while I led him into merely swaying together to the languid ballad.

"Slow dancing," I said.

"Is this whit ye call it?"

"Yes."

"It is strange."

"I know."

"Quite scandalous, I micht say. Is it common?"

"Yes."

"Indeed?"

"Yes."

"Curious."

"But the music would be a little different when dancing this way." I took his hand, stretching his easy arm forth and gently turned beneath his hovering fingers again.

"The music is different?"

"Yes."

"In whit manner?"

"There's a gentle rhythm to it," I said imagining the languid beat in my head to the soft song being sung now, and I ensued stepping into a gentle rumba.

"I see," he said as he suddenly remained motionless with fascination. "This sort of dance is quite, er, *personal*."

"It's called the rumba," I disclosed as I slowly circled around him, trailing my fingers over his lean waist while I passed in front of him.

"The rumba," he repeated questioningly. He snared me motionless as I arrived facing him again.

"Yes," I said. His hand stole around my neck, and he lifted my chin with his thumb.

"I understand quite clearly the meaning of this dance," he muttered closely.

"You do?" I sensed his lips sweeping lightly over mine, not quite kissing.

"Aye." His voice sounded absorbed, and I saw firelight catching the inspired wonderment on his half-darkened face as he closely gazed at me. A palm ran down my sleeve, and he took my hand in his. He started calmly walking away with me, leading us out of the concealing alley between the barracks through the crowd as music, dancing, drinking, and cheers continued erupting around us.

We paced toward our barrack, with Leif leading me up the staircase until we entered our room. He closed the door behind us, and I simply looked at him as he scratched his head while we were now standing alone together in our quarters.

"Mayhap, we shall remain indoors for the evening," he suggested as he advanced inside the room.

"Sure," I agreed easily, inclined to tidy up before going to bed anyway. Leif pulled the shutters over all the windowpanes to a close. He then paced toward the chair and sat, proceeding to remove his boots. I kicked off my boots also, and we comfortably started undressing ourselves. I easily removed my trousers once all the buttons to my waistcoat had been undone and I began unlacing my pair-of-bodies. Leif quickly tugged his shirt overhead, revealing his sculpted naked form after his breeches were withdrawn from him. He then began helping me unlace my pair-of-bodies over my short camisole styled shift. It was a bit of a relief to have the garment finally taken off me, and I placed it in the chair at the writing desk.

"Not so quick, lass," he said noticing me beginning to slip beneath the blankets, ready for bed.

"Why?" I asked curiously. He remained standing tall at the foot of the bed, hardly appearing ready to retire for the night.

"Come haur," he said, intimating for me to approach him.

"What for?"

"Merely come haur."

"All right," I said innocently, agreeing to get out of bed. I walked around the mattress toward him wondering what he was up to. "Now what?" I shrugged.

"Now ye may dance yer secret rumba fur me," he said. It sounded like a strong request coming from him, rather than a light joke.

"Right now?"

"Aye."

"With you naked just like that?"

"I reckon it is now quite appropriate."

I started laughing a little. I covered my mouth to subdue myself, but I just couldn't help it and kept laughing. Leif didn't seem to quite understand why I was so amused, but he was smiling too.

"Have I misunderstood the meaning of yer dance?" he asked, grinning at me.

"No," I said, calming myself as I gazed at him.

"Then, show it tae me again so that I may plainly see it."

"Okay." I willingly took his hand and placed it around my back. The color in his cheeks became apparent as I took my right hand in his and placed my left over his shoulder. I started softly singing *The Way You Look Tonight*, once made popular by Frank Sinatra, as I subsequently began stepping into the light rhythmic box steps of the dance with my hips naturally swaying side to side according to each step I took.

Obviously not knowing how to move accordingly, Leif simply remained motionless before me with his eyes transfixed to mine while I gently danced in a stationary spot before him. The music outside could still be heard with fiddles playing quickly again, but didn't interrupt the melody I was gently singing to him.

I held his stare as I slowly twirled beneath his extended fingers. The look on his face was sheer captivation and allure as I danced. He seemed fascinated, unknowing like a teenage boy who snuck his first peek inside an exotic dancer's bar, as I resumed repeating the first part of the dance. Suddenly, I was embarrassed by the attracted look in his eyes, and I dropped my gaze as I circled around him with simple steps. When I centered before him again, I decided to stop.

"Is that the entirety?" he asked, really enchanted.

"No," I said self-consciously.

"Pray, complete it," he encouraged. He was engrossed and was dissatisfied by my hesitation. "Continue."

"Okay," I muttered self-consciously. I was still willing to please him, and I started again. After the first series of duplicate box steps, I danced in front of him, I continued with an open break underarm turn. I repeated the motion, then progressed to a cross over break under arm turn, replicating the move three times. I parallel broke with him to the right and then again to the left. Stepping half a box, I opened and broke into an underarm turn and glided a walk around him. "There," I said bashfully, meeting the enticed expression in his eyes.

"That is it, then?" he asked, disappointed that I had finished.

"Yeah."

"Och."

"Why are you looking at me like that?"

"In whit manner?"

"I don't know. Like you are, I guess."

"Weel, I huvnae ever seen this sort of dance," he answered.

"Oh."

"It appeals tae me."

"It does?" I looked at him with surprise. "So, you like it?"

"Verily," he said in a low voice. "'Tis an irregular dance."

"I guess so," I regarded.

He sat on the edge of the bed and slid a hand around my waist. He drew me near between his muscular thighs, and now he gazed up into my eyes.

"Yoo're full of secrets, *rìbhinn*," he said. "However, ye are not permitted tae dance like that again with *anyone*. 'Tis forbidden. Is it understood?" His tone and the expression on his face turned entirely stern. He wasn't kidding. I felt a little unnerved by him for a second while staring back into his eyes.

"Yeah, sure," I replied genuinely, noticing the light beads of perspiration formed on his brow.

"Unless, 'tis with me," he said.

"Okay," I muttered, sensing his slightly calloused hands gliding around my naked thighs and over my buttocks as they began pushing my short shift above my abdomen.

He seized my gaze for a second longer before he sank his rapturous lips over my exposed navel, and a sudden burning need came over me as he kissed me there. My blood began warming and I strangely ached for him from within. He coerced me around him over the bed and caged me beneath him. He wedged my thighs apart with his knee and I sensed him hard and erect at my entrance. He invisibly took himself and stroked his swollen shaft between my cleft, spreading me open. Then in a single, voracious thrust he entered me, completely sheathing himself to the hilt.

AFTERWARD, we lay peacefully entwined in each other's arms, still connected in the aftermath of our lovemaking. He lifted his gaze to mine and stared at me as his fingers tenderly caressed my face and sank into my loose ringlets.

"What are you thinking?" I whispered as I gently stroked his long hair strands draping around his face before placing them behind his shoulders.

"That I am wholly gratified that ye belong tae me," he said softly.

"Oh," I whispered. "That's very sweet."

"I adore ye," he said in hushed tones. His lips came over mine again in a tender kiss. "Och!" he growled abruptly, interrupting our kiss, and suddenly disengaged from me, leaving me empty between my thighs.

"What's the matter?" I asked strangely as I observed him rear up on his knees, scratching vigorously at the golden tuft around his slightly flaccid penis.

"Och! I have become most uncomfortable of late," he informed me while continuing to energetically scratch himself.

"What are you talking about?" I shot up from the pillows alarmed, looking at him as he promptly turned his gaze down on himself. He sieved through the pretty yellow hairs amid his groin with his combing fingers.

"David Jones!" he cursed, annoyed.

"What is it?" I asked, aghast.

"I reckon I have become afflicted with phthiriasis," he said.

"What the hell!" I squealed, looking at him wide-eyed with appall.

"Calm yerself, *ceisdein*. 'Twill be alrecht," he said collectedly.

"Like hell!" I exclaimed and lunged toward his pubic hair to have a good look for myself.

"'Tis merely beasties. They wulnae kill ye!" he chuckled, making light of it. I glared at him instead, certainly unamused. But he was obviously amused by me since he kept chuckling.

"This is not funny!" I scolded seriously.

"I reckon 'tis on my head also."

"Are you serious?"

"Aye. Have a look fur me, then," he said. I leaned up on my knees and carefully examined his scalp.

"Unbelievable!" I gasped, horrified.

"Aye, it makes me scratch like the dickens."

"No kidding, Sherlock!"

"Sherlock?" he wondered quizzically.

"Never mind!"

"Lie yerself upon the bed," he instructed while laughing.

"No way." I shook my head, absolutely opposed. He chuckled louder.

"Lie, I say," he ordered laughingly, becoming more flushed in the face.

"You're not touching me!" I exclaimed adamantly. I suddenly jumped away from him. But his hands sharply snagged my ankles and tugged, whipping my legs from beneath me. I collapsed onto my stomach over the blankets as he easily forced me onto my back and yanked me down toward him. "Let me go! You're not touching me! You hear?" I squealed, trying to wiggle away from him.

"Ye best collect yerself, *ceisdein*, or I'll take a hand tae yer backside," he chuckled some more as he caged me with my legs kicking beneath him.

"What are you doing?" I panted while trying to free myself from him.

"I merely wish tae have a look at ye, that is all," he sighed ridiculously, finally curbing his laughter.

"Oh—okay," I realized and gave up thrashing.

"Now, remain still."

"Fine." I relaxed and allowed him to examine me. I horrendously shut my eyes at the hideous prospect of being infected while I felt his fingers carefully beginning to search between my spread thighs.

"Och, weel the nits are clearly seen," he noticed forthrightly.

"Ugh!" I cried, utterly repulsed. I shot out from under him and pounced off the bed to my feet onto the floor. "Oh my God! Oh my God!" I expressed ghastly, shaking, and shimmying myself in an appalling jog before the bed. I couldn't stop moving as I was completely freaking out. "This is awful! This is just absolutely awful!" I kept squawking. "I'm so repulsed! I can't believe it! *Ugh!* I want them off me! How could this have happened? Ooh this godawful place is so dirty! *Dirty! Dirty! Dirty!*" After a second I realized Leif was keeled over on the bed hysterically laughing so hard tears were streaming down his carmine face. "What's so funny?" I asked sharply. It took him a minute to compose himself enough to talk as I irritably observed him.

"I dinnae understand ye, lass," he said, still laughing hard.

"Why not?" I gave him a bizarre look.

"Ye are the soondest lass I ken. Ye have nae fear tossing yourself off rocks, or walking into deadly illnesses time and again! Or, throwing yerself about upon ice! Yet ye cry out and carry on as if the Devil has ye by the heels when ye merely have beasties upon ye!" he said laughingly.

"Well this lice crap can hurt you too!" I puffed excitedly. He looked at me like I was crazy and started laughing hard all over again. "Oh fine! Laugh at me all you want at my expense!"

"Gladly!" he roared, hysterically hooting.

"I don't care!" I stomped my foot, disgruntled at him. "You shouldn't have done this to me!"

"I huvnae done aught tae ye!" he chortled pulling himself upright sitting on the mattress.

"Yes you did!" I accused.

"Whit do ye mean? Nearly the entire camp has been afflicted with it," he said, collecting himself as he wiped his laughing tears from his eyes.

"Really?"

"Aye," he said actually. "Ye have been quite preoccupied with those who truly need yer assistance whilst serving those imperiled men with the pox. This particular circumstance isnae perilous amongst the encamped haur. So, nae one is going tae tell ye tae cure him of it when everyone knows how tae manage it."

"I see." I hopelessly shook my head and gave a resigned sigh. "Great—now we're in the middle of a lice outbreak. What else can go wrong?" I denounced. "Oh wait—I shouldn't have put that out there for the universe to hear." I rapped my knuckles against the log wall at the head of our bed. Leif lifted his brow and gave me an odd look as he smirked.

"Och," he muttered smilingly as I watched him scratching his head.

"You know, everything has to be washed now."

"I realize."

"Everything—disinfected in boiling hot water."

"Aye."

"All the bedding too," I said, believing I felt an itch over my head now.

"Aye," he said merely, scratching his head some more.

"I have never in my entire life come down with a case of lice or crabs." I scratched my head finally, aware of a distinct itch on it for certain.

"Never?" Leif's eyes widened, looking rather shocked.

"Never," I replied undoubtedly.

"Och," he said, amazed. "I have been afflicted a number of times that I can nae longer count."

"Thank you for sharing," I said ironically. He chuckled again understanding me. "Of course, no one's ever thought of actually disinfecting the bedding with boiling water when they do laundry around here before even thinking of changing everyone's sheets!"

"Weel," he said, straightening from the bed to his feet. "I shall draw yer water and *disinfect* ye also. A run of cotton-weed soap will take care of it."

He winked at me, and I noticed the residual grin over his humored face. His finger lightly tapped the tip of my nose when he moved past me toward the chamber pot to relieve himself.

Twenty-Nine

It took a prolonged period of time to finally rid ourselves from the crabs and lice that had infested us. I tediously combed through the long hair over Leif's head extracting the nits, making sure that I had adequately covered all the areas of his crown to the nape of his neck. I was finally able to convince him to let me trim his hair as a future precaution that would save us a lot of time and effort, and might possibly help prevent the likelihood of easily contracting it again.

"How much will ye crop?" he asked as he skeptically eyed the sheers in my hand.

"Not too much," I assured while he held the hand-held looking-glass before his eyes. "I mean, I could just as well take it all off," I teased. He abruptly leaped from the chair and scowled at me.

"Ye will do nae such thing," he warned with appall.

"Why not? It would save a lot of hassle—plus, you'd really look like a G.I.," I taunted shamelessly.

"I dinnae ken whit a G.I. is but I dinnae agree with it," he said sharply, giving me a certain look. "Do ye understand?"

"Fine," I said. "You don't have to get your breeches tied up in a knot." I deprecated. He glowered at me again, and I nicely patted the chair in front of me. "C'mon—I won't hurt you. I promise."

"Och! Ye need a lashing across that bonnie backside of yers," he chided. The smirk over his face was quite visible, and I laughed.

"I promise I'll cut it to the length we had agreed on," I resumed honestly.

"Alrecht." He paced back toward the chair and sat. I subsequently began combing his damp, silky strands down his back past his shoulders. Then, I took the sheers in hand and carefully started snipping away at his hair as he remained silent and rigid before me in the chair.

When I had finished shaping the gilded strands around his head that now hovered noticeably shorter just above his shoulders, I examined my handy work and thought he appeared strikingly handsome as usual. *No harm, no foul.* So, I gazed at him and smiled.

"Is it despicable?" he asked uneasily.

"No. It's not," I assured.

"Hmph! We shall see about it." He lifted the handheld looking-glass into view and scrutinized his head.

"You look very nice," I commented sincerely.

"'Twill suffice," he considered thoughtfully as he continued gazing at himself in the looking-glass. When he was satisfied, he stood from his seat. "Thank ye, *ceisdein*." He turned and softly pecked a kiss over my brow. "Are ye alrecht?"

"Huh?"

"Ye appear a bit weary." He placed the looking glass on the seat of the chair and put his hands over my shoulders, looking curiously at me.

"Oh, no, I'm all right," I said.

"I ken that we have had a terribly endless nicht. Ye must be quite weary. Mayhap, rest fur ye now is in order," he urged. It occurred to me now that I was quite tired. It sounded like a good idea to have a nap.

"Okay," I agreed.

"Very weel." He leaned and pressed his lips over mine in a quick kiss. When he straightened from kissing me, he lightly caught my chin between his fingers with a warmhearted wink. "I shall return later tae have tea with ye."

"Okay."

"Alrecht then." He moved away from me toward the door while brushing his hand over his shoulder, removing some of the faint remaining cut strands of hair. Gathering his waistcoat in hand, he easily swung it around his back as he pushed his arms through the armholes and buttoned it all the way down the front before disappearing behind the chamber door.

At that moment, I decided to pace toward the freshly laundered bedding and threw myself over the pillows ready for a long-awaited nap.

LATER, after napping, I noticed Leif coming through the door to our room and shutting it as I was arranging my latest medical records while sitting at the desk. He was staring at me as he paced deeper into our room and sat in the chair at the table, puffing on his pipe, still gazing at me.

"Why are you looking at me?" I inquired insecurely when I peered up from my work.

"I reckon ye appear irregular with cropped hair," he observed with a discerning eye. His smoking pipe drooped between his lips when he released it as he began removing his boots.

"You don't like it?" I asked uncertainly. I lightly stroked the cow-lick curls naturally flipping up at the ends of my new jaw-length, bobbed haircut that conceivably was a long way fashion forward.

"I do quite fancy it. Yoo're bonnie nae matter how shortly

cropped yer tresses are," he said surely, admiring me from across the room.

"Thank you," I said. I stood from my seat at the desk and paced across the room to gather the handheld looking glass from the only night stand by his bedside. I gazed thoughtfully at the razor cut pixy bangs above my brow that I had given myself, and admired the pair of matching crystal rosette pins on each side of my head holding a portion of hair back. "I think I appear rather avant-garde," I muttered to myself.

"Avant-garde?" Leif overheard.

"Yeah," I said, turning to look at him. He stood tall from his chair and began removing his waistcoat, as he was strangely looking at me.

"Aye, ye raither do appear unorthodox, indeed. However, ye are not tae blame fur it given the beasties of which ye had tae rid yerself. Ye are far too bonnie a lass tae pass as a lad nae matter how ye shall arrange yer hair—even in those abhorrent breeks ye fancy having upon yerself," he said absolutely. I smiled at him. He really wasn't fond of my beloved trousers. Still, he tolerated them fair enough.

"Thanks," I said giving him an appreciative look.

"Yoo're a bonnie *sìthiche*, certainly." He tossed his waistcoat over the back of the chair.

"What's that?"

"A wee folk. 'Tis whit I reckon of ye, of coorse."

"What's a wee folk?"

"A fairy."

"A *fairy*?" I looked strangely at him, replacing the looking-glass down on the nightstand.

"Aye," he said indifferently.

"Oh."

"Ye are certainly wee," he said ironically.

"Amazing—I had no idea," I replied sarcastically.

"Yet, ye are."

"Well, anyone is small compared to you—you're a giant like Paul Bunyan!" I replied ironically.

"Who is Paul Bunyan?"

"A folklore legend who was a giant lumberjack."

"Och," he chuckled. "Ye are wee nae matter."

"Thank you. You're so informative." I winked and smirked flippantly at him. His brow suddenly lifted high on his head and he abruptly snagged my wrist, surprising me.

"Come haur ye shameless nymph!" he said, pulling me near and firmly sat me over his lap. He grasped his pipe from his lips. "Now ye listen haur. Yoo're fortunate that I grant ye my patience, and I reckon 'tis because I adore ye. Otherwise make nae mistake about it—I would turn ye across my knee and give yer crease a guid lashing."

I could feel the smile on my face growing very wide as I tried looking at him without laughing. He perhaps sounded serious, but he had an indulgent grin on his face too.

"You're funny," I admitted, stifling a giggle.

"Am I?" he responded smilingly.

"Um-hm." I nodded. He peered at the small clock ticking on the pine mantelpiece then placed his smoking pipe over the letter desk beside him.

"In that case, it seems I micht have a bit of a moment tae teach ye a proper lesson." He abruptly stood scooping me high off his lap into his arms, completely catching me off guard.

"What sort of lesson?" I gasped laughingly.

"The sort that will remind ye how tae mind yer tongue." He suddenly flung me, and I simultaneously squealed as I went slightly airborne over the bed. He quickly pounced over me as I suddenly sank on my back into the mattress. I found myself swiftly enclosed by him as he hovered above me. We laughed a little together perceiving amusement in each other's eyes. "Now, ye must cite tae me whit ye have learnt once I'm through with yer instruction."

"So what's the lesson?" I asked, staring back up at his looming gaze. His eyes sparkled and mischief was recognizable on his face.

"The first aspect of yer lesson regards fine tuning that ear of yers," he said frankly.

"Okay?" I gave him a doubtful look.

"Ye must mind whit yer husband tells ye tae do," he specified.

"Sure," I said flippantly.

"Now," he started thoughtfully. "I bid ye first kiss me reit haur." Leif pointed to his chin.

"Easy enough." I lifted my lips to his chin and kissed it.

"And reit haur." He tapped a finger over his right jaw.

"Fine." I simply placed a kiss upon it.

"And haur." He tapped his left jaw. I ensued giving him a peck there also. "Haur," he continued, pointing to his brow. Of course, I obliged. "Quite importantly not tae disregard haur." He touched the tip of his finger to his pursed lips. I leaned up and pressed my lips gently over his. "Weel done," he said.

"Is that it?"

"Scarcely."

"What next?"

"Ye must now repeat efter me."

"Yes, Your Grace." I looked at him quizzically.

"I'm earnest," he said seriously in spite of the slanted grin over his easy-going expression.

"Fine," I agreed facetiously.

"Repeat efter me now—I shall be a guid lass and mind my tongue not tae sauce my husband," he said frankly. I laughed out loud, entertained.

"You think I'm sassy?" I laughed, amused.

"Quite." He was sure of it even though he was completely smiling.

"My goodness—how silly." I couldn't help laughing some more.

"Certainly, it is."

"I don't sass," I said really.

"Yoo're most certainly saucy," he countered factually.

"If that's what you think, even though I'm really not—just so that you know the truth about me."

"I reckon I quite clearly already ken the truth about ye, *àille dhubh.*" He arched an eyebrow, and the smirk on his face made me laugh.

"And if I don't repeat what you say, then what?"

"Then I shall punish ye!" he roared as he playfully swooped down over my neck tickling me with biting kisses. He unforgivingly delighted me with nipping lips all over my neck, and I laughed hysterically. After a moment, he slightly reared up, and I caught his entertained gaze as I wheezed, catching my breath.

"That's not fair," I said breathlessly, still smiling at him.

"Of coorse, it is most fair."

"I can't escape from you."

"I ken," he chuckled. "Ye deserve it." He leaned in close, pressing his lips over mine as my breath began settling. He continued kissing me with soft, warm little kisses over my chin and neck. His lips trailed back up to mine, and we began kissing each other with warmth and affection—and, growing heat.

An unexpected knocking audibly came from behind the door, and Leif broke from my lips.

"Damnation! Not at the moment," he muttered, annoyed at the interruption. "Aye?" he answered with vexation, still hovering soundly over me.

"I beg your pardon, Your Grace, it is Major Rogers." The voice was muffled behind the door.

"Aye, major, whit is it?" Leif inquired as he continued gazing at me. He grimaced, expressing displeasure.

"Colonel Monro requests a brief," Rogers informed him.

"Aye—thank ye. I shall meet promptly," Leif replied.

"Very well, Your Grace," Rogers said. Footsteps immediately started from behind the door and diminished down the steps.

"*Damnation*," Leif hissed, scowling. He lightly kissed my lips and raised himself from me. "Dinnae reckon yer lesson with me is completed, wife," he warned, giving me a slightly playful glance as he moved to collect his boots.

"Well, now you've got me shaking with fear," I said tongue-in-cheek.

"Och! Ye do indeed need a bit of discipline," he chuckled briskly as he sat in one of the two chairs by the desk, shoving one foot down into a boot. I gave him a quirky grin and an amused look crossed his face. He smirked knowingly and I giggled. He dropped his glance from me to the next boot he was fitting over his foot. A pause ensued, and I crisscrossed my legs while sitting on the edge of the bed, watching him. He straightened from his seat and grasped his waistcoat draped over the back of the chair.

"Leif?" I started.

"Aye, my angel?" he said while focusing on buttoning the waistcoat over his chest.

"I have a bad feeling," I disclosed sincerely. His eyes shot up from the buttons to me.

"A bad feeling?" he questioned attentively.

"Yes," I said, seriously holding his gaze as he suddenly paused fastening his waistcoat.

"Whit do ye mean?"

"The mission up the lake, I mean."

"Och," he realized with a faint sigh. He seemed slightly relieved that it wasn't something else. "I dinnae wish fur ye tae worry."

"But I *am* worried. It's a high-risk operation and I'm really concerned," I said. A faint sigh escaped him again, and a regrettable look came over his face. He crossed the floor toward me and sat close on the bed. He placed his hands evenly on each spread knee, and fixed his eyes steadily to mine.

"I wish ye waur never privy tae such information," he said.

"I don't want you to go," I said anyway.

"I ken. I have a duty, however. I must go. All will be weel, *ceisdein*. Yoo'll see," he said earnestly.

"No—that's not good enough," I replied quickly.

"Pray, dinnae be unreasonable with me, Sylvie," he said unemotionally.

"I'm not being unreasonable," I disagreed, steadily holding his gaze.

"I reckon that ye are. It is hard enough upon me that I must mind ye haur at every corner, that I can scarcely perform my proper duties as an efficacious officer tae Monro. Ye must understand," he said, seriously looking at me.

"Oh, I didn't realize I was constantly under your feet tripping you up like a toddler. Excuse me, I'm sorry," I said with offense. I suddenly shifted off the bed to my feet and started away from him. He swiftly snagged my wrist and gently spun me around to face him, pulling me back directly in front of him as he remained sitting on the bed.

"That is not whit I meant," he said in a uniform voice.

"It sure sounded that way," I said levelly too, trying to hide my emotions.

"I meant that having ye haur is pleasant and terrible fur me at the same moment. I dinnae fancy the notion of parting from ye at any time knowing whit awaits out yonder this fort. It concerns me, greatly. Nonetheless, I have a duty that I must honor." His palm slipped down from my wrist, and he gently held my hand.

"I understand," I said truthfully.

"Guid," he said.

"It's just that I have a really bad feeling about it," I continued unhappily.

"Aye, battle never permits pleasant sentiments."

"Yeah—that's true. I still don't want you to go, though. I don't think you should go. I know the way war can happen—and, I'm afraid for you," I said. Leif paused briefly, staring intently into my eyes.

"Ye ken the way of war," he echoed.

"Yes."

"Due tae yer father," he remembered, while his staring eyes were searching mine.

"Yes," I said as the first and second Gulf War came to mind. But I couldn't tell him about those things. "I'm now aware of how badly it's going." He remained quiet—not responding. I couldn't read his face as I stared back at him and it felt like a large pebble got stuck in my throat, leaving my wits suddenly scattered as I looked at him also.

"Ye mustn't worry, *ceisdein*. 'Twill be alrecht," he insisted after a moment.

"Don't tell me that."

"But I must," he assuaged.

"No, you don't."

"Why must I not?" He gave me a perplexed look.

"Because I know what I'm talking about, that's why," I said expressly.

"Dinnae be this way. 'Tis unpleasant."

"Of course it's unpleasant. What do you expect?"

"I dinnae understand why yoo're being trooblesome at present," he said, growing weary.

"Okay, I'll tell you why—because the insurgents are tough and illusive. Logistics are complicated and unpredictable. High command is out of touch and tyrannical, all the while leading us into a quagmire that will bring you back to me in a body bag. I hate war. I hate the military. It never ends. I get it. So, who cares?"

"I see..." he said after a second. "Weel, I do certainly care." I suddenly looked at him, realizing the stunned look on his face as it seemed he was trying to understand me. He was silent for a moment, assuming from my irrational outburst.

"Then if you care, you have to listen to me and not go," I said. He brought a hand to his brow and rubbed it hard with frustration. I also noticed his face seemed a little red when he pulled his palm away and looked straight at me again.

"Alrecht, calm now. Yoo're out of sorts, as yoo've worked yerself intae a state quite weel," he said unmoved.

"How can I stay calm when you and Finley are basically going to go out on a kamikaze mission? You're going to get yourselves killed, and you're telling me to calm down? That's ridiculous!"

Leif suddenly stood from his seat over the bed and towered over me, finally letting go of my hand.

"Ye are being quite petulant," he said, appearing aggravated.

"Petulant?" I repeated, rather annoyed also.

"Aye. Now that will be enough," he said, controlled with exasperation as he began finishing buttoning the rest of his waistcoat.

"I'm not finished though."

"Aye, ye are as I am through with this discussion."

"But—"

"That is quite enough, I say," he interjected frigidly. He was stilted with visible annoyance. "Hold yer tongue, lass. I let ye say yer piece, and now ye are quite through. I have important matters tae attend with Monro and the other officers, and I shall promptly see tae it. We shall discuss this nae further. Ye best understand." His tone was even and calibrated, and I could see that patience had worn thin with him. He was cool and not pleased. Leif rigidly bowed his head to me, and I stood staring at him, surprised that he would take such a tone with me. He turned away and paced toward the door. Reaching for the handle, he pulled the door open and stepped out into the outdoors, vanishing behind it when he shut it closed.

Well! I was sheerly incensed after he essentially shut me down and told me to be quiet. He just left me alone standing there like a moron. I never expected a time he would ever turn his back and walk out on me. I was stunned, and it made me angry.

I remained in the room irritated for a moment longer. Then, I decided to dress and attend matters in the infirmary, preferring not to dwell on how much he had irritated me while I distracted myself with my own duties.

AFTER DINNER, Leif and I entered our room together in noticeable silence. I was not particularly in a sociable mood, although I discerned he wanted to speak. Instead, I went to the chamber pot without a word. When I was finished, I noticed him sitting comfortably smoking his pipe while going over correspondences at the desk. I didn't understand how he could be so composed over the issue between us, and it silently miffed me.

I started undressing, silently ranting in my head as I finally removed my attire down to my shift. I began retrieving the pair of pretty hair pins from the sides of my head and unwittingly caught his image staring at me in the small free standing looking-glass before me. Paying no attention to him, I placed the pins on the stand and reached for my comb laid on it. I started running the teeth through my jaw-length, bobbed, cowlick curls and over my bangs. I lightly worked the tangles out and noticed in the looking-glass that his attention had returned to the correspondence in front of him.

When I had shortly finished, I put the comb back over the stand and sensed his eyes briefly on me again as I strode toward the bed. Turning the covers back, I blew out the candle on his bedside, crawled into bed and turned away from him with my back facing him. I closed my eyes, trying to sleep.

After several minutes with my eyes closed, parchments were heard being shuffled over the desk, and the sound of the chair scooted over the pine floor. Boots paced evenly across the room and ceased at the armoire. Clothes quietly rustled, then I heard him relieving himself in the chamber pot. Soon he returned advancing closer, and the mattress tilted as his weight came over it. I ensued taking my pillow and blanket as I promptly removed myself from bed. Irate, I silently placed my items precisely splayed on the floor and lay over it, managing to wrap myself in the blanket as best I could on the hard floor for the night.

It wasn't the ideal place to sleep, I suddenly recognized. The floor was too hard and made my bones uncomfortable. Still, I shifted a little, trying to discover the most doable position to tolerate sleeping on the unyielding support.

"Whit in Heaven's name are ye doin', lass?" Leif asked with a dubious voice. I turned and suddenly saw his big head peering over the edge of the bed from above. The candlelight he had placed on the other side of him glowed behind his fair hair, and I could discern the unbelievable expression on his face.

"What does it look like I'm doing?" I remarked evidently.

"I dinnae reckon I ken," he said.

"Well, I'm trying to sleep if you don't mind," I said.

"I do mind," he contradicted curiously.

"Well, I'm sorry about that," I disregarded and flipped to my other side, not facing him.

"Ye wulnae sleep upon the floor," he determined with an absurd tone.

"Yes I will. Nighty-night."

"Och!" he scoffed. "Do ye not reckon yoo're being quite foolish now?"

"Nope. Not at all."

"Preposterous! Yoo're being inane."

"Am not."

"I can plainly see that yoo're quite peevish as a child at present," he said matter-of-factly.

"Actually, I think I'm being quite fair."

"Nae—yoo're contrary."

"Am not."

"Aye, ye are."

"Oh! Just leave me alone, why don't you? So, I can get some sleep, thank you very much."

"Och!" he gasped outrageously. "Nae. I'll not leave ye be. Ye mind me and git yerself in this bed reit now."

"No," I said flat-out.

"Do it," he advised, sounding serious.

"Or what?" I was very unimpressed.

"Or, I shall git off this haur bed this very moment and haul yer crease intae bed fur ye!"

I suddenly swung my gaze over my shoulder and glared despicably at him. His brow lifted, and he distinctly looked at me. I quickly got the idea he wasn't kidding.

"Fine!" I griped, blatantly disgruntled as I came to my feet. I whipped up my blanket off the floor, and he scooted over making room for me. "You're unbelievable!" I accused as I was getting into bed again.

"Nae, yoo're the one quite *unbelievable*," he refuted distinctly. I huffed as I made myself comfortable against the pillows. He started shifting close to me.

"Don't touch me," I warned absolutely. His brow suddenly lifted high on his head again.

"I wulnae lay a hand upon ye," he said incredibly.

"Good. 'Cause I mean it."

"Aye, I can perceive it quite weel."

"Good for you—now, goodnight." I rolled away from him on my side. But he just as soon clasped a sturdy hand over my shoulder and pulled me back to face him again.

"Now, I reckon this churlish behavior is quite enough," he said mildly—although, I could distinguish the earnestness on his face. I couldn't help feeling a slight grin creep across my face regardless of my aggravation. An eyebrow arched over his eye. He looked confused despite the shallow grin over his lips. "Whit is amusing?" he asked frankly.

"No one's ever called me churlish before," I said.

"I find it difficult tae believe," he considered, appearing faintly amused. I shrugged indifferently in any case.

"I'm still not your friend anymore right now, though," I said.

"Och! Yoo're nae longer my friend then, is it?" he questioned with raised brows. He seemed surprised that I would ever say such a thing to him.

"Yeah. Just because you made me smile doesn't mean anything."

"Och, it disnae?"

"Nope."

"Hmph," he considered lightly. "Weel, I reckon ye mustn't truly care if I go then." I gave him a quick look. "Weel?" he questioned me. "If we are not friends as ye merely say, then whit does it matter if ye care whether I go upon the mission or not?"

"But I do care about you, Leif," I admitted truthfully.

"Yet ye say yoo're not my friend."

"Of course I'm your friend. I'll always be your friend. I'm just upset right now."

"I ken."

"You know?"

"Aye, I merely desired tae hear ye say it tae me. That is all," he said with an ironic glare.

"Good grief," I mocked.

"Aye," he responded alike. He shifted upward, sitting with his back against the pillows, and continued gazing down at me. "Now, shall we discuss again whit is trooblin' ye?"

"Yeah," I said of course. I decided to stir, also sitting up against the pillows. We sat close to each other, and I observed his hands comfortably enfolded over his blanketed lap.

"As ye wished," he started, holding my gaze steady to his, "I have given ye some thought."

"Oh yeah?" I said merely.

"Aye," he said. "I realize it is quite hard upon ye living haur. It isnae cheerful as it is at *Taigh Gràs* whaur very little concerns ye. Thaur is much we face that is perilous haur in camp—and, ye are also faced with these same perils, presently. It is hard enough fur lads tae bear the harshness of garrison living. It isnae an ideal situation fur lasses and bairns in the least bit. So, I ken that it is simply quite trying fur ye tae be haur with me. Ye are a mere lass incapable of being used tae living haur in this manner like the lads... and, I'm concerned that this place is beginning tae bear down upon ye. The fact remains that I cannae successfully carry out my task tae Fort Carillon whilst at the same moment I am most disquieted about ye. So, I spoke tae Fin about the matter."

"You did?" I responded with surprise.

"Aye."

"What did he think about it?"

"In short, he believes, in this case, I shouldnae go with the force."

"Oh."

"So, I decided tae see Monro about the matter."

"What did he say?"

"He had little words regarding it as he was indeed not pleased."

"Oh..." I immediately felt bad that Colonel Monro was disappointed in Leif.

"He claims that I shall be a risk tae the mission as I am not concentrated upon my duties. Thus, he has replaced me. So, I shall not go," he informed me. I sensed disappointment in his voice also. I felt worse that he believed that I was getting in his way.

"I see..." I said. But, a real sense of relief came over me, though, and I couldn't help feeling immensely better about his safety.

"So... ye neednae worry any longer," Leif said. I understood that he had gone out of his way to appease me, and it wasn't an easy thing for him to do. I knew that he had obligations to fulfill, and that he had responsibilities to the men in the garrison. So, I was aware that this was a big deal for him to have done for me.

"I'm sorry for the trouble I've caused," I said honestly.

"Aye." He nodded a bit.

"But, thank you," I said truly. I turned toward him and wrapped my arms around his neck, embracing him. "Thank you.

Thank you so much." I sensed his palms come around my back, holding me secure against his chest.

"Aye, lass," he muttered. I released him a little and gave him a gentle peck over his lips then hugged him again. "'Tis alrecht, *ceisdein*. Everything is alrecht."

"What about Finley? He won't be going either, right?" I asked as I released him from my embrace.

"Nae, he is tae go with the lads," he confirmed.

"Oh..." I looked at Leif with intense disconcertion. "I was hoping he wouldn't go either."

"Waur ye?"

"Yeah—I just don't want anything bad happening to either one of you. I don't know what Elizabeth or I would ever do if that should ever happen," I said.

"Yoo're minding us both, are ye?" he asked, gazing warmheartedly at me.

"Someone has to," I said.

"Hmph," he responded simply. "Weel, ye dinnae have tae worry about him. Fin can fend fur himself weel enough. He will be alrecht—and, I shall remain haur with ye now. So, ye neednae concern yerself anymore over me or Fin. Alrecht?" His expression was genuine, and he calmed me.

"Okay," I acknowledged. But I was still worried for Finely as I also wished he wouldn't be going on the mission, and it seriously disturbed me that he was going to go. I wanted to tell Leif about my continued concern over Finley, because I was so troubled by it. But I thought if I had pressed Leif on the issue regarding my concern for his brother, that I would have been pushing my wishes too hard with him, and that I would spark another disagreement with Leif which would not have guaranteed altering the decision for Finley to go on the mission; the decision for him was made, and as I gazed into Leif's eyes, I knew there was nothing I could do to change that fact. So, I let it go and no longer pressed the issue, still worried.

"Are we reconciled now?" Leif asked.

"Yeah," I said.

"Guid," he said, satisfied. "I dinnae desire it any other way."

"Me neither," I agreed.

"Now we may sleep. 'Tis been a tiresome day." He reached a hand toward the tin lantern on the stand next to his bedside and adjusted the door to dim the light. I slid down beneath the blankets, and he shifted himself close beside me. I was comforted by the fact that we were no longer on edge with each other, and knowing he would not be going on the military operation. But my final thoughts before I shut my eyes for the night, however, lay with Finley. I couldn't help but pray to God for his security and safe return.

I t rained several days and nights straight for almost a week, delaying the hazardous maneuver to Fort Carillon. Later, one early evening before the sun had completely set, the skies finally cleared and the air was balmy and humid. The grounds grew lively into the night with a celebration for the five companies that were to set sail north up Lake George to Lake Champlain in order to carry out the mission across enemy lines to destroy the sawmills at the French fort. I felt more unsettled than usual, since the men were about to dispatch for the field. For all our sakes I prayed for their safe return.

The fort was full of drinking, gambling, talking, and laughing as men were simply having a good time tonight. I decided as well to have a couple glasses of flavorful Madeira stored here in camp for officers to settle my unease, and after the third glass I was feeling quite fine. While strolling around the grounds within the fort, I noticed Leif and some other men seated outside at a lantern lit table, shuffling cards as they sat on crates and small casks. Finley removed himself from the group of cousins and sat close on a barrel smoking a pipe as I approached them.

"Are ye out this time 'round, Fin?" Leif asked as Angus continued shuffling the deck of cards.

"Aye. My arse is beaten enough already," Finley replied. Chuckles sputtered around the table.

"Alrecht, then—reckon 'tis merely the five of us lads instead," Cole said.

"Aye," Leif replied, taking a swig of rum from his mug. Since I noticed the empty space beside him, I decided to fill it and eased myself between him and Derek. The men all at once looked at me, joining them as Angus began dealing the deck of cards, and he suddenly stopped dealing the cards to the players. Regardless, I tossed my ante into the pile with the rest of the coins and automatically tapped the table for him to continue passing a card to me.

"Whit are ye doing, *ceisdein*?" Leif asked strangely. They were all looking weirdly at me, I noticed, as my eyes shifted around them encircling me.

"Playing—obviously," I said.

"But, this is a lad's game," he said evidently, indicating the surrounding company.

"So?" I shrugged, discerning the quizzical look on his face and the uncertain expressions on everyone else's.

"I reckon ye dinnae ken how tae play, and the lads haur dinnae have the patience fur me tae teach ye reit now," he condescended gently.

"Well, what's the game?" I asked.

"'Tis *poque*," he informed me.

"Oh, well that's all right—you don't have to teach me. I already know how to play poker," I said easily. Everyone was quiet for a minute, looking at me and Leif with strange uncertainty.

"Do ye?" Leif responded questionably.

"Yeah, I do," I said positively.

"Certainly?" he asked again, looking at me with astonishment.

"Yes," I said really.

He briefly considered it. "Alrecht, then," he allowed, appearing to humor me. "Deal my lass cards then, Angus." The men momentarily exchanged curious glances as Angus quietly resumed dealing out the right number of cards to each player. In this version of play, each player was given three cards to start. Now with the cards finally dealt, everyone looked at their hand. *Ok—I thought—not too bad*; I had a straight—*let's see how this goes...*

Derek, seated to Angus's left, opened the first bet with three sovereigns. Everyone around the table matched his bet including me, but Fearghus raised the bet two crowns more and everyone matched it. Cole raised ten guineas after that, and everyone remained in the game, expanding the winnings to a hearty sum. Then, Leif raised two guineas more and Angus along with Fearghus, folded. Soon, a crowd had gathered around our table intently watching us play. Several more betting rounds continued with us three remaining in the mix, until Leif upped the ante another three guineas. Cole folded, and now it was merely between Leif and me. I was down to my last florin when it was time for us to reveal our cards as I drew in a little breath with anticipation.

"*Oooh!*" the gathered crowd rumbled with impressiveness as our cards were shown. Leif's three king prial beat my straight of A-2-3. By the expression on his face, he was stunned over my hand of cards and a grin crossed his lips with open amusement. The players looked on wide-eyed, also amazed and entertained as muttering and chuckling broke out around the surrounding crowd of men.

"Guid game lads!" Angus roared cheerfully. The men agreed and laughed as some took easy swigs of ale from a sitting jug on a nearby cask.

"Yer lass knows how tae ruse like the rest of the arses at the table!" Roy said. Hearty laughter barreled forth around me.

"Weel done, Seamus!" Cole cheered.

"Aye," Leif replied with a smirk.

"Seems your lass is indeed a guid match!" Derek chuckled.

"I have already told him so!" Finley jeered from slightly behind Leif and mussed his loose hair all over his head. Leif's smirk slightly grew as he glanced with cautious humor at me. I spontaneously leaned toward him and brazenly planted my lips securely over his. Plenty of gasps and cheering roars howled around us as I kissed him. Once I released him from my kiss, I stood from my seat over a crate and straightened my waistcoat.

"Thanks a lot for the good game boys! A real pleasure! Gotta do it again some time," I said cheerfully. They suddenly looked at me with further surprise, but I didn't care as I turned to Leif and curtsied in front of him before departing from the concluded card game, leaving them all to their boisterous ways.

Music had already started playing, and the fiddlers and fifers were animated with life over a group of stretched tables as their stage. The bonfire was noticeably bright and high, and lit the entire courtyard as if the sun were shining. People were engaged, and I found a place beneath the cannon deck on a large bench to sit on the sidelines quietly watching the country folk dancing not too far away.

"Hallo, Your Grace," Hannah said, discovering me perched on the bench tucked out of the way. She was one of the cook maids and Corporal Jenkins' wife. A very friendly middle-aged woman, who was always tongue in cheek—nothing but a barrel of laughs all day, I thought. It was evident she was used to traveling military style with her husband and had little regard for genteel manners.

"Hi, Hannah. How are you?" I asked nicely.

"Well, I thank you."

"That's nice."

"How do you fare in this heat?" she asked.

"It's not my favorite," I admitted.

"Aye. Hot as the dickens' inferno, I say."

"Yeah."

"Be that as it will, never ceased the flow of spirits amongst these besotted men," she laughed.

"No. I guess not," I laughed too.

"Well, I thought to bring you the good stuff." She passed me a large mug full of Madeira. "'Tis the last of it till new provisions arrive."

"Oh, that's very nice—thank you, Hannah," I said gratefully, receiving the offer.

"Indeed! Bottom's up then!" she laughed brusquely, then turned away from me, disappearing into the animated crowd ahead. The mug felt weighty, I noticed, as I held it. I glimpsed into it, unable to see a thing in the dark, where I sat beneath the cannon deck, wondering how much liquid was actually inside. It seemed she might have given me the whole bottle. It was much too full for me to finish, I thought. Still, I drew the rim to my lips ready to enjoy at least a portion of it. After all, it was pretty darn flavorful, and I couldn't let it all go to waste.

About halfway down the pike into my mug of wine, while enjoying the music and viewing the dancers, Leif was detected moving through the crowd toward me. The torchlight caught his gleaming pearly teeth, though shadows obscured his face. He easily strode toward me in his typical swagger in breeches and boots with his mug in hand. I had a fleeting vision of him looking quite like a cowboy superimposed on my grandfather's Wyoming ranch walking over a midnight prairie beneath the glowing moon. He made himself comfortable sitting next to me on the bench and took a refreshing swig of rum from his mug. I ensued taking several more sips of wine from my own mug and met his accommodating gaze.

"That was quite a game ye put on thaur, *mo ghaol*," he remarked.

"You think so?" I replied casually.

"Aye," he said.

"Well, you didn't do badly yourself," I said equally. He chuckled giving me a humored look. I smiled at him and drank some more wine, noticing my mug had begun feeling lighter right now. In fact, it felt a lot lighter, and I realized how much warmer I was feeling than I had been earlier. "Gosh!" I suddenly expressed, uncomfortable as I began fanning my hand over my face. "It's boiling out here tonight. Don't you feel like you're on fire?" Leif strangely looked at me and chuckled a little.

"Aye, 'tis indeed warm outdoors, but I reckon it micht be the spirits having more of an effect upon ye instead."

"Holy-moly! I feel like I just walked through the gates of Hell!"

Leif abruptly puffed with a startled expression as he looked at me. Still, I drank more from my mug, because it tasted so good and I was thirsty.

"Yoo're quite a bird," he said, glimpsing curiously into my mug. "Was it full?"

"Yeah."

"Och! Yoo're into trooble now. Yoo've never had much in one sitting. 'Tis nearly completed."

Suddenly, I started laughing. "Do you suppose I'm drunk?" I giggled, nudging him in the ribs.

"Boozed ye mean?"

"Yeah."

"Aye, I reckon so." He squarely took my mug right out of my hand and placed it beside himself on the other side where he was sitting. "That will quite be the end of yer drink, lassie." I suddenly began laughing again.

"Who do you think you are? My dad or something? Telling me I can't have my drink!" I scolded laughingly. I waved a shameful finger before his eyes. His brow lifted high, and he started chuckling too.

"When the cat is away, the mice do play," he reprimanded. But I discerned the broad smile stretched ear to ear on his face.

"You're a real funny guy. You know that?"

"Mercy!" he exclaimed. He decisively set his drink down next to my confiscated mug beside him. "Come dance with me, and wear it off before the Almighty Lord has nae mercy upon yer soul in the morn." He clasped my hand and suddenly whirled me onto my feet, merging us into a lively Scottish country dance already in progress.

When the dance was finally over, I quickly moved from the dance area off to the side, panting elatedly, with Leif closely following me, and feeling much too hot also.

"Oh my gosh! I'm melting!" I expressed excitedly and started unbuttoning my waistcoat to remove it.

"Aye!" Leif agreed, delighted from dancing. He also quickly began unfastening his waistcoat and tugged it over his square shoulders off his sturdy frame. He placed it over the bench next to our mugs beneath the cannon deck. I finally removed my waistcoat also, and he retrieved it from me, draping it over his. Slightly cooler in our white linen shirts, he then seized my arm and eagerly returned us to the dance area. Shortly after we arrived again, step dancing had ensued, replacing the folk dancers. A significant circle of enthusiastically clapping spectators had been created while nine fiercely step dancing men clogged their heels into the ground. "I'm better than any of those lads," Leif touted shamelessly.

"Really?" I questioned doubtfully, giving him a taunting smirk.

"Aye," he responded arrogantly.

"Prove it then," I said. He turned his enlivened gaze to mine and gave me a figuring look.

"Alrecht, I shall." He promptly paced away from me into the competing circle and joined the stepping men.

The fiddles and fifes were fast, and the dancing feet kept pace with the rhythm in the balmy humid night air. The music was upbeat and fun. The tempo moderately increased and their driving heels quickened as they shuffled and stomped. They tapped and kicked high and low around their twirling ankles. My attention bounced between the men as they competed with each other. I compared them to Leif as he was vigorous and noticeably stood out from the rest while he skillfully managed his tapping toes to the rhythm of the music. I was thoroughly impressed by him as the tempo kept gradually increasing. One by one, contenders began dropping by the wayside, beaten and out of breath.

As the competition continued, it finally came down to Leif and one other guy. They robustly pounced, raising the stakes with fancier footwork for the other to challenge. Leif's skipping toes became so fast they seemed to blur into one undistinguishable motion. Suddenly, Leif's competitor ceased as he bent over with his hands on his waist gasping for air. The crowd went wild with cheers for the winner. The defeated man respectfully bowed to Leif, the champion, and the challenger easily parted ways with him.

Leif paced exhaustedly through the cheerfully applauding crowd, locating me as he approached in my direction. He noticed me clapping enthusiastically for him as he neared me.

"That was really good!" I said utterly amazed, aware of his heaving breath as he now stood close.

"Ye reckon so?" he panted quickly. I could see that he was profusely perspiring in the firelight.

"Yeah!" I said absolutely. He chuckled between panting, enlivened by my response.

"I dinnae reckon I micht have done so weel, if ye hudnae asked me tae prove it tae ye," he gasped.

"Now *that*, I don't believe," I joked.

"'Tis true," he wheezed, chuckling a bit more.

"All right," I said resolutely as I abruptly turned from him and stole the tricorn hat off the head of some poor, unsuspecting, swaying drunkard next to me and tipped it over my brow as I placed it on my head.

"Whit have ye in mind now?" Leif inquired curiously, smiling regardlessly.

"I've got a trick up my sleeve too," I said, directly looking at him as I made sure he noticed my wink at him. He gave me a strange look, and I started away from him.

"Whaur are ye going?" he asked.

"I'm gonna show you. Just stay here and watch," I said, looking back at him as I was already moving through the cluster of people without him. I headed toward the makeshift stage where the band was still playing and hopped over the bench onto the stretched tables. I approached a fiddler. He noticed me and ceased playing for a moment as the other musicians continued mindlessly along.

"Howdy!" I said obligingly.

"Aye!" he replied spiritedly.

He seemed friendly enough, I quickly assessed, so I pursued to ask, "I wonder if you wouldn't mind letting me share your fiddle a bit seein' as I can play too, and I haven't got mine here ta join ya? It'll only be for a little bit, that's all."

"Aye, t'be sure," he said willingly with a pungent smell of too much alcohol on his breath. "What's your name lad?"

"You can just call me Billy," I said, spontaneously making up a name.

"Aye, Billy. Well, have at it. I need a wee respite, nonetheless." He easily handed me his fiddle and bow.

"What's your name?" I asked as I received his instrument from him.

"James," he said.

"Well, much obliged to ya James," I replied freely, mimicking the country accent my grandfather spoke.

"Aye," he responded easily. He jumped unstably off stage to the ground and plopped himself over a tree stump as he yanked up the ale jug at his feet to take a swig from it. I subsequently decided to pursue the other band members as they were concluding the last melody. Since the two fifers were on break too, which left three fiddlers and a man on a single snare drum, I approached them with a request. They were kind enough fellows, as it seemed, and obliged me by agreeing to follow my lead.

So, with the receptive crowd still around, I started fiddling a catchy tune with heart, gathering the crowd's attention. After an improvised intro, the rest of the band mimicked the melody and pattern. They all had good ears, I recognized as we were playing together. The structure of the music was quickly established, allowing me to take my variation. It was an upbeat bluegrass way of playing, I knew they had never heard before. But the sitting fiddlers' feet were moving, and all eyes from the audience were on us with heads lightly bobbing.

It was customary to hear shouts among the crowd expressing approval or disapproval during a performance instead of applause, and as we finished playing music, we noticeably heard nothing. But I didn't have any inhibitions as a result of all the wine I had consumed while gazing at the audience staring back at me.

"Have not heard a fiddle played like that before!" a faceless guy hollered at me from the crowd.

"Aye! Whit about anither!" another man shouted from the gathered faces around me.

"Aye! We want to hear it again!" someone else expressed loudly.

"So, it was fair enough for y'all then?" I said audibly back to the crowd.

"Aye!" a number of loud voices replied.

"Where did ye pick up a fiddle like that, lad?" an Irishman yelled at me.

"Never mind!" I shouted back. "But, I'll play y'all some more if y'all like!"

"Aye!" members of the crowd yelled.

"All right then!" I responded. "Now let me just tell ya a little 'bout this next tune I'm gonna do for ya'll. Now, my grandpa and my pa loved ta fiddle. That's how I basically learned how to play when I was small—probably just like anyone else here learned ta do. This next one I'm gonna play for y'all was written and sung by a man my grandpa and pa liked very much named Mister Johnny Cash. It's about a man who was cursed since he was mocked by his cruel daddy."

"Now there! I done had me a cruel da also!" a nameless soldier audibly expressed.

"I too! Went and knocked his teeth out clear 'cross the Thames!" another guy yelled from the crowd.

"If ye care ta know what I reckon of my da—then here it is!" Suddenly many of us were staring at a man with breeches down his knees indiscriminately showing off his bare buttocks as he bent over for all to see. Goading cheers and boisterous laughter erupted loudly all around.

"Well then I s'pose all ya lads here are unkind then too!" I said audibly back to them.

"Ye best believe I'm damned unkind!" a guy roared from the onlooking surrounding men.

"Then this one goes out ta y'all!" I yelled back at them, and they hooted cheers at me. I turned to the guy on the snare drum and stomped a beat pattern with my foot. He proceeded following my lead. I then placed the fiddle to my chin and started ripping into a quick rhythmic melody. A moment of repeating it, I cued the fiddlers behind me to follow along. After an introduction of listening to each other and their improvised understanding for the feel of the music, we were all in good jumping harmonizing synchronicity. At that point I drew the fiddle from my neck and started animatedly singing the country tune, *A Boy Named Sue* to the interested audience.

It was a comical song, and laughter from the audience burst out everywhere! So, then I continued singing...

As I proceeded with the gritty jocular lyrics, a racket of audible laughter and cheering erupted across my captivated audience. Now, I had their toes really tapping and hands clapping! So, I went on...

The humored crowd roared, cheering loudly! It seemed I had everyone's attention, and I was really enthused. My inhibition at this time was nonexistent as I swung the fiddle to my chin again and resumed fiddling the rest of the song to the end. Bellowing applause spewed forth from my audience until the moment my new bandmates were done.

"Let us hear another from ya, lad!" a crowd member hollered.

"Aye, give us anither witty one!" a second nameless soldier cried.

"All right!" I answered obligingly. "Hope none of y'all been in jail! 'Cause that's what this next one's about!"

"No surprise, lad, but plenty of us come from gaol!" some faceless guy boasted.

"Then you might relate ta this next fella I'm gonna sing about! Don't worry though—this one's gonna keep your toes tappin' too!"

"Play it then!" an eager fan shouted.

"Aye, whit are ye bidin' fur?" Angus recognizably chimed in suddenly situated near me in the crowd.

I turned to the fiddlers accompanying me and readied my instrument. I instantly started introducing them to the rhythm of a new tune which quite resembled the way a fiddling jig might sound, but the melody was true grit Western style. The band was quick, and once they got the hang of it again, I drew the fiddle from my neck and started another Johnny Cash song called *Folsom Prison Blues*.

Again, I held my audience captive with entertainment, and I fiddled really well during a solo. The crowd was stomping! Then, I drew the fiddle away from my chin and resumed singing the next verse. After, I fiddled my heart out a second round and cheers roared out into the air! It was a good old time!

Then, I coached the band straight into another exciting fiddling tune and began a Chuck Berry ditty: *It's My Own Business*.

I swerved the fiddle to my chin again and diddled out the rest of the spanking tune. As I was finishing out the melody, heads were bobbing and toes were tapping. An outburst of excited applause emitted around me and the band. It was hard to quit on an enthusiastic crowd, so I turned to the band behind me and said breathlessly to them, "Follow me again, boys!"

"Aye!" they replied simultaneously with enthusiasm. I started again playing the fiddle. This time I slightly slowed the tempo for this next song, *Can't You See* by The Marshall Tucker Band. This next melody had a more soulful sway to it. A good tune merely enough for me to catch my wind in this oppressive muggy night air. As the band had a swift ear, they quickly followed me. Toward the end of the song, I suddenly put the fiddle down and got the crowd clapping in sync with me to the beat as I stomped and clapped, singing the final chorus twice to the end of the song.

"All right now!" I shouted enthusiastically and swept up the fiddle. "Here's one for all you boys who can't stop thinkin' about the girl you love!" Cheers and whistles burst out. I tapped a beat with my foot in front of the drummer. He followed me, then I instructed a new melody to the fiddlers. The band ensued, and I started the intro on my fiddle. After the intro, I twirled the fiddle from my neck and started a country version of *Sweet Child of Mine* by Guns N' Roses.

I sang the song, and then I burned on the fiddle over the solo riff. *Oops!*—popped a string! But the men howled, rowdily cheering.

Whew! We brought it to a finish, and I was steaming hot with perspiration in this night time humidity. Plus, the ground seemed kind of wobbly. I figured I was done playing for the enthusiastic crowd and took my proper stage bow. I couldn't remember the last time I had played so hard! It was definitely years ago. But it was loads of fun tonight!

"Thank ya boys! You're mighty kind!" I said enthusiastically to everyone.

"Where are yer goin', lad?" some Irishman shouted among the wildly cheering onlooking men.

"It's quittin' time boys! It's too damn hot out here!" I hollered back as I leaped off stage. I noticed James passed out in the corner where he had decided to break. I mindfully tucked his fiddle and bow in a protected area near him where it wouldn't receive damage, then worked my way, pushing through the crowd, looking for Leif. I couldn't easily locate him as I moved past the merry-making soldiers.

"Jesus, Mary and Joseph!" Leif gasped unexpectedly as he suddenly appeared behind me when he snagged my arm and spun me around to face him. I stopped short as I stared at him with a really big smile. "Yoo're incredulous! What an utter abomination!"

"No it wasn't!" I burst out laughing completely amused by his outrageously entertained, shocked expression.

"Yoo're scandalous!"

"I am not!" I laughed, smiling back at the smile spread widely over his humored face, contradicting his contempt.

"How in Heaven's name did ye ever learn tae manage that sort of presentation?" The whites of his eyes were incredibly large, and his teeth gleamed in the moonlight.

"From back home," I said frankly. He gawked outlandishly at me with a smile spread clear across his face.

"Whit a stir ye have caused! I dinnae believe my eyes! The lads enjoyed ye!" he said extraordinarily.

"I guess so!" I laughed. "Can you believe it?"

"I cannae!" He laughed also, shaking his head. "I dinnae reckon I quite ken whit tae do with ye. Yoo're full of outlandish surprises in every which manner I turn!"

"At least I'm not a bore to you then!" I teased unreservedly.

"I cannae indeed say so."

"Good! Gotta keep you on your toes then! I got ya! Pow!" I laughed freely as I mimicked shooting him with my finger gun.

"Och! Yoo're *far* too wicked, *lad*!" he teased and unexpectedly clasped my waist with his powerful hands.

"*Whoa!*" I squealed simultaneously with surprise as I found myself being tossed over his shoulder like a sack of potatoes.

"I reckon yoo've had yer fill of amusement fur tonecht. 'Tis high time tae get yer crease intae bed," he ordered, as my head was really swimming right about now.

"Alrighty pawtna! Yeehaw! *Ohh*, I hope I don't upchuck!" I expressed dizzily while he hauled me past Finley, Cole, and Derek, still seated on casks where I'd left them after the poker game earlier. They were in the middle of enjoying drinks and conversation as we were approaching them. I tipped my hat to them as Leif passed with me lugging over his shoulder. "Nighty-night boys!" I yelled to them, and their eyes suddenly bugged out with jaws dropped wide open.

As Leif continued carrying me over his shoulder through the courtyard, I recognized that we were near our barrack as I gazed upside down at his pacing boot heels. He easily paced up the staircase with me and entered our room, promptly closing the door at his back.

"Now then," he said finally while pitching me lightly over the bed onto my back.

"Howdy, howdy, howdy!" I laughed, ridiculously amused, waving the hat in my hand before his hovering eyes as I gazed up at him.

"Let me have *that*," he said, snatching the hat from my fingers while giving me an absurd look. His eyes sparkled with lightheartedness, and his cheeks were noticeably ruddy. "I shall see that it is returned tae its proper owner." He casually flung the hat into the air, and it landed evenly in the chair across the room.

"Well, now you're just a fancy shooter, arenchya?" I said giggly, referring to his good aim over the chair.

"Whit sort of dialect is that ye speak?" he asked, giving me a quizzical look.

"It's cowboy talk," I laughed.

"Is it?" he responded unknowingly.

"Yup!"

"Yoo're entirely disgraceful!"

"Oh well," I said flippantly, shrugging my shoulders. "Nothin' can be done about it now."

"I should have never let ye out of my secht! Yoo're incredulous!"

"So are you!"

"Not quite."

"Oh *please*! Don't give me that malarkey! I saw the way you hot-footed it across the ground," I said, really amazed. A light chuckle eluded him. "Never seen *that* before."

"Is that reit?"

"Yeah. You were like a jitter bug quicker than a Mexican jumping bean!"

"Pardon?" He gave me a kooky look, still smiling though.

"I said you were like a jitter bug," I repeated. He laughed, obviously humored. I think he had literally visualized a dancing bug jittering around. I started really laughing too, because I could see on his face that was exactly what he was thinking.

"Tell me again the latter part of whit ye said," he requested, still chuckling.

"That you were quicker than a Mexican jumping bean?"

"Aye."

"Well, you were!"

"Whit in Heaven's name is that?"

"A bean from Mexico that jumps because it has got a worm inside of it," I said offhandedly. Leif suddenly paused, bizarrely looking at me as if I were an alien with green antenna sprouting from my head.

"I beg yer pardon?" he responded peculiarly with a quirky looking grin.

"Because it's got a worm in it—that's what makes the bean jump!" I repeated. He suddenly burst out hysterically laughing, and his face flushed deeply. His head dropped to my breast and shook as he heartily laughed. The thick, silky, gilded strands over his head tickled my chin, amusing me also. He lifted his head, returning his mirthfully chuckling gaze to mine, and wiped the bit of tears that had welled in his eyes.

"Yoo're boozed!" he snorted hilariously.

"I know!" I admitted and started laughing irrationally.

"Och! Yoo're indeed in a sinful state!"

"But you know?"

"Aye?"

"That's exactly how you tapped your feet—just like one of those beans!"

"I have never heard of such a thing! Whaur do ye get such foolish notions into that wee mind of yers?"

"Did you learn to dance like that by people shootin' at your toes? 'Cause it was *real* fancy!"

"Nae." He laughed again, outright amused.

"Well it was some real nice footwork you were puttin' on out there. I betchya could dance your way outta shootin' saloon!" I laughed more also, attracted by his humorous response to me.

"A saloon?"

"Yeah, you know—one of your gunfightin' taverns."

"Och, aye."

"Yeah, I've seen the way you wield a gun! You think you're Wild Bill Hickok, don't you?"

"Who is he?"

"A really good gunslinger from the Old Wild West, a really long time ago."

"From how long ago?"

"Oh gosh—I guess from more than well over a century and a half ago."

"That long ago?"

"Yeah."

"He's weel dead and gone, then?"

"I guess that all depends on your point of view," I said, suddenly laughing hysterically.

"Och! Yoo're foolish!"

"But, do you want to know something?"

"Tell me then."

"Well, come to think of it," I said simmering a bit from laughter as I intently stared at him. "You actually do kinda resemble Hickok, except your nose is straight and his sloped, and you're much more handsome."

"How would ye ken?"

"From pictures that I've seen of him."

"Whaur micht ye have seen his image?" Leif asked, still chuckling. I noticed the curious expression on his face as his grin lingered.

"In print."

"Och."

"And you know what else?"

"Whit else?"

"He'd hold both his guns like this, and shoot at the bad guy real fast. *Pow! Pow! Pow!* Just like that—and knock 'em dead on his feet right there," I said, motioning simultaneously with my finger pistols before Leif's eyes. "Bad guys always shook in their boots with fear whenever they knew Hickok was in town, 'cause they could never take him down in a gunfight."

"So he was skilled at dueling?" Leif asked smilingly, captivated by what I was telling him.

"Um-hm."

"Ye certainly do ken how tae charm me, *àille dhubh*," he snorted, and we just kept laughing senselessly together. It seemed the more he laughed, the more I laughed. We just kept bouncing off each other feeding into one another's nonsensical amusement. Eventually, Leif wiped the tears from his eyes and stared at me with a big open smile. His sparkling ultramarine eyes held mine, and I noticed the deep ruddiness in his cheeks again.

"You've had a lot to drink too," I jeered.

"Aye, yet I can manage myself fine unlike my undisciplined wife," he taunted, still on the verge of chuckling all over again.

"Those are some *Devil* ballads ye ken," he said. I liked seeing the smirk on his face; it was charming and allured me. But, the half serious arching eyebrow over his eye rather missed the mark and failed to suggest a proper scolding.

"Well, they don't come close to any of the conversations I've heard floating around you guys," I said flippantly.

"Nonetheless, yoo're a wee devil presently."

"Then, if I'm so bad, what does that make you?"

"I have never claimed tae be an angel," he said frankly. A fiendish look suddenly came over his expression.

"Oh," I giggled. "Then, I guess I should be really scared of you, shouldn't I?"

"Ye figure swift, lass," he said.

"But, I'm not afraid of you." I gave him a dismissive look.

"Weel," he said thoughtfully, pursing his lips. "Ye ought tae fear me, since yoo're not awaur of how *wicked* I can be, if I so choose."

"Really?" I doubted him as I equally gazed at his lighthearted expression.

"Are ye begging fur me tae prove myself tae ye once more?"

"Only if that makes you feel better."

He raised his brow and an inspired smirk settled easily on his face. "I'm going tae roger ye reit now," he said as a matter of fact. I gasped unexpectedly.

"No you're not!" I laughed.

"Indeed I am." He straightened fully from me and began tearing off his boots.

"I don't believe you!" I giggled.

"Merely observe," he responded categorically.

"You're awful!"

"Ye dinnae yet ken how awful. I'm filled tae Hell with spirits. Yoo're saucy, and I want tae poke ye guid," he said. He meant it as I could plainly see the blatant waywardness expressed on his face, and it only made me laugh some more. "Do ye see how disobedient ye are?"

"I'm not disobedient!" I continued laughing as I recognized him now unfastening his breeches and dropping them to the floor.

"This disobedient laughter of yers will soon cease once I'm through with ye." He reached behind his back and tugged his linen shirt over his head. He tossed the shirt over the back of the chair as he towered at the edge of the bed before me now entirely naked.

"Wow! I guess you do *mean* business," I joked, noticing his readiness as I stared at his erection.

"Ye dinnae ken the merest bit of it." He suddenly grasped my leg and yanked off my boot.

"Man oh man! You are so *funny*!" I started laughing nonsensically again as I felt him tugging off my other boot.

"I'm quite glad that ye reckon so," he chuckled, appearing rather devilish. He skillfully unbuttoned the front flap to my trousers and eagerly pulled them off me.

"I think you need to go to Confession," I continued joking.

"Confession? Fur whit?"

"For what you want to do to me!"

"But it is my reit as yer husband!"

"I've never heard of that right before."

"Of coorse ye have."

"Nope!"

"Curious. But it is indeed my reit, and I shall!"

"Oh boy!"

"And, it is ye who need tae see a priest, as ye have conducted yerself in a most sinful manner tonecht."

"You're silly!" I laughed. "You're the one who needs to confess, because you think that you can just take what you can get from me just like a sacking Viking!"

"Aye! *Vikingr* men are amongst my ancestors and I'm going tae heed my fate—I'll take my booty haur weel and guid, *àille dhubh*," he said gruffly. He crouched forward and I hopped backward, slightly eluding him, laughing as my back suddenly stopped against the pillows. He crawled over the mattress with a menacing eyebrow arched high. He crept over me and caged me beneath him as I stared up at him, aware of the sinister, humored look obviously expressed on his face.

"What are you doing?" I responded unevenly despite myself, smiling back up at him. He didn't answer as he purposefully wedged my legs apart with his knee, positioned himself and I moaned with pleasure as he pushed himself into me with fervor.

AFTERWARD, my heart was racing and my head was spinning. The air around me was stifling, and suddenly I felt much too hot. The room seemed to swirl right before my eyes. I felt Leif gently kissing my brow when he disengaged from me. He slid off me, rolling onto his back beside me, and drew me close against him with an arm wrapped securely around my waist. Suddenly, I had a spell of extreme wooziness and I wasn't feeling well at all.

"Oh God!" I gasped nauseously.

"Whit is the matter?" he asked concernedly, simultaneously releasing his embracing arm from me. He shifted upward to look at me and his brow furrowed.

"No!" I suddenly sat up from him and stumbled out of bed. I dashed unsteadily toward the chamber pot, uncertain if I was going to make it. Leif invisibly caught my arm stabilizing me and swiftly helped me cross the rustic room in the direction I needed to go. As soon as I had arrived at the chamber pot, not soon enough, I dropped to my knees lurching over it and horribly regurgitated all that I had drunk and eaten. It was a very ungraceful event that seemed never ending. "*Ohhh,*" I moaned awfully.

"Och, lass—whit a pity ye are," he said sympathetically while carefully rubbing my back.

"Ohh, this is so *terrible*," I groaned uncomfortably, sickened. I abruptly heaved uncontrollably again into the pot.

"Yoo're as bad as a sailor reit now, I shall have ye ken," he said as I kept gagging.

"I'm sure," I coughed, trying to catch my breath for a second. "I can't believe I'm barfing," I whimpered.

"Aye, if that is whit ye call it. Yoo're doing a fine work of it."

"Ugh!"

"'Tis a consequence of over indulgence in booze."

"I have never been smashed in my *entire* life. Do you know that?" I said turning my terrible gaze up to his. "I have always been a really, *really* good girl!" I suddenly became emotional, and just started illogically crying. "I have *always* been a good girl—a *good* girl."

"Aye, I reckon that is so," Leif said. I suddenly lurched and heaved again into the pot.

"I never *ever* got into an ounce of trouble when I was growing up—not *ever*," I wept as I was vomiting.

"I dinnae reckon ye did."

"Now look at me!"

Leif's face became indiscernible in my watery gaze as tears streamed down my face. I kept heaving, and after a moment my heaving turned dry until my clinching stomach had finally relaxed and calmed.

"Aye, now look at ye," he said sedately. "Have ye completed retching now?"

"I think so." I seemed to have felt a little better now, but still couldn't stop myself from crying.

"Alrecht, then." He suddenly scooped me up into his powerful arms and carried me back to bed.

"I'm a responsible person, you know?" I sobbed into his neck.

"I ken."

"I never do stupid things like this. I don't just get smashed. I've never been wasted before—it's awful! Oh God, I feel so gross! I feel like a trashed, dumb-ass fraternity boy or some floozy, party chick who flaps her tits in every guy's face," I blubbered. Leif chuckled lightly.

"Och, come now—yoo're not at all a cocky lad or a wretched tavern wench."

"Being drunk is not a load of laughs."

"Aye, but it was a load of laughs earlier before now, was it not?"

"Yeah, but it's not worth the agony," I cried ridiculously. He snorted a little.

"Some say it is however."

"Not I—absolutely not."

"Och, weel, ye see that is because yoo're indeed a guid lass." He placed me with care over the mattress and crawled over it, laying himself beside me. "Now, now, yoo'll be alrecht later, *mo ghaol*."

"I hope so. I really do hope so."

"Ye will. Although the morrow wulnae come easily first." He kept himself propped on his elbow close beside me and wiped my moistened eyelashes with the pad of his thumb.

"I have done everything right my whole life, you know?"

"Aye."

"I was always a very responsible person—even as a kid. I was a serious girl—didn't fool around and get pregnant like so many other girls, no sir. I was even a virgin when I first got married, did you know that?" I sniveled senselessly.

"Weel, I, er, I—weel, I micht have reckoned ye had been chased, of coorse," he stammered.

"And that's a fact. Ooh, I had opportunities of course, but I didn't want to just throw myself at some knucklehead, because I was going to wait until I loved someone and he loved me back. It was my choice because that's how *I* wanted it to be. You know what I mean? I have only been with two men! *Only* two men my whole life—and I was married to both of them—that's you and Matt of cour—"

"Shh—alrecht now, that micht be enough, 'tis alrecht, *ceis-*

dein," Leif hushed affectionately, gently stroking my teary-eyed face. "Yoo're quite weary and out of sorts. I regret that I wisnae awaur of how much wine ye waur taking and missed preventing ye from having much of it soon enough."

"I'm sorry."

"Fur whit reason?"

"For getting drunk ."

"It isnae yer fault. I should have watched ye."

"I don't want you to be upset with me."

"Och, I am not the slightest angered by ye." He made himself comfortable, laying back again among the pillows and pulled me snug against him. "It is far too late fur the both of us. Rest yer weary head now." He kissed my temple and reached over the night-stand to adjust the lantern light. He then comfortably crooked an elbow behind his head and began resting. I noticed him close his eyes, so I closed mine also and tried relaxing just as he had urged me to do. It wasn't long after before I had finally fallen to sleep.

Thirty-One

I'm not certain what time I had awakened the next day, except it seemed that it might have been around noon when I finally opened my eyes to a splitting headache that felt like a cruel migraine. The blinding sunlight unbearably shone through the window over the letter desk where Leif was presently seated writing correspondences. The entering sunlight painfully hurt my eyes, and I immediately turned away from the window. I shoved a pillow over my aching head and moaned as my body felt weighty and debilitated. I probably couldn't have moved out of bed even if I had wanted to. Everything seemed foggy, and my mind was dull.

"Guid afternoon, *àille dhubh*," Leif greeted calmly. His voice sounded muffled through the pillow over my head.

"Hi," I mumbled. I sensed his weight come over the edge of the mattress next to me. He lightly slapped my backside, and I moaned again from the sheer pain of my splitting headache.

"How do ye fare?"

"I feel like I've been hit by a bullet train at full speed."

"Och, that disnae soond favorable."

"It's murder."

"In that case, let me have a look at ye."

"No. I don't want you to," I grumbled beneath the pillow. Suddenly, my protective cushion came off my head. "*Aww*," I whined as he carelessly tossed it to the foot of the bed. I sluggishly turned in my complete exhaustion to face him with squinting eyes. He clasped my chin with his forefinger and thumb, briefly examining me as his eyes rolled over my face.

"I reckon that yoo'll be quite alrecht," he assured.

"I have a huge hangover."

"Aye, yoo're under the wrath of grapes."

"Interesting way of putting it."

"Yoo're forswunk."

"Is that what you call it?"

"Aye."

"Well whatever it's called, I've been hammered in the head."

"I ken the feeling."

"Remind me next time never to touch another ounce of alcohol," I complained.

"If ye waur a laddie, I would seize the whipping board and lay it guid upon yer crease," he said point blank.

"Don't worry, I'll stick to tea for a long while," I replied dryly.

"Aye, I reckon yoo've been punished weel enough," he assessed.

"It's totally unfair," I pouted.

"Whit is unfair?"

"It's not fair that you don't feel the way I do. You had a lot to drink too—and it was rum, not wine."

"Och," he said indifferently. "I'm a man who can quite hold his own booze, unlike the wee thing ye are, who can barely sip a bit of Madeira without a snigger." He gave my hip a couple of light, arrogant slaps. "Aye, ye stay with tea, and yoo'll remain fairer off fur the time being."

"Oh, stop gloating in my misery," I said in a crotchety voice.

"I am not gloating," he chuckled.

"You're not?"

"Nae."

"Is that why you're laughing then?" I glowered at him, and he laughed a bit more.

"I am merely amused because I reckon yoo're quite charming," he said.

"Charming?" I gave him a ridiculous look.

"Aye."

"You think I'm charming?"

"Aye."

"Right now?"

"Aye."

"Ugh! I don't understand you." I sighed hopelessly, and he chuckled again.

"Haur now," he said, reaching for my dressing gown over the chair in the corner, then placed it before me. "Let us git a bit of food inside ye."

"But I'm not hungry," I said as he stood from the bed and paced across the floor toward the small dining table in the middle of the room.

"Nonetheless, 'twill help settle ye," he advised. I sluggishly sat up from the pillows and clumsily fumbled, slipping my arms through the sleeves of my dressing gown to cover my nudity. "I'm certain that ye are raither parched."

"Yes, I'm really thirsty, actually," I acknowledged as he returned to me with an already-prepared cup of tea.

"It is chilled, but 'twill quench yer thirst fair enough." He proffered the cup for me to take.

"That's perfectly fine, thank you," I replied gratefully. I carefully took the tea from him while leaning my back against the pillows supported by the earthen wall behind me. I placed the rim of the cup to my lips, and instead of dainty sips, I gulped all of it down as Leif returned to the table. He easily prepared a plate of food for me and strode back to the bed, placing the full plate before my crisscrossed legs. "Thank you," I said as he naturally took the emptied cup from my fingers.

"Aye," he responded simply. He moved toward the table again and refilled my cup, then placed it over the little nightstand within my reach by the bed. I took up a piece of bread and buttered it. I brought it to my lips and took a nibble, noticing that Leif was partly dressed in a shirt and breeches. It was warm inside our room, indicating that it was even hotter outside today. His neckcloth was removed, and his shirt was open low, exposing the light blonde hairs at the top of his chest.

"How long have you been up?" I inquired, observing him preparing a plate of food for himself.

"I awakened long before daybreak tae bid Fin and the lads' success, and safe return," he said as he cut a large piece of butter and smothered his bread with it.

"Oh, I didn't get a chance to say goodbye to him," I realized regretfully.

"It is quite understandable as ye waur in nae condition tae do so. Therefore, I reckoned tae let ye sleep instead," he said easily, pacing toward me with a full plate of food for himself.

"Oh…" I was very disappointed that I had missed Finley before he left on the mission and felt significantly regretful about it.

"Ye may greet him upon his return. He will be pleased tae see ye," Leif appeased, seating himself beside me on the bed as we faced each other.

"Okay. I'll be glad to see him, too, when he returns," I said, feeling a little better at the thought. I placed my scarcely nibbled piece of bread over my plate and gathered my teacup to satisfy more of my thirst, quickly finishing my second cup.

"Does it ail ye much?" he inquired sympathetically, noticing me rubbing my aching brow.

"Um-hm," I muttered, nodding a little. He gathered my cup from my hand and stirred from the bed, headed for the table, and poured more tea into it. After refilling my cup, he returned to me. Proffering it to me once more, I gladly took it from him, ready to sip.

"I must say tae ye that I have never knoon a soul tae entertain in the manner in which ye did last nicht," Leif said as he returned, sitting comfortably over the bed.

"Oh really?" I responded vaguely.

"Indeed," he said, cautiously smiling at me.

"I hope I didn't do anything too terrible," I wondered, feeling muddled over my memory of last night.

"Terribly entertaining, I shall say."

"Well, that's comforting."

"Tae be sure about it, 'twas quite scandalous."

"Sorry."

"I perceive yer remorse by yer ailing head. 'Tis fortunate that no one quite recognized that 'twas Her Grace's performance."

"I'm never having another drink in my life," I vowed groggily. He chuckled a little.

"Ye merely say that at present," he replied, appearing distantly amused.

"I mean it."

"Yoo're out of sorts. Ye dinnae ken whit ye mean reit now."

"I feel like I've been mowed over by a big rig, and I don't want to ever feel like this again. That much I *do* know."

"Weel, I dinnae ken whit a big rig is, yet I reckon yoo've learnt yer lesson not tae foolishly booze like the lads."

"Yeah, that's for sure."

"Whit is done is done. Every lad has a tale tae tell once he has been boozed, if he is able tae recall it. I reckon yoo're sadly presently part of that lot."

"Yes, it is a sad situation," I agreed ironically despite returning his mildly amused grin. I thoughtfully watched him, in the haze of my hangover, tear off a piece of his salted meat between his teeth and fingers. "Okay, you obviously know my drunken story. It's only fair that you should tell me one of yours."

"Och! I dinnae reckon so," he declined, shaking his golden head with a skeptical smile.

"Oh c'mon," I begged. "Please? It'll make me feel better." He gave me a doubtful look. "Please?"

"Alrecht," he agreed after a moment of consideration. "But, only if ye eat more from yer plate. Ye must first fill yer stomach." I glanced at the normal portion of food still standing on my plate in front of me with unhappiness.

"All right," I sulked. I forced myself to take several bites of oat porridge and molasses. As he quietly watched me eating, I eventually consumed the entire serving, finished my wedge of buttered bread, and sipped the last of my tea. I replaced the emptied cup over the stand, then stared at him with expectation as he completed the last of the reeking cheese he favored, and that was popular here—and of which I still refused to eat. His lips mildly tilted upward as he noticed me eagerly waiting.

"Alrecht, I shall merely tell ye a single tale, and that is all," he said finally, waving a warning finger at me.

"Okay," I agreed fairly.

"Very weel, this particular instance occurred whilst I was a lad in my youthful twenties," he started. "I had returned tae Scotland tae visit fur Christmas week from France."

"All right," I said, eager to hear his story.

"Weel, I went tae the tavern with Fin and the lads fur a bit of merriment. Efter a usual bout of whisky and gaming, some other lads began serenading. So, I went tae join the lads serenading, who were standing upon a bench by a table whaur a large fellow was seated kissing a wench. Weel, now, I had my fill of the guid drink, ye see, and so had the other lads as we waur all quite merrily belting out our jolly melody.

"Yet, I reckon that I micht have had a bit more tae drink than I ought tae have taken, fur suddenly it seemed I was atop a ship rocking and swaying over the deep blue sea. Weel, as I was merrily serenading with my lads, I had swayed too far and toppled clear off the bench from the group. I landed reit onto my crease upon the hard floor."

"You're kidding me!" I suddenly laughed, very much amused.

"Nae, I fear I'm quite sincere," Leif said, lightly chuckling at himself.

"You're lucky you didn't crack your head or break your tailbone in the fall," I said smilingly in spite of my being serious.

"Aye, weel, I reckon that nearly occurred."

"Oh no!"

"In my spill, I had unintentionally struck the man seated at the nearby table being entertained by his wench from behind and knocked his whisky clear out of his hand. It drenched his boots, and he was none too pleased about it."

"Uh-oh, what happened?"

"I shall tell ye—I was a lad then weighing thirteen stone—not like the man I am presently at fifteen stone. So, the angry fellow turned about, facing me, and when I stumbled tae my feet, our eyes met. He appeared something fierce with a black beard and a patch over one eye. Och! One Eye was an ugly wretch with a deep scar directly over his brow—fat and mean looking too, at eighteen stone. Thus, as the tale goes, he was also in the midst of kissing his tavern wench when I struck him, and dinnae favor the interruption caused by me in the least bit."

"Oh-no! Then what?" I asked, captivated.

"He cursed me—mocked me because of my wee size and clean breeches—wondering why I wisnae in a kilt instead. Some other things he said I shan't repeat as it isnae fit fur yer ears tae hear. I dinnae reckon anyone would dispute the notion that I was a lad quick with words, so I returned the favor. I hurled some raither ugly slights of my own his way and a number of witty phrases of which he was too dimwitted tae fathom. So, I jested about his lack of wit also due tae his dimwittedness. I recall mocking his teeth as his front ones whaur missing, and I also jeered about his gut— saying it was fit fur loving swine—tae put it in polite terms."

"Oh!" I gasped with surprise. "Did you really say that?"

"Aye, something of the sort," Leif said, smirking as he remembered.

"That's terrible!"

"Weel, One Eye dinnae agree with it either. He started at me with swinging fists. He told me that he was going tae bash my teeth out. Yet, I ducked from his fist, headed straight fur my nose. I reckon I was raither fortunate then."

"Yeah, I'd say so."

"Aye. Yet, I continued tae mock him with fitting words as a result of him missing his swing tae my head. I dinnae care about hurling slights at him and boxing him—I dinnae fear him in the merest when he yanked forth his large fists tae pound me. Although, I ken that I ought tae have been fearful. I was too boozed with whiskey and ready tae beat his crease—had my fists out quite like his ready tae slam him guid." Leif formed a solid fist and gesticulated just as he fiercely would have boxed One Eye. "But, Robert, anither uncle of mine, suddenly appeared betwixt us and pulled me back from One Eye as Robert had my cousins restrain me."

"Really?"

"Aye. He reckoned I was apparently nae match fur One Eye."

"And then what?"

"Robert offered the man a few humbling words upon my behalf. Then, One Eye relented from killing me."

"Just like that? He backed off?"

"Aye."

"Well, what did your uncle say to him? Do you know?"

"Nae," Leif said simply, shaking his head a little. "But, Robert was an officer of the Watch, so I reckon that micht have had a bit tae do with it."

"Well, yeah, I guess that would have had something to do with it," I surely agreed as I unbelievably smiled at him. "You're lucky you're uncle was there to prevent you from looking like One Eye."

"I realize so. I would have certainly been murdered otherwise." He ridiculously shook his head at himself.

"Lucky for you."

"Most indeed."

"I can't believe you got into a bar fight." I lightly shook my head with amusement.

"All sense is lost once a lad is liquored weel."

"No kidding."

"I retched weel over the street before I could make my way back home with Fin and the lads."

"Nice," I said satirically.

"I understand ye," he snorted. "I awakened the next morn feeling as if a spike had been driven through my head."

"That sounds familiar."

"Indeed it does. Och! I was thus terribly forswunk. I certainly met the wrath of my pleasure. Whit misery! I thought that I shall never have anither drink fur all time tae come, but whit is a man tae drink when he's in need tae quench his thirst? So, I thought a compromise was in order—that I shall henceforth mind my drink as it will certainly not mind me and lead me tae trooble," Leif expressed casually. I suddenly started laughing slightly, but not too hard like I had wanted since my head was so sensitive to pain. He observed my amusement with a smile. "Ye understand my meaning now, do ye not?"

"Yes, of course I do," I said, laughing lightly.

"That is guid."

"I've certainly learned my limitation. I'm glad I don't have to worry about you getting your teeth punched out, and you won't have to ever worry about me putting on another music concert."

"I believe that is quite reasonable." He winked at me, and I grinned in response.

"Besides," I started lightly. "I really like that all of your teeth are still in your head. I wouldn't have married you otherwise."

"Och!" he chuckled. "Whilst I do consider it most fortunate

that they remained in my head, if I had lost them, nonetheless, I reckon that ye wouldnae have had much tae say about the matter, as I still would have taken ye fur my own."

"Oh, well, in that case, lucky for me that I'm not looking at you having *castle teeth* right now because that's what I would've nicknamed you," I joked back. He started laughing, and his face cheerfully flushed.

"Yoo've got too much of a quick tongue, *ribhinn*," Leif said, chuckling.

"So do you, I'm told." I winked back at him.

He smiled again. "A sharp tongue can land ye in a heap of trooble, so ye best be warned, lassie. I speak from generous experience as a lad." He waved a cautious finger at me with an arched eyebrow and a smirk. I smiled widely at him and didn't say anything else. He gave me a knowing look while reaching for my used plate and collected it over his. "I am most earnest. Ye must heed me. Now," he began again as he also seized my emptied teacup, "ye must have anither cup of tea before ye return tae rest."

That actually sounded like a very good idea. A lazy day was the best thing for me, I agreed.

"Okay," I said, realizing that I felt a bit better than before now that I was slightly rehydrated and fed.

"Alrecht, haur ye are," he said, holding a freshly poured cup of lukewarm tea for me to take.

"Thank you," I replied politely, taking it from him.

"Aye," he responded naturally.

"What are you going to do now?"

"I must complete my correspondence. Then, I shall join ye tae rest fur a wee while as I, too, am a bit weary. Afterward, I shall leave ye tae observe how weel the lads have progressed rebuilding the outer buildings."

"All right," I replied, sipping a lot from my cup.

When he straightened from me, I watched him stride back toward the writing desk, glad that I was going to have a relatively relaxing day. He returned to his seat at the desk by the bright window, and I continued drinking my tea while watching him write. Shortly, when I had enough to drink, I carefully placed the teacup on the nightstand and made myself comfortable reclining on the thin mattress again.

I rested on my side facing him and resumed quietly, watching him scratch the nib of the quill over parchment as he slightly slouched over the desk. My eyelids soon felt heavy again, and soon I found myself drifting off toward slumber.

FIVE DAYS LATER, General Webb arrived at the fort. Apparently, it was his first visit to the outpost. He met with Colonel Monro and his officers in extended briefings. He also toured the fort and made his assessments. While he was quite orderly and seemingly in control of his faculties on this occasion, he politely remembered me and seemed to have had no hint of remembering the traumatic episode we had experienced with him earlier at Fort Edward. Instead, he conducted himself with grave tact as most other unemotional, hard-faced military officers did. So, his visit proceeded in typical, even fashion.

The next day, Leif found spare time to escort me on a walk around the grounds near the edge of the lake. The land around the south end of the lake had been cleared where the fort had been positioned. We wandered toward the east bend of the shoreline past the road to Fort Edward beyond a rocky knoll. We arrived at a stream and settled in front of it over a boulder.

The sun was beaming hot, and the air was heavy with humidity. It seemed that summer was closely upon us. I peered out over the lake from the running stream rushing by us and noticed the sky was a rich, bright, light-toned cobalt blue, partly interrupted by white cumulus clouds that were slowly drifting like suspended cotton puffs stretched across the high horizon.

The lack of a breeze made the heat almost unbearable, but the bubbling water glimmering beneath the sun offset the feeling of discomfort. So, I tugged off my boots and stockings as Leif had done, rolled up my trousers, and dangled our feet into the stream while perched over the boulder jutting out into the clear water. The cold water felt good, rushing over my feet as I idly swirled my toes. I sensed Leif watching my swimming feet as we enjoyably sat quietly together under the radiant sun.

"When we return tae Boston, I shall see that ye have all the pleasantries ye wish in order that ye mayn't be reminded of this place," he said calmly while staring at my moving toes.

"That's very sweet of you, Leif, but you don't have to compensate for anything. I'm okay, really. As long as I'm here with you, then everything is all right," I said, turning my eyes to him. His eyes moved from my feet and met mine, and they were noticeably blue, quite like what the sky looked like today. His gilded head glowed beneath the bright, gleaming sun, I also noticed. He was handsome as usual and appeared rugged by the two months we had been camped here at the fort in the forest.

"The wilderness is thick and vast. 'Tis unpleasant haur fur ye, I ken. Yoo've lost yer bonnie tresses tae show fur it." He gently buried his fingers among my very short, bobbed curls and easily combed them through.

"It's hair, it'll grow back," I said.

"Yet, ye remain with cheer." He grinned at me.

"Well, I'd rather laugh than cry whenever life gives me a bowl of lemons. A spoonful of sugar for lemons goes a long way, I think," I said.

"Indeed," he remarked. "Yoo're vantage is appealing." His hand was still caressing the back of my hair, then slid to the nape of my neck. He leaned and placed a dedicated kiss on the edge of my jaw. "A pity we dinnae have the discretion of trees surrounding us this time," he muttered.

"I guess that is a little bit of a disappointment, isn't it? Considering we got shot at," I murmured jokingly when he released me.

"Aye," he chuckled a bit. He romantically looked at me, but then his expression curiously altered as he gazed past me. His brow drew together, and he seemed uncertain or confused at first. He stirred, withdrawing his feet from the stream, and straightened to stand, towering tall above me as he looked at the lake toward the north of us. Suddenly, grim alarm washed over his expression.

"What is it?" I asked, glancing over my shoulder and following his line of sight. Boats were approaching and I also stood from the bubbling brook, looking out over the lake water, noticing their scant amount.

"They have returned too soon... Thaur are a few of them also," he observed, remotely speaking to himself. Of the two gunboats that had set sail and twenty whaleboats, Monro had ordered up the lake for the mission to Fort Carillon, both the gunboats were seen advancing with only two whaleboats rowing in tandem. "Dress yer feet, *ceisdein*, we must go," he said hastily and suddenly darted for his stockings over the pebbles. We quickly covered our toes and shoved our feet back inside our boots.

I hurriedly followed him away from the stream as he rapidly paced ahead of me back over the rocky clearing around the lakeshore. As my heart was racing hard with growing anxious apprehension while we were immediately making our way through the distance, I knew what Leif was initially thinking or hoping. My own thoughts and angst were running parallel to his, and I nervously held faith and prayed...

When we finally arrived near the docks, the boats were anchoring with a crowd of waiting men aiding the sailors as they roped the boats to the docks. There was confusion and disorder everywhere around the area, with many men shouting while they rushed to assist each other. One of the gunboats looked significantly damaged from fire and freshly smelled of smoke and char. I caught a glimpse of sailors being helped off the rigs and saw a lot of clotting blood over one's face, leading me to believe that he had just recently sustained his wound. The other man I'd also seen had relatively fresh, massive blood stains over the front of his shirt and knee-torn breeches, causing me to wonder what had happened.

"I beg ya pardon, Your Grace," Molly, one of the laundresses, interrupted out of the blue from behind me.

"Yes!" I said unexpectedly, preoccupied with alarm, as I suddenly swung around to face her.

"It is Betsy," she said, appearing very alarmed also.

"Yes?" I said, completely unaware.

"Her baby is coming, and it won't come out!" she cried, utterly fearful.

"What?" I responded distressingly as I looked at her.

"The baby—it will not come!" she cried again.

"Where is Betsy now?" I asked directly.

"She is in Corporal Edwards' barrack chamber," she sobbed.

"All right, I'm coming," I said determinedly. "Just a second," I insisted and quickly located Leif among the crowd of men. I tapped on his shoulder, calling his name, and he swiftly turned his distracted attention to me.

"Aye?" he responded abstractedly with dour unease on his face.

"I have to go to Betsy. Molly just informed me that the baby is trying to come," I notified nervously.

"Is it?" He was hasty and preoccupied.

"Don't worry, I'll handle it," I assured him without a second thought. What other choice did I have? I had to be confident despite my unfamiliarity with managing this emergency alone. I was about to turn away from him, ready to leave for where I needed to go, but he abruptly caught my hand in his.

"I shall be thaur tae assist ye when I can," he said.

"Okay," I said, and his hand slid from mine. He resumed assisting the men disembark, and I hurried out of the way off the dock. I hastened back inside the fort and headed toward our barracks for my medical bag. Once I had it in hand, I rushed around the fort toward the garrison gardens.

I speedily located Molly and followed her inside Corporal Edwards' barrack chamber. It had been cleared out of the men occupying the room aside from Edwards. When I arrived, Betsy appeared to be in full labor, screaming and crying hysterically in pain and fear. It was her first birth, apparently, so she really had no idea what to expect. Except, all she knew was that she was consumed in pain.

"How long has she been this way?" I asked the four maids surrounding her, who were also her friends, trying to ease her discomfort.

"I am uncertain," young Corporal Edwards interjected as he stood in the corner with his hands propped on his waist, appearing significantly terrified. I discerned the deep furrow in his brow as he anxiously rubbed his jaw. He was breathing quickly, and I knew he was sincerely concerned for her by the mere look of him.

"I believe about seven hours or so, Your Grace," Molly guessed.

"All right, I need fresh towels and boiling water. Hurry!" I ordered directly to anyone in the room who might oblige.

"I shall await outdoors," Corporal Edwards said nervously, and I simply nodded at him in accord.

"I shall retrieve your water, Your Grace," Sarah responded promptly and disappeared from the room. I spotted an ewer filled with fresh water and washbasin. I urgently scrubbed my hands with soap and water, then quickly wiped my fingers dry on one of the fresh towels I had brought with me.

As Betsy was moaning and screaming with each labor pain, I approached and examined her between her thighs to see how far she had dilated. She seemed fairly well expanded, and I probed her with my fingers to make sure the baby was not in breech or transverse but in the correct head-first delivery position. Thank God the baby was in the proper position, I had promptly discovered after my probing.

She wailed exceptionally in distressing agony with each contraction, whimpering and moaning regularly in between. It seemed she might have been having trouble pushing. So, I had a quick idea. I called Corporal Edwards' attention from the threshold as he guarded the entrance to the room and informed him that I needed his assistance, regardless of his uncertainty and the lack of color on his face. I instructed him to sit behind Betsy and slightly prop her with his strength, which was more stable than any of the other maids helping me. Then, I told a couple of the maids to take each of Betsy's legs to bend them at her knees and push against her for resistance as I coached Betsy to push with each birth pain.

Sarah soon returned with fresh towels and boiling hot water. So, I hastily instructed her to separate the water into another unspoiled vessel and submerged my clippers inside one of the pots with the raging water.

In about a half hour, the baby began effectively crowning, indicating the hard effort was working. After a few really good thrusts, the head had fully emerged, without the need for an episiotomy. In a couple of forceful pushes, a shoulder came forth followed by the other, and then the rest of the infant appeared with ease.

The complexion of the infant was first observed and it appeared normal as I meticulously rubbed a clean towel over the baby, removing blood and vernix from it. It coughed and instantly cried. The water had cooled significantly in the buckets, and I dabbed a towel in one of the tepid pots to continue wiping the baby clean. From all accounts of my examination, the infant appeared hearty and strong as it was alert and wailing with good reflexes.

"Congratulations, Betsy," I said elatedly as I clipped the umbilical cord and carefully swaddled the lovely newborn.

"Is the babe well?" Betsy inquired anxiously, full of anguish.

"Yes, of course, your beautiful little son is very well," I said. I carefully placed the baby over her breast for her to love and behold.

"Oh, my prayers have been answered! Praise be to our Lord, Jesus Christ!" she cried breathlessly.

"Amen," the four maids and Corporal Edwards said with humble gratitude.

"I have a son. I have a son," she repeated, completely amazed.

"You certainly do. Have you thought of a name for your baby boy?" I asked as I began cleaning Betsy from the afterbirth.

"I shall call him Ethan, after his father and my departed husband, and Christopher, after my new husband, Corporal Edwards, who has sworn to rear him as his own," she expressed with contented tears.

"That sounds lovely," I said. Corporal Edwards sat close to Betsy on the bed with his eyes focused on the newborn. He seemed enthralled and mesmerized at the new little human being now cradled in his mother's arms. He lifted a hand and gently caressed the baby's swaddled crown. A sense of serenity came over the couple as they both admired the sweet infant together. Viewing the admiring couple, it seemed to me that Corporal Edwards would be a good father to the baby. "I will come to visit you and the baby every day to see how you both are doing," I said as I began cleaning my bloodied hands in the wash basin.

"Aye, Your Grace, thank you most kindly," Betsy replied calmly.

"Anyone you allow to change the baby must do it with hands that have first been thoroughly washed with soap and water," I instructed seriously as the maids began removing the stained sheets and scrubbed over bloody locations on the floor with soapy scouring brushes.

"Aye, Your Grace," Betsy acknowledged attentively.

"Do *not* allow anyone who has not first washed his or her hands to merely touch the baby, do you understand?"

"As you say, Your Grace."

"Good. We want to prevent the spread of infection to the baby and to you as much as possible," I said absolutely. "Does everyone else here understand what I've just said?"

"Aye, Your Grace," Molly said dutifully. I continued to give each person a specific look until everyone attending readily gave me affirmative answers.

"Good. Those instructions go for all of you as well," I stipulated.

"Aye, Your Grace," they all said nearly in unison.

"All right, then," I said satisfactorily while I fitted my freshly washed clippers back inside my surgeon's bag.

When I had completed tending to my new patients, I exited the barracks, returning outside. I paced through the garrison gardens under a spell. I was riveted by what I had just witnessed and helped to achieve. The miracle of birth was truly a *miracle*. It is a phenomenon that observes what is important and sacred on a root level to all of life. It put into perspective the genesis of living, and highlighted the point of our existence.

I passed through the garrison barracks in utter mesmerization as this revelation enlightened my being. I was so grateful and thrilled that I had the opportunity to witness and assist in achieving this wonder firsthand by myself and that it had happened with such unforeseen ease under these prevailing hardships that were inescapable to all of us here. I walked through the fort walls toward the officer barracks, believing Betsy was the bravest woman I knew. She risked her life by bringing another human life into this world, and for that, I thought she was a heroine.

Advancing toward the steps leading to our quarters, I climbed the steep, wooden staircase and turned the brass door handle as I arrived on the upper landing. When entering our room, I noticed Leif standing at the window overlooking the lake. It was underexposed inside, but the daylight entering the window illuminated him, and he projected from the surrounding dimness. He didn't stir as I closed the door behind me. Instead, he remained standing there like a marble sculpture with a hand hidden in his pocket and the other with an elbow propped over the windowpane as his thumb and forefinger clutched his square chin. He was stoic and unresponsive when I mindfully advanced inside our room. The appearance of suspension was embedded on his face as he seemed deeply entrenched in thought. I could easily perceive a dark nebula hovering over his being as he clearly appeared dejected.

My walk on cloud nine suddenly evaporated...

I set my medical bag in the corner beneath the coat rack pegs beside the door. Thoughtfully pacing toward him, I arrived, standing next to him, and looked up at his distant expression. I carefully placed a hand high on the side of his upper arm to acquire his attention.

"Aye, *ceisdein*?" he responded unexpectedly, startled to suddenly see me. However, his tone remained gentle despite the unmistakably disturbed look on his face that conveyed a combination of anger and regret.

"What happened?" I ventured carefully, suddenly noticing his eyes. They were red and glazed. "Oh no!" I gasped abruptly, flinging my palm to my mouth, instantly knowing something unspeakable had gone wrong.

"Fin didnae return," he solemnly informed me, then his eyes shifted away from me and resumed gazing out the window.

"What?" I faltered.

"He is lost fur guid this time," he said in a somber tone.

"What do you mean? That's impossible!" I gasped. My eyes suddenly started welling as I realized the grave look on his face. He pinched the corner of his eyes and silently wiped them with the back of his hand with one brisk stroke, never changing the detached expression impressed on his face. "Are you sure?" I asked with a trembling voice, stunned.

"Aye, I'm quite certain." His eyes stayed fixedly, staring out the window as he kept them averted from mine.

"How could he not come back?"

"They couldnae retrieve him from the waters."

"Oh my God…" My vision blurred, and now I could no longer clearly see him. I blinked, and teardrops quietly slipped forth, trailing down my cheeks.

"He took a musket ball in the head and went overboard. The lads tried retrieving him as they waur under heavy attack by Huron. But the lads caught arrows and musket balls themselves and fell over also. They waur speared like fish and drowned."

"Oh God…" I wiped my fingertips over the teardrops rolling down my cheeks and slid a consoling arm around his waist, unable to hold back my weeping. His hand came over my shoulder as I attempted to lend him all the comfort he wished to take from me.

We merely stood there in front of the window, silently grieving in our own separate way: he was quiet, no longer speaking to me. Inanimate, he stood rigid as if carved into stone. In spite of his posture, he leaned on me somewhat when I felt his solid weight pressing against me. I fathomed a portion of the unspoken devastation he was certainly feeling and withholding as he was repressing his remorseful emotions in front of me; half his world had suddenly collapsed with the loss of his closest ally found within the bloodline of his brother. I understood very well the emotional place he had newly discovered himself to be in. The recovery from having lost someone dear to him would never land him in the same emotional place before this tragedy happened, and I mourned for him.

"I promised Elizabeth that he'd come back safe," I choked, covering my face in his chest with intense sorrow. Leif didn't respond as I thought of her at the same time. I knew exactly how she would be once she discovered this devastating news as I thought of myself in her place. All I could feel was awful, inexplicable sadness for her as more tears kept uncontrollably streaming down my face. Tremendous guilt consumed me also; I felt responsible after I'd promised Finley's safe return to her.

Despite my emotions, I forced myself not to come any more

unglued than I already had, as best as I could for Leif's sake. He didn't seem inclined to let his grief loose and allow his emotions to escape him. So, I strove to settle myself from any more tears as I wiped the droplets from my eyes. He gently squeezed my shoulder, and I pulled my embracing arms tighter around his chest, sealing myself close to him. Quieting myself, I understood his silence.

Standing by the window together, we supported each other in our unspoken mourning while looking out over the silver lake. I wondered how he and Elizabeth were ever going to get by without Finley being in their lives from now on.

"Elizabeth will learn of this tragedy from me upon our return tae Concord as it ought tae be," Leif said at length in a morose voice. I nodded my head in acknowledgment and took a deep breath as I cleared my eyes again with my fingers.

His hand slipped from my shoulder, and I finally turned my gaze up to him. He appeared official and reserved as he repressed his emotions. He turned his head away from the window and finally met my gaze. I recognized for the first time the solidity that is often ascribed to military men who have closely known death, and it had seeped into Leif's hardened eyes.

"I am so unimaginably sorry for what's happened to Finley, Leif," I choked. "I'm so sorry..."

"I, too," he replied, stone-faced except for the redness in his eyes, which only gave an inkling of the sorrow he surely had been feeling. But, his brow slightly furrowed as he happened to notice something overlooked on my torso. "Ye have bluid upon yer shirt." He lightly touched his forefinger to the area just below my breast.

"Oh," I said, glancing down at his pointing finger, realizing the large stain. "It's from Betsy's delivery."

"Och, aye," he remembered. "I regret that I wisnae able tae assist ye as I had intended."

"It's okay."

"Waur ye able tae manage?"

"Yes, everything went well."

"Guid. The lass is alrecht then?"

"Yes, she's just fine."

"And the bairn?"

"He's great—nice and strong."

"Och, she has a laddie?"

"Yeah."

"Very guid news." The expression on Leif's face changed a little and seemed to distantly soften. "Yoo're clever. I kent that ye would be able tae achieve it upon yer own, and ye did merely that." Despite the oppressive weight of our depressed moods, he seemed really proud of me as his gloomy expression slightly eased with a remote grin. He clasped my chin and gently stroked the side of my cheek with the pad of his thumb. When he released me, he attempted a fuller smile despite the dejection in his eyes.

"Thank you," I said softly. All of a sudden, a knocking came from the door.

"Aye?" Leif responded.

"I beg yer pardon, Your Grace, 'tis Captain Walsh."

"Aye?"

"I am seeking Her Grace's assistance in hospital if ye will so permit."

"Aye," Leif replied calmly.

"Thank ye, Your Grace. Whaur micht she be found?"

"My wife is preoccupied presently but will promptly arrive in hospital."

"Aye, Your Grace."

Then, steps were heard swiftly diminishing over the platform down the staircase. Leif returned to looking at me.

"I shall escort ye," he said.

"All right," I agreed.

WHEN WE ARRIVED at the hospital barracks, there were several men who had returned from the mission with serious injuries from multiple arrowheads and musket balls impaled in their flesh. One man trembling as he lay on a cot, pale as a white sheet, appeared as if he had seen evil incarnate as utter fear was clearly impressed on his face. General Webb and Colonel Monro stood at the side of the cot, interviewing the terrified man. I approached them with Leif at my side, listening to the soldier talk with chattering teeth. His skin seemed visibly moist, and he shivered uncontrollably as if he had just come from prolonged exposure to the depths of arctic waters. He was in a state of shock, and I noticed a large contusion high on his brow, curving over the hairline. His scalp had been split open and needed immediate suturing. I swiftly drew a blanket over him and monitored his pulse.

"When—w-we had merely arrived... at Sabbath Day Point... Indians came from out of the wood... everywhere..." the poor soldier told Webb and Monro with chattering teeth.

"Did no one stand to fire back upon them?" Webb inquired uneasily. The expression on Webb's face was stark alarm, I observed when I glanced at him.

"The first three boats did not... they were surprised... but we did," he said, shivering. There seemed to have been no abdominal injury, I noted, as I continued examining this poor man. "We fell back... Huron pursued us in boats... Th-they t-ook prisoners... I a-amongst th-them. The rum th-they s-stole from us, they drank... *Oh!* Th-they took *no m-mercy*! They are cruel! *So cruel! Savages!*" The soldier burst out crying hysterically.

"He's getting too excited," I said, concerned for this soldier. "He should be interviewed later." Colonel Monro and General Webb simply looked at me.

"Mayhap, Her Grace micht wish tae take leave fur a moment as we render the details of our status," Colonel Monro suggested plainly.

"Aye, such information may be found unpleasant to your ears,

Duchess," General Webb interjected, supporting Monro's sentiments.

"Micht ye care tae bide a moment till this discussion is completed, Sylvie," Leif urged more delicately.

"No, it's all right. I'm just saying that he's in no state to describe to you the recount of his experience because he's in shock, and his condition could deteriorate if you insist on continuing," I said soundly.

"A point weel regarded, madam, however—" Monro was suddenly interrupted as the panic-stricken soldier abruptly took hold of Webb's sleeve while he continued nonsensically rambling. The action startled Webb.

"They c-com-mitted great cruel-ties to our men!" the soldier cried.

"What sort of cruelties?" Webb asked with a particular look on his face.

"They... they t-took our men..." the soldier sobbed uncontrollably. The look and sound of terror were duly expressed all over his face.

"Whit did they do?" Monro asked directly.

"The Indians p-put th-them in cauldrons... and boiled them! Th-they flayed their flesh from the bone once they were cooked... upon which they ate a portion of them! We escaped our captors before 'twas us they cooked by stealing c-canoes and floated down the lake... Just the few of us men were able to flee. P-presently—we have only arrived," he bawled hideously. I abruptly gasped, horrendously appalled by his story.

"*Christ!*" Webb expressed suddenly, struck with horror.

"I have never heard of a thing like this!" Monro stated with sheer disbelief.

"I wish it were not true, c-colonel! Oh, how I shall pray to our Lord God to receive the souls of our fallen b-brave brethren in Heaven," the soldier cried.

"Christ have mercy," Leif said unbelievably beneath his breath, though he appeared emotionless and rather stone-faced.

"Indeed! It is an atrocious and evil act of the likes I have never knoon," Monro said gruesomely.

All aghast, simultaneous looks of grisly, grotesque terror quickly bounced between Leif, Monro, and Webb. Webb, in particular, seemed intensely more shaken as his ashen face went macabrely wry with horridly widened eyes. With the color of his face suddenly drained, a nervous look came over him. He promptly removed the grip that the frightened soldier had over his arm and drew forth a handkerchief from his waistcoat. He quickly dabbed away the light beads of perspiration that had abruptly emerged above his lip and brow. Leif's face was set hard as if chiseled in stone with his jaw clinched and brow deeply furrowed. He appeared revoltingly appalled and frozen in his stance. Monro's distinctly repulsed and severely alarmed expression reflected the speechlessness imprisoning us all as we tried to grasp the unthinkable concept of what we had just heard.

"I wonder if we are not in Hell as we speak," Webb finally uttered as he trembled slightly. He looked at Monro. "I shall take a bit of rum now as we proceed to meet."

"Aye," Monro agreed. He then turned to me before departing. "If Her Grace will be so merciful by tending tae these poor souls returned tae us. We shall be most grateful and in yer debt."

"Yes, of course," I said undoubtedly.

"Thank ye fur yer mercy," Monro said and politely bowed his head to me. Webb also gestured in the same manner, and the two men started their way toward the door out of the barrack chamber.

I immediately began medical treatment on the shocked soldier while Leif remained silently, standing still as a statue watching me work. I had rubbed a strong lavender-based salve mixed with chamomile over the soldier's chest to help calm his nerves. Afterward, I examined his head wound and then began preparing the contusion on his scalp for suturing by carefully cleansing it with soap and water. Next, I continued disinfecting it with Angelica root water before applying a mild local anesthetic that I had concocted made of cloves. When I had finished sterilizing the wound, I circumstantially glanced up at Leif as I was suturing the soldier's scalp. Leif stared transfixed at the soldier in thought with a deeply distressed look on his face.

"I seem to think that he's delusional," I disclosed disturbingly as I returned to looking at the sutures I was now placing over the soldier's injured head.

"Delusional?" Leif questioned as I sensed his eyes turning to me.

"The mind can play terrible tricks on a person's perception as a result of having been traumatized during an earlier event," I said.

"Yet, it appears that he has been quite startled in this recent affair," Leif observed.

"Yes, except he might not know fact from fiction now due to whatever he may have experienced in this last event," I replied.

"Do ye mean tae say that ye reckon he's gone mad, and that ye dinnae believe his words?" Leif asked incredibly.

"Who knows what he really saw out there in those woods? It's kinda hard to believe that cannibals really exist, don't you think? I mean, look at him—he's catatonic right now," I said realistically. My patient's breathing had finally grown regular, and he began to doze while lying on the cot as I worked on him.

"How can anyone contrive such a compelling tale as morbid flesh-eating savages devouring a man?" Leif inquired abominably.

"I suppose for some, the stress of witnessing what goes on on the battlefield can mentally break a person. You, of all, recognize that."

"Aye," Leif acknowledged.

"Yeah, and so such a person could just make up any kind of story because it's probably the only way that individual can cope with the adversity with which he or she was too terrified to face. I mean, for goodness sake, look at Webb—he rattles around like a bucket of loose screws," I said. Leif's brow lifted somewhat in response to my bluntly spoken opinion.

"Aye," he considered thoughtfully, nodding a bit. "Yet, my belief tells me that this lad haur knows precisely whit he saw, and whit he saw was true."

"Yes, I'm sure he believes what he saw was real, but that doesn't mean it's true." Leif released a heavy sigh as he seemed to realize something just now.

"I understand this is a most unpleasant topic tae discuss. But, the Algonquins are knoon fur their flesh-eating and torture," Leif said factually.

"Really?" I replied unusually.

"Aye."

"Well, I've never heard of it."

"Haven't ye?"

"No."

"It is most certainly true, and a weel knoon fact they commit such evil atrocities."

"Well, this is news to me."

"Mayhap, we shan't discuss this matter any further as I can plainly perceive that yoo're quite out of sorts presently," he yielded. He was right; I was completely unnerved by everything as I tried concentrating on finishing the last stitches over the soldier's head.

"Yeah," I said disconcertedly. "It's been too hard of a day." I snipped the end of the thread to the last stitch and tossed the needle into a tin cup of saline solution that I'd made earlier.

"Aye," Leif agreed gloomily. "When ye have concluded yer business haur I shall prefer tae retire early fur the evening."

"Yes, of course." I couldn't have agreed more. I was surely ready to finally end this day I wished had never come in the first place.

But, if there was any glimmer of brightness to this horrible day, for a second, my mind returned to the birth of Betsy's new infant son. That recollection helped soften the harsh blow for me as I disturbingly thought of Finley never being among us again.

THAT NIGHT, Leif was restless and couldn't sleep. Instead, he sat himself in a chair by the window and glumly gazed out into the darkness.

I supposed he had remained there in that hard, wooden chair for the whole night since when I opened my eyes the next morning, I found him still seated in the same place. I don't think he even got up to merely use the chamber pot during the middle of the night. Finley was undoubtedly on his mind, and I wasn't certain how Leif was going to proceed through this terrible life-altering event with the loss of his brother because they were very close. I knew that all I could do was to be with him and support him however I could in his way of grief.

As my sleepy eyes began focusing on him sitting by the window in the gloomy gray, overcast morning, he seemed unemotional and removed from the present while appearing extremely engrossed in thought. I stirred from bed and paced across the floor toward him. He didn't respond to my movement until I gently eased my fingers into his loose hair and caressed the nape of his neck. He glanced up at me from the chair, and although his eyes appeared abstracted, depressed, and distressed, he still grinned at me a little.

"Guid morn, my angel," he said despondently.

"Good morning," I replied gently. "Have you been here all night?"

"Aye, I couldnae sleep," he said.

"I understand..." I empathized. "Let me fix you some tea." He subtly nodded at my suggestion without a word. I withdrew from him for the table and started preparing tea for him. When it was soon prepared, I returned to him, passing him the filled cup.

"Sit by me," he requested as he took the teacup from me.

"Sure," I agreed. I retrieved the one chair from the table and drew it close next to his. I sat beside him, and he covered my hand with his as he drew it to hold on his knee.

While Leif barely drank his tea, we sat with each other in silence at length and merely stared out the window over the silver lake surrounded by grey-toned wilderness beneath a cloudy sky, mourning Finley.

LATER, six more panic-stricken survivors staggered inside the fort and, to everyone's great unsettlement, corroborated the first surviving soldier's story. I was horrified by the gruesome stories they had told and couldn't begin to comprehend the macabre war acts they had described that the Indians had committed against the soldiers. It was chilling and unheard of. Except, I remember hearing ghoulish press stories emerge out of Iraq once the second Gulf War began of how terrorists were capturing American affiliates and journalists and beheading them for all to see on social media. It fundamentally astounded me when I first learned of such a thing taking place, and I couldn't possibly conceive of how these heinous acts could ever be committed in an era that was supposed to be considered exceedingly sophisticated and civilized. It made me reconsider the idea that civilization was really as evolved as we perceived ourselves to be. I actually couldn't answer that question now. Part of me truly believed "yes," while the other part resoundingly said "no."

Webb was noticeably shaken by the latest events and took to consuming a large amount of rum as he sat at the table with Monro while eating in the dining chamber. He ordered Monro to quarter all the regulars within the fort walls when I unwittingly overheard aspects of their conversation while passing by an open window along the backside of Monro's office. I decided to stop and discreetly tune in on their conversation out of curiosity.

"Also, have provincials construct trenches about the camp on Titcomb's Mount," Webb directed with a grave tone.

"Aye, we cannae risk the enemy setting cannon upon it," Monro agreed.

"Indeed," Webb said.

"Aye," Monro echoed. "And my reinforcements? I shall need them with merely eleven hundred men haur at present."

"Of course, they will arrive immediately," Webb promised.

"Guid. Montcalm has more than eight thousand at his command, and thaur is nae question that I need men tae match his attack," Monro said.

"I'm very well aware. You will have reinforcements as promised," Webb said.

"Alrecht then," Monro replied adequately.

"Now, if you will excuse me, I am in need of a respite," Webb insisted conclusively.

"As ye wish, general," Monro responded. Suddenly, the chairs resonated over the wood floor, and the men began to step through the room. I moved away from the window with uncertainty, understanding that something ominous was looming, as I resumed my path to check on Betsy and her baby.

AFTER YESTERDAY, men around the base were on edge and alert more than usual. At dawn the following morning, Webb and his accompanying men made a hasty exit back south to Fort Edward. Monro enacted Webb's orders effective immediately, and the base bustled into motion with men relocating from the garrison gardens to reside within the fort walls. Leif was designated to oversee the construction project on Titcomb's Mount while repairs to one of the two gunboats were underway. The following days ran very long with preparations now in progress. With all the measures suddenly being enacted around the base, it was obvious that a looming strike was imminent.

A chill came over me, and my blood froze throughout my veins. It was difficult not to acknowledge what was happening here. Urgency flooded the camp. Perhaps, as I had hoped, all vital preparations being conducted were supporting the notion that there was still enough time for the men to better position themselves to launch a great offensive attack against the enemy when reinforcements soon arrived. But something in my gut kept my unease close, and I wondered what was going to befall us next.

Every day that followed, the atmosphere was stifled with oppressive heat. The air was heavy and muggy. It was a summer heat wave like I had never felt before and reminded me of the tropics—or, more precisely, being mercilessly stuck inside a humidifier with no way out.

The heat seemed much worse inside quarters than it did when simply being outside beneath the beating sun since the air became stagnant inside. If I could have stripped down to only wearing my shift outside, I would have gladly done so—if I could have gotten away with it in public without causing a scandal.

As I splashed my face with cold water from the washbasin over the small dresser in our room, the cool water felt refreshing against my warm skin. When I finished, I lightly patted the towel over my face and placed the cloth back beside the basin. It was dark outside now, and I wondered about the time. I paced across the room to the writing desk where Leif normally kept his timepiece when it wasn't on him and found it by the inkwell. I reached for it and unclasped it to read the time by candlelight.

It seemed the whole camp decided to bunk outdoors tonight because of the heat trapped inside the quarters. Plenty of chatting and languid voices from the courtyard floated up through the windows inside the room. Several large moths, taking on the size of something out of the tropics, fluttered through the windows, attracted by the lanterns' light set over the table and nightstand. Other creepy-crawlies, incited by the ripe nocturnal environment, including some strange-looking flying beetles and loathsome mosquitoes, entered the room.

Spoiled by the arid desert of the likes in Southern California, and the rest of the southwest which could not support such large and plentiful insects, I grew up never taking kindly to bugs. So, I quickly moved through our second story quarters shutting all the windows allowing no further pests to enter, sacrificing the cooler night air to gradually temper the heat inside.

"Whit are ye about, *àille dhubh*?" Leif inquired curiously as his voice suddenly came from the blinding darkness outside just as I was pulling the last window shutter closed in front of the writing desk. He startled me, since he was invisible in the dark.

"Where are you?" I asked, surprisingly.

"I'm reit before ye," he said simply. Honing in on his voice, my eyes suddenly adjusted from the candlelight in the room to the surrounding pitch blackness and found him seated over a barrel smoking his pipe on the cannon deck a few feet away, staring directly at me.

"Oh!" I realized, suddenly seeing him also joined by his cousins Angus, Cole, Derek, Lachlan, Liam, Roy, Bearnard, and Fearghus, all enjoying smokes and ale.

"Ye will perish indoors with all of the windows shut," Leif said.

"Yeah, but I can't stand all the disgusting bugs that keep coming inside. They bother me way *too* much," I replied annoyedly.

"They'll not harm ye," he said, dismissing my grievance.

"Oh yeah? These mosquitoes just took a chunk outta my arm. See?" I rolled up my sleeve and shoved my arm out the window into the darkness, showing him my poor, bitten forearm. A sudden light chuckle eluded him.

"Silly bird," he muttered in a senseless tone. The men snorted a little in agreement with him. "Pray, keep the windows open fur a while longer yet tae release the heat indoors, or I shall have us sleep outdoors as all the other lads tonecht."

"Well, I suppose in that case, it won't matter where we sleep tonight since inside will be just the same as outside with all the bugs then," I said peevishly as I obligingly re-opened the second half of the shutter.

"Aye, simply do as I say," he said, disregarding me. "Once yoo're through, rub some of that charmed salve of yers upon yer arm, then join me and the lads outdoors fur now."

"I guess I will," I accepted, silently continuing to mope over the irksome heat. I moved from the window and proceeded to reopen all the windows. I missed having screens over the windows like in my modern era, but we were fortunate enough to have a mosquito net over our bed. I checked the net once more, making sure there were no gaps in between for any bug to sneak inside. Now satisfied with it, I rubbed a calamine concoction over my arms that I had made to prevent skin irritation from bug bites. When I had finished, I started out of our room and went down the staircase.

Moving alongside the barracks toward the end, I climbed a flight of stairs that took me to the top of the cannon platform behind our building. Along the way, I passed many men relaxing with rum and ale as they gambled while seated on the deck behind the parapet. I found Leif and the guys doing the same thing outside our bedroom window as I approached them. Leif noticed me and pulled an empty crate next to himself for me to sit. As I made my way near him to take a seat, something caught my eye when I happened to glimpse beyond the embrasure directly behind us.

"What's that?" I asked unknowingly as I remained standing, staring curiously out into the darkness over the lake.

"Whit is it?" Leif asked, attentive to me.

"There's fire, it looks like," I answered observantly.

"Whaur?" he responded curiously and stood from his seat on the crate.

"Over there." I pointed to the appearance of three large fires on the west end of the lake, seemingly not too far away. Leif's cousins immediately stood up also and looked out past the other embrasures nearby.

"*Damnation!*" Leif hissed alertedly and quickly snatched up his large spyglass leaning against the parapet. He pulled the segments open and peered through the spyglass in the direction of the orange glowing light flickering in the distance. Studying the image for a minute, he then sharply retracted the telescope. "I must see Monro, ye lads remain and keep watch," he said, suddenly turning around from the parapet.

"Aye," Angus and his fellow companions agreed preparedly.

"What is it?" I asked Leif with concern.

"Ye neednae worry. I shall return momentarily," he urged and suddenly took off jogging over the deck. A sentry standing about halfway down the length of the platform apprehended Leif and said something while pointing out over the lake to him. Leif acknowledged him, then continued hurriedly over the platform. In a second, he vanished in the darkness as his audible footsteps quickly paced around the bend where he was headed down the staircase. I turned back toward the orange glow and stared for a second longer.

"What's going on?" I posed the question to anyone left around me who would answer.

"Ye must not be concerned, lass," Angus assuaged.

"Mayhap, Her Grace micht be interested in a game of cards," Derek recommended as he began shuffling a deck of cards over the crate.

"Aye, soonds fair, I shall join also," Fearghus encouraged and took a seat again over one of the crates. The men looked at me, and I knew they were trying to distract me with something less troubling to think about. Without really responding, I simply moved toward one of the surrounding crates and sat on it. Angus and Cole resumed looking out past the parapet, and Derek started dealing a round of cards to me.

Halfway into the game of Pinochle, I decided that I could no longer concentrate and excused myself from playing further. I returned standing and started pacing back along the platform toward the staircase where Leif had gone down. When I arrived at the top landing overlooking the stairs, a large body of military personnel was seen from my vantage point moving through the courtyard. They were all seen entering the fort as Leif suddenly emerged, galloping up the staircase toward me on his return.

"What's going on?" I asked as he arrived, towering next to me on the top landing.

"It appears Webb's reinforcements have newly arrived," Leif answered with a dour look on his face. I glanced down below as fresh troops were streaming into the courtyard, and a pervasive sense of tension palpably rose on base. He proceeded to pass me, and I turned quickly, following him until we arrived back at his cousins.

"Whit is the word from Monro?" Angus inquired.

"He has dispatched two scouting boats," Leif informed him. He drew forth his spyglass again and looked through it across the water.

"Then we wait," Angus said.

"Aye," Leif said as he was peering through his spyglass. "Webb's reinforcements have newly arrived," he told his surrounding cousins.

"Och! That's guid," Fearghus said, sounding relieved.

"How many men?" Cole asked.

"About a thousand men," Leif answered, abruptly collapsing his spyglass and turning his eyes to his cousins. He seemed agitated.

"A thousand!" Angus echoed suddenly with disapproval.

"We need far more than that!" Fearghus said alarmingly.

"Aye," Leif agreed.

"Webb can afford the men. Why has he sent so few?" Derek asked.

"He fears the vulnerability of his fort," Leif answered grimly.

"But, our post defends Fort Edward if Webb will permit it. Does he not see that primarily?" Bearnard expressed arguably.

"Which regiment has he sent tae join us?" Angus interrupted.

"Two hundred from the Royal American Regiment and eight hundred provincials under Colonel Frye," Leif informed them.

"Och," Angus said. "Frye is a knowledgeable warrior."

"Still, we need more men," Liam said uneasily.

"Monro has dispatched couriers tae Webb and Loudoun. We shall see whit either will do fur us men haur. Thaur is still time yet. Merely hold fast, lads," Leif said gravely. He then turned his eyes on me, and I looked back at him. It was hard to gauge his expression in the moonlight, and I wished that I could clearly see him to know what he was likely thinking. I suddenly felt too wired to rest, although it was very late, and I was weary from the day. An ominous feeling settled over me and fell like a rock to the pit of my stomach. I turned from Leif, pacing a couple of steps beyond him, and peered over the high parapet at the dancing orange glow along the lakeshore afar. I didn't know if my eyes were playing tricks on me or if the three large isolated fires were seemingly advancing at a snail's pace. I sensed Leif stepping quietly behind me and standing close.

"Are they moving?" I asked.

"Aye," he answered calmly.

"The flames seem really large, don't they?" I scrutinized them observantly.

"Come," he said, urging me away from viewing any more out the porthole. He stooped with his back against the rampart and steered me between his knees, intimating for me to sit with him on the platform. I placed myself sitting in front of him with my back against his chest as he easily stretched his legs out alongside me. The mounted cannon close by concealed us as we sat quietly for a moment together. His arms slid around my waist while he caressed and held me close to himself. I eased my fingers over his as they moved up over my breast above my heart in his embrace.

"I shall not let any harm come tae ye," he guaranteed softly against my ear. I sensed his lips press over the nape of my neck.

"Then you better stay alive," I told him with an adamant tone.

"I swear it," he vowed. I leaned my head back on his shoulder, and he rested his stubbled jaw against my cheek. A pensive silence ensued between us as the men's voices carried in the air all around us.

"They're coming, aren't they?" I inquired, finally breaking the silence between us.

"Aye," Leif replied.

"Are you scared?" I asked.

"I cannae permit myself tae be fearful," he answered. It became quiet between us again, and this time, the silence stayed. We sat holding each other for an indeterminate time, and I glanced up at the black sky. It was flooded with brightly shining stars. The Milky Way stretched as a massive cream nebula across the dark canopy above our heads. The universe appeared endless as countless shooting stars rained down over the atmosphere like combusting sparklers. I thought about the dimension of time again, and for the first time, I couldn't recall the faces of my parents. I closed my eyes and tried to remember their images. My brother and sister-in-law, Kyle and Dakota, were also foggy in my mind. Everyone else who was once close to me could no longer be seen. A cold fear seeped within my veins, and I shuddered. Leif's arm tightened around me and secured me in his encircling embrace.

"Everything will be alrecht," he whispered into my ear.

"I hope so," I replied, feeling otherwise.

"Have faith." He leaned his lips against my ear and gave me a soft, reassuring kiss.

Thirty-Two

I must have dozed for a little while because I had awakened to find myself having been neatly tucked into a corner of the parapet, hearing the voices of Leif and Angus talking alone together. It was still dim out, but dawn was beginning to break across the sky. I turned my vague attention in their direction and recognized them sitting over a couple of casks in a collection near the standing cannon, sharing a bottle of rum.

"Any word on the scouts?" Angus inquired.

"None thus far," Leif replied.

"Mayhap, they have been captured," Angus suspected.

"Aye, they ought tae have returned long by now," Leif said and straightened to his feet. He moved from the cask and drew open his spyglass. He peered through it passed the casement. He silently scoped the scene for a lengthy minute like a precision robot. "Och! *Christ*! Come have a look at this!" he expressed abruptly, alerted, fixing his telescope on a particular location in the distance. Angus erected himself from his seat over his cask, setting the rum bottle down on top, and stepped toward Leif. He also drew forth his spyglass and brought it up to his eye to look out ahead. It took him a second to fix onto Leif's sited location.

"*Damnation!*" Angus remarked alarmingly.

"Aye, ye see it then?" Leif responded in the same tone.

"*Bloody Hell*!" Angus observed with a chill in his voice. That's when I decided to stir from my restful spot and paced over to the next casement to see what they were looking at.

"*Damn their blood!* Look at all of them!" Leif stated.

"*David Jones!*" Angus cursed.

"They appear tae ride low," Leif noticed, keenly peering through his telescope.

"Aye," Angus noticed also.

It was difficult to distinguish what they were initially seeing afar over the lake. The water was silent and still. It appeared sleek, like a vast single sheet of black glass beneath the growing daylight. Then, in the distance, my naked eye began discerning tiny shapes emerging over the still water.

"The boats are adjoined," Angus continued noticing.

"Aye, they have got cannon with them," Leif perceived and quickly collapsed his spyglass, stepping away from the rampart. "I must warn Monro." He swiftly took off running along the deck in the opposite direction toward the ramp and vanished. I moved toward Angus and carefully edged near him to stare out across the lake from his position. I sensed him slightly pull away from his spyglass and glance at me. I glimpsed back at him and clearly perceived the gravity in his expression. He didn't say anything to me and glanced back into the telescope he was holding. I returned gazing over the water also, wondering what he and Leif had seen.

Dawn was now shortly upon us as the darkness was nearly completely gone. The images had grown larger and more distinct over the water. Angus pivoted his spyglass, slowly panning the vast vista from one point to the next. He suddenly seized onto something and focused on the western shoreline of the lake, then raced to the end of the rampart, peering through the last casement. I looked out from the opening where I remained in the direction where his interest was now abruptly captured. But I couldn't see anything unusual, because of the far distance and the obscuring forest. So, I shifted my attention back to the lake and could now clearly see an advancing flotilla spanning the water like an armada. There were far too many vessels to count, and my pulse began rising. Leif suddenly reappeared behind me breathing slightly heavy. He whipped out his spyglass before his gaze again and looked out toward the lake.

"How many boats do you think there are?" I asked him as he stood close behind me looking through his spyglass.

"Presumably four or five hundred," he observed.

"Oh my God," I gasped.

"Seamus!" Angus called suddenly.

"Aye!" Leif responded, and walked hurriedly toward him.

"Git a look over haur," he told Leif. Leif took up his scope and looked.

"*God in Heaven!* How many do ye reckon?" Leif responded with further alarm still looking through his telescope.

"Mayhap, close tae two thousand," Angus estimated as he also continued looking through his telescope.

"Or more," Leif approximated while looking out in the same direction.

"Aye," Angus agreed.

"Inform Monro, presently! He is about tae dispatch anither currier tae Webb," Leif ordered sharply.

"Aye!" Angus said quickly and abruptly whizzed over the deck down the ramp in the opposite direction from us.

I glimpsed back across the lake. The vanguard was approaching over the calm water like a silent blade over ice. But then minuscule human voices were heard echoing throughout the canyon beyond, over the water. It oddly sounded animated—perhaps even cheerful. Musket fire *popped* off afar like distant firecrackers, and drum rolls thumped audibly like a heartbeat, bringing the surrounding basin to life. Abruptly, battle horns trumpeted, resonating among the mountains. The vision of a vanguard swelling of hundreds of canoe-rowing Indians and a fleet of French bateaux came into view by the naked eye.

The atmosphere was already muggy and warm at the start of this morning. But the sky was brilliant—clear of the merest cloud—and the bluest cerulean I'd ever seen. In the slow motion of the enemy's oncoming threatening advance over the glassy water, and the way the crystal-clear blue sky appeared behind them among the pristine beauty of the valley unexpectedly brought me back to a moment in time that flashed before my eyes as I stood before the television watching a popular morning show in sheer disbelief and horror when two planes crashed into both World Trade Center Towers. The same hyper-suspended animated feeling of fundamental ghastly terrorizing horror shrouded in surrealism struck my awareness right now, and it impaled me from the gut to the pit of my soul. Without question, a sudden innate feeling came over me; I realized our fate and knew we were doomed.

I began trembling and backed away from the rampart, unexpectedly tripping backward over a crate behind me. I crashed square on my bottom and swiftly felt Leif seizing my arm as he promptly helped me back to my feet.

"Are ye alrecht, *ceisdein*?" he asked with a startled look on his face.

"Yes, I'm fine," I said, realizing I wasn't hurt.

"Take care. Ye appear weary tae me," he scrutinized concernedly. "Let's go—yoo've merely slept a couple of hours. Ye must rest properly now." He took my hand in his and started leading me away as he walked me back across the cannon platform intending to return me to our quarters without my objection. When we arrived inside with the front door still ajar behind him, he paused and gently placed a palm on the side of my face while looking earnestly at me. "Pray, rest now, and sleep," he said.

"I will," I agreed.

"I shall return later tae mind how ye are faring," he said.

"Okay," I responded, nodding accordingly.

"Remember tae latch the door efter me, and keep it so till I return."

"I will."

"Alrecht then." Subsequently, he turned back across the threshold, returning outside. His boots audibly galloped down the staircase as I moved to shut the door and lock it.

I paced toward the bed feeling very tired and tugged off my boots, then collapsed on the blankets, fixing the mosquito net closed around me in bed. The air was lightly moving and gently pushing the coarse, homespun linen curtains back and forth over the open windows. The faint sound of them whipping in the air and snagging slightly over the splintered windowsills easily lulled me into a nap.

WITHOUT WARNING, I was jarred awake by a loud and sudden musket shot powerfully erupting from somewhere close outside. More shots quickly ensued, and gunfire was suddenly being traded. I instantly got out of bed and went to the window overlooking the courtyard in the direction shots were being fired. It seemed nothing directly threatening was taking place within the fort, so I surmised that the exchange was happening close outside the walls in the direction of the garrison gardens. However, more shots opened in the air from a different direction southeast from here, slightly farther away, where some of our troops were stationed on the rocky hill of Titcomb's Mount several hundred yards away.

As I returned my attention to the courtyard, I spotted a man standing out among the others dressed in French colors, carrying a white flag and a leather correspondence tube. He stood with our guards surrounding him at the front gate. Leif emerged from Monro's office out into the quad and walked determinedly across the way toward the guarded French soldier. He delivered a rolled piece of parchment to the Frenchman. The French soldier took the parchment from Leif and secured it inside the leather tube. Leif stood among his men and observed the French soldier turn away as he was escorted off the premises by our redcoats. Then, Leif returned through the courtyard, pacing toward Monro's office at the end of our barracks, and stepped inside the open doorway.

After a minute, he returned outside along with Colonel Frye, Angus, Cole, Roy, Fearghus, and two other captains. They exchanged a few words and then separated. Subsequently, Leif started heading in my direction toward our barrack, and his boots pounded as they easily stepped up the staircase toward our quarters. I moved away from the window as he made his way upward to unlock the door and pulled it open for him just as he arrived at the threshold.

"Och, yoo're awake," he said, a little surprised to see me.

"Yeah," I said, stepping aside for him to enter our room.

"How did ye ken it is I?"

"I saw you coming up the stairs."

"Och," he realized as he proceeded inside. He closed the door, and I went to the table to pour a tin cup of previously boiled water to drink.

"Would you like some too?" I offered while filling a cup.

"Aye," he said. I handed him the filled cup and started pouring one for myself. He chugged it down in easy gulps before I barely took my first sip. I set my cup aside, sensing he wanted more, and refilled his cup. He swiftly drank from it again and set the emptied cup over the table. "That will be all, thank ye, *ceisdein*."

There were a lot of sounds coming from outside through the open windows. It seemed like a gigantic crowd had amassed around the grounds among a lot of unintelligible chatter echoing everywhere throughout. I gulped some of my water down too, wondering what was happening.

"So, what's going on?" I asked after finishing the water in my cup.

"The French have landed," Leif answered. He paced toward the window at the back of the room near our bed and glanced across the rampart, now guarded by many of our soldiers.

"I heard gunshots," I said.

"Aye, thaur was musket fire out by the garrison gardens and over by the entrenched camp on the mount," he said. The chatter outside abruptly became discernible. The noise didn't come from our men as it instead came forth in very poorly spoken French.

"Vous etes un homme mort, Iglismôn!"

"Je prendai votre cuir chevelu!"

"Iglismôn, je vous capturez! Vous n'obtenez aucun logement avec moi!"

"Je tranche votre tête! Je cuisiner et manger vous pour un bon repas!"

I gasped, instantly covering my mouth with alarm and unnerved by the chilling taunts thrown by unexpected surrounding Indians near the fort. They whooped and hollered, saying horridly threatening things: "*You dead man, Englishman! I take your scalp! I slice your head! I cook you for good meal!*" Leif's jaw appeared chiseled, set stern on his face as he tightened his lips into a line. The muscles over his jaw throbbed as he ground his teeth with sealed lips, enhancing his tight demeanor. He was provoked and appeared sharply angered, though he was controlled.

Without warning, loud pounding came from the roof directly above us. My eyes nervously shot upward, looking precisely overhead. It immediately seemed the roof was being mercilessly torn apart.

"What's that?" I asked, briskly startled.

"Our men are removing shingles from all barracks so that we shall not burn," he informed me, swiftly turning his gaze to me again as I looked up at the rafters. The wood shingles, in fact, were light and dry and would take a spark like kindling, flashing into sudden flames.

"Oh..." I said aridly. He paced away from the window, and my gaze dropped from the ceiling to him as he moved toward the table where I was standing. He stood before me, placing a hand over my shoulder, and his face softened slightly as he gazed at me.

"I fear I must ask ye tae assist the lads in hospital. Some of them took musket balls," he said.

"Oh! Yes, of course," I stammered with concern.

"Thank ye, *mo ghaol*."

"There's no need," I replied and turned to quickly ready my medical bag. In a second I had snatched it up and left our room with him as I followed him to the hospital among the commotion.

As men began trickling into the hospital with musket ball wounds, I realized there was no time to think, capitulate to fear, or contemplate the events taking place around us. I had to act and proceed with saving lives. I understood that this was probably the way my father felt and had to be as he performed as a M.A.S.H. surgeon in the field. So, I quickly fell into a focused professional zone as I began treating the wounded.

A soldier seeking Leif suddenly found him in the infirmary while he was momentarily talking with me. It was determined that Leif was needed elsewhere and had to leave me at that moment. I could perceive in his unspoken expression wondering whether I'd be all right here in the hospital alone while I worked. I assured him that I'd be fine, so he promptly left with the soldier.

MUCH LATER, around dusk, Leif arrived back at the hospital. He appeared dusty and grimy like everyone else around here on base. It was exceedingly hard to stay clean in conditions like this since we were continually exposed to the elements. Also, now that our situation was strained by imminent danger caused by the French simply splashing one's self with soap and water was a luxury.

"Don't come any closer," I warned nervously as Leif proceeded toward me.

"Whit is the matter?" he asked, alerted.

"The guy over there," I said, pointing to the isolated soldier restlessly sleeping in the corner of the room. "He has a fever."

"Does he?" Leif shortly ceased moving any closer with an uncertain look on his face.

"Yeah—he's one of the new guys, and he's exhibiting symptoms. I think we're going to have another outbreak," I fathomed uneasily. The expression on Leif's face suddenly became intensified with acute alarm.

"Yoo're telling me he's got the po—"

"*Shhh!*" I interrupted sharply. "You're gonna cause *hysteria* around here! As if there's not enough, we already have to contend with! We certainly don't need mass panic on our plate too, do we?"

"Certainly not!" he realized shortly with a startled look. I stood from the patient I had just finished suturing and scrubbed my hands down with one of the last remaining bars of soap on the grounds. Afterward, I paced to a corner in the cabin where it was dimly lit. I ensued removing my apron and tossed it inside a soiled laundry bag. My soiled bloodstained trousers followed as I intended to discard them also.

"Whit are ye doing, lass?" Leif asked unexpectedly with an indecent look on his face.

"Will you let me have your shirt, please?" I asked, stepping out of my trousers, and throwing them into the laundry bag.

"Fur whit reason?" He was shocked as he had no clue what I was doing by the unseemly expression he was giving me.

"Your shirt is much longer than mine and will cover me better," I said reasonably.

"Merely replace yer breeks over yer crease, and ye wulnae have trooble with yer shirt!" he said with a very displeased tone as he was about to lunge for my contaminated trousers to give them back to me.

"I'm a goddamn walking *biohazard,* and I'm not going to infect you with illness because of my contaminated *shit* clothes!

Now hand me your damn shirt!" I told him, close to my wits' end for the evening. He suddenly went silent, gawking at me with his mouth gaping in sheer astonishment over the use of my language. He forgot about reaching for my trousers on the floor and merely glowered at me with complete disapproval. "C'mon! Before we start pushing up daisies here would be nice, thank you very much!" I said impatiently, waving my fingers at him to hurry up and give me his shirt before I was discovered by someone else.

"That will be enough!" he snapped while giving me a blatant unheard-of look. "Ye very weel watch yer tongue with me, lass!" The expression on his face was utter appall mixed with displeasure as he stood right before me, trying to hide my indecency.

"Fine. I'm sorry. But really, I don't want you to get sick!" I expressed honestly. He looked at me without responding, but I discerned the stern, irritated look on his face. He moved to shield me completely as I continued removing my ruined shirt, and he began untucking his own shirt from his breeches. I tossed my contaminated articles into the laundry bag with the rest of the soiled clothing when he pulled his shirt overhead completely off himself and gave it to me. It was covered in dirt, and the aroma of his usually musky scent combined with smoke and tobacco. Despite the filth incrusting his shirt, however, it was still a safer bet than the bloodied, bio-infested clothing I was wearing.

"Thank you," I said as I pulled his shirt over my head.

"Aye," he replied sedately, noticing his article of clothing draping over me like a nightgown. He briefly cocked an eyebrow and shook his head with an unbelievable expression. I wasn't sure if he was in agreement with me now or not.

"These things need to be burned," I said, indicating the bag of hazardous clothing.

"I dinnae reckon that we can do that now," Leif said as he stood bare-chested before me.

"Why not?" I gave him an absurd look.

"All of the firewood has been dumped into the lake."

"How come?"

"Pardon?"

"Why? I mean."

"It was done tae prevent fire."

"Oh," I realized. "Well, all that in the bag over there is hazardous. No one should touch it, or whoever does will become ill. So, what can I do with it, then?" He fleetingly scanned the cabin.

"Thaur," he said, pointing to the corner opposite us by a collection of empty casks. "Merely place it thaur and leave it. Nae one will see it. Not even the laundresses will collect it as they are nae longer permitted inside this hospital."

I glanced over the location where he was suggesting and scrutinized the area, seeing that my choices were next to nil. The location was quite unnoticeable, and if, for certain, the maids were not allowed inside here to rummage the area for soiled laundry to hold and transfer, then it seemed as good a place as any to leave the soiled linens and clothing, given the dire situation upon us.

"But, I'll need a maid at least to help me with the patients," I reminded.

"Yoo'll have one," he assured. "Merely instruct her the area over thaur is forbidden."

"Right," I said and snatched up the burlap sack. I hid it among the casks, disguising it from view, and turned to wash my hands in the washbasin once more.

"Yoo're going tae scrub the skin reit off yer hands if ye keep at it the way ye do," Leif said as he curiously observed me.

I merely smirked at him. "Cleanliness is next to Godliness," I said ironically.

"Aye," he considered with a wan look.

"Besides," I continued while now shaking my hands dry since there weren't any clean towels around to use, "there are way too many microbes that love to settle on the hands to make anyone who comes in contact with them very sick if hands aren't kept clean."

"Microbes?" He grimaced, not understanding my meaning.

"Yeah, germs. *Germs* are the reason why people get sick. So, if we take care to wash our hands, then we reduce the chances of transmitting them from one person to the next and minimize the likelihood of illness," I explained, pacing toward him again, ready to leave the hospital. Leif lifted his own fingers into view and stared curiously at them. They were appallingly filthy, and my eyes widened. I was shocked because I'd never seen his hands so dirt-ridden as they were now. "Your hands are perfect petri dishes right now. You better wash them very well, or you're not allowed to touch me," I warned half-jokingly, trying to temper his agitated demeanor. An eyebrow arched over his eye, and a piqued expression came over his face.

"Och! I'll tooch ye as I please weel and guid—and if ye dinnae quit that saucy gab of yers, I'll poke ye with one of my soiled fingers reit now and see how ye like it," he sneered in a discreet manner with his brogue coming through strong.

"No, you won't!" I mocked, even though I was shocked.

"Press me," he said. My eyes widened as I noticed the way his smirk crossed his lips mirrored the brow raised high over his head in a look of warning. "Now, let us return tae our chamber as yoo've impolitely rid me of my shirt."

He turned and began exiting through the room. I started following him out of the hospital barracks outside into the crowded courtyard draped in his oversized shirt. It otherwise would have been a huge spectacle if I had drawn the attention of others by being recognized and dressed in this manner. But so much other activity was happening around us as we rapidly moved through the scene, my appearance didn't seem to matter right now to anyone.

I followed Leif up the stairs into our quarters, aware of our disgruntled state of mind as we began tidying ourselves. When we had completed making ourselves relatively neat and presentable again, he escorted me down into the officers' dining quarter, and we took our evening meal.

I sat quietly next to him as he and the other officers, including Monro, discussed the status of our situation. The conversation was severe and intense at times as the men discussed the French General Montcalm's strategy and the manner in which our fort should respond. The picture was clear, as I had fathomed by the evidence around me, that unless God graced us with some form of miracle via the act of nature or the additional arrival of appropriately numbered reinforcements, it very well seemed time was not on our side as we faced French incursion.

That night in bed, Leif remained dressed in his shirt, breeches, and boots as he held me close to him. The roof over our heads had been disassembled, and I saw through the rafters. The stars shined as brightly as they had done the night before. The moon was out, and the beams glowed over us in incandescent blue light. I lay awake for a moment, too tired to talk, but I just looked up into the Milky Way. Leif wasn't going to sleep tonight, I sensed. Although he didn't say it, I knew that he was merely holding me until I fell asleep before he would continue conducting his business around the fort.

THE NEXT DAY, I snacked on oat bread and tea in the officers' dining chamber below on the first floor while Leif and the officers were talking. I felt better having a ceiling overhead for complete shelter while eating, unlike our room, in case of flying debris that might injure us. I drew my teacup to my lips and quickly emptied it. I stood from the dining table to refill it and started toward the back of the cabin to gather the teapot on the tray resting over the stand. Without warning, an abrupt explosion blasted into the air at distinctly close range, muting my ears, startling the *Hell* out of me, and causing the teapot to slip from my grip. It crashed helplessly to the floor, spilling all that was left inside as the ground shook and the building rocked.

As a result of having grown up in Los Angeles and after having experienced countless earthquakes close to magnitude seven, I instinctively threw myself under the dining table with my pulse suddenly racing. I tucked my head between my crouched knees, covering it with my hands, anticipating destruction.

The room suddenly returned still, and not a peep came from the men still sitting at the table around me. After a second, a chair audibly scooted over the wood floor. I glimpsed from my tucked position and recognized Leif's face looking upside down at me beneath the table.

"'Tis alrecht, *ceisdein*," he said calmly.

"What the hell was that?" I asked, fearfully looking at him.

"'Twas our cannon blast," he said sedately, excusing my bad language.

"Oh," I realized, somewhat shaken.

"Ye may come forth. Thaur isnae anything tae fear," he persuaded while extending a hand to me.

"There's not?"

"Nae." He motioned with his hand for me to come out from beneath the table. As I took his palm, another sudden cannon blast violently erupted. I automatically jumped at the unexpected sound, knocking my head hard against the edge of the table as I was making my way from beneath it.

"Ouch!" I rubbed the sharp pain over my head with my hand.

"Ooo! Do take care," he advised while assisting me from under the table.

Returning to my seat next to him, the surrounding men stared at me with relative concern. Rendered a little self-conscious, I ignored their questioning stares and dusted off my shoulders as Leif poured a small amount of ale into my cup. I took the cup and raised it, acknowledging the staring men before taking a sip of the alcohol. They reciprocated the gesture and easily drank theirs. When throats cleared, conversation effortlessly resumed between them, among more cannon fire roaring in timed intervals.

Dust stirred from the ceiling and kicked around in the air with each shelling. The building shook, and the thought of it fatiguing due to this repeated disturbance and crumbling down on top of us abruptly entered my mind. As I continued listening to them discussing, I learned that the only road out from here connecting us to Fort Edward had been blocked by a substantial portion of the French party, cutting off communication and stranding a group of Massachusetts provincials on the strategic hill, Titcomb's Mount, near the fort. The enemy had already begun laying out trenches under a half mile from here with weaponry being positioned at our west wall. Hence, the eruption of cannon fire commenced first from our post over advancing enemy lines. The siege had begun...

FOLLOWING two days of continual deafening cannon fire exploding from the fort, along with sniping back and forth, the scene was a battle zone. The sound of sudden mortar explosions everywhere perpetually frightened me. I was nerve-racked as I moved around the courtyard to concentrate on taking care of the injured in the infirmary.

Until today, the explosions became calamitous as the enemy opened fire with bombs blasting at the fort. With our own guns firing rounds non-stop for thirty hours now, the cannons were fatiguing and exploded on the gunners, killing or severely maiming the platoon squads with amputations or third-degree burns. Injured men started streaming inside the hospital. They were coming to me with feet, legs, hands, or arms blown right off. It was becoming an overwhelming situation as I, the only attending physician, rushed, pacing myself in triage from patient to patient, trying to stabilize the wounded.

Plenty of mortally wounded men were dying left and right on me as I strove, working on them to save their lives, knowing full well there was absolutely nothing I could do to spare them without modern medical tools and supplies or assistance from other physicians and nurses. I didn't have the opportunity to really think about it, but I believed if I could not save one life, then I was going to try my hardest to save the other. I rotated around the hospital like a whirlwind, damned determined to save these men from dying.

I worked through the entire night and well into dawn without a wink of sleep. When the morning lit the surrounding scene, the room was full of injured men on cots and on the dust-covered floor. Some slept, and plenty of others painfully moaned. Several others became deceased. Still, more injured men kept coming to me.

When things seemed to have lulled for a moment, I relieved Sarah, the maid assisting me, to break for a moment since she had been up with me working the same duration. She was leaving through the doorway, the same instance I recognized Leif entering the cabin. Our eyes met from a distance at the opposite end of the room before he superficially scanned the abundant injured men reclining all over the place. I strode toward him with my clothes all bloodied, relieved to see him and wondering what was currently occurring outside the fort. He had scarcely slept in three days now, and the weariness was showing in his eyes. Still, he stood tall and strong as he briefly gazed around the location, surveying all the surrounding bodies. Soot and dirt had settled over his face and clothes from the blasting cannons, which kicked all kinds of particles everywhere into the air. He looked beleaguered and utterly exhausted.

"It appears yoo're in order haur," he observed, impressed.

"Yeah," I said reasonably. He scanned the blood all over my clothes.

"I came tae fetch ye tae eat presently. I reckon ye must be hungry," he said.

"Yes, I am, really," I said, realizing suddenly that I was starved. "But, I just sent Sarah out for a break. Someone should be here, though, to take care of everything."

"Merely tell the lass tae hasten and that ye wulnae be long absent," he said plainly.

"Right," I responded and quickly scrubbed my hands clean in the basin. We stepped out into the busy courtyard, and I luckily spotted Sarah at the well, drawing water only feet away. Leif waited for me at the hospital doorway as I hurried over to advise her. She politely acknowledged my directions, and I hastened back to Leif, telling him that I was ready to leave my position. Then, he and I started walking toward the officer's barrack, ignoring my heavily soiled clothes.

"Are you alright?" I inquired carefully, noticing him as we walked together through the courtyard.

"I am slightly weary, that is all," he replied merely.

"Oh," I muttered, knowing there was more to it. But I didn't think it was opportune for me to further inquire because he was already intensely pressed. He was abstracted, and even though he didn't openly show it, I could easily see that he was extremely stressed.

We entered quietly together inside the dining quarter. Leif indicated that he wasn't going to join in eating, since he said for me to help myself to the venison pottage in the pot sitting on the table. Instead, he passed through the cabin toward the doorway at the other end of the room and entered Monro's adjoining office. Left to fill my bowl with pottage, I sat alone at the table and began to eat. The door to Monor's office was left ajar, and I could hear the discussion taking place between him and his officers behind the artillery fire happening all around in the background.

"They have a second battery line now operating, and they are digging their approach reit haur," Leif reported, presumably pointing to a map.

"That is merely three hundred yards from our west curtain," Colonel Monro recognized with a critical tone.

"Aye," Leif said with the same severity.

"They will pursue another parallel trench, in that case," Monro observed. "We have tae prevent them from setting a battery thaur, or they will breach it."

"I have men firing upon them as we speak," Leif said.

"Men have found shrapnel coming over bearing the Royal mark," Angus said.

"They are from guns captured at Oswego," Frye notified.

"Damn the bastards using our own guns against us!" Monro said with vehement disdain. "*Damnation!* I want those men tae take out that new trench! Do ye hear me?" A fist slammed hard down over a table and resonated.

"Git it done now, captains," Leif ordered sharply. Bootsteps promptly scurried over the floor out of the office toward the opposite direction, leading outdoors.

"Men are weary, Colonel," Frye warned.

"As we all are. So what?" Monro returned sharply.

"We are three nights now without sleep. Some of the men grow stupefied and have shouted in surrender to Montcalm's men," Frye said.

"Have they now?" Monro replied irately.

"Aye," Frye said.

"Ye tell them that any man caught abandoning the fort will be hanged fur sedition. Any man caught advocating surrender will also be hanged fur treason. Ye let them know reit *now* that all cowardice acts will meet this fate. Is that clear, Lieutenant Colonel?" Monro expressed intolerably.

"Indeed, Colonel," Frye replied gravely.

"Mayhap, if we grant the men a two-hour respite at different intervals whilst maintaining our defense, the men may be sustained tae persevere with less tiredness," Leif proposed.

"We cannae afford any lapses. The men stand as they are," Monro commanded.

Suddenly, the conversation was interrupted by new footsteps entering the office from outdoors.

"Aye?" Monro said impatiently to the new individual.

"'Tis another message from Montcalm," the man answered. I could hear Monro's hand grabbing the parchment.

"Thaur is bluid upon it," Leif observed.

"Aye," Monro noted. A silence pervaded the office for a distended moment.

"Hold the courier till I have given my response," Monro commanded the messenger. The messenger's feet quickly resonated, returning outside.

"What is it?" Frye asked.

"It is Webb's correspondence in response tae my correspondence which I had dispatched tae him four days ago," Monro grimly informed his men.

"It has been intercepted," Leif said.

"Aye," Monro replied.

"Whit does Webb write?" Leif inquired. There was a pause between them, and the parchment was heard rustling. I imagined that the paper was being opened to be read.

"Webb expresses that he disnae think it prudent tae assist us," Monro stated fatally when he resumed speaking.

"*Bloody Hell!* Why not? He promised the men!" Leif retorted.

"He wulnae break his forces at Edward fearing the militia wulnae arrive haur in time," Monro said.

"Yet, there was time for him to do as he had promised prior tae now unless he knew something we did not," Frye snapped.

"He means tae be reinforced from the south, though Laird Loudoun assured us more men," Monro said.

"Aye, weel then if Webb was promised reinforcements from Loudoun, whaur in damnation are they?" Leif questioned.

"If we fall, the French will have a splendid road to launch a successful attack upon Fort Edward," Frye noted.

"Aye, then whit? Albany? They will take the whole frontier!" Leif replied alarmingly.

"Given whit we face, as is expressed in Webb's letter, he suggests under grave circumstances we micht consider the best terms fur capitulation," Monro dourly informed his men.

"Permit me tae see the correspondence?" Leif requested immediately.

"Aye," Monro said, sounding pensive. The parchment could be heard being transferred from hand to hand. Then, a moment of silence ensued again.

"Montcalm—his accompanying note advises surrender as well," Frye observed at length with a grim voice.

"We shall not," Monro said certainly.

"Aye, we shall fight honorably," Leif supported with conviction. I leaned in my chair a little and could see through the crack of the door Monro quickly scribing over parchment.

"Git this tae the currier." Monro briskly held out the note to Leif. Leif took the correspondence and whisked out the door into the courtyard.

"Whit is our artillery standing?" Monro asked Frye.

"We have half the cannon," Frye reported.

"Are ye certain?"

"Aye."

"*Crap!* Alrecht, git an engineer tae survey."

"Aye." Frye turned toward the doorway and vanished outdoors. Monro, by chance, discovered me through the cracked doorway, finishing my bowl of pottage. He removed himself from his desk and carefully closed the adjacent door to his office so that I could no longer see or listen to his conversation with his men. At that moment, I stood from my seat at the dining table, feeling very gloomy about our situation, and decided to leave the room now that I had finished eating.

As I was exiting the dining quarter out into the daylight, Leif simultaneously arrived, closely standing before me.

"I reckon ye ought tae rest now fur a bit," he said.

"No—I can't. There are too many men injured. I have to make my rounds," I replied uneasily.

"Yet, yoo're weary and must rest," he insisted bluntly.

"How can I rest with all that's going on? All I'll do is just sit around obsessively worrying about everything. It's better for me just to keep concentrating on what I know how to do," I insisted in return, perturbed.

"Very weel, then," Leif consented abruptly, even though he didn't fully agree. "Let's go," he said at his own behest and hastily escorted me back across the courtyard, returning me inside the hospital. He promptly left me there and returned to conduct his own business elsewhere.

The day turned long with the French's inexorable bombing campaign. Men continually arrived impaled with shrapnel, severed limbs, second or third-degree burns, musket balls, and arrowhead wounds impaled in their flesh. But our troops kept pounding back from the fort against the enemy with grapeshot, mortars, and howitzers.

FIVE DAYS now without sleep for the men fighting here. It was a complete war zone as men ran in every direction, holding down the stronghold. By sundown, however, the outlook among the men began to change. They were growing pervasively despondent, and morale sunk low, which permeated the garrison with misery. Collectively tired, dejected, and stressed, some men were hysterical, out of control with fear, and hurled themselves over the fort walls. Or, they were rendered to the true point of stupefaction that they suddenly stopped fighting and walked around or sat, dazed and confused like zombies. Chaos was close at hand, with the smell of mutiny hovering in the air.

At this point, against my preference, Leif decidedly came for me in the hospital and steadfastly told me that I could no longer care for the men. He was adamant and directed me back inside the officers' dining quarter, where I was to remain indefinitely. As the evening grew later, since there was no longer a roof over our own sleeping quarters to protect us from flying debris, I supposed that I was going to have to spend the night inside the dining cabin with him and some of the other officers as they stood around discussing matters.

I began growing sleepy as the men continued arguing among each other about how to proceed. *Who knows what the hell is going to happen next?* It seemed the whole place was going to blow up to high Heaven! And there wasn't a *damn* thing anybody could do about it! *God, please help us all here!*

I decided to move to the corner of the room away from the men around the table and found a spot over the floor by the wall to lean up against as I sat in order to finally rest. I tiredly sat on the floor, listening to what the men were saying. The conversation was animated and suddenly flared up with further heated discourse. It unexpectedly caught my attention and kept me from sleeping.

"Listen!" Monro interrupted angrily. "Angus, take yer men and survey the damage."

"Aye, sir," Angus responded readily.

"And give me the standing of our defense," Monro commanded.

"Aye, sir," Angus replied again and abruptly turned out of the cabin.

"I also must ken the standing of the entrenched camp," Monro said to Frye.

"Aye," Frye concurred and briskly vanished into the humid

gun-firing night. Meanwhile, Leif, Roy and Fearghus remained discussing with Monro.

Due to heavy exhaustion, I found that I could no longer keep my eyes open despite their heated discussion, so I drifted to sleep.

WHEN I HAD AWAKENED, it was still dark outside. Angus and Frye had returned, and the men were still convening over our dismal situation. I guess I must have dozed for a couple hours at a time because they were now confirming status reports from around the fort.

"Portions of the west bastions facing the enemy's batteries are breached," Angus reported.

"Whit about the bomb-proofs?" Monro inquired.

"Heavily damaged," Angus said.

"I see," Monro responded pensively. "How many cannon have we got left?"

"Merely five," Angus informed Monro. The men grumbled and cursed. "All but a few cases of ammunition left also." And apparently, according to Frye, reports from the entrenched camp weren't any favorable since the troops from Massachusetts experienced huge casualties from friendly fire.

"The men say they will not stay any longer—they are all worn out. They tell me they would rather be shot in the head by the enemy than parish in the trenches," Frye said miserably. Monro didn't respond except stare contemplatively into space with his jaw ominously clenched. "The enemy has also sited their breaching battery," Frye continued. Monro cast his eyes to the floor but didn't show any other signs of the weight he was carrying. He only remained unanimated in silence for a grave moment.

"Shall we continue tae fire tae the end of our stock?" Fearghus asked at length.

"If we do, they may think we are still well armed and fire their batteries that will breach our west curtain," Frye said.

"The French will then rush us. Who knows how our men micht react under their weary condition," Leif warned.

"Montcalm informed us that not even he can control his Indians," Angus mentioned with further concern.

"Then whit are we tae do?" Fearghus questioned disastrously.

"Tell the men tae cease fire. Tell all officers tae assemble in my office at first lecht," Monro commanded, downtrodden. The tone in his voice was the only indication of his compressing revelation, and everyone in the room went silent. Monro turned from his men, paced toward the back of the cabin, and disappeared behind the door to his office. The rest of the men stood around not really saying anything else while appearing glum and desolate as they only looked at each other. After a moment, they started disbanding from the cabin when Leif finally approached me, and I stood from my place on the floor.

"We shall retire now," he said drearily. He was so worn looking. He was bleak in the eyes with soot and smoke powder all over his face and clothes, and I on the other hand was numb since I felt as tired as he appeared. I followed his lead pacing outside from the cabin toward our barrack and climbed up the staircase to our room.

"What's going to happen?" I asked with uncertainty when we entered our skeletal quarters.

"We shall ken fully in the morn. But fur now, let ye and I rest if we may," he said.

<h1 style="text-align:center">Thirty-Three</h1>

The next morning, I lay in bed waiting for Leif to return from the officers' meeting with Monro. They deliberated for a long time. I was growing more restless as time passed with nothing to occupy my mind from this situation. So, I couldn't help but remove myself from bed and anxiously pace around the room for a while until I grew tired enough to sit at the writing desk for a moment. I gazed out the window beside me at the smoke billowing around the fort walls before ultimately returning to bed and simply lying there, trying to pass the time.

Finally, I decided to get to my feet again and poured myself a cup of old boiled water. As soon as I had put my lips to my cup, I heard knocking on the door. I set the cup over the table and rushed to unlatch the door. Leif paced inside and began removing his shirt while walking to the washbasin. He looked slightly recharged now that he had some hours of sleep, but the negative look still hovered over his expression.

"So what's going on?" I inquired curiously.

"We have sent a flag of truce tae Montcalm," Leif answered as he splashed water over his cheeks from the basin.

"We're surrendering?" I asked with surprise. Despite the fact that I had sensed the end coming, I never thought we would actually yield. But I was silently relieved that this was the end result over imminent chaos and death.

"Aye," Leif said. I observed him lathering his hands and spreading soap suds around his square jaw.

"So, are they going to take us prisoner?" I asked worriedly.

"Nae."

"Then what's going to happen? Are we going back to Boston?"

"Once we have completed negotiations. Mayhap, we may make the best terms possible fur our return, I pray," he informed me, taking up his straight edge. He proceeded to scrape off the long stubble now grown over his cheeks. "I must make haste and properly dress as thaur will be nae time tae do it later. Once ye have filled yer stomach with bread, ye must do the same, *ceisdein*."

"All right," I replied unquestionably. I began toward the table and sat quietly as I dipped a lone piece of tough bread into my cup of water to soften it. I quietly watched him as he skillfully shaved the light hair from his face as I ate. The room was silent from the merest verbal exchange between us as he proceeded like an android, making himself tidy at last.

Soon, he had finished and proceeded to replace his soiled breeches for fresh ones. Within ten minutes after dressing, he appeared pristine again with a cleanly shaven face, attired in a crisp white linen shirt, scarlet waistcoat, coat, and fresh beige breeches. His boots thumped over the pine-planked floor as he approached me and gave a quick peck over my brow.

"Latch the door efter me. I shall return sometime later," he instructed.

"Okay," I said. He turned from me, starting toward the door and I stood, following him. Crossing the threshold into the hot sunlight, he stepped down the staircase and I closed the door, locking it behind him.

When I had decided that I had taken enough stale bread and

water, I started washing the grime off my face and cleansing myself as best as I could with the last tiny bit of soap that we had. Afterward, I retrieved my last collection of unsoiled clothes and began dressing in my trousers, petite linen shirt, waistcoat, and caraco jacket. Once I had finished combing and straightening my bobbed ringlets and pixie bangs, I placed my pair of crystal hair pins on one side of my head, then continued waiting in the room for his return. I glanced at the small clock over the mantelpiece and saw that it was getting closer to noon. Since there was nothing else left for me to do, I decided to occupy my time by arranging our belongings and packing them into our traveling trunk.

Finally, after a couple of hours had passed, Leif knocked on the door again. I hastened across the room to open it. When he entered, he seemed resolved and stern with gravity as if a decision had been reached. His eyes scanned the room, and he quickly noticed our packed belongings on the floor by the wall near the entrance.

"Yoo've anticipated me," he said approvingly.

"I just thought I'd make it easier so that we both wouldn't have to pack our things," I said dutifully.

"Guid," he said stoutly. "Bide haur whilst I gather our belongings and ready the horses."

"All right," I responded simply. I decided to take a seat at the letter desk and waited for him while he completed the task.

Left alone in the room again while he was readying our horses, I found myself surprised that we were about to leave this place so soon, like night and day, after everything that had happened. My mind rushed toward Finley, and I was staggered as I thought about him. My eyes began to water as I sat alone in the room. It was bizarre how we could so quickly pick up and leave this place without Finley being with us. I didn't understand how it could be possible that we'd never see him again, and I was left suspended in surrealism and deep sadness as I awaited our departure.

What am I going to tell Elizabeth when I see her again? What will she say to me...? I promised her that I'd bring them both back to us. Oh, Finley... She's going to blame me for not keeping my promise to her and bringing you back to her? Now, I can't do that at all for her... I know how she's going to feel when she learns the truth from Leif about you being gone. I feel so guilty for promising her that I'd keep you safe... God help us... I'm praying for your soul and for Elizabeth, who's left behind now. What's going to happen to her? I think she's going to hate me...

When Leif returned with our things packed and readied for us to leave, I abruptly cleared my face so he wouldn't question me and followed him out of our room outside under the beating hot sun as we went down the flight of stairs, leaving our barracks at last. The entire garrison at the fort, along with about a hundred camp-following women, maids, and children, had assembled in the courtyard. They surrounded the flagpole, where now a large white flag was whipping in the wind in place of the Union flag.

Leif gripped my arm and guided me through the crowd toward the front gate, where the officers had assembled on their horses. It was a sad day of defeat for everyone today. The men from the Massachusetts regiment were not professional soldiers and bore the brunt of the battle. They looked broken and unimaginably battered, covered in grime, soot, and blood. The British regulars, despite their experience, appeared the same—ripped from head to toe. The scent of fire and gun smoke filled the air. Black plumes were billowing into the atmosphere from the fire burning on the bastion walls surrounding us.

"Up on yer horse now," Leif said to me, suddenly calling my dismayed attention from the beleaguered troops back to what I was supposed to be doing. I slipped my foot into the stirrup and hauled myself over Oakley. Then, Leif adroitly hurled himself up over Blaze. Soon, the front line of officers, with me next to Leif, began moving out the front gate.

After exiting the fort, a line of leading French officers surrounded by a sea of their soldiers and warring Indians were seen a short distance ahead and met us as we approached them. Suddenly, the tiny hairs on the nape of my neck stood, and an icy chill shivered over my skin. The sheer numbers of the French enemy in the thousands were frightening, but the war-painted Indians standing around among them held vile looks that instilled more fear to freeze over me because I suddenly realized on an intrinsic level that all rules to war engagement were nonexistent according to them: this was guerilla warfare—something at which they were adeptly skilled. I got the clear sense that they weren't finished harming as they stared loathsomely at us when we advanced toward the French side.

Mounted staunchly in full military dress, Monro and his officers fearlessly arrived directly facing the proud leading French general and his band of mounted officers. The flag bearer in our group bravely held the Union flag tall as it snapped in the wind above our heads, while we looked at the enemy's royal flags of King Louis XV animated in the air also. Officers from both sides began dismounting, and the men faced each other with Colonel Monro and the French general directly in front of all the warriors on both sides. Monro removed his hat and tucked it soundly underarm. The leading French general also withdrew his hat with an appropriate flamboyant bow. When he straightened, the two foes locked resilient eyes with each other.

"Colonel Monro," the French commander began addressing Monro in a calm, thick accent, "I am General Montcalm, Marquis de Saint-Veran, Commander and Chief of His Most Christian Majesty's forces of New France."

"General Montcalm," Colonel Monro acknowledged tactfully.

"It is an honor to make your acquaintance," General Montcalm said graciously. Monro stiffly bent his head in mere courtesy to the general. "You have served most honorably and have directed a siege agreeing to the best-practiced order. You have brought homage to your men. They have shown great valor. Thus, you must be commended." Montcalm then signaled to his aide-de-camp. His aide-de-camp proceeded in unraveling a rolled parchment and began reading aloud the articles of capitulation that Monro and Montcalm had both agreed on and signed.

According to General Montcalm's compliment to Colonel Monro, in the pledge, we were free to return to Fort Edward with safe passage by French escort. All our men were granted the ability to retain their own arms and personal belongings. The garrison was also able to keep the colors and was allowed to have one cannon as a memento for their bravery. Furthermore, those who were too sick and injured to travel would remain here at Fort William Henry and be cared for by the French, then return home. In exchange, our men must remain out of battle for a year and a half, and all French POWs held in British captivity must be returned to Fort Carillon by November. Also, all the artillery and ammunition, war stockpiles, and provisions remaining at Fort William Henry were forfeited. Finally, one officer of ours must remain with Montcalm as insurance until his troops that are assigned to escort us home safely return to the French side. That officer, I was sad to learn, was our own Captain Roy James MacLeod, one of Leif's cousins.

With all that said and done, both men civilly acknowledged each other: Monro rigidly but politely dipped his head, and Montcalm made a showy bow. Then, all the officers mounted back onto their horses. But before the meeting dissolved, Montcalm maneuvered his horse toward Leif while I remained slightly behind him, and he paused before him.

"My cousin, Duc de Monteith," Montcalm addressed very politely.

"My cousin, Marquis de Saint-Veran," Leif acknowledged accordingly. *Cousins?* This silently came to me as a further surprise.

"I regret that we met under unfriendly circumstances, and I am remorseful for the death of your brother. He fought intrepidly in the water. I have written to our cousin, King Louis, of your valiant brother in my correspondence. You are much like him. I pray that you and I shall meet again in more pleasant times in France. Until then, may our Lord Jesus Christ bless your welfare," Montcalm expressed sincerely.

"Thank ye, cousin. May our Heavenly Father bless yer welfare as weel," Leif responded solemnly. Then, they both properly bade each other farewell. Montcalm began veering away from us, and his troops yielded to the side as he passed between them with his aide-de-camp along with several other officers following him. Afterward, we were led by French soldiers inside the entrenched camp where we were to stay until tomorrow, when we would finally travel south back to Fort Edward.

As we were settling into camp, the area didn't seem close to being secured by French guards as would have been expected. Instead, the area was porous for anyone to filter in or out. There was a pervasive and tangible sense of shuddering fearfulness that infiltrated and swept through the camp. Leif and the other men were visibly on edge and uptight, and the women and children quivered with uncertainty as Indians were trickling inside the area. They roamed the grounds, scoping and casing the area until they easily found something they wanted and started harassing people for it. They were threatening people who wouldn't release their belongings to them with violence as they pillaged them. It was a terribly fearful feeling to hear women and children crying and men being punched and beaten throughout the camp if they didn't comply with the Indians' demands.

I was seated on a crate hidden from view behind Leif and the other men as they stood closely around, acutely alerted. Suddenly, a nearly naked Indian painted in intimidating black war paint from head to chest approached our horses next to us, intending to take them. He put his hands on Oakley's reins and was reaching for Angus's horse as his two other accomplices were closely behind him, ready to assist stealing from us. My heart suddenly jumped to my throat when I realized what was happening the second Leif invisibly whipped out his dirk, catching the Indian off guard. He had the long, vicious blade pressed against the Indian's neck as he was aiming to steal Oakley, ready to slice through the Indian's jugular in one easy motion.

Pistols from the Scotsmen abruptly showed in the air, and tomahawks from the Indians flung up high, ready to strike. My breath caught with my pulse sharply racing as I jumped to my feet and froze behind the Scotsmen. Without warning, it was an unpredictably precarious situation like in a gun-toting Wild West saloon or an urban gangster house, where an unexpected disagreement could suddenly bring forth a surrounding flash of arms, and everything could instantly go bad in one irresponsible move.

"Le cheval est à moi et pas pour vous de prendre," Leif said in perfect French to the Indian caught beneath the chin by his nasty blade. His tone was icy and lethal. It instantly appeared he was going to kill the Indian. The three Indians seemed quickly surprised to hear a redcoat speaking French. I could see some of the looks on the Scotsmen's faces, and they were hard and uncompromising, appearing as committed as the Indian raiders detestably staring them down close in front of them.

"Nous prenons ou vous meurent," threatened the scary-faced Indian in broken French who was standing with his tomahawk raised before Angus' head. Angus' pistol pointed directly between the Indian warrior's eyes without a flinch.

"Je vais vous envoyer en enfer première," Leif returned venomously, soundly unintimidated—telling the Indian that he would send him to Hell first.

"Iglismôn va mourir, vous verrez," the third Indian said rancorously, prepared to swing his axe with two adjacent pistols aligned at his temples held by Fearghus and Lachlan.

"Pas avant vous," Leif said heartlessly, on the verge of slicing the Indian's throat he kept fixed under his blade. The Indian winced, and it appeared that the tip of the lethal blade had slightly edged into his skin.

"Je prends votre cuir chevelu avec moi," said the Indian on the end of Leif's dirk with dry vehemence, threatening to take Leif's scalp regardless.

"Je vais en profiter pour voir vous essayez," Leif goaded frigidly. "Je vais prendre votre tête et le nourrir à la Diable." The tone in Leif's voice was icy, calculated, and determined as he told the threatening Indian who would take his scalp that he would feed the Indian's head to the Devil. It was a side of Leif I had never witnessed before, and if I were the enemy, he was now locking eyes with, I would have felt shivers run down my spine. Judging from his toxic voice alone, he was surely set to kill, and I thought all Hell was instantly about to break loose.

One of the Indians said something in their native language, and suddenly, they stood down, lowering their weapons with their eyes remaining fixed on the Scotsmen, still holding pistols at their heads, ready to blow them to smithereens. Leif scarcely withdrew the piercing dirk from the brave's throat when he carefully backed away from Leif. A perfect, petite, ruby-red droplet abruptly formed just above the jugular on the Indian's neck as he slowly stepped away from the extended blade. The Indian stared at Leif, looking as if he had been unexpectedly spooked while Leif maintained his broad, intrepid, fixed stance directly in front of him and his threatening Indian companions.

The Indians slowly began moving away from us while odiously staring down the surrounding Scotsmen, still poised to blow their heads off as panic was beginning to stir widely around camp. When the plundering individual Indian warriors were leaving us, one of them noticed me protected behind the Scotsmen. He fixed intentional eyes on me among the hate in his expression as he proceeded to walk past us. Leif's head precisely turned toward that particular Indian. He locked an impenetrable glare on the Indian as he walked by, watching him with despising intentions of his own, it seemed.

Suddenly, a pistol shot off into the air, causing immediate attention and screams from frightened women and children. Monro's gun was smoking from the warning he gave. The next shot, he vowed, was going to cause damage as he and his regulars were going to take charge.

Immediately after Monro's gunshot, French soldiers hastily appeared, running inside the encampment, and started clearing the Indians out of the site. But Leif and his cousins and fellow companions, along with every other person here, remained tense and nervous. The men appeared unconvinced that our status here was guarded and under control.

"They mean tae bide about," Angus said up-tightly as they were starting to sit over crates and barrels again with pistols remaining drawn.

"Aye," Leif said as he stayed standing next to me, panning the area with observant eyes.

"It appears like bloody trooble," Fearghus noted preparedly.

"Aye—fur tonecht, at least," Lachlan said.

"The French cannae control them. 'Tis also going tae be *bloody Hell* getting out of haur in the morn—perhaps all the way down tae Fort Edward," Leif said uneasily.

"Aye, the bastards mean harm," Bearnard determined disdainfully.

"They outnumber us by far. I reckon we must discuss how we are tae ride then, if we mean tae keep our scalps," Leif ordered in that case.

"Guid notion," Angus agreed. The men huddled as Leif started illustrating a mode of action in the dirt in case a confrontation occurred. They were anticipating a worst case scenario and said something about dropping formation, splitting up the lines, flanking right and left to engage the enemy in order to have a chance at saving our lives. They went on conferring their exit strategy as I glanced around myself at the anxious people in camp. But I didn't gather all that was being said between Leif and his men, since my attention turned toward the eerie calls the Indians pursued taunting us with. The Indians loitered around the perimeter of our camp waiting for the merest opportunity to enter the grounds again.

"Are ye listening tae me, Sylvie?" Leif questioned sharply. I suddenly returned my attention to him, realizing he was talking to me as he simultaneously laid a hand on my arm.

"What?" I said unknowingly.

"Ye must ride tight with me at all times. Do ye understand?" he instructed sternly.

"Absolutely," I said unquestionably.

"Ye must not stray, but remain tight with me. Do *exactly* as I say, alrecht?" he repeated severely.

"Yes, of course, I will," I promised indisputably.

"Alrecht, then, lads," he continued satisfactorily and returned talking to his companions. When they had devised their plan, they broke from each other and had the rest of the officers informed on how to march with Monro's consent.

There was good reason for all the jittery nerves in camp as night set in; the Indians remained on the outskirts, continuing to menace and harass us with tormenting calls that echoed spine-chillingly all around in the pitch black, moonless night. I doubted anyone dared shut their eyes to sleep, not knowing what the evening would bring despite the numerous men in our camp taking turns to keep watch throughout the night.

AT DAYBREAK, we began mounting our horses, preparing to leave the entrenched camp with French troops ready to escort us off the premises all the way toward Fort Edward. As Leif and fellow officers moved around, ordering the regulars to fill in the columns to march out, I remained attentively perched on Oakley, waiting where Leif had positioned me slightly behind Monro and his own horse poised in the vanguard. Then, alarmingly, countless Indians began flooding inside all around us, dangerously armed with fierce tomahawks, bows and arrows, guns, and knives. Fear and anxiety quickly permeated as they demanded the men in our camp to give up their arms and started stealing our equipment. They were stealing clothing, alcohol, weapons, and whatever else they could get their hands on from everyone. I glanced around everywhere to see widespread disorder beginning to break out around me. To my absolute shock and alarm, Indians attempted to seize every Black person along with all the women and children and take them as if they were just baggage to pillage too.

As I was watching all this occurring, I unexpectedly sensed a sudden hand come forcefully over my forearm, and I swiftly turned my attention to see an unfamiliar face. My eyes instantly locked onto the glower of a frighteningly black war-painted Indian as he attempted to pull me off my horse. I keenly sensed that he did not want the horse but me instead. I naturally reacted, wrenching my arm from his snatching grip, when he abruptly went flying completely down to the ground, face first, with unanticipated force. Leif came out of the blue atop Blaze and violently kicked the Indian from behind. At the same instant, Monro fired his pistol into the air, inciting near panic from everyone.

Suddenly, French guards rushed around us, attempting to assemble some semblance of order inside the camp again, but things were on the brink of disarray. Leif promptly fell into line and positioned his horse tight with mine, nearly trampling the fallen Indian he had kicked as the Indian lay dazed on the ground. The order was quickly given by Monro, and with me closely alongside Leif's leading fellow officers, we filed and ranked into lines.

Immediately, we started moving out of the encampment with French troops escorting us as they marched beside us. With a long column of people following behind us, we started south over the road to Fort Edward as Fort William Henry, still smoking from fire, began falling behind us in the distance.

Within minutes, we had moved past the clearing and entered the road surrounded by dense forest.

As we marched onward, a disturbance was heard coming from farther behind us as we continued along the road riding our horses. Leif turned his attention, looking past the ranks behind us. He swiftly returned, looking ahead, and informed Monro of something that was inaudible to me. So, I curiously turned my head to see what commotion was taking place, and I was horrified; the back end of the column was unprotected by the French, and people started screaming as Indians were falling upon them. The Indians were attacking! People were being hacked and scalped! Cries were growing more audible and confusion and commotion were spreading throughout the column. It seemed order was quickly falling apart at the seams.

My heart catapulted to my throat, arresting me with cold terror as I realized what was happening before my very own eyes. Upheaval down the row advanced. I spotted Corporal Edwards endeavoring to protect Betsy with her newborn baby in her arms when he was viciously tomahawked in cold blood from behind and his scalp cleaved off the top of his head. Betsy released a shrilling, horrendous scream, then was heartlessly seized by the murderous Indian. She was pulled out of the line with her newborn and dragged to the side of the road into the brush, swiftly vanishing into the woods by the hand of her captor. I noticed Leif out of the corner of my eye and looked at him, catching Colonel Monro's signal to him. Leif, in turn, motioned to his fellow officers down the ranks, and formation began to break accordingly.

Suddenly, a hollering *"whoo-whoo!"* sounded blindly from behind the trees, and the men quickly seized their arms, turning left and right, poised to fire as they flanked the forest. Then, an unseen arrow abruptly struck a regular in the neck, bringing him to his knees. Immediately, the air filled with flying arrows. Men started dropping left and right as they were suddenly pierced by arrowheads. Then, thousands of howling Indians at once emerged from the trees, running toward us, aiming to rip us to shreds with slicing tomahawks. Muskets all around began bursting out as they fired off at the oncoming slewing war party. Order instantly disintegrated, and the French escorting us tried to restore the situation by controlling the Indians. But their efforts were futile; there were just too many Indians attacking! Mayhem broke out and swarmed all over the place! Killing, scalping, and dragging people off into the woods was happening as people were trying to defend themselves!

General Montcalm was seen far behind down the road, galloping fast on his horse toward the havoc when Leif instantaneously grabbed my arm and yanked me off my horse. He swiftly started off wildly tugging me through the pandemonium, dodging us through the battle. We zigzagged erratically, running around over the road, trying to avoid death. An abrupt musket ball whizzed by my ear and my breath suddenly caught, with my pulse crazily skyrocketing out of control. All at once, an Indian with his weapon raised to deliver a mortal slash upon Leif unexpectedly came out of left field. Leif pulled the trigger, and I hollered as the pistol ball immediately pierced the Indian in the eye, spewing blood. The Indian directly dropped to the ground, and Leif continued moving, trampling right over the body without a thought. I tripped over it as he solidly towed me after him. He recklessly jerked me to my feet, hastening us along, and jarred me around like a rag doll over the ground. Weapons were flying, and shots were firing, bayonets kept stabbing while tomahawks hacked with chaos and panic all around.

In the midst of turmoil, a blur of violence surrounded me, and it was hard to tell which way the perils were coming from; at any moment, we could be shot, stabbed, or scalped and killed. Randomly weaving through trees now, Leif hurled us over an embankment, and we uncontrollably slid several yards down a mossy mound concealed by a grove of giant ferns. Suddenly straightening ourselves and turning around, we haphazardly faced a hollowed-out log camouflaged in moss and hidden beneath the ferns.

"Git inside!" Leif ordered frenetically as he was out of breath while he started shoving me toward the log. I unexpectedly looked at him. "Git inside!" he repeated.

"But, you can't fit!" I responded franticly, noticing the size of the opening as I tried catching my breath.

"Ye must git inside *now*!" he insisted without question and was pressing me over the shoulder to bend me inside the hollow.

"No!" I said extremely terrified, and he paused, attempting to put me inside the log.

"Do as I say, Sylvie!" he said impatiently, clearly alarmed.

"Where are you going to go?" I asked nervously.

"I must return tae the lads," he answered shortly.

"But you can't just leave me here all alone!" I replied, fearfully clutching onto his sleeve.

"Nae harm will come tae ye if ye do as I say! Now git in thaur!" he insisted with frustration.

"But what if you don't come back?" I panicked. He pried my clutching hand loose from his sleeve and firmly clasped my shoulders, fixing me to look directly up at him.

"I vow that I shall return," he swore. I stared exactly into his eyes, sheerly beside myself with trepidation. "Ye must remain collected, and do as I say." His tone suddenly became measured.

"*Please don't go, Leif!*" I begged.

"I have given ye my oath. I shall come back tae git ye," he said with firm conviction in a calibrated tone. "Now git yerself inside the log and remain thaur. Dinnae show yerself till I return fur ye. Do ye clearly understand me?" The look on his face and the tone in his voice struck me with such harsh gravity that I realized right away that I had no choice but to resign.

"All right," I said nervously.

"I shall come back fur ye," he assured again. I nodded and began complying by sticking my feet first inside the hollow log. At once I hurried myself hidden inside the broken tree trunk, and Leif released the fern covering the opening. The green bough bounced, obscuring my view as Leif immediately scurried away from me back over the slope and disappeared.

What seemed like a never-ending distance until we inadvertently discovered this undisclosed location must have really only lay seconds away since the sound of gunshots and war cries could clearly be heard close beyond the ridge. The panting from my own breath echoed in the tight enclosure surrounding me, and the intense beating of my rapidly thumping heart pounded loudly in my ears. Tremendously worried for Leif, I was tempted to slide out of the hole to peer over the ridge merely to see if I could get a glimpse of him in the middle of the chaos, but I promised to stay put and safely remain. So, I didn't move.

As time seemed to stand still abruptly while I waited in the log, it was killing me not knowing what was happening out there while the battle raged on.

But all of a sudden, the gunfire and war cries had ceased, and the air fell deathly silent. I waited hidden, closely attentive, with my ears alert to the merest sound coming from outside. There was nothing...

I THOUGHT I would discern Leif momentarily approaching, but as many minutes passed while I kept waiting—and waiting—I became panic-stricken. So many horrible, unthinkable thoughts began entering and swarming around inside my head. *Maybe Leif's hurt out there dying on the battlefield, and there's nothing I can do!* Suddenly, the small space I was confined to was closing in on me, and there seemed to be no air, making it difficult for me to breathe. It became too claustrophobic for me in here. For the second time in my life, I thought I was beginning to experience an anxiety attack, so I witlessly started wiggling myself out of the hollow tree.

When I came out into the open, I frantically continued crawling on my hands and knees beneath the giant overhanging fern branches until I shortly reached the base of the embankment where I abruptly stopped. I took a moment to catch my breath and gauge my orientation.

When I came to my feet, I hurriedly climbed the slope back over the ridge. Arriving over the crest, I rushed through the trees and could detect in the distance the aftermath strewn out over the road in the wake of the frenzied melee.

It was dead calm as I walked out onto the road. Bodies were scattered everywhere on the ground. Countless people had been hacked and scalped to death. Injured men were moaning and whimpering in unimaginable pain. Some seemed barely alive and passed over into death as I horrifiedly moved with caution around the ghastly scene. Many of the victims were from the Massachusetts regiment, with British regulars distributed in between. There were also a few women who had suffered the same atrocious fate. I couldn't begin to believe what I was seeing as I frenetically scanned the area for any sight of Leif.

Where on earth could he be? He should've gotten me from the log by now. He should have been back already.

He was nowhere to be seen—not anywhere between the trees or on the road...

I started fearing the worst.

I carefully meandered my way up the path among the dead, looking for him—desperately hoping not to find his face with the others on the ground.

He should have come for me by now...

Utterly terrified, my emotions overcame me, and my vision became obscured by welling tears while I continued walking around in complete disorientation, sheerly panicked. Frantically realizing that I might not ever see him again, my heart sank to the pit of my stomach with the same catastrophic misery I had known too well once before. But this time, it felt colossally worse.

As I was wiping tears from my eyes, I discerned movement up ahead. A surprising glimmer of hope, perhaps...? Until, I suddenly realized it was an Abenaki warrior noticing me advancing along the road as he was plundering from the dead men.

I immediately stopped in my tracks. He paused and stood from the deceased man he was stealing from. A chill swept over my skin, causing goosebumps and cold shock to run down my spine as my blood curdled and coursed like frigid ice water through my veins. My pulse shot up again and I started stepping backward as I simultaneously noticed a few more Huron warriors plundering from the dead also at a distance. The Abenaki warrior began moving toward me. I instantly spun around and took off running like a road-runner in the opposite direction, terrorized out of my mind. I sensed him swiftly moving behind me as I heard his whooping cry signaling others.

With Fort William Henry still smoldering not too far in the distance ahead, I aimed to reach the French encampment, hoping for possible protection. I dashed a good distance and believed that I could potentially save myself when I was completely blindsided from the right. I was knocked entirely off my feet onto my back and tackled by another undetected Abenaki warrior. I struggled fiercely beneath him, striving to get away. He whipped me around abruptly, taking fast hold of the hair over the crown of my head, and ferociously jerked me up to my knees as he stood behind me. I winced at the sharp pain on my scalp and blindly clawed his wrists. All at once, I felt a long, sharp blade come coldly over the front of my neck. I sensed my death about to occur right here and now as my throat was about to be slit.

"Je sera vous hanter la journé que vous meurent sur cette terre, et je vais continuer à suivre vous dans l'au-delà. Je vous maudire avec aucune pitié," I swore on my soul to curse him. Simultaneously, the Abenaki, who had originally spotted me from afar, had just arrived with four others and faced the warrior on the verge of slicing my throat. The one who spotted me said something to my attacker in a hostile tone, and they seemed to argue aggressively for a moment when suddenly, an unexpected musket fired from behind them. The two stopped talking, and the six Abenaki surrounding me turned to see who fired the shot. One of them said something abrupt, and the Abenaki who seemed to stop my death seized me from my potential killer. He sharply yanked me to my feet with his hand securely clinched around my arm, and he forced me to follow him with his band into the woods.

A few more shots rang out behind us as we dodged among the trees. I recognized the one now gripping me fast around my arm from before when he attempted to remove me from my horse earlier before we left the encampment. I tussled with him, trying to break from his grip as he compelled me to follow them. I was determined not to go anywhere with them. So, I clenched my teeth down onto his arm, and he suddenly howled. He flinched angrily, abruptly releasing me and shoving me backward down to the ground as he snatched his bitten arm.

I started scurrying away from him, but he instantaneously grabbed my neck and started choking me with one hand. He quickly drew forth a knife, and I saw the dangerous blade glinting above my pounding heart. I held my breath and closed my eyes in terror. The blade sharply ripped open the front of my riding jacket and tore into my shirt, slicing my stays and exposing my breast. I felt the tip of the raw blade firmly pressing against my bare skin between my breasts just above my stays. My breath grew short and fast as I anticipated with stark fear what was about to happen.

"Vous venez, ou je vous tuer maintenant," he threatened. I opened my eyes and stared into the committed dark brown eyes looking back at me. He was certainly going to kill me right here if I didn't go with him.

"Oui, Je viendrai," I choked aridly, agreeing to comply rather than being stabbed to death. He withdrew the knife and released the grip around my neck. I suddenly wheezed, coughing as air filled my lungs again. He took my arm and pulled me to my feet before he started walking again with the other five in the party, I was forced to pace with them through the forest, wondering where they were taking me, including how far I was being made to go.

We climbed over rocky terrain as we passed around the back side of Fort William Henry at quite a distance, heading north. As I was made to walk farther away from where Leif had left me, the rational side of my brain began considering the high likelihood that he was alive; he was a savvy and prudent man. He was resourceful and an experienced, resilient soldier who knew how to guard and fight. Furthermore, because I hadn't seen him lying on the ground back there on the road, I decided to wipe the dreadful idea of his possible death clear out of my mind just to keep from sobbing.

Comforted by the choice to believe he was unharmed, it occurred to me that once he had discovered me missing, he would look for me. *But how is he going to know where to find me?* I internally began freaking out even further because I could be anywhere in this wilderness, and he might never know where I have gone. *He'll never find me if they keep taking me farther away from the fort...*

We finally arrived at the edge of the lake, where there were canoes behind the fort. My captors indicated for me to get inside one of them. When I realized they were intending to take me across the water, I panicked so much more with deep misgiving. If they took me across the water, Leif would never know where I could possibly be in this vast, untamed wilderness. I didn't know what to do to prevent this from happening to me. So, I suddenly decided that I had to urinate and asked the Abenaki warriors in French if I could privately do so.

The Abenaki possessing me guided me to an area of undergrowth. He stood there watching me, and I knew that privacy was not going to be afforded to me. Having no choice, as I desperately needed to relieve myself and praying that he would not assault me, I dubiously proceeded, unbuttoning my trousers. I squatted, and as I was relieving myself, I thought to discreetly untie the loose ribbon to my hat dangling around my neck over my back when he glanced away in response to one of his warrior companions talking to him. My hat slipped quietly from my back into the vegetation by the canoes, and I hoped it would remain as a clue for Leif when he came searching for me, hopefully in this location. When I had finished urinating, I stood to re-button my trousers around my waist, but my captor faced me again and impatiently reached for me, grabbing my arm. He forced me out of the bushes before I completed closing the top button around my waist and steered me back toward the canoes where the others remained, waiting for me to get inside.

"I have a husband," I ventured to say in French to the one holding my arm and coercing me into the vessel.

"Your master—dead," he returned shortly in broken French as he moved, sitting closely behind me at the front of the canoe.

"He's alive, and he'll come for me," I expressed nervously, striving to convey my utmost conviction of it without fear as I prayed that it would be true.

"Silence! You no speak!" he ordered strictly at the back of my head.

Please let Leif be alive! Please let him find me! I repeatedly prayed to God as I faced the large body of water now around me when the craft moved out over the lake with me trapped inside by six well-armed Abenaki warriors.

MY ABENAKI CAPTORS paddled north up the lake for a long while, switching off their oars at various intervals and coasting occasionally. It seemed that we had covered a long distance without my captors ever breaking. Fort Carillon lay ahead of us just beyond dusk when we entered the channel into Lake Champlain and passed it a fair distance by full sundown. Moonlight lit the rest of the way. My hopes for Leif rescuing me began to dim with the sunlight when my hostage detainers finally beached the canoe on the shoreline of the lake to camp the night.

I sat among them, not wanting to bat an eyelid to sleep, although I was utterly exhausted from the traumatic ordeals of today. They conversed in their language, seemingly referring to me as eyes turned and hands pointed occasionally in my direction. I wondered what they were saying and what they ultimately had planned for me. It seemed an argument regarding me had broken out again between the one who was originally going to slice my throat on the road and the one who forced me into the woods with them, currently guarding me with certain protectiveness. Regardless, I merely kept hoping and praying to God for a miracle that Leif would somehow find me before anything bad happened to me. My hope was the only thing keeping me from crumbling under raw fear while witnessing the other Abenaki braves intervene between the arguing two by speaking also, and after a moment, it seemed the disagreement had been somewhat settled between them.

AT FIRST LIGHT the next morning, I was made to hike through the forest for hours. My last meal was thirty-six hours ago, and my stomach cramped with hunger. But my captors were determined to push onward and broke for rest only a few times for several minutes without eating. The terrain was tough and unstable at times as we moved through the mountains. At one point in our journey, I had grown so beaten from fatigue that I had to stop and collapse, sitting on the ground in the hot air. My possessor then unsympathetically grabbed my upper arm, yanked me up to my feet again, and indicated in French for me to piggyback over him.

"Non!" I refused in French, preferring to walk. I didn't want him touching me, and I certainly didn't want to rely on him; that required our bodies to be so closely engaged. But as I stepped to continue, my legs suddenly gave way, and my possessor caught me from descending to the ground when he grabbed me by the arm again. I jerked my arm from his stabilizing clasp, not wanting to be touched at all by him, and collapsed onto the ground.

"I carry you now!" he ordered intolerantly in French and abruptly turned me over his back as he whipped my legs around his waist with the assistance of his companions, tossing me over his back. Threatened, fearful, too weak to defy him, and with no other alternative, I allowed myself to rest over his bare back without any more complaint as he started carrying me through the rocky terrain in the forest.

As the men further trekked through the wilderness, I kept wondering how much farther we had to travel in this godawful heat and humidity until we arrived at wherever it was they were taking me, praying that I wouldn't ultimately suffer by their hand.

NIGHT FELL UPON US AGAIN, and we camped. Nerve-racked with fearful anxiety, I ate little fish they had provided me and scarcely closed one eye to sleep as I kept wondering how Leif would ever find me now—begging for him to still be alive as I also prayed for no harm to come to me.

It remained uncomfortably hot and muggy well through the night and into the following morning. As the sun rose, we started out trekking again between the trees. Another day came with minimal food and water intake that I could fetch with my hands in streams whenever my captors decided to break for short intervals. I was suffering from tiredness and found myself being carried by my detainer again today across the terrain.

Finally, at the height of the next day, we arrived at a rushing stream near a picturesque waterfall where their village was situated. *This must be their home*, I thought as I noticed all the wigwams and the settled Abenaki population casually moving around them.

As we entered the community, my captors were greeted enthusiastically by members of this society with whoops and hollers all around. To my surprise, I recognized ten other prisoners who had been taken from Fort William Henry also. Most of them were camp followers, with three men from the Provincial regiment scattered among them. They all had trepidation and uncertainty on their faces. I'm sure they were wondering what was to become of them, just as I was thinking the same thing concerning myself.

The scent of burning smoke filled the air as if a roast were cooking over an open fire. But there was something different about the aroma—one that I didn't recognize. Led by the one guarding me, we paced with the five other warriors deeper inside the community. With growing attention surrounding us as we passed through the village, I happened to notice the origin of the smoke. A huge bonfire was roaring in the center of the village, and I unwittingly detected, to the staggering horror of my eyes, a lifeless body tied to a stake engulfed in flames. I automatically gagged uncontrollably with dry heaves at the mere sight of the British soldier tied at the stake, charred beyond recognition as large flames continued engulfing him. Another screaming male captive was bound to another post near the charred soldier and was in the middle of having his heart torn out from his bare chest. Terrorized, I averted my eyes and nearly fainted but was prevented from collapsing to the ground as a result of my captor's firm grip around my arm as he was leading me through the village.

We abruptly stopped short when my guard sat me over a log in the shade beneath a tree as I continued heaving. He was promptly given a bowl of freshly ground red pigment by one of the women in the village, and he waited until I could gag no more. When my dry heaves subsided, he then pulled me to my feet so that I stood directly in front of him and began marking me with red paint over my face. When he had finished, he guided me to the beginning of a long line of villagers separated into two parallel lines, at which point I was made to walk through. At first, I thought that I would be degraded, mocked, or ridiculed in some way, but all they did was gently tap me on the shoulder as I walked between the lines of people. When I came out at the other end, they all loudly cheered and clapped.

After a moment when their excitement waned, the villagers encircled me along with the two warriors that had laid claim and argued over me. People stared at me with onlooking interest as the village elder emerged from his wigwam with assistance from two elderly women on each side. He appeared to be an ancient wise man of what age I couldn't easily discern. As he approached us, he came to feebly stand propped on an elevated platform in front of the encircling people gathered around us.

The sachem looked at me and at the two warriors to whom he commenced speaking in their Abenaki language. He seemed to ask a question. The one who had nearly sliced my throat open quickly jumped to respond to the question in an angry tone. He accusingly pointed at his companion, who had interrupted him from killing me as he disagreeably spoke to the sachem. When he finished speaking, the elderly sachem turned to the other man who had preserved my life and questioned him also. My defender spoke up with a firm, less-winded explanation—all the while, I wondered what was being said between them. When this man had finished speaking, the sachem fell silent and seemed to consider the two men standing directly before him. After a thoughtful moment, he then resumed speaking to them both—first to one and then to the other. Once the sachem had finished speaking, my potential killer snarled with apparent dissatisfaction and abruptly turned away from the sachem, leaving the gathering altogether. Seemingly unfazed by his disgruntled demeanor, the sachem returned, looking at the warrior who had saved my life, and calmly ended the discussion with several remaining words to him. The sachem lifted his palm ceremonially toward us, and the meeting seemed to be completed.

At that moment, my guard began leading me toward a group of three women. The women took me away from him and guided me down toward the nearby stream. I was reluctant about them touching me as they began removing my boots and clothes, but quickly understood that I had no choice except to follow their directions as they were impatient with me. After they successfully undressed me, they threw my belongings into the rushing water and I watched with misgiving as my clothes vanished into the moving stream.

When they started bathing me, I glanced up beyond the trees and noticed with apprehension the ten others captured from Fort William Henry. They were bound together by a rope around their necks and with their hands tied down in front. They were suddenly being marched toward a different location in the village by a group of Abenaki men. I wondered where they were being taken as I watched them being led away. For some reason, I didn't believe the place they were being forced to go to was going to be a hospitable one, and I regretted their situation as much as my own with deep concern because I had recognized their faces. Since their fate was uncertain also, I silently prayed for their wellbeing like I was also doing for my own while I felt cool water gushing over my bare shoulders as it was being poured over me.

Bewildered and apprehensive, one of the three women scolded me for looking at the captured individuals vanishing behind the trees and wigwams, and I supposed also for not paying attention to the three of them washing me. I suddenly averted my eyes from those captured and returned my attention to what was happening to me, realizing that one of the women wanted to wash my face. The woman took up her soaking rag and began wiping my face clean of red paint as the others continued scrubbing my body with their coarse linen rags until they were satisfied.

After they had cleansed me, the women had me dressed in deer-skin and moccasins. They each had a turn combing my short curls. When they were satisfied with my appearance, they led me back to the heart of the village inside one of the wigwams. I was ordered to sit quietly with one of the women as the other two had left. The space inside the wigwam was considerably large, I noticed. I remained sitting over a sizable bearskin rug covering the earth with the woman closely keeping watch over me in silence. Inside was simply furnished with one bed made of spruce boughs covered with bearskin. A collection of rustic tools for hunting, skinning, and fixing things were placed orderly against the wall at one end of the room.

It seemed a long time had passed while I was kept sitting alone with this woman watching me. I was growing weary, but stayed quietly seated wondering how I could escape from here. I didn't think it was going to be soon or easy for me to flee without being noticed and recaptured. So, I wondered how I was going to manage it with the least likely peril from these people and from the wilderness beyond.

While I was thinking about what was going to happen to me next and how I meant to escape from here—if I could—at last, the warrior who had preserved my life and coerced me to come here entered the wigwam. The woman watching me promptly left without a mere exchange of words with my captor. Now, suddenly finding myself alone in a confined area with him, my heart began racing. He slowly approached me, and I instinctively leaped backward, bumping the wall at my back, starkly uncertain of him and what he was going to do to me.

"Fear me not," he said calmly in French. He carefully motioned for me to remain calm with his palm. Yet, I was anything but calm since I didn't know what he had in mind. He knelt before me at a slight distance and carefully placed a bowl of unleavened bread and creamed corn on the mat beside the bear rug in clear view for me to see.

"Why have I been brought here?" I risked communicating with him.

"I bring food. You eat now," he said instead in a non-threatening manner. Despite my being starved for a mere morsel to eat, I hesitated to take anything from him. The frightening black war paint had been removed from his face and chest, revealing his actual handsome appearance. His burnt sienna complexion was clear of any scars. His face was chiseled with hooded, slightly almond-shaped eyes, and he appeared to be a young man in his early twenties. He was bare-chested, lean, and muscular, and the threatening presence he had assumed with me earlier seemed dispelled as he now looked at me without menace. His brown eyes locked onto mine. "You eat," he repeated in a stern tone, pushing the bowl closer toward me. "Fear me not. No fear me. Eat."

"Why am I here?" I ventured insecurely again instead of taking the food.

"Wife died bring son to me," he revealed with an even tone in broken French. All of a sudden, I shuddered with heightened panic.

"My husband—did you see him?" I asked shakily. "I have a husband. Did you see him?" Alarmed, I had to know. Webb's voice rang loud in my head: *His Grace—your lord, madam, is slain upon the field!*"

"Oui," he disclosed. I gasped and abruptly raised my trembling palm to my mouth, fighting uncontrollable tears beginning to well in my eyes; not only was I at a loss for words, I was essentially lost. "My brother fight him."

"Oh my God," I gasped unbelievably again, sharply filled with shock and sorrow since I couldn't help but to believe him as I gazed at his impassive expression. He was convincing as he stared unmoved at me, and I couldn't help myself when misery and vulnerability took me over; not only was I endangered now, but I was certain that he had recognized Leif from when Leif prevented him from stealing my horse when we were first encamped by the

French—not to forget the following day when he attempted kidnapping me as we were waiting to leave for Fort Edward. I knew this new man I was staring at had recognized me from that first occurrence because I certainly recognized him despite his appearance being cleared from the terrifying black war paint over his face. And knowing that this man looking at me now remembered what Leif looked like gave me the daunting feeling that he had, in fact, seen my husband on the battlefield and witnessed his slaughter.

"I, Aranck. Take you. Master of you," he informed me, directly looking at me.

"Non!" I told him for certain in French, overriding my nerves. I instantly cleared my vision with my fingers, unclear if he was going to harm me since I defied him despite his current docile disposition toward me. However, it was swiftly understood by me, determined by the way he had kidnapped and forced me here with him, that he might reject my defiance and injure me if I didn't comply with him. Except, I suddenly didn't know if he would actually act cruelly or not now, given the way he was looking at me with calmness in his eyes. Nevertheless, he still commanded an air of unyielding ferociousness, which kept me more than skeptical of him. I was beyond frightened of him as it seemed he was trying not to threaten me any longer when he cautiously approached closer and stood directly in front of me. "I have a husband," I informed him again through my shaky voice, desperately wanting to believe that Leif was still alive more than anything and trying to convince this new man to leave me alone.

"Old master no more. You mine," Aranck persisted.

My heart skipped a beat and plunged to the pit of my stomach when my nerves suddenly unraveled, causing my eyes to water, though I was striving my hardest to remain unshaken and clear minded. I swiftly wiped my slipping teardrops from my cheeks, not wanting him to see me unnerved any more than I'd already become, since it seemed he was lacking compassion for me by the glare he was giving me now. So, I quickly understood revealing my tearful distress was not going to help my situation with him as I read the detachment in his eyes. He didn't pity me—at all—and it didn't seem he was going to grant me any leeway for my emotions in the least, which only heightened my fear of him and the situation I found myself in further.

Unexpectedly, noise from outside was detected. It sounded like loud commotion and whooping hollering was heard from many different voices.

"Eat," he encouraged calmly again, ignoring me and the outdoor shrieking. I shook my head, reluctant to trust him. "Eat. You eat."

"Non," I replied.

"Eat," he insisted again.

I shook my head again, opposing him. I perceived that he wasn't going to relent and thought he might force me to comply when he started stepping even closer toward me. There was nowhere for me to escape when I reacted to avoid him as I jumped backward, further pressing my back into the wall behind me and fearfully looked at him.

"Obey me," he said mildly when he stopped short immediately before me. He lifted a hand toward me, and I flinched when I thought he was going to strike, but instead I sensed his calloused fingers lightly stroking my cheek. My heart raced and my breathing became short as alarm gripped me, knowing what he was likely expecting from me as he gazed intently at me.

Suddenly the skin hanging in front of the doorway whipped open, and one of the women who had washed me said something hasty to Aranck, alerting him. He abruptly swung around, facing the woman behind him, and immediately followed her out of the wigwam, leaving me alone.

I quickly wiped my eyes, clearing my vision, realizing now that I was alone in the wigwam with no one guarding me; perhaps, this was my chance to escape, as my instinct to run from here sharply seized me. But I was starved for food and couldn't think about escaping until I at least shoved a morsel into my mouth. So, I swiftly moved toward the clay bowl containing the creamed corn and plate with unleavened bread placed on the mat before me on the ground, disregarding that Aranck had given the food to me since he was no longer here to observe me eating it. I knelt before the food and hastily stuffed the creamed corn and bread into my mouth, eating all of it in a New York minute.

After my last bite of food, without any forethought, I pushed myself up to my feet, severely anxious to vanish out of sight from here without ever being detected. Peeking around the deerskin flap, I peered outside the opening of the wigwam to see if I had the slightest chance of escaping without being noticed. My instinct took me over, preventing any reasoning from entering my mind as I was determined to flee without considering the consequences.

As I scanned the outdoor location through the flap covering the entrance, I discerned that Aranck and the women were nowhere in sight among the crowd that had gathered outside at the center of the village, away from the wigwam. There was alarming excitement in the crowd everywhere. It seemed an unwelcome disturbance was taking place, and the whole village was fueled by excitement.

Noticing everyone in the community preoccupied with the commotion, I quickly turned back inside, taking up the last small portion of bread in my hand, and sneaked outside with it, knowing this was going to be the last bit of food supply I was going to have to take with me on my journey. As I made my way outside from the wigwam, hastened around the back side of it, and started between the other structures, men were whooping war cries, and I noticed some women were sobbing while the rest of the population seemed to have unexpected expressions of confounded curiosity as they meandered through the village toward the center during my undetected attempt to escape.

Careless of what was taking place around me, I started moving away from the crowd in the opposite direction, not knowing if I would ultimately be able to safely find my way back to Fort William Henry. I had no idea how I was going to navigate through this thick wilderness all alone without any skills or means for survival. But at this point, I didn't care. Rationality was not at the forefront of my mind as much as my instinct to save myself from being held captive was. All I knew was that I had to try escaping back to where I belonged, fully aware that I very well could die out here trying to rescue myself from a life unknown with the Abenaki. I simply wanted to go home, and I was willing to risk my life in order to return, leaving this nightmare behind me completely. I had already been taken captive once, and I wasn't inclined to experience it for a second time. I just felt that I had to get away—and if I was lucky to survive—I'd figure out the rest later… but only if I lived.

My heart was beating hard and fast in my chest as if it were about to burst through while I mindfully began creeping my way toward the path exiting the village. But I suddenly arrested my steps when hearing a man's voice unexpectedly carrying at full volume over the crowd speaking in perfect French.

Seized by this voice, my heart skipped a beat, and my breath caught as I found myself immediately returning from where I had just left in the village. Pressing my way through the crowd in the direction of his voice as he spoke, I gasped, instantly recognizing Leif as my eyes landed on him through the onlooking villagers.

"I am Prince Leif Charles Seamus MacLeod FitzJames Stewart, Duke of Monteith, grandson of King James the Second of England, Ireland, and Scotland. I am cousin to His Most Christian King, King Louis of France and Navarre, cousin to General Montcalm, Marquis de Saint-Veran!" Leif roared so that all could hear his thunderous introduction. "I am from the clans MacLeod of MacLeod and the Royal House of Stewart! I have fought many battles with my kinsmen and live to fight more!"

"Warrior Son of Great Fathers, why you come to Abenaki?" the elder sachem was heard saying impersonally to Leif in French as I pushed through the front of the gathering. My eyes gravitated immediately to perceive Leif standing at the center of everyone before the sachem, appearing impermeable and uncharacteristically savage. He was bare-chested like the male population around and fully armed with cross-belts, holding his broadsword, musket, tomahawk, and pistols. His breeches were tattered and torn over the thighs and knees—and stained with blood and mud. I unexpectedly discerned, to my greatest disbelief and horror, the monstrous appearance of four freshly decapitated Abenaki heads —two at each side—dangling by the hair among his clutching fists.

"I have come to claim whit has been stolen from me!" he hollered.

"What do you claim?" the sachem demanded unsympathetically as he stood gazing at Leif and perceived the decapitated heads dangling in his merciless hands.

"I claim my wife!" Leif returned in fury. The sachem didn't respond but unwaveringly stared at Leif in the eyes, appearing stone-faced. "These heads," Leif continued audibly as he raised them for everyone to perceive, "I have taken in honor of my brother's death committed by yer kinsmen on the waters of Lake George as he fought, as I, for King George of England! I have taken twenty scalps and eight heads and have let them rot upon the earth as I honor my brother and search for my wife!

"My cousin, French General Montcalm, made peace with the British Colonel Monro efter an honorable battle only tae be betrayed by yer kinsmen! In that betrayal, men of yer clan have stolen my wife! I have come tae reclaim whit has been stolen from me! I shall fight fur whit is mine till she is returned tae my possession!" He roared turbulently, shaking the heads and tossing them down to the dirt. They landed with weighty *thuds* to the ground and rolled slightly toward the feet of closely surrounding observers. People stared with impressed looks on their faces and moved frightfully back a bit as the Abenaki heads came slightly close to the onlookers' feet.

I moved hastily toward Leif from the crowd. He sharply turned his glance, noticing movement among the surrounding people, and our eyes immediately locked onto each other. His face was scarlet in the fit of anger. The emotion on his face instantaneously splintered once our eyes finally met again, and I could suddenly perceive his silent realization. Though still terrified, I automatically ran toward him inexplicably alleviated, joyous, and grateful beyond belief and more than what the world could ever imagine—to suddenly realize that he wasn't slain but was alive and ferociously well—struck me with exaltation to the core of my soul.

Remaining guarded as I arrived at him, he abruptly threw out a hand toward me, seizing me by my arm and securing his hold on me.

"Non! You may not take leave," the sachem said adamantly. Suddenly, some Abenaki men armed with clubs and tomahawks stepped alertedly toward us. "Another claim her for his own."

"Nae one lays claim tae whit I own but I!" Leif responded forcefully in French, whipping forth his tomahawk, prepared to fight—observing that a confrontation was imminent. The sachem stood quietly, contemplating for a moment as my Abenaki captor contested loudly to the sachem. The sachem said something in their native language, and then Aranck turned hardened eyes onto Leif.

"She must choose," the sachem ordered sternly. "Release her! She stands amidst Aranck and Warrior Son of Great Fathers." He abruptly motioned to Aranck, standing at the front edge of the gathering, to enter the circle of congregated villagers so that the three of us remained standing directly before the sachem and every other onlooker who had gathered. Leif seemed to hesitate for a moment as he briefly glimpsed at the surrounding villagers encircling us. His hand reluctantly withdrew from my arm when he returned, looking at the sachem as Aranck stood on the opposite side of me. Then, casting a look directly at me, the sachem urged me to make my choice. I easily placed my hand over Leif's glistening forearm from fresh blood stains and perspiration and tightly held onto him.

"I want my husband, the Duke of Monteith," I said tremulously as I spoke in French, fearing that confrontation was close to breaking out and that Leif would also be captured and burned at the stake like the other officer had been if not tortured alive first.

"Warrior Son of Great Fathers, cousin of King Louis of France and General Montcalm, le Marquis de Saint-Veran, claim what is yours and go in peace," the sachem said, simply settling the matter. I couldn't believe what I just heard and suddenly felt myself breathing again when I realized Leif and I were going to be released without incident. I was shocked; I believed our release would have met certain death after having faced Hell by torture.

I glanced at Aranck, noticing his imperceptible expression as Leif securely grabbed my arm again. Aranck protested loudly and cursed the decision. He abruptly turned out of the gathering in visible anger as he shoved his way through the surrounding villagers to leave the congregation. My attention suddenly turned to Leif as he instantly began tightly pulling me by the arm with haste away from the crowd, guiding me out of the village. We passed along the longhouse and wigwams without any harm coming our way as community members merely stood by watching us depart their premises.

Thirty-Four

Leif and I toiled through the mountains without incident for about an hour when suddenly I stopped walking resulting from the inability to physically go any further. I suddenly collapsed in the mud between the trees. Leif sharply arrested his steps and promptly adjusted his belts and weapons. When he was finished, he leaned and gathering my hand up into his.

"Come now, *ceisdein*, hold fast fur me," he encouraged calmly and lifted me over his back. I draped my arms over his shoulders and rested my chin on the perspiring curve of his neck with my cheek against his. He resumed hiking laboriously through the woods, carrying me nonstop along the way. The heat was unbearable with the humidity so high. I didn't know how he could sustain carrying me through the wilderness with the weight of his arms included.

"I'm sorry you have to carry me," I said guiltily.

"I shall manage," he said. I began reflecting on this whole ordeal and quietly became emotionally upset.

"I'm so happy you found me," I sniffled.

"I, too," he said, huffing with each step he took along the way.

"I thought I was never going to see you again," I wept softly.

"I meant tae tear the earth open from Heaven tae Hell till I found ye," he grunted while carrying me.

"How'd you know where they had taken me?" I asked, wiping my fingers over my teary eyes, trying to clear my vision.

"Efter we warred off the Indians near Fort William Henry, I returned whaur I had put ye and found ye missing... So, I went lookin' fur ye thaur about with the help of the lads. Liam spotted ye being carried off by Indians from the road and shot his musket at them from afar. Yet, it was Angus who had discovered yer hat beyond the French encampment at the shore of the lake and saw Indians stealing over the water with ye inside their canoe... So, we fitted ourselves in the next vessel and followed ye. I tracked ye as far north as their village when I discovered ye being bathed in the river by their women," he explained as he concentrated on his steps over the uneven terrain. "I would have taken ye back from them sooner, yet I was surrounded by villagers as I hid in the wood and 'twas too perilous then fur me tae take ye away. Therefore, I awaited a most opportune moment tae seek ye out and recapture ye from them. Yet, they sheltered ye, and I couldnae git tae ye. So, at that moment, I entered the village and was going tae fight fur ye as I perceived nae other recourse."

"Oh... I'm so glad it didn't come to fighting," I realized, as he would have surely been killed.

"I'm most grateful tae have our skins also."

"I'm so lucky you found me. I was so scared."

"Quite fortunate fur me as weel," he said.

"I didn't think they'd let us go easily, though. I'm extremely surprised."

"'Tis presumed that we shall perish in the wood."

"They rather have us dead in spite of letting us go?"

"'Tis less mouths fur them tae feed in one respect. Whether I was slain by them or released into the wilderness, I am a dead man tae them despite my bloodline. If I waur not kin tae Montcalm or the king of France, then they would have burnt me at the stake fur certain. Instead, as it is, their releasing us into the wood will be our torment and their vindication according tae them."

Words could not express how relieved and happy I was to be with him again, and I couldn't help the tears streaming down my cheeks. "Shh, now. 'Tis alrecht. Yoo're with me now again, safe and soond."

I *was* back with him, safe and sound, and I was comforted by this fact. I wrapped my arms around his shoulders, securing myself against him as I never wished to part from him again, and pressed my cheek against his while clearing my vision, settling myself from weeping any further.

We became quiet with each other as he actively hiked through the forest in this blistering, stifling heat with me over his back. My vision started clearing after a moment, and I found myself suddenly very tired—emotionally and physically. I could barely keep my eyes open at one point and felt them beginning to close as his steps rocked me. After a minute, I finally could no longer strive to stay awake when I succumbed to my sheer exhaustion and drifted to sleep like a baby, cradled by him on his back.

I WAS ABRUPTLY JARRED to consciousness as he mindfully placed me down on the cool ground beneath the shading towering trees. Looking around, I discovered us inside a huge thicket of vegetation closely resembling corn lilies, except this was all skunk cabbage surrounding us. It reeked horrendously. Especially when the oils invariably got on our skin and clothing—there was no difference between us and the skunks. At least, however, we were sure to keep all the bears and anything else with saber teeth and claws away from us, I thought.

Leif decided to finally give himself a break from his hard hike when he set me down on the ground. He brought his fingers to his lower lip and blew a series of sharp whistles imitating a sing-song descending pitch that sounded like *whoit whoit whoit*—just like a cardinal. Suddenly, the woodland echoed with a *what-chee*, and Leif responded with the same call. Then, Angus, Fearghus, Cole, Lachlann, Bearnard, Derek, and Liam simultaneously showed themselves within the thicket at a distance and started approaching us.

Leif adjusted his weapons again and swiftly scooped me up from the ground into his robust arms. Utterly drained from strength and still half asleep, I lethargically rested my head on his shoulder as he started moving toward his cousins, meeting them across the thicket.

"Och, thank Heaven, ye found her," Angus said with relief as he observed me in Leif's arms when they all met each other at the edge of the thicket.

"Aye," Leif replied.

"She appears worn out," Fearghus said.

"She needs food and water," Leif said.

"Then let's go, lads," Bearnard urged hastily, and the men began pacing through the woods around the grove. After several long minutes of continued trudging, soon rushing water resonated throughout the forest. The men headed in that direction until we soon arrived at the banks of a running stream. They found a concealed place behind some large protruding rocks and decided to camp the night there.

Leif carefully placed me down over a patch of fallen leaves, and I rested, feeling atypically weak. The men hacked off low-lying branches from the undergrowth and whittled the tips into points for spears. I watched Leif patiently wade in the stream as he had his spear poised for the plunge. Suddenly, he drove the spear down into the water. He pulled it out of the stream with a very large, pretty rainbow trout stuck flopping at the end. He paced toward the smoldering campfire and placed it down over the hot coals.

Cole and Derek caught more trout—enough to feed all of us quite well.

The men sat around minding their meal over the fire without much conversation. They were tired and looked haggard and beat up. Their faces were sweaty and dirty, and their hair was disheveled, straggly, and appeared greasy from their perspiration. Like the others, a beard had begun to grow over Leif's jaw, and I could clearly see the fierce Viking in him. They all resembled wild Nordic nomadic tribesmen, and the surrounding wilderness suddenly propped them into an unusual anthropological contextual scene from the Dark Ages.

When the fish was ready to eat, Leif came over and gave me a prepared piece cooked around a stick. I sluggishly pushed myself up to sit so that I could eat. I took the stick from him and quickly started satiating my hunger. Leif sat near me eating, also as the others remained together, eating off to the side around the campfire. We ate quietly together, and the feeling between us I sensed was unusual. He ate silently, chewing his food without even looking at me. He seemed distracted by something brooding in his mind, and the gloomy look on his face made me secretly question. But then again, none of the men seemed to be in a good mood in this torrid heat as they devoured their fish and washed it down with water from the stream without any of their typical banter. Instead, they were quiet and seemed very stressed while they appeared to be on the lookout for any little thing that alerted them. I was sure, like me, they were more than ready to leave the area for safer territory.

After having gone without food for a while, I ravenously scarfed down my fish, clearing every morsel from the bones. Almost immediately, when I was done eating, my stomach took a turn for the worse, and my mouth began to water. I suddenly shot up from my seat on the ground with queasiness and made a weak dash to the stream. I pitched over a rock head above the water, heaving up everything I had just consumed, and the water dutifully washed away the unpleasant mess. I dipped my hand below the water's surface, collecting fresh water, and swished my mouth out. After a moment, while cleansing my mouth from the unpleasant taste, I sensed Leif approaching my side.

"Are ye alrecht?" he inquired properly.

"I think I ate too fast," I said, sitting up from the rock.

"Och," he replied. "Shall I collect ye anither fish then?"

"No, it's alright, thank you. I'll be okay," I said, looking up at him from my hunch position over the rock. He nodded without speaking. The expression on his face seemed different. I suppose he appeared unusually stern and dour. It struck me as a little odd, but I didn't address it. Instead, he took my arm, helping me off the rock and back onto my feet.

"Ye must git tae sleep now," he urged, and I certainly agreed. I was exhausted and looked forward to being able to sleep again among sound company. The sun was setting and the forest became a dark, uncertain place at twilight. I moved over a pile of leaves and lay finally to rest. But Leif didn't choose to lie beside me tonight as he normally did until I fell asleep. Instead, he walked over toward his cousins and joined them around the smoldering fire pit that had been extinguished a minute ago. They were intermittently talking with each other in Scottish in low, somber tones. I picked up the distinct feeling that Leif was being distant from me. I had sensed it earlier today as he hardly spoke to me the whole way on our hike down to this point. I didn't like the way it made me feel, and I wondered about what was bothering him.

"Leif?" I said, interrupting him from his companions while they were speaking. They stopped talking with an air of uncomfortable silence, and he turned, looking in my direction.

"Aye?" he said in an unfriendly tone.

"Aren't you tired? Don't you want to lie down?" I asked considerately.

"I shall lie when I am ready, nae sooner," he said curtly and turned his attention back to his cousins without any other consideration. His surly tone made me uncomfortable. Apparently, there was something wrong brewing inside him that I was unaware of. I didn't know what it could be that was irking him, but suddenly, I was feeling a little angry, too, because of his abrupt tone with me. I sensed things between us had somehow gone awry, and I didn't know how or why. But whatever it was that was troubling him, I knew that I was going to have to face it head-on with him before it became worse between us for whatever reason.

I SLEPT SOLIDLY that night under a bright moon and stars. At dawn I had awakened to discover Leif simultaneously rousing from slumber a slight distance away from me. He apparently had chosen not to sleep close to me this time, I quickly noticed—which made me feel diminished, sad, and annoyed.

When everyone else had awakened, we immediately started out on foot again through undulating territory. It was another brutally hot day, and the heat only seemed to escalate everyone's irritability. And although I had slept well, I was still left drained from the days before. So, I straggled along the path at my own manageable pace behind the group.

Rather seemingly out of duty instead of kindness, Leif lagged along with me. He didn't speak or even look at me as we walked. Instead, like a horse with blinders, he kept his eyes fixed ahead on the narrow foot trail without a mere hint of acknowledgment toward me. I was mulling it over in my head: not so much as a simple *"Good morning"* or *"How are you feeling?"* Not merely a *"Hello"* had he offered me. Needless to say, I was growing increasingly annoyed with his pouty, pissed-off attitude.

Finally, I had about reached the end of my rope with him. I was just about to address whatever the hell was on his mind when the men decided to take an early break in this already sweltering morning heat at a creek to drink from their canteens and relieve ourselves. Except, I found that I could not approach the matter in private with all of them around. And as it appeared while we were breaking from our hike, the men were engaged and spoke well enough with each other while I, on the other hand, seemingly had been outcasted from the group like an untouchable. Well, this only chapped my hide even further, and I was going to let Leif know about it.

IT WASN'T until sometime much later in the morning when my temper had finally reached its boiling point and had gotten the better of me after being completely ignored by him. I suddenly stopped walking over the very narrow foot trail we were now slightly descending. Leif also ceased his steps following mine and glowered at me. I put my hands on my hips, ready to have it out, as I equally glared back at him, though I was still quite exhausted from days prior and from the sweltering heat encompassing the early day.

"What's your problem?" I asked bluntly.

"Pardon?" he replied callously with a raised brow, appearing caught off guard by my abrupt tone. The color already over his face from the heat flushed further, turning it crimson with clear vexation.

"Yeah, what's your deal?" I responded irritatedly.

"Micht ye try speaking properly fur once so that one micht understand yer meaning?" he returned sharply, being critical of me. I felt my blood pressure suddenly shooting up.

"Fine, let me spell it out for you—I want to know what that stick up your ass is since you're being such an asshole to me now," I said pointedly. Out of nowhere, his hand swung around my arm, latching too hard, squeezing me tight. I winced a little unexpectedly, caught by surprise. Leif suddenly jerked me aside off the trail with him. He instantly turned, looking over his shoulder, voicing something audible in Scottish to his cousins moving on the trail a moderate distance ahead. Their heads turned in our direction, and Angus yelled back in Scottish as he also raised his bayoneted musket in acknowledgment while they kept moving down the path. Within a minute, they were out of earshot. That's when Leif spun his boorish attention back to me.

"How *dare* ye speak tae me with that sort of tongue, woman!" Leif shouted angrily at me with a cutting glare, visibly piqued without question.

"How dare you behave in such a way toward *me*!" I shouted back at him. "What the hell have I done to you to make you act like such a *cock* toward me? *Nothing*—that's what!"

"Dinnae be presumptuous! Ye have done plenty tae try my patience, lass, and I'll have it *nae mair* from ye!" he snarled, seething at the seams.

"Oh, is that right?"

"Most indeed!"

"Please, oh *Great-One*, tell me what I've done?"

"Ye have disobeyed me fur the last time!"

"*Disobeyed?*" I echoed outrageously.

"Aye! I told ye tae remain put whaur I hid ye! But, ye chose tae do differently and entirely disobeyed me!"

"Oh my God! You are absolutely unbelievable! What am I? A dog or something like that you own?" I shouted, absolutely appalled. "News flash, buddy! I'm not some kind of *possession* that can be owned! Nobody *owns* me! *You* don't own me! I belong to no one but myself!" All of a sudden, his face went livid-scarlet, and I could have sworn steam was coming out of his ears. He set his jaw tight and square, and a second hand clamped down harshly around my other arm, cutting off circulation as he locked me directly in front of him.

"***I do own ye! Ye ur mine! Ye belong tae me and me alone!***" he exploded ferociously in a deep, thunderous voice, showering me with saliva during his fuming outburst.

"People aren't meant to be *owned*! People aren't meant to be bought and sold, traded, or taken like some kind of market commodity! We're all human beings! *You don't own me!* You can't tell me what I can and cannot do!" I yelled back just as angrily. He was starkly outraged and frightened me as he wildly held onto my arms. I struggled to get out of his binding grip, but he kept me immovable.

"***I do own ye! Yoo're my wife!***" He raged violently like a wild storm, simultaneously shaking me in his unyielding clasp as he gritted his teeth on the verge of completely losing control. He was so enraged; his brogue had become extremely thick that I could barely understand him.

"Just because I'm your wife doesn't mean you are my *owner*!"

"It does so mean *precisely* that!"

"I'm in charge of myself! You're not my boss!" I screamed.

"I am yer ***laird and master***! Ye are my ***possession*** tae do tae ye as I shall, and ye will ***obey me***! If I teel ye tae sit, ye will do it! If I teel ye tae stand, ye will do it! I shall teel ye whit tae do, when tae do it, whit tae say ur how tae say it, and ye will do it! And, if it pleases me, I shall—"

"*No way!* You're outta your damn mind! I'm sick and tired of you telling me how I should be! Stop bossing me around! I'm not some dumbass!" I interrupted, yelling at him. "I'm my own person! I'm not a slave to anyone! I have a mind, and I can think for myself without being told what to do! You can't program me like I'm a goddamn *computer*!"

"*I made ye a duchess! Yoo're my wife! Ye will honor me!*" The vein in the middle of his forehead popped out and pulsed as he shook me again. He yanked me around this time so hard that my neck whiplashed.

"I didn't ask you to marry me!"

"It wisnae yer responsibility!"

"Who said it was yours? You didn't have to do it!"

"Ye needed shelter and protection that only a man can provide!"

"I don't *need* you! Where I come from, I can provide very well for myself!"

"Ye arenae amongst wherever damnation yoo're from! Yoo're haur now wi' me! And that is the way it will forever remain!"

"Not if I can help it! You bullied me into marrying you! That's all you've ever done! And I'm not going to let you do it to me anymore!"

He suddenly released me and shoved his hand in his breeches pocket. He angrily whipped out my cycle beads so that I could see that he had them in plain sight. He violently hurled them into the air across the way toward the roaring creek beside us. They sank into the rushing water and instantly vanished. I suddenly looked at him in shock. I had discovered the beads missing when I was packing our things for us to leave the fort and I had no clue where they had gone missing until now.

"What the hell did you do that for?" I shouted angrily.

"Ye have *deceived* me!" he accused vehemently, going nuclear.

"Bullshit! I've done nothing of the sort! I've never lied to you! It takes two to make a marriage! It's not all about *you*! I have a say in it, too! Especially if all you're going to do is treat me like a sex slave and screw the hell outta me all the time without ever considering me!"

"Yoo're my property! 'Tis my *reit* tae bed ye whenever ur wherever I wish! I'll roger ye any which way I please! And, if I seed ye with my bairn then ye will bear it!"

"Like hell! It's my body! It belongs to me, not you! You never asked me if I wanted to risk my life being pregnant and having kids! It's my choice to want to or not since I'm the one who can die!"

"Whit sort of crap are ye retching! I dinnae have tae *ask ye*! It is expected of ye! Yer duty is tae me! Yoo're *my wife*! I consistently risk my life fur ye! And all ye can do is think about yerself! Goddamn it all, Sylvina! Ye ur a mere impudent, spoilt child!"

"How dare you! You conceited, thick-skulled, self-centered, lowbrow, savage barbarian, Neanderthal, misogynist pig!"

"Very weel, if that is whit ye believe of me!"

"It *is* what I think of you!"

"Then, ye dinnae ken a damned thing! Ye are profoundly disrespectful!"

"And you're profoundly a pompous ass!"

"Ye watch yer tongue with me riet now, ur I'll slap ye witless!"

"You can't talk to me that way!"

"Indeed, I can talk tae ye *that* way! And I shall, as I'll have ye listen tae me reit now!"

"You're the biggest bullying, numbskull, knuckle-dragging brute on the planet!"

"The trooble wi' ye is that ye believe that ye can carry yerself any which way ye damned weel choose, and do as ye will and please without any consideration! Ye go about the place as if ye are a man! And clearly, ye are not!"

"What? Just because I don't have a cock like you, that means I don't have a brain?"

"Yoo're not a *man*! If ye could get that notion through that *ninny* skull of yers, we would all be better off!"

"You male chauvinist! I have a very extensive education! I can think for myself!"

"Be that as it will! It disnae prevent ye from being *ravished*!" he hollered vehemently. I sharply broke off as it dawned on me all at once right now.

"Oh, is that what this is all about? You're freaking out because you think that some other guy might have screwed me?" I screamed, disastrously appalled.

"Now that ye have pleasantly broached the topic! Did he roger ye?" He stared wildly at me as I was unexpectedly stunned and couldn't readily respond. "*Did he roger ye?*" he reiterated savagely.

"Fuck you!" I shouted at the top of my lungs and sent my hand flying for his face. He swiftly blocked my arm in midair with one slamming blow, preventing it from reaching his head. "You motherfucking bastard!" I screamed with all my might. Suddenly, as if I didn't think his face could get any more crimson, his color deepened almost purple and his eyes sharpened like daggers with an abrupt surge of vicious ire. He was seething. He was breathing heavily, and I didn't know what was going to happen.

"Ye despicable *cunt*!" he roared violently and suddenly raised a brutal hand above my face. I flinched, but he didn't strike. Instead, I found myself unexpectedly shoved to the ground as I tumbled backward onto my bottom. ***"Did he roger ye?"*** he detonated again. I could see him looking ballistic at me with downright disgust.

"So what am I now? *Damaged goods?* What does it matter to you? I'm just your fuck buddy! You don't really care about me at all! By the way his name is Aranck, and if he did do it to me, you wouldn't want me any more anyway! Right?" I bellowed back from the ground.

"If I didnae want ye, I would have left ye with the dirty redskin!" he blasted.

"That's not true! You only came for me because you deem me your possession!"

"Ye are my possession! Ye are my property and I own ye!"

"Fucker!" I resonated and suddenly got to my feet again. "This has everything to do with your shitty-ass macho pride! You don't love me!" I charged at him with flailing arms. He grabbed me and held me at bay as I kept swinging my fists in all directions, wanting to whale upon him in any way that I could. But I was prevented because he was just too large and overpowering.

"Ye dinnae listen!" he roared.

"It's my fault?"

"Aye, it is yer fault! If ye would have minded me as ye whaur told, ye wouldnae have been stolen from me, and I wouldnae have had tae come all this treacherous way tae find ye!"

"How convenient of you to blame me when you're the one who fucking left me! I hate you!" I rang out as I kept aimlessly swinging my arms around. "I hate you! I wish we never met! I hate that I know you! I hate that I ever met you! You left me, and all you can think about is your stupid honor! All you want me for is to keep your bed warm at your beck and call with my ass in the air so that you can just fuck me whenever you want! Well, you fuck off!"

"*Christ* woman! Ye dinnae ken how much I want tae knock some sense into yer head reit now! I feel I want tae beat ye tae death! Ye made yerself vulnerable by not listenin' tae me! And now we have every goddamned Indian about blazin' doon the trail coming efter us! *Bloody Hell*! Whit will it take fur ye tae understand me! This is not the end of it! Och, nae indeed! I'm gonnae see tae it that ye git *weel and guid* whit is coming tae ye from me! Ye will be *punished* fur this abomination!"

"I hate you!" I shouted again.

He scowled hard-heartedly and stood unyieldingly before me, clenching his jaw—fixed with fury.

"I'm gonnae ask ye again—did he roger ye?" His voice suddenly turned rough and cold. I could see that he was striving very hard not to lose control altogether.

"Fucking bastard!" I jarred my knee up, aiming for his crown jewels. He blindly knocked my leg back down with his fist and shoved his leg between my thighs, separating them like a cop about to frisk a thug—thwarting any more efforts from me.

"Do that again, and I'll knock yer bonnie white teeth doon yer throat!"

"You're an idiot! Get your goddamn shitty-ass hands off me!"

"I shall not!"

"You can't blame me for this! If you hadn't disregarded me in the first place, then we wouldn't be here!"

"Ye best believe that I am damned weel *angry* at ye, and I *do* blame ye fur this entire occurrence! It was ye who refused tae follow my orders!"

"I'm not one of your military grunts that you can just order around!"

"Indeed yoo're not—they have got the wits tae follow orders whaur ye will not!"

"You pea-brained gorilla!"

"If ye had stayed whaur I had put ye, then I wouldnae have had tae traipse about Kingdom Come in the depths of enemy territory tae find ye!"

"Take your hands off me!"

"And look at ye! *Naked*! Dressed in skins like one of them! It disgusts me! Thaur I find ye so amongst them—taken by the same filthy redskins that spilt my brother's bluid and tore him tae pieces and devoured him like an animal fur food! We could have protected one anither then, do ye not ken? He micht be alive today if ye hudnae distracted me from my duties! *Bloody Hell*, woman! The notion that those foul Indians would take ye and make ye wife tae one of their own or profit by sellin' ye tae a slave trader. *Damnation!* Do ye not reckon that I have a reit tae be outraged?" He lost control and shook me so hard that my head whiplashed back and forth like a rag doll, hurting my neck.

"Don't you dare! I told you that you and Finley shouldn't go! But you refused to listen to me! It's not my fault! You should have listened to me! But you just think because I'm only an *emotional woman* that I haven't anything of real value to say! So go to Hell! You're a hypocrite! You racist, dirty rotten *slave owner*!"

He suddenly stopped speaking and glared vehemently at me, panting fiercely like a wild bull. I was so angry I swerved my arm again up toward his jaw. He snatched my claw with his powerful hand and swayed me back down to the mud, pitching on top of me, locking me between his thighs beneath him as he tried controlling my furious struggle to whale upon him. Immovably holding my wrists, he pinched them into the earth, cutting off my circulation as we both screamed at each other at the top of our lungs. He was animated with further outrage now that he was yelling full blast at me in Scottish as I was cursing him out quite well in English.

After a minute, I had become so winded that I couldn't keep up with his tirade. Forced to unintelligibly listen to his scouring rant, I waited until he was finished. When he was done, he panted heavily over me, glaring into my eyes. He started taking deep breaths, striving to gain some semblance of control over himself as he remained heavy on top of me. We glowered at each other, out of breath, not speaking. I was trying very hard to calm down, too. But it was very difficult.

"If ye hate me so, then go," he said, breathing hard and quivering. "Go. Return tae the Indian. He will have ye, I ken... I shan't stand in yer way... I shall nae longer have ye if ye hate me." Leif's voice cracked, and suddenly, his eyes seemed to fill with pain. I sensed his grip loosening over me. Within an instant, he seemed defeated. The wrath that had engulfed him suddenly disintegrated, but the passion in his eyes remained. He moved off of me and sluggishly recovered to his feet. I watched him turn his back to me as he started walking away. He returned over the path, moving in the direction where the others had gone.

I sat up from the mud, stunned, watching him walk farther and farther away from me without ever looking back. If I thought he had abandoned me inside the hollowed tree trunk near the fort, then what I felt now was his true rejection. I almost didn't know how to cope. I suddenly stood from the dirt, trembling.

I watched in stillness and in shock until he shortly vanished beyond the trees. He gave me the out—to no longer be with him. But I didn't feel that I actually wanted to take it—he was leaving me for sure. *What am I going to do...? Just stand here?*

Of course, I had no intention of going back to the Abenaki village. That was crazy! I wouldn't dream of making that choice. I suddenly darted out from the vegetation onto the trail. I perceived that he had already gone too far ahead. I started following in the direction he had gone—shaking and scared.

I STRAGGLED BEHIND, trailing Leif for quite a distance, weathered, tired, scared, hungry, thirsty, and still angry. He never simply glanced over his shoulder to check to see if I was following —obviously still fuming, too.

I didn't realize how far everyone else had traveled until they were finally sighted about a hundred and fifty yards ahead. His cousins turned, looking back behind themselves, noticing Leif approaching them, and they slowed to stop, waiting for him to catch up to them. They also noticed me lagging farther behind him. When he arrived at them, they said something inaudible to him, and he responded and kept walking past them. They glanced back at me after that exchange between them, aware something unfortunate had happened between us. Fearghus briefly said something to the cousins, and all but he resumed walking with Leif. As they started walking after Leif, Fearghus faced my direction and started heading toward me. He took his time pacing back over the narrow footpath and arrived to me sooner than I could have met him halfway.

"May I walk with ye, lass?" he inquired modestly. I was aware that he noticed how tired and out of sorts I was, to my embarrassment.

"Yes, thank you, Fearghus—if you don't mind?" I responded, clearing the tears from my eyes.

"Not at all," he said kindly. He was always very kind, and once again, he was proving how nice he was. He walked with me in silence. It was an uncomfortable silence at first since he fully knew that something bad had happened between Leif and me. Still, he kept my slow, feeble pace and mindfully helped me along the trail.

All the while, I hiked, my mind fixated on the terrible confrontation that had just happened between me and Leif. I couldn't believe that it had escalated to a physical point. I had never been in an altercation like that with anyone before in my life. It was truly unfortunate. I remained so upset about it that I was left feeling angry and distressed with tears. I was beside myself with regret. It seemed our relationship had been greatly damaged; I didn't know *how* or *if* Leif and I could repair it and ever be the same again.

As it seemed Fearghus was my only sympathizing companion, he assumed to be a spokesperson on my behalf by urging the guys to break often to keep me from collapsing during our trek through the mountains. It was a long, arduous journey, and the state of my exhausted condition slowed the men in this roasting summer heat. It seemed to take us forever to get to our next campsite, where we could finally rest until tomorrow. We were so far north in Vermont above Crown Point, New York, that I wondered if we'd ever make it back to Boston intact.

AT LAST, as the sun was beginning to set, we arrived on the final mountain ridge, and Lake Champlain was visible through the trees at a distance in the middle ground against New York's Adirondacks. But it would take us another day before we reached the shore.

We moved over the crest and hiked down a moderate gradient until we had arrived at rushing water. To my relief, I was glad they decided to stop here for the night. I went to the stream to quench my dying thirst as much as possible while they began setting up camp with a fire pit and fishing. But when I had satisfied myself with enough water, I noticed Leif had distanced himself from the group. He sat over a bolder away from everyone else. His shoulders slumped as he was digging a long twig into the silt, making a mindless little hole in the ground. Sometimes, he gazed at the turbulent stream in front of him. He didn't want anything to do with me, I knew, and I moved away from the place I was drinking water feeling quite dejected.

Fearghus took Leif's initiative and thoughtfully made a pallet of leaves for me to rest over on the ground, for which I was grateful. I was more than ready to relax now; it was too much of a day, and I was completely worn out. I approached Fearghus as I mechanically moved toward the bed of leaves, stealing a glimpse over my shoulder at Leif's melancholy figure fixed like a stone sculpture sitting on the rock in the coming darkness.

"Dinnae worry, lass. Give him time—he'll come about, ye will see," Fearghus said politely as he observed me noticing Leif. I wasn't so sure about having his confidence.

"Thank you, Fearghus. You're very kind," I said nevertheless.

"Thank ye, lass," he responded. "I reckon the fish is prepared tae eat now. I shall bring ye bit."

"Thank you very kindly," I replied gratefully.

"Indeed, lass." He went toward the guys around the fire, tearing at their pieces of fish, and I decided to sit my weary self over the leaves in solitude.

This time, as I ate alone, I had to make a conscious effort to slowly eat my food to prevent myself from getting nauseated. Leif sat eating with the rest of the men, but he didn't talk as his cousins moderately conversed with each other. Instead, he kept silent and remained glum.

When I had finished eating, I lay down over the leaves with my back facing everyone. I was dead tired like I had never been before, but my brain kept flashing images of the turmoil that had happened between me and Leif today. I couldn't shake the compounding emotions I was feeling, and tears began to roll from my eyes, mutedly, until I fell asleep.

❄

THE NEXT MORNING at the brink of dawn, we left our campsite and started trekking the rugged terrain again. But now we were moving down the mountain which made the effort slightly less rigorous, even though the sun and the humidity steamed the earth and made us extremely uncomfortable by causing us to profusely perspire. Fearghus remained my hiking partner, while Leif stayed clear of me the whole morning. Except for Fearghus looking out for me as we hiked over unpredictable terrain, everyone else ignored me like Leif. I was feeling bad over it all. Obviously, they had closed ranks, and I didn't think it was fair. But I still didn't have the drive or desire to attempt talking with Leif about anything just the same.

It wasn't until much later in the day, at dusk, that we finally reached the edge of Lake Champlain. The men seemed scarcely at ease as they retrieved the French bateau they had hidden in the cove. They shoved it out into the water. With little consideration, Leif faintly acknowledged my existence as he wordlessly seized me and lifted me inside the boat before the rest of the men got into the vessel. Derek and Cole pitched the sail, and it caught the wind, blowing us out over the water. The sun went down upon us as we glided south. The moon was large and full, lighting our way over the black water. I was surprised that Leif chose to sit next to me, considering how he shunned me with not even a word or a glimpse of acknowledgment from him the entire day.

As we sailed over the lake, the boat bobbed gently and pacified me to a considerable extent while water sloshed over the sides. I was extremely exhausted and my mind began to empty as I listened to the waves breaking against the hull, and soon I gave into my tiredness as I could hardly keep my eyes open any longer.

WHEN I HAD AWAKENED, daybreak was already upon us, and I discovered that I had been sleeping soundly with my head resting on Leif's shoulder. I suddenly straightened, and he shifted from me without a word. The bateau took us beyond Crown Point and Fort Carillon, past Lake Champlain, and we were now already halfway down Lake George. It wasn't until well after sundown we returned to the end of the lake and docked the boat.

When we landed onshore, we entered the French encampment now at Fort William Henry. It was crawling with missionaries who were tending to the wounded British and French soldiers. After entering the fort, Leif and his cousins shortly met with Montcalm's second in command, Brigadier Francoi-Gaston, chevalier de Levis, who was managing the aftermath of the siege. He civilly offered us food and shelter for the night and returned to us our horses that he had kept stabled while Leif and his cousins went searching for me.

When Leif and his cousins were preparing our departure from here for the next day, he opened one of his saddlebags attached to Blaze and whipped out a clean shirt that he had found.

"Haur," he said coldly, giving it to me. It was the last decent article of clothing that either one of us had left.

"Thanks," I said. He didn't say another word after giving me the shirt. I tossed the billowy garment over my head and modestly covered myself. He then retrieved an extra shirt from Angus and properly covered his bare chest. Another night would pass without him or anyone else speaking to me as all of us together camped under the stars near the fort. This time, at least, everyone seemed slightly less on edge since, for the moment, we were unlikely to be ambushed by the French or their Indian allies.

THE NEXT MORNING, as everyone was preparing to leave Fort William Henry for Fort Edward, I decided to finally approach Leif as he was saddling the bags over our horses. I felt apprehensive. Still, I had to speak with him. No one else was around and it was just the both of us in each other's company, so it was a good time to do it, I believed.

"Hi," I said hesitantly as he was buckling the saddlebags around Blaze. He turned his eyes to mine for the first time since our argument.

"Hullo," he said calmly and returned, looking at the bags he was fixing.

"May we speak for a moment first before we go?" I inquired carefully. He paused what he was doing and briefly stared at his hands over the horse's belts.

"Aye," he said, agreeing, and shifted his eyes back to me. It felt awkward between us, and I hesitated a little out of fear.

"I don't hate you... You need to know that's the truth," I said, feeling awful that I had ever said it. His face suddenly softened, and he seemed unguarded now. I could perceive the hurt materializing in his eyes as we gazed at each other.

"Weel..." He cleared his throat. "That is guid tae ken... I certainly dinnae hate ye either."

"That's good," I said sedately, agreeing also. A moment of uncomfortable silence ensued between us as we stood face to face, gazing at each other. I broke off my gaze and glimpsed at the dirt I was nervously picking from beneath my fingernails. "And," I started, looking back up at him, "you don't have to worry—I wasn't raped. Nothing like that ever happened to me with him. That's the truth, too." Leif leaned against his horse with his elbow up on the side of his saddle as if some of his strength unexpectedly had been sapped from him. He bent his head, covering his face with his hand, and took a moment in silence. He started to shake a little. After a minute, he withdrew his palm covering his face and lifted his head. He was flushed and rubbed his hand over his moistened eyes and cheekbones, clearing his expression.

"Guid," he said finally with a cracked voice.

"I'm so sorry this ever happened between us. I don't want it to be like this—and I'm really hoping that it won't last." As I was telling him this, my fortitude at once evaporated, and I uncontrollably became overwhelmed with emotion; my vision flooded with quiet tears. "But, I think you must understand my perspective too... because I was extremely frightened when you just left me out there all alone in the log—especially after you promised that you'd never leave me... You said you'd come back, but you didn't... so I became very, *very* scared." I paused, covering my eyes with my fingers, finally sobbing out everything bad that had ever happened to me in my life. I looked at him again through my watery gaze and wiped away some of my flooding tears. "I thought you were dead, Leif," I expressed breathlessly. "It brought me back to that same unimaginable moment of being alone again when I lost Matt. All of those same horrible, devastating feelings came rushing back. Except, this time it felt much, *much* worse—with you... and I didn't know what to do—even though you told me to stay there. I was just so scared. I thought I'd never see you again—because I thought you were dead."

Leif pinched his eyes again, and his lashes moistened further. He subtly nodded his head without a spoken word, seeming thoughtful to what I was saying.

"I did keep my promise tae ye, Sylvie. I returned fur ye," he said hoarsely after a pause. "But, I regret that ye whaur frightened... I understand yer fear."

"I just don't think that I could handle it again if you were gone," I sniffled miserably. "I can't go through that again..."

He nodded his head a tad some more in acknowledgment. "I was frightened too when I found ye missing." His voice was croaky; his eyes were bloodshot from fatigue and welling now with visible tears as he strove to keep his composure when he drew in a deep breath. "I didnae ken whit had happened tae ye, and I was struck with utmost fear." He cleared his throat again. "When I discovered ye missing, I straight away went lookin' fur ye without a mere thought." He blinked, and several silent tears dropped from his eyelashes. He took his hand, briefly wiping his eye with an open palm, then flipped it around to wipe the other eye. "I didnae care whaur my journey finding ye would lead me because I was going tae bring ye back tae me if it was the very last thing I was ever going tae do." I stared at him, listening, feeling worse. "Do ye ken how many men I have killed tae have ye back, Sylvie?" I meekly shook my head in response. "I have killed twenty men in my effort finding ye...

"I lost track of ye at one moment... in the mountains when a band of Ottawa waylaid us. I thought reit then that I had lost ye fur guid. I had nae notion how far intae perilous country they had taken ye... This land is vast and treacherous... Nonetheless, I would travel the distance just tae have ye back. I didnae sleep fur three nichts. I tracked ye by day and by moonlight—that is how I discovered ye as soon as I did. Yet, I would have scoured the earth and continued tae kill countless men who stood in my way tae get ye back tae me.

"I believed ye when ye told me that ye waur not a spy fur France or Spain—even when Fin was certain that ye waur. Loudoun is anither one—do ye ken why he didnae get tae treat ye the way he wanted tae when ye waur first delivered tae him?"

"No," I sniffled, staring meekly at him.

"It is because I prevented him from harming ye. Loudoun gave us orders tae turn ye loose upon the French and send ye tae Fort Carillon efter he was first done with ye. But I took ye back because I believed ye. I merely wish fur ye tae believe me too."

His voice was cracking as he kept speaking, and all the anguish in his eyes was visible. I had never seen him this way before. The tone in his voice was so different. It was like he had been destroyed. All his visible fury was gone, and he looked like an empty shell exposed. I stayed standing in front of him, quietly listening, completely shaken by everything catastrophic that had happened since Finley's death. I just didn't realize until now how absolutely unselfish Leif truly was. He desperately acted and unconditionally put his life on the line for me. He valiantly came all the way into enemy territory, miles and miles away north, to rescue me from the Abenaki. I had no clue what it took for him to do that, and I had not shown any real gratitude to him for saving me like I should have done.

"Then, when I finally discovered ye in the village, I wanted tae burn it down tae the ground with everyone in it... I am yer protector, Sylvie... Ye are my wife—and, thus, it remains." His eyes streamed tears, but he was still relatively composed. "'Tis true. Yoo're quite correct about whit ye said." He wiped his eyes again.

"What did I say?" I couldn't remember it all at this point.

"I shouldnae blame ye fur Fin's demise. Ye have nae part in it." He shifted a little from Blaze, watching his fingers on one hand mindlessly playing with the buckle straps on the saddlebag. He took his other hand and cleared his vision again. "And, 'tis also true whit ye said about my pride—it is hurt." He kept staring at his slowly fiddling fingers over the straps. He wouldn't look at me any more right now.

I couldn't stop the tears coming from my own eyes as I quietly remained standing before him; I was simply hurting too much. His voice became really low, making it hard for me to hear.

"*Dear God*, Fin is now gone, and I thought that I had lost ye also... Can ye not see whit is occurring tae me because of ye?" I merely looked at him through my watery gaze. "Ye huvnea the merest notion of the agony pressed upon me. Have ye?" he inquired with such a low voice; I thought it was a rhetorical question. "Yoo're the pulse of my heart. I'm tormented—yoo're wrenching my soul asunder, Sylvie."

The very same thing was happening to me also; I thought I would die from the grief. Tears escaped the corners of his eyes, rolling over his cheekbones just like mine. His fingers erased them from his pain-stricken face. He cleared his throat again, and then he didn't say anything. His hand also stopped moving over the horse's straps. "I cannae withstand it." His voice dropped so low that I almost didn't hear him.

I stepped closer toward him and carefully slid my palm over the back of his hand on the saddle. He didn't respond.

"I'm sorry, Leif. I'm so, *very* sorry. I didn't mean to hurt you. I don't ever *want* to hurt you," I wept breathlessly. "I'm really, really sorry." I entwined my fingers in his. His fingers contracted over mine, and he delayed looking at me. But when he did, our eyes met, and the look was deeply sincere and raw.

"I forgive ye," he said with a gravelly voice.

"You do?" I asked uncertainly.

"Aye," he replied in a soft tone.

"Thank you," I responded humbly in my own soft voice. It became quiet for a moment between us, and we both took the opportunity to dry our tears and collect ourselves.

"I ask fur yer forgiveness as weel. I said some things tae ye in the fit of anger that waur not polite. I apologize."

"Thank you. Well—understanding your point of view, I would have been quite angry too," I recognized.

"I reckon that ye quite whaur." A wan little grin eased his flushed face a bit. I smiled a little, too, in response.

"Yes, well," I said, still clearing my face, "I certainly forgive you too."

I pressed my hand firmly on his, and he squeezed my fingers, wrapping his palm around mine. He pulled me close, and we embraced each other. We were back together like before, holding each other like we used to. Leif was connected to me again; he gently stroked the side of my face, and I felt good about us once more. My sense of security and the love he exhibited toward me had returned. Things between us seemed refreshed and normal again—almost.

WE MOUNTED our horses and caught up with the others waiting for us at the edge of Fort William Henry. Leif and I rode side by side along the way, going south toward Fort Edward, and it felt more comfortable journeying with each other this time. But I sensed the dust had not yet completely settled between us. Unfortunately, things had been said and done that had caused emotional wounds, and there was a residual cloud from it hanging in the air between us. We had hurt each other, and there was a level of restriction now existing from him. The harm was fresh and deep—and would need time to heal, I recognized. And, even though we had apologized, the pain we had caused each other exposed a measure of truth that was unmistakable between us and could not be disregarded.

Thirty-Five

Riding on horseback now was such a blessing from all the arduous hiking we had done on foot. I was so glad to be finally sitting for the rest of the way home.

It started sprinkling on us as we traveled along the road. The light droplets felt good on my head and face while falling from the dark gray sky. The earth was beginning to cool and the rain gave us a break from the staggering sauna-like heatwave that had been relentlessly upon us for weeks. But by the time we had arrived at Fort Edward very late at night, it was pouring torrential rain on us.

I was shocked to see the fort overrun by a sea of men, appearing in the thousands, camped outside the fort walls. It seemed nearly half the existing colonial militias from the thirteen colonies were all here. We dismounted and closely meandered our way around people as we entered the fort and walked through the courtyard. Drenched from the rain, we finally entered inside and discovered the officers' barracks were nearly as crowded without a room to spare.

We unexpectedly encountered General Webb as he was nervously roaming around the dining quarter. He was startled at first to see us but was instantly pleased to learn that we had survived the French siege. He said that Colonel Monro had also survived and had arrived six days ago with a small contingent of five hundred survivors—the largest group to have arrived that endured the attack. Webb continued to explain the reason for the enormous number of men stationed here. Apparently, it was a result of the governors of New York, Connecticut, and Massachusetts who had received his urgent call for help to send to Monro. However, they had received notification not in time to assist, and the response was too late as troops were only now streaming in by the thousands.

After the brief updates, Webb very kindly offered for us to bunk in his office for the rainy night. The offer was gladly taken.

TWO DAYS LATER, we rode into Albany at last and twilight was just now upon us. It was a good feeling to be back in civilization again. We entered a nondescript, modest tavern inn, and I wondered why the guys had chosen to stay here for the night instead of at the Rasmussens' house as we had usually done before.

"I reckon it best we do not disturb the family this time, and this is the only place in town that has vacant quarters that soldiers have not yet taken," Leif explained as he was paying the innkeeper. It seemed like a courteous enough establishment; I supposed—at least for the soldiers who were gladly served up food and liquor by the bar maids.

Arriving from outdoors, drinks plus dinner were highly anticipated by Leif and his cousins. I noticed that the men were still distant with me and were eating in strained silence, which was uncomfortable for me to experience. Everyone but Fearghus, who continued to remain demurely polite toward me, and Leif, making sure that I had enough to eat and drink, still treated me as if I were nonexistent. Even Leif only kept to the basics as he refrained from his usual affection toward me while he occasionally refilled my mug and put more food on my plate. I was aware that they were all still displeased with me as I was sitting there in my buckskins, modestly covered by Leif's shirt. I was clearly made to feel ashamed.

I felt that I should say something to make it better. But I didn't know what to say or even if I should attempt it out of fear of possibly making the situation worse since it was obvious that the men were all incredibly angry at me.

"Um," I spontaneously heard myself start apprehensively in spite of my fear, breaking the glum silence. Eyes promptly turned on me with sullen expressions. "This is perhaps overdue, I'm sure, but I just want to finally say thank you to all of you for assisting my husband in my safe return. I know it was a dangerous thing for you to have done, and I want to let you know that I really appreciate what you did—so thank you. I'm very much appreciative. It won't ever be forgotten."

Blank expressions surrounded me at the table. Everyone seemed caught off guard by my unexpected apology and stared unresponsively at me for a second. They briefly glanced at each other without saying a word, appearing stumped.

"Er, aye, of coorse... We could never leave Seamus disappointed," Angus said expressionlessly. The uncomfortable silence ensued again. But now it seemed more strained, and everyone resumed eating awkwardly as they remained unspoken for the rest of the meal.

DINNER COULDN'T HAVE BEEN DONE and over with soon enough, I thought. It was such a relief to enter the privacy of our room—although it was as tight as a cloister cubicle. I was too exhausted to nearly not have the presence of mind to undress. I took off my moccasins and soiled attire and dropped onto the bed with little strength left from the day, once I had placed a clean shift over my body, which Leif had acquired for me.

"Oh it feels so good to be on a bed again," I said tiredly as my head sank into the pillow.

"Aye," Leif agreed. His tone was sober, I noticed. He seemed brooding as he set his bayoneted musket in the corner by the bed and unbuckled his pistol belts from his waist. He removed his broadsword from his baldric and leaned it in the same corner where he had placed his bayoneted musket. He took his unbuckled pistol belts, dropping them onto the chair, while keeping his sword belt in hand and meditatively folded it in half, not undressing any further.

"Aren't you going to get some rest now too?" I asked wearily, noticing him.

"Efter a moment," he said and faced me. He stepped toward me and stopped short at the edge of the bed.

"What are you doing?" I asked, sensing something wrong.

"Weel, it appears that we have some unsettled business tae mind," he said earnestly.

"What are you talking about?" I asked, puzzled.

"I need ye tae mind me, Sylvie."

"Mind you? I don't get it. Why are you standing there like that?"

"I need tae lay a matter tae rest," he said, slightly swinging the belt at his side.

"What do you mean?"

"I reckon I must have a word prior to my disciplining ye."

"*Disciplining* me?" I echoed confusedly, suddenly sitting up in bed.

"Aye," he said, pulling up a Shaker chair from the corner of the room and sitting directly in front of me. He put the strap across his muscular thighs, holding it secure on both ends. "The matter betwixt us is not yet entirely settled, and it must be laid tae rest before we carry on."

"What?" I inquired skeptically, noticing the strap pulled taut across his large thighs.

"I mean tae complete this business before we retire," he said flatly. I couldn't believe what he was thinking! I stared shockingly at him, feeling suddenly afraid.

"You can't be serious," I questioned, feeling dry in my throat as I swallowed hard.

"I am quite earnest." He was *dead* serious, and my heart began beating fast.

"So, you think whipping me is going to make everything better? Because, I can pretty much guarantee you that it's going to make everything one hundred times worse between us," I said nervously.

"I ken that ye say so since yoo're frightened, and ye micht be cross with me efter it is done. But, ye will come tae see that I have guid cause and yoo'll understand." His tone was mild, but his face was stern as heck.

"No! Are you *crazy*?" I responded, becoming excited. "You can't! It's totally illegal and you can go to jail for it."

"'Tis perfectly legal. It is within my reit as yer husband."

"I don't care! It's way outta bounds!"

A faint sigh came from him, and he thoughtfully pursed his lips. His shoulders slumped, taking an easier posture with me.

"That is precisely whit I mean fur ye tae learn. The fact being that ye dinnae care," he said reasonably.

"No—I *do* care. But this is *crazy*! I'm not going to let you just *hit* me like some ignorant piece of trash!"

"However, ye dinnae behave as though ye *do* care, Sylvina."

"But I care! I *really* do! Trust me—I'm telling you the truth. This is all unnecessary!" I couldn't believe that the very person I trusted with my life and who I loved, the one I considered my best friend and closest confidant, was going to betray me. I couldn't believe that he intended to commit the worst act imaginable that could ever be brutally committed by the one who was supposed to guard and cherish me—aside from being murdered.

Leif leaned carefully over his knees, assuming an even more calm approach.

"Ye are awaur that Loudoun thinks ye tae be a spy, do ye not?" he said carefully.

"Yes," I replied insecurely.

"Aye, that is reit," Leif said. "He has his sights set upon ye. He will do anything tae git his hands upon ye, as ye weel ken—in spite of me no less—and, now, it is quite personal betwixt him and me," Leif explained, suddenly looking dour once more. "So, when I had learnt that ye had been seized and marched tae Fort Hill and discovered ye in Loudoun's office thaur," his face was becoming red again from the sheer anger of thinking about it, "I wanted tae call him out fur a duel reit then and thaur. That is how outraged I was. The notion of him manipulating his way with ye in order tae take ye in spite of me... it is enough tae make me challenge him in such a manner. If I waur not already in jeopardy with the Crown, I would have certainly done so tae kill him immediately," He broke off, clinching his jaw, then collected himself again. "Instead, I decided it was more prudent tae keep alive and take better aim at ridding him fur guid off of the continent by political means.

"However, the concern is that Laird Loudoun is more friendly with King George than I—and he is awaur of my father's loyalty and affection fur his father, King James, and the French Crown... Still, I have a friend in Master William Pitt. Therefore, thaur micht be some hope yet regarding Loudoun's exile from the colonies altogether... Now that Loudoun knows that ye and I are wed, it would be easy fur him tae accuse me of treason. Did ye ken that?"

"No—I didn't," I said guiltily, turning my eyes down to my clean shift covering my knees.

"And, ye of coorse ken whit the punishment fur that is, do ye not?" I meekly nodded my head, feeling shame. "Aye," he said. "Thus, do ye suppose that it pleases me tae have learnt that the reason fur yer seizure was over the fact that ye had called an English officer a foul name?"

I didn't know he had known that part of it, and I unexpectedly stared at Leif, feeling more disgraced.

"I didn't know he was an officer," I muttered dishonorably. Leif arched an eyebrow. "No, I guess you wouldn't be pleased about that—either."

"Indeed I was not. I reckon the name ye used was '*dipshit*,' was it not?" He gave me a very disapproving look. I was further startled that he would have ever remembered the word.

"How do you know that's what I said?" I questioned nervously.

"Word travels fast."

"Yes—but that man was badly mistreating a poor little boy who was starving for food! He accused him of stealing, except I had paid for the food!" I justified quickly.

"Whilst I do indeed pity the lad, and perceive yer generosity tae him a noble deed, nonetheless, due tae yer lack of restraint, ye have pit me at further odds with Laird Loudoun."

"I'm sorry, I had no idea," I said genuinely.

"Apparently ye did not—which is the reason why ye must think before ye act, Sylvie," Leif said carefully. He paused for a moment, looking at me with a discerning eye. "Now, getting tae the most recent matter at hand. Yoo're awaur that we waur almost killed trying tae find ye in the highlands thaur in Algonquin territory?"

I glanced down at my nails nervously, picking at each other, utterly shamefaced. "I know, I'm really sorry about that, I feel really bad about it. I realize now I should've listened." I suddenly returned my eyes to his. "But, that's why I also apologized to the guys, because I realized that I had put them in danger too, and I didn't want them to think that I didn't care—because I do care. I would have said sorry to them earlier, but everyone was so mad at me, I just didn't know when to tell them."

Leif nodded with some consideration. "Weel, I respect that ye did tell them so."

"Well—so, good, I'm glad that you do. Then, can we please just simply put this all behind us now?" I stared at him with a very worried look. A light sigh came from him again as a sympathetic expression faintly crossed his face.

"I reckon if it waur merely ye and I, Sylvie, I micht contemplate not saying anither word about it. But, thaur are the other men tae consider in this circumstance. Ye risked them too, Sylvie, by giving them nae choice but tae follow me across enemy territory tae find ye. Ye put us all intae peril." He broke off, and his eyes landed on my crossed calves as I sat crisscrossed style on the bed. Then, he darted a razor look back to me. "I wanted tae raise Hell with the Indian who stole ye from me." He paused again, fixedly staring at me as his face became red all over again. I was unable to hold his gaze and looked down at the quilt. "Ye micht recall whit Monro said he would do if he caught deserters leaving the fort. Do ye recall that?" I nodded a little. "Weel, whit did he say then?"

"He said he'd hang them."

"Aye, precisely. If a man amongst us had done whit ye did, he would have suffered some sort of consequence. He micht have been flogged, or tarred—seared with a torch or hot iron. Or, he would have been downright shot if not hanged."

"Oh," I said with a hollow voice, returning my eyes to his.

"Now, I ken that yoo're not accustomed tae many ways. I have traveled a fair number of places about the world, and I realize those places I have visited have different traditions. But I have never met any lass—surely not one from this haur colony also—who quite shares your mannerism. So, I reckon ye must come from a home— whaur I dinnae ken—that has afforded ye quite a liberal upbringing as a lad that is not typically customary tae our ways haur." He shot me a pointed look. "And, I presume not even the Indian lasses are so free in their ways as weel... Surely, indeed, not one lass from Pennsylvania, I am certain, would behave in the manner in which ye do." He went silent again for a minute. My heart suddenly sank. "Therefore, I may be more lenient upon ye by considering yer innocence."

There was a long silence that followed. Until, I noticed him stand at the edge of the bed directly in front of me. He was gently swinging the belt lightly back and forth, and it slapped his muscular thigh.

"Alrecht now," he said. "Best git this over and done with—the sooner the better. Yoo've crossed my orders far enough and have caused grave harm."

"No! It's uncouth!" I burst out and scrammed off the bed to the other side of it, facing him.

"I must see tae it that ye are correctly punished, Sylvina. I told ye whit was going tae become of ye. Do ye recall it?"

Oh, I *recalled* it for sure. I threw myself off the other side of the bed, completely away from his reach, anticipating his move.

"Aye, weel," he said with a there-you-have-it tone. "I mean tae see it through."

"Over my dead body!"

"Dinnae tempt me." He swung the opposite end of the leather belt into his other hand and pushed the ends toward each other. The straps bowed apart. He pulled it taught again and the straps *snapped* loudly together.

"Like Hell! You've got another notion coming to you instead if you hit me, *pal*," I responded tremulously while radically wagging my finger at him.

"Shall I cleanse yer mouth out with soap too now?" he threatened. I suddenly bit my lip. "Ahh, I didnae reckon so," he said again and started pacing around the bed.

When Leif got beyond the halfway point, I bolted beneath the bed and flung myself to the other side. I stood facing him again, out of reach. He narrowed his eyes and scrutinized me for a moment as he remained still. I could see him thinking about what he was going to do. It came to mind that if he wanted to pulverize me, he could do it. There wasn't anything whatsoever that I could do to prevent him from doing so. He was tall, strapping, six foot three inches, two hundred pounds, against my five foot six inches, one hundred twenty pounds. Furthermore, I thought again over the fact that he could wield a forty-two-inch, five-and-a-half-pound, two-handed Claymore with one hand as if it were as light as a twig. It made the basket broadsword he carried in uniform appear light as a feather in contrast.

"Now listen haur, Sylvina—" he started.

"No, you listen! I already said I'm sorry!" I exclaimed suddenly. "It's not like I *intended* any of that on purpose! I promise—I'll never ever, *ever* do it again! I mean it—never, ever!"

"That is the entire purpose of this whole matter," he said logically. "I must see tae it that ye wulnae do it again—because ye micht disobey me once more." Rather than coming for me, he opted to talk some more and sat in the other chair facing opposite me. "Now, I realize that I have been quite permissive with ye fur some time yet, and it is because I reckon that ye have been permitted tae go about yer ways as ye please. Again, although I dinnae ken from whaur it is exactly ye come amongst the colonies, I understand that ye have been granted such privileges. I also recognize that such discretion has been granted tae ye, as I suspect ye have been accustomed tae a setting whaur one's survival is of little consequence. But, I must tell ye—life is serious, Sylvie. It is not a diversion fur amusement purposes. Thaur are consequences tae one's behavior—and those consequences involve life and death. Whit ye do or say not only affects how we micht manage our way in life, but it can also git us killed. Yer words or actions can also affect others in the same manner. So, that is why it is terribly imperative fur ye tae think before ye behave. And, when I tell ye tae do something, ye must obey me because it is fur yer own guid as weel as fur the guid of others.

"I am awaur that ye are trepidatious tae have tae learn this bold lesson. Yet, it is important fur ye tae ken the severity of the damage ye have caused, so that ye are certain not tae do it again. I am a man already in a perilous position, and I cannae afford any mistakes. How can I protect ye if I am dead?" he explained. I stared at him on the verge of tears.

"I'm so sorry. I didn't mean to," I said shakily.

"I ken ye would never intend tae cause me harm, Sylvie. But, ye micht simply do so unwittingly as yoo've already done thus far twice since we' have been wed. The reason fur yer repeated mistake is because ye dinnae believe me when I tell ye that certain matters hold peril." He paused momentarily, steadily looking at me. "Ye are indeed quite educated fur a lass… Yoo're intelligent—thaur is nae a doubt about it… and, I ken that yoo're in the habit of having yer own mind. I also ken," he arched a serious eyebrow, "that ye dinnae take kindly tae having tae abide by yer superior that is I. But, ye must learn tae listen tae me, yer husband, as I ken whit is best fur us both. And, taking into account that ye have imperiled the other men… I must punish ye upon their behalf as weel."

"Okay, okay, okay—alright," I said cautiously. "You're one hundred percent correct. I completely understand what you're saying. I was absolutely in the wrong. I'll listen to everything you have to say and follow exactly what you tell me to do from now on. No questions asked, even if I disagree."

"Guid." He stood from his seat on the chair and gently swung the strap against his thigh. "Now come from about the bed, and let's see tae it. Better git it done promptly."

"Are you crazy? I just *told* you that I was going to follow exactly what you say and that I wouldn't question you about it! How many times do I have to say that I'm sorry to you?"

He sighed heavily, totally frustrated, and rubbed his brow, showing it.

"Alrecht, now, that will be quite enough. Ye still yet arenae listening tae me. Now, ye listen tae me weel and guid. I understand that ye reckon yoo're remorseful, and I believe that ye quite are. However, that is merely because ye presently perceive my threat. Ye must repent in order tae reconcile the error of yer ways by accepting yer punishment, Sylvina. 'Tis the only course tae amend yer transgression—by accepting yer discipline. 'Tis yer debt." He suddenly revealed a look of embarrassment. "I can tell ye from personal experience that a guid whip across the crease places matters clearly intae perspective." I backed away farther from him with the bed in between us being the only thing protecting me so far. "I'm quite certain that ye have noticed how the lads arenae pleased with ye either, and they will remain so till this is done. 'Tis as I told ye earlier how yoo've thoughtlessly placed them at risk also. They deserve whit is owed tae them for their trooble." He took a deep breath.

"This is very bad psychology you're using," I argued.

"I dinnae ken whit psychology is, but I reckon that I am being quite reasonable with ye," he said.

"No, you're not! You're not using good judgment!" I replied.

"According tae my reason, I most certainly am using the best judgment," he specified. "Yoo're going to have tae brave the consequence fur yer transgression, Sylvina. Now, be a guid lass, come haur from about the bed, lift yer shift, and bend over."

"No! I'm not going to let you *hit* me!" I objected strongly. I didn't care how he substantiated it. I wholeheartedly did not believe in physical abuse—especially when it came to a man versus a woman. I was thoroughly offended and seriously terrified. I lifted a nervous finger to him and wildly shook it. "Don't you dare take one step toward me! You do, and I'll—"

"Or whit?" He gave a challenging look.

"I'll—I'll make sure that you'll be *really* sorry if you lay a single finger on me!" I threatened firmly.

"Is that reit?" His golden eyebrows shot up. "Weel, ye look haur, lass, I'll come reit over thaur this very minute and turn ye across my knee tae leather yer crease if ye dinnae come tae me now."

"You're gonna have to make me 'cause I am *not* gonna subject myself to any kind of brutality!"

"How did I ken that ye would be so intolerably obstinate." He sardonically shook his head and started across the bed to get me. There was not much leeway in the room. I sprang toward the tall armoire in the corner and forcefully squeezed myself behind it.

"Keep away from me!" I shouted. In a couple of easy steps taken, he now stood at the crack between the furniture and wall, eyeing me hidden through the slit. It occurred to me this was probably not the best hiding choice, since I had trapped myself in the corner. He grinned insufferably and began pushing the heavy, solid oak armoire away from the wall. I squashed myself as tightly as I could in the corner to stay clear of him. He grunted some while moving the heavy piece of furniture. But, in no time, the space had widened, and his hand snagged my wrist. I pounded my fist repeatedly on his arm to no avail as he tugged me out from behind the armoire. "I'm gonna scream my head off, you know!"

"I reckon so—before I lay a hand upon ye, I'm certain of it. But more so, I ken, once I have at ye. I expect that all of Albany will hear ye. Ye have the breath fur it. But that is quite alrecht—yoo'll survive. I promise."

I dug my heels into the floor as he pulled me. Little good did that do except burn the bottom of my bare feet. I kicked him in the shin and hurt my toe. I wrenched my wrist, pinched his skin, and pounded his arm, to no consequence—unfortunately. He unceremoniously spun me around and tossed me onto the bed, face down, leaning a solid hand into my back, fixing me still. I squirmed frantically and luckily shot out beneath his grasp across the bed onto the floor away from him like a cat pouncing out of a water puddle.

"You big sadistic oaf! You keep your hands off me!"

"I intend tae do it, Sylvina! All ye have tae do is abide by me, and it will be an easy task."

"Oh yeah—easy for you, of course!" I mentally did a quick scan of the room.

"If ye dinnae cooperate, then I shall lash ye past the half dozen till ye tire. And, I assure ye that ye will relent far sooner than I."

"Matt would never have done what you're trying to do to me right now!"

"Weel, now I am not Matt. Am I not?"

"That's the problem—he was civilized! And you're obviously a *barbarian*!"

"Weel, I would bet my fortune that if ye had gravely transgressed against Matt the way ye have transgressed against me, he micht have likely punished ye as weel."

"No, he wouldn't have!"

"Aye, he indeed would have."

"You don't know that!"

"I do ken it."

"No, you don't! Because he would've never struck me! That's not the kind of man he was!"

"Be that as it will. I am certain that any man in my position would do whit is expected of him tae exercise his duty in this regard."

"He would never hit me!"

"That is why yoo're spoilt."

"I'm not spoiled!"

"Yoo're going tae ken some humility, Sylvina."

"Humility?"

"Aye."

"Are you kidding me?"

"Do I appear as though I am jesting?"

"Like I said, Matt would never beat me for any mistakes I might have made!"

"Och! He was a saint now, was he? Pardon me fur being a demon! But he spoilt ye like the dickens. Yoo're disobedient and saucy. Now, git over haur."

I zoomed to the door and tried the handle. It flung open—thank God! I beelined through the corridor over the landing. Leif was hot on my tail, and I flew down the staircase overlooking everyone socializing in the tavern. Attention all around was suddenly drawn in my direction as I rapidly descended the staircase. I flew around the bar and started zigzagging around tables with him close behind me. I accidentally sideswiped a barmaid as she was carrying a large tray of dirty dishes back to the kitchen and ungracefully toppled over her, sending her to the floor beneath me. Dishes wildly crashed, breaking all over the floor, clearly resonating throughout the room.

"*Och!* Yoo've done it now, lass!" Leif said with definite displeasure in his voice while towering directly above me.

Before I had the chance to move, in one big swoop, he hauled me up and swung me over his shoulder like a sack of potatoes.

"Put me down this instant! You backward, uncivilized lout!" I shouted, kicking and punching him over his back and shoulders as he started carrying me away back toward the staircase. He ignored my thrashing around. "You crazy barbarian!" I shouted again.

Hardly deterred, he made his way up the staircase with me, throwing myself unruly in every direction as he bound me securely over his shoulder. I accidentally banged my head against the wall as he rounded the corridor, hurting myself. But within a minute, he returned me inside our room. The door *clicked* shut, this time making sure he had latched it. He threw me over the bed again, and I pounced back up on the mattress with my hands visibly prepared for self-defense.

"Come any closer, and I'll karate chop you!" I hissed wrathfully.

"I dinnae ken whit a karate chop is, but I reckon that I can hold my own against it." He glowered at me.

"I'll never *ever* forgive you for this! You uncouth, prehistoric primate! You psychopathic—moron! You horny pervert!" I seethed. "You're totally enjoying this! I can see it!"

Leif pulled up the belt, tugging it tight in his hands, and slowly arched it back and forth.

"I dinnae ken the meaning of those words. But, since I am able tae forgive ye fur all that yoo've done tae me, then I reckon yoo'll be able tae forgive me also—once yer crease is nae longer black and blue." He tightened his lips and glowered at me again. Although, I also detected a scarce, wan smirk on his face. "And, as for my enjoyment of this, ye have tried my patience far enough. Now, ye deserve whit is coming tae ye." He gave me a stern look again and snapped the belt. "Now, git over haur."

"You're gonna have to make me first!"

"As ye wish."

"Stay away, or I'll—"

"Or whit?"

"I'll—I'll—you'll regret it! You just better stay away!"

"Not by any means. Now git."

OH, I was stark raving livid at Leif Charles Seamus MacLeod FitzJames Stewart! If ever the Furies existed, the deities sure paid me a good visit tonight! In all my days of living, I was never so angry at anyone as I was with him. Curse Leif Charles Seamus MacLeod FitzJames Stewart and his evil Scottish ass! He could go straight to Hell and stay there for all I cared! I'd be so lucky if I never had to look upon his wicked face again! *How dare he lay a finger on me!*

It was a terrible, hideous night. All I could do afterward was lie awake in bed on my stomach in burning pain, cursing Leif's soul to the Devil. At least he didn't escape injury from me, however, while trying to achieve his point. I had a piece of him, too—brief though it was—following the first stinging crack of the strap over the flesh of my bare bottom. A short struggle occurred, which landed him a nice fat lip and a bloody nose. Not to mention the four attractive gashes running down the side of his face and the serious teeth impressions torn into his forearm. Unfortunately, that was only accomplished to serve his purpose to further lash me until his heart was content and I had reached the end of my struggle, leaving me to feel like I was nearly left at death's door as I thought I'd black out.

Leif had enough insight, however, to leave the room after he was done. He didn't return for a couple of hours later once I'd already blown out the candle in the lantern. He also had the brains not to attempt climbing into bed with me and instead slept on the floor near the opposite side of the bed. In that case, I couldn't even see him. A very good thing! Motionless in bed, I heard him on the floor, briefly shifting around. He took a really deep breath and sighed before relaxing.

Much too angry, upset, and physically uncomfortable, I found it quite difficult to sleep. I lay in bed, unable to shake from my mind what Leif had done to me, and my anger just continued to mount. At one point, I had grown so furious over all of this that I nearly had the mind to simply get out of bed and walk over to him on the floor to deliver a merciless kick in his groin. But doing that would have just further escalated the situation. So, the thought left my mind.

As I was forced in misery to just lie there, however, I started thinking. To my displeasure, I began considering that maybe there might have been some validity to his perspective. Perhaps I had been taking things too lightly; I really never thought about it until now. It wasn't as though I was intentionally flippant about matters. I just supposed that I somehow viewed living in this place as less threatening, in a strange paradoxical twist, than existing in my own era. Life in my own society was overpopulated, highly complex, and moved at lightning pace with little time to reflect or consider others—generally speaking.

There were multifaceted integrated issues vitally influencing every country. My own father was a U.S. military veteran, and he would sometimes tell us about his war experiences. So, I was aware that wars took place and the effects that were rendered on soldiers, their families, and the aftermath left on both friendly and foe populations. I had witnessed the Oklahoma City bombing, the first World Trade Center bombing, the wars in Bosnia, the genocide in Uganda, the war in Somalia, the September eleventh World Trade Center Massacre, and the ensuing wars in Iraq and Afghanistan—and all the natural disasters that had occurred in between. So, I knew that suffering existed. But, all of that had been witnessed through the lenses of the media via television, periodicals, or the internet and essentially removed me from the actual experience of those tragedies.

I suppose, the more I thought about it, the fortune of high technologies pervasively used had shielded my whole society from certain unpleasant truths. It created a protective bubble for us to live inside, where we went about our insulated daily lives isolated from others, even within our own communities, including the rest of the world. In addition, if we were ever faced with our own personal problems, there was always room for escape, allowing us—if we wanted to—to indefinitely ignore the problem ailing us by diverting our attention onto more pleasant subjects.

There was nowhere for me to run or hide now; I was stuck here with Leif's sorry ass. I couldn't take refuge with my parents, cry on my girlfriend's shoulder, hop on the web for social support, chat on social media with friends, divert myself with my electronic devices, listen to music on a whim, watch TV, escape with a movie, or dive on my cellphone just to talk to my brother from any given location. I couldn't even get inside my car and just drive indefinitely to any irrelevant place. There was nowhere for me to turn to receive pity and comfort.

Pity. Was I pitying myself this whole time? It dawned on me that, conceivably, maybe I was. I supposed I hadn't actually realized it before. Where I came from, everything was so effortless;

when we wanted anything, we could get it on a whim if we could afford it.

People really didn't seem to *need* each other, pertinent to their very own survival in the postmodern world. It was strange, really; the world was hyper-connected via information, communication, and commerce on a swift, continual basis but detached from macro inter-human connectedness. But microcosmically, everyone still loved their families and close friends because that was what was important to them. Here, however, everyone needed one another because their very lives depended on it; it didn't matter what the scenario was. People counted on each other—from a political, social, and economic level all the way down to the close familial circle.

So, I started thinking about Leif and scowled angrily. It was so important where I was from not to be needful of other people—particularly for women. It was incumbent upon them to receive the highest level of education possible in order that they could achieve economic and social autonomy from others—particularly from men. We learned to place our value in the number of degrees earned, the amount of work we did in our chosen fields of profession, and the number of things that could be acquired by us while simultaneously being married and having a family too, because that was the meaning of our successful independence. But now I had realized that my success was determined by the happiness of my personal relationships. Furthermore, the reality of the matter was that my personal truth had changed, and that it now began and ended with Leif.

I resented that I was giving Leif any credit at all. I carefully turned from my stomach onto my side embittered by the physical pain he had caused me.

Still, he was a real living breathing man who bled just like any other man existing in the twenty-first century. A dead man in 2017 was no different than a dead man in 1757. He was so real to me; probably the realist person I'd ever known and had reminded me in some remote way of Matt, although they were categorically different in terms of their personalities, appearances, and backgrounds. Because of this, my current surroundings seemed to fade into insignificance. The environment in which I found myself was idyllic compared to the smoggy skies and grid-lock traffic congestion in which I was formerly immersed. But a bomb was a bomb. It didn't matter if it was launched from a howitzer by men in redcoats or launched by pilots flying F-22 Raptor stealth fighter jets high in the sky; death and destruction were all the same. The only difference was the capacity of magnitude to create annihilation: a single mortar exploding at a time versus weapons of mass destruction detonating simultaneously at any given time from any single place around the globe. It didn't matter if it were muskets firing a shot as opposed to fully automatic machine gun rifles spraying countless riddling bullets everywhere. Still, death was death no matter what the scale or what era in which it took place.

I suppose this is why I was so intensely upset: the fact that Leif bled real blood, and we did, in fact, have a deep-seated, inexplicable bond with each other, which eerily collided my two disconnected realities together. The image of Leif's face sharply entered my mind, the way he looked when I saw him for the first time in days when he stood there at the center in the Abenaki village. He was haggard, blood-stained, and worn from tirelessly searching for me. He fearlessly fought and killed men because I had been kidnapped. He raged with anger and fear, believing that I had been hurt, and his expression knotted from the pain of my verbal abuse, made me feel worse.

Maybe... maybe I did cross the line. I guess it was irresponsible of me to have not remained hidden where he had told me to stay. If I had, I wouldn't have been kidnapped.

He was right; I should have stayed. My actions nearly got him killed, and my heart froze with panic at the thought of losing him.

Furthermore, it wasn't the first time he had risked his life for me, I distinctly remembered, and my stomach churned with dread.

I further put him at risk with Lord Loudoun, which, as he hinted, could get him killed. It would kill me if anything bad were to ever happen to him. I suddenly sat up in bed wanting to tell him that I was sorry again and to offer him a place in bed. The sudden weight on my bottom electrified the pain of his awful deed all over again, and I just as quickly changed my mind. I angrily tossed my head back into the pillows, silently griping and bitching.

Granted, I thought unhappily, there was more that had to be considered. Very disgruntled about it, I had to admit that he was right—again. I had come from a place that allowed me full freedom to exercise my life the way I saw fit according to me. I could say or do anything I wanted with little or no consequence to anyone. If I got into a disagreeable discussion with a stranger on the streets of LA or New York City, who cared? That stranger would always remain a stranger, and we'd simply move on with our daily lives, disregarding that we had ever met with relatively no consequence to me or to the other person, despite our expressed unfriendly opinions toward each other. I supposed it was because society was just too big and busy for people to actually care about bothering with another person who was perceived to be of no importance to them.

But that didn't apply to living here. This place was completely different. Apparently, deeds and words truly mattered very much; they established the crux of a person's integrity within the community, no matter how small or large the society might be. Compared to my flexible mammoth society, this one was small, tight-knit, quaint, and rigid with strict customs. It was certainly not a "woman's" world—not anything close to the Women's Liberties Movement mentality that was so inherently ingrained in my culture. Here, men and women were correspondingly boxed in within their respective sexual roles between homemaker and provider—nothing else. People lived their lives according to what was expected of them, not according to their individual aspirations.

But I had to admit, even though I really did not want to, that I supposed Leif didn't truly have to marry me. Instead, he could have merely abandoned me to the whims of others like Lord Loudoun, for instance, or just selfishly kept me around for himself and done to me as he pleased without any consideration. I'm now convinced that I easily could have had a much harder time and probably could have fallen into some form of indentured servitude if not flat-out slavery. Except, he wasn't like that. No, instead, he showed me much kindness and chose to make me his wife, which offered me sanctuary and significant social standing: something I know I otherwise would not ever have been afforded under any normal circumstance here.

He made it clear: *I am a duchess*. What a very odd idea... I didn't believe in holding titles. The concept of aristocracy, in general, was unattractive to me and foreign. Still, since this was my new lot in life, admittedly there was responsibility in my new position which belonged to me and which I had not fully grasped until now. It was a difficult adjustment for me to have to make; it went against my natural inclination to freely be my own person and to be inherently respected for the independence that I would have found by my peers in my society.

Still, I had no choice but to recognize where I was now, as I also suddenly realized simultaneously that I was coming to terms with the fact that I would probably never enjoy the freedoms of my former life that I had so easily taken for granted ever again. Although this society was small and seemingly simple, social interconnections remained complex, highly visible, and potentially dangerous to one's autonomy or life. A good word or deed went a long way in this place, and vice-versa for anything done wrong.

The place where I was from centered upon the individual and valued uniqueness. That was quite different from this era, which valued and accepted uniformity in conformity. I suppose that I did have to rethink my alternative mode of behavior with respect to

Leif; what I perceived as normal was evidently not according to his condition or perspective.

I guess... I guess that I should have paid closer attention to what I had said to that dog-face officer in Boston. I thought now that I should probably be more mindful about what I say or do in the future since, apparently, my actions could adversely affect Leif's high-wire balancing act with his close political ties. The thought of his head being lopped off for treason over something I mistakenly might have done turned my stomach.

And what about all that? Tyranny, imperialism, monarchies, totalitarianism, and the Divine Right of Kings? One king over another? Hannovers versus Stewarts? England versus France and Spain? Who controlled which territories and on what part of the globe? How was I involved in any of this? My national identity began with the American Revolution. Before that, everything else in history seemed sort of obscured. All these names, places, dates, dogmas—so much to remember—were slightly glossed over in history classes; they were just a bunch of names and dates in books and seemed rather trivial to me. Compared to the rise of Communism and Socialism manifested in Hitler's evil Third Reich, Stalin's brutal Soviet regime, and the Cold War in general, I supposed it was all the same. The bottom line was the struggle for power over others and the right for one to exist freely from oppression. It's a situation that seemingly keeps repeating itself in history.

So, as I angrily continued putting things into perspective, I guess it was actually relevant which king ruled and what side of the political fence one chose to sit on in order to survive; and, when I looked at it through this lens, then I supposed it was misguided of me to have originally thought that this period in time was less aggressive than my own time when in fact it was proving to be quite the opposite: literally dangerous and cut-throat.

I heard Leif breathing steadily but lightly from his blind spot on the floor. I guess he couldn't sleep either. *Good—I couldn't be happier!*

＊

I DIDN'T SLEEP a wink last night since I was caught up between episodes of wrath and rationalization. I stayed in bed pretending to keep my eyes shut, still seething when Leif got up off the floor early this morning. I didn't bother granting him a single spoken word as he moved to the washbasin and began shaving his Grizzly Adams beard and mustache off his face. When he was finished, he dressed and quietly left the room.

In about three hours he had returned with parcels in hand. He noticed me lying in bed awake and paced to the foot of the bed. He set the parcels down over the quilt, easily untied the strings, and unfolded the fabric wraps.

"I have replaced yer riding attire along with yer favored breeks. I reckon yoo'll find them tae yer liking." He spread the nicely fashioned attire over the bed for me to see. "Once yoo've dressed, come have a morsel tae eat. The lads are awaiting as we must take our leave not before long."

I slowly moved out of bed, feeling every aching muscle in my bottom, angering me to the hilt all over again. Ignoring his existence, I strode to the washbasin on the dresser and started refreshing myself with soap and water. Afterward, I began taking my time to dress. When I was nearly finished, I paced around the room, tying the ribbons just so over the front of my riding jacket, fussing over them as I tried to tie them into perfect bows. Once satisfied, I then worked on my hair as I flipped my bobbed curls up at the ends around my head and messed with the placement of my pixie bangs over my brow while viewing myself in the looking glass. Stalling for time as I examined my appearance in the looking glass, I wasn't certain about encountering the other guys, and I wished there was some way for me to get out of it.

"'Twill be alrecht, Sylvie. The lads wulnae bite ye as yoo've done yer poor husband." Leif winked at me and smirked with his slanted fat lip. "Now, keep yer pecker up." He lightly tapped the end of my nose, and I quickly slapped his finger down. "Ooo! Yoo're fortunate that we huvnae the time. Otherwise, I would roger ye weel and guid reit now." He winked at me again, and his busted lip twinged. I glowered at him, not the least bit amused. He shook his head and left the room, leaving me to myself.

HOW ON EARTH could he be right again? The fellows kindly welcomed me back into the fold with gentle morning greetings. Like the Ice Queen, however, I coldly kept my eyes off Leif as he sat with everyone at the table over cider, bread, salted venison, and cheese. As far as I was concerned, Leif had dropped off the radar far from the face of the planet. I swore to myself that it would be a cold day in Hell before possibly acknowledging his mere existence again.

Considering the fresh, fragile state of my rump, I chose to nibble a bite of venison pottage and sip a bit of sweet lemon water while standing at the bar. Cole and Fearghus came up to me as I stood there eating alone. Fearghus slipped a brotherly arm around my shoulder, and Cole compassionately looked at me with his caterpillar eyebrows.

"May we ask if yoo're alrecht, as we hope that ye are, lass?" Cole asked.

"Aye, it soonded as if ye waur being slain," Fearghus said, seeming sincere by the expression on his face. I felt my ears and face become hot and shot them both a sharp look.

"Yeah, well, I guess I've accidentally married the *Terminator*," I commented frigidly, trying to keep my cool. Cole's caterpillars lifted high on his brow.

"The *Terminator*?" Cole snorted.

"Yeah, he just goes around killing everyone," I answered irritably.

"Now thaur Seamus, ye didnae have tae nearly murder yer

poor wife tae git yer meaning tae her. A simple talkin' tae would have sufficed tae gain her understanding, would ye not have reckoned so?" Cole said.

I fired a dagger look at Leif. He was careful not to meet my gaze and instead meticulously focused on the piece of bread he was buttering without answering.

"She ought tae consider herself fortunate fur merely a blackened backside. Nae harm in that," Angus said with a mouth stuffed with venison.

"Aye, nae harm in that at all. I've knoon some women folk that have received far harsher punishment than a blistered crease from their men," Derek said after swallowing the food in his mouth.

"Aye, her bonnie white teeth still remain in her head," Liam said.

"Aye," Bearnard agreed as he took a swig from his mug.

"Micht ye care tae join us with a seat at the table, lass?" Lachlan asked, grinning.

"No, thank you," I said with self-respect. Snickering easily went around between the cousins at the table.

It proved not to be so bad, though, as I stood there eating something for my morning meal. There was some light banter that went back and forth between them about it. Leif was smart, however, to remain quietly eating his food throughout the teasing. I resentfully started thinking that he might have been right all along—even though I still wanted to inflict some sort of severe bodily injury on him just to satisfy myself.

RIDING on Oakley was absolutely out of the question. I didn't know how I was going to manage it as I stood there in front of her hard leather saddle, skeptically eyeing it. It was going to hurt like hell as I suddenly realized what I was literally going to be up against. Leif thickly folded his blanket and inserted it over my saddle. If he was suddenly feeling guilty, compassionate, or just looking for some kudos, he was barking up the wrong tree and sure as heck wasn't going to get any kind of positive acknowledgment from me, no matter how thoughtful he meant to be. I feebly pulled myself over Oakley into the saddle and painfully eased onto the cushion he had created for me without wanting help from him.

It was a grueling ride maneuvering our way back over the Mohawk trail bound for the Berkshires. Every step Oakley took transmitted another blow to my already sensitive rump, and I wasn't sure how much more of this I was going to be able to take. Boston seemed to lie forever in the distance at this rate, and I thought I might just break down and cry from the pain. It seemed the men had developed a particular code of silent chivalry for my benefit as they paced the trek nice and slowly with abundant rest stops in between along the way. They took the opportunity to relieve themselves, refill canteens with water, allow the horses to refresh by the streams, or merely stretch their limbs. Since we were somewhat safer back in the British wilderness on our way home, I supposed they could afford some concession on my behalf, for which I was silently grateful.

Leif and I rode apart from each other, never once exchanging a word the entire time on the path. Once again, it was Fearghus coming to the rescue, keeping me polite company as we continued along the way. Due to all the breaks taken, we didn't make much headway out of New York. The men had set up camp just before sundown in a pasture around a small lake where the altitude began to elevate. Utterly beaten, quite literally, in addition to the ride, my temper had not come close to being assuaged. So, as soon as Leif had put up the tent, I decided to turn in for the evening and entered it. He followed me toward the tent, but I turned just before he entered and whipped the canvas, opening closed squarely in his face before he reached inside of it.

He may sleep outside with the rest of the animals!

❄

THE NEXT DAY, we bumped around for several hours, making our way now higher up in the Taconic Mountains. The going was rougher this time around, and I constantly kept shifting in my saddle. Finally, I couldn't take it anymore. *To Hell with it all!* I decided to come down off my horse. Noticing me, everyone drifted to a stop, and I simply started walking instead without worrying about further slowing the train down.

"I shall walk with her, Fearghus," Leif suggested quietly to my companion before he was about to dismount from his horse and pace with me.

"Aye," Fearghus acknowledged and stayed planted on his horse.

"Then, we shall meet ye at the fort," Angus said.

"Aye," Leif agreed.

"Alrecht then, dinnae tarry fur long if ye intend tae make it by nichtfall. Or we shall come looking fur ye thinking something ill befell ye," Angus said.

"Aye," Leif said. He swung down from Blaze and started walking beside me instead of Fearghus. The others started lightly galloping away, turning into obscured spots bouncing over the road. Leif and I were now left behind in the forest alone together as we proceeded walking in silence.

Well, well, well... So, he's going to walk with me, huh? So be it. Hell will have to freeze over first before I'd utter a single syllable to him: the atrocious, sadistic, knuckle-dragging, brutal ape!

Funny, though... he didn't look very much like a beast as the radiant sun beamed down on him, setting him aglow like an angel between the trees. Still, I closed myself off to him and froze my heart believing that I wanted nothing more ever to do with him. So, I just limped along, ignoring his presence.

After twenty minutes or so into our walk over the path, I sensed that he wanted to say something to me, but I continued imagining he was nonexistent. Observing me, he remained quiet instead as we continued pacing along.

"Yoo'll be more comfortable tomorrow, I imagine," Leif said offhandedly at length as he kept an eye on me.

"Your imagination has malfunctioned seeing how you've nearly crippled me," I shot back, unable to help my angry feelings.

"If I had crippled ye, ye wouldnae be walking now," he replied.

"Oh, you're so merciful then, aren't you?" I scowled at him. He took a deep breath and sighed as he rubbed his brow.

"I recognize that ye are vexed at me. Yet, ye must understand why 'twas done. Still, it disnae please me that I had tae swing my strap at ye," he said.

"Oh? And how do you suppose it makes me feel? Or do you care at all?"

"I do care." He raised his eyebrows, appearing genuine about it.

"You've got a funny way of showing it," I derided sullenly. "You seem pretty good at beating people up." I glowered at him. He chuckled a little, to which I was surprised, and I frowned angrily at him. "Did I say something funny?"

"Weel, nae," he said, sounding unfazed by my bad attitude. "Merely, I have never had tae discipline anyone myself till now— not even a soldier ever."

"Congratulations. There's a first time for everything, I suppose. You must be really proud of yourself."

"I'm not proud of it."

"Well, you got something out of it—I'm sure."

He looked at me, unguarded. "I shall have ye ken that I have had my fair share of being on the other end of the stick," he said. I looked at him with sudden surprise; it was hard to imagine anybody being able, or having the guts, to crack a disciplining stick over his backside. But then again, I just as quickly remembered that particular story involving him and a barn as a kid he'd once told me about.

"Still, I bet you were tough as nails as a kid, and no one could make you cry for anything while you got a whupping," I said resentfully. He chuckled and glanced down at his walking feet.

"That isnae true," he said, returning his gaze to me.

"That's very hard to believe," I said.

"'Tis true, however, I had my crease whipped countless times as a laddie by my uncles or by the schoolmaster fur getting into mischief and jesting about in the school chamber. I liked tae jest a bit in the school chamber, making the other lads laugh. It wisnae admirable—I got plenty scolded fur it."

"*Hmph*, interesting," I remarked, keeping my eyes on the road ahead of us.

"Not tae mention the time I burnt the barn down tae the ground... Ye recall that I told ye about that occurrence."

"Yeah, I remember that story."

"Aye, weel, I got a fairly bad licking fur that one. It left me quite blistered. I wisnae able tae sit upon my backside fur a week efter that occurred." I just gave him a mean glare without a word. "Thaur was also the time I got my crease beaten fur using all of the chicken eggs fur target practice with my sling. Also, fur stealing my Uncle Iain's pistole tae shoot pheasants up in the tree, which spooked the horse my cousin, Risteard, was shoeing, and he got kicked in the head fur it. And, I got beaten fur the time I decided as a jest tae throw a basket of toads intae my Uncle Cailean's chamber whilst he was upon the chamber pot. Also, fur jesting about by snatching the chair from beneath my much older cousin, Coinneach, as he was about tae take his proper seat at the dining table, which made him fall flat on his crease upon the floor." Leif paused momentarily.

"Well... I suppose it's kinda expected for a boy who's nothing but a handful to get a spanking every once in a while. But, I'm a grown woman, so I don't think it can be compared," I scowled at him again.

"Weel, my father wisnae particularly an affectionate man, but he was sensible and just. In all the time I had spent living with him, he had punished me merely once."

"You don't say?" I gave Leif a skeptical look.

"Aye, indeed—and he had done so when I was far older than a wee lad."

"Is that right?"

"Aye."

"How old?"

"I was seventeen years of age. I was grown, mind ye."

"What happened?" I asked despite my sour mood.

"Weel, being a lad with a quick tongue, I found myself quite admired amongst the lads in King Louis' Court. 'Tis common fur lads tae want tae impress one anither with wit and experience, ye ken... Yet, this particular incident pertained tae a lass—a young lady new tae Court at the time had come tae wait upon the queen. She was a bonnie lass from Ireland—innocent tae France and its ways. Her name was Miss Imer. Many of the other lads reckoned she was quite bonnie also... A bit of time had passed since her new arrival, and Miss Imer and I took kindly tae one anither fair enough. Like most lads who seek nothing but the enjoyment of feminine company, I had it in mind tae kiss her... and as we waur kissing, a friend of mine discovered us in the garden.

"Weel, lads like tae goad each other into proving their manly standing amongst one anither—and so, I expressed tae my chums some information that had taken place with the lass that in truth didnae occur beside the kiss."

"Is that right?" I said interestingly with a disapproving glare.

"Unfortunately, 'tis true," he replied with some visible embarrassment.

"So, you were a schmuck," I said unmoved.

"Whit is a schmuck?"

"A guy who does things like that."

"Och... aye, weel, I wisnae thinking about whit I was doing at the time. I merely invented the tales tae impress the lads—and I had succeeded, fur I became further weel liked amongst them."

"Good for you," I said sarcastically, keeping my eyes off him and looking straight ahead.

"Nae," he said negatively, shaking his gilded head. "It wisnae guid fur me, or fur the lass since she began receiving many unsolicited overtures from various lads. Her aunt, Lady Henrietta, was none too pleased about it and blamed me fur it—rightfully so she did." I gave him a sidelong glance. "So, Lady Henrietta decided tae discuss the matter with my father."

"Really?" I said sarcastically.

"Aye."

"Who can blame her? I would've boxed your ears myself." Leif chuckled briskly. I frowned at him.

"I dinnae doubt that ye would have done so," he said ironically. "Aye weel, my father wisnae the least bit pleased about whit I had done either, and he addressed King Louis at Court efter his birthday feast. He revealed all whit had occurred tae the king. My father decided tae ask the king's permission tae punish me reit thaur in everyone's presence at Court... Of coorse, the king, taking it as mere entertainment, granted my father permission. So, my father grabbed me by the ear and pulled me front and center into the hall whaur all could see. I was told then tae face the lass I had slighted, raise the tail of my coat, and yank my breeches tae my knees. I was instructed tae kneel over, and father ensued, delivering a series of thrashing, burning whips from his stinging cane upon my crease."

"Did he?" I inquired, finding myself interested in his story despite myself.

"He most certainly did. My father had a heavy hand, and it hurt like the dickens. I had not been beaten like that since I was a wee lad by my uncle fur burning down the barn—I had forgotten how it felt tae be struck against my bare hide at that age... It took all my micht not tae wail from the mere pain of each blow. I was truly humiliated. And, when he was done, he told me in front of King Louis' Royal Court that it was my responsibility tae think before I spoke—that nae son of his would dishonor himself by disgracing the honor of anither through ill deeds. In this case, 'twas the spread of lies against a lass—fur if I did so then I would have nae honor, and I would know nothing but shame... and he said thy word was thy bond—the only true measure of a man's virtue.

"So, efter I was leathered quite weel, I was made tae apologize tae His Majesty King Louis and his Court, and personally tae Miss Imer and Lady Henrietta fur all tae hear. The next day I was sent tae work at a tannery fur six months. Efter that, I was installed intae King Louis' guard—and that is how I came intae military life."

"Oh," I said quietly. Leif kicked a pebble in the trail and watched it bounce a couple of times ahead of us. I suddenly realized his point of view and the place from where he had come. Albeit I strongly disagreed with his disciplinary method, I understood his intention loud and clear and that the meaning of his punishment did not stem from a malicious heart. Instead, it was done out of sympathy to prevent me from making similar mistakes in the future and to ensure that I might have an easier life experience than he.

"Now ye ken, *àille dhubh,* that I wisnae spared the rod much either," he said. He turned his eyes down toward me, and I looked up from the road meeting his ultramarine gaze.

"Spare the rod, spoil the child," I remarked essentially, feeling a little more at ease.

"Aye." He subtly nodded his head.

"That's what my mother used to say sometimes," I said.

"She must have been a wise woman."

"Yes, she was. But her technique dealt with doling out time-outs instead of spankings."

"Whit are time-outs, once and fur all?"

"Well, instead of being beaten to death, my mom—*and* my

dad, I'll have you know—would have me sit in the corner of the room on what they called the 'naughty stool' until I had explained to them what I had done wrong and apologized for it. I also had to promise that I'd never do it again—whatever it was that I'd done wrong."

"Indeed?" He gave me a strange look and chuckled faintly.

"Yes," I said matter-of-factly.

"Therefore, did ye keep yer promise?"

"Yes, of course."

"Hmm..." He thoughtfully eyed me. "Then, ye must not have done anything terribly wrong till now." I frowned at him, contrary.

"Even if you think so, you could have relied on psychology and exercised some restraint," I reprimanded.

"I reckon that I did use reason. And, as fur exhibiting restraint, I reckon that I did that also," he said bluntly.

"Oh, you don't say? Amazing how I'm hobbling now like an impaired hobbit, and you're telling me that you demonstrated self-control?" I looked at him in sheer disbelief.

"Aye," he said obviously.

"How can you say that?"

"I dinnae come into bed with ye afterward. Do ye recall so?" I squinted my eyes at him, giving him a nasty look.

"What's that supposed to mean?"

"It means that I dinnae come into bed with ye tae do whit I wanted tae do tae ye," he said.

"And what *exactly* did you want to do?" I pressed dryly, feeling my temper rising again.

"Roger ye, of coorse," he said. "I truly wanted tae. Ye waur beastly. Yet, I didnae want tae harm ye."

"So you enjoyed it, did you?" Ooo, I was starting to boil up inside again as I gave him an appalling look.

"Weel, I wouldnae say exactly so."

"What does that mean—*exactly*?"

"It means instead I didnae tooch ye, since I didnae consider it quite fair tae take ye whilst ye waur out of sorts as ye waur," he said.

"Ooh, wow—I guess that was *noble* of you. I suppose, in that case, you deserve the Medal of Honor for not raping me in addition to battery," I said coldly. "You listen to me, *Conan The Barbarian*—you don't know how lucky you are that you didn't attempt getting into bed with me, or you'd surely be missing a prized asset belonging to that anatomy of yours that you admire so much!" So angry again, I forcefully hauled myself back into the saddle despite the pain and quickly galloped off, leaving him behind.

Leif hastily hopped onto Blaze and caught up alongside me as I discovered him pacing close to me. He snagged my reins, yielding Oakley to a stop. He blocked his horse in front of mine, forcing me to face him. He heaved a heavy sigh, still holding my reins.

"I regret having mentioned it, but I was merely endeavoring tae make amends," he said. "I dinnae wish fur us tae remain miserable once we return tae Boston. I would prefer us tae be merry with one anither as we waur henceforth."

"Well, since you've made it so clear that you're my master, why don't you just make me?" I faked a ridiculous smile of contentment. "There! Is that better?" Before he could respond, I slipped off my horse on the opposite side so that I didn't have to look at him and started limping ahead on the trail.

"Why must ye be immensely obstinate?" he questioned with a hopeless tone. I heard him dismount Blaze and begin following me. He swiftly arrived at my side and strode with me, holding the reins to both horses trailing behind us. I kept my eyes off him with my lips shut and continued moving on. "Sylvie—I understand that yoo're cross. Yet, it rumples my spirit so." His tone suddenly sounded quite docile. He stopped walking. But I kept going. "I merely wish fur ye tae understand me, that is all." Something jarred me when he just said that, and I halted my steps. I turned to face him.

"Likewise," I said with an unmoved tone. He paused, simply looking at me.

"Fair enough," he said, steadily holding his eyes to mine.

"Good," I said tightly.

"Are we agreed now?" he inquired cautiously. He suddenly looked rather shy or uncertain—maybe both since I couldn't easily discern. I put my hands on my hips and considered him for a moment.

"I suppose so," I said with residual resentment.

"Fine," he said quietly. The shy look on his face became more apparent. Then, I knew he was a little embarrassed too, but I didn't know why for certain—except maybe he felt a tinge ashamed for what he had done to me. "In that case, I wonder... weel, I want tae ken if... I desire tae share yer bed again if yoo'll have me." I gawked at him for a second and my response was staggered. "The ground feels too hard, ye see," he said awkwardly.

"But we're camping," I obviously pointed out.

"Aye—it is still harder yet," he said abashedly. Without answering, I simply turned away from him and resumed walking silently. He followed slightly behind me, not speaking further. I thought he was going to apologize, but he didn't. I shook my head at the audacity that he didn't and was on the verge of being outraged all over again. However, as I began to consider his request, maybe that was his way of apologizing to me. *Who knows? Because I surely don't. All I know is that I'm going to be miserable with Leif if something doesn't change for the good between us...* I walked for a good solid twenty-five to thirty minutes mulling over his request without further acknowledging him. Finally, I arrested my steps and spun around to face him. He ceased his pace also and stood gazing at me. I locked eyes with him, looking him square in the face.

"Fine," I said pleasantly. His brow lifted in question as he gazed at me. "We may share the same bed again, as you wish, Your Grace."

"Thank ye, Your Grace," he said with equal formality. I looked at him for a second longer, then passed him by as I stepped toward Oakley, remaining still slightly behind him. I slipped my fingers inside the depths of one of her saddlebags, pulled forth the second pistol stolen from his pistol box, and pointed it at close range directly at his groin.

"But," I hissed, gritting my teeth hard as though they might shatter, "*Leif Stewart—Duke of Monteith*—if you ever, *ever*, lift so much as a *finger* to me again, I'll blow your cock off straight to Hell! And, I will leave you for good. You will never see me again— ever. Do you understand me, highlander?"

He didn't flinch as he stood there like a stone pillar in suspended silence, holding his steadfast gaze to mine. Then, he deliberately stretched forth his palm right side up and wagged his fingers.

"Give the pistol tae me," he said evenly. But I was reluctant. He waved his fingers again. "Give the pistol tae me. Ye neednae worry. Pass it tae me now."

I hesitated but eventually gave him the gun. He uncocked the hammer and checked it. It wasn't loaded, but he still held his breath. He arched an eyebrow at me as he tucked it inside his saddlebag. He then bent over and unsheathed the dagger tucked inside his boot. He whisked it up before both our eyes. This time, I held my breath with some concern despite what he had just said to me. He turned the dirk around, and the blade caught the sunlight and illuminated it like a star as the tip sank into the flesh of his right palm. An orb of ruby-red blood formed on the center pad of his palm. He then distinctly made the Sign of The Cross over himself with his ruptured hand. He turned the blade around, and I noticed it dripping with blood.

"I vow upon our Heavenly Father and upon our Savior Jesus Christ and upon the Holy Spirit: with this blade, I shed my bluid for thee. To thee, I pledge willingly: I shall never raise a hand tae thee."

Leif shoved the threatening dagger back into the scabbard inside his boot. Then, he swiped a bit of blood off his open wound with a pinky and gently touched my bottom lip with it. My tongue automatically licked the blood off, and I tasted the iron that flowed within him. I looked at him, stunned. He shortly sucked his palm, then yanked a handkerchief from his waistcoat pocket and bound his hand. Afterward, he leaned again and drew forth the shielded dirk, passing it over to me.

"Thaur," he said as I stood stunned in front of him, holding the heavy blade. "'Tis yers tae slay me if ever I betray ye." His gaze was steadfast, intense, and solid. "I am a man of my word, Sylvie. I dinnae speak idly. I mean whit I say, and I do as I mean—always." He paused a second and arched an eyebrow. "Are we reconciled now at last, *àille dhubh*?"

"Yes—I believe we are," I said with a small voice.

"Guid," he said. "I dinnae care tae sleep alone anymore. Now, let us come along."

Thirty-Six

Angus kept a lookout for us on the rampart near the entrance as we arrived at an overcrowded Fort Massachusetts. He noticed us approaching and flagged us. Leif waved back, and Angus left the stockade to meet us.

"Yoo've arrived soondly," Angus said to Leif as he dismounted from his horse when he arrived at us.

"Aye," Leif said, stepping toward my horse now and taking me by the waist to help me down.

"Glad tae see that yoo're both in a fair state," he remarked approvingly while watching Leif assist me without any complaint. He wanly grinned at Angus, and Angus reciprocated with his own grin.

"The place appears overrun," Leif said.

"Aye, 'tis futile entering inside. The lads are camped over haur instead," Angus said. He led us to where the others had settled several yards from the fort on the meadow near the shore of the river.

It was a long and tortuous ride today, and I was glad the day was over. I was more than happy to place myself to rest on the blanket inside the tent. The ground was cushioned by thick grass, and it felt comfortable as I lay stretched over it on my stomach. I didn't mind so much when Leif entered the tent to sleep beside me and slid his arm around my waist to cuddle when we fell asleep.

"*MO GHAOL*," Leif muttered softly as he gently nudged my shoulder, rousing me from a sound slumber.

"Hm?" I muttered sleepily.

"Yoo're dreaming aloud," he whispered.

"Really?" I yawned.

"Aye."

"Oh, sorry."

"Are ye alrecht?"

"Yeah, of course."

"Guid. Ye sounded quite vexed in yer dream."

"I kept telling you to hurry up and take your shower, or we'd be late. But you didn't take one," I murmured groggily, still half asleep.

"Och... A shower?" he inquired curiously.

"You know—like rain coming from a pipe inside a house or something, so that you can easily bathe instead of using a tub."

"Och," he said, still sounding uncertain. "I shall make certain tae remain bathed—when I can. Yoo're too feisty when yoo're cross."

"I'll take that into account."

"Thank ye," he said softly.

"Sure."

"Whit was the rest of yer dream concerning, nonetheless? It seemed strange."

"We were supposed to meet Kyle and Dakota for dinner, but you were making us late because you wouldn't shower," I murmured drowsily.

"Och... I apologize," he muttered when he yawned.

"You should because you really are smelly, by the way."

"I dinnae reckon that ye carry the fragrance of roses either, lass." His tone was ironic and I couldn't help my little giggle.

"You're so terrible."

"Admittedly. Yet, your fragrance is not offensive tae me," he said sincerely.

"Thank you. But I could use a bath, too," I agreed.

"Now, who is Dakota?"

"My brother's wife," I answered.

"I see..." His tone turned sympathetic, and he became quiet.

"Did I say anything else?" I wondered sleepily.

"Aye, ye mentioned power having gone out due tae a snow-storm," he curiously informed me. "Ye waurnae pleased about it, and ye spoke profanity."

"Oh..."

"I reckon we are going tae have tae mind that profane speech yoo've taken a fancy tae. I'm surprised by the words ye ken." He really didn't approve, given the disdain in his voice.

"Is that right?" I remarked cynically.

"Indeed it is," he attested without any hint of amusement. "I ken whit 'fuck' is, and it carries the same filthy notion as *swive*—a damned dirty word fur certain." I suddenly felt embarrassed and shrank a little from shame. "Yet, I must ken the meaning of the other disgraceful words I have heard ye say."

"Like what?" I asked guiltily.

"Tell me whit 'bullshit' means?"

"It's a bad way of calling something bogus or ridiculous."

"I see... Now, tell me whit does 'dipshit' truly mean?"

"It means someone who is completely inept."

"Och... Misogynist?"

"Um—it's a man who hates women in general."

"My word..." he responded, sounding pensive. "Yet, that isnae true of me, fur I raither fancy women."

"Yes, I know. I was just angry."

"Whit did ye mean by primate, then?" he asked.

"Well, it's a creature belonging to an order of animals which have large brains and complex hands and feet."

"That definition disnae soond quite so terrible compared tae the way ye first said it tae me."

"That's because I called you a prehistoric primate, which is basically the same as calling you an ape."

"I say! That isnae flattering."

"No—it's not."

"Whit is a male chauvinist?"

"It's a man who believes women are subordinate to men because men are intellectually superior to women."

"*Humph!*" he replied, sounding disagreeable. "As fur a 'psychopathic moron'? I believe those whaur the words?"

"You have a good memory."

"I recall every word yoo've ever spoken tae me from the time we primarily met."

"Seriously?"

"Aye."

"Wow—you're like an elephant. Supposedly, they never forget anything."

"Certainly?"

"Um-hm."

"How verily curious... Yet, I huvnae finished. Tell me whit it means—'psychopathic moron'."

"It means someone who is violently and socially impaired."

"That is terrible."

"I would agree."

"And, a 'horny pervert'?" he inquired. I giggled unevenly despite my embarrassment.

"Um, that would be someone who's easily sexually aroused and is a sexual deviant."

"Fur Heaven's sake! Does it truly?" He sounded bitterly amused.

"Yes," I murmured with abashment.

"Ye said that I couldnae order ye about like a computer. Whit did ye mean?"

"Well, I meant that you couldn't just order me around like you could program a machine. You see, a computer is an electronic device that processes information according to data given to it," I answered, not caring about divulging the definition to him, perceiving that it didn't really matter at this point anyway.

"Och..." he replied, sounding confused and uninformed. "Whit does that mean, however?"

"It just means a thing that can't think for itself," I simplified.

"I see. Whit about 'sadistic'? Clarify it."

"Well," my voice dropped a little from further humiliation, but I was unable to stifle the giggle that escaped me. "That word basically describes, um—it describes a person."

"Whit sort of person?"

"A person who gains sexual gratification from inducing pain on others."

"Atrocious! Ye indeed ken how tae knock hard with words—ye portrayed me weel in poor lighting," he said, seriously surprised.

"I'm sorry," I said sincerely.

"Forgiven."

"Ye also said that I am a racist. Whit does that mean?"

"A racist is someone who holds extreme prejudices against certain ethnic groups of people as they are viewed inferiorly."

"Och..." He became quiet for a moment and I sensed him contemplating. "Ye must promise me tae watch yer tongue henceforth," he resumed.

"Okay," I sighed.

"Is it a promise?"

"Yes," I replied drowsily.

"Guid." He gently kissed the side of my head as wolves howled throughout from somewhere in the background, and it became silent between us as we listened to them. He scooted himself close to me and wrapped an arm around my waist, drawing me snugly against him as I began drifting back to slumber.

WE PUSHED HARD ONWARD since leaving Fort Massachusetts. Leif wanted to make good time reaching Concord, so he even bypassed the route south along the Connecticut River to pay a visit to the sharecroppers and soldiers quartered on our and Finley's properties in Northampton. He had grown quiet and despondent like the rest of the guys as we made our way across the country. He seemed distinctly more demoralized and absorbed in his thoughts the closer we came toward Concord. I was very aware of the reason why: his mind centered on Finley as did mine, and I felt the dismal weight on his shoulders. I pitied the solitary grief he was feeling and would not reveal to anyone. I worried about anticipating him delivering the horrible news to Elizabeth. The toll was heavy; I knew from my own personal experience that this was a circumstance that could truly break a person. The pendulum could literally swing either way, depending upon the person, and no one could ever predict how a person might be affected and transformed through such an experience by losing a loved one to death. So, I precisely felt Leif's silent lamenting pain and wanted nothing more but to have the miraculous ability to simply dissolve it away from him.

LATE AFTERNOON on the fifth day, we finally rode into Concord. Everyone was silent from miles back as depression settled heavily on us. I forgot about the much decreased residual pain over my bottom as the Buckingham mansion appeared against the hills in the background. It was a slow and steady progression as we approached the green-pastured property.

Within minutes, figures emerged from the nice house, noticing our advancement over the road. It was Elizabeth and her girls. Elizabeth turned toward them, and the girls took off, running eagerly back inside the house. Shortly, Elizabeth's brother, Earnest, and his wife, Anne, along with their father, Mr. Buckingham, had appeared outside with the girls. Amity had also emerged from the front door into the hot, steaming sunlight with Mercy beside her. Elizabeth had already begun walking hurriedly toward us, and Leif dismounted from his horse, ready to greet her. The other men followed as they dismounted their horses also, and so did I as we proceeded to meet her.

I perceived her seeking Finley among us as we came closer over the field from the road. She was anticipatory, eagerly delighted to finally see him again. But it was almost immediately that the potential happiness in her face suddenly dispelled into uncertainty and panic—as if she already knew when she saw us without him.

"Where's my Finley?" she asked suddenly in a trembling voice, looking starkly alarmed as we arrived close to her.

"I regret, Beth, tae inform ye—" Leif started morosely.

"Nay!" she gasped spontaneously, interrupting him as he moved to place a consoling hand upon her shoulder. "It cannot be! Where is he? I do not see him. Did he choose to see *Taigh-Bheinn* before returning to me, then?"

"Nae. He didnae," Leif said solemnly.

"Then, where might he be?" she insisted quickly, appearing extremely distressed.

"He wulnae be returning. Yet, his soul, I pray, has been commended tae God in Heaven," Leif responded soberly with the stiffest upper lip I'd ever seen.

"Pray, do not tell me that I mayn't see him!" she stammered all at once, breaking down sobbing hysterically. She collapsed fully to the ground. "*Nay!*" she cried uncontrollably, releasing a guttural wail that seemed to come from her soul. I rushed from Oakley toward her and held her while she slumped to the ground, comforting her. She wailed like I had never heard anyone else weep before. She was inconsolable, but I just kept embracing her, rocking her a little, trying to soothe and calm her. Leif leaned, clasping one of her arms, and we both assisted her to her feet. We all slowly paced with her toward the house, where her stunned family remained observing. Her brother and his wife approached us and assisted her from us, taking her inside the mansion.

The children had become excited in a horrible way, as they were inquiring where their father was while they witnessed their mother in hysterics. They began sobbing, too, not fully understanding what was happening to their mother and confused about the situation. Elizabeth's father instructed the maids to take the questioning children away from their Uncle Leif and me. They quickly interceded and removed the children from our presence, guiding them back indoors, away from us.

"Forgive me, Your Grace, it is most upsetting news," Mr. Buckingham said regrettably to Leif, clearly distraught.

"Indeed," Leif agreed gravely.

"The Lord has blessed us still, for it is good to see that you are well," Mr. Buckingham said, turning to me.

"Thank you, Mister Buckingham. You as well," I replied somberly.

"Thank you. Welcome home to you both, indeed. I am most pleased that you have made a safe return," Mr. Buckingham said sincerely with a grim look.

"Thank ye, Master Buckingham," Leif replied politely.

"Pray, won't you come indoors and be at home? There are fresh linens already laid and a pleasant roast in the kitchen that awaits," Mr. Buckingham said.

"Thank ye, Master Buckingham," Leif said.

"You are most welcome," Mr. Buckingham replied respectfully. He turned to the cousins. "Sirs, please come indoors. Refresh yourselves as you are indeed welcome also." He signaled the stablehands to take our horses. Then, Mr. Buckingham led us inside his house.

Whimpering echoed through the halls, filling the place with sadness as a maid took over, leading me and Leif through the house while the cousins were led by Mr. Buckingham and his son and wife into the dining room. Once Leif and I arrived at the staircase, we were led away from the others as we followed the maid up the steps and were guided to our room.

When Leif and I entered our bedroom, we quietly began tidying ourselves with little words shared between us. Any words expressed to each other came forth soft and glum while I mechanically cleaned myself and donned a fresh bedgown. As I was lightly struggling to slip my toes into the new slippers Leif had purchased for me back in Albany, I thought to say, "Perhaps I should see how Elizabeth is coping."

"Aye, that will be guid of ye," he said quietly as he was despondently tucking his fresh white shirttail inside his breeches like an android.

"All right," I replied softly. I took a few steps through the room toward the door and decided to cease. Before leaving, I glanced over my shoulder at his melancholy face. "Will you be all right?" I inquired with concern.

"I shall be," he assured grimly. I hesitated and looked skeptically at him. "Ye ought tae mind how Elizabeth is faring. I reckon she needs yer assistance." His tone was encouraging even though the look on his face remained morose. But he needed someone for emotional support, too, I thought. Or was it better to leave him alone? "Go now," he insisted mildly.

"All right," I agreed, still feeling torn. I turned toward the door anyway and left the room with him inside, alone to himself.

I made my way through the halls and entered Elizabeth's bedroom. She was sobbing horribly on her bed among the pillows. Her sister-in-law, Anne, was tending to her beneath the canopy of her bed.

"Oh! Sylvina, you have come... Thank you. You are most kind," she whimpered, noticing me entering her bedroom and approaching her. She briskly wiped her tears with a dainty hand-kerchief, trying to clear her appearance. But the tears kept streaming down her flushed face. "You may presently take your leave, Anne. I thank you greatly," she told her.

"Indeed, you are welcome. I shall mind the children presently," Anne said gently before greeting me on her departure as she was about to leave the room, then closed the door behind her.

"Pray, will you not sit with me upon the bed, Sylvina?" Eliza-beth invited me as she sniffled awfully.

"Yes, of course," I responded compassionately. I placed myself over the quilt beside her and embraced her. I gently rubbed her back, coddling her with sympathy as she continued sobbing.

"Forgive me, for I am out of sorts," she wept.

"You don't have to apologize for anything, Elizabeth. If anyone needs to apologize—it's me. I'm so, so incredibly sorry, Elizabeth. I thought I could do it... I thought... I thought that I could bring them both back to us," I lamented with tears forming in my eyes, feeling racked with sheer guilt.

"I don't perceive how you could have managed it, Sylvina."

"I thought I could, though."

"How?"

"I'm not sure how. I didn't give it any thought, really. I was just convinced that I could do it—to bring them back safely. I thought that I would've had the ability to keep them safe from danger if I was there with them to advise them."

"You could not keep them safe from their duty to protect us. I tried to explain this to you before you took your leave."

"I know you did. I realize it now. I don't know what I was thinking. It was stupid of me. I was extremely foolish to think that I could have had anything to do with controlling the outcome of what happened. I'm incredibly sorry. I wouldn't blame you if you hated me now."

"Why do you say such a thing?"

"Because I think you might, since I couldn't keep my promise to you."

"Aye, 'twas foolish of you to believe that you could ever make such a promise to me—to guard our husbands when it is only God who can grant them refuge."

"Then, I regret that I didn't pray hard enough when I thought I had."

"Nay. I do not despise you, Sylvina. You are my sister. I admire your fondness for our husbands—that you would risk yourself for them demonstrates your devotion to them and reveals my own cowardice."

"What? You are not at all a coward. How could you even say that? It was braver of you to remain here and be a mother to your husband's children while you prayed for him. What else could you have possibly done for him?"

"I am uncertain. Yet I do esteem your bravery. Once you had departed from us, my desire to join you was compelling... if merely to remain in Fin's presence... I do not know how I shall ever presently manage without him. I never believed the day would come that I would never lay eyes upon him once more before our elder years," she whimpered as she dabbed her tears away from her eyelashes.

"I understand completely," I consoled softly.

"Aye, I suppose that you do," she sniffled.

"I feel that it's extremely important for you to understand that you are the brave one between us because of your faith. Your constant love and support of Finley gave him strength to persevere through his separation from you while he fought in this war—and the fact that you gave him strength through your selflessness is brave and admirable. Finely knew your heart, Elizabeth. He knew that you loved him."

"I knew his heart also. He was a very good husband. He was

truly dear to me... I shall miss him greatly. How did you ever muddle through when Mathew departed?"

"I was heartbroken... For a long time, I couldn't overcome the emptiness I felt when he passed away. I missed him all of the time... and I went through life like an empty shell. Except, I realized that I had responsibilities in my life that couldn't be ignored—so I just focused on those as I continued living each day... I suppose it just takes time before it's possible to see past the pain. But, having faith in something lends some strength, I've found."

"Aye, I shall continue to seek my strength through our Savior, Jesus Christ... Only, I am ever more distressed now that mother has passed as well."

"Did she?" I was shocked to hear this unexpected news since it suddenly occurred to me that I hadn't seen Mrs. Buckingham with the other family members on our arrival.

"Aye, she has passed away also," Elizabeth wept.

"What on earth happened?" Mrs. Buckingham seemed in stellar health when I last saw her, so this came to me as a big shock.

"She suddenly had a fit and was taken from us when we were enjoying the garden together last month."

"Oh, no—I'm so terribly sorry, Elizabeth." This was horrible news on top of everything else for certain, and I found it difficult to swallow while sympathetic tears kept coming forth from me, too.

Elizabeth continued sobbing out her despair for a length of time, and all I could do to comfort her was simply remain by her side as I quietly wept with her. After an emotional hour, she calmed and fell asleep from the strain as I consoled her.

So, I cleared my appearance and decided at this time to quietly leave her in peace to rest when I left her bedroom seeking Leif instead. I returned to our bedroom, but discovered that he wasn't there. When I went downstairs, I checked several rooms where I thought he might be located. As I discovered Mr. Buckingham and his son, Earnest, faintly conversing over Madeira in the sitting room without Leif, I began wondering where he might have gone; he was nowhere to be found now.

"Mayhap, he is sitting upon the veranda with the other lads, madam," Mr. Buckingham suggested kindly.

"Yes, thank you, I'll look there," I replied solemnly. I paced toward the back of the house and entered out onto the spacious veranda. The guys were all out there seated on the steps and in chairs. They were smoking and drinking ale, talking lightly without much to really say. The air among them was lamentably toned down, depressed and despondent as they sat around each other. Their heads turned in my direction as they heard me approaching them. They shifted in their seats and politely stood when I came near.

"Has anyone seen Leif?" I inquired as they noticed me.

"I cannae say that I have, lass," Cole said.

"I reckon having seen him go fur a walk about a half hour ago across the green," Angus said. "I dinnae believe he has yet returned."

"Oh," I realized. "Thank you."

"Aye," Angus said quietly.

I stepped off the veranda away from them and moved down onto the stone path leading me through the garden. The porch vanished as I wound my way through the garden and strolled off the path out over the open green clearing. I recognized the emerald hill not too far in the distance that was once blanketed with snow, and I remembered the carefree sled ride Leif and I had taken over it last November. It was strange to think that was almost a year ago. It felt like yesterday, yet at the same time seemed so long ago. Remembering that moment filled me with warmth and affection for that innocent time. I wished right now that we could return to that naive period when everything seemed so idyllic and optimistic despite my homesickness.

The frozen pond we had accidentally slid over near the foot of the hill now sparkled flecks of gold as it rippled beneath the hot, humid sun. I circled the refreshing water, catching a glimpse in the distance of lodging soldiers freely exiting and entering the guest house where my fate had been inevitably sealed with Leif. I simply stared at that house now as I kept walking, amazed at how much time had gone by.

After a few minutes, I found myself now aimlessly wandering through the woods. I wasn't sure where I was going, but I just kept walking, hoping to find Leif somewhere out here.

Finally, I spotted him through the trees, crouched on the ground with his back leaning against a thick tree trunk. His knees were raised near his chest, supporting his elbows with his head buried over his crossed arms. He was trembling, and I heard him weeping as I quietly came close. It crushed my heart to see him broken down like this, alone by himself in emotional distress. It was the only time I had ever known him to crumble and basically lose himself in despair as I unavoidably felt the depth of his grief.

I carefully stepped and knelt in front of him, but his head remained buried over his clutched arms. He shook with such sorrow that he wasn't even aware I had closely arrived before him. My palm slipped over his quaking shoulder and tenderly caressed it.

"Ye shouldnae have discovered me," he croaked.

"If you prefer to be alone, I'll understand," I empathized and began removing my hand from his shoulder. Without lifting his troubled head to look at me, his hand moved over mine and firmly grasped it in place.

"I dinnae wish fur ye tae perceive me in such a state, fur I am not a weak man," he choked.

"Of course, you're not weak," I said softly, trying to quiet him as I knelt beside him. I slid my fingers from his clasping hand and wrapped both arms around his neck, soothing him. "It's okay... it's all right," I comforted as I leaned my cheek over his silky head.

"I should have prevented him from going upon the mission by

protesting the charge. It was a folly attempt..." he said, stifling his irregular breathing.

"It's not your fault, Leif," I replied.

"Aye, it is."

"No—it's not. You can't blame yourself for what happened. It's no one's fault. It was out of your control. You mustn't blame yourself at all. It's not your fault." I pressed my lips on his gilded crown, attempting to assuage him as I stroked his back while soundly embracing him. He eased up a little, taking me into his arms, and enfolded me in his own powerful embrace. He buried his heavy head inside the curve of my neck and shoulder and tightly held onto me.

His tears soaked against my skin as I firmly held him for an indefinite period. I could feel the density of his body as he allowed himself to rest against me while we embraced. My fingers gently moved through his hair while placing comforting kisses over his tearful head, wanting nothing more but to evaporate his pain.

I quietly shushed him, repeatedly kissing his distressed brow and after a moment, he began settling from his weeping when he finally lifted his gaze to mine. His face was flushed crimson with his cheekbones glistening and eyes irritated red. I carefully placed my palms on the sides of his cheeks and stroked a thumb over the moistness around his eyelashes, drying them.

"It's okay," I hushed, delicately pressing my lips over his damp cheekbone just below his eye. "I'm so sorry for the loss you're feeling," I whispered against his skin. I kissed his damp eyelid, and his eyelashes tickled my lips. I felt his large hands lightly come over the sides of my face. He pulled me slightly away from his face and steadied his eyes on mine. Holding my gaze, he stared at me for a moment without speaking. His thumb faintly traced the outline of my bottom lip as he stared back into my eyes. Then, he leaned, and I sensed his lips press over mine in a supple, genuine kiss. I gently kissed him back with affection, and he returned to kissing me in the same way until I sensed his caressing lips increase with further intent.

He began gently kissing me with augmenting heat and coerced me backward onto my back against the earth with the weight of his body, locking me beneath him. He released me from his kiss and closely hovered, just gazing at me without a word. His face was deeply ruddy, I noticed, as he intimately remained above me. He stared entranced at me and gnashed his jaw. His breathing was unusual, I also noticed—fierce and irregular—and he was trembling. It seemed he was striving quite hard to restrain something potent, latent, and unknown within him.

"What's wrong?" I asked, realizing his strange expression. Whatever it was he was fighting within him, it made him appear a bit frightening.

"I... I desire very much tae be with ye—yet—" he broke off, speaking with difficulty.

"But what?" I inquired.

"I fear—I fear that I cannae help myself if yoo'll permit me," he struggled to express.

"Oh," I responded in a small voice with some uncertainty. "It's okay—"

"Yoo're bonnie," he choked, interrupting me.

"Leif, it's okay if you—" Before I could finish, he stifled me with an overpowering kiss filled with burning heat emitting from his desire. With an invisible hand, he impatiently groped the buttons on his breeches loose and took my wrists, shackling them in his grip. He pressed them firmly into the cool earth surrounding my head. I wasn't exactly agreeing with him; I was simply trying to say that I understood his grief. But, before I realized it, he had turned up my skirts. He separated my thighs with his knee, duly positioning himself when I felt him powerfully entering me, sheathing himself to the hilt in one solid, voracious thrust, causing me to gasp.

"Wait," I said breathlessly. He groaned and clenched my wrists tighter into the dirt.

"Forgive me," he heaved, pushing himself as far as he could reach the end of my depths. I wrenched against him, trying to ease the robust pressure from his overwhelming thrust, as I felt the tip of his stone-hard shaft ramming against my cervix. But he caught my knees firm against his chest, crimping me, and plunged even deeper, forcing the wind from me, striking the back of my uterus.

"*Uhh!*" I cried out in sharp pain. "Wait," I gasped, pulling myself away from him. But, he had me locked beneath him. He pressed my wrists further into the cool, soft earth, cutting off my circulation, and rammed himself harder inside the same exact location, causing me to cry out again. "Leif!" I gasped.

"Merely be with me... Receive me as I am," he groaned.

"Wait," I said under my breath.

"I am yer laird and master," he said with bated breath that burned my brow. "Do ye recall my telling ye so?"

"Yes, I remember," I winced shakily, struggling to correct his formidable position deep within me.

"Then, repeat it tae me," he demanded in a low voice that nearly sounded threatening.

"You're my lord. You're my master," I uttered, giving into his demand as I hoped he'd reduce his powerful thrust.

"That I am." He clamped down with more fervor and whaled another pounding blow.

"I can't!" I gasped, cringing from the piercing pain.

"I shall never forsake ye," he panted unevenly. "Swear tae me that ye wulnae ever forsake me." He surged again, this time pounding my cervix so hard it felt like he had broken into my womb. I took a deep breath, and he plunged even farther. It felt as though he was going to tear right through my belly, and the aching burned.

"*Ahh!*" I cried.

"I believed that I had lost ye. Do ye understand? I believed that ye waur gone. I shan't lose ye, *àille dhubh*. Yoo're going tae understand entirely," he continued unevenly, "and ye are going tae ken completely, without question whit I am tae ye... that I shall own every part of yer being when I am done with ye, whether ye permit it or not." I struggled again, and he pummeled more, fiercely foraging a new threshold within my depths. I moaned from the aching invasion. I tried wrenching myself from him, resisting. But he only grunted, jolting me as he thrust even deeper, grabbing my unfettered attention. "I mean tae have ye ken that we are forever bound nae matter whit occurs," he uttered coarsely. "Ye belong tae none other but me... The whole of ye belongs tae me. Ye will submit tae me and ken in yer soul that I possess ye." His tone was gentle and warm. But the words were intimidating. It seemed he was warning me and reminding me about what had happened between us, inspired by retribution from all the torment he was feeling and all the strife that I had caused him in recent days.

"Leif, I can't," I gasped.

"Will it," he commanded.

It was sweltering outside, and the added heat consuming him made it unbearable for me to essentially exist. Beads of sweat sparkled all over his face like tiny crystals, dripping like dew droplets over my brow, and I tasted the salt as they fell upon my lips. Ignoring my plea, he continued ramming me with such intense force that I thought I would disintegrate. With each surge, he delivered a blow that hammered a rock-solid, uncompromising punch that stabbed like an iron rod inside my uterus.

He was pulverizing me. The motion was endless. He discounted me as I moaned and complained while grinding me with each impacting blow repeatedly. I suddenly ceased being except at the moment of each strike, where I only came to consciousness at the sharp, intrusive pain he was inflicting upon me. I was rendered incapable of fighting him or the pain; he was controlling me, driving me to collapse over the summit of some kind of concrete submission as he worked his will over me. Then, the pain oddly began mixing with emerging pleasure. My breath caught as I suddenly seized, and the flesh within me spastically convulsed around the attacking intrusion of his penis. I moaned and shivered as my vaginal walls pulsed. Disregarding it, he kept moving, impaling me repeatedly with each obliterating blow.

"I can't take it!" I shrieked.

"Ye can. Receive me completely by willing it," he groaned. "Take whit I am giving tae ye. Take it. 'Tis all that I am giving tae ye without reservation. All of it."

He clenched my wrists even tighter—grunting during his aggressive concerted effort—and pressed himself remorselessly harder on me, forcing me into the earth. My wrists felt like they were going to shatter while he worked himself inside me. He was unyielding in his restraint over me, welding me to him, fixing me to his will while seeking mine.

"Leif—" I began to beg.

"Nae," he rejected. "Ye answer me now."

"What do you want to know?"

"Tell me whit am I tae ye?"

"I've already told you!"

"Ye huvnae told me a thing. Whit am I truly tae ye?"

I didn't answer him, and the pain quickly mounted further. He wouldn't stop. Instead, he continued with no indication of ever subsiding, demanding my answer. I felt myself caving, and I thought I would die. All at once, my whole body unexpectedly arrested, opposing the pain, and quaked with pleasurable seizures. He released my knees, and my hips involuntarily rose to meet him. My thighs swung tightly around his hips, welcoming the contradiction of pain and pleasure. My body strove to maintain the incredible euphoric sensation and completely betrayed me as I tightly wrapped my legs around his hips.

Every thrust he committed against me hit like a piercing shock of burning electricity as I felt it searing inside my belly, and I recoiled from it, believing he was going to rip right through me. I squirmed, but the attack persisted on an endless cycle of uncontrollable shuddering ecstatic contractions resulting from each penetrating plunge. My hips continued betraying me, greeting the stinging infringement despite my negative reaction. He turbulently endeavored in dripping sweat while he pushed me deeper into the surrounding earth, pinning me staunchly bound in his grip.

Each sudden thrust began delivering an elevating sensation that was indescribable as he demanded my answer. He wasn't going to quit; time and again, he repeated the question, bearing down on me as if he meant to break me in half.

"Oh God!" I wailed breathlessly as I was vehemently launched off the edge of pain into pristine pleasure beyond the apex of submission. "Oh God!" I wept. "Okay... Okay... Oh God! I'm dying... Leif! *Uhh!* Leif...! Please! I love you... I truly do! I'm lost without you... I love you more than life. My greatest joy. I won't ever leave you...You have me. Forever—you have me... all of me. I'm yours..." He grabbed my hair and yanked my head back, forcing me to lock eyes with his.

"At last ye say so. Thus ye understand me, do ye not?" he growled victoriously.

"Yes."

"Listen tae me well now. Dinnae ever dispute the truth. Ye belong tae me. Yoo're mine—all of ye—as I had vowed ye would be. Ye loove me, and I loove ye. We are forever bound. Ye may never forget this truth as ye receive all that I have tae give tae ye. Take it. Take every bit of me that I am offering—without fear or guilt. Take all that I am and wholly receive me without mercy. Ye wulnae doubt me as I mean fur ye tae ken my happiness, fur I shall bestow joy upon ye as I runneth over with it. I swear it. Now be with me."

My flesh profoundly pulsed all around him. He unhanded me and dropped his entire weight over me. I could scarcely breathe as he wrapped his arms around me. He encased my body and penetrated me even deeper, determinedly hunting his way through me.

I suddenly screamed loudly when I felt him inside of my belly and electrifying it; his extreme ferocity was inextricable. He sharply smothered my mouth with his, choking me, hurting my lips, and scratching my face with his sandpaper jaw. He pumped harder, more violently, as though chiseling me apart to reach the core of my essential being and take hold of it like he was already physically doing to my body.

Then, suddenly, he tapped into a hidden reserve. From the pulverized dust from my annihilation rushed a geyser responding to the ferocious passion of want and need. I flung my arms around his soaking back. I tightly gripped him, wanting to drown inside of him as I pushed my hips against his groin and met him with every punch.

I bit his lip and tasted the warm ore in his blood. His teeth clamped down on my neck, and he sucked, painfully bruising my skin. My hands entered beneath his drenched shirt, and my nails scoured through the sweat from the nape of his neck to the small of his back. He suddenly reared up and roared. He barbarically returned to me as the both of us frantically ripped and shredded, tearing at each other's flesh in an incinerating yearning to be fused as one.

The atmosphere burned, and it felt as though we were inside an inferno as my screams tangled with his. Deep in the fire engulfing us, we melded together and finally lost ourselves in each other at the ultimate culminating moment that seemed to change us from being singular to being fundamentally fused as one union while we soared into each other's heart. At that moment, I felt him burn right through me when he erupted into my core as the searing heat of his essence blazed a trail inside of me.

IN A DAZE, I sluggishly came back to myself while resting over Leif's rapidly beating chest, dripping wet from his seed escaping between my thighs. His chest rose and fell with every calming breath he strove to take. His skin still burned past the torn shirt ripped from his chest. After a distended moment, the sound of his heart now pounded exceedingly slow in my ear as we stayed pasted together, not wanting to disrupt the last of our hazardous union. I felt his palm splay over my back and gently stroke me as he braced me tightly with the other.

I barely leaned my head up from his, and our eyes met. His stroking hand came over my cheek and caressed my face. "I love you," I told him softly as his thumb lightly brushed my lips.

"I loove ye," he returned. "I have always loov'd ye, Sylvie." I smiled at him. "I shall never cease loving ye." Wrapping a gentle hand around the back of my head, he drew my lips down over his, bestowing an affectionate kiss. I returned, gazing at him, and his lips languidly curved into a slight grin as he softly grunted at a remote thought.

"What?" I inquired quietly.

"Do ye not understand my joy?" he asked gently.

"Tell me."

"I own ye," he said humbly. I didn't say anything. "'Tis a glorious revelation. Yet, whit is most profound is that it seems that I cannae own ye without submitting my soul tae ye."

"I suppose that is the way it can only ever work between us," I considered thoughtfully.

"So it appears."

"Well…"

"Aye?"

"I guess that means we're a balanced union, then."

"Hmm. An appealing notion, *mo ghaol*."

"I'll always love you, Leif—always." I lightly kissed his lips, sealing the element of my truth. He guided my head back down on his muscular chest, and I tucked my brow inside the curve of his neck.

"Let us remain reit haur fur a moment longer. I dinnae care tae return tae the hoose at present," he said.

"Me neither." I felt him kiss the side of my head as he locked me tight in his arms. The air was hot and muggy, but a breeze swelled over us and rustled the surrounding shading leaves high above, cooling the perspiration on our skin to some relief.

I closed my eyes, listening to him breathing, and felt the wind escaping him. It wafted over my cheek as his arms clenched me in place while I comfortably lay over him, continuing to keep us peacefully adjoined.

THE NEXT MORNING, I awoke injured and disabled, with every muscle in my body badly aching. I could hardly walk in order to make my way to visit the chamber pot in the privy closet and move to the washbasin afterward. Perhaps this is what it felt like to be hit by a bullet train at full speed and miraculously survive. My insides felt like they had been put through an industrial blender. However, I considered when my eyes landed on the blunt force object that had done this to me as it lay flaccid against the thigh of its owner lying in bed that it was strange how it looked so harmless right now and yet had the power to do so much damage. The owner of it awoke, hearing me as I hobbled over the floor, crossing the room back toward the bed.

"Och, poor lass," he said, observing me with a look closely resembling gloating conceit. How considerate of him to stretch a helping hand toward me from the mattress and assist me back into bed, I thought. "It appears yoo've had a rough ride, lass."

I narrowed my eyes at him and scowled as I tried carefully adjusting myself comfortably on the bed against the pillows.

"I suppose you'd know all about it," I glowered. He smiled some more. "*Ugh*, how could you do this to me?" I moaned as I sank feebly back into the pillows.

"It wisnae easy," he said.

"Oh, my goodness." I rolled my eyes, dismissing him over his apparent strength and size. He arched an eyebrow and licked the ugly sore on his lower lip that I had aptly given him.

"And whit do ye call this?" He also pointed to the deep bite mark where the skin had been broken over his shoulder.

"Well... I guess you rather do look pretty beat up too," I admitted, feeling a bit smug myself. "Can't say that you didn't have it coming to you, though."

"I'm not complaining," he said and winked at me. "I reckon I shall stand and take whit I git and git whit I deserve with pleasure." He reached around my waist and pulled me down close to him. "Come haur ye shameless creature."

"You've gotta be *kidding* me," I said, shrinking from him. "Talk about cruel and unusual punishment. I feel like I've been put through an industrial grinder and stampeded by a mountain herd of cattle. In case you haven't already noticed, but I can scarcely walk—that's how unbelievably sore I am. I think I've had enough lessons from you. So, no, thank you."

He stifled a chuckle and, with disregard, pulled me back toward him.

"I promise that I shall very much take care," he coaxed and tugged me inescapably beneath him.

"You don't understand the meaning of the word '*no,*' do you?" I replied softly, sensing his knee separate my thighs. He smiled at me.

"Aye," he said, nodding his golden head a tad.

He gently entered me and proved, however, to be as cautious as a man of his size could possibly be, cupping me with great fragility. He kept saying gentle words to me in Scottish in such a manner that was glorifying, which I understood was reconciliation for his harsh actions. His deeply tender persistence nevertheless continued reminding me of the enduring lesson he had initially impressed upon me with brutal force.

This time, he merely shook in my embrace as he erupted and completely expelled himself, filling me again with his essence. He tried not to stir or thrust while arriving at his climax in order not to hurt me more than he already had. Instead, he trembled constrained, succumbing to the moment as it was granted to him and disintegrated until the end.

Afterward, while still engaged, he gently rolled me over him and held me close. He stroked my bare back and shoulders across the older bruises that had begun vanishing, which were left from the physical altercation that had occurred between us in Vermont nearly two weeks ago.

"I dinnae ken how I would ever manage tae continue living if I had lost ye," he said, tenderly caressing his lips over one of the bruises. "I dinnae ever wish tae lose ye, Sylvie."

"I don't ever want to lose you either," I said against his neck. He sank his fingers among my bobbed ringlets and caressed the back of my head on his chest, resting near his throat. I could feel his pulse throbbing normally against my brow, and the beating of his heart filled my ear. Falling still and quiet, it seemed time would wait for us now, and we rested uninterrupted in peace, drifting back into slumber.

PART SIX

Home

I was glad now that we were finally home again in Boston at *Taigh Gràs*. News had traveled fast about the massacre at Fort William Henry. As a result, Lord Loudoun had earned himself a worse reputation among the people here. People around here were already angry over Lord Loudoun's quartering edict and took issue with it. But after the fall of Fort William Henry, people believed Massachusetts Bay Colony should no longer participate in the war, since it had not only provided the most provincial troops for the war, it also lost the most men as a result.

Now that it is October, almost a month and a half since the trauma experienced at Fort William Henry, it was a little over a year since I had arrived during the summer here in this era. It was difficult for me to believe that I had been here for that long, as it seemed like only yesterday, I had come here instead.

The storm fell hard tonight with pounding rain. It was lightning, and thunder loudly crashed throughout the sky as I was preparing myself for bed. I sat at the dressing table combing my bobbed curls, but the static electricity in the air kept my hair frizzy. Leif entered our bedroom, closing the door behind him. He noticed me fussing over my pixie bangs as he came close and stole a caressing palm around my neck.

"Whit are ye doing?" he asked.

"I'm just trying to fix my hair, but it's sticking out everywhere because of the static electricity in the air due to the storm. My hair isn't behaving," I sighed.

"Och, weel yoo're still bonnie," he disregarded and gave a kiss on my cheek. Just then a huge flash of lightning flashed in all the windows, setting off a large crashing sound of thunder. I suddenly jumped at the sound and moved away from the dressing table by the window.

"Whit's the matter?" he asked, noticing me.

"I don't want to get struck by lightning. It's not safe by the windows," I answered.

"Och," he replied, and his lips curled upward, appearing humored. "Weel, 'tis late now nonetheless. Ye ought tae be asleep in bed, *mo ghaol.*"

"Yes, it is late," I agreed and climbed into bed beneath the blankets. Leif strode toward the bench at the foot of the bed and sat as he proceeded to remove his boots. "How was your meeting with Governor Pownall?"

"Och, 'twas as weel as expected. He is most displeased with Laird Loudoun and refuses any troops fur the winter offensive His Lordship is planning," Leif said as he stood and began undressing for bed.

"What offensive?" I asked.

"He means tae take Fort Carillon efter all," he said as he tugged his linen shirt over his head, revealing his well-sculpted chest.

"Oh," I replied despondently as I observed him coming over the bed and entering beneath the down blankets.

"Dinnae fret. 'Twill be alrecht," he assuaged.

"How do you know?"

"I shall continue my correspondence with Prime Minister Master Pitt in London and inform him of Laird Loudoun's mismanagement of the war. Also, Governor Pownall shares my opinion about His Lordship along with the other governors. Governor Pownall will also correspond with Master Pitt regarding the matter with Loudoun, and I shall hope that thaur may be a resolution," he explained.

"I see," I realized as I sensed him wrap a bare arm around me and pull me close to him. "Does His Lordship still want me arrested?" I asked uneasily.

"I reckon he has other pressing matters at the moment," Leif responded gently against my temple, then pressed his lips against it.

"So, he'll forget about me then?" I felt his warm breath caressing my ear as I thought about Lord Loudoun's persistence regarding me and hoped to be left alone by him.

"He is in Albany at present, no less, fur the winter. Therefore, I doubt that he will be any consequence tae us haur. Thaur is nae need fur ye tae concern yerself over His Lordship. He has nae business with ye. I shall duel him first before he takes ye from me."

"I don't want you dueling anyone."

"Dinnae fret any longer, truly. He is awaur of the risks that involve me pertaining tae yer regard. The warrant fur ye has been voided now that we are wed. Any matter he has with ye may be addressed by me."

"Still... I don't want anything bad happening to you."

"Fear not, alrecht? I mean tae have him recalled from the colonies," Leif disclosed calmly.

"That would be so great to have him gone from here," I responded wishfully.

"Aye. He is a danger tae us all haur. If he had it in mind, he would have every man hanged fur treason fur going against his directive," Leif said. "I shall see tae his end if it is the last thing I ever do." I nodded quietly in acknowledgment. I felt his lips warmly come against the back of my head as he gave me a little kiss.

"Aside from the obvious reasons, why else do you and he loathe each other?" I inquired curiously.

"Thaur is ill will betwixt us since his clan betrayed the House of Stewart in favor of the current Hanoverians," he informed me. "Loudoun raised troops tae fight Jacobites and capture Prince Charles. However, Prince Charles escaped tae France. Afterward, Loudoun maintained his troops in the Highlands and terrorized the countryside. He also publicly named me a Jacobite. He did it believing 'twould dishonor me so that I would be accused and tried fur treason. So, in addition, tae my military service, I was forced tae pledge my allegiance tae the English Crown if I wished tae keep my lands and titles—as weel as my own head."

"Oh, wow," I muttered.

"Now ye fully ken how I have come tae serve the Crown," he said.

"My goodness," I replied softly. I shifted and turned toward him. I propped myself up on my elbow and faced him. "Do you really think that you can get him recalled?"

"Aye. I believe so," Leif said.

"I hope you succeed," I wished. He lifted his palm and his fingers lightly stroked my pixie bangs to the side over my brow. A languid grin warmed his face, and I smiled affectionately at him in return. His thumb and forefinger caught my chin, and he carefully pulled my lips over his.

"Come haur," he uttered softly and turned me over to fit me perfectly, spooning against him. "Enough of this political speak. Close yer eyes presently and sleep. Pleasant dreams, *ceisdein*."

"Pleasant dreams, Leif," I whispered back. He reached an arm overhead to the side to adjust the lantern light. It was now dark amid the flashes of lightning and thunder roaring throughout. We quietly listened to the pouring rain pounding on the windows around the room as we began falling to sleep, and peace began descending upon us.

THE NEXT MORNING, I awoke feeling rather queasy again. I decided this morning to have a light breakfast with Leif and Amity. As I spread strawberry preserves over my small oat bannock, I felt that I couldn't eat it. My stomach was bothering me. So, I took a sip of ginger tea hoping that it would help settle my stomach. It didn't seem to help this time. I decided nevertheless to eat a portion of my bannock, because I needed to have eaten something to satiate my morning hunger. I glanced at Leif as he contentedly ate and read the latest news from the *Gazette*. He appeared engrossed as I took one more bite from my strawberry preserve-covered bannock. After the last bite, however, I felt that I couldn't eat anymore and was suddenly even more nauseous.

"Excuse me," I said abruptly as I quickly removed myself from the morning table.

"Aye," Leif replied, appearing puzzled when I hastily moved away. I rushed out of the dining room through the corridor toward the first-floor privy closet. Not soon after entering the closet, I bent over the chamber pot and heaved all that I had just eaten plus more. After a moment when I had finished vomiting, I was uncontrollably trembling as I straightened from the pot.

"Oh my God," I said under my breath, feeling extremely worried like never before.

"Whit is the matter?" Leif inquired as I suddenly realized him standing at the threshold behind me, startling me a little. He appeared significantly concerned as his steady eyes held mine.

"I'm feeling under the weather," I said as I mindfully moved past him from the closet doorway into the corridor.

"Yoo're not feeling weel?" he inquired with care as he started pacing closely beside me in the hallway. The steep worry was clear in his voice.

"No," I responded equally fearfully while continuing through the passageway, intending to head toward the bedroom in order to rest on the bed for a while. Leif gently slipped a palm over my shoulder, urging me to cease pacing. I instantly seized my steps through the hallway and turned, facing him.

"Yoo're ill?" he questioned. The look of alarm was visible on his face as his hand slid down my sleeve, and he noticed my nerves when he took my hand into his. "Yoo're tremulous as a leaf."

"I know. I can't help it," I replied, nervously looking at him.

"But yoo're never ill. I shall promptly call upon the surgeon," he eagerly suggested.

"No! You don't need to do that," I protested.

"Whyever not?"

"Because I think I'll be okay."

"How are ye certain?" he asked, seriously looking at me. I gave a little relenting sigh as I couldn't control my shivering.

"I'm shaking because I'm scared," I said unevenly.

"Aye, I can plainly see your fear," he replied. "Now tell me why I shan't call upon the surgeon?"

"You shouldn't because I know what it is."

"Do ye?"

"Yes."

"Then, whit has put ye in such a state?"

"You have," I said with a wan little smile.

"I am puzzled." His brow furrowed as he couldn't fathom my meaning.

"I—I'm pretty sure that I'm pregnant," I disclosed. Leif's eyes immediately grew large as his brow lifted high.

"Pregnant?" he echoed. The expression on his face instantly changed from severe concern to elated expectation. "Yoo're bairned?" he repeated cautiously.

"Yeah." I nodded.

"Och!" The intense worry in his disposition instantly transformed to extreme surprise and he gave me a sudden heartened look of unexpected joy.

"I know," I said, understanding his surprise.

"Praise God!" he said elatedly as he immediately took me into his arms, embracing me. "How are ye certain?"

"Well, I haven't been feeling that well lately, and now I can't seem to hold anything down after I eat something," I expressed tremulously.

"Is that how ye truly ken?" he asked curiously, easing me away from his chest a little in order to look into my eyes.

"Among everything else, I also missed my cycle. I'm tired a lot, and my breasts are really tender—and I feel really warm like I have a fever, but I don't have one," I revealed quietly.

"Och," he realized understandingly while also appearing amazed. The symptoms were similar to the last time I was pregnant. So, I knew for certain that I had become pregnant again. Leif held me around my waist and drew me close into his strong arms again. I embraced him also and felt his lips affectionately press on top of my head. "I am greatly pleased by this news," he said happily against my crown.

"I'm glad," I whispered against his chest. He slightly released me from his arms when his thumb and forefinger gently clutched my chin as he lifted my lips to his.

"Mayhap, ye micht rest now," he suggested.

"Yes, I think that's a good idea," I agreed.

"Guid," he said with an agreeable expression. "I have matters tae which I must attend, yet I shall return about noon tae see how ye fare."

"All right," I responded as I sensed him fully releasing me from his embrace.

"Haur," he uttered. I suddenly felt him scooping me off my feet high into his arms, and he carefully started through the corridor, heading for the staircase.

"It's okay, I can walk," I joked.

"Ye quiver as a leaf, however. I shall place ye upon the bed whaur ye may rest undisturbed," he insisted instead, appearing rather serious over the fact I wasn't feeling well.

When Leif entered our bedroom, he gently placed me in bed against the down pillows. He pulled the warm blankets over me and turned toward the fireplace. He stoked the flames, then placed a fresh log over the dim coals. The log soon caught fire after he worked the coals, and I observed him turn from the hearth when he had finished with the burning fireplace. He approached me in bed and leaned a soft kiss over my lips, causing me to smile a little.

"I shall take my leave presently and shall return not before long," he uttered between our kisses.

"Okay," I acknowledged softly. He straightened from me, then turned toward the threshold where he vanished behind the door.

I couldn't stop from shuddering, so I pulled the blankets tauter around me. The room started to grow warmer, and my trembling began subsiding. I was truly glad that Leif was happy about the prospect of becoming a father, but I was simultaneously scared to death to give birth in this time period. I needed to see a modern-day obstetrician with monthly check-ups to make sure the pregnancy was developing normally and ultimately safely deliver the baby. Not having this advantage more than frightened me. It terrified me. As I continued pondering my new physical state, I had calculated that I must have been close to six weeks along in my pregnancy when I realized, to my surprise, that the moment of conception was undoubtedly when we were in Concord before arriving back in Boston. In a couple of months, my flat stomach was going to start becoming round, and I lay in bed this morning feeling a mixture of feelings from terror to bliss all at the same time.

Thirty-Eight

Thanksgiving had come with visiting Elizabeth and our nieces at her family's house in Concord. It was nice to see the Buckinghams again and to know how they were faring. Elizabeth seemed to be coping with the tragic circumstances surrounding her husband's death with the aid of her sister, Suzanna, and sister-in-law, Anne. It seemed that while Elizabeth was coping, she had plenty to occupy her attention with her responsibilities to her children. But when I caught her alone at times away from company, she showed moments of melancholy and grief—and my heart went out to her. It was easy to perceive that her heart still lay with Finley as she continued wearing widow's weeds, vowing never to replace her sad attire even when the appropriate mourning period had ended.

Still, knowing the Buckinghams were a resilient family, our Thanksgiving visit ended as well as could have been expected, though Finley was sorely missed by us all. I often prayed for Elizabeth in my own moments of solace, praying that she would overcome this devastation somehow as time passed. I continued praying that she would eventually be granted peace as she remembered Finley's life with joy by recognizing his survival through their children.

Time, I knew, would be her blessing.

DECEMBER HAD COME SO SOON after Thanksgiving, and now snow blanketed Boston in silence. I was sleeping comfortably among the pillows when I awoke this morning, feeling Leif's large hand gently stroking my slightly rounded stomach. It seemed that I was completing my first trimester without any noticeable concerns. The nausea had subsided, and although I felt like napping occasionally during the day, I generally felt better. My concerns over delivering the baby also waned somewhat since it seemed far enough into the future.

"What do you think it will be?" I asked sleepily as I gazed at Leif's gently caressing palm over my belly.

"I reckon a lass," he said as he raised his gaze from his palm. I glanced from his hand and met his sparkling ultramarine eyes.

"I think it's a boy," I guessed.

"Do ye now?" he responded, smiling affectionately at me.

"Yeah," I responded sleepily. "I bet if you put your ear over my stomach, you could probably hear the heart beating."

"Do ye reckon?" he responded with a surprise.

"Yes, I think so," I said.

"Alrecht, then. Let us see." He shifted the blankets off me a bit and carefully lifted my shift. I observed him place his ear against my bare, rounded belly, and he listened quietly for a moment.

"Och! Indeed, I can hear it!" he expressed, completely amazed. He turned his grinning gaze toward mine. I smiled at him, and he leaned back against the pillows while keeping his gentle palm splayed possessively over my stomach. "Whit does it feel like fur ye?" he asked interestedly.

"It feels like a little fish," I said.

"Curious. I seemed tae have also heard many bubbles," he chuckled a little. I laughed a little, too. "Come haur, *cuisle mo chridhe*," he said and gently tugged me close to him, fitting me snugly against his chest. It grew quiet between us as we rested comfortably with each other this morning.

"You know," I started pensively.

"Aye?" He languidly glanced at me.

"I was pregnant once before," I began.

"Aye, I recall ye telling me so," he remembered.

"Yeah." I nodded a bit with my head against his chest. "Remember that I told you how Matt passed away?"

"Aye."

"Well, I was five months pregnant when it happened."

"Aye," Leif responded attentively.

"We were both crossing the street together when a drunk driver came barreling through the street... Matt suddenly pushed me out of the way so that I wouldn't get hit. I fell down hard in the street... and Matt got run over—and I miscarried. I lost the baby," I remembered remorsefully.

"Och, *mo ghaol*, whit a terrible occurrence. My commiseration," he said tenderly as he spoke against my head. He delivered a sympathetic kiss to the top of my brow.

"I don't want anything bad to happen this time," I said, worrying about the potential for an accident to occur to me.

"Dinnae fret. Yoo're safe haur with me. Naught ill will befall ye," he promised.

"I hope not," I prayed.

"Naught will," he promised again. I raised my gaze to his crystal blue eyes, and he lifted his lips to mine in another soft kiss. I wanted to believe him—that I was safe and nothing wrong would happen to me or the baby—and I prayed that he was right. Matt protected me with his life, and so had Leif. I felt safe and extraordinarily happy with Leif. Much like the way I had felt with Matt, I didn't want that love, happiness, and security to ever vanish from me; I knew that I wouldn't have the strength to withstand such a tragedy with Leif. My bond with him felt incomprehensibly stronger. So, I leaned and warmly pressed my lips on his. His hand slipped around me, and he gently rolled me off him onto my back as he began kissing me back with warmth and yearning. I sensed his knee separating my thighs, and the heat between us grew, warming my blood that was already searing due to the life growing inside of me when he solidly entered and filled me from within.

CHRISTMAS WAS QUICKLY APPROACHING on the calendar and I spent most of my time tutoring Amity and arranging for our Christmas Eve dinner ball again this year. Amity was making good gains in her studies as we had resumed her education once we'd returned from Concord back in the fall after our return from Fort William Henry. She was learning how to read and write, and it wouldn't be long now until I could start introducing her to more difficult subjects. It was exciting to see her grasp the material she was learning. She was a bright girl, I believed, and I was certain that one day she would successfully demonstrate independence.

I sat at the letter desk in my bedroom making a list of guests who would attend our Christmas dinner and the food which we needed for the menu this season. As I was thinking about what should be placed on the dinner menu, I glanced out the window and saw snow falling from the gray sky. The maples, birches, and dogwoods were barren again, and the evergreens were coated with fresh snow. My mind reverted to last Christmas, and I thought about how much I had enjoyed the time. I realized then that I had been here for over a year now, and I was mesmerized by how much time had quickly passed. I also remembered the time before last Christmas. It was approaching two Christmases ago when I had last seen my family, and I began wondering about them again. I wondered about their well-being and how they were spending their days. It had been so long since I last saw them now, and I felt a slight bout of homesickness exude into my consciousness, beginning to turn my happy thoughts into wistfulness.

I removed myself from the letter desk and paced toward my dresser. I knelt and opened one of the bottom drawers where I kept my most personal belongings. Rummaging through my collection of things toward the bottom back of the drawer, my hand seized onto a small velvet pouch. I withdrew it from the drawer and pulled the closure open. I slipped my fingers into the pouch, withdrew my long-hidden cell phone, and gazed at it momentarily as I remembered it. Out of curiosity, I pressed the "on" button, and to my utter surprise, the screen illuminated. Except, I thought that was exceedingly strange as I stared flummoxed at it since my last memory of it was of it having fully discharged and dead to the touch. But somehow, it had oddly recharged to its fullest percentage, and I patently stared at it in utter confusion.

"How is this possible? It should be dead. I don't understand..." I muttered to myself.

With the screen now lit, I went ahead and typed in my passcode, and the apps fell into view. However, I noticed that the time and date still didn't register. But I tapped on my picture album app, and all of my photos and videos remained stored. I quickly checked my contacts and music, and it seemed my whole former life had still been perfectly stored—down to my credit cards, personal phone number, and address.

I decided to tap on my photo app again, and my album appeared. I scrolled through the photos and found pictures of my family and friends. Completely joyful to see their images again, I expanded the pictures of my parents and selfies that I had taken with my brother and Dakota simply to remember them as I gazed longingly at their captured faces. While continuing to scroll through the picture index, I found images of Matt and me enjoying our hike in Griffith Park. There were many images of Matt and me together enjoying ourselves. I had rediscovered the wedding pictures of us, and I fondly scrolled through them.

After taking a moment to gaze through the images, I closed the photos and opened the video section. I found videos of our wedding and the guests that had attended. I decided to open one of the videos and play the one of Matt and me dancing the first dance at our wedding to one of his favorite songs: *Kiss from a Rose* by Seal. As I watched the video, I realized that so much had fundamentally changed and that was a life lived a long time ago.

Suddenly, the door to the room opened, and Leif strode into our bedroom, closing the door behind him. My attention was unexpectedly disrupted and I dropped the phone inside the drawer as my knee accidentally bumped its edge when I hastily shut it closed.

"Oh my gosh! You startled me," I gasped with my hand over my pounding heart.

"Forgive me, *ceisdein*. I didnae intend tae frighten ye," he said sincerely as I nervously got to my feet. "Whit is it?" he inquired, observing me.

"Nothing," I said abruptly as I tried striding calmly back toward the letter desk.

"Certainly?" he questioned. I noticed his eyes narrow as he gave me a doubtful look.

"Yeah, sure," I replied quickly.

"Are ye breaking yer oath tae me then?" he asked suspiciously. He gave me a certain stern look that I knew was very earnest.

"What? No! Not at all, Your Grace," I responded uneasily.

"Then tell me whit it is that has made ye ill at ease," he requested measuredly. I took a little breath and released a bit of a sigh.

"Well, there isn't anything wrong. I mean, there wasn't a problem—but I guess there is one now—depending on the way you perceive it," I stammered, trying to collect my thoughts as I swept my short ringlets away from my face, tucking them behind my ear.

"Whit are ye gabbin' about, lass?" Leif asked with a puzzled expression. His tone was impatient, and I didn't want him suspicious of me. I took a larger breath and released a full sigh this time.

"Okay," I said, realizing that now I was going to have to finally disclose to him the complete truth about everything. "Okay, all right—I have something to tell you at last, but I really think that you should sit down before I tell you."

"Ye require that I sit fur whit ye must say?" he asked with a confused look.

"Yes," I said seriously. He seemed hesitant to take a seat. "Please," I insisted.

"As ye wish," he agreed. He paced across the room and sat on the bench at the foot of the bed. "Yoo're concerning me, at present," he said disconcertingly. "Are ye faring weel?"

"Yes, I actually feel quite fine. There's no need to worry about me or the baby. Everything's fine," I said positively.

"Then, whit is it that unsettles ye?" He steadily gazed at me with severity, and I felt intimidated to reveal anything to him.

"Okay... How am I going to tell you this?" I thought aloud as I put my hands on my round belly and gently rubbed it up and down. "Wait a minute, I have an idea," I said eagerly as a sudden thought occurred to me, which might alleviate some of the strain I was feeling to tell him the truth about me. I paced back toward the letter desk and gathered a blank loose-leaf parchment. I started folding it in half. Then, I folded it a few more times until I was satisfied with what I had constructed. I turned toward Leif and held up the constructed parchment.

"Do you know what this is?" I asked him as I held it before him to see.

"Why, a piece of parchment that ye have crafted," he said, interested, though his brow was furrowed, making him appear perplexed.

"Do you know what the structure is called?" I asked, regardless.

"Nae," he said simply, shaking his head also.

"Of course, not—why am I asking you that?" I said to myself. "Okay, it's called a paper airplane," I informed him.

"I see," he said unknowingly, but appearing very attentive to me.

"Watch," I replied. I promptly retracted my arm and launched the paper plane into the air. It effortlessly soared across the room until it crashed into the door to the bedroom and fell to the floor.

"Och! That is quite clever!" he responded remarkably, appearing really captivated now.

"Yeah, well, where I come from children make them all the time to play with," I imparted.

"Is that so?"

"Yes."

"I see. It is quite clever."

"Yes, well, the idea of it is based on a real concept. You see, where I come from there are very large contraptions called airplanes that resemble a simple paper airplane like the one I just showed you. Except, unlike paper, they're made of metal, and transport people from place to place at long distances," I explained.

"I beg yer pardon?" He looked startled at me.

"It's true," I said, disregarding his startled expression. I could tell by the look on his face that he wasn't going to believe me at all, and that I might cause him to worry about my emotional or mental state—which promptly began worrying me. "Okay..." I started again more thoughtfully. "Remember when I said that I would never lie to you, right?"

"Aye, that is reit," he recalled without question.

"Well, there are things about me that you don't know, because I've kept them secret," I said carefully as I held his steady gaze.

"Aye, I'm awaur of it," he said insightfully.

"Well, I'm not sure how I can tell you this without alarming you," I prefaced.

"Merely tell me and then we shall see how I respond," he exhorted.

"All right. But you have to promise me *never* to tell a single living soul—ever—of what I'm about to tell you," I insisted.

"Very weel. I shan't," he promised.

"All right," I replied satisfactorily. "Okay, here it goes... I'm not from these colonies."

"Yoo're not?" He had an extremely doubtful look on his face now.

"No."

"Then, from whaur do ye come?" he asked nevertheless.

"Well, I'm going to tell you—that in fact, I'm not from this century," I started. Leif's brow deeply furrowed and now he suddenly seemed very concerned. "It's true."

"Then, from whit century do ye belong?" he asked inquisitively, although I could also see the questionable look on his face.

"I'm from the twenty-first century. I was born in nineteen eighty-four," I finally revealed to him.

"I beg yer pardon?" he asked briskly, looking flabbergasted at me.

"My birthdate is December twenty-fourth, nineteen eighty-four," I told him. He didn't respond except silently stare at me as the expression on his face abruptly became unreadable. "Okay, this is going to sound so crazy. But, it's true," I continued to venture. "You see, somehow, I got caught up in a temporal warp, and it delivered me here to this time period after I got into a car crash. I can't figure out how it happened, though, but I quantum leaped—and now, I'm here with you," I explained, feeling myself becoming excited over finally telling him. However, I could clearly perceive him gazing at me with sheer concern and disbelief. Still, I continued telling him, "I'm from a place called California—Los Angeles, to be specific. It's a city within the state of California.

And California is part of a collection of fifty states called the United States of America. That's the country where I'm from. You see, one day, not too long from now, these colonies are going to unite and rebel against the Crown because they will feel that they've been mistreated, and there's going to be a revolution. The colonies will call themselves the United States of America. A war is going to happen between Great Britain and the colonies here—and the colonies will win," I rambled. Leif stared at me, utterly dumbstruck, and suddenly I stopped talking.

He thinks I'm crazy...

"Yet, England is a most mighty country, *ceisdein*—far mightier than these colonies could ever meet tae challenge her."

"For now, yes, I know. But you watch—it's going to happen. The colonies will defeat England."

"By whit means?"

"France and Spain are going to help the colonies."

"When shall this occur?" he asked measuredly, appearing utterly confounded.

"Seventeen seventy-five will be when the first battle between England and the colonies will take place. But the colonies won't declare independence from England until seventeen seventy-six," I answered. "I know this because I'm from the future, and this is my country's history." Leif drew in a deep breath and sighed, appearing very doubtful and categorically alarmed. He started straightening from the bench and stood tall before me. His hands gently came over my shoulders as he calmly gazed at me with worry.

"Forgive me, *mo ghaol*. I ken that yoo're not a witch, however, yoo're not making any sense whitsoever as one micht. I plainly realize yer delicate state, and I reckon that ye have become distressed due to it and that ye must rest," he carefully suggested as I perceived the resignation and sheer disbelief on his face.

"No! I feel just fine. And, you're right, I'm absolutely not a witch. I knew you wouldn't believe me, but I'm telling you the truth. Here! I can prove it!" I replied eagerly before he could respond and removed myself from standing in front of him. I hastily returned to my dresser drawer and opened it. Reaching inside, I promptly pulled forth my cell phone and waved it in plain sight for him to see. "See? I can prove it to you."

His brow suddenly lifted high on his head, and his eyes widened as he no longer appeared doubtful but unexpectedly surprised with a strange look. "Whit is it that yoo're presenting tae me?" he inquired, simultaneously appearing baffled and even more alarmed as I waved my phone in the air.

"It's my phone. It's called a cellphone—a telephone," I answered as I approached him.

"Pardon?" He gazed at me with a very uncertain look now regarding the phone as I arrived, standing closely before him.

"See?" I replied, finally proving it to him.

"Aye—I do see it," he expressed, nonplussed.

"So, I'm telling you the truth."

The expression on his face suddenly transformed as his eyes bounced from me to the phone in my hand. He nodded his head a little with a severely furrowed brow while also now gazing pensively at me, clearly appearing thunderstruck.

"I'm telling the truth."

"I—I believe ye." He paused for a second longer, staring with confusion at the phone in my hand. I could perceive that he didn't know what to say in response. So, he simply stood there before me in silence, thinking and staring at it in bewilderment. "Whit is done with it?" he asked after a fleeting moment, extremely baffled —appearing almost frightened.

"It's used for speaking with people from long distances," I disclosed. Leif returned to the foot bench and sat again. I followed him and stood close to him. "You see, if you had one I could call you on it, and then we could hold a conversation with each other from afar."

"From afar?"

"Yes."

"Och..." he responded as his eyes turned upward from the phone, still looking dumbfounded at me. I decided to sit next to him on the bench.

"Here, you can see it," I suggested as I closely presented the phone for him to observe. He curiously gathered it among his large fingers and began to examine it.

"Whit sort of material is it?" he inquired strangely, still looking extraordinarily stunned.

"The protective case for it is made of a material called plastic," I said. He turned the phone over in his examining fingers, and carefully scrutinized it.

"Whaur is a plastic derived?"

"It comes from another material called petroleum, and that comes from deep within the ground," I informed him.

"Och..." he replied cluelessly.

"Here, let me see it for a moment," I urged. He proffered the phone to me, and I retrieved it from his grip. I proceeded in removing the case from it so that he could clearly see the phone for himself. Then, I passed it back to him, and he began more carefully examining it all over again.

"Of whit sort of material is it made?" he inquired once more, sheerly mystified.

"It's made of glass and aluminum," I informed him.

"'Tis a very fine instrument," he uttered remarkably. He subsequently fell quiet for a lengthy moment as he studied my phone in his hand. "Forgive me for saying ye waurnae weel," he expressed finally, clearly shocked.

"It's okay," I replied understandingly.

"I have often wondered why ye have never caught a simple chill and how ye could survive the pox without a mere mark," he expressed wondrously.

"I've been vaccinated as an infant against many diseases. So, I'm not susceptible to a lot of illnesses. I was vaccinated against smallpox as an adult because I had volunteered my medical services to poor immigrant communities once. That's what I wanted to tell you when we were at Fort William Henry, but I felt that I couldn't at the time," I revealed.

"I see..." he said simply, turning his blank gaze from the phone to me again.

"I've been wanting to tell you about myself for such a long time, but I just didn't know how to tell you without seeming crazy and scaring you."

He nodded contemplatively in response.

"I thought you would send me away to an insane asylum or something if I told you," I continued.

"A sanitarium?"

"Yes."

"I would never send ye away from me."

"Well... I wasn't so sure. It's a pretty big tale to believe."

"Even so, I would have never sent ye away—ever."

"But you would have called the physician."

"Aye. I would have done so—tae call upon the physic tae examine ye. Yer welfare is my utmost concern."

"I know..." I drifted momentarily as I gazed at the staunch sincerity on his face. "Now, you can see that I'm not crazy."

"Yoo're not mad," he agreed as he shook his head a little. I smiled a bit at him. He grinned a little too. But it was a nervous grin. I could perceive him contemplating and I wondered what was going through his mind.

"Would you like to see something?" I asked.

"Aye," he replied innocently, unable to conceal his bafflement as it was transparent on his face.

"All right," I said, taking the phone from him and typing in my passcode as he intently watched me. All the apps fell into view, and I tapped on the photo app. My photo album came into sight, and I expanded the photos. "See?" I started again as I passed the phone back to him for him to hold. "These are my parents. They live in California, too." I showed him their images.

"Och..." Leif replied, closely studying the image of them together. "This isnae a painting," he quickly recognized.

"No, it's called a photograph. The camera captures the image through the exposure of light," I explained. "The camera won't be invented until about a hundred years from now, though. But it will look a lot different from this one. Instead, the first cameras will look rather large and bulky."

"Remarkable," he expressed cluelessly as he gazed intently at the close-up photograph of my parents sitting outside in their backyard by their swimming pool. "These are yer parents, then?" he realized meditatively.

"Yes," I responded.

"They are a handsome pair," he remarked, mesmerized by their images.

"Thank you."

"Yer mother is bonnie and quite fair."

"Her father is of German descent, and her mother was French Canadian."

"That is how ye have come tae ken French, of coorse. I recall ye telling me a bit about yer parents when we first wed."

"Yes."

"And, yer father is quite swarthy. He's a Negro," Leif noticed.

"Yeah, his parents are from Puerto Rico—a United States territory that was won in the Spanish-American war," I disclosed freely.

"Hence your knowledge of Spanish," he surmised.

"Yes," I said, nodding a bit.

"How very curious," he uttered pensively as he kept staring at the picture. "Ye waur never a spy."

"No," I said ridiculously, shaking my head. He turned his glance up from the phone and looked categorically amazed at me. "Here, I want to show you something else," I said, and I leaned closer to him as I pressed the video album. "I've got pictures that move."

"Whit do ye mean?"

"I'll show you." I tapped on the video I had taken of my parent's cocker spaniel, Doolittle, as she lunged for the slice of pizza in my hand. The picture began to move with sound emitting from the phone. I was recorded laughing and scolding Doolittle for trying to steal my slice of pizza from me. When the video ended, I glanced back at Leif, and our eyes met again. Pure amazement was expressed completely on his face, rendering him speechless for a moment again.

"This is miraculous," he expressed finally, awestruck.

"No, it's not. It's just advanced technology," I replied.

"How does it operate in that case?" he asked fascinatingly, referring to the phone.

"Well, it's basically a computer, and it's programmed to function. I don't know how it works specifically because I'm not a computer scientist, but it uses a battery to power it. Except, the charge from the battery doesn't last long—only about a couple of days or so—before it no longer works. That's why I don't understand how the battery is fully charged now without a source of electricity to recharge it. It's impossible for it to be working right now—I'm absolutely stumped—because the last time I checked it, the battery was completely discharged, and the phone was unresponsive," I rambled, nonplused.

"Och..." Leif replied, trying to understand what I was saying. "Yet, it operates presently."

"Yeah, but it won't last," I said.

"I see," he responded, still greatly puzzled by it all. His thumb accidentally touched the video of me and Matt dancing at our wedding, and the video started playing. It called Leif's attention to it, and his gaze shifted from me down to the illuminated screen in his hand.

"That's Matt," I informed him in a soft voice.

"Och…" Leif said as he kept watching the video playing. "The pair of ye appear merry."

"Yeah," I admitted. "That was captured during our wedding reception."

"I see… Yoo're extraordinarily bonnie."

"Thank you." When the short video had ended, Leif lifted his gaze from the phone to look steadily at me again. He stared intently at me for a moment without speaking, appearing intensely pensive.

"I have been hard upon ye," he said sincerely with an extremely serious expression on his face.

"I understand, though," I replied truthfully.

"I understand presently as weel," he said genuinely. I gently smiled at him, and he nodded a little.

"Let's try something for a moment," I suddenly suggested. I slipped my hand over his to gather the phone from him. I switched the phone to camera mode and held it up before us.

"Whit are ye doing?" he asked curiously.

"You'll see," I replied as I activated the video mode. "Okay now it's filming. Say something."

"Whit shall I say?"

"Anything you want."

"My words elude me."

"All right, I'll go first then—I love you with all my heart, Leif," I said and gave a nice kiss on his cheek.

"Och, alrecht, I see now." He grinned a little. "Sylvie, ye are the lecht of my soul and the ballad of my heart. I shall forever adore ye with all of my loove," he said and returned a kiss on my cheek. I pressed the button, and the camera stopped recording.

"Okay, now watch," I said as I pulled the phone into our view. I tapped the playback button, and the video started to play. Leif sat quietly, struck with enthrallment and mesmerization as he viewed the moving images of us just recorded. When it had finished playing, he gazed at me with continued marvel and was speechless for a long moment.

"Let's do anither," he expressed finally, completely impressed.

"Okay," I agreed, smiling at him. So, we made a couple more selfie videos to his thorough enjoyment. It was gratifying for me also to observe him entirely engaged in this novel instrument that I helped him to discover.

"Alrecht, now instruct me—how micht I make it so that the image remains still?" he desired interestedly.

"Sure, of course. The phone is pretty user-friendly once you get the hang of it," I replied readily.

"Och," he responded unknowingly, and I began showing him how to use the features on the phone. The only apps that worked were the photo app, the camera, the voice recorder, music, and word processing apps. The others were futile, since they needed a connection to the internet, I had explained to him as he cluelessly gazed at me. After several minutes, he seemed to have gotten some idea of how to navigate the photo app once I instructed him.

"This is truly remarkable," he said fascinatingly while toying with my phone.

"It is, isn't it?" I agreed freely, watching his fingers scroll through the stored images. After several more minutes went by while observing Leif discover the phone, I decided to leave him alone with it and started from the bench with the intention of completing our Christmas dinner menu.

"One moment," he said suddenly. He lightly snagged my wrist in his grip, arresting my steps.

"Yeah?" I replied curiously.

"Dinnae take yer leave from me as of yet," he requested politely. "I shall like tae ken everything from whence ye came."

"Of course," I agreed openly. So, I sat back down on the bench next to him and began telling him everything about where I was from and what happened the night I had disappeared. I told him all about my family and what it was like growing up in a sprawling metropolitan city like Los Angeles. I told him about my brother and how his wife and I met as college students. I told him all about the schools that I had gone to as a child and the family vacations that we had taken as we visited places all around the country.

I told him about the history of the United States and about the structure of my country, how the government was organized and divided into three separate but equal branches, and how citizens voted to send citizens to represent them in the government. I told him about President Lincoln and the civil war that the country would endure. I also told him about the two world wars in which America became involved and won. And, I revealed to him how the world was ordered between capitalism and communism after the Second World War.

I continued to tell him about the Cold War and how America won without firing a single shot. I told him about complex architectural accomplishments that lined major cities in the United States. I revealed to him the sophisticated telecommunication and transportation accomplishments that had taken place.

"Ye mean tae tell me that men travel by air vessels tae far off lands raither than by sailing ships as they do presently?" Leif asked in complete astonishment.

"Well, people still travel by ocean. But, yes, that's what I was trying to make you understand when I constructed the paper airplane," I answered.

"Whit else?" he inquired attentively.

"Well, we have launched people into outer space where they fly high above the Earth and orbit around it like the moon," I revealed. Leif stared at me, gaping in utter fascination.

"Truly?" he replied with a flabbergasted expression.

"Yes. And, the United States is the only country that landed people on the moon. Neil Armstrong planted our flag there. That was accomplished in the nineteen sixties," I continued.

"How is it possible?" he questioned.

"It's possible," I said. "Soon, the United States will be sending people to Mars. The idea is to colonize it." I didn't think that his eyes could have grown any wider but they now became huge orbs. I continued telling him all about the advancements made in medicine and how we cure and prevent certain diseases on a genomic level as he simply stared at me with captivation.

"How is it possible that ye are haur sitting directly beside me at present?" he asked.

"I don't know. But, it's possible—obviously, because I'm here," I said wondrously.

"Aye, ye are," he fathomed scarcely. He started asking me a million questions as he was extremely curious about where I was from. I sat next to him, answering all of his questions and revealing more about what occurred in the future. We continued discussing for hours, and it became late in the day. It wasn't much longer when the sun began setting. At this moment, Leif tucked the phone in his breeches pocket, and we finally left the bedroom for the dining room to have our early evening meal together in a deeper understanding of each other, as my biggest burden had been unloaded from me at last.

I AWAKENED in the middle of the night, hearing a soft song being sung that I'd remembered. The melody was *Songbird* by Fleetwood Mac. As my drowsy vision began adjusting in the darkness, I recognized the glow of my phone in Leif's palm as he rested against the pillows. It illuminated his face in soft blue hues as he listened quietly to the lyrical song emitting from its speakers.

"I see that you've found my song list," I observed sleepily as the melody finished.

"Aye. 'Tis a bonnie ballad," he stated.

"It is," I agreed.

"Yet, I dinnae recall the musical instrument I heard incorporated in the ballad."

"It's a piano—sort of like a harpsichord."

"Och, aye," he recognized. I rolled to my side to face him, and he turned his captivated gaze to me while he remained propped against the pillows.

"May I see the phone for a moment?" I asked.

"Aye, of coorse," he replied easily and passed it to me.

"I'm not sure if you'll like this version, but this song reminds me of when I was little. My parents used to dance to this song when I was really young," I said as I scrolled through my music collection.

"Och," Leif replied simply as he waited patiently for me to search for what I was looking.

"Here it is," I said as I found *The Way You Look Tonight*. I pressed play, and the melody came through the speakers.

"Och, I reckon that I recall this ballad. Ye serenaded it tae me whilst at the fort. Merely presently 'tis a lad serenading," he remembered.

"Yeah," I replied, remembering also.

"Whit instruments play it? 'Tis charming."

"The guitar, the bass, piano, drums, and violins."

"I see..." he said softly as he continued listening to the song. When the song had ended, he turned his gaze toward mine and said, "I very much enjoyed that ballad. 'Tis raither merry."

"Yes, it is," I agreed. I then scrolled down my list and found another song he might likely enjoy.

"This song is also a favorite of mine," I revealed, also as I pressed my finger over the song *For All We Know* sung by The Carpenters. The melodic music began to play and it was hypnotizing. I lightly sang along, and Leif smiled intriguingly at me as he listened intently.

"I favor that ballad also," he remarked pleasantly when the song and I had finished.

"I'm glad that you liked it." I smiled at him and observed the intrigue and affection in his eyes. He then gathered the phone from where I had placed it close between us among the pillows and moved it carefully toward the nightstand next to his bedside, where he placed it. Afterward, he shifted among the pillows and closely faced me again.

"Therefore, this is common music in yer period?" he asked innocently.

"There are all sorts of genres of music that people like to listen to. But, yes, that is a sample of popular music of my time. Some of the songs I have on my phone were recorded before I was born and were popular when my parents were young. And some of the songs remind me of when I was small, when my parents used to listen to them. Others were popular during my generation," I answered.

"I see. 'Tis quite different than whit I am familiar," he said as he softly spoke to me.

"I know," I replied gently also.

"Ye come from a bonnie family," he complimented.

"Thank you. We loved each other very much."

"Hmm... How pleasant."

"Yeah."

"Ye must long tae return tae your family."

"I still miss them."

"I reckon so..."

"I mean, at first, when I came here, that was all I wanted to do —was to return home every waking moment. I was so scared and very homesick..."

"I understand the sentiment."

"I think about them sometimes."

"Certainly, ye must..." Leif gazed meditatively at me, but the expression in his eyes was also affectionate and warm.

"But now—things are vastly different because I have you... So, I don't miss them as much as I did at first," I said truthfully. He nodded a little without grinning as he seriously gazed at me.

"Ye have sacrificed tremendously tae be living haur in this

period with me... Yet, I desperately long fur ye tae feel at home with me, Sylvie," he said in a very gentle tone.

"I do feel at home with you. Wherever you are—as long as we're together, then I am right at home. I belong with you."

"And, I belong with ye."

"I can't see my life without you, Leif."

"Nor can I perceive my life without ye. Ye are my heart."

"You are my heart, too."

"We possess one anither. Do ye realize that is true?"

"Yeah—I know."

"I loove ye, Sylvie," he said straightforwardly as he bound my eyes to his.

"I love you too," I whispered back. I gently smiled at him, and I could see his lips finally curl upward in the dim firelight. His fingers lightly came over my brow as he stroked my pixie bangs to the side.

"Yoo're like Laird MacLeod's fairy maiden, but yoo're my *sìthiche*," he said softly. I felt his fingers gently stroking the side of my cheek, and I smiled endearingly at him. "Tell me more about yer parents," he requested.

"Well, I think I've told you everything," I said as I tried remembering.

"Och."

"Did I tell you that my mom was an attorney by profession?"

"A barrister?"

"Yeah."

"I believe not. Was she now?"

"Yeah. She's retired from practicing."

"Intriguing..."

"And, my dad was a M.A.S.H. surgeon."

"Whit does that mean?"

"He was a surgeon that worked for a mobile army surgical hospital."

"Och, I see. I reckon that yer father must have been proud of ye for having been a physic, fur ye have become a surgeon like he."

"I suppose so," I replied modestly.

"Yer mother too must have been proud tae have such an intelligent daughter," he said sincerely. I smiled at him in response. Leif smiled warmly in return, and I loved the way his fingers felt against my skin as he tenderly stroked my cheek. It fell quiet between us for a moment, and we simply stared at each other, not saying anything else as we were just happy to share in the moment of each other's company.

"Thanks for listening to me," I whispered to him.

"Indeed, *mo ghaol*. I shall always regard whit ye have tae say tae me."

"I feel really relieved now that you know everything about me."

"I am pleased that ye have told me all thaur is tae ken. I can only imagine the burden ye waur bearing by holding such a great secret." He shifted a little, and I felt his lips warmly press over mine. "We must guard yer telephone so that nae one ever discovers it, lest we are accused of sorcery."

"I know," I agreed, absolutely.

"I shall keep it hidden with my most treasured possessions," he said seriously.

"All right." I yawned tiredly as I was now fighting to remain awake for us to continue speaking.

"After the thaw, I shall also desire tae discover whaur exactly ye vanished," he said. "We shall journey tae see this place."

"That would mean a lot to me. I have no idea how it happened, and I'd really like to know how I got here."

"We shall discover how ye whaur transported through time tae come haur. Thaur must be a reason fur how it occurred, as the topic has piqued my interest."

"That would be great to figure out how it happened. I just hope that we can understand it—maybe there's a way to go back and forth through time. Or maybe not. I don't know... I just don't ever want to become lost again," I said as I yawned sleepily.

"Aye, I dinnae wish fur that tae occur tae ye again, either. Although, I am certain God permitted me tae find ye."

"I think our meeting is a blessing too."

"Aye," he said. I yawned again, and I was helplessly beginning to fall to sleep as I struggled to keep my eyes open. "Ah, yoo're weary now," he noticed. "Come haur." He carefully pulled me against him and fitted me close. I sensed his arm come around me, and his palm gently rested over my swollen belly. My stomach churned and the baby settled more comfortably as I rested on my side. "Och! The bairn moves!" he expressed amazedly.

"Yeah. The baby is doing well," I said gladly. Another yawn escaped me, and I felt Leif's lips press softly over my temple. "Guidnecht, my angel."

"Goodnight," I whispered back, then my eyes closed.

"Ye are my greatest possession—the pulse of my heart, and I adore ye with all of my soul," he uttered gently against the back of my head. "*Mo leannan.*"

"My beloved," I whispered faintly, translating his beautiful words.

"Aye." His lips gently pressed against the back of my head, and I slipped my fingers among his, contracting them as I meant never to let him go. His palm tightened over mine in return, and he held me close in his secure arms.

Thirty-Nine

After I had disclosed everything about myself to Leif, I felt an inexplicably huge burden lifted from me. Talking with him now came more easily, and our bond became even tighter.

This Christmas we had a trimmed tree again that embellished the drawing room for the season like before, as arrangements had been made for our Christmas Eve dinner ball. I sat at the dressing table, fixing my ringlets that had grown somewhat longer, almost touching my shoulders, while Leif completed polishing his timepiece.

"Happy birthday and Merry Christmas, *mo ghaol*," he said softly against my ear as he leaned close to give me a warm kiss on my neck after tucking his timepiece into his waistcoat pocket.

"Thank you and Merry Christmas to you too," I said lovingly when I observed him kiss my neck in the looking glass. I noticed a small, nicely designed mahogany box coming around my shoulder held between his fingers. "What is this?" I expressed surprise at receiving the box from him.

"A gift fur ye upon yer birthday," he said.

"Thank you so much!" I replied as I happily glanced down at

the box in my hand. I opened it and discovered a pair of beautiful, deep sapphire and pearl earrings. "Oh, my goodness!" I gasped. He smiled and gently clutched my chin between his thumb and forefinger, turning my gaze upward to meet his. He raised my lips to meet his, giving me a benevolent kiss. When he withdrew his lips from mine, I retrieved the beautiful earrings from the box and hooked them into my pierced ears.

"They are splendid upon ye," he remarked while closely observing me in the looking glass.

"Thank you," I replied, feeling very happy.

"I have commissioned several portraits of ye," he informed me.

"You have?

"Aye. The first begins efter Christmas week."

"That's exciting."

"I am eager fur it," he said while gazing at each other in the looking glass now. "Yoo're splendid."

"Thank you. You look very handsome," I said, smiling at him. His expression brightened even more with an easy grin creasing his cheeks.

"Shall we presently meet our guests as they will soon arrive?"

"Yes." I stood from the dressing table and slipped my palm into his. We left the bedroom together with my fingers gently linked around his muscular arm, and we enjoyed our guests during this festive Christmas dinner.

A WEEK LATER, the sound of the bell tower and gunfire rang in the New Year. The brightly shining moon, I noticed, was exceedingly large as if it were on a nearby collision course with Earth. It seemed fantastic as it lit the surrounding landscape in an illuminating blue monochromatic scheme. As I stood there next to Leif in the midnight snow gazing at the bonfire our servants had set for themselves to usher in the New Year, I marveled at the world around me and gave thanks to God. Miracles happen all the time and can be perceived if a soul's open to receive them, I thought, as I gazed up into the starry heavens above. I could feel the growing life inside of me moving as my blood coursed heatedly through my veins like the mantle coursing through Earth. I realized most potently tonight that Leif and I were bonded through our souls to the bone, in blood, and by the flesh.

"Happy New Year," I said as I turned my gaze to him.

"Och, tae ye as weel, *mo ghaol*," he replied. His lips pressed upon my brow, and I slipped my arm around his lean waist beneath his coats. He stole an arm around my shoulder and carefully pulled me close to him while we observed the servants celebrating around the roaring flames. We remained apart from them in the midnight snow, quietly watching the fire also while it crackled and popped in the freezing night air, illuminating the surrounding silent binding snow—and it was joy to be here with the man I soulfully loved.

THE MONTHS SEEMED to be flying by. I could hardly believe that March had already arrived, and I was completing my second trimester without any apparent difficulty, to my relief. I was comfortable at this stage in my pregnancy of expecting our first child, and I started nesting, happily focusing a large portion of my attention on decorating our infant's nursery.

After I had finished my lessons with Amity, I decided to take a break and relax on the settee in the sunroom with a book. While reading I had grown tired and decided to rest my eyes for a while. The next thing I remembered was feeling the gentleness of Leif's lips over mine in a kiss which awakened me.

"Oh, hi," I said drowsily as I sat up in the settee.

"Hullo, *mo ghaol*," he said. "How are ye faring?"

"Great."

"Whit guid news."

"Where are you coming from?"

"I have merely arrived from meeting with the governor."

"Oh," I replied simply as I shifted from my place on the settee to stand. He kindly proffered his hand and helped me to my feet.

"I care for a walk. Micht ye join me?" he asked.

"Sure," I agreed.

"Grand. I shall fetch our capes, and return shortly."

"Okay." I motioned to Amity, sitting comfortably on the sofa near me, where she was engrossed in her knitting project. She glanced up at me from her work, and I told her that her uncle and I were going for a walk. She nodded with a sweet smile and continued contentedly working on her project.

Within a minute, Leif returned with our capes, and we stepped out into the early, fresh, cool spring air through the floral garden. We strolled toward the Common, enjoying each other's company and admiring the thaw that was upon us now. The sun shined brightly, and the sky was clear and light cerulean blue. The trees were beginning to bloom their sap-green leaves, and the days were growing long again. Abundant Lilac bushes were soon to blossom with purple and periwinkle hues and fill the air with their intense, heady, sweet perfume again. The honeysuckles would soon flower in force, luring hummingbirds all around to feed on their nectar. The pond we had skated on was no longer frozen in ice and now rippled in the breeze, glinting like golden glitter under the sun between the trees. We walked among the trees around the pond's shoreline and listened to the sparrows chirping high among the boughs.

"Recall my telling ye that I had met with the governor today?" Leif started.

"Yeah?" I replied curiously.

"Weel, we discussed our correspondences regarding Prime Minister Master Pitt," he informed me.

"Oh," I realized.

"It seems Master Pitt is changing coorse upon the war effort."

"He is?"

"Aye."

"In what way?"

"He has relieved the Earl of Loudoun of his duties," Leif said. I suddenly arrested my steps. I turned, facing Leif, and glanced up at his ultramarine eyes, shocked. "Aye," he replied as he stopped walking also and gazed back at me.

"I can't believe it. Are you serious?" I asked unbelievably.

"Most earnest. He soon will be returning tae England. New leadership is forthcoming. The Earl of Loudoun will face his shame in front of the Crown," Leif said.

"We don't have to worry about him anymore?"

"Nae longer."

"I can't believe it... You did it," I replied amazingly.

"Not without the governor's assistance."

"Yes, of course," I acknowledged. "I have to say that I'm not only absolutely shocked, but I'm so completely relieved."

"As am I."

"I can't believe this has happened... I'm so glad he's leaving. I just can't believe it—it's been so long," I said, throwing my arms around his neck in a big embrace, entirely impressed with what he'd done.

"I too am quite pleased, *mo ghaol*," he responded. I sensed his arms coming firmly around me, securing our embrace. This was the end of Lord Loudoun's ability to exert totalitarian control over the colonies, antagonize the population here, and threaten Leif through me. "Now, we may be at peace," Leif said softly against my cheek.

"I'm so glad beyond words," I said against his neck. He released his embrace around me a little and gazed directly into my eyes. I felt his confident palm ease within my cape and gently caress my round belly, and movement was detected from within as the baby gave me a healthy kick.

"Och!" Leif chuckled with surprise. "We have a hearty bairn."

"Yes, we do."

"I am most pleased at whit the future holds fur us," he expressed in a warm, gentle tone as I felt his lips brushing against mine.

"So am I," I replied tenderly.

"Pulse of my heart." His soft lips came over mine. "*Mo leannan*," he said to me between our kiss, and my heart fluttered with inexplicable endearing warmth for him.

The world was aglow under the bright warm spring sun. Suddenly a hummingbird appeared before us and hovered. We stared at it in awe as it stared back at us while suspended right before our eyes, lingering for a moment as if to say hello. Then, as soon as it had appeared, it darted off into the enveloping sky and vanished, leaving us mesmerized.

Somewhere behind us, we left all that we had once known and embarked on a new vision that was to come. Our gazes shifted from the sky where the bird had flown and turned upon the sparkling water before us as it rippled in the light breeze, knowing we held the future in our womb. It seemed that what was to follow was bright and full of marvels. At that moment, I felt all was right with the world. And it was.

Thank You For Reading

Are you curious to know more about Leif and Sylvie? The next novel, *The Pulse of My Heart*, will continue their story.

Join the author's email list to receive newsletters whenever E. C. Roderick publishes a new book and for exclusive sneak peeks and author news.

Thank you; I appreciate your interest in my books!

Join the author's mailing list:

Acknowledgments

First and foremost, thank you to my husband, Alan, who believes in everything I do. Without your support, this story would have never been written. I'm immensely grateful to you for encouraging me in all of my creative endeavors and for inspiring me to create them. I love you. Also, thank you to my family, who have given me the same wonderful support. I love all of you.

Thank you immensely to the beta readers who read the manuscript. Your input was highly regarded and strengthened this story, for which I'm entirely grateful.

A huge thank you to my editor, Candy Leondard, for your attention to detail so that the manuscript read smoothly and for all of your encouragement. You're incredibly appreciated.

Also, a wonderful thank you to Mary Ann Smith for creating the perfect cover for this story. I can't tell you enough how grateful I am for our collaboration.

Finally, but certainly not least, thank you incredibly to readers like you. I treasure that you took a chance on a new emerging author like me and have followed this story from the beginning. Without you, I would not be able to bring more stories for you to enjoy and continue my love for writing while being with my family.

Thank you!

About the Author

E. C. Roderick is an emerging author of romance fiction. Her award-winning historical time-travel romance debut novel, TAKEN, which is also a number one Amazon bestseller, begins the saga of Leif and Slyvie. Once a classically trained fine artist, E. C. Roderick taught fine art to both adults and children for many years and found it rewarding. While she enjoyed the creativity inherent in the art process, she discovered her love for writing.

As she raises her family with her husband, finding the necessary space and time to paint has become challenging. Consequently, she focuses on creative writing whenever she has the opportunity. This particular medium for creativity has proven equally rewarding for her, as she delights in developing strong characters and their environments for readers to enjoy.

When E. C. Roderick takes a break from writing, she enjoys spending time with her family and going for long walks with her husband on the beach in southern California.

Connect with the author: